• THE Naked AND THE Dead

THE Naked AND THE Dead

NORMAN MAILER

AN OWL BOOK

HOLT, RINEHART AND WINSTON / NEW YORK

Grateful thanks are expressed to the publishers and copyright owners for permission to reprint lyrics from the following songs:

Betty Co-ed, by Paul Fogarty and Rudy Vallee. Copyright, 1930, by Carl Fischer, Inc., New York, and used with their permission.

Brother, Can You Spare a Dime? Words by E. Y. Harburg, music by Jay Gorney. Copyright, 1932, by Harms, Inc., and used with the permission of Music Publishers Holding Corporation.

Faded Summer Love, words and music by Phil Baxter. Copyright, 1931, by Leo Feist, Inc., and used with their permission.

I Love a Parade, words by Ted Koehler, music by Harold Arlen. Copyright, 1931, by Harms, Inc., and used with the permission of Music Publishers Holding Corporation.

Show Me the Way to Go Home, words and music by Irving King. Copyright, 1925, by Harms, Inc., and used with the permission of Music Publishers Holding Corporation.

These Foolish Things Remind Me of You, by Jack Strachey, Hold Marvel and Harry Link. Copyright, 1935, by Bourne, Inc., and used with their permission.

Published by Holt, Rinehart and Winston,
383 Madison Avenue, New York, New York 10017
Published simultaneously in Canada by Holt, Rinehart and
Winston of Canada, Limited.

Library of Congress Cataloging in Publication Data
Mailer, Norman.
The naked and the dead.
"An Owl Book."
1. World War, 1939-1945—Fiction. I. Title.
[PS3525.A4152N34   1981]   813'.54   80-25751
ISBN 0-03-059043-4

First published in hardcover by Rinehart and Company in 1948.
First Owl Book Edition—1981.
Printed in the United States of America
1 3 5 7 9 10 8 6 4 2

I would like to thank William Raney, Theodore S. Amussen, and Charles Devlin for the aid and encouragement given me at various times in the writing of this novel.

To my Mother and Bea

PART ONE

Wave

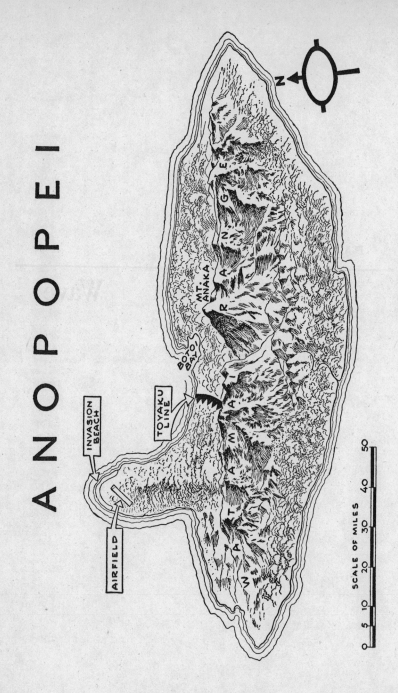

1

N OBODY COULD sleep. When morning came, assault craft would
be lowered and a first wave of troops would ride through the surf
and charge ashore on the beach at Anopopei. All over the ship, all
through the convoy, there was a knowledge that in a few hours some
of them were going to be dead.

A soldier lies flat on his bunk, closes his eyes, and remains wide-
awake. All about him, like the soughing of surf, he hears the murmurs of men dozing fitfully. "I won't do it, I won't do it," someone
cries out of a dream, and the soldier opens his eyes and gazes slowly
about the hold, his vision becoming lost in the intricate tangle of
hammocks and naked bodies and dangling equipment. He decides
he wants to go to the head, and cursing a little, he wriggles up to a
sitting position, his legs hanging over the bunk, the steel pipe of the
hammock above cutting across his hunched back. He sighs, reaches for
his shoes, which he has tied to a stanchion, and slowly puts them on.
His bunk is the fourth in a tier of five, and he climbs down uncertainly
in the half-darkness, afraid of stepping on one of the men in the
hammocks below him. On the floor he picks his way through a
tangle of bags and packs, stumbles once over a rifle, and makes his
way to the bulkhead door. He passes through another hold whose
aisle is just as cluttered, and finally reaches the head.

Inside the air is steaming. Even now a man is using the sole fresh-water shower, which has been occupied ever since the troops have come on board. The soldier walks past the crap games in the unused salt-water shower stalls, and squats down on the wet split boards of the latrine. He has forgotten his cigarettes and he bums one from a man sitting a few feet away. As he smokes he looks at the black wet floor littered with butts, and listens to the water sloshing through the latrine box. There has been really no excuse for coming, but he continues to sit on the box because it is cooler here, and the odor of the latrine, the brine, the chlorine, the clammy bland smell of wet metal is less oppressive than the heavy sweating fetor of the troop holds. The soldier remains for a long time, and then slowly he stands up, hoists his green fatigue pants, and thinks of the struggle to get back to his bunk. He knows he will lie there waiting for the dawn and he says to himself, I wish it was time already, I don't give a damn, I wish it was time already. And as he returns, he is thinking of an early morning in his childhood when he had lain awake because it was to be his birthday and his mother had promised him a party.

Early that evening Wilson and Gallagher and Staff Sergeant Croft had started a game of seven card stud with a couple of orderlies from headquarters platoon. They had grabbed the only empty place on the hold deck where it was possible to see the cards once the lights were turned off. Even then they were forced to squint, for the only bulb still lit was a blue one near the ladder, and it was difficult to tell the red suits from the black. They had been playing for hours, and by now they were in a partial stupor. If the hands were unimportant, the betting was automatic, almost unconscious.

Wilson's luck had been fair from the very beginning, but after one series in which he had taken three pots in a row it had become phenomenal. He was feeling very good. There was a stack of Australian pound notes scattered sloppily and extravagantly under his crossed legs, and while he felt it was bad luck to count his money, he knew he must have won nearly a hundred pounds. It gave him a thick lustful sensation in his throat, the kind of excitement he received from any form of abundance. "Ah tell ya," he announced to Croft in his soft southern voice, "this kind of money is gonna be the

4

ruination of me yet. Ah never will be able to figger out these god-dam pounds. The Aussies work out everythin' backwards."

Croft gave no answer. He was losing a little, but, more annoying, his hands had been drab all night.

Gallagher grunted scornfully. "What the hell! With your kind of luck you don't have to figure your money. All you need is an arm to pick it up with."

Wilson giggled. "That's right, boy, but it's gonna have to be a mighty powerful arm." He laughed again with an easy, almost childish glee and began to deal. He was a big man about thirty years old with a fine mane of golden-brown hair, and a healthy ruddy face whose large features were formed cleanly. Incongruously, he wore a pair of round silver-rimmed glasses which gave him at first glance a studious or, at least, a methodical appearance. As he dealt his fingers seemed to relish the teasing contact of the cards. He was day-dreaming about liquor, feeling rather sad because with all the money he had now, he couldn't even buy a pint. "You know," he laughed easily, "with all the goddam drinkin' Ah've done, Ah still can't remember the taste of it unless Ah got the bottle right with me." He reflected for a moment, holding an undealt card in his hand, and then chuckled. "It's just like lovin'. When a man's got it jus' as nice and steady as he wants it, well, then he never can remember what it's like without it. And when he ain't got it, they ain't nothin' harder than for him to keep in mind what a pussy feels like. They was a gal Ah had once on the end of town, wife of a friend of mine, and she had one of the meanest rolls a man could want. With all the gals Ah've had, Ah'll never forget that little old piece." He shook his head in tribute, wiped the back of his hand against his high sculptured forehead, brought it up over his golden pompadour, and chuckled mirthfully. "Man," he said softly, "it was like dipping it in a barrel of honey." He dealt two cards face down to each man, and then turned over the next round.

For once Wilson's hand was poor, and after staying a round because he was the heavy winner, he dropped out. When the campaign was over, he told himself, he was going to drum up some way of making liquor. There was a mess sergeant over in Charley Company who must have made two thousand of them pounds the way he sold a quart for five pounds. All a man needed was sugar and yeast and some of them cans of peaches or apricots. In anticipation he felt a warm mellow glow in his chest. Why, you could even make it with less. Cousin Ed, he remembered, had used molasses and raisins, and his stuff had been passing decent.

For a moment, though, Wilson was dejected. If he was going to fix himself any, he would have to steal all the makings from the mess tent some night, and he'd have to find a place to hide it for a couple of days. And then he'd need a good little nook where he could leave the mash. It couldn't be too near the bivouac or anybody might be stumbling onto it, and yet it shouldn't be too far if a man wanted to siphon off a little in a hurry.

There was just gonna be a lot of problems to it, unless he waited till the campaign was over and they were in permanent bivouac. But that was gonna take too long. It might even be three or four months. Wilson began to feel restless. There was just too much figgering a man had to do if he wanted to get anything for himself in the Army.

Gallagher had folded early in that hand too, and was looking at Wilson with resentment. It took somebody like that dumb cracker to win all the big pots. Gallagher's conscience was bothering him. He had lost thirty pounds at least, almost a hundred dollars, and, while most of it was money he had won earlier on this trip, that did not excuse him. He thought of his wife, Mary, now seven months pregnant, and tried to remember how she looked. But all he could feel was a sense of guilt. What right did he have to be throwing away money that should have been sent to her? He was feeling a deep and familiar bitterness; everything turned out lousy for him sooner or later. His mouth tightened. No matter what he tried, no matter how hard he worked, he seemed always to be caught. The bitterness became sharper, flooded him for a moment. There was something he wanted, something he could feel and it was always teasing him and disappearing. He looked at one of the orderlies, Levy, who was shuffling the cards, and Gallagher's throat worked. That Jew had been having a lot of goddam luck, and suddenly his bitterness changed into rage, constricted in his throat, and came out

6

in a passage of dull throbbing profanity. "All right, all right," he said, "how about giving the goddam cards a break. Let's stop shuffling the fuggers and start playing." He spoke with the flat ugly "a" and withered "r" of the Boston Irish, and Levy looked up at him, and mimicked, "All right, I'll give the caaads a break, and staaart playing."

"Pretty fuggin funny," Gallagher muttered half to himself. He was a short man with a bunched wiry body that gave the impression of being gnarled and sour. His face, in character with this, was small and ugly, pocked with the scars of a severe acne which had left his skin lumpy, spotted with swatches of purple-red. Perhaps it was the color of his face, or it might have been the shape of his long Irish nose, which slanted resentfully to the side, but he always looked wroth. Yet, he was only twenty-four.

The seven of hearts was showing. He looked cautiously at his two buried cards, discovered both of them were also hearts, and allowed himself a little hope. He hadn't had a flush all night, and he told himself he was due. "Even *they* can't fug me this time," he thought.

Wilson bet a pound, and Gallagher raised him. "All right, let's make this a decent pot," he growled. Croft and Levy came along, and when the other man dropped out, Gallagher felt cheated. "What's the matter?" he asked. "You going chickenshit? You're only gonna get your fuggin head blown off tomorrow." His statement was lost in the skittering of the money onto the folded blanket upon which they were playing, but it left him with a cold shuddering anxiety as though he had blasphemed. "Hail Mary, mother of . . ." he repeated quickly to himself. He saw himself lying on the beach with a bloody nub where his head should have been.

His next card fell, a spade. Would they ship his body home, he wondered, and would Mary come to his grave? The self-pity was delicious. For an instant he longed for the compassion in his wife's eyes. She understood him, he told himself, but as he tried to think of her, he saw instead a picture of '. . . Mary, mother . . .' which had remained in his memory from some postcard reproductions of religious paintings he had bought in parochial school. What did

7

Mary, *his* Mary, look like? He strained to remember, to form her face exactly in his mind. But he could not at this moment; it eluded him like the melody of a half-recalled song that kept shifting back into other, more familiar tunes.

He drew a heart on the next card. That gave him four hearts and there would be two more chances to pull the fifth heart. His anxiety eased and then was translated to a vital interest in the game. He looked about him. Levy was folding his hand even before the round of betting started, and Croft was showing a pair of tens. Croft bet two pounds, and Gallagher decided that he had the third ten. If Croft's hand didn't improve, and Gallagher was certain it wouldn't, then Croft would be playing right into his flush.

Wilson giggled a little and fumbled sloppily for his money. As he dropped it onto the blanket he said, "This yere's gonna be a mighty big pot." Gallagher fingered his few remaining bills and told himself this was the last opportunity to come back. "Raise you two," he muttered, and then felt a kind of panic. Wilson was showing three spades. Why hadn't he noticed it before? His luck!

The bet, however, was only called, and Gallagher relaxed. Wilson didn't have the flush yet. It was at least even between them, and Wilson might have no other spades in the hole; he might even be trying for something else. Gallagher hoped they both wouldn't check to him on the next round. He was going to raise until his money gave out.

Croft, Staff Sergeant Croft, was feeling another kind of excitement after the next row of cards was turned up. He had been drifting sullenly until then, but on the draw he picked up a seven, which gave him two pair. At that instant, he had a sudden and powerful conviction that he was going to win the pot. Somehow, he *knew* he was going to pull a seven or a ten for a full house. Croft didn't question it. A certainty as vivid as this one had to mean something. Usually he played poker with a hard shrewd appreciation of the odds against drawing a particular card, and an effective knowledge of the men against whom he played. But it was the margin of chance which existed in poker that made the game meaningful to him. He entered everything with as much skill and preparation as he could bring to

8

it, but he knew that things finally would hang also on his luck. This he welcomed. He had a deep unspoken belief that whatever made things happen was on his side, and now, after a long night of indifferent cards, he had a potentially powerful hand.

Gallagher had drawn another heart, and Croft figured him for a flush. Wilson's three spades had not been helped by the diamond he had drawn, but Croft guessed that he had his flush already and was playing quietly. It had always struck Croft how slyly Wilson played in contrast to his good-natured, easygoing air.

"Bet two pounds," Croft said.

Wilson threw two into the pot, and then Gallagher jumped him. "Raise you two." That made it certain Gallagher had his flush, Croft decided.

He dropped four pounds neatly on the blanket. "And raise *you* two." There was a pleasurable edge of tension in his mouth.

Wilson chuckled easily. "Goddam, this is gonna be a big pot," he told them. "Ah ought to drop out, but Ah never could git out of the habit of peekin' at that last card."

And now Croft was convinced that Wilson had a flush too. He could see that Gallagher was uncertain — one of Wilson's spades was an ace. "Raise you two," Gallagher said a little desperately. If he had the full house already, Croft told himself, he'd raise Gallagher all night, but now it would be better to save some money for the last round.

He dropped two more pounds on the pile over the blanket, and Wilson followed him. Levy dealt the last card face-down to each of them. Croft, containing his excitement, looked about the half-dark hold, gazed at the web of bunks that rose all about them, tier on tier. He watched a soldier turn over in his sleep. Then he picked up his last card. It was a five. He shuffled his cards slowly, bewildered, wholly unable to believe that he could have been so wrong. Disgusted, he threw down his hand without even checking to Wilson. He was just beginning to feel angry. Quietly, he watched them bet, saw Gallagher put down his last bill.

"Ah'm makin' an awful mistake, but Ah'll see ya," Wilson said. "What ya got, boy?"

9

Gallagher was truculent as though he knew he were going to be beaten. "What the fug do ya think I got — it's a flush in hearts, jack up."

Wilson sighed. "Ah hate to do this to ya, boy, but Ah got ya in spades with that bull." He pointed to his ace.

For several seconds Gallagher was silent, but the dark lumps on his face turned a dull purple. Then he seemed to burst all at once. "Of all the mother-fuggin luck, that sonofabitch takes it all." He sat there quivering.

A soldier in a bunk near the hatch raised himself irritably on one elbow, and shouted, "For Chrissake, Jack, how about shutting up and letting us get some sleep."

"Go fug yourself," Gallagher yelled.

"Don't you men know when to quit?"

Croft stood up. He was a lean man of medium height but he held himself so erectly he appeared tall. His narrow triangular face was utterly without expression under the blue bulb, and there seemed nothing wasted in his hard small jaw, gaunt firm cheeks and straight short nose. His thin black hair had indigo glints in it which were emphasized by the light, and his gelid eyes were very blue. "Listen, trooper," he said in a cold even voice, "you can just quit your pissing. We'll play our game any way we goddam please, and if you don't like it, I don't figure there's much you can do, unless you want to mess with four of us."

There was an indistinct muttered reply from the bunk, and Croft continued looking at him. "If you're really looking for something, you can mess with me," Croft added. His speech was quiet and clearly enunciated with a trace of a southern accent. Wilson watched him carefully.

This time the soldier who had complained made no answer at all, and Croft smiled thinly, sat down again. "You're lookin' for a fight, boy," Wilson told him.

"I didn't like the tone that boy was using," Croft said shortly

Wilson shrugged. "Well, let's get goin' again," he suggested.

"I'm quitting," Gallagher said.

Wilson felt bad. There just wasn't any fun in it he decided,

10

to take a man for all the money he had. Gallagher was most of the time a nice fellow, and it made it doubly mean when you took a buddy you'd slept in the same pup tent with for three months. "Listen, boy," he offered, "they ain't no point in bustin' up a game 'cause a man goes broke. Lemme stake you to some of them pounds."

"Nah, I'm quitting," Gallagher repeated angrily.

Wilson shrugged again. He couldn't understand these men like Croft and Gallagher who took their poker so damn hard. He liked the game, and they wasn't gonna be much of a way to pass the time now till morning, but it wasn't *that* important. A stack of money spread before you was a good feeling, but he'd rather drink. Or have a woman. He chuckled sadly. A woman was a long way off.

After a long while, Red got tired of lying in his bunk and sneaked past the guard to go up top. On deck, the air seemed chill after being so long in the hold. Red breathed it deeply, and moved about cautiously for a few seconds in the darkness until the outline of the ship formed for him. The moon was out, limning the deck-housings and equipment with a quiet silver sheen. He stared about him, aware now of the muted wash of the propellers, the slow contained roll of the ship which he had felt down below in the vibration of his bunk. He felt at once much better, for the deck was almost deserted. There was a sailor on watch at the nearest gun but in comparison to the hold this was isolation.

Red walked over to the rail and looked out to sea. The ship was hardly moving now, and all the convoy seemed to be pausing and nosing its way through the water like a hound uncertain of the scent. Far off against the horizon the ridge line of an island rose steeply, formed a mountain, and fell away again in one descending hill after another. That was Anopopei, he decided, and shrugged. What difference did it make? All islands looked the same.

Blankly, without any anticipation, he thought of the week ahead. Tomorrow, when they landed, their feet would get wet and their shoes would fill with sand. There would be one landing boat after another to be unloaded, crate after crate to be toted a few yards up the beach and dropped in a pile. If they were lucky there would be

11

no Jap artillery, and not too many snipers left. He felt a tired dread. There would be this campaign and then another and another, and there would never be an end to it. He massaged his neck, looking dourly at the water, his long thin body sagging at every joint. It was about one o'clock now. In three hours the guns would start and the men would bolt a hot nauseating breakfast.

There was nothing to do but to go from one day into the next. The platoon was lucky, for tomorrow anyway. They'd have recon working on the beach detail for a week probably, and the first patrols where all the trails were strange would be made already, and the campaign would have dropped into a familiar and bearable rut. He spat again, kneading with his blunt scarred fingers the knurled swollen knuckles of his other hand.

In silhouette against the rail, his profile consisted almost entirely of a large blob of a nose and a long low-slung jaw, but in the moonlight this was misleading for it did not show the redness of his skin and hair. His face always seemed boiled and angry except for his eyes, which were quiet, a pale blue, marooned by themselves in a web of wrinkles and freckles. When he laughed his teeth showed, big and yellow and crooked, his rough voice braying out with a contemptuous inviolate mirth. Everything about him was bony and knobbed, and although he was more than six feet tall, it was unlikely that he weighed one hundred and fifty pounds.

His hand scratched his stomach, explored about for a moment or two and then halted. He had forgotten his life belt. Automatically he thought of going back to the hold for it, and was angered at himself. "Goddam Army gets you so you're afraid to turn around." He spat. "You waste half your time trying to remember what they told you to do." Still he debated for a moment whether he should fetch it, and then grinned. "Aaah, you can only get killed once."

He had told that to Hennessey, a kid who had joined recon only a few weeks before the division's task force had loaded ship for this invasion. "A life belt, that's something for Hennessey to worry about, a life belt," he said to himself now.

They had been up on deck together one night when an air raid sounded, and they had squatted under a life raft, watching the ships

12

in convoy lashing through the black water, the crew at the nearest gun standing tensely by the breech. A Zero had attacked and a dozen searchlights had tried to focus on it. Hundreds of tracer arcs had lined red patterns through the air. It had all been very different from the combat he had previously seen, without heat, without fatigue, beautiful and unreal like a color movie or a calendar picture. He had watched in absorption, not even ducking when a bomb had exploded in a livid yellow fan over a ship a few hundred yards away.

Then Hennessey had destroyed his mood. "Jesus, I just remembered," he had said.

"What?"

"I ain't got any air cartridges in my life belt."

Red had guffawed. "I'll tell you what. When the ship goes down, you just ride a nice fat rat to shore."

"No, this is serious. Jeez, I better blow it up." And in the darkness he had fumbled for the tube, found it, and inflated the belt. Red had watched him with amusement. He was such a kid. The way they turned them out now, all the kids wanted to obey the rules. Red had felt almost sad. "You're all set for everything now, huh, Hennessey?"

"Listen," Hennessey had boasted, "I ain't taking any chances. What if this boat should get hit? I ain't going into the water unprepared."

Now, in the distance, the shore of Anopopei slid by slowly, almost like a huge ship itself. Naw, Red thought, Hennessey wouldn't go into the water unprepared. He was the kind of kid who would put away money for marriage before he even had a girl. It was what you got for following the rule book.

He drooped his body over the rail, and looked down at the water. Despite the lethargy of the ship, the wake burbled rapidly. The moon had passed behind a cloud, and the water looked dark and malevolent, terribly deep. There seemed an aureole about the ship which extended fifty yards from the side, but beyond that was only blackness, so vast, so dense, that he could no longer determine the ridge line of Anopopei. The water churned past in a thick gray foam, swirling and shuddering along the waves the ship formed in its passage. After a time Red had that feeling of sad compassion in which one seems to understand everything, all that men want and fail to get. For the first time in many years he thought of coming back from the mines in the winter twilight with his flesh a dirty wan color against the snow, entering his house, eating his food in silence while his mother waited on him sullenly. It had been an acrid empty home with everyone growing alien to one another, and in all the years that had passed, he had never remembered it except in bitterness. And yet now, looking at the water, he could have some compassion for once, could understand his mother and the brothers and sisters he had almost forgotten. He understood many things, remembered sad incidents, ugly incidents, out of the years he had knocked around, recalled a drunk who had been robbed on the steps leading up to Bowery Park near Brooklyn Bridge. It was a type of understanding which could have come to him only at this moment, culled from all his experience, the enforced restlessness of two weeks on shipboard, and the mood of this night as they moved toward the invasion beaches.

But the compassion lasted for only a few minutes. He understood it all, knew he could do nothing about it any longer, and was not even tempted. What was the use? He sighed and the acuteness of his mood slipped out with his breath. There were some things you could never fix. It was too mixed-up. A man had to get out by himself or he became like Hennessey, worrying over every gimcrack in his life.

He wanted none of it. He'd do no man harm if he could help it, and he'd take no crap. He never had, he told himself proudly.

For a long time he remained staring at the water. He had never found anything. All he knew was what he didn't like. He snorted, listening to the wind cling to the ship. All through his body he had the sense of every second sliding past, racing toward the approaching morning. This was the last time he would be alone for months, and he savored the sensation. He had always been a loner.

There wasn't anything he wanted, he told himself again. Not a buck, not a woman, not a one. Just let there be Two-bit Annie around the corner when he felt like company. There wasn't anybody else would have him anyway. He grinned and gripped the rail, feeling

14

the wind lap against his face, inhaling the swollen vegetal smells it carried from the island across the water.

"I don't care what you say," Sergeant Brown told Stanley, "you can't trust any of them." They were talking to each other in low voices from their adjoining bunks. Stanley had been careful to pick them together when they first came on board. "There isn't a woman you can trust," Brown decided.

"I don't know, that isn't the whole damn truth," Stanley muttered. "I know I trust my wife." He didn't like the way the conversation was going. It was feeding a few worms of doubt in his mind. Besides he knew Sergeant Brown didn't like anybody to disagree with him.

"Well, now," Brown said, "you're a good kid, and you're smart, but it just don't pay to trust a woman. You take my wife. She's beautiful, I've shown you her picture."

"She's really a good-looking dame," Stanley agreed quickly.

"No doubt about it, she's beautiful. You think she's gonna sit around and wait for me? No, she ain't. She's out having herself a good time."

"Well, I wouldn't say that," Stanley suggested.

"Why not? You ain't going to hurt any feelings of mine. I know what she's doing, and when I get back I'm going to have a little accounting with her. I'm going to ask her first, 'Been having any dates?' and if she says, 'Yes,' I'll get the rest out of her in two minutes. And if she says, 'No, honey, honest I haven't, you know me,' I'm just going to do a little checking with my friends and if I find she's been lying, well, then I'll have her, and, man, maybe I won't give her some lumps before I kick her out." Brown shook his head in emphasis. He was about medium size, a trifle fat, with a young boyish face, a snub nose, freckles, and reddish-brown hair. But wrinkles had formed about his eyes and there were several jungle ulcers on his chin. At a second glance, it was apparent that he was easily twenty-eight years old.

"It certainly would be a dirty deal for a guy to get when he does go back," Stanley offered.

Sergeant Brown nodded soberly, and then his face turned bitter. "What do you expect? Do you think you're going to go home a hero? Listen, when you get home folks are going to look at you and say, 'Arthur Stanley, you been gone a long time,' and you'll say, 'Yeah,' and then they'll say, 'Well, things've been pretty rough here, but I guess they're going to improve some. You're sure lucky you missed it all.' "

Stanley laughed. "I haven't seen much," he said modestly, "but I do know that those poor civilians don't begin to know the score."

"Man, but they don't," Brown said. "Listen, you've seen enough combat at Motome to have an idea. Why, when I think of my wife fooling around probably right this minute, while I'm lying here sweating out tomorrow, I begin to get mad . . . mad." He cracked his knuckles nervously, fingered the steel pipe between their hammocks. "It ain't as if tomorrow is gonna be so bad although they'll have recon working its ass off, but a little work ain't gonna kill us." He snorted. "Hell, if General Cummings was to come up to me tomorrow and say, 'Brown, I'm putting you on unloading detail for the duration,' you think I'd bitch? In the pig's hole I would. I've seen enough combat to last ten men, and I'll tell you this invasion tomorrow if we was to be shelled from the ship to the beach and back couldn't begin to equal Motome. That was one day I *knew* I was gonna be dead. I still don't see how I got through it."

"What happened?" Stanley asked. He flexed his knees carefully to avoid kicking the man in the bunk above him, only a foot above his head. This story he had heard a dozen times when he was first assigned to recon, but he knew Brown liked to tell it.

"Well, from the beginning when they assigned the platoon to Baker Company for that rubber boat deal, it was a cinch we were screwed, but what could you do?" He went on, telling a story of how they had set out in rubber boats from a destroyer several hours before the dawn, had been caught in an ebb tide and seen by the Japanese. "Man," Brown said, "maybe you think I wasn't keeping a tight asshole when those Japs started firing at us with an AA battery. There wasn't any of our boats that didn't get hit some and start sinking, and in the one next to us was the Company Commander, Billings was his

16

name I think, and the poor bastard had just broken down completely. He was crying and moaning and trying to fire off a flare so the destroyer would open up and give us some cover, but he was shaking so much he couldn't hold the flare gun in his hand.

"And in the middle of all that, Croft stands up in their rubber boat, and he says, 'Why, you ornery sonofabitch, give me that gun.' Billings gives it to him, and Croft stands up in plain sight of all those Japs on the beach, fires the gun twice, and then loads it."

Stanley shook his head in commiseration. "That Croft is quite a guy," he said.

"Quite a guy! Listen, he's made of iron. He's the one man I'd *never* cross. He's probably the best platoon sergeant in the Army and the meanest. He just doesn't have any nerves," Brown said bitterly. "Out of all the old guys in recon, there ain't one of us whose nerves ain't shot. I tell ya, I'm scared all the time, and Red is too. And Gallagher, he's only been with us six months but he was in on the rubber boat deal and he counts too I suppose, he's scared, and Martinez is the best little scout you could ever want but he's even more scared than I am, and even Wilson although he don't let on much is none too happy. But Croft — I tell you Croft loves combat, he *loves* it. There ain't a worse man you could be under or a better one, depending on how you look at it. We lost eleven guys out of seventeen in the platoon, counting the Lieutenant we had then, some of the best guys in the world and the rest of us weren't good for anything for a week, but Croft asked for a patrol the next day, and they assigned him to A Company on TDY until you and Ridges and Toglio came in as replacements and we had enough men to make up a squad."

By now, Stanley was interested in only a facet of this. "Do you think we'll get enough replacements to fill out the platoon?" he asked.

"As far as I'm concerned," Brown said, "I hope we never get the replacements. Until then, we're just an odd squad, but if we ever get up to T/O we'll still only be two squads of a lousy eight men apiece. That's the trouble with being in an I and R platoon, you're just those two undersize cavalry squads, and they send you out on missions where you really need an honest-to-God infantry platoon."

"Yeah, and we get screwed on the ratings too," Stanley said. "In any other platoon in the regiment you and Martinez would be staffs, and Croft would be a tech."

Brown grinned. "I don't know, Stanley," he said, "if we get the replacements, there's still a corporal open. You wouldn't sneeze at that, now would you?"

Despite all his efforts, Stanley felt himself reddening. "Ah, hell," he muttered, "who am I to be thinking of that?"

Brown laughed softly. "Well, it's something to think about."

Furiously, Stanley told himself that he would have to be more careful with Brown in the future.

A psychologist in a famous experiment rang a bell every time he gave food to a dog. Naturally, the dog's saliva flowed at the sight of the food.

After a time the psychologist took away the food, but continued to ring the bell. The dog kept on salivating to the sound of it. The psychologist went one step further: he took away the bell and substituted many kinds of loud noises. The saliva continued to form in the dog's mouth.

There was a soldier on the ship who was like the dog. He had been overseas for a long time, and he had seen a great deal of combat. At first the sound of a shell and the impact it made were very much connected to the fear he felt. But after many months, he had known too much terror, and by now any sudden sound would cause him panic.

All this night he had been lying in his bunk and shuddering at the sound of quick loud voices, or at a change in the throbbing of the ship's engines, or at the noise of a piece of equipment when someone kicked it along the floor. His nerves were pitched tauter than he could ever remember, and he lay sweating in his bunk, thinking with dread of the morning to come.

The soldier's name was Sergeant Julio Martinez, and he was the scout of the I and R platoon of headquarters company of the 460th Infantry Regiment.

18

2

AT 0400, a few minutes after the false dawn had lapsed, the naval bombardment of Anopopei began. All the guns of the invasion fleet went off within two seconds of each other, and the night rocked and shuddered like a great log foundering in the surf. The ships snapped and rolled from the discharge, lashing the water furiously. For one instant the night was jagged and immense, demoniac in its convulsion.

Then, after the first salvos, the firing became irregular, and the storm almost subsided into darkness again. The great clanging noises of the guns became isolated once more, sounded like immense freight trains jerking and tugging up a grade. And afterward it was possible to hear the sighing wistful murmur of shells passing overhead. On Anopopei the few scattered campfires were snubbed out.

The first shells landed in the sea, throwing up remote playful spurts of water, but then a string of them snapped along the beach, and Anopopei came to life and glowed like an ember. Here and there little fires started where the jungle met the beach, and occasionally a shell which carried too far would light up a few hundred feet of brush. The line of beach became defined and twinkled like a seaport seen from a great distance late at night.

An ammunition dump began to burn, spreading a rose-colored flush over a portion of the beach. When several shells landed in its midst, the flames sprouted fantastically high, and soared away in angry brown clouds of smoke. The shells continued to raze the beach and then began to shift inland. The firing had eased already into a steady, almost casual, pattern. A few ships at a time would discharge their volleys and then turn out to sea again while a new file attacked. The ammo dump still blazed, but most of the fires on the beach had smoldered down, and in the light which came with the first lifting of the dawn there was not nearly enough scud to hide the shore. About a mile inland, something had caught fire on the summit of a hill, and

19

back of it, far away, Mount Anaka rose out of a base of maroon-colored smoke. Implacably, despite the new purple robes at its feet, the mountain sat on the island, and gazed out to sea. The bombardment was insignificant before it.

In the troop holds the sounds were duller and more persistent; they grated and rumbled like a subway train. The hold electric lights, a wan yellow, had been turned on after breakfast, and they flickered dully, throwing many shadows over the hatches and through the tiers of bunks, lighting up the faces of the men assembled in the aisles and clustered around the ladder leading up to the top deck.

Martinez listened to the noises anxiously. He would not have been surprised if the hatch on which he was sitting had slid away from under him. He blinked his bloodshot eyes against the weary glare of the bulbs, tried to numb himself to everything. But his legs would twitch unconsciously every time a louder rumble beat against the steel bulkheads. For no apparent reason he kept repeating to himself the last line from an old joke, "I don't care if I do die, do die, do dy." Sitting there, his skin looked brown under the jaundiced light. He was a small, slim and handsome Mexican with neat wavy hair, small sharp features. His body, even now, had the poise and grace of a deer. No matter how quickly he might move the motion was always continuous and effortless. And like a deer his head was never quite still, his brown liquid eyes never completely at rest.

Above the steady droning of the guns, Martinez could hear voices separating for an instant and then being lost again. Separate babels of sound came from each platoon; the voice of a platoon leader would buzz against his ear like a passing insect, undefined and rather annoying. "Now, I don't want any of you to get lost when we hit the beach. Stick together, that's very important." He drew his knees up tighter, rolled back farther on his haunches until his hipbones grated against the tight flesh of his buttocks.

The men in recon looked small and lost in comparison to the other platoons. Croft was talking now about the landing craft embarkation, and Martinez listened dully, his attention wavering. "All right," Croft said softly, "it's gonna be the same as the last time we practiced it. They ain't a reason why anything should go wrong, and it ain't goin' to."

Red guffawed scornfully. "Yeah, we'll all be up there," he said, "but sure as hell, some dumb sonofabitch is going to run up, and tell us to get back in the hold again."

"You think I'll piss if we have to stay here for the rest of the war?" Sergeant Brown said.

"Let's cut it out," Croft told them. "If you know what's going on better than I do, *you* can stand up here and talk." He frowned and then continued. "We're on boat-deck-station twenty-eight. You all know where it is, but we're goin' up together just the same. If they's a man here suddenly discovers he's left anythin' behind, that'll be just t.s. We ain't gonna come back."

"Yeah, boys, don't forget to take your rubbers," Red suggested, and that drew a laugh. Croft looked angry for a second, but then he drawled, "I know Wilson ain't gonna forget his," and they laughed again. "You're fuggin ay," Gallagher snorted.

Wilson giggled infectiously. "Ah tell ya," he said, "Ah'd sooner leave my M-one behind, 'cause if they was to be a piece of pussy settin' up on that beach, and Ah didn't have a rubber, Ah'd just shoot myself anyway."

Martinez grinned, but their laughter irritated him. "What's the matter, Japbait?" Croft asked quietly. Their eyes met with the intimate look of old friends. "Aaah, goddam stomach, she's no good," Martinez said. He spoke clearly, but in a low and hesitant voice as if he were translating from Spanish as he went along. Croft looked again at him, and then continued talking.

Martinez gazed about the hold. The aisles between the bunks were wide and unfamiliar now that the hammocks were lashed up, and it made him vaguely uneasy. He thought they looked like the stalls in the big library in San Antonio and he remembered there was something unpleasant about it, some girl had spoken to him harshly. "I don't care if I do die, do die," went through his head. He shook himself. There was something terrible going to happen to him today. God always let you know things out of His goodness, and you had to

21

. . . to watch out, to look out for yourself. He said the last part to himself in English.

The girl was a librarian and she had thought he was trying to steal a book. He was very little then, and he had got scared and answered in Spanish, and she had scolded him. Martinez's leg twitched. She had made him cry, he could remember that. Goddam girl. Today, he could screw with her. The idea fed him with a pleasurable malice. Little-tit librarian, he would spit on her now. But the library stalls were still a troop hold, and his fear returned.

A whistle blew, startling him. "Men for boat-deck fifteen," a voice shouted down, and one of the platoons started going up the ladder. Martinez could feel the tension in everyone around him, the way their voices had become quiet. Why could they not go first? he asked himself, hating the added tension which would come from waiting. Something was going to happen to him. He knew that now.

After an hour their signal came, and they jogged up the ladder, and stood milling outside the hatchway for almost a minute before they were told to move to their boat. The decks were very slippery in the dawn, and they stumbled and cursed as they plodded along the deck. When they reached the davits which held their landing boat, they drew up in a rough file and began waiting again. Red shivered in the cold morning air. It was not yet six A.M., and the day had already the depressing quality which early mornings always had in the Army. It meant they were moving, it meant something new, something unpleasant.

All over the ship the debarkation activities were in different stages. A few landing craft were down in the water already, filled with troops and circling around the ship like puppies on a leash. The men in them waved at the ship, the flesh color of their faces unreal against the gray paint of the landing craft, the dawn blue of the sea. The calm water looked like oil. Nearer the platoon, some men were boarding a landing craft, and another one, just loaded, was beginning its descent into the water, the davit pulleys creaking from time to time. But over most of the ship men were still waiting like themselves.

22

Red's shoulders were beginning to numb under the weight of his full pack, and his rifle muzzle kept clanging against his helmet. He was feeling irritable. "No matter how many times you wear a goddam pack, you never get used to it," he said.

"Have you got it adjusted right?" Hennessey asked. His voice was stiff and quivered a little.

"Fug the adjustments," Red said. "It just makes me ache somewhere else. I ain't built for a pack, I got too many bones." He kept on talking, glancing at Hennessey every now and then to see whether he was less nervous. The air was chill, and the sun at his left was still low and quiet without any heat. He stamped his feet, breathing the curious odor of a ship's deck, oil and tar and the fish smell of the water.

"When do we get into the boats?" Hennessey asked.

The shelling was still going on over the beach, and the island looked pale green in the dawn. A thin wispy line of smoke trailed along the shore.

Red laughed. "What! Do ya think this is gonna be any different today? I figure we'll be on deck all morning." But as he spoke, he noticed a group of landing craft circling about a mile from them in the water. "The first wave's still farting around," he reassured Hennessey. For an instant he thought again of the Motome invasion, and felt a trace of that panic catching him again. His fingertips still remembered the texture of the sides of the rubber boat as he had clung to it in the water. At the back of his throat he tasted salt water again, felt the dumb whimpering terror of ducking underwater when he was exhausted and the Jap guns would not stop. He looked out again, his shaggy face quite bleak for a moment.

In the distance the jungle near the beach had assumed the naked broken look which a shelling always gave it. The palm trees would be standing like pillars now, stripped of their leaves, and blackened if there had been a fire. Off the horizon Mount Anaka was almost invisible in the haze, a pale gray-blue color almost a compromise between the hues of the water and the sky. As he watched, a big shell landed on the shore and threw up a larger puff of smoke than the two or three that had preceded it. This was going to be an

23

easy landing, Red told himself, but he was still thinking about the rubber boats. "I wish to hell they'd save some of that country for us," he said to Hennessey. "We're gonna have to live there." The morning had a raw expectant quality about it, and he drew a breath, and squatted on his heels.

Gallagher began to curse. "How fuggin long we got to wait up here?"

"Hold your water," Croft told him. "Half the commo platoon is coming with us, and they ain't even up yet."

"Well, why ain't they?" Gallagher asked. He pushed his helmet farther back on his head. "It's just like the bastards to have us wait up on deck where we can have our fuggin heads blown off."

"You hear any Jap artillery?" Croft asked.

"That don't mean they ain't got any," Gallagher said. He lit a cigarette and smoked moodily, his hand cupped over the butt as though he expected it to be snatched away from him any moment.

A shell sighed overhead, and unconsciously Martinez drew back against a gunhousing. He felt naked.

The davit machinery was complicated, and a portion of it hung over the water. When a man was harnessed into a pack and web belt and carried a rifle and two bandoliers and several grenades, a bayonet and a helmet, he felt as if he had a tourniquet over both shoulders and across his chest. It was hard to breathe and his limbs kept falling asleep. Climbing along the beam which led out to the landing craft became an adventure not unlike walking a tightrope while wearing a suit of armor.

When recon was given the signal to get into its landing boat, Sergeant Brown wet his mouth nervously. "They could've designed these better," he grumbled to Stanley as they inched out along the beam. The trick was not to look at the water. "You know, Gallagher ain't a bad guy, but he's a sorehead," Stanley was confiding.

"Yeah," Brown said abstractedly. He was thinking it would be a hell of a note if he, a noncom, were to fall in the water. My God, you'd sink, he realized. "I always hate this part," he said aloud.

He reached the lip of the landing craft, and jumped into it, the

24

weight of his pack almost spilling him, jarring his ankle. Everyone was suddenly very merry in the little boat which was swaying gently under the davits. "Here comes old Red," Wilson yelled, and everybody laughed as Red worked gingerly along the beam, his face puckered like a prune. When he reached the side he looked over scornfully at them and said, "Goddam, got the wrong boat. They ain't no one stupid-looking enough here to be recon."

"C'mon in, y'old billygoat," Wilson chuckled, his laughter easy and phlegmy, "the water's nice and cold."

Red grinned. "I know one place on you that ain't cold. Right now it's red-hot."

Brown found himself laughing and laughing. What a bunch of good old boys there were in the platoon, he told himself. It seemed as if the worst part were over already.

"How's the General get into these boats?" Hennessey asked. "He ain't young like us."

Brown giggled. "They got two privates to carry him over." He basked in the laughter which greeted this.

Gallagher dropped into the boat. "The fuggin Army," he said, "I bet they get more fuggin casualties out of guys getting into boats." Brown roared. Gallagher probably looked mad even when he was screwing his wife. For an instant he was tempted to say so, and it made him laugh even more. In the middle of his snickering he had a sudden image of his own wife in bed with another man at this exact moment, and there was a long empty second in his laughter when he felt nothing at all. "Hey, Gallagher," he said furiously, "I bet you even look pissed-off when you're with your wife."

Gallagher looked sullen, and then unexpectedly began to laugh too. "Aaah, fug you," he said, and that made everyone roar even more.

The little assault craft with their blunt bows looked like hippopotami as they bulled and snorted through the water. They were perhaps forty feet long, ten feet wide, shaped like open shoe boxes with a motor at the rear. In the troop well, the waves made a loud jarring sound beating against the bow ramp, and already an inch or

25

two of water had squeezed through the crevices and was sloshing around the bottom. Red gave up the effort to keep his feet dry. Their boat had been circling for over an hour and he was getting dizzy. Occasionally a cold fan of spray would drop on them, shocking and abrupt and a trifle painful.

The first wave of soldiers had landed about fifteen minutes ago, and the battle taking place on the beach crackled faintly in the distance like a bonfire. It seemed remote and insignificant. To relieve the monotony Red would peer over the side wall and scan the shore. It still looked untenanted from three miles out but the ornament of battle was there — a thin foggy smoke drifted along the water. Occasionally a flight of three dive bombers would buzz overhead and lance toward shore, the sound of their motors filtering back in a subdued gentle rumble. When they dove on the beach it was difficult to follow them, for they were almost invisible, appearing as flecks of pure brilliant sunlight. The puff their bombs threw up looked small and harmless and the planes would be almost out of sight when the noise of the explosions came back over the water.

Red tried to ease the weight of his pack by compressing it against the bulkhead of the boat. The constant circling was annoying. As he looked at the thirty men squeezed in with him, and saw how unnaturally green their uniforms looked against the blue-gray of the troop well, he had to breathe deeply a few times and sit motionless. Sweat was breaking out along his back.

"How long is this gonna take?" Gallagher wanted to know. "The goddam Army, hurry up and wait, hurry up and wait."

Red had started to light a cigarette, his fifth since their boat had been lowered into the water, and it tasted flat and unpleasant. "What do you think?" Red asked. "I bet we don't go in till ten." Gallagher swore. It was not yet eight o'clock.

"Listen," Red went on, "if they really knew how to work these kind of things, we woulda been eating breakfast now, and we woulda got into these crates about two hours from now." He rubbed off the tiny ash which had formed on his cigarette. "But, naw, some sonofabitchin' looey, who's sleeping right now, wanted us to get off the goddam ship so he could stop worrying about us." Purposely, he spoke

26

loud enough for the Lieutenant from the communications platoon to hear him and grinned as the officer turned his back.

Corporal Toglio, who was squatting next to Gallagher, looked at Red. "We're a lot safer out in the water," Toglio explained eagerly. "This is a pretty small target compared to a ship, and when we're moving like this it's a lot harder to hit us than you think."

Red grunted. "Balls."

"Listen," Brown said, "they ain't a time when I wouldn't rather be on that ship. I think it's a hell of a lot safer."

"I looked into this," Toglio protested. "The statistics prove you're a lot safer here than any other place during an invasion."

Red hated statistics. "Don't give me any of those figures," he told Corporal Toglio. "If you listen to them you give up taking a bath 'cause it's too dangerous."

"No, I'm serious," Toglio said. He was a heavy-set Italian of about middle height with a pear-shaped head which was broader in the jaw than the temple. Although he had shaved the night before, his beard darkened all of his face under his eyes except for his mouth, which was wide and friendly. "I'm serious," he insisted, "I saw the statistics."

"You know what you can do with them," Red said.

Toglio smiled, but he was a little annoyed. Red was a pretty good guy, he was thinking, but too independent. Where would you be if everybody was like him? You'd get nowhere. It took co-operation in everything. Something like this invasion was planned, it was efficient, down to a timetable. You couldn't run trains if the engineer took off when he felt like it.

The idea impressed him, and he pointed one of his thick powerful fingers to tell Red when suddenly a Jap shell, the first in half an hour, threw up a column of water a few hundred yards from them. The sound was unexpectedly loud, and they all winced for a moment. In the complete silence that followed, Red yelled loud enough for the whole boat to hear, "Hey, Toglio, if I had to depend on you for my safety, I'd a been in hell a year ago." The laughter was loud enough to embarrass Toglio, who forced himself to grin. Wilson capped it by saying in his high soft voice, "Toglio, you can figger out

27

more ways to make a man do something, and then it turns out all screwed up anyway. Ah never saw a man who was so particular over nothin'."

That wasn't true, Toglio said to himself. He liked to get things done right, and these fellows just didn't seem to appreciate it. Somebody like Red was always ruining your work by making everybody laugh.

The assault boat's motors grew louder suddenly, began to roar, and after completing a circle, the boat headed in toward shore. Immediately the waves began to pound against the forward ramp, and a long cascade of spray poured over the troops. There was a surprised groan and then a silence settled over the men. Croft unslung his rifle and held one finger over the muzzle to prevent any water from getting into the barrel. For an instant he felt as though he were riding a horse at a gallop. "Goddam, we're going in," someone said.

"I hope it's cleaned up at least," Brown muttered.

Croft felt superior and dejected. He had been disappointed when he had learned weeks before that recon was to be assigned to the beach detail for the first week. And he had felt a silent contempt when the men in the platoon had shown their pleasure in the news. "Chickenshit," he muttered to himself now. A man who was afraid to put his neck out on the line was no damn good. Leading the men was a responsibility he craved; he felt powerful and certain at such moments. He longed to be in the battle that was taking place inland from the beach, and he resented the decision which left the platoon on an unloading detail. He passed his hand along his gaunt hard cheek and looked silently about him.

Hennessey was standing near the stern. As Croft watched his white silent face, he decided that Hennessey was frightened and it amused him. The boy found it hard to be still; he kept bobbing about in his place, and once or twice he flinched noticeably at a sudden noise; his leg began to itch and he scratched it violently. Then, as Croft watched, Hennessey pulled his left trouser out of his legging, rolled it up to expose his knee, and with a great deal of care rubbed a little spittle over the irritated red spot on his knee. Croft gazed at the white flesh with its blond hairs, noticed the pains with which

Hennessey replaced his trouser in the legging, and felt an odd excitement as if the motions were important. That boy is too careful, Croft told himself.

And then with a passionate certainty he thought, "Hennessey's going to get killed today." He felt like laughing to release the ferment in him. This time he was sure.

But, abruptly, Croft remembered the poker game the preceding night when he had failed to draw his full house, and he was confused and then disgusted. You figure you're getting a little too smart for yourself, he thought. His disgust came because he felt he could not trust such emotions, rather than from any conviction that they had no meaning at all. He shook his head and sat back on his haunches, feeling the assault boat race in toward land, his mind empty, waiting for what events would bring.

Martinez had his worst minute just before they landed. All the agonies of the previous night, all the fears he had experienced early that morning had reached their climax in him. He dreaded the moment when the ramp would go down and he would have to get out of the boat. He felt as if a shell would swallow all of them, or a machine gun would be set up before the bow, would begin firing the moment they were exposed. None of the men was talking, and when Martinez closed his eyes, the sound of the water lashing past their craft seemed overwhelming as though he were sinking beneath it. He opened his eyes, pressed his nails desperately into his palms. "Buenos Dios," he muttered. The sweat was dripping from his brow into his eyes, and he wiped it out roughly. Why no sounds? he asked himself. And indeed there were none. The men were silent, and a hush had come over the beach; the lone machine gun rapping in the distance sounded hollow and unreal.

A plane suddenly wailed past them, then roared over the jungle firing its guns. Martinez almost screamed at the noise. He felt his legs twitching again. Why didn't they land? By now he was almost ready to welcome the disaster that would meet him when the ramp went down.

In a high piping voice, Hennessey asked, "Do you think we'll be getting mail soon?" and his question was lost in a sudden roar of laughter. Martinez laughed and laughed, subsided into weak giggles, and then began laughing again.

"That fuggin Hennessey," he heard Gallagher say.

Suddenly Martinez realized that the boat had ground to a stop. The sound of its motors had altered, had become louder and a little uncertain, as if the propeller were no longer biting the water. After a moment he understood that they had landed.

For several long seconds, they remained motionless. Then the ramp clanked down, and Martinez trudged dumbly into the surf, almost stumbling when a knee-high wave broke behind him. He walked with his head down, looking at the water, and it was only when he was on shore that he realized nothing had happened to him. He looked about. Five other craft had landed at the same time, and the men were stringing over the beach. He saw an officer coming toward him, heard him ask Croft, "What platoon is this?"

"Intelligence and reconnaissance, sir, we're on beach detail," and then the instructions to wait over by a grove of coconut trees near the beach. Martinez fell into line, and stumbled along behind Red, as the platoon walked heavily through the soft sand. He was feeling nothing at all except a conviction that his judgment had been delayed.

The platoon marched about two hundred yards and then halted at the coconut grove. It was hot already, and most of the men threw off their packs and sprawled in the sand. There had been men here before them. Units of the first wave had assembled nearby, for the flat caked sand was trodden by many feet, and there was the inevitable minor refuse of empty cigarette packs and a discarded ration or two. But now these men were inland, moving somewhere through the jungle, and there was hardly anyone in sight. They could see for a distance of about two hundred yards in either direction before the beach curved out of view, and it was all quiet, relatively empty. Around either bend there might be a great deal of activity, but they could not tell this. It was still too early for the supplies to be brought in, and all the troops that had landed with them had been quickly dispersed. Over a hundred yards away to their right, the Navy had set up a command post which consisted merely of an officer at a small folding desk, and a jeep parked in the defilade where the jungle met the beach. To their left, just around the bend an eighth of a mile away, the Task Force Headquarters was beginning to function. A few orderlies were digging foxholes for the General's staff, and two men were staggering down the beach in the opposite direction, unwinding an eighty-pound reel of telephone wire. A jeep motored by in the firm wet sand near the water's edge and disappeared beyond the Navy's CP. The landing boats which had beached near the colored pennants on the other side of Task Force Headquarters had backed off by now and were cruising out toward the invasion fleet. The water looked very blue and the ships seemed to quiver a little in the mid-morning haze. Occasionally one of the destroyers would fire a volley or two, and half a minute later the men would hear the soft whisper of the shell as it arched overhead into the jungle. Once in a while a machine gun would start racketing in the jungle, and might be answered soon after with the shrill riveting sound of a Japanese light automatic.

Sergeant Brown looked at the coconut trees which were shorn at the top from the shelling. Farther down, another grove had remained untouched, and he shook his head. Plenty of men could have lived through that bombardment, he told himself. "This ain't such a bad shelling, compared to what they did to Motome," he said.

Red looked bitter. "Yeah, Motome." He turned over on his stomach in the sand, and lit a cigarette. "The beach stinks already," he announced.

"How can it stink?" Stanley asked. "It's too early."

"It just stinks," Red answered. He didn't like Stanley, and although he had exaggerated the faint brackish odor that came from the jungle, he was ready to defend his statement. He felt an old familiar depression seeping through him; he was bored and irritable, it was too early to eat, and he had smoked too many cigarettes. "There ain't any invasion going on," he said, "this is practice. Amphibious maneuvers." He spat bitterly.

Croft hooked his cartridge belt about his waist, and slung his rifle. "I'm going to hunt for S-four," he told Brown. "You keep the men here till I get back."

"They forgot us," Red said. "We might as well go to sleep."

"That's why I'm going to get them," Croft said.

Red groaned. "Aaah, why don't you let us sit on our butts for the day?"

"Listen, Valsen," Croft said, "you can cut all the pissin' from here on."

Red looked at him warily. "What's the matter?" he asked, "you want to win the war all by yourself?" They stared tensely at each other for a few seconds, and then Croft strode off.

"You're picking the wrong boy to mess with," Sergeant Brown told him.

Red spat again. "I won't take no crap from nobody." He could feel his heart beating quickly. There were a few bodies lying in the surf about a hundred yards from them, and as Red looked a soldier from Task Force Headquarters began dragging them out of the water. A plane patrolled overhead.

"It's pretty fuggin quiet," Gallagher said.

Toglio nodded. "I'm going to dig a hole." He unstrapped his entrenching tool, and Wilson snickered. "You just better save your energy, boy," he told him.

Toglio ignored him and started digging. "I'm going to make one too," Hennessey piped, and began to work about twenty yards from Toglio. For a few seconds the scraping of their shovels against the sand was the only sound.

Oscar Ridges sighed. "Shoot," he said, "Ah might as well make one too." He guffawed with embarrassment after he spoke, and bent over his pack. His laughter had been loud and braying.

Stanley imitated him. "Waa-a-aaah!"

Ridges looked up and said mildly, "Well, shoot, Ah just cain't help the way Ah laugh. It's good enough, Ah reckon." He guffawed again to show his good will, but the laughter was much more chastened this time. When there was no answer, he began to dig. He had a short powerful body which was shaped like a squat pillar, for it tapered at neither end. His face was round and dumpy with a long slack jaw that made his mouth gape. His eyes goggled placidly to increase the impression he gave of dull-wittedness and good tem-

32

per. As he dug, his motions were aggravatingly slow; he dumped each shovelful in exactly the same place, and paused every time to look about before he bent down again. There was a certain wariness about him, as though he were accustomed to practical jokes, expected them to be played on him.

Stanley watched him impatiently. "Hey, Ridges," he said, looking at Sergeant Brown for approbation, "if you were sitting on a fire, I guess you'd be too lazy to piss and put it out."

Ridges smiled vaguely. "Reckon so," he said quietly, watching Stanley walk toward him, and stand over the hole to examine his progress. Stanley was a tall youth of average build with a long face which looked vain usually and scornful and a little uncertain. He would have been handsome if it had not been for his long nose and sparse black mustache. He was only nineteen.

"Christ, you'll be digging all day," Stanley said with disgust. His voice was artificially rough like that of an actor who fumbles for a conception of how soldiers talk.

Ridges made no answer. Patiently, he continued digging. Stanley watched him for another minute, trying to think of something clever to say. He was beginning to feel ridiculous just standing there, and on an impulse kicked some sand into Ridges's foxhole. Silently, Ridges shoveled it out, not breaking his rhythm. Stanley could feel the men in the platoon watching him. He was a little sorry he had started, for he wasn't certain whether the men sided with him. But he had gone too far to renege. He kicked in quite a bit of sand.

Ridges laid down his shovel and looked at him. His face was patient but there was some concern in it. "What you trying to do, Stanley?" he asked.

"You don't like it?" Stanley sneered.

"No, sir, Ah don't."

Stanley grinned slowly. "You know what you can do."

Red had been watching with anger. He liked Ridges. "Listen, Stanley," Red shouted, "wipe your nose and start acting like a man."

Stanley swung around and glared at Red. The whole thing had gone wrong. He was afraid of Red, but he couldn't retreat.

"Red, you can blow it out," he said.

33

"Speaking of blowing it out," Red drawled, "will you tell me why you bother cultivating that weed under your nose when it grows wild in your ass-hole?" He spoke with a heavy sarcastic brogue which had the men laughing before he even finished. "Good ol' Red," Wilson chuckled.

Stanley flushed, took a step toward Red. "You ain't going to talk to me that way."

Red was angry, eager for a fight. He knew he could whip Stanley. There was something which he was not ready to face, and he let his anger ride over it. "Boy, I could break you in half," he warned Stanley.

Brown got to his feet. "Listen, Red," he interrupted, "you weren't spoiling that damn hard to have a fight with Croft."

Red paused, and was disgusted with himself. That was it. He stood there indecisively. "No, I wasn't," he said, "but there ain't any man I won't fight." He wondered if he had been afraid of Croft. "Aaah, fug it," he said, turning away.

But Stanley realized that Red would not fight, and he walked after him. "This ain't settled for me," he said.

Red looked at him. "Go blow, will ya."

To his amazement Stanley heard himself saying, "What's the matter, you going chickenshit?" He was positive he had said too much.

"Stanley," Red told him, "I could knock your head off, but I ain't gonna fight today." His anger was returning, and he tried to force it back. "Let's cut out this crap."

Stanley watched him, and then spat in the sand. He was tempted to say something more, but he knew the victory was with him. He sat down by Brown.

Wilson turned to Gallagher and shook his head. "Ah never thought old Red would back down," he murmured.

Ridges, seeing he was unmolested, went back to his digging. He was brooding a little over the incident, but the satisfying heft of the shovel in his hand soothed him. Just a little-bitty tool, he told himself. Pa would git a laugh out of seein' somethin' like that. He became lost in his work, feeling a comfortable familiarity in the labor.

34

They ain't nothin' like work for bringin' a man round, he told himself. The hole was almost finished, and he began to tamp the bottom with his feet, setting them down heavily and evenly.

The men heard a vicious slapping sound like a fly-swatter being struck against a table. They looked around uneasily. "That's a Jap mortar," Brown muttered.

"He's very near," Martinez muttered. It was the first thing he had said since they had landed.

The men at Task Force Headquarters had dropped to the ground. Brown listened, heard an accelerating whine, and buried his face in the sand. The mortar shell exploded about a hundred and fifty yards away, and he lay motionless, listening to the clear terrifying sound of shrapnel cutting through the air, whipping the foliage in the jungle. Brown stifled a moan. The shell had landed a decent distance away, but . . . He was suffering an unreasonable panic. Whenever some combat started there was always a minute when he was completely unable to function, and did the first thing that occurred to him. Now, as the echo of the explosion damped itself in the air, he sprung excitedly to his feet. "Come on, let's get the hell out of here," he shouted.

"What about Croft?" Toglio asked.

Brown tried to think. He felt a desperate urgency to get away from this stretch of beach. An idea came to him, and he grasped it without deliberation. "Look, you got a hole, you stay here. We're gonna head down about half a mile, and when Croft comes back, you meet us there." He started gathering his equipment, dropped it suddenly, muttered, "Fug it, get it later," and began to jog down the beach. The other men looked at him in surprise, shrugged, and then Gallagher, Wilson, Red, Stanley and Martinez followed him, spread out in a long file. Hennessey watched them go, and looked over at Toglio and Ridges. He had dug his hole only a few yards away from the periphery of the coconut grove, and he tried to peer into the grove now, but it was too thick to be able to see for more than fifty feet. Toglio's foxhole on his left was about twenty yards away but it seemed much farther. Ridges, who was on the other side of Toglio, seemed a very great distance away. "What shall I do?" he whispered to Toglio.

He wished he had gone with the others, but he had been afraid to ask for fear they would laugh at him. Toglio took a look around, and then crouching, ran over to Hennessey's hole. His broad dark face was sweating now. "I think it's a very serious situation," he said dramatically, and then looked into the jungle.

"What's up?" Hennessey asked. He felt a swelling in his throat which was impossible to define as pleasant or unpleasant.

"I think some Japs sneaked a mortar in near the beach, and maybe they're going to attack us." Toglio mopped his face. "I wish the fellows had dug holes here," he said.

"It was a dirty trick to run off," Hennessey said. He was surprised to hear his voice sound natural.

"I don't know," Toglio said, "Brown's got more experience than I have. You got to trust your noncoms." He sifted some sand through his fingers. "I'm getting back in my hole. You just sit tight and wait. If any Japs come, we've got to stop them." Toglio's voice was portentous, and Hennessey nodded eagerly. This was like a movie, he thought. Vague images overlapped in his mind. He saw himself standing up and repelling a charge. "Okay, kid," Toglio said, and clapped him on the back. Crouching again, Toglio ran past his own hole to talk to Ridges. Hennessey remembered Red's telling him that Toglio had come to the platoon after the worst of the Motome campaign. He wondered if he could trust him.

Hennessey squatted in his hole and watched the jungle. His mouth was dry and he kept wetting his lips; every time there seemed to be a movement in the bushes, his heart constricted. The beach was very quiet. A minute went by, and he began to get bored. He could hear a truck grinding its gears down the beach, and when he took a chance and turned around, he could see another wave of landing craft coming in about a mile from shore. Reinforcements for us, he told himself, and realized it was absurd.

The harsh slapping sound came out of the jungle and was followed by another discharge and another and another. That's the mortars, he thought, and decided he was catching on fast. And then he heard a screaming piercing sound almost overhead like the tearing squeals of a car braking to avert a crash. Instinctively he curled flat

36

in his hole. The next instants were lost to him. He heard an awful exploding sound which seemed to fill every corner of his mind, and the earth shook and quivered underneath him in the hole. Numbly he felt dirt flying over him, and his body being pounded by some blast. The explosion came again, and the dirt and the shock, and then another and another blast. He found himself sobbing in the hole, terrified and resentful. When another mortar landed, he screamed out like a child, "That's enough, *that's enough!*" He lay there trembling for almost a minute after the shells had stopped. His thighs felt hot and wet, and at first he thought, I'm wounded. It was pleasant and peaceful, and he had a misty picture of a hospital bed. He moved his hand back, and realized with both revulsion and mirth that he had emptied his bowels.

Hennessey froze his body. If I don't move, I won't get any dirtier, he thought. He remembered Red and Wilson talking about "keeping a tight ass-hole," and now he understood what they meant. He began to get the giggles. The sides of his foxhole were crumbling, and he had a momentary pang of anxiety at the thought that they would collapse in the next shelling. He was beginning to smell himself and he felt a little sick. Should he change his pants? he wondered. There was only one other pair in his pack, and he might have to wear them for a month. If he threw these away, they might make him pay for them.

But no, that wasn't true, he told himself; you didn't have to pay for lost equipment overseas. He was beginning to get the giggles again. What a story this would make to tell Pop. He saw his father's face for a moment. A part of him was trying to needle his courage to look over the edge of his hole. He raised himself cautiously, as much from the fear of further soiling his pants as from an enemy he might see.

Toglio and Ridges were still beneath the surface of their slit-trenches. Hennessey began to suspect he had been left alone. "Toglio, Corporal Toglio," he called, but it came out in a hoarse croaking whisper. There was no answer; he didn't ask himself whether they had heard him. He was alone, all alone, he told himself, and he felt an awful dread at being so isolated. He wondered where the others were. He had never seen combat before, and it was unfair to leave him alone; Hennessey began to feel bitter at being deserted. The jungle looked dark and ominous like a sky blacking over with thunderclouds. Suddenly, he knew he couldn't stay here any longer. He got out of his hole, clutched his rifle, and started to crawl away from the hole.

"Hennessey, where you going?" Toglio shouted. His head had suddenly appeared from the hole.

Hennessey started, and then began to babble. "I'm going to get the others. It's important, I got my pants dirty." He began to laugh.

"Come back," Toglio shouted.

The boy looked at his foxhole, and knew it was impossible to return to it. The beach seemed so pure and open. "No, I got to go," he said, and began to run. He heard Toglio shout once more, and then he was conscious only of the sound of his breathing. Abruptly, he realized that something was sliding about in the pocket his pants made as they bellied over his leggings. In a little frenzy, he pulled his trouser loose, let the stool fall out, and then began to run again.

Hennessey passed by the place where the flags were up for the boats to come in, and saw the Navy officer lying prone in a little hollow near the jungle. Abruptly, he heard the mortars again, and then right after it a machine gun firing nearby. A couple of grenades exploded with the loud empty sound that paper bags make when they burst. He thought for an instant, "There's some soldiers after them Japs with the mortar." Then he heard the terrible siren of the mortar shell coming down on him. He pirouetted in a little circle, and threw himself to the ground. Perhaps he felt the explosion before a piece of shrapnel tore his brain in half.

Red found him when the platoon was coming back to meet Toglio. They had waited out the shelling in a long zigzag trench which had been dug by a company of reserve troops farther along the beach. After word had come that the Jap mortar crew had been wiped out, Brown decided to go back. Red didn't feel like talking to anybody, and unconsciously he assumed the lead. He came around a bend in the beach and saw Hennessey lying face-down in the sand with a deep rent in his helmet and a small circle of blood about his head. One of his hands was turned palm upward, and his fingers clenched as though he were trying to hold something. Red felt sick. He had liked Hennessey, but it had been the kind of fondness he had for many of the men in the platoon—it included the possibility that it might be ended like this. What bothered Red was the memory of the night they had sat on deck during the air raid when Hennessey had inflated his life belt. It gave Red a moment of awe and panic as if someone, *something*, had been watching over their shoulder that night and laughing. There was a pattern where there shouldn't be one.

Brown came up behind him, and gazed at the body with a troubled look. "Should I have left him behind?" he asked. He tried not to consider whether he were responsible.

"Who takes care of the bodies?"

"Graves Registration."

"Well, I'm going to find them so they can carry him away," Red said.

Brown scowled. "We're supposed to stick together." He stopped, and then went on angrily. "Goddam, Red, you're acting awful chicken today, picking fights and then backing out of them, throwing a fit over . . ." He looked at Hennessey and didn't finish.

Red was walking on already. For the rest of this day, that was one part of the beach he was going to keep away from. He spat, trying to exorcise the image of Hennessey's helmet, and the blood that had still been flowing through the rent in the metal.

The platoon followed him, and when they reached the place where they had left Toglio, the men began digging holes in the sand. Toglio walked around nervously, repeating continually that he had yelled for Hennessey to come back. Martinez tried to reassure him. "Okay, nothing you can do," Martinez said several times. He was digging quickly and easily in the soft sand, feeling calm for the first time that day. His terror had withered with Hennessey's death. Nothing would happen now.

When Croft came back he made no comment on the news Brown gave him. Brown was relieved and decided he did not have to blame himself. He stopped thinking about it.

But Croft brooded over the event all day. Later, as they worked on the beach unloading supplies, he caught himself thinking of it many times. His reaction was similar to the one he had felt at the moment he discovered his wife was unfaithful. At that instant, before his rage and pain had begun to operate, he had felt only a numb throbbing excitement and the knowledge that his life was changed to some degree and certain things would never be the same. He knew that again now. Hennessey's death had opened to Croft vistas of such omnipotence that he was afraid to consider it directly. All day the fact hovered about his head, tantalizing him with odd dreams and portents of power.

PART TWO

Argil and Mold

1

IN THE EARLY BRIEFINGS of his staff, Major General Edward Cummings, commander of the troops on the island, had described Anopopei by saying it was shaped like an ocarina. It was a reasonably accurate image. The body of the island, about a hundred and fifty miles long and a third as wide, was formed generally in a streamline with a high spine of mountains along its axis. On a line almost perpendicular to the main body of Anopopei, the mouthpiece, a peninsula, jutted out for twenty miles.

General Cummings's task force had landed on the tip of this peninsula, and in the first few days of the campaign had advanced almost five miles. The initial wave of assault troops had splashed out of their boats, run up the beach, and entrenched themselves at the edge of the jungle. Subsequent waves passed their position and filed through the brush along trails the Japanese had cut previously. There was little resistance the first day or two, for the majority of Japanese had been withdrawn from the beach when the Navy shelling began. The early advances were only briefly delayed by a minor ambush, or a temporary defense position set up along a ravine or across a trail. The troops pawed forward gingerly a few hundred yards at a time, sending out many patrols to examine the ground ahead before each company moved up. There was no front line for several days at least. Little groups of men filtered through the jungle, fought minor skirmishes with still smaller groups, and then moved on again.

43

Cumulatively there was a motion forward, but each individual unit moved in no particular direction at any given time. They were like a nest of ants wrestling and tugging at a handful of bread crumbs in a field of grass.

On the third day the men captured a Japanese airfield. It was a minor affair, a quarter-mile strip of cleared jungle with a small hangar recessed in the brush and a few buildings already destroyed by the Japanese, but the Pacific communiques included it, and radio announcers mentioned the victory toward the end of their news broadcasts. The airfield had been taken by two platoons who circled the jungle about it, routed the sole machine-gun squad still defending the clearing, and radioed back to Battalion Headquarters. The nightly defense positions of the General's troops had some coherence for the first time. The General established a front line a few hundred yards beyond the airstrip, and listened that evening to the Japanese artillery bombarding the field. By midmorning the next day his troops had moved forward another half mile up the peninsula, and the front had broken again into sluggish separate globules of mercury.

It seemed impossible to maintain any sort of order. Two companies might start in the morning with perfect liaison between their flanks, and by nightfall would be bivouacking a mile apart. The jungle offered far more resistance than the Japanese, and the troops tried to avoid it wherever they could, threading their way along creekbanks, forging trails through the comparatively uncluttered wilderness of natural coconut groves, and moving with pleasure through the occasional clearings of kunai grass. The Japanese in response would shell the clearings at unpredictable hours, so that the troops avoided them finally, and blundered through the uncertain avenues which thinner patches of jungle might provide.

In the first week of the campaign the jungle was easily the General's worst opponent. The division task force had been warned that the forests of Anopopei were formidable, but being told this did not make it easier. Through the densest portions, a man would lose an hour in moving a few hundred feet. In the heart of the forests great trees grew almost a hundred yards high, their lowest limbs sprouting out two hundred feet from the ground. Beneath them, filling the space, grew other trees whose shrubbery hid the giant ones from view. And in the little room left, a choked assortment of vines and ferns, wild banana trees, stunted palms, flowers, brush and shrubs squeezed against each other, raised their burdened leaves to the doubtful light that filtered through, sucking for air and food like snakes at the bottom of a pit. In the deep jungle it was always as dark as the sky before a summer thunderstorm, and no air ever stirred. Everything was damp and rife and hot as though the jungle were an immense collection of oily rags growing hotter and hotter under the dark stifling vaults of a huge warehouse. Heat licked at everything, and the foliage, responding, grew to prodigious sizes. In the depths, in the heat and the moisture, it was never silent. The birds cawed, the small animals and occasional snakes rustled and squealed, and beneath it all was a hush, almost palpable, in which could be heard the rapt absorbed sounds of vegetation growing.

No Army could live or move in it. The men skirted the jungle forests, and moved through second-growth brush, past smaller woods of coconut trees. Even here they could never see for more than fifty or a hundred feet ahead, and the early stages of the operation were conducted by groping movements of tiny groups of men. The peninsula was only a few miles wide at this point, and the General had two thousand men stretched across it, but there was little connection between them. Between one company of a hundred and eighty men and another, there was room for any number of Japanese troops to slip through. Even when the terrain was comparatively clear, the companies would not often try to set up a partial line. After a week of fumbling through the jungle, the military concept of a connected line could seem no more than a concept. There were Japanese left everywhere behind the front troops, and all through the jungle, in every part of the area that the General had captured on the peninsula there were subsidiary ambushes and skirmishes, until the mouthpiece of the ocarina seemed covered with burs. There was an intense and continuous confusion.

The General had expected this, had even made his allowances for it. Two-thirds of his force of six thousand men were kept in the rear working on supplies, and threshing the jungle in security

45

patrols. He had known from intelligence reports before the campaign began that the Japanese had at least five thousand men against him, and of these, his men had not come in contact with more than a few hundred. The Japanese commander, General Toyaku, was obviously holding them for a protracted defense. As if in assurance, the scattered air reconnaissance that was granted Cummings occasionally from Army Headquarters, brought back photos which showed a powerful defense line set up by Toyaku on a front which ran from the main mountain range of Anopopei to the sea. When Cummings came to the base of the peninsula he would have to pivot his troops through a ninety-degree arc to the left and face the defense line Toyaku had built.

For this reason, Cummings did not mind the leisureliness of his advance. Once his troops had reached the Toyaku Line it would be essential to keep them well supplied, and for that he would need a road which could keep pace with his men. On the second day after the invasion, the General had reasoned quite correctly that the main battles with the Japanese would occur miles away. He had immediately diverted a thousand men to building a road. They started on an improved trail which the Japanese had used for motor transport from the airfield to the beach, and the division engineers widened it, sodding the top surface with gravel from the beach. But beyond the airfield the trails were rudimentary, and after the first week still another thousand men were assigned to the road.

It took them three days to build each mile, and the front troops drew constantly ahead. By the end of three weeks the division task force had moved fifteen miles up the peninsula and the road reached only halfway to them. Along the rest of the route, supplies were carried up by pack trains, and almost a thousand more men were occupied with that.

The campaign progressed uneventfully from day to day, no longer being mentioned in news broadcasts. The division's casualties were light, and the front had finally achieved some form. The General watched the constant activity of men and trucks out of all the bivouacs in the jungle adjacent to the beach, and contented himself temporarily with cleaning out the Japanese who were left in the rear,

46

with building the road, and with moving his front forward at an easy and calculated rate. He knew that in a week or two, at most a month, the actual campaign would begin.

2

TO THE REPLACEMENTS, everything was new and they were miserable. They seemed to be wet all the time, and no matter how they set up their pup tents, they would always blow down during the night. They could find no way to anchor their short tent pins in the sand. When the rain started they could discover no alternative to drawing up their feet and hoping their blankets would not become drenched again. In the middle of the night they would be awakened for guard, and would stumble through the moonlight to sit numbly in a wet sandy hole, starting at every sound.

There were three hundred of them and they all felt a little pathetic. Everything was strange. Somehow they had not expected to do labor details in a combat zone, and they were bewildered by the contrast between the activity of the day when trucks and landing craft were constantly in motion and the quiet of evening when everything was so peaceful. Then it was cooler, and out across the water the sunset was usually beautiful. Men would be smoking their last cigarettes before dark or writing letters or attempting to secure their tents with a piece of driftwood. The sounds of battle were muted at night and the distant crackling of small-arms fire, the remote echoes of the artillery seemed detached from them. It was a confusing period, and most of them were pleased when they were assigned to their companies.

But Croft was not. He had been hoping against his better judgment that recon would be given the eight replacements they needed, and to his disgust they had been assigned only four. It was the culmination of a series of frustrations for him since the platoon had landed on Anopopei.

47

In the beginning, the first annoyance was that they saw no combat. The General had been forced to leave half his division behind to garrison Motome, and as a result he had brought to Anopopei only a fraction of the officers and personnel from Division Headquarters. These men were merged with the bivouac of headquarters company of the 460th Regiment, and the Combined Headquarters was established in a coconut grove on a low sandy bluff overlooking the sea.

Recon had been assigned to set it up. After working on the beach for only two days, they were diverted to the bivouac, and spent the rest of the week in clearing the brush, laying barbed wire around the perimeter, and leveling an earthen floor for the mess tents. After that, their duties had been routine. Each morning Croft had assembled the platoon and reported to work on the beach detail or the road gang. A week went by and then another without any patrols.

Croft fretted. The labor details irked him, and although he had employed the same efficiency with which he managed all the platoon's activities, he was sullen, bored with the unchanging pattern of each day. He was seeking for an outlet to his resentment and the replacements provided it. Before they were assigned, he had noticed them on the beach every day, had watched them fold their pup tents and be counted off for labor details. And like an entrepreneur considering improvements, he had been calculating what kind of patrols he could manage with a full seventeen men.

When he learned that recon had been given only four new men, he was infuriated. It brought them up to thirteen, but since the paper strength of the unit was twenty men this gave him no balm. On Motome, the headquarters squad, consisting of seven men, had been assigned permanently to the regimental intelligence section, and for all practical purposes were out of the platoon. They never went on patrols, they never shared guard or labor details, they took their orders from other noncoms, and by now he no longer knew all of them by name. On Motome the riflemen in the platoon had gone out sometimes with three or four men on a patrol which needed twice as many. And all that time there had been seven additional men in his platoon over whom he had no authority.

48

To increase his anger he discovered that a fifth man had been assigned to the platoon, but had been diverted already to headquarters squad. After evening chow, he stalked over to the orderly room tent and started an argument with the Headquarters Company Commander, Captain Mantelli.

"Listen, Cap'n, you're gonna give me that other man in headquarters squad."

Mantelli was a light-haired man with glasses, and a high-pitched merry laugh. He held his hands before his face in a mock attitude of defense as Croft burst in on him.

"Hold on, Croft," he laughed. "I ain't a goddam Jap. What the hell do you mean busting in here and tearing down this orderly room?"

"Cap'n, I been shorthanded too long, and I ain't gonna take it any more. I'm tired of taking the men out and risking their ass, when there's seven men, seven men goddammit, just sitting around in headquarters, being orderlies and to hell knows what for you officers."

Mantelli giggled. He was smoking a cigar which looked incongruous on his thin face. "Croft, suppose I was to give you those seven men? Who the hell would hand me a piece of toilet paper in the morning?"

Croft gripped the desk and glared down at him. "It's one thing to kid around, Cap'n, but I know my rights and the platoon ought to get that fifth man. All they'll use him for over at Operations 'n' Intelligence is to sharpen pencils."

Mantelli giggled again. "Sharpen pencils. *Goddam!* Croft, I don't think you got a good opinion of me." The evening air was blowing in from the beach, rustling the pyramidal tent flaps. At the moment there was no one else in the orderly room. "Listen," Mantelli went on, "I know it's a damn shame your platoon's short, but what can I do?"

"You can give me that fifth man. He's assigned to the platoon, and I'm the platoon sergeant. I want him."

Mantelli scraped his feet on the dirt floor of the tent. "What do you think happens over at Operations? Colonel Newton walks in,

49

and by God there's a piece of work ain't done, and he sorta sighs, and says, 'Things are going too slow here,' and damn if I don't hear about it. Croft, wake up, you ain't important, the only thing that counts is to have enough clerks to keep a headquarters going." He rolled his cigar tentatively in his mouth. "Now that we got the General and all his staff right in our bivouac, so you can't spit without hitting a court-martial, they need even more men out of your platoon. If you don't shut up I'll put you to cleaning typewriter ribbons."

"Cap'n, I don't care. I'm gettin' that other man if I gotta go see Major Pfeiffer, Colonel Newton, General Cummings, I don't give a damn. The platoon ain't gonna be hanging around the beach forever, and I want all the men I can get."

Mantelli groaned. "Croft, if you had your way, you'd be picking through the replacements as if you were buying horses."

"You're damn right I would, Cap'n."

"Oh, Jesus, you guys never give me a minute's rest." Mantelli leaned back and kicked the desk once or twice with his foot. Out through the tent flaps he could see the beach framed through a clump of coconut trees. Far in the distance an artillery piece fired once.

"You gonna give me that extra man?"

"Yeah . . . yeah . . . yeah." Mantelli squinted. On the sand, not a hundred yards away, the replacements were erecting their pup tents. Far off in the harbor a few Liberty ships at anchor were disappearing in the evening haze. "Yeah, I'll give him to you, the poor sonofabitch." Mantelli flipped through a few sheets of paper, ran his finger down a column of names, and underlined one of them with his nail. "His name's Roth, and his MOS is clerk. You'll probably make a hell of a rifleman out of him."

The replacements remained on the beach for another day or two. The evening after Croft had talked to Captain Mantelli, Roth walked forlornly through the replacement bivouac. The man with whom he was bunking, a big good-natured farm boy, was still over at another tent with his friends, and Roth didn't want to join them. He had gone along the previous night and, as it usually happened, he had felt left out of things. His bunkmate and his bunkmate's friends were all young, probably just out of high school, and they laughed a lot at stupid jokes and wrestled with each other and swore. He never knew what to say to them. Roth felt a familiar wistful urge for somebody he could talk to seriously. He realized again there wasn't anyone he knew well among the replacements — all the men with whom he had come overseas had been separated from him at the last replacement depot. Even then, it wasn't as if they had anything special about them. They were all stupid, Roth thought. All they could think about was getting women.

He stared gloomily at the pup tents scattered over the sand. In a day or two he would be sent up to his new platoon, and the thought gave him no joy. A rifleman now! It was such a dirty trick. At least, if they hadn't told him he was going to be a clerk. Roth shrugged. All the Army wanted you for was cannon fodder. They even made riflemen out of men like himself, fathers, with poor health. He was qualified for other things, a college graduate, familiar with office work. But try and explain it to the Army.

He passed a tent where a soldier was pounding some stakes into the sand. Roth paused, and then recognized the man. It was Goldstein, one of the soldiers who had been assigned with him to the reconnaissance platoon. "Hello," Roth said, "you're all occupied, I see."

Goldstein looked up. He was a man of about twenty-seven with very blond hair and friendly serious blue eyes. He stared intently at Roth as if he were nearsighted, his eyes bulging slightly. Then he smiled with a great deal of warmth, cocking his head forward. Because of this and the staring concentration of his eyes he gave an immediate impression of great sincerity. "I'm just fixing my tent," Goldstein said now. "I was thinking and thinking about it today, and I finally decided what the trouble was. The Army never designed tent pins to be used in sand." He smiled enthusiastically. "So I cut some branches off a bush, and I'm making stakes out of them now. I bet it'll hold up in any kind of a wind." Goldstein's speech was always earnest but a little breathless as if he were afraid of being interrupted. Except for the unexpectedly sad lines which ran from his nose to the corners of his mouth, he would have looked like a boy.

51

"That's quite an idea," Roth said. He couldn't think of anything to add, and he hesitated for a moment, and then sat down on the sand. Goldstein kept working, humming to himself. "What do you think of our assignment?" he asked.

Roth shrugged. "It's what I expected. No good." Roth was a small man with an oddly hunched back and long arms. Everything about him seemed to droop; he had a long dejected nose and pouches under his eyes; his shoulders slumped forward. His hair was clipped very short and it accentuated his large ears. "No, I don't care for our assignment," he repeated a little pompously. Altogether, Roth looked like a frail mournful ape.

"I think we were pretty lucky," Goldstein said mildly. "After all, it isn't as if we're going to see the worst kind of combat. I hear a headquarters company is pretty good, and there'll be a more intelligent type fellow in it."

Roth picked up a handful of sand and let it drop. "What's the use of kidding myself?" he said. "The way I look at it, every step in the Army turns out to be worse than you expected, and this is going to be the worst of all." His voice was deep and sepulchral; he spoke so slowly that Goldstein became a little impatient for him to finish.

"No, no, you're too pessimistic," Goldstein told him. He picked up a helmet and began to use it as a mallet on one of the stakes. "If you'll excuse me for saying so, that's no way to look at it." He pounded several times with the helmet and then whistled sadly. "Very poor steel in these," he said. "Look at the way I dented it just hitting in a stake."

Roth smiled a little contemptuously. Goldstein's animation irritated him. "Aaah, it's all very well to talk," he said, "but you never do get a break in the Army. Look at the ship we came over on. They had us packed in like sardines."

"I suppose they did the best they could," Goldstein suggested.

"The best they could? I don't think so." He paused as if to edit his woes and select the most telling ones. "Did you notice how they treated the officers? They slept in staterooms when we were jammed in the hold like pigs. It's to make them feel superior, a chosen group. That's the same device Hitler uses when he makes the Germans think they're superior." Roth felt as if he were on the edge of something profound.

Goldstein held up his hand. "But that's why *we* can't afford to have such an attitude. *We're* fighting against that." Then, as if his words had rubbed against a bruised part of his mind, he frowned angrily and added, "Aaah, I don't know, they're just a bunch of Anti-Semiten."

"Who, the Germans?"

Goldstein didn't answer right away. ". . . Yes."

"That's one approach to it," Roth said, a little pontifically. "However, I don't think it's as simple as that." He went on talking.

Goldstein did not listen. Gloom had settled over him. He had been cheerful until a moment ago, and now suddenly he was very upset. As Roth talked, Goldstein would shake his head from time to time or make a clucking sound with his tongue. This had no relation to what Roth said. Goldstein was remembering an episode which had occurred that afternoon. Several soldiers had been talking to a truck driver and he had heard their conversation. The truck driver was a big fellow with a round red face, and he had been telling the replacements which companies were good and which were not. As he meshed his gears and started to pull away he had shouted back, "Just hope you all don't get in F Company, that's where they stick the goddam Jewboys." There had been a roar of laughter, and someone had yelled after him, "If they stick me there, I'm resigning plumb out of the Army." And there had been more laughter. Goldstein flushed with anger recalling it. But more, he felt a hopelessness even in his rage, for he knew it would do him no good. He wished he had said something to the boy who had answered the truck driver, but the boy didn't matter. He was only trying to be smart, Goldstein thought. It was the truck driver. Goldstein saw again his brutal red face, and despite himself he felt fear. That *grobe jung,* that peasant, he said to himself. He felt an awful depression: that kind of face was behind all the pogroms against the Jews.

He sat down beside Roth and looked off moodily at the ocean. When Roth finished talking, Goldstein nodded his head. "Why are they like that?" he asked.

53

"Who?"

"The Anti-Semiten. Why don't they ever learn? Why does God permit it?"

Roth sneered. "God is a luxury I don't give myself."

Goldstein struck the palm of his hand with his fist. "No, I just don't understand it. How can God look down on it and permit it? We're supposed to be the chosen people." He snorted. "Chosen! Chosen for *tsoris!*"

"Personally, I'm an agnostic," Roth said.

For a time Goldstein stared at his hands, and then he smiled sadly. The lines deepened about his mouth, and he had a sarcastic indrawn look on his lips. "When the time comes," he said solemnly, "they won't ask you what kind of Jew you are."

"I think you worry too much about those things," Roth said. Why was it, he asked himself, that so many Jews were filled with all kinds of old wives' tales? His parents at least were modern, but Goldstein was like an old grandfather full of mutterings and curses, certain he would die a violent death. "The Jews worry too much about themselves," Roth said. He rubbed his long sad nose. Goldstein was an odd fellow, he told himself; he was enthusiastic about almost everything to the point of being a moron, and yet just start talking about politics or economics or about anything that was current affairs, and like all Jews he would turn the conversation to the same topic.

"If we don't worry," Goldstein said bitterly, "no one else will."

Roth was irritated. Just because he was a Jew too, they always assumed he felt the same way about things. It made him feel a little frustrated. No doubt some of his bad luck had come because he was one, but that was unfair; it wasn't as if he took an interest, it was just an accident of birth. "Well, let's stop talking about it," he said.

They sat watching the final brilliant striations of the sunset. After a time, Goldstein looked at his watch and squinted at the sun, which was almost entirely below the horizon. "It's two minutes later than last night," he told Roth, "I like to keep track of things like that."

"I had a friend once," Roth said, "who used to work at the weather bureau in New York."

54

"Did he?" Goldstein asked. "You know I always wanted to do work like that, but you need a good education for it. I understand it takes a lot of calculus."

"He did go to college," Roth admitted. He preferred a conversation like this. It was less controversial. "Yes, he went to college," Roth repeated, "but just the same he was more lucky than most of us. I'm a graduate of CCNY and it never did me any good."

"How can you say that?" Goldstein asked. "For years I wanted to be an engineer. Think of what a wonderful thing it is to be able to design anything you want." He sighed a little wistfully and then smiled. "Still I can't complain. I've been pretty lucky."

"You're better off," Roth assured him. "I never found a diploma any help in getting a job." He snorted bitterly. "Do you know I went two years without any job at all. Do you know what that's like?"

"My friend," Goldstein said, "you don't have to tell me. I've always had a job, but some of them are not worth mentioning." He smiled deprecatingly. "What's the use of complaining?" he asked. "Taken all together, we're pretty well off." He held out his hand, palm upward. "We're married and we have kids — you have a child, don't you?"

"Yes," said Roth. He drew out his wallet, and Goldstein peered through the evening light to discern the features of a handsome boy about two years old. "You've got a beautiful baby," he said, "and your wife is very . . . very pleasant looking." She was a plain woman with a pudgy face.

"I think so," Roth said. He looked at the pictures of Goldstein's wife and child, and returned the compliments automatically. Roth was feeling a gentle warmth as he thought of his son. He was remembering the way his son used to awaken him on Sunday mornings. His wife would put the baby in bed with him, and the child would straddle his stomach and pull feebly at the hairs on Roth's chest, cooing with delight. It gave him a pang of joy to think of it, and then, back of it, a realization that he had never enjoyed his child as much when he had lived with him. He had been annoyed and irritable at having his sleep disturbed, and it filled him with wonder that he could have missed so much happiness when he had been so close to it.

55

It seemed to him now that he was very near a fundamental understanding of himself, and he felt a sense of mystery and discovery as if he had found unseen gulfs and bridges in all the familiar drab terrain of his life. "You know," he said, "life is funny."

Goldstein sighed. "Yes," he answered quietly.

Roth had a flush of warmth for Goldstein. There was something very sympathetic about him, he decided. These thoughts he had were the kind of things you could tell only to a man. A woman had to be concerned with her children, and with all the smaller things. "There are lots of things you can't tell a woman," Roth said.

"I don't think so," Goldstein said eagerly. "I like to discuss things with my wife. We have a wonderful companionship. She understands so much." He paused as if to find a way to phrase his next thoughts. "I don't know, when I was a kid of about eighteen, nineteen, I used to have a different idea of women. I wanted them, you know, for sex. I remember I used to go to prostitutes, and I would be disgusted, and then after a week or so I would want to go again." He gazed at the water for a moment, and then smiled wisely. "But being married made me understand a lot about women. It's so different from the way you think of it when you're just a kid. It's . . . I don't know, it isn't so important. Women," he said solemnly, "don't like it the way we do. It doesn't mean as much to them."

Roth was tempted to ask Goldstein some questions about his wife, but he hesitated. He was relieved by what Goldstein had said. The private aches, the self-doubts he had known when he heard soldiers talking about their affairs with women were a little soothed now. "That's true," he admitted gladly. "Women just aren't interested in it." He felt very close to Goldstein as if they shared a deep knowledge. There was something very nice, very kind, about Goldstein. He would never be cruel to anybody, Roth thought.

But even more, he was certain that Goldstein liked him. "It's very nice, sitting here," Roth said in his deep hollow voice. The tents had a silver color in the moonlight and the beach glistened at the water's edge. Roth was full of many things he found difficult to utter. Goldstein was a kindred soul, a friend. Roth sighed. He supposed a Jew always had to go to a fellow Jew to find understanding.

The thought depressed him. Why should things be that way? He was a college graduate, educated, far above nearly all the men here, and what good did it do him? The only man he could find who was worth talking to sounded a little like an old Jew with a beard.

They sat there without talking for several minutes. The moon had gone behind a cloud, and the beach had become very dark and quiet. A few muted noises of speech and laughter from the other pup tents filtered through the night. Roth realized he would have to return to his tent in a few minutes, and he dreaded the prospect of being awakened for guard. He watched a soldier come walking toward them.

"I guess that's Buddy Wyman," Goldstein said. "He's a nice kid."

"Is he coming to that reconnaissance platoon with us?" Roth asked.

Goldstein nodded. "Yes. When we found out we were both going to the same place we decided to bunk together if they let us."

Roth smiled sourly. He should have known. He moved aside as Wyman crouched to come into the tent, and waited for Goldstein to introduce them. "I think I saw you when they got us all together," Roth said.

"Oh, sure, I remember you," Wyman said pleasantly. He was a tall slim youth with light hair and a bony face. He dropped on one of the blankets and yawned. "Boy, I didn't think I'd be talking that long," he apologized to Goldstein.

"That's all right," Goldstein said. "I got an idea on how to fix the tent, and I think it's going to stay up tonight." Wyman examined it, and noticed the stakes. "Hey, that's swell," he said. "I'm sorry I wasn't here to help you, Joe."

"That's okay," Goldstein said.

Roth felt as if he were no longer wanted. He stood up and stretched his body. "I guess I'll be taking off," he said. He rubbed his hand along his thin forearm.

"Stay around awhile," Goldstein said.

"No, I want to get some sleep before guard." Roth started walking back to his tent. In the darkness, his feet dragged. He was thinking that Goldstein's friendliness did not mean very much. "Just a surface part of his personality. It doesn't go deep."

Roth sighed. As he walked, his feet made soft slushing sounds through the sand.

"Sure. Listen," Polack said, "there's all kinds of ways of beating a game." He extended his long pointed jaw at Steve Minetta and grinned. "They ain't a way you can't figure out to get around something."

Minetta was only twenty, but his hair had receded far enough to give him a high forehead. He had developed a thin mustache which he trimmed carefully. Once he had been told he looked like William Powell, and he combed his hair to increase the resemblance. "Naw, I don't agree with you," he said. "Some raps you can't beat."

"What're you talkin' about?" Polack wanted to know. He twisted about in his blankets, and turned to face Minetta. "Listen," he said, "once in the butcher shop, I'm drawin' a fowl for this old biddy, and I try to get away with one of the two pieces of fat around the belly." He paused dramatically, and Minetta laughed at the grin on Polack's big lewd mobile mouth.

"Yeah, so what?" Minetta asked.

"Well, she's watching me real close, and when I start to wrap up the fowl, she says, 'Where's the other piece of fat?' I look at her and I say, 'You don't want it, lady, it's diseased. It'll ruin the taste of the whole chicken.' She shakes her head and says, 'Never mind, young man, I want it.' So what could I do, I give it to her."

"How'd you beat the game there?" Minetta wanted to know.

"Hah, before I give it to her, I cut open the bile sack on the liver. That chicken must have tasted like shit."

Minetta shrugged. The moon cast enough light into the tent for him to see Polack's face. He was grinning, and Minetta decided Polack was comical with the three teeth missing on the left side of his mouth.

Polack was perhaps twenty-one but his eyes were shrewd and bawdy, and when he laughed his skin was wizened, tough, like the

58

skin of a middle-aged man. Minetta felt a little uncomfortable with him. Secretly he was afraid to match his knowledge against Polack's.

"Stop throwing it," Minetta said. Who did Polack think he was telling the story to?

"No, it's the truth,' Polack said in a hurt voice. He always dropped the "h" when he said "think" or "the" or "truth."

"Yeah, it's da troot,' Minetta said, mimicking him.

"You havin' a good time?" Polack asked.

"I can't complain," Minetta said. "You talk like something out of a comic book." He yawned 'Anyway, one thing nobody ever beat was the Army."

"I ain't done so bad," Polack said.

"You're doing bad till the day you get out of it," Minetta told him. He clapped his hand against his forehead, and sat up. "The goddam mosquitoes," he said. He rummaged underneath his pillow, a towel wrapped about a soiled shirt, and drew out a small bottle of mosquito lotion. As he rubbed it over his face and hands he grumbled. "What a way for a guy to live." He propped himself on an elbow and lit a cigarette. He remembered he was not supposed to smoke at night, and for a moment debated with himself. "Aaah, fug it," he said aloud. Unconsciously his hand shielded the cigarette, however. He turned toward Polack and said, "Boy, I don't like to live like a pig." He pounded his pillow smooth. "Sleeping on top of your own filthy clothes, wearing dirty clothes to sleep. Nobody lives like that."

Polack shrugged. He was next to the youngest of seven brothers and sisters, and until he went to an orphanage he had always slept with a blanket spread out on the floor near a coal stove in the center of the room. When the fire died down in the middle of the night the first child to become chilled would get up and fill the stove again. "It ain't so bad wearin' dirty clothes," he told Minetta, "it keeps the bugs off ya." He had washed his own clothing since he was five years old.

"Ain't that a hell of a choice?" Minetta asked. "Smell your own stink or get carried away by the bugs." He was thinking of the clothes he used to wear. He was always known as the best dresser on the block, the first kid to pick up the new dance steps, and now he had a shirt which was two sizes too big for him. "Hey, did you hear that joke about Army clothes?" he asked. "It comes in two sizes, too large and too small."

"I heard it," Polack said.

"Aaah." Minetta remembered the way he would spend an hour in the middle of an afternoon dressing himself carefully, and combing his hair several times. It gave him pleasure to do that even when he had no place to go. "You tell me how to get out of the Army, and I'll say you can beat every game."

"There's ways," Polack said.

"Sure, you can go to heaven too, but who does?"

"There's ways," Polack repeated mysteriously again, nodding his head in the darkness. Minetta could just make out his profile, and he decided that he looked like a cartoon of Uncle Sam with his hooked broken nose and his long jaw slanting back to his receded gums.

"Well, what way?" Minetta asked.

"You ain't got the guts for it," Polack said.

"I don't see you getting out," Minetta persisted.

Polack's voice was rasping and humorous. "I like it in the Army," he said.

Minetta was becoming irritated. It was impossible ever to win an argument with Polack. "Aaah, fug you," he said.

"Yeah, fug you too."

They turned away from each other and settled down in their blankets. A mist was blowing in from the ocean, and Minetta shivered a little. He thought of the reconnaissance platoon to which they had been assigned, and wondered with a little quiver of fear if he could take combat. He started to drowse, and thought dreamily of returning to his block wearing his overseas ribbons. It would be a long time, he realized, and the fear of combat came back again. He heard a battery fire a few miles away, and pulled the blanket over his shoulder. It gave him a cozy sensation. "Hey, Polack," he said.

"Wha . . . at?" Polack was almost asleep.

Minetta forgot what it was he wanted to say, and on an impulse he asked, "You think it'll rain tonight?"

60

"Cats and dogs."

"Yeah." Minetta's eyes closed.

That same night Croft was discussing the new arrangement of the platoon with Martinez. They were squatting on the blankets inside their pup tent. "That Mantelli's a funny wop," Croft said.

Martinez shrugged. Italians were like Spanish, like Mexicans. He didn't like this kind of conversation. "Five new men," he mumbled thoughtfully. "Goddam big platoon." He smiled in the dark and clapped Croft on the back lightly. It was rare for Martinez to show any affection. After a moment he muttered, "Recon lots of fighting now, huh?"

Croft shook his head. "Damn if I know." He cleared his throat. "Listen, Japbait, they's something I want to talk about to ya. I'm gonna divide us into two squads again, and I been thinkin' I'm gonna keep most of the old men in one squad and set up the other one with you and Toglio."

Martinez fingered his delicate aquiline nose. "The old squad with Brown?"

"Yeah."

"Red, Brown's corporal?" Martinez asked.

Croft snorted. "I wouldn't pick Red on a bet. That boy can't take any orders so how the hell could he give 'em?" He picked up a stick and lashed it against his legging. "Naw, I thought of Wilson," he said, "but Wilson can't even read a map."

"Gallagher?"

"I would have liked to make Gallagher, but he just blows his top in a tight spot." Croft hesitated. "I tell you, I picked Stanley. Brown's been batting my ear about how good Stanley is. I figured he'd be the best man to work with Brown."

Martinez shrugged. "Your platoon."

Croft broke the stick in two. "I know, Stanley is the biggest goddam brown-nose in the platoon, but at least he wanted the job, which is more than you can say for Red or Wilson. If he ain't any good, I'll bust him, that's all."

Martinez nodded. "Only pick, I guess." He looked at Croft.

61

"You say I have squad with goddam men who are . . . who are *new?*"

"That's right." Croft slapped Martinez on the shoulder. He was the only man in the platoon whom Croft liked, and he felt an anxious, almost paternal care for Martinez, which was at odds with the rest of his nature. "I'll tell you, Japbait," he said roughly, "you been through more than any other man in the platoon including me. The way I figure it, I'm going to use the squad of old men for most of the patrols because they know what to do. That new squad is going to get the easy ones for quite a while. That's why I want you to have it."

Martinez paled. His face was expressionless but one of his eyes winked nervously several times. "Brown, bad nerves," Martinez said.

"The hell with Brown. Ever since the rubber boats he's been missing all the shit storms. It's his turn. You need a rest, man."

Martinez fingered his belt. "Martinez goddam good scout, okay," he said proudly. "Brown good boy, but his nerves . . . no fuggin good. I'm with old squad, okay?"

"The new one's gonna have it easier."

Martinez shook his head. "New men, no know me. No fuggin good, don't like it." He tensed himself with the effort to put his feelings into English. "Give order . . . trouble. Don't listen to me."

Croft nodded. The argument had validity. And yet he knew how frightened Martinez was. Sometimes at night Croft could hear him groaning from a nightmare. When he put his hand on Martinez's back to awaken him, Martinez would spring up like a bird startled into flight. "You really sure, Japbait?" Croft asked.

"Yes."

Japbait was a good old boy, Croft thought. There were good Mexicans and bad Mexicans, but you couldn't beat a good one. "A good man'll hold on to his job," Croft said to himself. He felt a surprising flush of warmth for Martinez. "You're a good old sonofabitch," he told him.

Martinez lit a cigarette. "Brown scared, Martinez scared, but Martinez better scout," he said softly. His left eye still quivered nervously. And as if his eyelid were transparent, it seemed to reveal his heart beating behind it in anguished sudden ambush.

62

The Time Machine:

JULIO MARTINEZ

SHOEING THE MARE

A small slim and very handsome Mexican with neat wavy hair, small sharp features. His body had the poise and grace of a deer. And like a deer his head was never quite still. His brown liquid eyes always seemed nervous and alert as if he were thinking of flight.

Little Mexican boys also breathe the American fables, also want to be heroes, aviators, lovers, financiers.

Julio Martinez, age of eight, walks the festering streets of San Antonio in 1926, stumbles over pebbles, and searches the Texas sky. Yesterday he has seen an airplane arching overhead; today, being young, he hopes to see another.

(When I am big I build fly-planes.)

Short white pants which reach the middle of his thighs. His white open shirt shows slim brown boy-arms, his hair is dark and clustered with ringlets. Cunning little Mex.

Teacher likes me, Momma likes me, big fat Momma with the smell; her arms are great and her breasts are soft; at night in the two little rooms there is the sound of Momma and Poppa, shlup-shlup, shlup-shlup, giggle in your pillow. (When I am big I build fly-planes.)

The Mexican quarter is unpaved, and little wood lean-tos sag in the heat. You can always breathe earth-powder, always smell the kerosene, the cooking grease, always sniff the mangy summer odor of spavined horses drawing carts, barefooted old men sucking at pipes.

Momma shakes him, talks in Spanish. Lazy one, get me a pepper and a pound of pinto beans. He grasps the coin, which is cold against his palm.

Momma, when I am big I fly plane.

63

You are my good smart boy (the wet pungent smack of her lips, flesh smells), now get what I have sent you for.

There are many things I will do, Momma.

She laughs. You will make money, you will own land, but now you hurry.

Little Mexican boys grow up, have hair creep like minuscule vines across their chins. When you are quiet and shy it is hard to find girls.

Ysidro is your big brother; he is twenty and slick dresser. His shoes are brown and white and his sideburns are two inches long. Julio listens to him.

I screw good stuff. Big girls. Girls with plat'num blonde. Alice Stewart, Peggy Reilly, Mary Hennessey. Protestant girls.

I screw *them* too.

Ysidro laughs. You make love to your hand. Later you will be smart. You will learn to play a woman like a guitar.

Julio makes love when he is fifteen. There is a little girl on the earth-pressed street who wears no bloomers. Ysabel Flores, dirty little girl. All the boys she makes love to.

Julio, you are sweet sweet sweet.

Under the tree behind the empty house in the dark. Julio, like the dogs, okay?

He feels the sweet sick nausea. (Protestant girls like me, I will make much money.) Ysabel, when I am big I buy you many dresses.

Her wet velveted body relaxes. She lies down on her spread-out dress, her premature breasts lolling in the summer heat. Dresses? she asks. What color will they be?

Julio Martinez is big boy now, big financier; he works in a hashhouse. Counterman. The foul rich barbecue smell, the garlic molten in the hot dogs on the griddle. Joe and Nemo, Harry and Dick, White Tower. Grease on a sizzling plate and the crumblings, the rancid fat, all to be scraped with the spatula. Martinez wears a white jacket.

64

Texans can be impatient. Hey, you boy, hurry up that chili.

Yes, sir.

Prostitutes look through him. Lots of relish, boy.

Yes, miss.

The cars flare by in the electric night, his feet ache on the concrete floor. (I will make much money.)

But there are no jobs with much money. What can a Mexican boy do in San Antone? He can be counterman in hashhouse; he can be bellhop; he can pick cotton in season; he can start store; but he cannot be a doctor, a lawyer, big merchant, chief.

He can make love.

Rosalita has a big belly; it is almost as big as the belly of her father Pedro Sanchez. You will marry my daughter, Pedro says.

Sí. But there are prettier girls than Rosalita.

It was time you were married anyway.

Sí. (Rosalita will grow fat, and children will run through the house. Shlup-shlup, shlup-shlup, giggle in your pillow. He will dig ditches on the roads.)

You are the first with her in any case.

Sí. (It was not his fault. Sheik, Ramses, Golden Trojan. Sometimes it was even two dollars out of the twenty he made in a week.)

I will talk with Señora Martinez.

Sí. If you wish.

The night is dull with woe. Rosalita is sweet but there are girls sweeter. He walks along the dirt-impacted streets. They are beginning to pave them now.

Tired? Restless? Knock up a dame? Join The Army.

Martinez is a buck private in 1937. He is still a private in thirty-nine. Nice shy Mex kid with good manners. His equipment is always spotless, and that's sufficient for the cavalry.

There are details. You weed the officers' gardens, you can be houseboy at their parties. You groom a horse after you ride it; if it is a mare you swab out its dock. The stables are hot and fermy. (I will buy you many dresses.) A soldier strikes a horse across the head.

That's the only way that dumb four-legged sonofabitch knows. The horse neighs with pain, lashes out with its feet. The soldier strikes it again. Sonofabitch kept tryin' to throw me today. Treat a horse like a nigger and it'll act up right.

Martinez steps out from his stall, is seen for the first time. Hey, Julio, the soldier says, keep your mouth shut.

The instinctive quiver. (Hey, you boy, hurry up that chili.)

The nod, the grin. I do that, Martinez says.

Fort Riley is big and green and the barracks are of red brick. The officers live in pretty little houses with gardens. Martinez is orderly for Lieutenant Bradford.

Julio, will you do a good job on my boots today?

Yes, sir.

The Lieutenant takes a drink. Want one, Martinez?

Thank you, sir.

I want you to do a real good job on the house today.

Yes, sir, I do that.

The Lieutenant winks. Don't do anything I wouldn't do.

No, sir.

The Lieutenant and his wife leave. Ah think yore the best boy we eveh had, Hooley, Mrs. Bradford says.

Thank you, ma'am.

When the draft starts Martinez makes corporal. The first time he drills a squad he is so frightened he can barely sound the commands. (Fugged if I'll take an order from a Mex.) Squad left, left by squads. To the rear, march; to the rear, march. (You men must understand your responsibility. There is nothing more difficult in the world than to be a perfect noncom. Firm and aloof, firm and aloof, those are the keywords.) COL-umn RIGHT. The shoes tamping on the red clay, the sweat drips down. Hut, hup, hip, hor, hut, hup, hip, hor. (I screw white Protestant girls, firm and aloof. I WILL BE GOOD NONCOM.)

Squad halt! PaRADE rest!

Martinez is in the cadre for General Cummings's infantry division, goes overseas as a corporal in recon.

There are discoveries. Aussie girls can be made. The streets of Sydney, the blonde girl with the freckles who holds his hand. I think you're awful cute, Joolio.

You too. The taste of Aussie beer, and the Aussie soldiers hitting him for a buck.

Yank, got a shilling or two?

Yank? Okay, he mumbles.

The blonde prostitutes to whom he makes love. Oh, what a roll you got, Joolie, what a bloody bloody roll. Gi' it to me, again.

I do that. (I screw Mrs. Lieutenant Bradford now, I screw Peggy Reilly and Alice Stewart, I will be hero.)

Martinez looks at a blade of grass. BEE-Yowww, BEE-Yoww. The whip of the bullet is lost crying in the wilderness. He crawls, slithers behind a stump. BEE-Yowwww. The grenade is heavy and dull in his palm. He lofts it into the air, hugs his head in the deep secret embrace. (Momma's arms are great and her breasts are soft.) BAAA-ROWWWWWMM.

Did ya get the sonofabitch?

Where the hell is he?

Martinez inches forward. The Jap lies on his back with his chin jerked toward heaven. The white tripe of his gut makes a flower on the field of red.

I got him.

You're a good old bastard, Martinez.

Martinez made sergeant. Little Mexican boys also breathe the American fables. If they cannot be aviators or financiers or officers they can still be heroes. No need to stumble over pebbles and search the Texas sky. Any man jack can be a hero.

Only that does not make you white Protestant, firm and aloof.

3

AN ARGUMENT was about to break in officers' mess. For the last ten minutes Lieutenant Colonel Conn had been conducting a tirade against labor unions, and Lieutenant Hearn was getting restless. It was a bad place to hold one's temper. The mess had been set up with a great deal of haste, and it was not really big enough to feed forty officers. Two squad tents had been connected, but even then it was rather cramped, not nearly roomy enough to hold six tables, twelve benches, and the equipment of the field kitchen at one end. Moreover, the campaign was too young for the food to show any real improvement over the enlisted men's mess. A few times the officers had had pie or cake, and once there had been a salad when a crate of tomatoes was purchased from a merchant ship off the peninsula, but the average meal was pretty bad. And since the officers were paying for their meals out of their food allowance, it made them a little bitter. At every course there would be a low murmur of disgust, carefully muted because the General was eating with them now at a small table set off at one end of the tent.

At midday, the annoyance was greater. The mess tent had been erected in the least prepossessing area of the bivouac, several hundred yards from the beach, without any decent shade from the coconut trees. The sun beat down and heated the inside until even the flies ambled sluggishly through the air. The officers ate in a swelter, sweat dripping from their hands and faces onto the plates before them. At Motome in the division's permanent bivouac the officers' mess had been set up in a little dell with a brook trickling over some rocks nearby, and the contrast was galling. As a result there was little conversation, and it was not exceptional for a quarrel to start. But at least in the past it had not cut across too many ranks. A captain might argue with a major, or a major with a lieutenant colonel, but no lieutenants had been correcting colonels.

Lieutenant Hearn was aware of that. He was aware of a great many things, but even a stupid man would have known that a second lieutenant, indeed the only second lieutenant in Combined Headquarters, did not go around picking fights. Besides, he knew he was resented. The other officers considered it a piece of unwarranted good fortune that he should have been assigned to the General as his aide when he had joined the outfit only toward the end of the Motome campaign.

Beyond all this, Hearn had done little to make friends. He was a big man with a shock of black hair, a heavy immobile face. His brown eyes, imperturbable, stared out coldly above the short blunted and slightly hooked arc of his nose. His wide thin mouth was unexpressive, a top ledge to the solid mass of his chin, and his voice was sharp with a thin contemptuous quality, rather surprising in so big a man. He would have denied it at times but he liked very few people, and most men sensed it uneasily after talking to him for a few minutes. He was above all the kind of man other men love to see humiliated.

It would only be common sense for him to keep his mouth shut, and yet for the last ten minutes of the meal, the sweat had dripped steadily into his food, and his shirt had become progressively damper. More and more he had been resisting the impulse to mash the contents of his plate against the face of Lieutenant Colonel Conn. For the two weeks they had been eating in this tent, he had sat with seven other lieutenants and captains at a table adjacent to the one where Conn was talking now. And for two weeks he had heard Conn talk about the stupidity of Congress (with which Hearn would agree, but for different reasons), the inferiority of the Russian and British armies, the treachery and depravity of the Negro, and the terrible fact that Jew York was in the hands of foreigners. Once the first note had been sounded, Hearn had known with a suppressed desperation exactly how the rest of the symphony would follow. Until now he had contented himself with glaring at his food and muttering "stupid ass," or else staring up with a look of concentrated disgust at the ridgepole of the tent. But there was a limit to what Hearn could bear. With his big body jammed against the table, the scalding fabric of the tent side only a few inches away from his head, there was no way he could avoid looking at the expressions of the six field officers, majors and colonels, at the next table. And their appearance never changed. They were infuriating.

69

There was Lieutenant Colonel Webber, a short fat Dutchman, with a perpetual stupid good-natured grin which he interrupted only to ladle some food into his mouth. He was in command of the engineer section of the division, reputedly a capable officer, but Hearn had never heard him say anything, had never seen him do anything except eat with ferocious and maddening relish whatever slop had been delivered to them that day out of the endless cans.

Across the table from Webber were the "twins," Major Binner, the Adjutant General, and Colonel Newton, the Regimental Commander of the 460th. They were both tall thin mournful-looking men, with prematurely gray hair, long faces, and silver-rimmed eyeglasses. They looked like preachers, and they also rarely spoke. Major Binner had given evidence one night at supper of a religious disposition; for ten minutes he had conducted a monologue with appropriate references to chapter and verse in the Bible, but this was the only thing which distinguished him to Hearn. Colonel Newton was a painfully shy man with excellent manners, a West Pointer. Rumor claimed he had never had a woman in his life — since this was in the jungle of the South Pacific, Hearn had never had an opportunity to observe the Colonel's defection at first hand. But the Colonel was beneath his manners an extremely fussy man who nagged his officers in a mild voice, and was reputed never to have had a thought which was not granted him first by the General.

These three should have been harmless; Hearn had never spoken to them, and they had done him no harm but he loathed them by now with the particular venom that a familiar and ugly piece of furniture assumes in time. They annoyed him because they were part of the same table which held Lieutenant Colonel Conn, Major Dalleson and Major Hobart.

"By God," Conn was saying now, "it's a damn shame that Congress hasn't slapped them down long ago. When it comes to *them* they pussyfoot around as if they were the Good Lord himself, but try and get an extra tank, try and get it." Conn was small, quite old, with a wrinkled face, and little eyes set a trifle vacantly under his forehead as though they did not function together. He was almost bald with a patina of gray hair above his neck and over his ears, and his nose was large, inflamed, and veined with blue filaments. He drank a great deal and held it well; the only sign was the hoarse thick authority of his voice.

Hearn sighed and poured some lukewarm water from a gray enamel pitcher into his cup. The sweat was lolling doubtfully under his chin, uncertain whether to run down his neck or drip off the edge of his jaw. Caustically, Hearn's chin smarted as he rubbed the perspiration onto the forearm of his sleeve. About him, through the tent, conversation flickered at the various tables.

"That girl had what it takes. Oh, brother, Ed'll tell you."

"But why can't we lay that net through Paragon Red Easy?"

Would the meal never end? Hearn looked up again, saw the General staring at him for an instant.

"Goddam shame," Dalleson was muttering.

"I tell you we ought to string them up, every last mother's son of them." That would be Hobart.

Hobart, Dalleson and Conn. Three variations on the same theme. Regular Army first sergeants, now field officers; they were all the same, Hearn told himself. He derived a mild amusement from picturing what would happen if he were to tell them to shut up. Hobart was easy. Hobart would gasp and then pull his rank. Dalleson would probably invite him outside. But what would Conn do? Conn was the problem. Conn was the b.s. artist from way back. If there was anything you had done, he had done it too. When he wasn't mouthing politics, he was your friend, the fatherly friend.

Hearn left him for a moment, and reconsidered Dalleson. There was only one possibility for Dalleson, and that was for him to get enraged and want to fight. He was too big to do anything else, even bigger than Hearn, and his red face, his bull neck, his broken nose, could express either mirth or rage or bewilderment, the bewilderment always a transitory thing until he realized what was demanded of him. He looked like a professional football player. Dalleson was no problem; he even had potentialities for being a good man.

Hobart was easy too; the Great American Bully. Hobart was the only one who had not been a Regular Army first sergeant, but almost as good, he had been a bank clerk or the manager of a chain store branch. With a lieutenancy in the National Guard. He was what you would expect; he never disagreed with anyone above him and never listened to his subordinates. Yet he wanted to be liked by both. He blustered and cajoled, was always the good guy for the first fifteen minutes you knew him, with the rutted gross patois of the American Legion-Rotary-Chamber of Commerce, and afterward distrusted you with the innate, insecure and blinding arrogance of his stamp. He was plump and cherubic with sullen pouting cheeks and a thin little mouth.

Hearn had never doubted these impressions for a moment. Dalleson, Conn and Hobart were always lumped together. He saw the differences, actually disliked Dalleson a little less than the others, recognized the distinctions in their features, their abilities, and yet they were equated in the sweep of his contempt. They had three things in common, and Hearn threw out all the other divergences. They were first of all red-faced, and Hearn's father, a very successful midwestern capitalist, had always been florid. Secondly, they all had tight thin little mouths, a personal prejudice of his, and third, worst of all, none of them for even an instant had ever doubted anything they had ever said or done.

Several people had at one time or another made it a point to tell Hearn that he liked men only in the abstract and never in the particular, a cliché of course, an oversimplification, but not without casual truth. He despised the six field officers at the adjacent table because no matter how much they might hate kikes, niggers, Russians, limeys, micks, they loved one another, tampered gleefully with each other's wives at home, got drunk together without worrying about dropping their guard, went joyously through their income-bracket equivalents of shooting up a whorehouse on Saturday night. By their very existence they had warped the finest minds, the most brilliant talents of Hearn's generation into something sick, more insular than the Conn-Dalleson-Hobarts. You always ended by catering to them, or burrowing fearfully into the little rathole still allowed.

And the heat by now had banked itself in the tent, was almost licking at his body. The mutter, the clatter of tinware against tinware rasped like a file against his brain. A mess orderly scurried by, putting a bowl of canned peaches on each of the tables.

72

"You take that fellow . . ." Conn mentioned a famous labor leader. "Now, I know for a fact, by God —" his red nose wagging mulishly behind his point — "that he's got a nigger woman for a mistress."

Dalleson clucked. "Jesus, think of that."

"I've heard on good authority that he's even had a couple of tan little bastards off of her, but that I ain't going to vouch for. All I can tell you is that all the time he's pushing through these bills to make the nigger a King Jesus, he's doin' it for good reason. That woman is runnin' the whole labor movement, the whole country including the President is being influenced every time she wiggles her slit."

The labial interpretation of history.

Hearn heard the sharp cold accents of his own speech coming out of his chest. "Colonel, how do you know all that?" Beneath the table his legs were weak with anger.

Conn turned to Hearn in surprise, stared at him across the six feet separating their chairs, the perspiration tatted lavishly in big droplets on his red pocked nose. He was doubtful for a moment, uncertain whether the question was friendly or not, obviously bothered by the minor breach of discipline involved. "What do you mean, how do I know, Hearn?" he asked.

Hearn paused, trying to keep it within bounds. He was aware abruptly that most of the officers in the tent were staring at them. "I don't think you know too much about it, Colonel."

"You don't, eh, you don't, huh. I know a hell of a sight more about those labor bastards than you do."

Hobart jumped in. "It's awright to go around screwing niggers and living with them." He laughed, seeking for approbation. "Perfectly all right, isn't it?"

"I don't see how you know so much about it, Colonel Conn," Hearn said again. The thing was taking the form he had dreaded. Another exchange or two and he would have his choice of crawfishing or taking his punishment.

His earlier question was answered. When Conn was caught, he only pushed it a little further. "You can shut your mouth, Hearn. If I'm saying something I know what I'm talking about."

73

And like an echo, Dalleson getting in: "We know you're pretty goddam smart, Hearn." An approving titter flickered through the tent. They all did dislike him then, Hearn realized. He had known it and yet there was the trace of a pang. The Lieutenant beside him was sitting stiff, tensed, his elbow removed a careful inch from Hearn's.

He had pushed himself into this position, and the only thing to do was to carry it off. Alloyed with the outraged beating of his heart was fear and a detached, almost mild concern with what would happen to him. A court-martial perhaps?

As he spoke he felt a pride in the precision of his voice. "I was thinking, Colonel, that since you do know so much about it, you must have found out peeking through keyholes."

A few startled laughs answered him and Conn's face expanded with rage. The red of his nose extended slowly out to his cheeks, his forehead, the blue veins startling now, a cluster of purple roots which held his choler. He was obviously searching for speech like a player who has dropped a ball and runs in frantic circles trying to locate it. When he spoke it would be terrible. Even Webber had stopped eating.

"Gentlemen, *please!*"

It was the General calling across the length of the tent. "I won't have any more of this."

It silenced them all, cast a hush through the tent in which even the clacking of the tableware was muted, and then the reaction set in with a chorus of whispers and small exclamations, an uncomfortable self-conscious return to the food before them. Hearn was furious with himself, disgusted by the relief he had felt when the General intervened.

Father dependence.

Beneath the surface of his thoughts he had known, he realized now, that the General would protect him, and an old confused emotion caught him again, resentment and yet something else, something not so genuine.

Conn, Dalleson and Hobart were glaring at him, a trio of ferocious marionettes. He brought his spoon up, champed at the remote sweet pulp of the canned peach which mingled so imperfectly with the nervous bile in his throat, the hot sour turmoil of his stomach.

74

After a moment he clanked the spoon down, and sat staring at the table. Conn and Dalleson were talking self-consciously now like people who know they are being listened to by strangers on a bus or train. He heard a fragment or two, something about their work for the afternoon.

At least Conn would be having indigestion too.

The General stood up quietly, and walked out of the tent. It gave permission for the rest of them to leave. Conn's eyes met Hearn's for a moment and they both looked away in embarrassment. After a minute or so, Hearn slid off the bench, and strolled outside. His clothing was completely wet, the air caressing against it like cool water.

He lit a cigarette and strolled irritably through the bivouac, halting when he reached the barbed wire, and then pacing back underneath the coconut trees, staring morosely at the scattered clusters of dark-green pup tents. When he had completed the circuit, he clambered down the bluff that led to the beach, and walked along through the sand, kicking abstractedly at pieces of discarded equipment still left from invasion day. A few trucks motored by, and a detail of men shuffled in file through the sand carrying shovels against their shoulders. Out in the water a few freighters were anchored, yawing lazily in the midday heat. Over to his left a landing craft was approaching a supply dump.

Hearn finished the cigarette and nodded curtly to an officer passing by. The nod was returned, but after a doubtful pause. He was going to be in for it now, there was no getting away from that. Conn was a bloody fool, but he had been a bigger ass. It was the old pattern; when he could take something no longer he flared up, but that was weakness in itself. And yet he could not bear this continual paradox in which he and the other officers lived. It had been different in the States; the messes were separate, the living quarters were separate, and if you made a mistake it didn't count. But out here, they slept in cots a few feet away from men who slept on the ground; they were served meals, bad enough in themselves, but nevertheless served on plates while the others ate on their haunches after standing in line in the sun. It was even more than that; ten miles away men were being killed, and that had different moral demands than when men were killed

75

three thousand miles away. No matter how many times he might walk through the bivouac area, the feeling was there. The ugly green of the jungle beginning just a few yards beyond the barbed wire, the delicate traceries of the coconut trees against the sky, the sick yellow pulpy look of everything; all of them combined to feed his disgust. He trudged up the bluff again, and stood looking about the area at the scattered array of big tents and little ones, at the trucks and jeeps clustered together in the motor pool, the file of soldiers in green sloppy fatigues still filing through for chow. Men had had time to clear the ground of the worst bushes and roots, to establish a few grudged yards out of the appalling rifeness of the terrain. But up ahead, bedded down in the jungle, the front-line troops could not clear it away because they did not halt more than a day or two, and it would be dangerous to expose themselves. They slept with mud and insects and worms while the officers bitched because there were no paper napkins and the chow could stand improvement.

There was a kind of guilt in being an officer. They had all felt it in the beginning; out of OCS the privileges had been uncomfortable at first, but it was a convenient thing to forget, and there were always the good textbook reasons, good enough to convince yourself if you wanted to be quit of it. Only a few of them still kicked the idea of guilt around in their heads.

The guilt of birth perhaps.

There was such a thing in the Army. It was subtle, there were so many exceptions that it could be called no more than a trend, and yet it was there. He, himself: rich father, rich college, good jobs, no hardship which he had not assumed himself; he fulfilled it, and many of his friends did too. It was not true so much for the ones he had known at college. They were 4-F, or enlisted men, or majors in the Air Corps, or top-secret work in Washington or even in CO camps, but all the men he had known in prep school were now ensigns or lieutenants. A class of men born to wealth, accustomed to obedience . . . but that made it incorrect already. It wasn't obedience, it was the kind of assurance that he had, or Conn had, or Hobart, or his father, or even the General.

The General. A trace of his resentment returned again. If not for the General he would be doing now what he should have done. An officer had some excuse only if he were in combat. As long as he remained here he would be dissatisfied with himself, contemptuous of the other officers, even more contemptuous than was normal for him. There was nothing in this headquarters, and yet everything, an odd satisfaction over and above the routine annoyances. Working with the General had its unique compensations.

Once again, resentment, and the other thing, awe perhaps. Hearn had never known anyone quite like the General, and he was partially convinced the General was a great man. It was not only his unquestioned brilliance; Hearn had known people whose minds were equal to General Cummings's. It was certainly not his intellect, which was amazingly spotty, marred by great gaps. What the General had was an almost unique ability to extend his thoughts into immediate and effective action, and this was an aptitude which might not be apparent for months even when one was working with him.

There were many contradictions in the General. He had essentially, Hearn believed, a complete indifference to the comforts of his own person, and yet he lived with at least the luxuries which were requisite for a general officer. On invasion day, after the General landed on the beach, he had been on a phone almost all day long, composing his battle tactics off the cuff, as it were, and for five, six, eight hours he had directed the opening phases of the campaign without taking a halt, indeed without referring once to a map, or pausing for a decision after his line officers had given him what information they possessed. It had been a remarkable performance. His concentration had been almost fantastic.

Once in the late afternoon of that first day, Hobart had come up to the General and asked, "Sir, where do you want to set up headquarters bivouac?"

And Cummings had snarled, "Anywhere, man, anywhere," in shocking contrast to the perfect manners with which he usually spoke to his officers. For that instant the façade had been peeled back, and a naked animal closeted with its bone had been exposed. It had drawn a left-handed admiration from Hearn; he would not have been surprised if the General had slept on a bed of spikes.

But two days later, when the first urgency of the campaign was over, the General had had his tent location moved twice, and had reprimanded Hobart gently for not having picked a more level site. There was really no end to the contradictions in him. His reputation in the South Pacific was established; before Hearn had come to the division he had heard nothing but praise for his techniques, a sizable tribute for those rear areas where gossip was the best diversion. Yet the General never believed this. Once or twice when their conversation had become very intimate, Cummings had muttered to him, "I have enemies, Robert, powerful enemies." The self-pity in his voice had been disgustingly apparent and quite in contrast to the clear cold sense with which he usually estimated men and events. He had been advertised in advance as the most sympathetic and genial officer in a division command, his charm was well known, but Hearn had discovered quite early that he was a tyrant, a tyrant with a velvet voice, it is true, but undeniably a tyrant.

He was also a frightful snob. Hearn, recognizing himself as a snob, could be sympathetic, although his own snobbery was of a different order; Hearn always classified people even if it took him five hundred types to achieve any kind of inclusiveness. The General's snobbery was of a simpler order. He knew every weakness and every vice of his staff officers, and yet a colonel was superior to a major regardless of their abilities. It made his friendship with Hearn even more inexplicable. The General had selected him as his aide after a half-hour interview when Hearn had come to the division, and slowly, progressively, the General had confided in him. That in itself was understandable; like all men of great vanity, the General was looking for an intellectual equal, or at least the facsimile of an intellectual equal to whom he could expound his nonmilitary theories, and Hearn was the only man on his staff who had the intellect to understand him. But today, just a half hour ago, the General had fished him out of what was about to explode into a dangerous situation. In the two weeks since they had landed he had been in the General's tent talking with him almost every night, and that sort of thing would get around very quickly in the tiny confines of this bivouac. The General had to be aware of it, had to know the resentments this would induce, the danger to morale. Yet against his self-interest, his prejudices, the General held on to him still and, even more, exerted himself in unfolding the undeniable fascination of his personality.

Hearn knew that if it were not for the General he would have asked for a transfer long before the division had come to Anopopei. There was the knowledge of his position as a servant, the unpleasant contrasts always so apparent to him between the enlisted men and the officers. There was most of all the disgust for the staff officers he concealed so unsuccessfully. It was the riddle of what made the General tick that kept Hearn on. After twenty-eight years the only thing that interested him vitally was to uncover the least concealed quirks of any man or woman who diverted him. He had said once, "When I find the shoddy motive in them I'm bored. Then the only catch is how to say good-bye." And in return he had been told, "Hearn, you're so goddam healthy, you're nothing but a shell."

True, probably.

In any case it was not easy to find the shoddy motive in the General. He owned, no doubt, most of the dirty little itches, the lusts for things which were unacceptable to the mores of the weekly slick-paper magazines, but that did not discount him. There was a talent, an added factor, a deeper lust than Hearn had run across before, and, more than that, Hearn was losing his objectivity. The General worked on him even more than he affected the General, and Hearn loathed the very idea. To lose his inviolate freedom was to become involved again in all the wants and sores that caught up everybody about him.

But even so there was a wry isolated attention with which he watched the process unfolding between them.

He saw the General about an hour later in his tent. Cummings was alone for the moment, studying some air operations reports. Hearn understood immediately. After the first two or three days of the campaign, when no Japanese air attacks had developed on Anopopei, it had been decided at higher levels to remove the squadron of fighter planes that had been assigned to the campaign and had operated from another island over a hundred miles away. They had not been of great use but the General had been hoping that when the airfield he had captured was enlarged for the Air Corps, he could use that air support against the Toyaku Line. It had enraged him when the airplanes had been shunted to another campaign, and that had been the time when he had made his remark about enemies.

He was studying the theater air operations reports now to find out if any aircraft were being used needlessly. In another man it would have been absurd, a self-pitying castigation, but with the General it was not. He would absorb every fact in the report, probe the weaknesses, and when the time came and the captured airfield was ready, he would have a strong series of arguments, documented by the reports he studied now.

Without turning around, the General said over his shoulder, "You did a damn fool thing today."

"I suppose so." Hearn sat down.

The General moved his chair about slightly, and looked thoughtfully at Hearn. "You were depending on me to bring you out of it." He smiled as he said this, and his voice had become artificial, slightly affected. The General had many different types of speech; when he spoke to enlisted men he swore slightly, made his voice a little less precise. With his officers he was always dignified and remote, his sentences always rigidly constructed. Hearn was the only man to whom he spoke directly, and whenever he did not, whenever the down-to-junior-officer-level affectation slipped in, it meant that he was very displeased. Hearn had once known a man who stuttered whenever he was telling a lie; this on a more subtle level was as effective a clue. The General was obviously furious that he had had to come to Hearn's support in such a way that headquarters would talk about it for days.

"I guess I did, sir; I realized that afterward."

"Will you tell me why you behaved like such an ass, Robert?" Still the affectation. It was almost effeminate. The General had given Hearn when he first met him an immediate impression of very rarely saying what he thought, and Hearn had never had occasion to change his mind. He had known men who were casually like him, the same trace of effeminacy, the same probable capacity for extreme ruthlessness, but there was more here, more complexity, less of a congealed and overt personality to perceive comfortably. The General at first

80

glance did not look unlike other general officers. He was a little over medium height, well fleshed, with a rather handsome sun-tanned face and graying hair, but there were differences. His expression when he smiled was very close to the ruddy, complacent and hard appearance of any number of American senators and businessmen, but the tough good-guy aura never quite remained. There was a certain vacancy in his face, like the vacancy of actors who play American congressmen. There was the appearance and yet it was not there. Hearn always felt as if the smiling face were numb.

And his eyes gave him away. They were large and gray, and baleful, like glass on fire. On Motome there had been an inspection before the troops boarded ship, and Hearn had walked through the ranks behind the General. The men trembled before Cummings, stammered out their replies in hoarse self-conscious voices. Three-quarters of it, of course, came from talking to a general, but Cummings had been so genial, had attempted so fully to put them at their ease, and it had not worked at all. Those great eyes with the pale-gray irises had seemed almost blank, two ovals of shocking white. Hearn remembered a newspaper article which had described the General as having the features of a genteel intelligent bulldog, and the article had added a little lushly, "in his manner are combined effectively the force, the tenacity, the staying power of that doughty animal with all the intellect and charm and poise of a college professor or a statesman." It was no more accurate than a newspaper story ever was, but it underlined a favorite theory about the General which Hearn had. For that reporter he had been The Professor, as he had been The General, The Statesman, The Philosopher, to any number of different men. Each of those poses had been a baffling mixture of the genuine and the sham, as if the General instinctively assumed the one which pleased him at the moment, but beyond that was driven on, was handed a personality garment by the unique urges that drove him.

Hearn leaned back in his chair. "All right, I suppose I was an ass. So what? There's a kind of pleasure in telling somebody like Conn where to shove it."

"It was a completely pointless thing to do. I suppose you considered it some kind of indignity to have to listen to him."

"All right, I did."

"You're being very young about it. The rights you have as a person depend completely upon my whim. Just stop and think about that. Without me you're just a second lieutenant, which I suppose is the operative definition of a man who has no soul of his own. You weren't telling him *to shove it*" — the General's distasteful pronunciation of "shove it" italicized the phrase — "*I* was, in effect, telling him, and I had no wish to do so at the time. Suppose you stand up now while you're talking to me. You might as well start at first principles. I'm damned if I'm going to have people walking by and seeing you sit here as if this division were a partnership between you and me."

Hearn stood up, conscious of a sullen boyish resentment in himself. "Very well," he said sarcastically.

The General grinned at him suddenly with some mockery.

"I've heard the kind of filth Conn purveys for a good many more months than you have. It's boring, Robert, because it's pointless. I'm a little disappointed that you reacted on such a *primal* level." His voice flecked delicately against Hearn's mounting annoyance. "I've known men who've used filth until it became a high art. Statesmen, politicos, they did it for a purpose, and their flesh probably crawled. You can indulge your righteous rage but the things it comes out of are pretty cheap. The trick is to make yourself an instrument of your own policy. Whether you like it or not, that's the highest effectiveness man has achieved."

Perhaps. This was something Hearn was beginning to believe. But instead he muttered, "My range isn't as long as yours, General. I just don't like to be elbowed."

Cummings stared at him blankly. "There's another approach to it, you know. I don't disagree with Conn. There's a hard kernel of truth in many of the things he says. As for example, 'All Jews are noisy.' " Cummings shrugged. "They're not all noisy, of course, but there's an undue proportion of coarseness in that race, admit it."

"If there is, you have to understand it," Hearn murmured. "They're under different tensions."

"A piece of typical liberal claptrap. The fact is, you don't like them either."

82

Hearn was uneasy. There were . . . traces of distaste he could detect in himself. "I'll deny that."

Cummings grinned again. "Or take Conn's view of 'niggers.' A little extravagant perhaps, but he's more nearly right than you suspect. If anyone is going to sleep with a Negress . . ."

"A Southerner will," Hearn said.

"Or a radical. It's a defense mechanism with them, bolsters their *morale*." Cummings showed his teeth. "For example, perhaps you have?"

"Perhaps."

Cummings stared at his fingernails. Was it disgust? Abruptly he laughed with sarcastic glee. "You know, Robert, you're a liberal."

"Balls."

He said this with a tense rapt compulsion as if he were impelled to see how far he could rock the boulder, especially when it had pinched his toes just a moment before. This was by far the greatest liberty he had ever taken with the General. And even more, the most irritating liberty. Profanity or vulgarity always seemed to scrape the General's spine.

The General's eyes closed as if he were contemplating the damage wreaked inside himself. When he opened them, he spoke in a low mild voice. "Attention." He stared at Hearn dourly for a moment, and then said, "Suppose you salute me." When Hearn had complied, the General smiled slightly, distastefully. "Pretty crude treatment, isn't it, Robert? All right, at ease."

The bastard! And yet with it, there was an angry reluctant admiration. The General treated him as an equal . . . almost always, and then at the proper moment jerked him again from the end of a string, established the fundamental relationship of general to lieutenant with an abrupt startling shock like the slap of a wet towel. And afterward always his voice like a treacherous unguent which smarted instead of salving the pain. "Wasn't very fair of me, was it, Robert?"

"No, sir."

"You've seen too many movies. If you're holding a gun and you shoot a defenseless man, then you're a poor creature, a *dastardly person*. That's a perfectly ridiculous idea, you realize. The fact that you're

83

holding the gun and the other man is not is no accident. It's a product of everything you've achieved, it assumes that if you're . . . you're aware enough, you have the gun when you need it."

"I've heard that idea before." Hearn moved his foot slowly.

"Are we going into that attention business again?" The General chuckled. "Robert, there's a stubbornness in you which is disappointing to me. I had some hopes for you."

"I'm just a bounder."

"That's the thing. You are. You're a . . . all right, you're a reactionary just like me. It's the biggest fault I've found with you. You're afraid of that word. You've cast off everything of your heritage, and then you've cast off everything you've learned since then, and the process hasn't broken you. That's what impressed me first about you. Young man around town who hasn't been broken, who hasn't gone sick. Do you realize that's an achievement?"

"What do you know about young men around town . . . sir?"

The General lit a cigarette. "I know *everything*. That's such a fatuous statement that people immediately disbelieve you, but this time it happens to be true." His mouth moved into the good-guy grin. "The only trouble is, one thing remains with you. Somewhere you picked it up so hard that you can't shake the idea 'liberal' means good and 'reactionary' means evil. That's your frame of reference, two words. That's why you don't know a damn thing."

Hearn scuffled his feet. "Suppose I sit down?"

"Certainly." The General looked at him and then murmured in a completely toneless voice, "You're not annoyed, are you, Robert?"

"No, not any more." With a belated insight he understood suddenly that the General had been riding a great many emotions when he ordered him to stand up. It was so difficult ever to be certain what went on in the General's head. Through their whole conversation Hearn had been on the defensive, weighing his speech, talking with no freedom at all. And abruptly he realized that this had been true for the General also.

"You've got a great future as a reactionary," the General said. "The trouble is we've never had any thinkers on my side. I'm a phenomenon and I get lonely at times."

84

There was always that indefinable tension between them, Hearn thought. Their speech was forced to the surface through a thick resistant medium like oil.

"You're a fool if you don't realize this is going to be the reactionary's century, perhaps their thousand-year reign. It's the one thing Hitler said which wasn't completely hysterical." Outside the partially opened flap of the tent, the bivouac sprawled out before them, rank and cluttered, the raw cleared earth glinting in the early afternoon sun. It was almost deserted now, the enlisted men out on labor details.

The General had created that tension but he was involved in it too. He held on to Hearn for what . . . for what reason? Hearn didn't know. And he couldn't escape the peculiar magnetism of the General, a magnetism derived from all the connotations of the General's power. He had known men who thought like the General; he had even known one or two who were far more profound. But the difference was that they did nothing or the results of their actions were lost to them, and they functioned in the busy complex mangle, the choked vacuum of American life. The General might even have been silly if it were not for the fact that here on this island he controlled everything. It gave a base to whatever he said. And as long as Hearn remained with him, he could see the whole process from the inception of the thought to the tangible and immediate results the next day, the next month. That kind of knowledge was the hardest to obtain, the most concealed in everything Hearn had done in the past, and it intrigued him, it fascinated him.

"You can look at it, Robert, that we're in the middle ages of a new era, waiting for the renaissance of real power. Right now, I'm serving a rather sequestered function, I really am no more than the chief monk, the lord of my little abbey, so to speak."

His voice continued on and on, its ironic sustained mockery spinning its own unique web, while all the time the tensions inside him flexed and expanded, sought their inexorable satisfactions in whatever lay between Hearn and himself, between himself and the five thousand troops against him, the terrain, and the circuits of chance he would mold.

What a monster, Hearn told himself.

85

Chorus:

(The mess tent is on a low bluff overlooking the beach. In front of it is a low serving bench on which are placed four or five pots containing food. The troops file by in an irregular line, their mess gear opened and extended. Red, Gallagher, Brown and Wilson shuffle past to receive their rations. As they go by they sniff at the main course which has been dumped into a big square pan. It is canned Meat and Vegetable Stew heated slightly. The second cook, a fat red-faced man with a bald spot and a perpetual scowl, slaps a large spoonful in each of their mess plates.)

RED: What the fug is that swill?

COOK: It's owl shit. Wha'd you think it was?

RED: Okay, I just thought it was somethin' I couldn't eat. (Laughter)

COOK: (good naturedly) Move on, move on, before I knock-the-crap-out-of-you.

RED: (pointing below his belt) Take a bite on this.

GALLAGHER: That goddam stew again.

COOK: (shouting to the other cooks and KPs on the serving line) Private Gallagher is bitching, men.

KP: Send him to officers' mess.

GALLAGHER: Give me a little more, will ya?

COOK: These portions are scientifically measured by Quartermaster. Move on!

GALLAGHER: You sonofabitch.

COOK: Go beat your meat. (Gallagher moves on.)

BROWN: General Cummings, you're the best damn guy in the outfit.

86

COOK: You looking for more meat? You won't get it. They ain't no meat.

BROWN: You're the worst guy in the outfit.

COOK: (turning to the serving line) Sergeant Brown is now passing in review.

BROWN: As you were, men. Carry on, pip, pip. (Brown moves by.)

WILSON: Ah swear, don't you ration destroyers know another way to fug up this stew?

COOK: 'When it's smokin', it's cookin'; when it's burnin,' it's done.' That's our motto.

WILSON: (chuckling) Ah figgered you all had a system.

COOK: Take a bite on this.

WILSON: You got to wait your turn, boy. They's five men in recon is ahead of ya.

COOK: For you, I'll wait. Move on, move on. Who're you to block traffic?

(The soldiers file by.)

4

BY THE end of the first month of the campaign, the front-line troops had advanced to the base of the peninsula. Beyond it the island extended on either side, and about five miles from the junction of the peninsula with the mainland, the mountains of the Watamai Range ran along parallel to the sea. The Toyaku Line was drawn up to the left of the peninsula on a fairly straight line running from the cliffs of the mountain range to the ocean. As the General expressed it to his staff, he had "to make a left turn off the avenue of the peninsula into a narrow street which has figuratively a factory wall on its right, a ditch on its left [the sea], and Toyaku in front of us."

He conducted the pivoting operation with brilliance. There were many problems involved. He had to move his front line, stabilized at last, through a ninety-degree arc to the left, and it meant that, while the flank companies on the left who could anchor themselves by the sea would have to move only a half mile or so, the companies on the right would be obliged to wheel through a six-mile arc of jungle, and would be exposed through every hour of their march.

He had two alternatives. The safer plan was to have the battalion on his right flank drive straight inland until it reached the mountains. A temporary line could then be drawn up on a diagonal, and slowly he could have the right wing turn and drive along parallel to the mountains until his lines faced Toyaku. But that would take several days, possibly a week, and there might be a great deal of resistance. The other project, far more dangerous, was to move his right flank in a direct thrust to the mountain cliffs which abutted the Toyaku Line. That way, the entire front could be pivoted in a day.

But it was very dangerous. Toyaku undoubtedly would have a striking force ready to knife around the edge of the advancing troops, and turn their flank. During the entire day he would be pivoting his troops, the General would have an undefended right flank. He took the chance, and turned it into an advantage. On the day of the operation he withdrew a battalion from the road and kept them in reserve. He gave instructions to the commanders of the companies on the right flank to advance through the jungle without concerning themselves with their flank or rear. Their mission was merely to make the six-mile march through no man's land, and establish a defense position by that night at the mountain cliffs a mile away from the outposts of the Toyaku Line.

The General guessed correctly. Toyaku sneaked a company of Japanese troops around the flank while the movement was in progress, but the General met them with his reserve battalion, and encircled them almost completely. For several days an extremely confused battle went on in the jungle behind the division's new lines, but by the end of that time, all but a few stragglers of the company Toyaku had dispatched into the division's rear had been killed. There were more snipers behind the lines, and once or twice a pack train was ambushed, but these were minor incidents. The General did not concern himself with that. After the pivoting operation he was far too busy establishing his new line. In the first two days the men on the front hacked out new trails, and laid barbed wire, cut fields of fire through the jungle, and established telephone communications with their flanks and rear. A few minor Japanese attacks caused the General no great worry. Four days went by after the movement, and then five. With each day the General strengthened his lines, and increased the speed with which he built the road to the front. He knew it would take him two weeks at least before the road could catch up to his troops and until then he could only increase his defenses. A major attack by Toyaku could still embarrass him, but it was a gamble he had to take.

In the meantime he moved his headquarters bivouac. The division's task force had progressed almost twenty-five miles since the day they had landed, and by now the radio communication was difficult, the telephone wire had been extended seriously. He advanced the bivouac fifteen miles up the peninsula to another coconut grove just off the road. It was not as pleasant as the first headquarters had been on the beach, and the troops in headquarters company of the regiment had to spend several busy days clearing the brush between the trees, laying out barbed wire, digging new latrines, and setting up their tents and foxholes, but when they had finished the bivouac was not unlivable. It was much hotter, and little breeze filtered through from the jungle surrounding them, but there was a stream which ran just outside the oval encirclement of wire, and the men did not have to go far to bathe.

Subsequently the General had service company of the 460th bivouacking on the other side of the road from them. He knew that unless there was a disastrous retreat he would not have to move this bivouac for the rest of the campaign, and slowly, as time permitted, he began to build it up. A field shower was built for the officers, and the mess tents were erected, and squad tents were set up once again for the division staff offices. The ground through the bivouac was trimmed each morning, gravel walks were laid along the paths, and the motor pool had a culvert built of empty gasoline drums at the entrance to the road.

These elaborations gave Cummings a constant pleasure. No matter how many times he had seen it, the slow improvement of a bivouac was always satisfying. By the time his pivoting operation was a week old, he felt as if he had erected a small village. During the day there was constant activity with men working on improvements in the bivouac area, and trucks constantly moving in and out of the motor pools. On the other side of the road the maintenance shops were in operation in service company, and in the somnolent afternoons in the jungle he could hear their machine tools grinding. His own bivouac had been enlarged several times and by now the barbed wire around the perimeter enclosed an ellipse of earth almost two hundred yards long and more than half as wide, and in the area were over a hundred pup tents, a dozen pyramidal and squad tents, a row of twenty fly tents in which his officers were housed, three latrines, two field kitchens, over forty trucks and jeeps, and almost three hundred men.

Recon was a very small part of all this. With the five new replacements, the platoon had a total strength of fourteen men, and their arc of the bivouac consisted of seven pup tents extended in ten-yard intervals along a section of the perimeter. At night two men in the platoon would be awake at any hour, sitting in the two machine-gun emplacements that faced past the barbed wire toward the jungle; in the daytime the perimeter would be virtually deserted, with only one man left behind as the rest of the platoon went out to work on the road. Five weeks had gone by since invasion day, and with the exception of a few routine security patrols around the new bivouac, the platoon had seen no activity. It was approaching the rainy season, and it grew hotter each day, more trying to work on the road. By the time they had been in the new bivouac for a week, many of the men, including some of the veterans of the Motome campaign, were wishing for combat again.

After evening chow Red had washed up, and moved over to Wilson and Gallagher's tent. All day it had been extremely hot and sultry, even more unbearable than the days and nights before it, and Red was feeling irritable. The day, like every other day, had been spent working on the road.

Gallagher and Wilson were sprawled in their tent, smoking quietly without talking. "Whateya say, Red?" Wilson drawled at last.

Red wiped his forehead. "That kid Wyman! It used to be bad

enough bunkin' with a Boy Scout like Toglio, but that kid Wyman
. . ." He snorted. "They're gonna be sendin' 'em overseas soon with
a sugar tit."

"Yeah, the platoon seems all topside-bottom since we got the
replacements," Wilson complained. He sighed, and ran the sleeve of
his fatigue shirt over his chin, which was moist with perspiration.
"Weather's fixin to act up," he said quietly.

"More fuggin rain," Gallagher snorted.

Dark slated clouds were washing the eastern sky and mounting
thunderheads in the north and south. The air was leaden and moist,
hanging limp without a murmur. Even the coconut trees seemed
swollen and expectant, their leaves drooping languidly over the raw
chopped earth of the bivouac.

"That corduroy we put in is gonna be washed out," Gallagher
said. Red looked out across the area and scowled. The tents were sagging, and appeared gloomy and somber although the sun was still
shining with a dull red glow in the west.

"Just so we don't get our tails wet," Red said.

He debated for a moment whether to go back to his tent and
deepen the rain trench, which had almost overflowed in the previous
night's downpour, and then he shrugged. It was about time Wyman
learned how to do it. He crouched and dropped into the hole in which
Gallagher and Wilson were resting now. It was a hole about two feet
deep and about as wide and long as a double bed. Wilson and Gallagher slept side by side in it with two blankets between them and the
earth. Overhead they had anchored a ridgepole of bamboo on two uprights, had draped their combined ponchos over it, and staked the
ends to the ground on each side of the hole. It was possible to kneel
inside the tent without bumping one's head against the ridgepole, but
not even an eight-year-old child could have stood in it. From outside,
the shelter appeared to be no more than two feet above the level of
the ground. This tent was typical of almost all the pup tents in the
bivouac.

Red lay down between them, and stared out at the obtuse triangle of sky and jungle visible from the head of the tent. They had
dug the hole to fit their bodies, and Red's long legs dangled over

91

the rain trench at the entrance. When the rain blew in the open end, it collected in the trench, which was lower than any other part of the hole. Now it was still muddy.

"Next time you men dig a tent right, so a guy can get in it," Red said. He guffawed.

"If you men don' like it, get the hell out," Gallagher grumbled.

"That's your Boston hospitality," Red said.

"Yeah, we got no place for fuggin bums," Gallagher kidded heavily. The purple lumps on his face looked swollen and putrefactive in the dull light.

Wilson giggled. "Ah say only thing worse'n a damyankee is a fella from Boston."

"They wouldn't let *you* in a town where you had to wear some fuggin shoes," Gallagher snorted. He lit a cigarette and turned over on his stomach. "Got to know how to read and write if you want to come north," he said.

Wilson was a little hurt. "Listen, boy," he told him, "Ah may not be able to read eve'thin' so good, but they ain't a thing Ah cain't do if Ah set mah mind to't." There had been that time, he was thinking, when Willy Perkins had bought the first washing machine in town, and when it had gone on the bum, he'd taken it all apart and then fixed it. "They ain't a thing Ah cain't fix if it's piece of machinery," he said. He took off his glasses and wiped the perspiration from them with a corner of his handkerchief. "Once Ah remember there was a fella in town who had an English bicycle. American one wa'n't good 'nough for him. He lost some of the ball bearin's out of it, and they wa'n' none Ah could get to fit, so Ah jus' took an American ball-bearin' ring, and fit it to't." He pointed one of his thick fingers at Gallagher and added, "Rode as good after Ah fixed it as it ever did."

"Pretty clever," Gallagher sneered. "In Boston you could get any kind of ball bearing you wanted."

"A man's better if he can do without at times," Wilson muttered.

Red snickered. "I don't see where you're such a damn sight better doing without your pussy." They all laughed. "That's somep'n a man should never do without," Wilson admitted. He rubbed his hand reflectively against one of the earthen walls of the hole. "In Boston,"

Gallagher said, "if one of your buddies gets a piece, he lets you know about it." Immediately afterward he felt ashamed. He made a mental note to remember what he had just said when he went to Chaplain Hogan for confession. The resolution made him feel better. He was always forgetting the bad things he had done when he did go to confession. Sometimes when he would be trying to collect his bad thoughts before he saw Father Hogan, he could not remember any of them, and he would have to go in and say only, "Father, I have blasphemed."

Mary knew so little about him, Gallagher thought. She didn't even know the way he swore. But that was just a bad habit he had picked up in the Army, Gallagher told himself. He had used bad language before when he was with the gang, but that didn't count. He was just a kid then. He had never sworn when a woman was around.

Gallagher began to think of the gang. What a good bunch of guys they were, he told himself with pride. There had been the time they passed out pamphlets to get McCarthy elected in Roxbury. He had even made a speech afterward, saying that his victory was due to his loyal cohorts. And there was the time they had made that raid into Dorchester, and had taught the Yids a lesson. They had picked one kid about eleven who was coming home from school and they had surrounded him, and Whitey Lydon had asked, "What the hell are ya?" The kid had trembled and said, "I don't know." "You're a mockey," Whitey had told him, "that's what you are, a fuggin mockey." He had held the kid by his shirt, and said, "Now, what are ya?"

"I'm a mockey," the kid had said. He was about to cry.

"All right," Lydon had told him, "spell it. Spell 'mockey.' "

The kid had stammered, "M-o-c-c-i."

What a roar that had been, Gallagher thought. M-o-c-c-i. The dumb kid had been so afraid he must have crapped his pants. The goddam Yids. Gallagher remembered how Lydon had got on the police force. What a break that had been for him; with a little luck he could have got a job like that too. But of all the work he had done in his spare time for the Democratic Club, he hadn't got anything for it. What was wrong? He wanted to do big things. He would even have got a job in the post office if it hadn't been for that Alderman Shapiro and his fuggin nephew Abie or Jakie. Gallagher felt a deep resentment. There was always something to beat him. He felt his mute anger growing, and because it gave him a rich satisfaction to say it, he burst out suddenly, "I see we got a couple of fuggin Yids in the platoon."

"Yeah," Red said. He knew one of Gallagher's tirades was beginning and it bored him. "Yeah," he sighed, "they're sonsofbitches just like the rest of us."

Gallagher turned on him. "They only been in one week and already they're lousin' up the platoon."

"Ah don't know," Wilson murmured; "that Roth ain't much good, but the other fellow, that Goldstein or Goldberg or whatever the hell his name is, he ain't a bad boy. Ah was workin' with him today, and we got to talkin' about the best way to lay down a corduroy."

"I wouldn't trust a fuggin one of them," Gallagher said fiercely.

Red yawned and drew his feet up. "It's beginning to rain," he said.

A few drops were pattering on the tent. The sky was a unique color; it had the leaden-greenish surface of stained glass, but there was a sheen, too, as though an intense light were shining on the other side of the pane. "It's gonna rain like a sonofabitch," he said. He lay back again. "You guys got your tent anchored okay?"

"Ah reckon so," Wilson said. A soldier went running by outside, and the sound of his footsteps evoked a moody spirit in Red. It was the old sound, a man trying to get under cover before a storm. He sighed again. "All I ever done my whole life was get a wet ass," he muttered.

"You know," Wilson said, "ol' Stanley is really feelin' his piss now that he's in for corporal. Ah heard him tellin' one of the replacements all about the Motome invasion. 'It was rough,' Stanley said." Wilson chuckled. "Ah was glad to hear that Stanley thought so, 'cause Ah hadn't made up mah mind about it."

Gallagher spat. "Stanley ain't gonna give me any of his crap."

94

"Yeah," Red said. Gallagher and Wilson still believed he had been afraid to fight Stanley. To hell with them. When he had heard that Stanley was going to make corporal he had been amused and contemptuous; it had seemed just right. Stanley *would* be noncom material. "More men get to heaven by sucking first at the other end," he mumbled to himself.

Only it wasn't that simple. He realized abruptly that he had wanted to be chosen for corporal. He almost laughed aloud, a little bitterly, as if there would never be an end to the surprises in himself. The Army's got me, he thought. It was the old trap. First they made you afraid, and then they let you sew on ribbons. He would have turned it down if they had asked him . . . only he would have got a bang out of turning it down.

Some lightning flashed nearby, and a few seconds later the thunder seemed to explode overhead. "Man, that was close," Wilson said.

The sky was almost black now with the impending storm. Red lay back again. All his life he'd been turning down the stripes, and now . . . He tapped his hand several times on his chest, slowly, almost mournfully. He had always lived his life in himself, able to carry his belongings on his back. "The more things you own, the more things you need to keep you comfortable." It was an old axiom of his, but this once it was without much solace. He was running down. He had been a loner for a long, long time.

"The rain's starting," Gallagher said.

A vicious wind lashed at the tents. The rain came on softly, tapped against the rubber fabric of the shelter, and then began to drive harder. In only a few seconds it became furious with pellets like hail. The tents began to bend and strain. A few bursts of thunder sounded in the distance, and then a cloud shattered overhead.

The men in the tent winced. This would be no ordinary storm.

Wilson reached up and braced his weight against the ridgepole. "Goddam," he muttered, "that wind could cut a man's head off." The foliage beyond the barbed wire had already assumed a beaten look as if a herd of animals had trampled upon it. Wilson peered out for an instant and shook his head. The bivouac area was invisible, a void of green across which the rain streamed, beating upon the subdued grass and shrubs. The wind was tremendous. Wilson remained on his knees, feeling the violence of it dumbly. Although he had ducked back from the opening in the tent, his face was completely wet. There was no way to keep out the water which dripped quickly through every rip and seam of the tent fabric and blew in through the entrance like successive waves of surf. The rain trench had filled already, was flowing over onto their bedding. Gallagher gathered up their blankets, and the three men squatted under the flapping ponchos, trying to hold them down, and failing miserably in the attempt to keep their feet dry. Outside the water had risen in great puddles which kept spreading and sending out tentacles like enormous amoeba absorbing the earth. "Goddam, goddam," Wilson said.

Goldstein and Ridges were completely wet. When the rain had started, they had got out of their tent and pounded down all the stakes. Goldstein had crammed the blankets into the rubber bag of his jungle pack, and he crouched on his knees now inside the tent, trying to hold it down in the wind. "This is terrible," he shouted.

Ridges nodded. His ugly dumpy face was covered with drops of water, and his straight sandy hair had plastered itself in a spiral about his head. "Nuttin' to do but wait," he shouted back. His voice was lost in the wind, and Goldstein could hear nothing but "wait," which had a long wailing quality that pebbled his flesh with a sudden shudder. There seemed nothing in the universe but the gray violence roaring about them. Goldstein felt his arm wrenched cruelly as the ridgepole lashed upward with an abrupt vicious snap. He was so wet that his green fatigues looked black.

The bottom of the ocean would look like this, he told himself. There were subterranean storms that he had read about, and this must be like them. Apart from his awe, and his concern that the tent should remain up, Goldstein was watching the storm with a fascinated interest. Probably the world had been something like this when it first began to cool, he thought, and felt a deep excitement as if he were witnessing creation. It was silly to think about the tent in the same moment, but he could not help himself. He was convinced that it would remain standing; the stakes were three feet deep, and the soil was the clay type that could take extreme stresses. If he had only known a storm like this was coming, he could have built a shelter that would last through anything, and he could lie underneath it, completely dry without the slightest worry. Goldstein was annoyed at Ridges. He should have told him what kind of storms there were; he was a veteran and he should have been prepared. Already Goldstein was planning the next tent he would build. His shoes had filled with water and he worked his toes to warm his feet. Squeegee action, he thought; probably the man who invented the squeegee had an experience like mine.

Ridges was watching the typhoon with panic and acceptance. Mighty sponges o' God swelling, he said to himself. The foliage of the jungle was churning turbulently, and the leaden-green sky painted it with greens so varied and brilliant that Ridges thought it looked like the Garden of Eden. He felt the throbbing of the jungle as a part of himself, the earth, which had turned to a golden mud, seemed alive to him. He kept looking at the fantastic green of the jungle and then at the orange-brown earth, febrile and pulsing as though the rain were cutting wounds into it. Ridges flinched before the power of it.

The Lord giveth and He taketh away, Ridges thought solemnly. Storms were a basic part of his life; he had come to fear them, to bear with them, and finally to expect them. He saw his father's reddened wrinkled face with the sad quiet blue eyes. "I'll tell you, Ossie," his father had said, "a man works and he toils, he puts in his good sweat tryin' to pull out a livin' from the land, and when all his work is done, if the good Lord sees it fitten, it's taken away in a storm." Perhaps that was the deepest truth in Ridges's nature; it seemed to him that all his life, he and his father had struggled with barren land and insects and blights, had worked their fields with one aging mule, and often as not, their work had been ruined in one black night.

He had helped Goldstein pound in the stakes because you helped your neighbor when he asked for it, and Ridges had decided the man you bunked with, even if he was a stranger, was still your neighbor; but secretly he had felt that their attempts to secure the tent would be useless. God's ways were God's ways, he told himself, and a man did

97

not try to brook them. If the storm was meant to blow away their tent, it would do it even if they had a plow to hold it down. Now, because he did not know it was not raining in Mississippi, he prayed that the storm should not destroy his father's crops. They jus' been planted, Lord. Please don' wash them away. And even in his praying Ridges had no hope; he prayed to show that he was respectful.

The wind tore through the bivouac area like a great scythe, slashing the palm fronds from the coconut trees, blasting the rain before it. As they looked, they saw a tent jerk upward from its mooring, and then stream away in the wind, flapping like a terrified bird. "I wonder what's happening up at the front," Goldstein shouted. He had realized with a shock that there were other bivouacs like this, scattered for miles into the jungle. Ridges shrugged. "Holdin' on, Ah guess," he shouted back. Goldstein wondered what it looked like up forward; during the week he had been with recon, he had seen only the mile or two of road upon which they were working. Now he tried to conceive of an attack being made during this storm and winced before the prospect of it. All his energies had to be concentrated on the ridgepole, which he held with both hands. The Japs might even be attacking their area now, he thought. He wondered if anyone was on guard in the machine gun emplacements. "A smart general would start an attack now," he said.

"Reckon," Ridges answered quietly. The wind had lapsed for a moment, and their voices had a subdued uncertain quality as if they were talking in a church. Goldstein released the pole, and felt the strain flowing out of his arms. Fatigue products being carried away by the bloodstream, he thought. Perhaps the storm was practically over. In the hole, the ground was hopelessly muddy, and Goldstein wondered how they would sleep that night. He shivered; abruptly he had realized the chill weight of his sodden clothing.

The wind started again, and their mute tense struggle to preserve the tent began once more. Goldstein felt as though he was holding onto a door which a much stronger man was trying to open from the other side. He saw two more tents tear off into the wind, and he watched the men running to find shelter somewhere else. Wyman and Toglio, laughing and cursing, dropped into their hole. "Our tent just

98

went," Wyman shouted, his young bony face spread in a great grin. "Gee, this is something!" he roared, and the expression on his face was somewhere between delight and wonder as though uncertain whether the typhoon was a catastrophe or a circus.

"What about your stuff?" Goldstein shouted.

"Lost. Blew away. I left my M-one in a puddle of water."

Goldstein looked for his rifle. It was on a ledge above the hole, splattered with water and mud. Goldstein was disgusted because he had not wrapped it in his dirty shirt before the storm began. He was still a rookie, he told himself; a veteran would have remembered to protect it.

Water was dripping from Toglio's big fleshy nose. He moved his heavy jaw and shouted. "Think your tent'll hold?"

"Don't know," Goldstein roared. "The stakes will." The four men were cramped in the hole even though they were squatting on their heels. Ridges watched his feet sink into the mud, and wished he were not wearing shoes. Man's jus' more fussed tryin' to keep 'em dry than the whole thing's worth, he thought. A rill of water kept running into the tent along the ridgepole and trickling onto his bent knee. His clothing was so cold that the drops of water seemed warm. He sighed.

A tremendous gust of wind bellied under the tent, blew it out like a balloon, and then the ridgepole snapped, tearing a rent in the poncho. The tent fell upon the four men like a wet sheet, and they struggled stupidly under it for a few seconds before the wind began to strip it away. Wyman got the giggles, and began to feel around helplessly. He lost his balance and sat down in the mud, struggling feebly under the folds of the tent. "Jesus," he laughed. He felt as if caught in a sack, and he subsided into helpless laughter. Too weak to punch my way out of a paper bag, he said to himself, and this made everything seem even more ludicrous. "Where are you?" he shouted, and then the folds of the tent filled out again like a sail, ripped loose completely, and went eddying and twisting through the air. A little piece of the poncho had been left on one of the stakes, and it flapped in the gale. The four men stood up in the hole, and then crouched before the force of the wind. They could still see the sun just above

99

the horizon in one clear swatch of sky that seemed infinite miles away. The rain was very cold now, almost frigid, and they shuddered. Almost all the tents were down in the bivouac area, and here and there a soldier would go skittering through the mud, staggering from the force of the wind with the odd jerking motions of a man walking in a motion picture when the film is unwinding too rapidly. "Christ, I'm freezin'," Toglio shouted.

"Let's get out of here," Wyman said. He was covered with mud and his lips were chattering. "Goddam rain," he said.

They stumbled out of the hole, and began to run toward the motor pool where there would be some shelter in the lee of the trucks. Toglio staggered as though he had lost some necessary ballast and was being driven downwind without any way to control himself. Goldstein shouted to him, "I forgot my rifle."

"You don't need it," he bawled back.

Goldstein tried to halt and turn around but it was impossible. "You never can tell," he heard himself shout. They were running side by side, but it felt as if they were roaring to each other across a vast room. Goldstein had a moment of glee.

For a whole week they had worked on improving their bivouac. Every spare moment, there had been something new to set up. And now his tent was lost, his clothing and writing paper were sopping, his gun would probably rust, the ground would be too wet for sleeping. Everything was ruined. He had the kind of merriment a man sometimes knows when events have ended in utter disaster.

He and Toglio were blown into the motor pool. They collided as they tried to turn and went sprawling in the mud. Goldstein felt like lying there without getting up, but he put his hands against the ground, pushed and went staggering behind one of the trucks. Almost the entire company was in the trucks or bunched together in the lee of them. There were about twenty men clustered together behind the truck he had reached. They stood there shivering and huddled together for warmth, their teeth chattering from the icy rain. The sky was an immense dark bowl that crashed and quaked with thunder. All Goldstein could see was the green truck, and the wet green-black uniforms of the men. "Jesus," somebody said.

100

Toglio was trying to light a cigarette, but it soaked through and came apart in his mouth before he could get his matches out of his waterproof pouch. He threw it to the ground and watched it dissolve in the mud. Despite the fact that he was completely wet, the rain still hurt; every drop that went down his back was like a cold slug, shocking and loathsome. He turned to the man next to him, and shouted, "Your tent go down?"

"Yeah."

It made Toglio feel better. He rubbed his black unshaved chin, and felt intimate suddenly with all the men, liked them immensely with a burst of warmth. They were all good guys, good Americans, he told himself. It took Americans to stand something like this and laugh about it, he decided. His hands were cold, and he stuck them in the baggy pockets of his fatigue pants.

Red and Wilson, who were standing a few feet away, had begun to sing. Red's voice was deep and gruff, and Toglio laughed as he listened to them.

> *Once I built a railroad, made it run,*
> *Made it race against time*

they sang, and jogged up and down to warm their feet.

> *Once I built a railroad, now it's done,*
> *Brother, can you spare a dime*

Toglio found himself roaring with laughter. Red was a comic, he told himself, and began to hum with them

> *Once I built a tower to the sun,*
> *Bricks and rivet and lime,*
> *Once I built a tower, now it's done,*
> *Brother, can you spare a dime?*

Toglio joined in on the last line, and Red beckoned to him. The three of them kept singing as loudly as they could, their arms about each other for warmth. The wind had abated to some degree, and they could hear their voices clearly every now and then, but they sounded distant and a little unreal, like a radio in another room being turned up and down, up and down.

Once in khaki suits
Gee, we looked swell
Full of that Yankee Doodly Dum.
Half a million boots went sloggin' thru Hell,
I was the kid with the drum.
Say, don't you remember, they call me Al?
It was Al all the time.
Say, don't you remember, I'm your pal?
Buddy, can you spare a dime?

They started laughing as they finished, and Toglio yelled, "What do we sing next? How about 'Show Me The Way to Go Home'?"

"I can't sing," Red shouted. "My throat's too dry. I need a drink." He pursed his mouth and rolled his eyes, and Toglio laughed into the rain. What an ugly comical guy Red was. They were all good guys.

"Show me the way to go home," Toglio sang, and several other men began to sing with them.

I'm tired and I want to go to bed,
I had a little drink about an hour ago,
And it's gone right to my head.

The rain had become hard and steady, and Toglio had a wistful mellow feeling as he chanted the words. He was cold, and despite the bodies about him he kept shivering. He had an image of driving in a car on a winter twilight, approaching a strange town which beckoned to him with its warmth and lights.

Wherever I may roam,
On land or sea or foam,

102

You can always hear me singing this song,
Show me the way to go home.

It was almost dark, and in the lee of the truck underneath the coconut trees it was becoming difficult to see the men's faces. Toglio's mood deepened, became sad and gentle. He remembered how his wife had looked once trimming a Christmas tree, and a tear ran down his heavy fleshy cheeks. For a minute or so he felt completely removed from the war, from the rain, from everything; he knew that in a little while he would be having to consider where and how he would sleep, but for this brief moment he sang resolutely, wriggling his toes, letting all the soft sensuous memories that the songs evoked flow unresisting through his mind.

A jeep came wallowing through the mud and came to a halt about thirty feet from them. He saw General Cummings and two other officers dismount, and he nudged Red to stop singing. The General was bareheaded and his uniform was completely wet, but he was smiling. Toglio looked at him with interest and some reverence. He had seen the General many times in the bivouac area but this was the first time he had been so close. "You men, you men here," the General shouted as he came near them, "how do you feel . . . wet?" Toglio laughed with the others. General Cummings grinned. "It's all right," he shouted, "you're not made of sugar." The wind ebbed, and in a more normal tone he said to a major and lieutenant who were with him, "I do believe the rain's about to halt. I just telephoned Washington, and the War Department assured me it was bound to stop." The two officers laughed vigorously, and Toglio found himself smiling. The General was a swell guy, a perfect example of an officer.

"Now, men," the General said loudly, "I don't believe there's a tent that's still up in the area. As soon as the storm lifts, we'll try to bring up some ponchos from the beach, but I have no doubt some of you are going to be wet tonight. It's to be regretted, but you've been wet before. A bit of trouble has started up on the line, and some of you may spend the night in a far worse place." He paused for a moment, standing in the rain; then he added with a twinkle, "I as-

103

sume that none of you left a guard post when the storm broke. If any of you are here who shouldn't be, you better get the hell back as soon as I leave." There was a snicker from the men. Since the rain had eased, most of the company had drifted over toward the truck where the General was talking. "Seriously, men, from what we heard before the communications went out, I've an idea there are going to be some Japs inside our lines tonight, so you better keep an extremely alert guard. We're fairly far back from the front, but we're not that far back." He smiled at them, got back into his jeep, followed by the officers, and drove out of the area.

Red spat. "I knew we been havin' it soft too long. Two to one they send us out to catch a shit-storm tonight."

Wilson nodded, shaking his head angrily. "When you have it good it don' pay to bitch. All those replacements wantin' to see combat, they're gonna change they mind."

Toglio interrupted. "Gee, the General is a swell guy," he said.

Red spat again. "They ain't a general in the world is any good. They're all sonsofbitches."

"Listen, Red," Toglio protested, "where could you find a general like that who'd talk to a bunch of GIs? He's okay for my money."

"He's a crowd-pleaser, that's all he is," Red told him. "What the fug business has he got tellin' us his worries? I got enough of my own."

Toglio sighed and stopped talking. What a contrary guy Red was, he decided finally. It had stopped raining and he thought of going back to the remains of his tent. The idea depressed him, but Toglio would not allow himself to dawdle now that the storm was over. "Come on, we might as well fix up some way to sleep," he said.

Red grunted. "It won't do you any good. We're gonna be up on the line tonight." With nightfall, the air was becoming sultry again.

The General was worried. After the jeep pulled out of the motor pool he said to his driver, "Take us to headquarters battery of the one-five-one." He turned around to Major Dalleson and Lieutenant Hearn, who were squeezed together uncomfortably in the back seat.

"If their line isn't in to Second Battalion we'll be doing some walking before the night is over." The jeep passed through an opening in the barbed wire and turned right onto the road that led toward the front. The General scrutinized it morosely. The mud was very bad and it would become worse. Now it was slimy and the jeep skidded and weaved from one side of the road to the other, but in a few hours it would become hard and gummy like clay, and the vehicles might bog down to their hubs. He gazed dully at the jungle on either side of the road. They passed a few Jap corpses decomposing in a ditch and the General held his breath. No matter how familiar that smell had become, he could never bear it casually. He made a mental note to have a burial detail police the road once this trouble was over.

The night had come and with it a potential disaster. In the jeep motoring forward slowly through the darkness, Cummings had a sensation of being suspended in air. The steady drone of the motor, the silence of everyone in the vehicle, and the heavy wet rustling of the jungle seemed to strip him of everything but the quick absorbed functioning of his mind. Alone, settled by himself somewhere in space, he had to work this out. The storm had come with amazing rapidity, following in the wake of a Japanese attack. Ten minutes before the rain had begun, he had had a message from 2nd Battalion headquarters that a heavy fire fight had started before their lines. And then the telephone lines had been cut to pieces in the storm, his headquarters had been laid flat, and the radio would not function. He had no idea of what was happening at the front. By now Hutchins might have pulled back 2nd Battalion. The Japs, driven on with a kind of frenzy generated by the gale, could conceivably have penetrated his front line in any number of places. With no orders coming through to them, Lord knew what might happen. If only headquarters battery had its line open to the front.

At least he had moved a dozen tanks up two days ago to 2nd Battalion. They would never have been able to make it on the road tonight, nor, for that matter, could they advance now, but if necessary, a defense position could be organized around them tonight. What chaos there could be. The entire line might be a series of isolated hedgehogs by tomorrow. And there was nothing he could do until he got to a telephone line. Anything could develop. In two days he might be back where he was when he started the pivoting operation.

When he reached that telephone line, the decisions would have to be almost immediate. He reviewed the personalities of his line officers, remembered the distinguishing characteristics, if there were any, of different companies, even individual platoons. His acute memory re-issued a spate of incidents and strength figures; he knew effectively where every gun and every man on Anopopei was placed, and all this knowledge passed in an undigested flow through his head. At the moment he was an extremely simple man. Everything in him was functioning for one purpose, and from experience, with a confident unstated certainty, he knew that when demanded of him all this information would crystallize into the proper reactions. If he built up enough tension his instincts would not fail him.

And with all this there was an intense and primitive rage. The storm had thwarted him, and his anger took childish forms. From time to time a spasm of irritation washed over his concentration and muddied it. "Not a word about that storm," he would mutter to himself every now and then. "A meteorological corps which doesn't function. Army knew about it, but did they tell me? No report of the storm, none at all. What bungling or perhaps not bungling at all. They're trying to cross me."

At that moment the driver stalled the jeep in a rut. Cummings turned toward him. He could have shot him, but instead he mur-mured, "Come on, son, we have no time for that." The jeep motor started again, and they continued on.

His bivouac had been destroyed. That was the most painful fact of all. The dangers to the division occupied his mind, caused him a good deal of anxiety, but that was abstract. What hurt directly, per-sonally, was the shambles in which he had left the bivouac. He felt a sense of grief almost, remembering how the rivulets had washed away the gravel walks, the way his cot had turned over, become im-paled in the mud, the filth and wreckage of his tent. What a waste! It angered him again.

"You better turn on your lights, son," he said to the driver. "This is going to take too long otherwise." If any snipers were near it would

106

be like walking through a forest of thugs, carrying a candle. The General tensed pleasurably in his seat. Danger had a tang which made him appreciate the magnitude of his work. "You'd better cover the road on either side," he said to Hearn and Dalleson. They pointed their carbines out the open sides of the jeep, scanning the jungle. With the lights on, the foliage was silvery, more mysterious.

Lieutenant Hearn fingered the magazine on his carbine, removed it, clicked it into position again, holding the small rifle in his large hands, the muzzle pointed toward the jungle. He was in a complex mood with many elements of excitement and dejection. After all the order, all the well-timed advances, the front might now have exploded into anything, and in the meantime their jeep wandered around like a nerve seeking for a muscle or organ to function upon. The General had once said to him, "I like chaos, it's like the reagents foaming in the beaker before the precipitation of the crystals. It's a kind of savory to me."

Which was a crock of the well-known article, Hearn had decided at the time. The General didn't like chaos, or rather he didn't like it when he was in the beaker. The only ones who liked it were men like himself, Hearn, who really weren't involved.

Still, the General had reacted well. Hearn remembered the first apathy that had caught them all when the storm abated. The General had stared at his muddy cot for almost half a minute, and then had scraped off a small handful of muck, which he kneaded in his fingers. That storm had cut the legs from them all, and yet the General had responded, made his incredibly urbane speech to the men, while everything in all of them had demanded tucking up one's tail and slinking off for some cover. That was understandable, however; the General had had to recover the connotations of his command.

And now he was comprehensible too. Hearn knew from the tone of his politeness, the quality of his voice, that he was thinking of nothing at all but the campaign and the night ahead. It made the General another man, definitely the nerve end with no other desire than to find something to act upon.

It depressed Hearn even as it elicited his admiration. That type of concentration was inhuman, the process beyond his scope. He stared

107

glumly at the jungle before him, hefting the carbine in his hands again. It was possible that a Jap machine gun could be set up at the next bend in the road, or much more likely there might be a few Jap snipers with an automatic weapon or two. Their jeep would round the bend, be hit by a dozen bullets at once, and that would be the end of his petty history of unfocused gropings and unimportant dissatisfactions. And with him quite as casually would be lost a man who might be a genius, and an overgrown oaf like Dalleson, and a young nervous driver who was probably a potential Fascist. Like that. Turning a curve in the road.

Or, obversely, he might kill a man himself. It would be a question of throwing up his rifle, pressing the trigger, and a particular envelope of lusts and anxieties and perhaps some goodness would be quite dead. All as easy as stepping on an insect, perhaps easier. That was the thing, that was what caused this mood. Everything was completely out of whack, none of the joints fitted. The men had been singing in the motor pool, and there had been something nice about it, something childish and brave. And they were here on this road, a point moving along a line in the vast neutral spaces of the jungle. And somewhere else a battle might be going on. The artillery, the small-arms fire they had been hearing constantly, might be nothing, something scattered along the front, or it might be all concentrated now in the minuscule inferno of combat. None of it matched. The night had broken them into all the isolated units that actually they were.

He became conscious again of Dalleson's huge bulk against his own large body, and he stiffened a little. After a moment or two he fished a cigarette out of the breast pocket of his shirt and fumbled for a match.

"Better not smoke," Dalleson grunted.

"The jeep lights are on."

"Yeah," Dalleson grunted and was silent again. He shifted his seat slightly in the cramped rear of the jeep, and was annoyed at Hearn for taking up so much room, for smoking. Dalleson was nervous. He wasn't worried in the least about an ambush. If it came, he would meet it coolly and acquit himself well. What bothered him was

108

what they were going to do when they got to the 151st Artillery. He had the anxiety of a dull student who was going to enter an examination he dreaded. As the G-3, in charge of operations and training, Dalleson was supposed to know the situation as well as the General, if not better, and without his maps and papers Dalleson felt lost. The General might depend on him for a decision, and that would be fatal. He twisted again in the seat, sniffed gloomily at Hearn's cigarette smoke, and then bent forward and spoke in what he thought was a low voice, although it brayed out loudly, startlingly.

"I hope everything's okay when we get to the one-five-one, sir," Dalleson shouted.

"Yes," the General said, listening to the spinning humming sounds of the tires as the jeep splashed through the mud. Dalleson's bellow had grated on him. They had been driving for ten minutes with the headlights on, and his sense of danger had abated. He was worried again. If the line wasn't in, they would have to go riding through the mud for another half hour at least, and then there still might not be communications. The Japs might be breaking through at this moment.

There *had* to be communications. Without them . . . without them, it would be as though he were in the middle of a game of chess and someone had blindfolded him. He could guess what his opponent's next move would be and answer it, but it would be more difficult to predict the next move, and the next, and he might be making responses which were wasted, if not fatal. The jeep sloughed around a curve, and as it came out of the turn its headlights shone on the startled eyes of a soldier behind a machine gun in an emplacement by the side of the road. The jeep pulled up to him.

"What the hell do you guys mean coming down the road with your lights on?" he shouted. He saw the General and blinked. "Sorry, sir."

"It's all right, son. You're right, it's bad business, breaking one of my own orders." The General smiled, and the soldier grinned back. The jeep turned off the road into the lane which led to the bivouac of headquarters battery. Everything was dark in the area, and the General paused for a moment to orient himself. "The blackout tent is over there," he said, pointing, and the three officers set off and walked through the darkness, stumbling over the roots and shrubs of the imperfectly cleared ground. The night was very black with a tense quality about it that kept the officers from saying anything. They passed only one man in the fifty yards to the blackout tent.

The General pushed aside the flaps and groped with distaste inside the dark safety corridor. The tent had obviously blown down, been dragged in the mud, and then erected again. The inside walls were slimy. At the end of the safety corridor he pushed aside a second set of flaps and walked inside. An enlisted man and a captain were sitting at a desk.

The two men sprang to their feet. "Sir?" the Captain said.

The General sniffed. The air was extremely moist and foul. Already a few drops of sweat were forming on his forehead and back. "Where's Colonel McLeod?" he asked.

"I'll get him, sir."

"No, wait a minute," the General said. "Can you tell me if the line to Second Battalion is in from here?"

"Yes, sir, it is."

The General felt a deep relief. "Ring them for me, please." He lit a cigarette and smiled at Lieutenant Hearn. The Captain picked up the receiver out of a field telephone box, and cranked three times. "We have to relay it through B Battery, sir."

"I know," the General said shortly. It was the one subject on which the General ever showed annoyance; there was not a facet of the operations of the division with which he was not familiar.

In a minute or two, the Captain handed the phone to the General. "Second Battalion, sir."

"Give me Samson," the General said, using the code name for Lieutenant Colonel Hutchins. "Samson, this is Camel," he said, "I'm talking from Pivot Red. What's happening? Are your lines through to Paragon White and Paragon Blue?"

"This is Samson. Yes, our circuits are open." The voice was faint and distant and there was a buzzing in the earpiece. "Short," the General muttered.

"We've been trying to get you," Hutchins said. "We stopped the

110

attack on Paragon White B and C, and at Paragon Red E and G." He gave the co-ordinates. "Personally I think it was a feeler, and they're going to try again tonight."

"Yes," the General said. He was busy estimating the possibilities. They would have to be reinforced. First Battalion of the 459th, Infantry which he had been holding in reserve and working on the road, could be moved up in two hours, but he would have to leave at least a company and a detached platoon behind for reserves. The attack might come sooner than that. The General debated, and decided finally to move up only two companies from 1st Battalion, save the other two for covering any retreat which might be necessary, and strip headquarters and service companies of all available platoons. He glanced at his watch. It was eight o'clock now. "Samson," he said, "at about 2300, Potential White Able and Dog will reach you by convoy march route. They are to make contact with Paragon White and Paragon Red where they will be used according to opportunity. I'll direct that as the occasion demands." Everything was extremely clear to him at this moment. The Japanese would be attacking tonight, probably against the entire line, but certainly against the flanks. The storm would have delayed Toyaku's troops in reaching their assembly points, and chances were he would be unable to bring many tanks up. It could not be a probing attack, searching for weaknesses in the line. With the mud and the sluggish maneuvering that would involve, Toyaku would have to drive at a few points, and hope he could break them. This, the General felt, he could handle. "We're going to have some extremely powerful local attacks tonight," he said into the mouthpiece. "I want you to contact all line units and instruct them to hold their ground. *There is to be no general retreat.*"

"Sir?" The voice at the other end of the phone was doubtful.

"If the Japs can penetrate, let them. The companies on the flanks of any gap in the line are to hold their positions. I'll court-martial any officer who pulls back his unit for tactical reasons. Anything that gets through us will be handled by the reserve."

Dalleson was bewildered. The one decision he had made was that, with a newly established line and a few powerful Japanese thrusts on tap for the night, the safest thing would be to pull back the

111

troops a mile or two, and attempt to delay the attack until morning. He felt a deep gratitude now that the General had not asked his opinion. He had assumed immediately that the General was right and he was wrong.

Hutchins was speaking again. "What about me? Will I get any men?"

"Powerhouse will reach you at 2330," the General said. "You will deploy them between Paragon Red George and Paragon Red Easy at the following co-ordinates: 017.37 — 439.56, and at 018.25 — 440.06." The General assigned these positions from a mental image of his battle map. "As additional support, I'm going to send you a reinforced platoon from Paragon Yellow Sugar. They're to be used for pack train and lateral communication with Paragon White, and if possible afterward as rifle support at Paragon White Baker or Cat. We'll work that out as things go along. I'm going to set up a temporary CP here for the night."

Everything flowed out of him easily now, his decisions quick and instinctively just, he believed. The General could not have been more happy than he was at this moment. He hung up, and gazed for a moment at Hearn and Dalleson, feeling a quiet impersonal affection for them both. "Going to be a lot doing tonight," he murmured. Covertly, he noticed the artillery captain and the enlisted man looking at him almost in awe. With something like gaiety he turned to Dalleson.

"I promised Hutchins a reinforced platoon. I'm going to send up Pioneer and Demolition, but we'll have to add a squad to that from some other platoon."

"How about I and R, sir?"

"Fine, we'll give it to recon. Now, work out some march orders. Quickly, man!" He lit a cigarette and turned to Hearn. "I suggest you pick us up some cots, Lieutenant." Hearn was no bother to him at this moment.

In the battle that followed that night, Dalleson's suggestion to add a squad from recon to the pioneer and demolition platoon was the only contribution he made.

112

5

ROTH DREAMT that he was catching butterflies in a lovely green meadow when Minetta wakened him for guard. He grumbled and tried to go back to sleep, but Minetta kept shaking him. "All right, all right, I'm getting up," he whispered angrily. He rolled over, groaned a little, got on his hands and knees, and shook his head. "Three hours' guard tonight," he realized with dread. Morosely he began to put on his shoes.

Minetta was waiting for him in the machine-gun emplacement. "Jesus, it's spooky tonight," he whispered. "I thought I'd be on forever."

"Anything happen?"

Minetta gazed out at the black jungle before them. It was just possible to discern the barbed wire ten yards beyond the machine gun. "I thought I heard some Japs sneaking around," he muttered, "so keep your ears open."

Roth felt a sick fear. "Are you sure?"

"I dunno. The artillery's been going steady for the last half hour. I think there's a battle going on." He listened. "Wait!" A battery fired a few miles away with a hollow clanging sound. "I bet the Japs are attacking. Jesus, recon is gonna get caught right in the middle of it."

"I guess we're lucky," Roth said.

Minetta's voice was very low. "Yeah, I dunno. Being doubled up on guard ain't so good either. Wait, you'll see. Three hours on a night like this is enough to make you flip your lid. How do we know that the Japs won't break through, and before your shift is over they'll be attacking right here? We're only ten miles from the front. Maybe they'll have a patrol out here."

"This is serious," Roth said. He remembered the way Goldstein's face had looked when he was making his pack soon after the storm. Goldstein was up there now, seeing combat. Roth had an odd sensation. He might even be killed. Any of them — Red, Gallagher, Sergeant Croft, Wyman, Toglio, or Martinez or Ridges or Wilson; they were all up there now, right in the middle of it. Any one of them could be gone by tomorrow. It was horrible the way a man could be killed. He wanted to tell Minetta some of this.

But Minetta yawned. "Jeez, I'm glad this is over." He started to go and then turned back. "You know who you wake up?"

"Sergeant Brown?"

"That's right. He's sleeping on a blanket with Stanley over there." Minetta indicated the direction vaguely.

Roth muttered, "Just five of us on this part of the perimeter. Think of it, five men having to hold down a whole platoon's part of the perimeter."

"That's what I mean," Minetta said. "We ain't getting any break. At least there's a lot of men where the first squad is." He yawned quietly. "Well, I'm going," he said.

Roth felt terribly alone after Minetta left him. He gazed into the jungle, and got into the hole behind the machine gun as silently as he could. Something like this was beyond him, he told himself; he didn't have the nerves for it. This took a younger man, a kid like Minetta or Polack, or one of the veterans.

He was sitting on two cartridge boxes, and the handles cut into his bony rump. He kept shifting his weight, and moving his feet about. The hole was very muddy from the evening storm, and everything about him felt damp. His clothes had been wet for hours, and he had had to spread his blankets on the wet ground. What a way to live! He would have a cold by morning, he was certain. He'd be lucky if it wasn't pneumonia.

Everything was very quiet. The jungle was hushed, ominous, with a commanding silence that stilled his breath. He waited, and abruptly the utter vacuum was broken and he was conscious of all the sounds of the night woods — the crickets and frogs and lizards thrumming in the brush, the soughing of the trees. And then the sounds seemed to vanish, or rather his ear could hear only the silence; for several minutes there was a continual alternation between the sounds and the quiet, as if they were distinct and yet related like a drawing of some cubes which perpetually turn inside-out and back again. Roth began to think; there was some heavy thunder and lightning in the distance, but he did not worry about the threat of rain. For a long time he listened to the artillery, which sounded like a great muffled bell in the heavy moist night air. He shivered and crossed his arms. He was remembering what a training sergeant had said about dirty fighting and how the Japs would sneak up behind a sentry in the jungle and knife the man. "He'd never know at all," the sergeant had said, "except maybe for one little second when it was too late."

Roth felt a gnawing, guttish fear, and turned around to look at the ground behind him. He shuddered, brooding over such a death. What an awful thing to happen. His nerves were taut. As he tried to see the jungle beyond the little clearing past the barbed wire, he had the kind of anxiety and panic a child has when the monster creeps up behind the hero in a horror movie. Something clattered in the brush, and Roth ducked in his hole, and then slowly peeked above it, trying to discern a man or at least some recognizable object in the deep shapes and shadows of the jungle. The noise stopped, and then after ten seconds began again. It was a scratching urgent sound, and Roth sat numbly in the hole, feeling nothing but the beat of his pulse throughout his entire body. His ears had become giant amplifiers and he was detecting a whole gamut of sounds, of sliding and scraping, of twigs cracking, of shrubs being rustled, which he had not noticed before. He bent over the machine gun, and then realized that he didn't know whether Minetta had cocked it completely or left it half-loaded. It meant that he would have to pull back the bolt and release it in order to be certain, and he was terrified of the noise it would make. He took up his rifle, and tried to loose the safety lever quietly, but it clicked into place quite audibly. Roth flinched at the noise, and then gazed into the jungle, trying to locate the particular place from which the sounds were coming. But they seemed to originate everywhere, and he had no idea of their distance and what caused them. He heard something rustle, and he turned his rifle clumsily in that direction, and waited, the sweat breaking out on his back. For an instant he was tempted to shoot, blindly and furiously, but he remembered that that was very dangerous. "Maybe they don't see me either," he thought, but he did not believe it. The reason he did not fire was for fear of what Sergeant Brown would say. "If you fire without seeing anything

115

to aim at, you just give away the position of your hole, and they'll throw a grenade in on you," Brown had told him. Roth trembled. He was beginning to feel resentful; for some time he had been convinced that the Japs were watching him. Why don't you come on? he wondered desperately. By now his nerves were so taut that he would have welcomed an attack.

He pressed his feet into the thick mud of the hole, and, still looking into the jungle, picked some mud off his boots with one hand and began to knead it like a piece of clay. He was unconscious of doing this. His neck had begun to pain him from the tension with which he held himself. It seemed to him that the hole was terribly open and that there was not enough protection. He felt bitter that a man should have to stand guard in an open hole with only a machine gun before him.

There was a frantic scuffling behind the first wall of jungle and Roth ground his jaws together to keep from uttering a sound. The noises were coming closer like men creeping up, moving a few feet and then halting, before approaching another few feet. He fumbled around the tripod of the machine gun to find a grenade, and then held it in his hand wondering where to throw it. The grenade seemed extremely heavy, and he felt so weak that he doubted if he could hurl it more than ten yards. In training he had been told the effective range of a grenade was thirty-five yards, and he was afraid now that he would be killed by his own grenade. He replaced it beneath the machine gun, and just sat there.

His fear had to ebb after a time. For perhaps half an hour he had been waiting for the noises to develop into something, and when nothing occurred, his confidence began to come back. He did not reason that if there were Japs they might spend two hours in advancing fifty yards toward him; because he could not bear the suspense, a part of him assumed that they could not either, and he became convinced there was nothing in the jungle but some animals scurrying about. He lay back in the hole with his shirt against the damp rear wall, and began to relax. His nerves calmed slowly, rousing to a pitch of fear again every time some sudden noise came out of the jungle, but still becoming more and more composed like a receding tide. After an hour had passed he grew sleepy. He thought of nothing, listened only to the

116

profound pendant silence of the wood. A mosquito began to sing about his ears and his neck, and he waited for it to bite him so that he could crush it. It made him think that there might be insects in the hole with him, and his body began to crawl, and for a few moments he was certain an ant was traveling down his back. It recalled to him the roaches that had infested the first apartment he had had when he was married. He remembered how he had reassured his wife, "There's nothing to worry about, Zelda. I can tell you from my studies that the roach is not too vicious a pest." Zelda had got some idea that there must be bedbugs also, and no matter how many times he reassured her, "Zelda, roaches eat bedbugs," she would start up in bed, and grasp him with fear, "Herman, I know there's something biting me."

"But I tell you that's impossible."

"Don't tell me about your roaches," she would whisper angrily in the darkened bedroom. "If roaches take care of bedbugs they have to get into the bed to do it, don't they?"

Roth felt a mingled pleasure and wistfulness in remembering. Their life together had not been all that he had hoped. There were so many fights, and Zelda had a cruel tongue; he recalled how she had taunted him with his education and the fact that he could make no money. It had not been entirely her fault, he thought, but then it had not been his either. No one was to blame. It was just that you didn't get everything you had hoped for when you were a kid. He wiped his hands on his fatigue trousers with a slow thorough motion. Zelda had been a good wife in some ways. Their quarrels had become as difficult for him to remember as her face. He mused about her now, and in his mind she became another woman, many women. He began to construct a lewd fantasy in his mind.

Roth dreamt he was taking pornographic pictures of a model whom he had dressed as a cowgirl. She was wearing a ten-gallon hat, and a leather fringe about an inch wide across her breasts, and a leather holster and cartridge belt slung at an angle across her hips. He imagined now that he was telling her which way to pose and she was obeying with a tantalizing insouciance. His groin began to ache, and he sat there, brooding, dreaming.

After a time he became sleepy again, and tried to fight against it.

117

Some artillery was firing steadily a mile or two away, the sounds loud, then muffled, then loud again. It gave him a secure feeling. He hardly listened any longer to the jungle. His eyes kept closing, remaining shut for many seconds while he yawed away on the edge of slumber. Several times he was about to fall asleep when a sudden noise in the jungle would rouse him with a start. He looked at the luminous dial of his watch and realized with dismay that he had still an hour of guard. He lay back, closed his eyes with the full intention of opening them in a few seconds, and fell asleep.

It was the last he remembered until he awoke almost two hours later. It had begun to rain once more, and the gentle drizzle had soaked his fatigues and penetrated to the insides of his shoes. He sneezed miserably once, and then realized with dismay how long he had been asleep. "A Jap could have killed me," he said to himself, and the thought sent electric wakening shudders through his body. He got out of the foxhole and stumbled over toward where Brown was sleeping. He would have missed him but he heard Brown whisper, "What the hell are you thrashing around for like a pig in the brush?"

Roth was meek. "I couldn't find you," he whined.

"Hell of a note," Brown said. He stretched once in his blankets, and stood up. "I couldn't sleep," he said. "Too many goddam noises . . . What time is it?"

"After three-thirty."

"You were supposed to wake me at three."

Roth had been afraid of this. "I began to think," Roth said weakly, "and lost track of the time."

"Shit!" Brown said. He finished tying his shoes and walked out to the emplacement without saying anything else.

Roth stood still for a moment, his rifle strap chafing his shoulder, and then began looking for the place where he and Minetta were sleeping for the night. Minetta had pulled the blankets over him, and Roth lay down beside him gingerly, and tried to tug them away. At home he had always insisted on having the sheets tucked in tightly; now with the blankets drawn up over his feet he was miserable. Everything seemed wet. The rain kept falling on his exposed legs and he became very chilled. The blankets were midway between sopping and damp; they had a musty wet odor which reminded him of the smell of feet. He kept turning over, trying to find an accommodating place on the ground, but it seemed as if a root were always sticking into the small of his back. The drizzle teased him when he pulled the blankets off his face. He was sweating and shuddering at the same time, and he was convinced he would be sick. Why didn't I tell Brown he ought to be glad I stood an extra half hour of guard for him? he asked himself abruptly, and felt frustrated and bitter that he had failed to answer him. Wait, I'll tell him in the morning, he assured himself angrily. Of the men in the platoon he decided there was not one of them he really liked. They're all stupid, he said to himself. There wasn't a single one of them who was the least bit friendly to a new man, and he felt a spasm of loneliness. His feet were cold. When he tried to wriggle his toes, the hopelessness of warming them overwhelmed him. He tried to think of his wife and son and it seemed to him there could be no more perfect life than to return to them. His wife had a soft mothering look now in her eyes, and his son was staring at him with delight and respect. He thought of his son growing up, discussing serious things with him, valuing his opinion. The drizzle tickled his ear, and he pulled the end of the blanket over his head again. Minetta's body was warm and he huddled toward it. He thought once again of his infant son, and felt a swell of pride. He thinks I'm someone, Roth said to himself. I'll show them yet. His eyes closed and he loosed a long whispering sigh, immensely wistful in the soft drizzling night.

That fuggin Roth, Brown said to himself, falling asleep on guard and maybe getting us all killed. No man's got a right to do something like that; he lets his buddies down and they ain't a worse thing a man can do.

No, sir, Brown repeated, they ain't a worse thing a man can do. I may be afraid and I may have my nerves shot all to hell, but at least I act like a sergeant and take care of my duties. There's no easy way to get ahead; a man's got to pull his share, take his responsibilities, and then he gets what he earns. I've had my eye on Roth from the beginning. He's no good, he's lazy, he's shiftless, and he don't take an interest in anything. I hate these fathers who bitch because they finally

119

got caught. Hell, what about us who been sweating it out for a couple of years and Lord knows how long to come? We were fightin' when they were screwin' their wives, and maybe screwin' ours too.

Brown shifted his weight angrily on the cartridge boxes and looked out at the jungle, rubbing his hand reflectively over the bridge of his short snubbed nose. Yeah, what about us, he said to himself, sitting out here in a lousy hole in the rain, sweatin' out every goddam noise while those women are on the loose havin' their own sweet time?

I should have known better, marrying a two-timing bitch like that. Even when we were in high school, she was rubbing up against everything that wore pants. Oh, I know a lot more now, I know that it's a mistake to marry a woman 'cause you can't make her any other way, holding out on me for all that time, and even now I don't know if she was cherry. There ain't any such thing as a clean decent woman any more, when a man's sister will go up to him and tell him to mind his own business because she's fooling around and her husband's out of town, it's time for a man to open his eyes. There ain't a one of them a man can trust out of his sight; how many times have I picked up a piece from a married woman with kids, it's disgustin' the way they all act.

Brown took his rifle off his knees and laid it against the machine gun. It's bad enough with all a man's got to worry about out here, with guys like that fuggin Roth who fall asleep on guard, and trying to keep the details straight so no man has to work more than his share, and always wondering if today is the day you get it, so that you'd think a woman would have the decency to keep her legs closed, but, no, there isn't one of them that's worth a snowball in hell. All the time we're out here beating our meat for company, doing it till it's disgusting, but what the hell else is there? I oughta quit 'cause it breaks down your confidence, and I'd be feeling stronger, but how can ya without a goddam woman and nothing to think about? All the men do it. Sure.

And right now what is she doing, she's probably right in bed talking to a guy this very minute and they're figuring out what they're gonna do with the ten thousand insurance on me when I get knocked off. Well, I'm gonna fool them, I'm gonna live through the goddam

120

war and then I'm gonna get rid of her, and then I'm gonna make my mark. There'll be a lot of ways for a man to make some money after the war if he isn't afraid of some hard work and taking on some responsibility, and I'm not afraid. All the men say I'm a good noncom. I may not be as good a scout as Martinez and I may not have ice instead of blood in my veins the way Croft has, but I'm fair, and I take my job seriously. I'm not like Red, always goofing off, or thinkin' of a smart crack instead of working, I really try hard to be a good noncom 'cause if you succeed in the Army there isn't any other place you won't succeed. If you have to do something you might as well do it right, that's what I believe.

Some artillery fired continuously for several minutes, and Brown listened to it tensely. The boys are really getting it now, he told himself, sure as hell, the Japs are attacking and recon's bound to be in the middle of it. We're a hard-luck platoon, there's no doubt about it, I just hope nobody gets hurt tonight. He stared into the darkness. I'm real lucky being left behind, he told himself, I'm sure glad I'm not in Martinez's shoes. It's going to be real rough tonight, and I don't want any part of it. I've had my share of the close ones, running across a field with a machine gun ticking after me or swimming in the water that time the Japs had the AA gun turned on us is enough for any man to have to take. I'm proud I'm a sergeant, but there are times when I wish I was just a buck private and all I had to do was bitch like Roth. I've got to look out for myself because no one else will, and I've sweated this war out long enough not to get hit now.

He fingered one of the jungle ulcers on his mouth. I just hope to hell none of the boys get hurt tonight, he said to himself.

The truck convoy ground sullenly through the mud. It was over an hour since recon had left its bivouac area, but it seemed much longer. There were twenty-five men packed inside the truck and, since there were seats for only twelve, over half the men sat on the floor in a tangle of rifles and packs and arms and legs. In the darkness everyone was sweating and the night seemed incomparably dense; the jungle on either side of the road exuded moisture continually.

No one had anything to say. When the men in the truck listened they could hear the front of the convoy grinding up a grade before them. Occasionally the truck to their rear would creep up close enough for the men to see its blackout lights like two tiny candles in a fog. A mist had settled over the jungle, and in the darkness the men felt disembodied.

Wyman was sitting on his pack, and when he closed his eyes and let the rumble of the truck shake through him he felt as if he were in a subway. The tension and excitement he had felt when Croft had come up and told them to pack their gear because they were moving forward had abated a little by now and Wyman was drifting along on a mood which vacillated between boredom and a passive stream of odd thoughts and recollections. He was thinking of a time when he had accompanied his mother on a bus trip from New York to Pittsburgh. It was just after his father died, and his mother was going to see her relatives for money. The trip had been fruitless and, coming back on a midnight bus, he and his mother had talked about what they would do and decided that he would have to go to work. He thought of it with a little wonder. At the time it had been the most important night of his life, and now he was going on another trip, a far more eventful one, and he had no idea what would happen. It made him feel very mature for a moment; these were things which had happened just a few years ago, insignificant things now. He was trying to imagine what combat would be like, and he decided it would be impossible to guess. He had always pictured it as something violent, going on for days without halt. And here he had been in the platoon for over a week and nothing had happened; everything had been peaceful and relaxed.

"Do you think we'll see much tonight, Red?" he asked softly.

"Ask the General," Red snorted. He liked Wyman, but he tried to be unfriendly to him because the youth reminded Red of Hennessey. Red had a deep loathing of the night before them. He had been through so much combat, had felt so many kinds of terror, and had seen so many men killed that he no longer had any illusions about the inviolability of his own flesh. He knew he could be killed; it was something he had accepted long ago, and he had grown a shell about that knowledge so that he rarely thought of anything further ahead

122

than the next few minutes. However, there had been lately a disquieting uncomfortable insight which he had never brought to the point of words, and it was bothering him. Until Hennessey had been killed, Red had accepted all the deaths of the men he knew as something large and devastating and meaningless. Men who were killed were merely men no longer around; they became confused with old friends who had gone to the hospital and never come back, or men who had been transferred to another outfit. When he heard of some man he knew who had been killed or wounded badly, he was interested, even a little concerned, but it was the kind of emotion a man might feel if he learned that a friend of his had got married or made or lost some money. It was merely something that happened to somebody he knew, and Red had always let it go at that. But Hennessey's death had opened a secret fear. It was so ironic, so obvious, when he remembered the things Hennessey had said, that he found himself at the edge of a bottomless dread.

Once he could have looked ahead to what he knew would be bad combat with a repugnance for the toil and misery of it, and a dour acceptance of the deaths that would occur. But now the idea of death was fresh and terrifying again.

"You want to know something?" he said to Wyman.

"Yeah?"

"They ain't a thing you can do about it, so shut up."

Wyman was hurt and lapsed into silence. Red felt sorry immediately afterward, and drew out a bar of tropical chocolate, bent out of shape and covered with tobacco grains from the silt of his pockets. "Hey, you want some chocolate?" he asked.

"Yeah, thanks."

They felt the night about them. In the truck there was no sound except for an occasional mutter or curse as they hit a bump. Each vehicle by itself was making all the noises that trucks can make; they creaked and jounced and groaned over the bogholes, and their tires made wet singing sounds. But, taken all together, the line of trucks had a combined, intricate medley of vibrations and tones which sounded like the gentle persistent lapping of surf against the sides of a ship. It was a melancholy sound, and, in the darkness, the men sprawled uncomfortably on the floor, their backs propped against the knees of the man behind them, their rifles pitched at every odd angle or straddled clumsily across their knees. Croft had insisted they wear their helmets, and Red was sweating under the unaccustomed weight. "Might as well wear a goddam sandbag," he said to Wyman.

Encouraged, Wyman asked, "I guess it's gonna be rough, huh?"

Red sighed, but repressed his annoyance. "It won't be too bad, kid. You just keep a tight ass-hole, and the rest of you'll take care of itself."

Wyman laughed quietly. He liked Red, and decided he would stay near him. The trucks halted, and the men moved around inside, shifting their positions and groaning as they flexed their cramped limbs. They waited patiently, their heads dropping on their chests, their damp clothing unable to dry in the heavy night air. There was barely a breeze and they felt tired and sleepy.

Goldstein was beginning to fidget. After the trucks had remained motionless for five minutes, he turned to Croft and asked, "Sergeant, is it all right if I get out and take a look at what's holding us up?"

Croft snorted. "You can stay right here, Goldstein. They ain't none of us gonna be getting up and getting lost on purpose."

Goldstein felt himself flush. "I didn't mean anything like that," he said. "I just thought it might be dangerous for us to be sitting here like this when there might be Japs around. How do we know why the trucks stopped?"

Croft yawned and then lashed him in a cold even voice. "I tell you what, you're going to have enough things to worry about. Suppose you just set down and beat your meat if you're gettin' anxious. I'll do all the goddam masterminding." There was a snicker from some of the men in the truck, and Goldstein was hurt. He decided he disliked Croft, and he brooded over all the sarcastic things Croft had said to him since he had been in the platoon.

The trucks started again, and moved jerkily in low gear for a few hundred yards before they stopped. Gallagher swore.

"What's the matter, boy, you in any hurry?" Wilson asked softly. "We might as well get where we're goin'."

They remained sitting there for a few minutes, and then began

124

to move again. A battery they had passed on the road was firing, and another one a few miles ahead also had gone into action. The shells whispered overhead, perhaps a mile above them, and the men listened dully. A machine gun began to fire far away, and the sound carried to them in separate bursts, deep and empty, like a man beating a carpet. Martinez took off his helmet and kneaded his skull, feeling as though a hammer were pounding him. A Japanese gun answered fire with a high penetrating shriek. A flare went up near the horizon and cast enough light for them to see one another. Their faces looked white and then blue as though they were staring at each other across a dark and smoky room. "We're gettin' close," someone said. After the flare had died, it was possible to see a pale haze against the horizon, and Toglio said, "Something's burning."

"Sounds like a big fight going on," Wyman suggested to Red.

"Naw, they're just feeling each other out," Red told him. "There'll be a helluva lot more noise if something starts tonight." The machine guns sputtered and then became silent. A few mortar shells were landing somewhere with a flat thudding sound, and another machine gun, much farther away, fired again. Then there was silence, and the trucks continued down the black muddy road.

After a few minutes they halted again, and somebody in the rear of the truck tried to light a cigarette. "Put the goddam thing out," Croft snapped.

The soldier was in another platoon and he swore at Croft. "Who the hell are you? I'm tired of just waiting around."

"Put that goddam thing out," Croft said again, and after a pause, the soldier snuffed it. Croft was feeling irritable and nervous. He had no fear but he was impatient and overalert.

Red debated whether to light a cigarette. He and Croft had hardly spoken to each other since their quarrel on the beach, and he was tempted to defy him. Actually he knew he wouldn't, and he tried to decide whether the real reason was that it was a bad idea to show a light or because he was afraid of Croft. Fug it, I'll stand up to that sonofabitch when the time comes, Red told himself, but I'll damn sure be right when I do.

They had begun to move once more. After a few minutes they

heard a few low voices on the road, and their truck turned off and wallowed through a muddy lane. It was very narrow and a branch from a tree swept along the top of the truck. "Watch it!" someone shouted, and they all flattened themselves. Red pulled some leaves out of his shirt and pricked his finger on a thorn. He wiped the blood on the back of his pants and began searching for his pack, which he had thrown off when he first got into the truck. His legs were stiff and he tried to flex them.

"Don't dismount till you're told," Croft said.

The trucks came to a halt, and they listened to the few men circling around them in the darkness. Everything was terribly quiet. They sat there, speaking in whispers. An officer rapped on the tail gate and said, "All right, men, dismount and stick together." They began to jump out of the truck, moving slowly and uncertainly. It was a five-foot drop into darkness and they didn't know what the ground was like beneath them. "Drop the tail gate," someone said, and the officer snapped, "All right, men, let's keep it quiet."

When they had all got out, they stood about waiting. The trucks were already backing away for another trip. "Are there any officers here?" the officer asked.

A few of the men snickered. "All right, keep it down," the officer said. "Let's have the platoon noncoms forward."

Croft and a sergeant from the pioneer and demolition platoon stepped up. "Most of my men are in the next truck," the noncom said, and the officer told him to move his men together. Croft talked in a low voice to the officer for a minute and then gathered recon around him. "We got to wait," he said. "Let's stick around that tree." There was just enough light for them to notice it, and they walked over slowly. "Where are we now?" Ridges asked.

"Second Battalion headquarters," Croft said. "What've you been working on the road for all this time if you don't even know where you are?"

"Shoot, Ah just work, Ah don' spend mah time lookin' around," Ridges said. He guffawed nervously, and Croft told him to be quiet. They sat down around the tree and waited silently. A battery fired in a grove about five hundred yards away and it lit up the area for a moment. "What's the artillery doin' up this close?" Wilson asked.

"It's cannon company," someone told him.

Wilson sighed. "All a man does is sit around an' get his tail wet."

"It seems to me," Goldstein said formally, "that they're managing this thing very poorly." His voice was eager as if he were hoping for a discussion.

"You bitching again, Goldstein?" Croft asked.

The anti-Semite, Goldstein thought. "I'm just expressing my opinion," he said.

"Opinion!" Croft spat. "A bunch of goddam women have opinions."

Gallagher laughed quietly and mockingly. "Hey, Goldstein, you want a soapbox?"

"You don't like the Army any more than I do," Goldstein said mildly.

Gallagher paused, then sneered. "Balls," he said. "What's the matter, you want some gefüllte fish?" He stopped, and then as if delighted with what he had said, he added, "That's right, what Goldstein needs is some of that fuggin fish." A machine gun began to fire again; because of the night it sounded very close.

"I don't like the way you express yourself," Goldstein said.

"You know what you can do," Gallagher said. He was partially ashamed, and to drown it he added fiercely, "You can go blow it . . .'"

"You can't talk to me that way," Goldstein said. His voice trembled. He was in a turmoil, revolted by the idea of fighting, yet recognizing the deep necessity for it. The goyim, that's all they know, to fight with their fists, he thought.

Red stepped in. He had the discomfort a display of emotion always roused in him. "Let's take it easy," he muttered. "You guys'll be getting plenty of fight in a minute." He snorted. "Fightin' over the Army. As far as I'm concerned, it's been a goddam mess ever since they put Washington on a horse."

Toglio interrupted him. "You've got the wrong attitude, Red. It ain't decent to talk about George Washington that way."

Red slapped his knee. "You're a regular Boy Scout, ain't you, Toglio? You like the flag, huh?"

Toglio thought of a story he had read once, *The Man Without a Country*. Red was like the man in that, he decided. "I think some things aren't fit for kidding," he said severely.

"You want to know something?"

Toglio knew a crack was coming, but against his judgment he asked, "What?"

"The only thing wrong with this Army is it never lost a war."

Toglio was shocked. "You think we ought to lose this one?"

Red found himself carried away. "What have I got against the goddam Japs? You think I care if they keep this fuggin jungle? What's it to me if Cummings gets another star?"

"General Cummings, he's a good man," Martinez said.

"There ain't a good officer in the world," Red stated. "They're just a bunch of aristocrats, *they* think. General Cummings is no better than I am. His shit don't smell like ice cream either."

Their voices were beginning to carry above a whisper, and Croft said, "Let's keep it down." The conversation was boring him. It was always the men who never got anywhere that did the bitching.

Goldstein was still quivering. His sense of shame was so intense that a few tears welled in his eyes. Red's interruption frustrated him, for Gallagher's words had pitched Goldstein so taut that he needed some issue desperately now. He was certain, however, that he would start weeping with rage if he opened his mouth, and so he remained silent, trying to calm himself.

A soldier came walking toward them. "Are you guys recon?" he asked.

"Yeah," Croft said.

"Okay, you want to follow me?"

They picked up their packs and began walking through the darkness. It was difficult to see the man ahead. After they had gone a few hundred feet, the soldier who was leading them halted and said, "Wait here."

Red swore. "Next time, let's do it by the numbers," he said. Cannon company fired again, and the noise sounded very loud. Wilson dropped his pack and muttered, "Some poor sonsofbitches are gonna catch hell in 'bout half a minute." He sighed and sat down on the wet ground. "You'd think they had somepin better to do than have a whole squad of men walkin' around all night. Ah can't make up m' mind if Ah'm hot or cold." There was a wet heavy mist over the ground, and alternately they shivered in their wet clothing and sweltered in the airless night. Some Japanese artillery was landing about a mile away, and they listened to it quietly.

A platoon of men filed by, their rifles clanking against their helmets and pack buckles. A flare went up a short distance away, and in its light the men looked like black cutouts moving past a spotlight. Their rifles were slung at odd angles, and their packs gave them a humped misshapen appearance. The sound of their walking was confused and intricate; like the truck convoy, it resembled the whisper of surf. Then the flare died, and the column of men passed. When they were some distance away, the only sound that still remained was the soft metallic jingle of their rifles. A skirmish had started at some distance and Jap rifles were firing. Red turned to Wyman and said, "Listen to them. Tick-boom, tick-boom. You can't miss it." A few American rifles answered, their fire sounding more powerful, like a leather belt slapped on a table. Wyman shifted uneasily. "How far away do you figure the Japs are?" he asked Croft.

"Damned if I know. You'll see 'em soon enough, boy."

"Hell he will," Red said. "We're going to be sitting around all night."

Croft spat. "You wouldn't mind that, would you, Valsen?"

"Not me. I'm no hero," Red said.

Some soldiers walked past in the darkness, and a few trucks pulled into the bivouac. Wyman lay down on the ground. He was a little chagrined that he would spend his first night in combat trying to fall asleep. The water soaked through his shirt, which was already wet, and he sat up again, shivering. The air was very sultry. He wished he could light a cigarette.

They waited another half hour before receiving the order to move. Croft stood up and followed their guide while the rest trailed behind. The guide led them into a patch of brush where a platoon of men was grouped around six antitank guns. They were 37s, small guns about six feet long with very slender barrels. One man could

129

pull one gun without too much difficulty over level hard ground.

"We're going along with antitank up to First Battalion," Croft said. "We got to pull two of them guns."

Croft told them to gather around him. "I don't know how muddy the damn trail is going to be," he began, "but it ain't too hard to guess. We're going to be in the middle of the column, so I'm going to cut us into three groups of three men each, and they'll be one group restin' all the time. I'll take Wilson and Gallagher, and Martinez can take Valsen and Ridges, and Toglio, you got what's left — Goldstein and Wyman. We're scrapin' the barrel," he added dryly.

He went up to talk to an officer for a few seconds. When he came back, he said, "We'll let Toglio's group have the first rest." He got behind one of the guns and gave it a tug. "The sonofabitch is going to be heavy." Wilson and Gallagher started pulling it with him, and the other platoon, which had already divided into a few men on each gun, began to move out. They tugged the guns across the bivouac area, and passed through a gap in the barbed wire where there was a machine gun emplacement. "Have a good time, men," the man at the machine gun said.

"Blow it out," Gallagher answered. The gun was beginning to drag on his arms already.

There were about fifty men in the column, and they moved very slowly down a narrow trail through the jungle. After they had moved a hundred feet, they were no longer able to see the men in front of them. The branches of the trees on either side of the trail joined overhead, and they felt as though they were groping through an endless tunnel. Their feet sank into the deep mud and, after a few yards, their boots were covered with great slabs of muck. The men on the guns would lunge forward for a few feet and then halt, lunge forward and halt. Every ten yards a gun would bog down and the three men assigned to it would have to tug until their strength seeped from their fingers. They would wrestle the gun out of its rut and plunge it forward for fifteen feet before their momentum was lost. Then they would pull it and lift it for another few yards until it sank into a hole once more. The entire column labored and stumbled at a miserable pace along the trail. In the darkness they kept ganging up on each

130

other, the men on one gun sometimes riding it up onto the muzzle of the one ahead, or falling behind so far that the file at last broke into separate wriggling columns like a worm cut into many parts and still living. The men at the rear had the worst of it. The guns and men that preceded them had churned the trail until it was almost a marsh, and there were places where two teams would have to combine on one gun and carry it above the ground until they had passed the worst of the slime.

The trail was only a few feet wide. Huge roots continually tripped the men, and their faces and hands became scratched and bleeding from the branches and thorns. In the complete darkness they had no idea of how the trail might bend, and sometimes on a down slope, when they could let the gun roll a little distance, they would land at the bottom with the field piece completely off the trail. Then they would have to fumble in the brush, covering their eyes with their arms to protect them from the vines, and a painful struggle to bring the gun back on the path would begin.

Some Japanese might easily have been waiting in ambush, but it was impossible to keep silent. The guns squeaked and lumbered, made sucking sounds as their tires sank into the mud, and the men swore helplessly, panted with deep sobbing sounds like wrestlers at the end of a long bout. Voices and commands echoed hollowly, were lost in a chorus of profanity and hoarse sobbing, the straining sweating noises of men in great labor. By the time an hour had passed, nothing existed for them but the slender cannon they had to get down the track. The sweat drenched their clothing and filled their eyes, blinding them. They grappled and blundered and swore, advanced the little guns a few feet at a time with no consciousness any longer of what they were doing.

When one team was relieved by another, they would stagger alongside the guns trying to regain their wind, falling behind sometimes to rest for a little while. Every ten minutes the column would stop to allow the stragglers to catch up. During the halts the men would sprawl in the middle of the trail not caring how the mud covered them. They felt as though they had been running for hours; they could not regain their breath, and their stomachs retched emptily.

131

Some of the men began to throw away their equipment; one after another the men threw their helmets aside or dropped them on the trail. The air was unbearably hot under the canopy of the jungle, and the darkness gave no relief from the heat of the day; if anything, walking the trail was like fumbling through an endless closet stuffed with velvet garments.

During one of the halts, the officer leading the file worked his way back to find Croft. "Where's Sergeant Croft?" he shouted, his words repeated by the men along the trail until it reached Croft.

"Here, sir." They stumbled toward each other through the mud.

"How're your men?" the officer asked.

"Okay."

They sat down beside the trail. "Mistake trying this," the officer gasped. "Have to get through."

Croft, with his lean ropy body, had borne the labor comparatively well, but his voice was unsteady and he had to talk with short quick spates of words. "How far?" he asked.

"Have to go one mile . . . one mile yet. More than halfway there, I think. Never should have tried it."

"They need the guns bad?"

The officer halted for a moment and tried to speak normally. "I think so . . . there's no tank weapons there . . . up on the line. We stopped a tank attack two hours ago . . . at Third Battalion. Orders came to move some thirty-sevens over to First Battalion. Guess they expect attack there."

"Better get them through," Croft said. He was contemptuous because the officer had to talk to him. The man ought to be able to do his own job.

"Have to, I guess." The officer stood up and leaned for a moment against a tree. "If you get a gun stuck, let me know. Have to cross a stream . . . up ahead. Bad place, I think."

He began to feel his way forward, and Croft turned around and worked his way back to the gun he was pulling. The column was over two hundred yards long by now. They started to move, and the labor continued. Once or twice a flare filtered a wan and delicate bluish light over them, the light almost lost in the dense foliage through which it

132

had to pass. In the brief moment it lasted, they were caught at their guns in classic straining motions that had the form and beauty of a frieze. Their uniforms were twice blackened, by the water and the dark slime of the trail. And for the instant the light shone on them their faces stood out, white and contorted. Even the guns had a slender articulated beauty like an insect reared back on its wire haunches. Then darkness swirled about them again, and they ground the guns forward blindly, a line of ants dragging their burden back to their hole.

They had reached that state of fatigue in which everything was hated. A man would slip in the mud and remain there, breathing hoarsely, having no will to get to his feet. That part of the column would halt, and wait numbly for the soldier to join them. If they had breath, they would swear.

"Fug the sonofabitchin' mud."

"Get up," somebody would cry.

"Fug you. Fug the goddam gun."

"Let me lay here. I'm okay, they ain't a thing wrong with me, I'm okay, let me lay."

"Fug you, *get up!*"

And they would labor forward a few more yards and halt. In the darkness, distance had no meaning, nor did time. The heat had left their bodies; they shivered and trembled in the damp night, and everything about them was sodden and pappy; they stank but no longer with animal smells; their clothing was plastered with the foul muck of the jungle mud, and a chill dank rotting smell somewhere between leaf mold and faeces filled their nostrils. They knew only that they had to keep moving, and if they thought of time it was in so many convulsions of nausea.

Wyman was wondering why he did not collapse. His breath came in long parched shudders, his pack straps galled, his feet were ablaze, and he could not have spoken, for his throat and chest and mouth seemed covered with a woolly felt. He was no longer conscious of the powerful and fetid stench that rose from his clothes. Somewhere deep inside himself was a wonder at the exhaustion his body could endure. He was normally a sluggish youth who worked no more than he was obliged to, and the sensations of labor, the muscle strains,

133

the panting, the taste of fatigue were things he had always tried to avoid. He had had vague dreams about being a hero, assuming this would bring him some immense reward which would ease his life and remove the problems of supporting his mother and himself. He had a girl and he wanted to dazzle her with his ribbons. But he had always imagined combat as exciting, with no misery and no physical exertion. He dreamed of himself charging across a field in the face of many machine guns; but in the dream there was no stitch in his side from running too far while bearing too much weight.

He had never thought he would be chained to an inanimate monster of metal with which he would have to grapple until his arms trembled helplessly and his body was ready to fall; certainly he had never imagined he would stumble down a path in the middle of the night with his shoes sucking and dragging in slime. He pushed at the gun, he lifted it with Goldstein and Toglio when it became mired in a hole, but the motions were automatic by now; he hardly even felt the added pain when they had to pull it out by the wheel hubs. His fingers were no longer able to close, and often he would tug helplessly until his hands slipped away with the gun still mired.

The column was proceeding even more slowly than it had at the start, and sometimes fifteen minutes would elapse before a gun could be moved a hundred yards. Every now and then a man would faint, and would be left by the side of the trail to make his way back alone when he recovered.

At last a message began to carry back along the trail, "Keep going, we're almost there," and for a few minutes it served as a stimulant so that the men labored with some hope again. But when each turning in the trail discovered only another ribbon of mud and darkness, the men began to feel a hopeless dejection. Sometimes for as much as a minute they would not move at all. It became harder and harder to pitch themselves against the guns again. Every time they stopped they felt like quitting.

There was a draw they had to cross a few hundred feet before they reached 1st Battalion, and its banks sloped very steeply down to a little stony brook, then ascended again abruptly to about fifteen feet above the bottom. This was the stream the officer had mentioned.

134

When the men reached it, the column stopped completely, and the stragglers caught up. Each team of soldiers waited for the men and gun in front of them to cross the stream. In the night it was an extremely difficult business at best and took a long time. The men would go sliding down the bank trying to restrain their field piece from turning over at the bottom, and then they would have to lift it over the slippery rocks of the brook before attempting to wrestle it up the other side. The banks were slimy, and there was no foothold; time and again a team would force their gun up almost to the top of the draw only to slip back again futilely.

By the time Wyman and Toglio and Goldstein had to move their gun, a half hour had passed and they were a little rested. Their wind had returned and they kept shouting instructions to each other as they nosed the gun over the edge of the bank. It began to pull away from them, and they had to resist desperately to keep it from crashing to the bottom. The exertion drained most of the strength they had recovered, and after they had carried the piece across the stream, they were as exhausted as they had been at any time during the march.

They stopped for a few moments to gather whatever force was left in them and began the struggle up the bank. Toglio was wheezing like a bull, and his commands had a hoarse urgent sound as if he were wrenching them from deep inside his body. "Okay, PUSH . . . PUSH," he growled, and the three of them strove numbly to roll the gun. It resisted them, moved sluggishly and treacherously, and the strength began to flow out of their trembling legs. "HOLD IT!" Toglio shouted "DON'T LET IT SLIP!" They braced themselves behind the gun, trying to wedge their feet into the wet clay of the bank. "PUSH AGAIN!" he shouted, and they forced it upward a few more feet. Wyman felt a band was stretching dangerously inside his body and would snap at any moment. They rested again, and then shoved the gun another few yards. Slowly, minute by minute, they came closer to the top. They were perhaps four feet from the crest when Wyman lost the last reserves of his strength. He tried to draw some few shreds of effort from his quivering limbs, but he seemed to collapse all at once, and just lay stupidly behind the gun supporting it with no more than the weight of his sagging body. The gun began to slip, and he pulled away. Toglio and Goldstein were left at each of the hubs. When Wyman let go, they felt as though someone were pushing down against the gun. Goldstein held on until the sliding wheels pulled his fingers loose, one by one, and then he just had time to shout hoarsely, "WATCH IT!" to Toglio, before the gun went crashing down to the bottom. The three men fell after it, rolling in its wake. The gun struck some rocks at the bottom, and one of the wheels was knocked completely awry. They felt for it in the darkness like pups licking the wounds of their mother. Wyman began to blubber with exhaustion.

The accident caused a great deal of confusion. Croft's team was on the gun waiting behind them, and he began to shout, "What's holdin' you up? What's happening down there?"

"We had . . . trouble," Toglio shouted back. "Wait!" He and Goldstein succeeded in turning the gun on its side. "The wheel's shot," Toglio shouted. "We can't move the gun."

Croft swore. "Get her out of the way."

They tried, and couldn't budge it.

"We need help," Goldstein shouted.

Croft swore again, and then he and Wilson slid down the bank. After a while they were able to tumble the gun over enough times to move it down the creek bed. Without saying anything, Croft went back to his gun, and Toglio and the others climbed up the far bank and went staggering down the trail till they reached 1st Battalion's bivouac. The men who had arrived before them were lying on the ground motionless. Toglio stretched out in the mud, and Wyman and Goldstein lay down beside him. None of them spoke for ten minutes. Occasionally, a shell might burst somewhere in the jungle about them and their legs might twitch, but this was the only sign they gave of being conscious. Men were moving about constantly, and the sounds of the fighting were closer, more vicious. Voices kept coming to them out of the darkness. Someone would shout, "Where's the pack train for B Company?" and the answer would be muffled to the men lying on the ground. They hardly cared. Occasionally they would be aware of the sounds of the night; for a few instants they might concentrate on the constant thrumming that emanated from the jungle, but they always relapsed into a stupor, thinking of nothing once more.

136

Croft and Wilson and Gallagher brought their gun in a short while later, and Croft shouted for Toglio.

"What do you want? I'm here," Toglio said. He hated to move.

Croft came toward him in the darkness and sat down beside him. His breath was coming in long slow gasps like a runner after a race. "I'm going to see the Lieutenant . . . tell him about the gun. How the hell did it happen?"

Toglio propped himself on an elbow. He loathed the explanations that were to come, and he was confused. "I don't know," he said. "I heard Goldstein yell 'Watch out' and then it just seemed to rip out of our hands." Toglio hated to give excuses to Croft.

"Goldstein yelled, huh?" Croft asked. "Where is he?"

"Here I am, Sergeant." Goldstein's voice came out of the darkness beside them.

"Why'd you yell 'Watch out'?"

"I don't know. I felt suddenly as if I couldn't hold it any more. Something pulled it away from me."

"Who was the other man?"

Wyman roused himself. "I guess I was." His voice sounded weak.

"Did you let go?" Croft asked.

Wyman felt a trace of fear as he thought of admitting that to Croft. "No," he said. "No, I don't think so. I heard Goldstein yell, and then the gun started to come down on me. It was rolling back so I got out of the way." Already he was uncertain exactly how it had occurred, and a part of his mind was trying to convince him that he spoke the truth. With it, however, he felt a surprising flush of shame. "I guess it was my fault," he blurted out honestly, but his voice was so tired that it lacked sincerity, and Croft thought he was trying to protect Goldstein.

"Yeah," Croft said. A spasm of rage worked through him, and he turned on Goldstein and said, "Listen, Izzy."

"My name isn't Izzy," Goldstein said angrily.

"I don't give a damn what it is. The next time you pull a goddam trick like that, I'm going to put you in for a court-martial."

"But I don't think I let go," Goldstein protested weakly. By now,

137

he too was no longer sure. The sequence of his sensations when the gun had begun to pull out of his hands was too confused for him to feel righteous. He had thought that Wyman stopped pushing first, but when Wyman declared he was to blame, Goldstein had a moment of panic. Like Croft, he believed Wyman was protecting him. "I don't know," he said. "I don't think I did."

"You don't think," Croft cut him off. "Listen, for as long as you've been in the platoon, Goldstein, you've done nothing but have ideas about how we could do something better. But when it comes down to a little goddam work, you're always dicking off. I've had enough of that bullshit from you."

Once again Goldstein was feeling a helpless anger. A reaction he could not control, his agitation was even greater than his resentment and choked him so that he could not speak. A few tears of frustration welled in his eyes, and he turned away and lay down again. His anger was now directed toward himself and he felt a hopeless shame. Oh, I don't know, I don't know, he said.

Toglio had a mingled relief and pity. He was glad the onus of losing the gun was not his, and yet he was unhappy anyone should be blamed. The bond of common effort that the three men had known while struggling with the weapon was still with him, and he said to himself, poor Goldstein, he's a good guy; he just had hard luck.

Wyman was too exhausted to think clearly. After he declared it was his fault, he was relieved to discover he was not to be blamed after all. He was actually too depleted to think consecutively about anything, or indeed remember anything. By now, he was convinced it was Goldstein who had deserted the gun, and his main reaction was one of comfort. The image still most vivid to him was the agony he had felt in his chest and groin as they had started up the embankment, and he thought, I would have let go two seconds later if he didn't. For this reason, Wyman felt a dulled sense of affection for Goldstein.

Croft stood up. "Well, that's one gun they ain't going to rescue for a little while," he said. "I bet it stays there for the whole campaign." He was enraged enough to strike Goldstein. Without saying

138

anything more, Croft left them and went in search of the officer who had led the column.

The men in the platoon settled down and began to sleep. Occasionally a shell would burst in the jungle nearby, but they hardly cared. The battle had been threatening all evening like a thunderstorm which never breaks, and by now it would have taken a barrage to move them. Besides, they were too weary to dig holes.

It took Red longer to fall asleep than any of the others. For many years his kidneys had bothered him whenever he had too much exposure to dampness. They were throbbing now, and he turned several times on the wet ground, trying to decide if it would be less painful to sleep with his back against the moist earth or exposed to the night air. He lay awake for a long time thinking, his mood turning through a small gamut from weariness to sadness. He was thinking of a time when he had been caught in a small town in Nebraska with no jobs to be had, and had had to wait until he could catch a boxcar out of town. It had seemed very important to him then not to beg for something to eat, and he wondered if he still had that pride. "Oh, I've been tough in my time," he muttered to himself. "Lot of good it does me." The air was cold on his back, and he turned over. It seemed to him that all his life he had been sleeping in bare wet places, seeking for warmth. He thought of an old hobo saying, "Half a buck in your pocket and winter coming," and felt some of the gloom he had known on cold October twilights. His stomach was empty, and he got up after a while and rummaged through his pack. He found a K ration and chewed the fruit bar, washing it down with water from his canteen. His blanket was still wet from the evening storm, but he wrapped it about him and found a little warmth. Then he tried to go to sleep again, but his kidneys were aching too much. At last he sat up, fumbled in the first-aid kit on his cartridge belt, and withdrew the little paper bag of wound tablets. He swallowed half of them and drank about half the water remaining in his canteen. For a moment he thought of using them all, but then he remembered that he might be wounded and need them. It brought back his dejection, and he stared solemnly into the darkness, being able to discern after a time the bodies of the sleeping men around him. Toglio was snoring, and he heard Martinez mutter softly in Spanish and then cry out, "I no kill Jap, God, I no kill him." Red sighed and lay down again. What men sleep easy? he thought.

A trace of an old anger passed through him. I don't give a damn about anything, he said to himself, and listened uneasily to a shell sighing overhead. This time it sounded like the branches of a tree murmuring in a winter wind. He remembered once striding along a highway as evening came. It had been in the eastern coal-mining towns of Pennsylvania and he had watched the miners driving home in their battered Fords, their faces still dark with the day's accumulation of soot and coal dust. It had not looked anything like the mining country in Montana he had left years before, and yet it had been the same. He had walked along brooding about home, and someone had given him a ride and treated him to a drink in a noisy bar. That night had a beauty about it now, and he remembered for a moment the sensation of leaving a strange town on a dark freight. Things like that were only glints of light in the long gray day of those years. He sighed again as if to grasp something of the knowledge he had felt for an instant. Nobody gets what he wants, he said to himself, and this deepened his mood of pleasurable sorrow. He was growing drowsy, and he burrowed his head under his forearm. A mosquito began to whine near his ear and he lay still, hoping it would go away. The ground seemed crawling with insects. The little buggers are one thing I'm used to, he thought. For some reason this made him smile.

It was beginning to rain, and Red covered his head with the blanket. His body was slowly sinking into a weary slumber in which different parts of him fell asleep at separate intervals, so that long after he had stopped thinking, a portion of his mind could feel the quivering of an exhausted limb or a cramp in one of his limbs. The shelling was becoming steady, and a half mile away from him a machine gun kept firing. Almost asleep, he watched Croft return and spread out a blanket. The rain continued. After a time, he no longer heard the artillery. But even when he was completely asleep, one last area of his mind noticed what was happening. Although he didn't remember it when he awoke, he heard a platoon of men march by, and was conscious of some other men beginning to push the antitank guns to the other side of the bivouac. There's a Jap road leads into the bivouac, he said in his sleep. They're going to protect it now. Probably he was feverish.

He dreamed until he heard a voice shout, "Recon? Where's recon?" The dream ebbed away, and he lay there drowsily, listening to Croft spring to his feet and holler, "Here, over here!" Red knew he would have to be moving in a few minutes, and he burrowed deeper into his blankets. His body ached and he knew that when he stood up he would be stiff. "All right, men, on your feet." Croft was shouting. "Come on, get up, we got to move."

Red pulled the cover off his face. It was still raining and his hand came away wet from the top surface of the blanket. When he replaced the blanket in his pack, his pack also would become wet. "Aaaahhhhh-rr." He cleared his throat with disgust and spat once or twice. The taste in his mouth was foul. Gallagher sat up beside him and groaned. "Goddam Army, why don't they let a guy sleep? Ain't we done enough tonight?"

"We're heroes," Red said. He stood up and began to fold his blanket. It was sopping wet on one side and muddy on the other. He had slept with his rifle beside him, covered under the blanket, but it too was wet. Red wondered how long it had been since he was dry. "Fuggin jungle," he said.

"Come on, you men, snap it up," Croft said. A flare lit the wet ugly shrubs about them and flickered dully against their wet black clothing. Red saw that Gallagher's face was covered with mud, and when he felt his own face, his hands came away soiled. "Show me the way to go home," he hummed. "I'm tired and I want to go to bed."

"Yeah," Gallagher said. They made their packs together and stood up. The flare had gone out and they were blinded for a moment in the returning darkness. "Where we going?" Toglio asked.

"Up to A Company. They expect an attack there," Croft said.

"We sure are a hard-luck platoon," Wilson sighed. "At least we're done with them antitank guns. Ah swear Ah'd fight a tank with mah bare hands 'fore Ah'd rassle with one of them sonsofbitches again."

141

The squad formed a single file and began to move out. First Battalion's bivouac was very small and in thirty seconds they had reached the gap in the barbed wire. Martinez led them cautiously down the trail leading to A Company. His drowsiness vanished quickly, and he became alert. Actually, he could not see anything, but some sense seemed to guide him along the bends in the path so that he rarely stumbled or blundered off the trail. He was proceeding about thirty yards ahead of the other men and he was completely isolated. If some Japanese had been waiting in ambush along the path, he would have been the first to be trapped. Yet he had very little fear; Martinez's terror developed in a void; the moment he had to lead men, his courage returned. At this instant, his mind was poised over a number of sounds and thoughts. His ears were searching the jungle ahead of him for some noise which might indicate that men were waiting in the brush beside the trail; they were also listening with disgust to the stumbling and muttering of the men following behind him. His mind recorded the intermittent sounds of battle and tried to classify them; he looked at the sky whenever they passed through a partial clearing in order to find the Southern Cross and determine in which direction the trail was bending. Wherever he could, he made a mental note of some landmark they were passing and added it to the ones he had observed previously. After a time he kept repeating a jingle to himself which went, Tree over trail, muddy creek, rock on trail, bushes across. Actually there was no reason for him to do it; the trail led only from 1st Battalion to A Company. But this was a habit he had formed on his first patrols. He did it instinctively by now.

And another part of his mind had a quiet pride that he was the man upon whom the safety of the others depended. This was a sustaining force which carried him through dangers his will and body would have resisted. During the march with the antitank guns, there had been many times when he wanted to quit; unlike Croft, he had felt it no contest at all. He would have been perfectly willing to declare the task beyond his strength and give up, but there was a part of his mind that drove him to do things he feared and detested. His pride with being a sergeant was the core about which nearly all his actions and thoughts were bound. Nobody see in the darkness like Martinez, he said to himself. He touched a branch before his extended arm and bent his knees easily and walked under it. His feet were sore and his back and shoulders ached, but they were ills with which he no longer concerned himself; he was leading his squad, and that was sufficient in itself.

The rest of the squad, strung out behind, was experiencing a variety of emotions. Wilson and Toglio were sleepy, Red was alert and brooding — he had a sense of foreboding. Goldstein was miserable and bitter, and the tension of creeping down a trail in the black early hours of the morning made him gloomy and then sad. He thought of himself dying without friends nearby to mourn him. Wyman had lost his power to recuperate; he was so tired that he plodded along in a stupor, not caring where he went or what happened to him. Ridges was weary and patient; he did not think of what the next hours would bring him, nor did he lose himself in contemplation of his aching limbs; he just walked and his mind drifted slowly like a torpid stream.

And Croft; Croft was tense and eager and impatient. All night he had been balked by the assignment of the squad to a labor detail. The sounds of battle he had been hearing all night were goading to him. His mind was buoyed by a recurrence of the mood he had felt after Hennessey's death. He felt strong and tireless and capable of anything; his muscles were as strained and jaded as any of the men's, but his mind had excluded his body. He hungered for the fast taut pulse he would feel in his throat after he killed a man.

On the map there was only a half mile between 1st Battalion and A Company, but the trail doubled and curved so often that it was actually a mile. The men in recon were clumsy now and uncertain of their footing. Their packs sagged, their rifles kept sliding off their shoulders. The trail was crude; originally a game wallow, it had been partially enlarged, and in places it was still narrow. A man could not walk without being scratched by the branches on either side. The jungle was impenetrable at that point, and it would have taken an hour to cut one's way a hundred feet off the path. In the night it was impossible to see anything and the smell of the wet foliage was choking. The men had to walk in single file, drawn up close. Even at three

143

feet they could not see one another, and they plodded down the trail with each man grasping the shirt of the man before him. Martinez could hear them and judge his distance accordingly, but the others stumbled and collided with one another like children playing a game in the dark. They were bent over almost double, and the posture was cruel. Their bodies were outraged; they had been eating and sleeping with no rhythm at all for the last few hours. They kept loosing gas whose smell was nauseating in the foul dense air. The men at the rear had the worst of it; they gagged and swore, tried not to breathe for a few seconds, and shuddered from fatigue and revulsion. Gallagher was at the end of the file, and every few minutes he would cough and curse. "Cut out the goddam farting," he would shout, and the men in front would rouse themselves for a moment and laugh.

"Eatin' dust, hey, boy," Wilson muttered, and a few of them began to giggle.

Some of them began to fall asleep as they walked. Their eyes had been closed almost the entire march, and they drowsed for the instant their foot was in the air and awakened as it touched the ground. Wyman had been plodding along for many minutes with no sensation at all; his body had grown numb. He and Ridges drowsed continually, and every now and then for ten or fifteen yards they would be completely asleep. At last they would weave off the trail and go pitching into the bushes stupidly before regaining their balance. In the darkness such noises were terrifying. It made the men uncomfortably aware of how close they were to the fighting. A half mile away some rifles were firing.

"Goddammit," one of them would whisper, "can't you guys keep quiet?"

The march must have taken them over half an hour, but after the first few minutes they no longer thought about time. Crouching and sliding through the mud with their hands on the man in front became the only thing they really knew; the trail was a treadmill and they no longer concerned themselves with where they were going. To most of them the end of the march came as a surprise. Martinez doubled back and told them to be quiet. "They hear you coming for ten minutes," he whispered. A hush settled over the men, and they trod the last

144

hundred yards with ridiculous precautions, tensing every muscle whenever they took a step.

There was no barbed wire, nor any clearing at A Company. The trail divided in a quadruple fork which led to different emplacements. A soldier met them where the path broke up and led the squad along one of the footpaths to a few pup tents pitched in the middle of some foliage. "I got Second Platoon," he told Croft. "I'm just about a hundred yards down the river. Your squad can sleep in these holes tonight, and set up a guard right along here. They's two machine guns set up for you."

"What's doing?" Croft whispered.

"I dunno. I heard they expect an attack all up and down the line about dawn. We had to send a platoon over to C Company early tonight, and we been holding down the whole outpost here with less than a platoon." He made a rustling sound in the darkness as he wiped his hand against his mouth. "C'mere, I'll show you the setup," he said, grasping Croft's elbow. Croft slipped his arm free; he hated to have anyone touch him.

They went a few feet along the path, until the sergeant from A Company halted before a foxhole. There was a machine gun mounted in front, its muzzle just projecting through a fringe of bushes. Croft peered through the foliage and in the faint moonlight was able to see a stream of water and a strip of beach bordering it on either side. "How deep is the river?" he asked.

"Aw, it's four, five feet maybe. That water ain't going to stop them."

"Any outposts forward of here?" Croft asked.

"Nothing. And the Japs know right where we are. Had some patrols up." The soldier wiped his mouth again and stood up. "I'll show you the other machine gun." They walked along a stubbly path cut through the jungle about ten feet from the river's edge. Some crickets were chirping loudly, and the soldier trembled a little. "Here's the other one," he said. "This is the flank." He peered through the bushes and stepped out onto the strip of beach. "Look," he said. Croft followed him. About fifty yards to their right, the bluffs of Watamai Range began. Croft looked up. The cliffs rose almost verti-

145

cally for perhaps a thousand feet. Even in the darkness, he felt them hovering above him. He strained his eyes and thought he saw a swatch of sky where they ended but could not be certain. He had a curious thrill. "I didn't know we were that close," he said.

"Oh, yeah. It's good and it's bad. You don't have to worry about them coming around that end, but still we're the flank. If they ever hit here hard, there ain't much to hold them." The soldier drew into the bushes again and exhaled his breath slowly. "I'll tell you these two nights we been out here give me the creeps. Look at that river. When there's a lot of moonlight it just seems to shine, and you get jittery after a while looking at it."

Croft remained outside the jungle edge, looking at the stream that curved away at the right and flowed parallel to the mountains. It took a turn toward the Japanese lines just a few yards before the first walls of the bluff began, and he would be able to see everything on that side. To the left the stream ran straight for a few hundred yards like a highway at night, sunk between high grassy banks. "Where are you?" he asked.

The soldier pointed to a tree which projected a little from the jungle. "We're just on this side of it. If you got to get to us, go back to the fork and then take the trail at the far right going away from here. Yell 'Buckeye' when you come up."

"Okay," Croft said. They talked for a few more minutes, and then the other soldier hooked his cartridge belt. "Jesus, I'll tell ya, it'll drive ya crazy spending a night here. Just wilderness, that's all, and you stuck out at the end of it with nothing but a lousy machine gun." He slung his rifle and struck off down the trail. Croft looked at him for a moment and then went back to recon. The men were waiting by the three pup tents, and he showed them where the two machine guns were placed. Briefly he told them what he had learned and picked a guard. "It's three A.M. now," he told them. "There's gonna be four of us on one post and five on the other. We'll do it in two-hour shifts. Then the post that's only got four men will get the extra one for the next time around." He divided them up, taking the first shift at the flank gun himself. Wilson volunteered to take the other gun. "After Ah'm done, Ah'm gonna want to sleep right on through," Wilson

146

said. "Ah'm tired of gittin' up right when Ah'm havin' a good dream."

The men smiled wanly.

"An' listen," Croft added, "if any trouble starts, the men that are sleeping are to git up goddam fast and move to help us. It's only a couple of yards from our tents to Wilson's machine gun, and it ain't much further to mine. It shouldn't be takin' you all more than about three hours to reach us." Again, a couple of men smiled. "Okay, that's about it," Croft said. He left them and walked over to his machine gun.

He sat down on the edge of the hole and peered through the bushes at the river. The jungle completely surrounded him, and, now that he was no longer active, he felt very weary and a little depressed. To counteract this mood, he began to feel the various objects in the hole. There were three boxes of belt ammunition and a row of seven grenades lined up neatly at the base of the machine gun. At his feet were a box of flares and a flare gun. He picked it up and broke open the breech quietly, loaded it, and cocked it. Then he set it down beside him.

A few shells murmured overhead and began to fall. He was a little surprised at how near they landed to the other side of the river. Not more than a few hundred yards away, the noise of their explosion was extremely loud; a few pieces of shrapnel lashed the leaves on the trees above him. He broke off a stalk from a plant and put it in his mouth, chewing slowly and reflectively. He guessed that the weapons platoon of A Company had fired, and he tried to determine which trail at the fork would lead to them in case he had to pull back his men. Now he was patient and at ease; the danger of their position neutralized the anticipation for some combat he had felt earlier, and he was left cool and calm and very tired.

The mortar shells were falling perhaps fifty yards in front of the platoon at his left, and Croft spat quietly. It was too close to be merely harassing fire; someone had heard something in the jungle on the other side of the river or they would never have called for mortars so close to their own position. His hand explored the hole again and discovered a field telephone. Croft picked up the receiver, listened

147

quietly. It was an open line, and probably confined to the platoons of A Company. Two men were talking in voices so low that he strained to hear them.

"Walk it up another fifty and then bring it back."

"You sure there're Japs?"

"I swear I heard them talking."

Croft stared tensely across the river. The moon had come out, and the strands of beach on either side of the stream were shining with a silver glow. The jungle wall on the other side looked impenetrable.

The mortars fired again behind him with a cruel flat sound. He watched the shells land in the jungle, and then creep nearer to the river in successive volleys. A mortar answered from the Japanese side of the river, and about a quarter of a mile to the left Croft could hear several machine guns spattering at each other, the uproar deep and irregular. Croft picked up the phone and whistled into it. "Wilson," he whispered. *"Wilson!"* There was no answer and he debated whether to walk over to Wilson's hole. Silently Croft cursed him for not noticing the phone, and then berated himself for not having discovered it before he briefed the others. He looked out across the river. Fine sergeant I am, he told himself.

His ears were keyed to all the sounds of the night, and from long experience he sifted out the ones that were meaningless. If an animal rustled in its hole, he paid no attention; if some crickets chirped, his ear disregarded them. Now he picked a muffled slithering sound which he knew could be made only by men moving through a thin patch of jungle. He peered across the river, trying to determine where the foliage was least dense. At a point between his gun and Wilson's there was a grove of a few coconut trees sparse enough to allow men to assemble; as he stared into that patch of wood, he was certain he heard a man move. Croft's mouth tightened. His hand felt for the bolt of the machine gun, and he slowly brought it to bear on the coconut grove. The rustling grew louder; it seemed as if men were creeping through the brush on the other side of the river to a point opposite his gun. Croft swallowed once. Tiny charges seemed to pulse through his limbs and his head was as empty and shockingly aware as if it had

148

been plunged into a pail of freezing water. He wet his lips and shifted his position slightly, feeling as though he could hear the flexing of his muscles.

The Jap mortar fired again and he started. The shells were falling by the next platoon, the sound painful and jarring to him. He stared out on the moonlit river until his eyes deceived him; he began to think he could see the heads of men in the dark swirls of the current. Croft gazed down at his knees for an instant and then across the river again. He looked a little to the left or right of where he thought the Japanese might be; from long experience he had learned a man could not look directly at an object and see it in the darkness. Something seemed to move in the grove, and a new trickle of sweat formed and rolled down his back. He twisted uncomfortably. Croft was unbearably tense, but the sensation was not wholly unpleasant.

He wondered if Wilson had noticed the sounds, and then in answer to his question, there was the loud unmistakable clicking of a machine gun bolt. To Croft's keyed senses, the sound echoed up and down the river, and he was furious that Wilson should have revealed his position. The rustling in the brush became louder and Croft was convinced he could hear voices whispering on the other side of the river. He fumbled for a grenade and placed it at his feet.

Then he heard a sound which pierced his flesh. Someone called from across the river, "Yank, Yank!" Croft sat numb. The voice was thin and high-pitched, hideous in a whisper. "That's a Jap," Croft told himself. He was incapable of moving for that instant.

"Yank!" It was calling to him. "Yank. We you coming-to-get, Yank."

The night lay like a heavy stifling mat over the river. Croft tried to breathe.

"*We you coming-to-get, Yank.*"

Croft felt as if a hand had suddenly clapped against his back, traveled up his spine over his skull to clutch at the hair on his forehead. "Coming to get you, Yank," he heard himself whisper. He had the agonizing frustration of a man in a nightmare who wants to scream and cannot utter a sound. "We you *coming-to-get*, Yank."

He shivered terribly for a moment, and his hands seemed con-

149

gealed on the machine gun. He could not bear the intense pressure in his head.

"We you coming-to-get, Yank," the voice screamed.

"COME AND GET ME YOU SONSOFBITCHES," Croft roared. He shouted with every fiber of his body as though he plunged at an oaken door.

There was no sound at all for perhaps ten seconds, nothing but the moonlight on the river and the taut rapt buzzing of the crickets. Then the voice spoke again. "Oh, we come, Yank, we come."

Croft pulled back the bolt on his machine gun, and rammed it home. His heart was still beating with frenzy "Recon . . . RECON, UP ON THE LINE," he shouted with all his strength.

A machine gun lashed at him from across the river, and he ducked in his hole. In the darkness, it spat a vindictive white light like an acetylene torch, and its sound was terrifying. Croft was holding himself together by the force of his will. He pressed the trigger of his gun and it leaped and bucked under his hand. The tracers spewed wildly into the jungle on the other side of the river.

But the noise, the vibration of his gun, calmed him. He directed it to where he had seen the Japanese gunfire and loosed a volley. The handle pounded against his fist, and he had to steady it with both hands. The hot metallic smell of the barrel eddied back to him, made what he was doing real again. He ducked in his hole waiting for the reply and winced involuntarily as the bullets whipped past.

BEE-YOWWWW! . . . BEE-YOOWWWW! Some dirt snapped at his face from the ricochets. Croft was not conscious of feeling it. He had the surface numbness a man has in a fight. He flinched at sounds, his mouth tightened and loosened, his eyes stared, but he was oblivious to his body.

Croft fired the gun again, held it for a long vicious burst, and then ducked in his hole. An awful scream singed the night, and for an instant Croft grinned weakly. Got him, he thought. He saw the metal burning through flesh, shattering the bones in its path. "AII-YOHHHH." The scream froze him again, and for an odd disconnected instant he experienced again the whole complex of sounds and smells and sights when a calf was branded. "RECON, UP . . . UP!"

he shouted furiously and fired steadily for ten seconds to cover their advance. As he paused he could hear some men crawling behind him, and he whispered, "Recon?"

"Yeah." Gallagher dropped into the hole with him. "Mother of Mary," he muttered. Croft could feel him shaking beside him.

"Stop it!" he gripped his arm tensely. "The other men up?"

"Yeah."

Croft looked across the river again. Everything was silent, and the disconnected abrupt spurts of fire were forgotten like vanished sparks from a grindstone. Now that he was no longer alone, Croft was able to plan. The fact that men were up with him, were scattered in the brush along the bank between their two machine guns, recovered his sense of command. "They're going to attack soon," he whispered hoarsely in Gallagher's ear.

Gallagher trembled again. "Ohh. No way to wake up," he tried to say, but his voice kept lapsing.

"Look," Croft whispered. "Creep along the line and tell them to hold fire until the Japs start to cross the river."

"I can't, I can't," Gallagher whispered.

Croft felt like striking him. "Go!" he whispered.

"I can't."

The Jap machine gun lashed at them from across the river. The bullets went singing into the jungle behind them, ripping at leaves. The tracers looked like red splints of lightning as they flattened into the jungle. A thousand rifles seemed to be firing at them from across the river, and the two men pressed themselves against the bottom of the hole. The sounds cracked against their eardrums. Croft's head ached. Firing the machine gun had partially deafened him. BEE-YOWWWW! A ricochet slapped some more dirt on top of them. Croft felt it pattering on his back this time. He was trying to sense the moment when he would have to raise his head and fire the gun. The firing seemed to slacken, and he lifted his eyes cautiously. BEE-YOWWW, BEE-YOWWWW! He dropped in the hole again. The Japanese machine gun raked through the brush at them.

There was a shrill screaming sound, and the men covered their heads with their arms. BAA-ROWWMM, BAA-ROWWMM,

151

ROWWMM, ROWWMM. The mortars exploded all about them, and something picked Gallagher up, shook him, and then released him. "O God," he cried. A clod of dirt stung his neck. BAA-ROWWMM, BAA-ROWWMM.

"Jesus, I'm hit," someone screamed, "I'm hit. Something hit me."

BAA-ROWWMM.

Gallagher rebelled against the force of the explosions. "Stop, I give up," he screamed. "STOP! . . . I give up! I give up!" At that instant he no longer knew what made him cry out.

BAA-ROWWMM, BAA-ROWWMM.

"I'm hit, I'm hit," someone was screaming. The Japanese rifles were firing again. Croft lay on the floor of the hole with his hands against the ground and every muscle poised in its place.

BAA-ROWWMM. TEEEEEEEEN! The shrapnel was singing as it scattered through the foliage.

Croft picked up his flare gun. The firing had not abated, but through it he heard someone shouting in Japanese. He pointed the gun in the air.

"Here they come," Croft said.

He fired the flare and shouted, "STOP 'EM!"

A shrill cry came out of the jungle across the river. It was the scream a man might utter if his foot was being crushed. "AAAIIIIII, AAAIIIIIIII."

The flare burst at the moment the Japanese started their charge. Croft had a split perception of the Japanese machine gun firing from a flank, and then he began to fire automatically, not looking where he fired, but holding his gun low, swinging it from side to side. He could not hear the other guns fire, but he saw their muzzle blasts like exhausts.

He had a startling frozen picture of the Japanese running toward him across the narrow river. "AAAAIIIIIIIIIIH," he heard again. In the light of the flare the Japanese had the stark frozen quality of men revealed by a shaft of lightning. Croft no longer saw anything clearly; he could not have said at that moment where his hands ended and the machine gun began; he was lost in a vast moil of noise out of which individual screams and shouts etched in his mind for an instant. He could never have counted the Japanese who charged across the river; he knew only that his finger was rigid on the trigger bar. He could not have loosened it. In those few moments he felt no sense of danger. He just kept firing.

The line of men who charged across the river began to fall. In the water they were slowed considerably and the concentrated fire from recon's side raged at them like a wind across an open field. They began to stumble over the bodies ahead of them. Croft saw one soldier reach into the air behind another's body as though trying to clutch something in the sky and Croft fired at him for what seemed many seconds before the arm collapsed.

He looked to his right and saw three men trying to cross the river where it turned and ran parallel to the bluff. He swung the gun about and lashed them with it. One man fell, and the other two paused uncertainly and began to run back toward their own bank of the river. Croft had no time to follow them; some soldiers had reached the beach on his side and were charging the gun. He fired point blank at them, and they collapsed about five yards from his hole.

Croft fired and fired, switching targets with the quick reflexes of an athlete shifting for a ball. As soon as he saw men falling he would attack another group. The line of Japanese broke into little bunches of men who wavered, began to retreat.

The light of the flare went out and Croft was blinded for a moment. There was no sound again in the darkness and he fumbled for another flare, feeling an almost desperate urgency. "Where is it?" he whispered to Gallagher.

"What?"

"Shit." Croft's hand found the flare box, and he loaded the gun again. He was beginning to see in the darkness, and he hesitated. But something moved on the river and he fired the flare. As it burst, a few Japanese soldiers were caught motionless in the water. Croft pivoted his gun on them and fired. One of the soldiers remained standing for an incredible time. There was no expression on his face; he looked vacant and surprised even as the bullets struck him in the chest.

Nothing was moving now on the river. In the light of the flare,

153

the bodies looked as limp and unhuman as bags of grain. One soldier began to float downstream, his face in the water. On the beach near the gun, another Japanese soldier was lying on his back. A wide stain of blood was spreading out from his body, and his stomach, ripped open, gaped like the swollen entrails of a fowl. On an impulse Croft fired a burst into him, and felt a twitch of pleasure as he saw the body quiver.

A wounded man was groaning in Japanese. Every few seconds he would scream, the sound terrifying in the cruel blue light of the flare. Croft picked up a grenade. "That sonofabitch is makin' too much noise," he said. He pulled the pin and lobbed the grenade over to the opposite bank. It dropped like a beanbag on one of the bodies, and Croft pulled Gallagher down with him. The explosion was powerful and yet empty like a blast that collapses windowpanes. After a moment, the echoes ceased.

Croft tensed himself and listened to the sounds from across the river. There was the quiet furtive noise of men retreating into the jungle. "GIVE 'EM A VOLLEY!" he shouted.

All the men in recon began to fire again, and Croft raked the jungle for a minute in short bursts. He could hear Wilson's machine gun pounding steadily. "I guess we gave 'em something," Croft told Gallagher. The flare was going out, and Croft stood up. "Who was hit?" he shouted.

"Toglio."

"Bad?" Croft asked.

"I'm okay," Toglio whispered. "I got a bullet in my elbow."

"Can you wait till morning?"

There was silence for a moment, then Toglio answered weakly, "Yeah, I'll be okay."

Croft got out of his hole. "I'm coming down," he announced. "Hold your fire." He walked along the path until he reached Toglio. Red and Goldstein were kneeling beside him, and Croft spoke to them in a low voice. "Pass this on," he said. "We're all gonna stay in our holes until mornin'. I don't think they'll be back tonight, but you cain't tell. And no one is gonna fall asleep. They's only about an hour till dawn, so you ain't got nothin' to piss about."

154

"I wouldn't go to sleep anyway," Goldstein breathed. "What a way to wake up." It was the same thing Gallagher had said.

"Yeah, well, I just wasn't ridin' on my ass either, waitin' for them to come," Croft said. He shivered for a moment in the early morning air and realized with a pang of shame that for the first time in his life he had been really afraid. "The sonsofbitchin' Japs," he said. His legs were tired and he turned to go back to his gun. I hate the bastards, he said to himself, a terrible rage working through his weary body.

"One of these days I'm gonna really get me a Jap," he whispered aloud. The river was slowly carrying the bodies downstream.

"At least," Gallagher said, "if we got to stay here a couple of days, the fuggers won't be stinkin' up the joint."

The Time Machine:

A lean man of medium height but he held himself so erectly he appeared tall. His narrow triangular face was utterly without expression. There seemed nothing wasted in his hard small jaw, gaunt firm cheeks and straight short nose. His gelid eyes were very blue . . . he was efficient and strong and usually empty and his main cast of mind was a superior contempt toward nearly all other men. He hated weakness and he loved practically nothing. There was a crude unformed vision in his soul but he was rarely conscious of it.

No, but why *is* Croft that way?

Oh, there are answers. He is that way because of the corruption-of-the-society. He is that way because the devil has claimed him for one of his own. It is because he is a Texan; it is because he has renounced God.

He is that kind of man because the only woman he ever loved cheated on him, or he was born that way, or he was having problems of adjustment.

Croft's father, Jesse Croft, liked to say, "Well, now, my Sam is a mean boy. I reckon he was whelped mean." And then Jesse Croft, thinking of his wife who was ailing, a weak woman sweet and mild, might add, " 'Course Sam got mother's milk if ever a one did, but Ah figger it turned sour for him 'cause that was the only way his stomach would take it." Then he would cackle and blow his nose into his hand and wipe it on the back of his pale-blue dungarees. (Standing before his dirty wood barn, the red dry soil of western Texas under his feet.) "Why, Ah 'member once Ah took Sam huntin', he was only an itty-bitty runt, not big enough to hold up the gun hardly . . . but he was a mean shot from the beginning. And Ah'll tell ya, he just didn't like to

156

have a man interfere with him. That was one thing could always rile him, even when he was an itty-bitty bastard.

"Couldn't stand to have anyone beat him in anythin'.

"Never could lick him. Ah'd beat the piss out o' him, and he'd never make a sound. Jus' stand there lookin' at me as if he was fixin' to wallop me back, or maybe put a bullet in mah head."

Croft hunted early. In the winter, in the chill Texas desert, it used to be a cold numbing ride across twenty miles of rutted hard-baked road with the dust blowing like emery into the open battered Ford. The two big men in the front would say little, and the one who was not driving would blow on his fingers. When they reached the forest, the sun would still be straining to rise above the brown-red line of ridge.

Now, look, boy, see that trail, that's a deer run. They ain't hardly a man is smart enough to track down a deer. You set an' wait for 'em, and you set where the wind is blowin' down from the deer to you. You got to wait a long time.

The boy sits shivering in the wood. Ah'm fugged if Ah'll wait for any ole deer. Ah'm gonna track 'em.

He stalks through the forest with the wind on his face. It's dark, and the trees are silver-brown, and the ground is a deep-olive velvet. Where is that ole deer? He kicks a twig out of his way, and stiffens as a buck goes clattering through the brush. Goddam! Ole deer is fast.

Next time he is more cautious. He finds a deer track, kneels down and traces the hoofprint tenderly, feeling a thrill. Ah'm gonna track this old deer.

For two hours he creeps through the forest, watching where he places his feet, putting his heel down first, then his toes before he shifts his weight. When the dried thorny branches catch in his clothing, he pulls them free quietly, one by one.

In a little clearing he sees a deer and freezes. The wind is blowing gently against his face, and he thinks he can smell the animal. Goddam, he whispers to himself. What a big ole bastard. The stag turns slowly, looks past him from a hundred yards. Sonofabitch cain't see me.

157

The boy raises his gun, and trembles so badly the sights waver. He lowers it, and curses himself. Jus' a little ole woman. He brings it up again, holding it steadily, moving the front sight over until it points a few inches below the muscle of the foreleg. Ah'm goin' to git him through the heart.

BAA-WOWWW!

It is someone else's gun, and the deer drops. The boy runs forward almost weeping. Who shot him? That was mah deer. I'll kill the sonofabitch who shot him.

Jesse Croft is laughing at him. Ah tole you, boy, to set where Ah put you.

Ah tracked that deer.

You scared that deer into me. Ah heard ya footing it from a mile away.

You're a liar. You're a goddam liar. The boy throws himself at his father, and tries to strike him.

Jesse Croft gives him a blow across the mouth, and he sits down. You ole sonofabitch, he screams, and flings himself at his father again.

Jesse holds him off, laughing. Little ole wildcat, ain't ya? Well, you got to wait ten years 'fore you can whop your pa.

That deer were mine.

One that wins is the one that gits it.

The tears freeze in the boy's eyes and wither. He is thinking that if he hadn't trembled he would have shot the deer first.

"Yes, sir," Jesse Croft said, "they wa'n' a thing my Sam could stand to have ya beat him in. When he was 'bout twelve, they was a fool kid down at Harper who used to give Sam a lickin'." (Scratching the back of his gray scraggly hair, his hat in his hand.) "That kid would lick Sam every day, and Sam would go back and pick a fight the next day. Ah'll tell ya, he ended up by whoppin' the piss out of that kid.

"And then when he was older, about seventeen maybe, he used to be bustin' horses down to the fair in August, and he was known to be 'bout the best rider in the county. Then one time a fella all the way from Denison came down and beat him in a reg'lar competition with

158

judges and all. I 'member Sam was so mad he wouldn't talk to no one for two days.

"He got good stock in him," Jesse Croft declared to his neighbors. "We was one of the first folks to push in here, must be sixty years ago, and they was Crofts in Texas over a hunnerd years ago. Ah'd guess some of them had that same meanness that Sam's got. Maybe it was what made 'em push down here."

Deer hunting and fighting and busting horses at the fair make up in hours a total of perhaps ten days a year. There are the other things, the long flat sweeps of the terrain, the hills in the distance, the endless meals in the big kitchen with his parents and brothers and the ranch foremen.

There are the conversations in the bunkhouse. The soft reflective voices.

Ah tell ya that little gal is gonna remember me unless she was too goddam drunk.

Ah jus' looked at that nigger after that, an' Ah said, Boy, you no-good black bastard, an' Ah jus' picked up that hatchet an' let him have it right across the head. But the sonofabitch didn't even bleed much. You can kill an elephant about as fast as you can kill a nigger in the head.

A whoor is no damn good for a man, Ah gotta have it at least five six times 'fore Ah'm satisfied, and that ole business of stickin' it in once an' then reachin' for your hat jus' leaves me more fussed than it's worth.

Ah been keepin' an eye on that south herd leader, the red one with the spot 'hind his ear, an' he's gonna be gittin' mean when the hot weather comes.

The Education of Samuel Croft.

And always, day after day, the dust of cattle through the long shimmering afternoons in the sun. A man gets bored and it's uncomfortable falling asleep in a saddle. Thinking of town maybe. (Bar and a whorehouse, dry goods.)

Sam, you gittin' itchy?

159

A lazy somnolent pulsing in his loins. The sun refracts from the hide of his horse, bathes his thighs in a lazy heat. Yeah, some.

They're fixin' to start a National Guard outfit in Harper.

Yeah?

Ah figger they'll be some women hangin' round the uniforms, an' ya git to do a lot of shootin'.

Maybe I'll go down with ya. He wheels his horse to the left and rides out to turn back a straggler.

The first time Croft ever killed a man he was in a National Guard uniform. There was a strike on at Lilliput in the oil fields, and some scabs had been hurt.

They called the Guard. (The sonsofbitches started this strike come from up north, New York. They's some good boys in the oil fields but they got they heads turned by Reds, an' next thing they'll have ya kissin' niggers' asses.) The guardsmen made a line against the gate to the plant and stood sweating in a muggy summer sun. The pickets yelled and jeered at them.

Hey, drillers, they called out the Boy Scouts.

Let's rush 'em. They're jus' company scabs too.

Croft stands in line with his mouth tightening.

They're gonna rush us, the soldier next to him says.

The Guard lieutenant is a haberdashery salesman. If there're rocks being thrown you better lie down, men. If it should git real bad, fire a couple of rounds over their heads.

A stone lofts through the air. The crowd is sullen outside the gate, and every now and then one of them shouts some curses at the soldiers.

No sonofabitch'll talk to me that way, Croft says.

A rock strikes one of the soldiers, and they lie down on the ground and point their rifles above the heads of the advancing crowd.

Let's rip the place apart.

About ten men start to walk toward the gate. Some stones fly over their heads and scatter among the soldiers.

All right, men, the lieutenant pipes, fire over them.

160

Croft sights down his barrel. He has pointed his gun at the chest of the nearest man, and he feels a curious temptation.

I'll just squeeze the trigger a little bit.

BAA-WOWWW! The shot is lost in the volley, but the striker drops.

Croft feels a hollow excitement.

The lieutenant is cursing. Goddam, who shot him, men?

Guess they's no way to find out, Lieutenant, Croft says. He watches the mob retreating in a panic. Bunch o' dogs, he tells himself. His heart is beating, and his hands feel very dry.

" 'Member that gal, Janey, he married. Ah'll say one thing for her, she was a reg'lar ole tomcat," Jesse Croft said. (He spewed an oyster of phlegm, and ground it reflectively with his boot.) "Jus' the meanest little ole girl, Ah'll tell ya she was a mate for him till they busted up. They ain't one of the gals my boys've married that I woulda taken up against her. Ah'm an old man, but Ah'll tell ya, mah balls would git to itchin' when Ah'd look at her and jus' think of lovin' up to her." (Scratching his pants vigorously.) "Trouble with Sam he shouldn'ta married her. When a man can knock off a piece with a woman without slippin' her a weddin' ring, it don' pay to git any ideas about settlin' down with her. A woman that likes her nookie ain't gonna be satisfied with one man after she gits used to him." (Pointing his finger at the man he is talking to.) "Reckon that's a law of life."

Oh, give it to me, you sonofabitch, give it to me, I'LL KILL YOU IF YOU STOP.

Who's your man?

You're my man, you give it to me, give it to me, give it to me.

They ain't nobody can make love to you like me.

They ain't anybody, anybody, oh, you're just a goddam fuggin machine.

The long sliding of a belly against a belly.

I love ya better than any man ever could.

161

You do, baby, you do.

Ah'm jus' an old fuggin machine. (Crack . . . that . . . whip! Crack . . . that . . . WHIP!)

After they married, Croft rented a little house on the ranch from his father. He and Janey petered out for each other through a slow taciturn year, through a thousand incidents which they forgot while the effects still remained. At night they would sit by themselves in the parlor, listen to the radio and seldom talk. In a dumb instinctive way, Croft would search for an approach.

Want to go to bed?

It's early, Sam.

Yeah. And an anger would work in him. They had torn at each other once, had felt sick when they were close together and other people were with them. Now, in sleep their bodies intruded; there was always a heavy limb in the way. And the nights together working on them, this new change, this living together between them like a heavy dull weight, washing dishes and mouthing familiar kisses.

The buddy system.

But he wanted no buddy. In the quiet nights in the cheap parlor of this house set on the Texas plains, an undefined rage increased and increased. There were the things he did not know how to utter (the great space of the night), the fury between them balked almost completely now. There were the trips to town, the drinking bouts between them, the occasional kindling of their bodies in a facsimile of their earlier passion, only confusing and protracting the irreversible reaction.

It ended with him going to town alone, and taking a whore when he was drunk, beating her sometimes with a wordless choler. And for Janey it resulted in other men, ranch hands, once one of his brothers.

"It jus' don' pay to marry a woman with hot pants," Jesse Croft said later.

Croft found out in a quarrel.

And another thing, you go tomcattin' to town, and jus' hellin' around, well, don' be thinkin' Ah'm jus' sittin' around. They's things Ah can tell you too.

162

What things?

You want to know, don't ya? You got yore water hot. Jus' don' push me around.

What things?

She laughs. Jus' a way of talkin'.

Croft slaps her across the face, catches her wrists and shakes her. WHAT THINGS?

You sonofabitch. (Her eyes glaring.) You know what kind of things.

He strikes her so heavily that she falls.

That's one thing you ain't best in, she screams.

Croft stands there trembling and then wrenches out of the room. (Goddam whore.) He feels nothing and then anger and shame and then nothing again. At this moment his initial love, his initial need of her is full-throated again. (Jus' an ole fuggin machine.)

"If Sam coulda found any of the boys who was scooting up her pants, he'da killed 'em," Jesse Croft said. "He tore around like he was gonna choke us all with his hands and then he took off for town and threw himself about as good a drunk as Ah've seen him indulge. And when he got back he'd enlisted himself in the Army."

After that there were always other men's wives.

You must think I'm a pretty cheap woman going out with you like this.

Wouldn't say that. Everybody likes to have a good time.

That's it. (Drinking her beer.) That's my philosophy. Need to have a good time. You don't think a bit cheap of me, do you, soldier?

Hell, you're too good-lookin' a woman for me to think cheap. (Have another beer.)

And later. Jack don't treat me right. You understand me.

That's right, honey, I understand you. They roll together in bed.

Ain't nothing wrong with that philosophy, she says.

Not a damn thing wrong. (And . . . crack . . . that . . . WHIP!)

You're all fuggin whores, he thinks.

163

His ancestors pushed and labored and strained, drove their oxen, sweated their women, and moved a thousand miles.

He pushed and labored inside himself and smoldered with an endless hatred.

(You're all a bunch of fuggin whores)

(You're all a bunch of dogs)

(You're all deer to track)

I HATE EVERYTHING WHICH IS NOT IN MYSELF

6

THE BATTLE that began on the night of the storm carried over well into the next afternoon. The attack recon had repulsed was only one of many similar assaults that sputtered up and down the river for hours, and ended at last in a breathless and dreary stalemate. Almost every one of the line companies was involved at one time or another, and each time the pattern was repeated. A group of thirty or fifty or a hundred Japanese would try to cross the river against a squad or platoon of American soldiers, entrenched in foxholes with automatic weapons. That night the Japanese had struck first at Cummings's left flank near the water, and then at dawn had engaged the two companies near the mountain bluffs where recon held the extreme right flank. After both had failed, Toyaku attacked in early daylight the center of the line, and succeeded in giving one company a bad mauling, and forced another to retreat almost back to 2nd Battalion headquarters. The General, still at headquarters battery of the 151st, made a quick decision, confirmed the tactics he had decided upon the preceding night, and sent out orders that the center of the line was to hold its positions.

Toyaku was able to send four hundred men across the river and four or five tanks, before the General's artillery and counterattacks by companies on the edge of the gap made it too expensive to continue. At the most dangerous moment for Cummings, it was still no worse than the problem of ejecting the rump of a fat man who had broken a hole through the stuffing of a couch, and was now spluttering and wriggling his backside in an effort to escape. The General attacked with his reserves, concentrated all the division's artillery on a natural clearing into which the Japanese behind his lines had been forced, and with the aid of his tanks, which had been held in readiness at a point only a quarter mile from the Japs' deepest penetration, succeeded in puncturing the rump. It was the biggest battle of the campaign to date, and the most successful. By late afternoon of that day the Japanese striking force was shattered, and the survivors disappeared into the jungle again, and were either pinched off one by one during the week that followed or succeeded in making their way back across the river to their own lines. This was the second time the General had routed a force which had penetrated his lines, and he gave Hearn a little lecture about it. "This kind of thing is what I call my dinner-table tactics. I'm the little lady who allows the lecher beside me to get his hand way up under my dress before I cut off his wrist."

Tag ends of the battle spouted for a few days, and there were many local fire fights and patrol clashes, but the General, with what Hearn had to admit was unerring instinct, had cut through the subsidiary clashes, the confusing and contradictory patrol reports, to understand that the battle as far as Toyaku was concerned was over after his smash at the middle of the line had been absorbed. The General spent the next day in re-establishing the hole in his lines, and diverting again his reserve to its work on the road. Two or three days later, after a lot of patrol activity, he made an unopposed advance of over a mile, which brought his front elements within a few thousand yards of the Toyaku Line. He estimated it would take him another two weeks to bring the road up to his front, and in another week the Toyaku Line should be breached. He was exceptionally easy to get along with the week after the battle, and as a symptom of that, he was continually feeding Hearn his private military maxims. "Toyaku's through in an offensive sense," he told Hearn. "When the over-all strategy of your campaign is defensive you can figure on losing about a fifth of your force in counteroffensives, and then you've just got to dig in. Toyaku frittered it away. The Japanese brood their way through campaigns; they sit around restless until the tension gets too great and then they erupt. It's a fascinating paradox. They have that game of theirs, *go,* which is all feverish activity, all turning of flanks, and encirclements, and then when they fight they act like wounded animals who roar down clumsily when the flies become too goading. It's not the way to work it. In an army whenever you have unnecessary precautions, men guarding sectors which don't demand it, or being idle for some other reason than that they need the rest, then you've acted immorally as a commander. The less duplication, the less wasted effort, the greater it follows will be the pressure you exert on your opponent. And the greater will be the opportunities that arise for you."

As a corollary of this, he had set his headquarters troops to rebuilding their bivouac two days after the battle. The tents went up again, the gravel walks in the officers' portion of the bivouac were filled in again, and the General's own tent had a floor of duckboards. Officers' mess in this bivouac had a better location, but after the storm it was improved even more with secondary bamboo ridgepoles which held the sides straight. A consignment of fresh meat came in, and headquarters company's ration of it was divided equally. One half went to the one hundred and eighty enlisted men in the bivouac at the time, and the other half went to the thirty-eight officers in officers' mess. The General's electric refrigerator was uncrated, and was fed from the gasoline generator that created all the electric power for the bivouac.

Hearn was disgusted. And once again he was bothered by one of the minor enigmas about the General. The meat business had been a flagrant injustice, one which Hobart as the G-4 in command of assigning supplies would be quite capable of committing, but Hobart had not been responsible. Hearn had been in the General's tent when Hobart had come up with a grin and told Cummings that some fresh meat had come. The General had shrugged and then given some unmistakable suggestions on how it should be divided. It was incredible. The General with his undeniable perception must have known what the effect would be on the enlisted men, and yet he had disregarded the resentments it would cause. It could not have been to satisfy his belly, for Hearn watched him pick tastelessly at the fresh meat during

166

the meals that followed, and he almost always left his plate half filled. Nor could it have been from habit; the General was quite aware of what he was doing. He considered it effective. After Hobart had left, the General had looked at Hearn blankly, his great pale eyes quite expressionless, and then unaccountably he had winked. "Have to keep you happy, Robert. Perhaps if the meals are better you won't be indulging your temper so much."

"Very thoughtful of you, sir." And the General had roared suddenly with an odd choked mirth that began with a cascade of chuckles, progressed through a choking fit, and ended with him sitting upright in his chair and hawking his sputum into his silk monogrammed handkerchief.

"I think it's about time a recreation tent was set up for the officers' use at night," he said at last. "You're not too busy right now, Robert. I'll put you in charge of it."

An odd commission. But Hearn understood it finally. He told the first sergeant of headquarters company to give him a detail of men, had them clear the roots and grass from a plot of ground, cover it with gravel, and erect a squad tent. When it was up, a deep rain trench was dug all around it. A double entrance was contrived at the front to make it a blackout tent, and some strips of canvas from a discarded tent were used to drape over the lashed corners so that no light could leak out at night. When they had finished with that, Hearn spent an afternoon having them cut bamboo and erect a few writing tables, and two game tables. He had commanded them sullenly through the entire project, quite aware of their resentment toward him, always able to overhear the bitter muttered remarks that were meant for him. The General had given him this assignment because he knew he would hate it, and for that reason Hearn was determined to do a perfect job. He became very finicky about sloppy items in the tent's construction, and once or twice had an argument with the sergeant in command of the detail. All very fine, but that seemed a little too shallow a satisfaction for the General.

The lesson beneath the lesson appeared a little later. The soldier who had been assigned to the operation of the generator in the daytime had been given the officers' recreation tent as an additional chore.

167

He was supposed to furl the side flaps in the morning and let them down at night and fasten the sides. He was also, since the noise of the generator was considered too loud to be used at night, supposed to fill all the Coleman lanterns with kerosene, and light them.

Hearn went into the recreation tent one evening several days after it had been completed, and found it still dark. A few officers were groping around and swearing to each other. "Hey, Hearn," one of them called to him, "how about getting on the ball and giving us some light?"

He stalked over to the pup tent of the recreation tent orderly, and bawled him out. "What's the matter, Rafferty, do you have too many jobs to handle?"

"Jesus, Lieutenant, I'm sorry. I just forgot about it."

"Well, all right, hop to it, don't stand there looking at me." Hearn had found himself about to yell, "Get on the ball, man, will you," and after Rafferty got out of his tent and went jogging over to the motor pool to get some kerosene, Hearn had looked at him with disgust. Stupid ass, he thought, and immediately afterward, with a shock, he realized the trace of contempt he was beginning to feel for an enlisted man. It was slight, barely apparent, and yet it was there. They had tried to balk him when they were building the tent, they had indulged every tiny advantage they could. They had done it before they even worked with him, before they knew him; they had accepted him with an instinctive and immediate distrust, and he resented it.

Suddenly he knew the General's lesson. A new element had been added. In the past when he worked with enlisted men he had been tough because he considered his sympathies had no place in a particular job. When men worked they generally resented their leader. That was unimportant. He had not resented them.

And now there were the beginnings of resentment. The General's point was clear enough. He was an officer, and in functioning as an officer for a long enough time he would assume, whether he wanted to or not, the emotional prejudices of his class. The General was reminding him that he belonged to that class. He remembered Cummings's pale baleful eyes staring at him blankly, and then the inexplicable wink. "Have to keep you happy, Robert." It was a little clearer now. Hearn had known ever since he had been with the General that if he wanted to he could easily rise to a field officer's rank by the end of the war. And there was an ambition in him which responded to that, an ambition he distrusted. Cummings recognized it, Cummings had effectively told him then that if he wanted to, if he was strong enough to overcome the distastes and prejudices he felt toward officers, he could satisfy that ambition.

Understand your class and work within its limits. Marxist lesson with a reverse twist.

It disturbed Hearn deeply. He had been born in the aristocracy of the wealthy midwestern family, and although he had broken with them, had assumed ideas and concepts repugnant to them, he had never really discarded the emotional luggage of his first eighteen years. The guilts he made himself feel, the injustices that angered him were never genuine. He kept the sore alive by continually rubbing it, and he knew it. He knew also at this moment that out of all the reasons why he had begun to quarrel with Conn in officers' mess, one of the vital ones had been that he was afraid of not really caring enough about what Conn was saying. It was true of too many of his reactions. And since his direct self-interest could only move him back toward the ideas of his father, there was no other direction for him to turn, unless there was some other emotional basis for continuing in his particular isolated position on the Left. For a long time he had thought there was one, for even a longer period he had sustained his politics because his friends and acquaintances in New York assumed them as a matter of course, but now in the isolation of the Army, under the searching critique of the General's mind, his fingers were being pulled from the chinning bar.

He walked back to the recreation tent and went inside. Rafferty had filled the lamps and lit them, and already the evening influx of officers had begun. Two card games had been started, and several of the officers were beginning to use the writing tables.

"Hey, Hearn, you want to come in on some poker?" It was Mantelli, one of Hearn's few friends in the headquarters.

"All right." Hearn pulled up a chair. Since the tent had been set

169

up, Hearn had spent his evenings here in unstated defiance of the General. Actually he found it dull and uncomfortable, for it became tremendously hot inside and the air filled quickly with cigarette and cigar smoke, but this was a part of the continual sparring that went on between the General and himself. The General had wanted him to build the tent — all right, he would use it. But, tonight, after his realization about Rafferty, the idea of seeing the General gave Hearn an intimation of dread. There had been very few people he ever feared, but he was beginning to think he was afraid of the General. The cards came around to him, and he shuffled them and dealt, playing mechanically without much interest. He could feel himself perspiring already, and he stripped his shirt and hung it on the back of his chair. It went this way every evening. By eleven o'clock virtually all the officers were in their undershirts, and the tent stank of sweat and smoke.

"Those cards are gonna be hot for me tonight." Mantelli grinned, his small mouth twisted around a cigar.

The babel of chatter was dense already, saturated in the smoke. Somewhere, far off in the jungle, some artillery fired once, the sound thudding in Hearn's head like a jaded angry nerve. Division's nightly smoker, he muttered to himself.

He had played only a few hands with moderate luck when there was an interruption. The General for the first time had come into the tent. "Attention!" somebody bawled.

"At ease, gentlemen," the General murmured. He stared about the tent, his nostrils wrinkling faintly at the odor. "Hearn," the General called.

"Sir?"

"I need you." He waved his hand slightly, his voice brisk and impersonal. While Hearn was still buttoning on his shirt, he left the tent.

"Go ahead, run to poppa," Mantelli grinned.

Hearn was angry. Normally, the fact that the General had come to him would have been pleasing, but the General's voice had humiliated him. For a moment he actually considered remaining in the tent. "I'll get back that money later," he said to Mantelli.

170

"Not tonight, huh?" one of the other officers at the table gibed.

"My master's voice," Hearn said.

He finished buttoning his shirt, kicked his chair back into place, and walked through the tent. In one corner a few officers were drinking up one of their ration bottles of whisky.

He heard them singing and then he was fumbling with the folds of the double curtain at the blackout exit. After the lights inside, he was blinded as he emerged into the dark cool air, so blinded that he almost collided with the General, who had been waiting for him.

"Sorry, I thought you'd gone on ahead," Hearn muttered.

"It's all right." The General strolled slowly toward his own tent, and Hearn constrained his pace to keep from walking too fast. Had the General heard him say "My master's voice"? Aaah, to hell with him.

"What do you need me for, General?"

"We'll discuss that when we get to the tent."

"Yes, sir." Between them for the moment there was some antagonism. They walked on in silence, their feet crunching into the gravel walk. Only one or two men passed by them in the darkness; with the night, almost all activity halted in the bivouac. About them in the rough ellipse of their area Hearn could feel almost tangibly the ring of enlisted men sitting in their foxholes on guard. "Quiet tonight," he muttered.

"Yes."

At the entrance to the General's tent, another collision occurred. Hearn halted at the tent flaps to allow the General to precede him, and Cummings in turn put his hand on Hearn's back to indicate that he was to go first. They both started at once, and Hearn sideswiped the General, felt him recoil a foot or two from the weight of Hearn's big body. "Sorry." There was no answer for a moment, and in a little spasm of anger Hearn separated the flaps and walked in ahead. When Cummings followed, his face was extremely pale and his lower lip showed the indentation of two teeth. Either the collision had hurt him more than Hearn had thought or he was disturbed enough to pinch his lip. But why? It would be more characteristic for Cummings to find amusement in the situation.

171

Still defiant, Hearn sat down without permission. The General seemed about to say something and then was silent. He took the other chair, which faced his desk, shifted it slightly to face Hearn, and stared at him impassively for almost a minute. He had an entirely new expression on his face, one Hearn had never seen before. The bald gray eyes with their immense and startling white pupils seemed dulled. Hearn had the impression that he could touch the surface of Cummings's eyeballs, and the eyes would not blink. In the slight pinch of his mouth, the constriction of the muscles at all the vertices of his face, there seemed a curious pain.

With a little shock, Hearn wondered at the tensions that had made the General seek him out. It must have been humiliating. Even more, there was no artifice about it now, no suggestion of work for him on the General's clean furled desk. Hearn stared at the map of Anopopei that lay tacked to a large drawing board. The ocarina on which the General played his little tune.

Once again Hearn realized how barren was the General's tent. Wherever he was, on Motome, in his ship's cabin, or here, he never seemed to live in a place. The tent was so austere. The cot looked unslept in, the desk was bare again, and the third and unoccupied chair rested at perfect right angles to the larger of the two foot lockers. The tent floor was bare and clean, unmarred by mud. The light of the Coleman lantern threw long diagonals of light and shadow across all the rectangular objects of the tent, so that it looked like an abstract painting.

And Cummings still stared at him with that inexplicable gaze as if he did not know him at all. Like the pulse of their blood, some artillery sounded again in the distance. "I was wondering, Robert," the General said at last.

"Yes, sir?"

"You know, I don't know a damn thing about you really." The voice was flat and colorless.

"What's the matter, have I been stealing your whisky?"

"Perhaps you have . . . figuratively." What the hell did that mean? The General leaned back in his chair, the next question a little too casual. "How's the recreation tent going?"

172

"Fine."

"The Army still hasn't figured out a way to change the air in a blackout tent."

"Oh, it stinks over there all right." So the General had been lonesome for him. Poor little rich boy. "I can't complain, though, I've cleared a hundred bucks out of the poker games."

"In two nights?"

"No, three."

The General smiled thinly. "That's right, it was three nights."

"As if you didn't know."

The General lit a cigarette and extinguished the match with a slow wave of his hand. "I assure you, Robert, there are a few other concerns in my mind."

"I didn't say there weren't."

The General glared at him with a deliberate, self-conscious unveiling of his eyes. "You've got so damn much cheek you're going to die before a firing squad someday." The voice had been a suppressed bellow, and with acute surprise Hearn saw that the General's fingers were trembling. The suspicion of an idea almost defined itself in his head and then was lost like a piece of thread that misses the eye of a needle and wavers fragilely before collapsing.

"Sorry."

And this too seemed the wrong thing to say. The General's mouth was white again. Cummings leaned back in his folding chair, took a long puff of smoke, and then abruptly beamed at Hearn with a fatherly genial air, incredibly counterfeit. "You're still a little annoyed at me about the meat, aren't you?" he asked.

Annoyed. The General had used that word once before. An odd word at this time. Was he in the driver's seat now? It was a little eerie to feel that the General was coming to him, a little uncomfortable. And instinctively his mind clamped down, became grudging and aware as if soon he would be asked for something he did not want to grant. The General would never put a handle to their relationship. At times they had the easy tacit friendship that many generals had with their aides, field officers with their orderlies. And there were all the other moments when they were much closer — the discussions, the

173

occasional bits of gossip. There was also the antagonism between them. And he couldn't find the bone on which all this was grafted.

"I suppose I am annoyed," Hearn said at last. "The rooking the enlisted men got on their meat isn't going to make them love you any."

"They'll blame Hobart or Mantelli or the mess sergeant. That's hardly to the point anyway. You don't really care, you know that."

Damn if he'd give anything away free. "If I did, you certainly couldn't understand it."

"I imagine I could. I probably have a normal allotment of decent impulses."

"Hah."

"You don't think, Robert. The root of all the liberals' ineffectiveness comes right spang out of the desperate suspension in which they have to hold their minds."

Right spang out of it! It was almost pleasant to find a bit of midwestern earth in all the polished and refracted facets of the General's speech. "Name calling is always easy," Hearn muttered.

"Oh, think, man, will you? If you ever followed anything through to the end, not one of your ideas would last for an instant. You think it's important to win this war, don't you?"

"Yes, but I still don't get the tie-up with the meat."

"Well, then, follow me out in this. And you're going to have to take my word, for I've made a study. When I was your age, a little older, the type of thing that preoccupied me was what makes a nation fight well."

"I imagine it would be a kind of identity between the people and the country whether it's for good reasons or bad."

The General shook his head. "That's a liberal historian's attitude. You'd be surprised what a tiny factor that is." The lamp was beginning to sputter and he reached over to adjust the valve, his face lit rather dramatically for a moment by the light source beneath his chin. "There are just two main elements. A nation fights well in proportion to the amount of men and materials it has. And the other equation is that the individual soldier in that army is a more effective soldier the poorer his standard of living has been in the past."

"That's the whole works, huh?"

"There's one other big factor I've played with for a time. If you're fighting in defense of your own soil, then perhaps you're a little more effective."

"Then you come back to my point."

"I wonder if you know how complicated that is. If a man fights on his own soil, it's also a great deal easier for him to desert. That's one problem I never have to consider on Anopopei. It's true the other thing overweighs it, but stop and think about it. Fondness for a country is all very lovely, it even is a morale factor at the beginning of a war. But fighting emotions are very undependable, and the longer a war lasts the less value they have. After a couple of years of war, there are only two considerations that make a good army: a superior material force and a poor standard of living. Why do you think a regiment of Southerners is worth two regiments of Easterners?"

"I don't think they are."

"Well, it happens to be true." The General placed his fingertips together judiciously and looked at Hearn. "I'm not peddling theories. This is observation. And the conclusions leave me, as a general officer, in a poor position. We have the highest standard of living in the world and, as one would expect, the worst individual fighting soldiers of any big power. Or at least in their natural state they are. They're comparatively wealthy, they're spoiled, and as Americans they share most of them the peculiar manifestation of our democracy. They have an exaggerated idea of the rights due themselves as individuals and no idea at all of the rights due others. It's the reverse of the peasant, and I'll tell you right now it's the peasant who makes the soldier."

"So what you've got to do is break them down," Hearn said.

"Exactly. Break them down. Every time an enlisted man sees an officer get an extra privilege, it breaks him down a little more."

"I don't see that. It seems to me they'd hate you more."

"They do. But they also fear us more. I don't care what kind of man you give me, if I have him long enough I'll make him afraid. Every time there's what you call an Army injustice, the enlisted man involved is confirmed a little more in the idea of his own inferiority." He smoothed the hair over his temple. "I happen to know of an American prison camp in England which'll be a terror once we invade

175

Europe. The methods used will be brutal, and it's going to cause a stink eventually, but it happens to be necessary. In our own back yard we have a particular replacement depot where an attempt was actually made to kill the Colonel in command. You aren't capable of understanding it, but I can tell you, Robert, that to make an Army work you have to have every man in it fitted into a fear ladder. Men in prison camps, deserters, or men in replacement camps are in the backwaters of the Army and the discipline has to be proportionately more powerful. The Army functions best when you're frightened of the man above you, and contemptuous of your subordinates."

"Where do I fit into this?" Hearn asked.

"You don't yet. There are such things as papal dispensations." The General grinned at him, lit another cigarette. Almost entirely muted, a burst of laughter from the recreation tent filtered through the bivouac to them.

Hearn sat forward. "You take the man who's out on guard right now, and listens to that laughter. It seems to me there'd come a time when he'd want to turn his machine gun around."

"Oh, eventually. The time soldiers start doing that is when an army is about defeated. Until then, the hate just banks in them, makes them fight a little better. They can't turn it on us, so they turn it outward."

"But you've a big gamble there," Hearn said. "If we lose the war, you've produced a revolution. It seems to me in terms of your interest it would be better to lose the war by being overgood to the men, and avoid the revolution afterward."

Cummings laughed. "That would be one of your liberal weeklies, wouldn't it? You're an ass, Robert. We're not going to lose the war, and if we did, you don't think Hitler would grant a revolution, do you?"

"Then what you're saying is that you people can't lose the war either way."

"You people, you people," the General parroted. "That's a bit of Marxism, isn't it, the great big capitalist conspiracy. Just how do you know so much about Marxism?"

"I've played around with it."

176

"I doubt it. I doubt if you *really* have." The General pinched the butt of his cigarette reflectively. "You're misreading history if you see this war as a grand revolution. It's power concentration."

Hearn shrugged. "I'm a poor history student, I'm no thinker. I just think it's bad sense to have men hating you."

"Again I say it's not important if they're afraid of you. Robert, stop and think, with all the hate there's been in the world, there have been surprisingly few revolutions." He ticked his chin softly with his fingernail, a little sensuously, as if he were absorbed in the scraping sound of his beard. "You can even see the Russian revolution as a space-organization progress. The machine techniques of this century demand consolidation, and with that you've got to have fear, because the majority of men must be subservient to the machine, and it's not a business they instinctively enjoy."

Hearn shrugged again. This discussion had taken the form it invariably assumed. The more intangible and inchoate criteria he tried to use still had value, but to someone who thought like the General, his ideas would appear no more than sentiment, false sentiment, as Cummings had told him so many times. Still he made an effort. "There are other things," he said quietly. "I don't see where you can dismiss the continual occurrence and re-forming of certain great ethical ideas."

The General smiled slightly. "Robert, politics have no more relation to history than moral codes have to the needs of any particular man."

Epigrams and more epigrams. He felt a certain revulsion. "General, by the time you get done after this war, working out the next bigger *consolidation,* the American in the 'forties is going to have the same kind of anxiety that the Europeans had in the 'thirties when they knew the next war would finish them."

"Probably. The natural role of twentieth-century man is anxiety."

"Aaahr." Hearn lit a cigarette, and found with surprise that his hands were shaking. The General was transparent for this single moment. Cummings had begun this argument purposely, had re-established the poise, the unique superior adaptation he had been lacking, for whatever reason, when they had entered the tent.

"You're too stubborn ever to give in, Robert." The General stood

177

up and walked over to his foot locker. "To tell you the truth, I didn't ask you over here for a discussion. I thought perhaps we might have a game of chess together."

"All right." Hearn was surprised, a little uneasy. "I don't think I'll give you much of a battle."

"We'll see." The General set up a small folding table between them, and began placing the pieces on the board. Hearn had talked to him about chess once or twice, and the General had spoken vaguely of playing, but Hearn had discounted it. "You really want to play?" he asked.

"Certainly."

"If someone walks in, it'll be a pretty sight."

The General grinned. "Clandestine, eh?" He had finished arranging the pieces, and he picked up a red and a white pawn, hid one in each of his fists and then extended them for Hearn to choose. "I'm rather fond of this set," the General said genially. "It's hand-carved ivory, not really so dear as you'd think, but the man who made it is a pretty indisputably a craftsman."

Hearn, without comment, picked the red pawn, and after replacing them the General made the opening move. Hearn gave a conventional response, settled his head comfortably in his large hands, and tried to study the board. But he found himself nervous. He was feeling both excited and depressed; the conversation had troubled him, and he was bothered by the fact that he was playing chess with the General. It made everything between them more overt. There seemed something vaguely indecent about it, and he entered the game with a feeling that it would be disastrous for him to win.

He played through the first few moves rather carelessly. He was really not thinking at all, listening instead to the occasional muted rumble of the artillery, the steady absorbed flickering of the Coleman lantern. Once or twice he thought he heard the foliage soughing in the bivouac outside, and the sound made him gloomy. He caught himself staring at the rapt simple concentration on the General's face. His expression was similar to the one he had assumed on the beach invasion day, or on the night they had driven in the jeep, and again it was impressive in its force and direction.

178

Hearn woke up to realize he was in trouble after only six moves. Sloppily, without any real consideration, he had violated a principle by moving his knight twice before his development was completed. His position was not yet dangerous, the knight was only in the fourth rank, and its squares of retreat could be opened easily enough, but the General was opening with an odd attack. Hearn began really to study the game. By now the General could win by completing his development and extracting all the juice out of the slight positional advantage he would have on completion. But it would be a long contest, and the end game would undoubtedly be difficult. Instead the General was launching a pawn attack which would be very embarrassing if it failed, for Cummings's development would be backward, and his king's pawns would have to be opened.

Hearn pondered his responses, and lost himself quickly in the dizzying heights of chess, where he held the entire position in one portion of his mind while investigating the numerous answers the General might make to each move, and the correspondingly more complex replies he himself could manage. Then he would relinquish that approach and try to discern the variations that might arise from moving another piece.

Yet it was hopeless. With almost frightening skill, Hearn felt himself being harassed, then threatened, then strangled by the advance of the General's pawns. Hearn had been on his college chess team, and at different periods in his life he had been tremendously interested in the game. He was a good enough player to realize how very good the General was, good enough to understand something of a man's nature by the style in which he played, and the General had been brilliant in his conception, and coldly efficient in extracting every possible advantage from the slight superiority he had had at the beginning. Hearn conceded on the twenty-fifth move after losing a knight and a pawn in exchange for two pawns, and sat back in his chair fatigued. The game had caught him, piqued his interest, and he felt a sullen desire to play again.

"You're not bad," the General said.

"I'm fair," Hearn muttered. Now that the game was over, he was aware once more of the jungle sounds outside the tent.

179

The General was putting the pieces back in the box, seeming to cherish each one with his fingertips before placing it in its green plush container. "This is really my game, Robert. If I have a single passion, it's chess."

What did the General want of him? Hearn felt suddenly badgered; their discussion, this game, seemed to follow out of some inexorable want behind the well-groomed and unresponsive features of the General. An inexplicable mood caught Hearn, and his sense of oppression returned, magnified a little. The air in the tent seemed heavier somehow.

"Chess," Cummings stated, "is inexhaustible. What a concentration of life it is really."

Hearn's sullenness was increasing. "I don't think so," he said, listening to the accents of his own clear sharp voice with something like distaste. "The thing about chess that used to intrigue me, and ended by being just boring, is that there's nothing remotely like it in life."

"Just what do you think warfare is essentially?"

They were off again. Hearn wanted to avoid a discussion this time, he was weary of being maneuvered by the General. He felt stubborn. For an instant he felt like striking the General, seeing the gray hair suddenly messed, the General's mouth leaking blood. The impulse was powerful and momentary. When it left, he felt merely badgered again. "I don't know, but warfare certainly isn't chess. You might make a case for the Navy, where it's all maneuvering on open flat surfaces with different units of fire power, where it's all Force, Space and Time, but war is like a bloody football game. You start off with a play and it never quite works out as you figured it would."

"It's more complicated, but it comes to the same thing."

Hearn slapped his thigh with sudden exasperation. "By God, there're more pages to the book than you've read. You take a squad of men or a company of men — what the hell do you know about what goes on in their heads? Sometimes I wonder how you can have the responsibility of sending them out on something. Doesn't it ever drive you crazy?"

"That's where you're always missing the boat, Robert. In the

180

Army the idea of individual personality is just a hindrance. Sure, there are differences among men in any particular Army unit, but they invariably cancel each other out, and what you're left with is a value rating. Such and such a company is good or poor, effective or ineffective for such or such a mission. I work with grosser techniques, common denominator techniques."

"You're up so damn high you don't see anything at all. The moral calculus on anything is too involved ever to be able decently to make a decision."

"Nevertheless, you make the decisions and they work out or they don't."

There was something unclean about having a conversation like this, while somewhere out on the front a man might be rigid with terror in his foxhole. Hearn's voice was a little shrill as if that terror were somehow communicated to him. "How do you work out something like this? You have men who have been away from America for a year and a half. How can you calculate whether it's better so many be killed and the rest get home faster, or they all stay over here, and go to pot, and have their wives cheat on them. How do you tot up something like that?"

"The answer is, I don't concern myself with that." The General ticked his beard again with his fingernail. He spoke after a little hesitation. "What's the matter, Hearn? I didn't know you were married."

"I'm not."

"Leave a girl behind, get a Dear John?"

"No, there're no loose ends in back of me."

"Then why all this concern about women 'cheating'? It's in their nature to do that."

Hearn grinned with a sudden relish, a little amazed at his own audacity. "What's the matter, sir, speaking from personal experience?" He remembered immediately afterward that the General was married, apparently a piece of minor information, for the General had never spoken about it, and he had learned it from some other officer. He regretted the statement he had just made, however.

"Maybe from personal experience, maybe," the General said. His voice changed abruptly. "I'd like you to remember, Robert, that every

181

liberty you take is with my sufferance. I think you went a little too far."

"I'm sorry."

"You can shut up."

Hearn was silent, watching the General's face, which was remote. His eyes had contracted, looked almost as if they were supporting something about ten inches from his face. Two spots of white had formed beneath his lower lip, almost directly under the corners of his mouth.

"The truth is, Robert, my wife is a bitch."

"Oh."

"She's done just about everything she could to humiliate me."

Hearn was amazed, and then revolted. That self-pity had appeared again in Cummings's voice. You didn't go around telling things like that, at least not in that tone of voice. Apparently, there was the General and there was the General. "Well, I'm sorry, sir," he mumbled at last.

The Coleman lantern was dying, and its flickers threw long shifting diagonals of light through the tent. "Are you, Robert, are you really? Does anything ever touch you?" For that single instant the General's voice was naked. But he extended his arm and adjusted the lantern again. "You know you're really inhuman," the General said.

"Perhaps."

"You never grant a thing, do you?"

Was *that* what he meant? Hearn stared into his eyes, which were luminous at the moment, almost beseeching. He had an intuition that if he remained motionless long enough the General would slowly extend his arm, touch his knee perhaps.

No, that was ridiculous.

But Hearn stood up with a sudden agitated motion, and walked a few steps to the other end of the tent, where he stood motionless for a moment, staring at the General's cot.

His cot. No, get away from there, before Cummings grabbed that interpretation. He wheeled around, and looked at the General who had not moved, had sat like a large and petrified bird, waiting . . . waiting for what must be indefinable.

"I don't know what you mean, General." His voice fortunately was crisp.

182

"It doesn't matter." The General looked at his hands. "If you have to take a leak, Robert, for God's sake go outside and stop pacing around."

"Yes, sir."

"We never did finish that argument."

This was better. "Well, what do you want me to admit, that you're a God?"

"You know, if there is a God, Robert, he's just like me."

"Uses the common denominator techniques."

"Exactly."

Now, they could talk talk talk. And yet for the moment they were quiet. Between them at this instant was the uncomfortable awkward realization that they did not like each other at all.

The conversation wavered back again, passed through a minor discussion, flitted about the campaign. After a decent interval, Hearn left him and went back to his fly tent. But in the darkness, listening to the stiff starched rustle of the leaves on the coconut trees, Hearn found it difficult to sleep. Out around him spread the miles of jungle, the endless spaces of the southern heavens with their unfamiliar stars.

Something had happened tonight, but already it seemed exaggerated, out of proportion. He did not quite believe what he had heard. The scene was involuted now, something warped by a dream. Only he found himself laughing quietly on his cot.

The shoddy motive.

If you searched something long enough, it always turned to dirt. But even in his laughter Hearn had a picture of himself, saw his big body writhing slightly in mirth on his cot, saw his own shock of black hair, his features contorting in this curious convulsive mirth.

Once a woman who had been his mistress for a time had brought him a mirror in the morning, and said, "Look at yourself, you're just like an ape when you're in bed."

The mirth was a little exasperated now, his limbs almost feverish. Jesus, what a situation.

But when morning came, Hearn was no longer sure that anything had happened at all.

Chorus:

The second squad is digging a new latrine. It is midafternoon and the sun is lancing through a gap in the coconut trees and refracting brightly from the rough stubbled ground. Minetta and Polack are down in the trench, working slowly. Their shirts are removed and there is a wide band of moisture on their pants under their belts. Every ten or fifteen seconds a spadeful of earth lofts out of the hole and drops with a light pattering sound on the mound of soil beside the latrine.

MINETTA: (sighing) That lucky wop, Toglio. (He leans his foot against the shovel.) You think we're lucky being back here? Up there you can get wounded and go home. (He snorts.) All right, so he can't move his elbow so good.

POLACK: Who needs an elbow to screw with?

BROWN: (He is sitting on a stump beside the hole.) Yeah, let me tell you guys something. Toglio's going to go back and find his wife fooling around with anything that wears pants. There ain't a woman you can trust.

STANLEY: (He is sprawled beside Brown.) Oh, I don't know, I trust my wife. There's all kinds of women.

BROWN: (bitterly) They're all the same.

MINETTA: Yeah, well, I trust my girl friend.

POLACK: I wouldn't trust those bitches with a nickel.

BROWN: (picking eagerly at his snub nose) That's what I believe. (He talks to Minetta, who has stopped digging.) You trust your girl friend, huh?

MINETTA: Sure, I do. She knows when she's got something good.

BROWN: You think you can give her a better piece of ass than anybody else?

184

MINETTA: I ain't been beat yet.

BROWN: I'll tell you something, you're a kid. You don't know what a good piece means. . . . Tell me something, Minetta, you ever been laid with your shoes off? (Stanley and Polack roar with laughter.)

MINETTA: Haw, haw.

BROWN: I'll tell you what, Minetta. You just ask yourself a couple of questions. Do you think there's anything special about you?

MINETTA: That ain't for me to say.

BROWN: Well, I'll tell you, there ain't. You're just an ordinary guy. There's not a damn thing special about any of us, not about Polack or you or Stanley or me. We're just a bunch of GIs. (Brown is enjoying himself.) Okay. While we're home, and slipping a little meat to them every night, they're all lovey-dovey. Oh, they can't do enough for ya. But the minute you go away they start thinking.

MINETTA: Yeah, my Rosie thinks of me.

BROWN: You bet she does. She starts thinking of how good it was to have it steady. Listen, she's a young girl, and if she's as beautiful as my wife is, she's missing her good time. There's lots of guys around, lots of four-Fs and USO commandos, and pretty soon she lets herself be talked into going out on a date. And then she dances and starts rubbing up against a guy . . .

MINETTA: Rosie wrote me she don't go out to any dances. (Polack and Brown laugh.)

POLACK: He believes the bitches.

MINETTA: Well, I tested her plenty of times, and I never caught her in a lie yet.

BROWN: That just proves she's smarter than you. (Stanley laughs uncomfortably.) Listen, they're no different from you and me, especially the ones that've had their screwing. They like it just as much as men do, and it's a helluva sight easier for them to get it.

POLACK: (falsetto voice) I don't know why I'm not more popular with the girls . . . I'm such an easy lay. (They all laugh.)

BROWN: What do you think your girl friend is doing now? I'll tell you what. It's just about six A.M. now in America. She's wakin' up in bed with a guy who can give her just as much as you can, and she's giving him the same goddam line she handed you. I tell you, Minetta, there ain't a one of them you can trust. They'll all cheat on you.

POLACK: There ain't a fuggin woman is any good.

MINETTA: (weakly) Well, I ain't worrying.

STANLEY: It's different with me. I got a kid.

BROWN: The ones with kids are the worst. They're the ones who're bored and really need a good time. There ain't a woman is worth a goddam.

STANLEY: (looking at his watch) It's about our turn to dig. (He jumps into the hole and picks up a shovel.) Jesus, you guys are a bunch of goldbricks. Why the hell don't you do your share? (He shovels furiously for a minute, and then halts. He is sweating freely.)

POLACK: (grinning) I'm glad I ain't got to worry about one of those bitches cheating on me.

MINETTA: Aaah, fug you. You think you're pretty goddam good.

7

AFTER the night when the Japanese failed to cross the river, the first squad remained in its position for three days. On the fourth day, 1st Battalion advanced a half mile and recon moved up with A Company. Their new outpost was on the crest of a hill which looked down into a tiny valley of kunai grass; they spent the rest of the week digging new holes, stringing barbed wire, and making routine patrols. The front had become quiet. Nothing happened to the platoon, and they seldom saw any other men except for the platoon of A Company whose positions were on an adjoining hill a few hundred yards away. The bluffs of Watamai Range were still on their right, quite close, and in the late afternoon the cliffs hung over them like a wave of surf about to break.

The men in recon spent their days sitting in the sun on top of the hill. There was nothing to do except eat their rations and sleep and write letters and stand guard in their foxholes. The mornings were pleasant and new, but by afternoon the men were sullen and drowsy, and at night they found it hard to sleep, for the wind moved the grass in the valley beneath them and it looked like a column of men moving toward their hill. At least once or twice every night, a man on guard would awaken the entire squad and they would sit in their holes for almost an hour searching the field beneath them in the silver uncertain moonlight.

Occasionally, they would hear the crackling of some rifles in the distance sounding like a bonfire of dry twigs on an autumn day, and often a shell or two would arch lazily overhead, sighing and murmuring before it crashed into the jungle beyond their lines. At night the machine guns would be hollow and deep, and would hold the mournful boding note of primitive drums. Almost always, they could hear some noise like a grenade or a mortar or the insistent shrill tatting of a sub-machine gun, but the sounds were so far away and so muffled that in time they disregarded them. The week went by in an uncomfortable suspended tension which they felt only in their unvoiced fear of the towering mute walls of Watamai Range on their right.

Every day a ration detail of three men would trudge over to the hill on which the adjacent platoon of A Company was bivouacked, and return with a box of 10-in-1 rations and two five-gallon jerricans of water. The trip was always uneventful and the men did not dislike it, for the monotony of the morning was broken and it gave them a chance to talk to someone other than the men in their squad.

On the last day of the week, Croft and Red and Gallagher filed down their hill, wove through the six-foot kunai grass in the valley beneath them, emerged into a bamboo grove, and from there followed the trail that led to A Company. They filled their empty water cans, strapped them to pack boards, and talked for a few minutes with some of the men in A Company before starting back. Croft was leading them, and when he reached the beginning of the trail he halted, and motioned to Red and Gallagher to come forward.

"Listen," he whispered. "You men were making too goddam much noise coming down the hill. Just 'cause this is a short distance and you got a little weight on your back don' mean you're supposed to wallow round like a bunch of goddam pigs."

"Okay," Gallagher muttered sullenly.

"C'mon, let's go," Red muttered. He and Croft had hardly spoken to each other all week.

The three men filed slowly down the trail keeping a distance of ten yards between them. Red found himself treading warily, and he realized with a trace of anger that Croft's command was influencing him. He walked along for many yards trying to determine whether he was afraid of Croft's anger or his caution came from habit. He was still debating this when he saw Croft stop abruptly, and creep through some bushes on the side of the trail. Croft turned around and looked at Gallagher and him, and then waved his arm forward in a slow silent motion. Red looked at his face; Croft's mouth and eyes were expressionless but there was a poise and tension about his entire body which was imperative. Red crouched and moved up beside him. When the three of them were together, Croft held his finger to his mouth, and then pointed through a break in the foliage beside the trail. About twenty-five yards away there was a tiny hollow. It was actually no more than a small clearing, encircled by jungle, but in the middle of it three Japanese soldiers were sprawled on the ground, resting with their heads on their packs, and a fourth soldier was sitting beside them with his rifle across his lap, his chin resting on his hand. Croft looked at them for a long tense second, and then stared fiercely at Red and Gallagher. His jaw had tightened, and a small lump of cartilage beneath his ear quivered once or twice. Very carefully, he slipped off his pack board and laid it noiselessly on the ground.

"We can't get through that brush without making a noise," he whispered almost soundlessly. "Ah'm gonna throw a grenade, and then we all rush together. Y'understand?"

They nodded dumbly, stripping their packs. Then Red peered through the yards of brush that separated them from the draw. If the grenade failed to kill the Japs, all three of them would be exposed as they went charging through the brush. Actually he hardly thought of this; he rebelled against everything in the situation. It was unbelievable. He always had a similar reaction when he knew he would be in combat in a few seconds. It always seemed impossible he would move or fire his gun, expose his life, and yet he always advanced. Red was feeling now the anger that always followed this, a rage at his desire to avoid the moment to come. I'm as good as any man jack, he told himself numbly. He looked at Gallagher, whose face was white, and Red felt a surprising contempt although he knew that he was himself equally frightened. Croft's nostrils had dilated, and the pupils of his eyes looked cold and very black; Red hated him because Croft could enjoy this.

Croft slipped a grenade out of his belt, and pulled the safety pin. Red looked through the foliage again and stared at the backs of the Japanese soldiers. He could see the face of the man who was sitting up, and it added to the unreality; he felt as though something were choking him. The Japanese soldier had a pleasant bland face with wide temples and a heavy jaw; he looked cow-like and his thick hands appeared sturdy and calloused. Red had for a moment an odd detached pleasure, quite incongruous, which stemmed from the knowledge that he was unobserved. And yet all of this was mixed with dread, and the certainty that none of it was real. He could not believe that in a few seconds the soldier with the broad pleasant face was going to die.

Croft opened his fingers, and the handle of the grenade snapped off and spun a few feet away. The fuse in the grenade popped, and a sputtering noise destroyed the silence. The Japanese heard it, sprang to their feet with sudden cries, and moved a few steps uncertainly back and forth in the tiny circle of the draw. Red watched the expression of terror on one soldier's face, heard the sizzling of the grenade, the sound mixing with the ringing in his ears and the pounding of his heart, and then dropped to the ground as Croft lofted the grenade into the draw. Red grasped his tommy gun and stared intently at a blade of grass. He had time before the grenade exploded to wish he had cleaned his gun that morning. He heard a terrifying shriek, thought once of the soldier with the broad face, and then found himself afoot, crashing and stumbling through the brush.

The three of them halted on the edge of the draw and looked down. All four of the Japanese soldiers were lying motionless in the trampled kunai grass. Croft gazed at them and spat softly. "Go down and take a look," he told Red.

Red slid down the bank to the gully where the bodies lay sprawled. He could tell at a glance that two of the men were certainly dead; one of them reposed on his back with his hands clawed over the bloody mash of what had once been his face, and the other was crumpled on his side with a great rent in his chest. The other two men had fallen on their stomachs and he could see no wounds.

"Finish them off," Croft shouted down to him.

"They're dead."

"Finish them off."

Red felt a pulse of anger. If it'd been anyone else but me, the bastard would have done it himself, he thought. He stood over one of the motionless bodies, and brought the sights of his tommy gun to bear on the back of the soldier's head. He took a little breath, and then fired a burst. He felt nothing except the rising quivering motion of the gun in his hands. After he had fired, he noticed that it was the soldier who had been sitting with his rifle across his thighs. There was an instant in which he hovered on the lip of an intense anxiety, but he repressed it and strode over to the last soldier.

As he looked down upon him, Red felt a wash of many transient subtle emotions. If he had been asked, he might have said, "I didn't feel a goddam thing," but the back of his neck was numb, and his heart was beating rapidly. He had an intense distaste for what he was about to do, and yet as he stared at the body and pointed his sights at the man's neck, he was feeling a pleasurable anticipation. He tightened his finger on the trigger, taking up the slack, tensing himself for the moment when he would fire and the slugs would make round little holes in a cluster, and the corpse would twitch and shake under the force of the bullets. He pictured all those sensations, pulled the trigger . . . and nothing happened. His gun had jammed. He started to work the bolt when the body underneath him suddenly rolled over. It took Red almost a second to realize that the Jap was alive. The two men stared at each other with blank twitching faces, and then the Jap sprang to his feet. There was a fraction of a second in which Red could have knocked him down with the stock of his gun, but the frustration he had felt when the gun jammed, added to the shock he experienced when he realized the soldier was alive, combined to paralyze him completely. He watched the soldier stand up, move a step toward him, and then Red's muscles worked suddenly, and he hurled his gun at the Jap. It missed, and the two soldiers continued to stare at each other, not three yards apart.

Red could never forget the Jap's face. It was gaunt and the skin was drawn tightly over the eyes and cheeks and nostrils so that he had a hungry searching look. He had never seen a man's face so intensely; his gaze concentrated until he could detect every imperfection in the man's skin. He saw blackheads on the Jap's forehead, and a tiny postule on the side of his nose, and drops of sweat in the deep hollows under his eyes. Perhaps they stared at each other for half a second, and then the Jap unsheathed his bayonet, and Red turned and ran. He saw the other man lunging toward him, and Red thought inanely, Horror movie. With a great effort he shrieked over his shoulder, "Get him, GET HIM, CROFT!"

Then Red tripped, and lay motionless on the ground, half stunned. He was trying to ready himself for the flash of pain the knife would cause as it pierced his back, and he held his breath. He heard his heart beat once, and then once more. His alertness was returning, and he poised his body. His heart beat again, and again, and again. Abruptly, he realized that nothing was going to happen.

Croft's clear cold voice grated in his ear. "Goddam, Red, how long you gonna lay on the ground?"

Red rolled over and sat up. He repressed a groan with difficulty, but the effort made him shudder. "Jesus," he said.

"What do you think of your boy friend?" Croft asked softly.

The Jap was standing several yards away with his hands in the air. He had dropped the bayonet, and it lay at his feet. Croft walked over and kicked it away.

Red looked at the Japanese soldier, and for an instant their eyes met. Both men looked away, as if they had each been caught in something shameful. Red realized suddenly how weak he felt.

Yet even now he could not admit any weakness to Croft. "What took you guys so goddam long?" he asked.

"Got down as fast as we could," Croft said.

Gallagher spoke up abruptly. His face was white and his mouth

191

trembled. "I was gonna shoot the mother-fugger but you were in the way."

Croft laughed quietly, and then said, "Ah guess we frightened him more than you, Red. He damn sure stopped running after you when he saw us."

Red found himself shuddering again. He felt a grudged admiration for Croft, and with it a great deal of resentment at being in his debt. For a second or two he tried to find some way to thank him, but he could not utter the words.

"I guess we might as well head back," Red said.

Croft's expression seemed to change. A glint of excitement formed in his eyes. "Why don't you head on back, Red?" he suggested. "Gallagher and me'll follow you in a couple of minutes."

Red forced himself to say, "Want me to take the Jap?" There was nothing he wanted less. He found himself still unable to look at the soldier.

"No," Croft said. "Gallagher and me'll take care of him."

Red realized there was something odd about Croft at this moment. "I can take him okay," he said.

"No, we'll take care of him."

Red looked once at the bodies lying limp in the green draw. Already a few insects were buzzing over the corpse who had lost his face. Everything that had happened to him seemed unreal again. He looked at the soldier from whom he had fled, and already his face seemed anonymous and small. A part of him wondered why he had not been able to meet his eyes. Jesus, I feel pooped, he thought. His legs quivered a little as he picked up his tommy gun. He felt too tired to say anything more. "Okay, see you up on the hill," he muttered.

For some obscure reason, he knew he should not leave, and as he walked away down the trail he felt again the curious shame and guilt the Japanese soldier had caused him. That Croft's a bastard, he told himself. Red felt leaden, in fever.

When he had gone, Croft sat down on the ground and lit a cigarette. He smoked intently without saying anything. Gallagher sat beside him, looking at the prisoner. "Let's get rid of him and get back," he blurted suddenly.

"Hold your water," Croft told him softly.

"What's the use of torturin' the poor bastard?" Gallagher asked.

"He ain't complainin'," Croft said.

But then, as if he had understood them, the prisoner crumpled suddenly to his knees and began to sob in a high-pitched voice. Every few seconds he would turn to them, and extend his hands with plead-ing motions, and then he would beat his arms on the ground as if he despaired of making them understand. Out of the spate of words, Gallagher could distinguish something that sounded like "kood-sigh, kood-sigh."

Gallagher was a little hysterical from the abruptness with which the combat had begun and ended. His momentary compassion for the prisoner lapsed and was replaced by an intense irritation. "Let's cut out that 'kood-sigh' shit," he roared at the Jap.

The soldier was silent for a moment, and then began to plead again. His voice had a desperate urgency which rasped Gallagher's senses. "You look like a fuggin Yid with all that handwaving," he shouted.

"Let's keep it down," Croft said.

The soldier approached them, and Gallagher looked uncomfort-ably into his black pleading eyes. A powerful fishy stench arose from his clothing. "They sure can stink," Gallagher said.

Croft kept staring at the Jap. An emotion was obviously working through his mind, for the lump of cartilage under his ear kept puls-ing. Croft actually was not thinking at all; he was bothered by an in-tense sense of incompletion. He was still expecting the burst that Red's gun had never fired. Even more than Red, he had been anticipating the quick lurching spasms of the body when the bullets would crash into it, and now he felt an intense dissatisfaction.

He looked at his cigarette, and on an impulse he handed it to the Japanese soldier. "What're you doing that for?" Gallagher asked.

"Let him smoke."

The prisoner puffed at it eagerly, and yet self-consciously. His eyes kept darting suspiciously at Croft and Gallagher, and the sweat glistened on his cheeks.

"Hey, you," Croft said, "sit down."

The Jap looked at him with uncomprehending eyes. "Sit down." Croft made some motions with his hands, and the prisoner squatted with his back against a tree. "You got anything to eat?" Croft asked Gallagher.

"I got a chocolate bar from the ration."

"Let's have it," Croft said. He took the bar from Gallagher and handed it to the soldier, who looked at him with dull eyes. Croft made eating motions with his hand, and the prisoner, comprehending, ripped the paper away, and wolfed down the chocolate. "Goddam, he sure is hungry," Croft said.

"What the fug are you doin' it for?" Gallagher asked. He felt exasperated to the point of tears. He had been saving the candy for over a day, and its loss pained him; moreover, he was vacillating between irritability at the prisoner and a grudged compassion. "The dumb bastard sure is skinny," he said with the superior affection he might have used if he saw a mongrel dog shivering in the rain. But then immediately afterward he watched the last piece of chocolate disappear in the Jap's mouth, and he muttered angrily, "What a goddam pig he is."

Croft thought of the night the Japanese had tried to cross the river. He felt a shiver work its way through him, and he stared for a long time at the prisoner. He felt an intense emotion toward him which made him clench his teeth. But what it was, he could not have said. He removed his canteen and took a drink. He saw the prisoner watching him as he gulped down the water, and on an impulse he handed him the canteen. "Go ahead, drink," he said. Croft gazed at him as he swallowed with long eager draughts.

"I'm a sonofabitch," Gallagher said. "What got in ya?"

Croft did not answer. He was staring at the prisoner, who had finished drinking. There were a few tears of joy in the Jap's face and he smiled suddenly and pointed to his breast pocket. Croft extracted a wallet, and opened it. There was a picture of the Japanese soldier in civilian dress and beside him was his wife and two little children with

194

round doll faces. The Japanese soldier pointed to himself and then made two gestures with his hand above the ground to indicate how tall his children had grown.

Gallagher looked at the picture, and felt a pang. For an instant he remembered his wife and wondered what his child would look like when it was born. With a shock he realized that his wife might be in labor now. For some reason which he did not understand he said suddenly to the Jap, "I'm gonna have a kid in a couple of days."

The prisoner smiled politely, and Gallagher pointed angrily to himself and then held his hands extended and about nine inches apart. "Me," he said, "me."

"Ahhhhhh," the prisoner said. "Chiisai!"

"Yeah, cheez-igh," Gallagher said.

The prisoner shook his head slowly, and smiled again.

Croft came up to him, and gave him another cigarette. The Japanese soldier bowed low, and accepted the match. "Arigato, arigato, domo arigato," he said.

Croft felt his head pulsing with an intense excitement. There were tears in the prisoner's eyes again, and Croft looked at them dispassionately. He gazed once about the little draw, and watched a fly crawl over the mouth of one of the corpses.

The prisoner had taken a deep puff and was leaning back now against the trunk of the tree. His eyes had closed, and for the first time there was a dreamy expression on his face. Croft felt a tension work itself into his throat and leave his mouth dry and bitter and demanding. His mind had been entirely empty until now, but abruptly he brought up his rifle and pointed it at the prisoner's head. Gallagher started to protest as the Jap opened his eyes.

The prisoner did not have time to change his expression before the shot crashed into his skull. He slumped forward, and then rolled on his side. He was still smiling but he looked silly now.

Gallagher tried to speak again but was incapable of it. He felt an awful fear and for an instant he thought of his wife again. Oh, God save Mary, God save Mary, he repeated to himself without thinking of the meaning of the words.

Croft stared for almost a minute at the Jap. His pulse was slowing down and he felt the tension ease in his throat and mouth. He realized suddenly that a part of his mind, very deeply buried, had known he was going to kill the prisoner from the moment he had sent Red on ahead. He felt quite blank now. The smile on the dead man's face amused him, and a trivial rill of laughter emitted from his lips. "Goddam," he said. He thought once again of the Japanese crossing the river, and he prodded the body with his foot. "Goddam," he said, "that Jap sure died happy." The laughter swelled more strongly inside him.

Later that morning recon received an order to return to the rear. They folded their tents, stowed their ponchos in their jungle packs, filled their canteens from the water Red and Gallagher and Croft had brought back, and ate a ration while they waited for other troops to relieve them. About noon a squad from A Company moved into their outpost, and recon descended their hill and took the trail leading back to 1st Battalion. It was a long hike over a muddy lane in the jungle, and after a half hour they settled down into the tedium and weariness of trudging through the mud. A few of them were jubilant; Martinez and Wyman had a pressure removed from them, and Wilson was thinking about whisky. Croft was taciturn, reflective, and Gallagher and Red were nervous and irritable and started frequently at every unexpected noise. Red found that he was continually turning around to look behind him.

They reached 1st Battalion in an hour, and after a short rest they moved on along a lateral trail to 2nd Battalion. It was midafternoon when they arrived there, and Croft received orders for the squad to bivouac on the battalion perimeter for the night. The men cast off their packs, withdrew their ponchos and set up their pup tents again. There was a machine-gun emplacement in front of them and they did not bother to dig any more holes. They sat about resting and talking, and gradually they felt the tension of the past week coming back. "Goddam," Wilson said, "that sure was a lonely place they put us. Ah tell ya Ah jus' wouldn' wanta spend a honeymoon there."

Wilson was feeling restless. There was a tickle in his throat and his legs and arms felt drawn, overworked. "Man," he announced, "Ah

196

could sure use a nice big bottle of likker." He stretched his legs and yawned a little desperately. "Ah tell ya what," he said, "Ah heard they's a mess sergeant over here that makes a decent drink for a man." None of the men answered him, and he got to his feet. "Ah think Ah'm gonna take a little walk and see if Ah can manipilate some likker for us."

Red looked up irritably. "What the hell you gonna use for money? I thought you lost it all up on the hill." They had been playing poker every day.

Wilson was hurt. "Listen, Red," he confided, "they ain't ever a time when Ah been broke. Ah don't claim to be no poker player, but Ah'll bet ya they ain't many men who can say they busted me in a game." Actually he had lost all his money, but an obscure pride kept him from admitting it. At this moment, Wilson was not thinking of what he would do if he could find some whisky without having the money to purchase it. He was interested only in finding the whisky. Jus' lemme see some likker, he thought, an' Ah'll fin' a way to drink it.

He got up and walked away. In about fifteen minutes he returned grinning. He sat down beside Croft and Martinez, and began to poke at the ground with a twig he was holding. "Listen," he said, "they's a little ole mess sergeant here who's got a still out in the woods yonder. Ah was talkin' to him, and Ah manipilated him into settin' us a price."

"How much?" Croft asked.

"Well, Ah'll tell ya," Wilson said, "it's kinda high . . . but it's good stuff. He been usin' canned peaches and apricots and raisins with lots of sugar and yeast. He let me sample it, an' it's goddam good."

"How much?" Croft asked again.

"Well, now, he wants twenty-five of them pounds for three canteens full. Ah never could figger out them damn pounds, but Ah reckon it ain't much over fifty dollars."

Croft spat. "Fifty dollars, hell. It's all of eighty bucks. That's pretty steep for jus' three canteens."

Wilson nodded. "Yeah, but then what the hell, we're jus' gonna get our haids blown off tomorrow." He paused and then added, "Ah tell ya, we can get Red and Gallagher in on it, and then it jus' makes five pound apiece 'cause they'll be five of us. Five time five, twenty-five, ain't it?"

Croft deliberated. "You get Red and Gallagher in, and Martinez and me'll put up."

Wilson went over to talk to Gallagher, and left him with five Australian pounds in his pocket. He stopped to chat with Red, and mentioned the price. Red exploded. "Five pounds apiece for three lousy canteens? Wilson, you can get five canteens for twenty-five pounds."

"Now, you know you cain't, Red."

Red swore. "Where the hell's your five pounds, Wilson?"

Wilson took out Gallagher's money. "That's it, Red."

"It wouldn't be one of the other men's money, would it?"

Wilson sighed. "Honestly, Red, Ah don' know how the hell you can think those kind of things about a buddy." At the moment he was completely sincere.

"All right, here's five," Red growled. He still thought Wilson was lying, but it didn't really matter. He needed to get drunk anyway, and he did not have the energy to find some liquor for himself. His body stiffened for a moment in a duplication of the panic that had caught him when he was walking alone on the trail and had heard the shot from Croft's gun. "All we ever do is screw each other anyway, what the hell." He could not shake the death of the Japanese prisoner. It had been wrong somehow. When the Jap hadn't been killed the first time, he rated being taken in as a prisoner. But it was more than that. He should have stayed. The whole week up there, the night on the river, the killings. He sighed heavily. Let Wilson have his good time; it was getting hard to find.

Wilson collected the rest of the money from Croft and Martinez, picked up four empty canteens, and went off to see the mess sergeant. He paid the twenty pounds he had promoted, and returned with the four canteens filled. One of them he hid under a folded blanket in his pup tent, and then he joined the other men and unhitched the canteens from his belt. "We better drink 'em up fast," he said. "That alcohol might eat on the metal."

Gallagher took a swig. "What the fug is it made of?" he asked.

198

"Oh, it's good stuff," Wilson assured him. He took a long drink and exhaled pleasurably. The liquor flushed its way through his throat and chest and settled warmly in his stomach. He felt tendrils of pleasure winding through his limbs and a joyous warmth began to relax his body. "Man, that does me good," he said. With the drink inside him, and the knowledge that there would be more to follow, Wilson felt mellow, he had a desire to speak of philosophical subjects. "Y'know," he said, "whisky is the kind of thing a man oughtn't to do without. That's the trouble with the goddam war; a man cain't get off by hisself, and do the kind of things where he had a good time for hisself and don't hurt no one a darnn bit."

Croft grunted inaudibly and wiped the mouth of the canteen before he drank. Red sifted some dirt through his fingers. The liquor had been sweet and raw; it had rasped his throat and the irritation expanded through his body. He rubbed the side of his lumpish red nose and spat angrily. "No one's gonna ask you what you want to do," he told Wilson. "They just send you out to get your ass blown off." For an instant, he saw again the dead bodies in the green draw, the naked look of lacerated flesh. "Don't kid yourself," he said, "a man's no more important than a goddam cow."

Gallagher was remembering how the legs and arms of the Japanese prisoner had twitched for a second after Croft had shot him. "Just like wringing the neck of a fuggin chicken," he muttered surlily.

Martinez looked up. His face was drawn, and there were shadows under his eyes. "Why not you keep quiet?" he asked. "We see same things you do." His voice, almost always quiet and polite, had an angry strident note which amazed Gallagher and silenced him.

"Let's pass the canteen around," Wilson suggested. He tilted it upward, and drank the last inch. "Guess we got to open another one," he sighed.

"We all paid up for this," Croft said. "Let's see we drink the same amount." Wilson giggled.

They sat about in a circle, passing the canteen from time to time, and talking in slow indifferent voices which began to blur before the second canteen was finished. The sun was dropping toward the west, and for the first time that afternoon shadows were beginning to drift

199

from the trees and the black-green ponchos of their pup tents. Gold stein and Ridges and Wyman were sitting about thirty yards away talking in soft voices. Occasionally, a noise of some minor activity — a truck grinding up the lane that led to the bivouac or the shouts of some soldiers on a labor detail — would filter through the coconut grove. Every fifteen minutes a battery about a mile away would fire, and a part of their minds would wait for the sound of the explosion when the shells landed. There was nothing to look at but barbed wire in front of them and the thick brush of the jungle beyond the grove.

"Well, back to headquarters company tomorrow . . . let's drink to that," Wilson said.

"I hope we just dig that fuggin road for the rest of the campaign," Gallagher said.

Croft fingered his belt dreamily. The awareness and excitement he had felt after he killed the prisoner had faded on the march to an empty sullen indifference to everything about him. As he drank, the sullenness remained but there were changes taking place in him. His mind had become dulled and blurred, and he would sit motionless for minutes at a time without speaking, intent upon the curious whirling and tumbling that was going on inside his body. His mind kept yawing drunkenly like the underwater shadows that ripple about a piling. He would think, Janey was a drunken whore, and a dull clod of pain would settle in his chest. Crack that whip, he muttered to himself, and his mind eddied over the lazy sensual memories of striding a horse and looking down a hill into a sunlit valley beneath. The alcohol spread through his legs, and he recalled for an instant the entire complex of pleasant sensations he felt when the sun had heated his saddle, and the smell of the hot leather and the wet horse spread about him. The heat re-created the glare of the sunlight in the green draw where the Japanese bodies were lying, and as he thought of the look of surprise that almost came to the prisoner's face the instant before he died, a trickle of laughter began to flow in Croft, and dribbled between his thin tight lips like the frail saliva that bubbles from a sick man's mouth. "Goddam," he muttered.

Wilson was feeling exceptionally good. The whisky had filled his body with a rosy sense of complete well-being, and vague lewd sen-

200

sual images stroked his mind. His groin was filling, becoming tumescent, and his nose quivered with excitement as he remembered the fermy sweating smells of a woman in heat. "They ain't anythin' Ah wouldn' give to be lovin' it up with a woman now. Time Ah was workin' as a bellboy at the Hotel Main in town, they was a girl there she was workin' as a singer in some little old band that'd come to town, and she used to keep ringing for me to bring her up some drinks. Well, Ah was a young kid then, an' Ah was kind of slow to catch on, but they was one day Ah went up to her room and they she was bareass naked, an' jus' waitin' for me. Ah tell ya, Ah didn't go down and tend to business for all of three hours, and they wasn't hardly a goddam thing she wouldn' do for me." He sighed, and took a long drink. "Her and me jus' loved it up eveh afternoon for all of two months, and she tol' me they wan't a man could equal me." He lit a cigarette, and his eyes twinkled behind his spectacles. "Ah'm a good fella, anybody'll tell ya that. They ain't a damn thing Ah cain't fix, not a single piece of machinery eveh been able to lick me, but Ah'm a sonofabitch comes to women. They's lots of women tol' me they neveh found a man like me." He ran his hand over his massive forehead and through his pompadour of golden hair. "But it jus' plays hell on a man when he ain't got a woman." He took another drink. "Ah got a girl waitin' for me in Kansas don' know Ah'm married. Use to fool aroun' with her when Ah was at Fort Riley. That little ole gal writes me letters all the time, Red'll tell ya 'cause he been readin' 'em to me, and she's jus' waitin' for me to come back. Ah keep tellin' mah old woman that she better stop writin' me those kind of naggin' letters about the kids and why Ah don't send more money home, or Ah'm damn sure not gonna go back to her. Shi-i-i-it, Ah like that ole gal in Kansas better anyway. She cooks a meal for me that's fitten for a man to eat."

Gallagher snorted. "Fuggin cracker like you, all you got time to do is screw and eat."

"What the hell's better?" Wilson asked mildly.

"A man can get ahead, that's what," Gallagher said. "You work your ass off, you want something for it." He held his face numb. "I got a kid coming, probably being born right now while I'm drinking, but I never had a fuggin break, that's the goddam truth." He gave a little moan of anger, and then leaned forward tensely. "Listen, I remember there was times when I'd be going out alone for a walk and . . . I'd . . . I'd see things, and I'd know I was going to be something big." He paused bitterly. "But there was always something screwing me up." He stopped angrily, as if looking for words, and then looked off moodily.

Red was feeling very drunk and very profound. "I'll tell you guys something . . . none of ya are ever gonna get anything. You're all good guys, but you're gonna get . . . the shitty end of the stick. The shitty end of the stick, that's all you're gonna get."

Croft let out a roar of laughter. "You're a good bastard, Gallagher," he shouted sullenly, clapping him on the back. He felt a vast explosive mirth which embraced everything. "An' you're jus', jus' an old *cock-hound,* Wilson. You're the goddamnedest ole lecher . . ." His voice was thick and the others, even in their drunkenness, looked at him uneasily. "I bet you were born with a stiff rod."

Wilson began to cackle. "Ah've suspected it mahself."

They laughed together violently, and Croft shook his head as if to halt the uproarious whirl of his head. "I'm going to tell you men something," he said. "You're all good guys. You're all chicken, and you're all yellow, but you're good guys. They ain't a goddam thing wrong with you." He gave a tight smile which set his mouth awry, and then laughed again. He took a long drink. "Japbait here is the best goddam friend a man could have. Mex or no Mex, you can't beat him. Even ol' Red who's a dumb mean ol' sonofabitch, and I'm gonna shoot him someday, even ol' Red means all right in his own stupid way."

Red felt a pang of fear which alerted him for an instant as if a drill were probing one of his teeth. "Up yours, Croft," he said.

Croft laughed with intense merriment. "See what I mean," he pointed out.

Red relapsed into a moody somnolence. "You're all good fuggin guys," he said, waving his arm vaguely through the air.

Croft giggled suddenly. It was the first time the men had ever heard him make such a sound. "Like Gallagher said, that dumb ol' sonofabitch floppin' around in the dirt like he was a chicken with its neck jus' been wrung."

202

Wilson cackled with him; he did not know why Croft was laugh ing, but it did not concern him. Everything about him had become diffused and uncertain and pleasant. He felt only an encompassing warmth for the men with whom he drank; in the languorous swirls of his mind they existed with him as something superior and amiable. "Ol' Wilson'll never let you all down," he chuckled.

Red snorted and rubbed the edge of his nose, which had become numb. He felt a savage irritation at a combination of things too numerous and subtle for him to determine. "Wilson, you're a good buddy," he said, "but you're no goddam good. I'll tell ya somethin', the whole bunch of us are no damn good."

"Red drunk," Martinez said.

"You're fuggin ay," Red shouted. Liquor seldom made him happy. It recalled in his mind a monotonous suite of dingy barrooms and men drinking quietly, looking with resignation into the bottom of their shot glasses. For an instant he could see again the opaque rings of the glass base. He closed his eyes and the rings seemed to flow into his brain. He felt himself sway drunkenly, and he opened his eyes, and sat upright fiercely. "Fug ya, all of ya," he said.

They paid no attention to him. Wilson looked around and saw Goldstein sitting alone at the next tent, writing a letter. Abruptly, it seemed shameful to Wilson for them to drink without including any- one else in the squad. For a few seconds he watched Goldstein scribbling busily with a pencil, moving his lips soundlessly as he wrote. Wilson decided that he liked Goldstein but he was vaguely irri- tated that Goldstein did not drink with them. That Goldstein's a good fella, he said to himself, but he's kind of a stick-in-the-mud. It seemed to Wilson that Goldstein was missing a very fundamental understand- ing of life.

"Hey, Goldstein," he roared, "come over here."

Goldstein looked up, and smiled diffidently. "Well, thanks, but I'm writing a letter to my wife now." His voice was mild, but it had an expectant fearful quality in it as if he knew he would be abused.

"Aw, forget that ol' letter," Wilson said, "it'll wait."

Goldstein sighed, stood up, and walked over. "What do you want?" he asked.

Wilson laughed. It seemed an absurd question to him. "Ah, hell, have a drink. What do ya think Ah asked ya for?"

Goldstein hesitated. He had heard that the liquor made in the jungle stills was often poisonous. "What kind is it?" he temporized. "Is it real whisky or is it jungle juice?"

Wilson was offended. "Man, it's just good liquor. Y' don' ask questions like that when a man offers ya a drink." Gallagher snorted. "Take the goddam drink or leave it, Izzy," he said.

Goldstein reddened. Out of fear of their contempt he had been about to accept, but now he shook his head. "No, no, thank you," he said. To himself, he thought, What if it should poison me? That would be a fine way, to leave Natalie to get along as best she can. A man with a wife and child can't take chances. He shook his head again, looking at their hard impassive faces. "I really don't want any," he said in his mild breathless voice, and waited with apprehension for their answer.

All of them showed contempt. Croft spat, and looked away. Gallagher looked righteous. "None of *them* drink," he muttered.

Goldstein knew that he should turn around and go back to his letter, but he made a feeble attempt to justify himself. "Oh, I drink," he said. "I like a little sociable drink once in a while, before meals or at a party . . ." He trailed off. A part of his mind had known with a certain bitter understanding that he was in trouble the moment Wilson called him, but that had served only to send random disconnected warnings which he was incapable of obeying.

Wilson looked angry. "Goldstein, you're chicken, that's what you *are*." Out of his superiority and well-being, he felt a condescending annoyance at anyone who was too stupid to appreciate the chance he had given Goldstein.

"Aaah, go write your letter," Red bellowed. He was in an ugly mood, and Goldstein's expression of humiliation and bewilderment offended him. He felt contempt that Goldstein could not hide his feelings; more, he had had a bitter amused knowledge from the moment Wilson had offered Goldstein a drink. He had known exactly what would happen and it gave him an ironic pleasure. Deep inside him he was feeling a trace of sympathy for Goldstein, but he smothered it.

"A man ain't worth a damn if he can't even take care of himself," Red muttered.

Goldstein turned around abruptly and walked away. The circle of men who were drinking drew closer, and there was an almost tangible bond between them now. They opened the third canteen.

"It was jus' a mistake," Wilson said, "to try an' be nice to him."

Martinez nodded. "Man pay for liquor, drink it. No free drinks."

Goldstein tried to become absorbed in his letter again. But he found it impossible to write. He kept brooding over what the men had said and what he had answered, and he kept wishing that he had given the replies he was thinking of now. Why do they give me all this aggravation? he wondered, and for a moment felt like weeping. He picked up his letter and read it through again, not quite able to concentrate on the words. After the war he was planning to open a welding shop, and he and his wife had been discussing it in letters ever since he had been overseas. Just before Wilson had called him, Goldstein had not been writing. He had held his pencil in his hand, and he had thought with excitement and joy of what it would be like with a shop of his own, becoming an established man in the community. He had not been daydreaming about the shop; he had the place picked out, and he had figured very nicely how much money he and his wife would save if the war lasted one year or at most two —he was very optimistic about its ending soon — he had even calculated how much they could save if he were to make corporal or sergeant.

It was the only pleasure he had since he had left the States. At night in his tent he would lie awake and plan for his future, or think of his son, or try to imagine where his wife would be at that moment. And sometimes, if he decided that she would be visiting her relatives, he would attempt to create their conversation, and would shake with suppressed glee as he remembered the family jokes.

But now he could not bury himself in those thoughts. As soon as he would try to hear the light cheerful sound of his wife's voice, he would become conscious of the bawdy laughter of the men who were still drinking at his left. Once his eyes filled with tears and he shook his head angrily. Why did they hate him so? he asked himself. He had

205

tried so hard to be a good soldier. He had never fallen out on a hike, he was as strong as any of them, and he worked harder than most of them. He had never fired his gun once when he was on guard, no matter how tempted he had been, but no one ever noticed that. Croft never recognized his worth.

They were just a bunch of Anti-Semiten, he told himself. That was all the goyim knew, to run around with loose women, and get drunk like pigs. Deeply buried was his envy that he had never had many women and did not know the easy loud companionship of drink. He was tired of hoping to make friends with them; they didn't want to get along with him, they hated him. Goldstein smacked his fist against his palm in exasperation. How can You permit the anti-Semites to live, God? he asked. He was not religious, and yet he believed in a God, a personal God with whom he could quarrel, and whom he could certainly upbraid. Why don't You stop things like that? he asked bitterly. It seemed a very simple thing to accomplish, and Goldstein was irritated with the God he believed in, as if he were a parent who was good but a little thoughtless, a little lazy.

Goldstein picked up his letter and began to write again. "I don't know, honey, I get so sick at the whole thing at times I want to quit. It's a terrible thing to say, but I hate the soldiers I have been put with, they're a bunch of *grobe jungen*. Honestly, honey, it's hard to remember all the fine ideals. Sometimes even with the Jews in Europe I don't know why we're fighting. . . ." He reread what he had written, and then crossed it out violently. But he sat there for a minute or two with a cold fear.

He was changing. He realized it suddenly. His confidence was gone, and he wasn't sure of himself. He hated all the men with whom he lived and worked and he could never remember a time in the past when he hadn't liked nearly everyone he knew. Goldstein held his head for a moment, and then laboriously began to write again. "I have an idea that is pretty good. Maybe we should try to do some work with the junk yards. There is lots of things they have there that need only a little welding to be able to work even if they don't look so good . . ."

206

Wilson was getting restless. He had been sitting in one place for several hours now, and his mood of contentment was beginning to lapse. His drinking sessions always followed a similar pattern: for the first few hours he would feel happy and benevolent, and the more he drank the more superior he felt to anyone who was not drinking. But after a time he would feel a need for some external excitement and he would become bored and a trifle sober. He would fidget, become a little agitated, and then abruptly he would leave the bar or the house where he was drinking, and wander away to accept whatever adventures might occur. Many times he would wake up the next day in the bed of a strange woman, or in the gutter, or on the sofa in the parlor of his small frame house. And rarely would he remember what had happened to him.

Now he emptied the last few drops of the third canteen and sighed noisily. His voice had become very thick. "What in the hell are we gonna do now, men?" he asked.

Croft swayed to his feet and laughed again. He had been chuckling to himself all afternoon. "I'm gonna sleep," he announced.

Wilson shook his head, and leaned forward, holding Croft's leg. "Sergeant — Ah'm gonna call ya sergeant 'cause you're so goddam chicken — sergeant, you got no call to be hittin' the sack 'cause it ain't even gonna be dark for an hour yet, maybe two."

Gallagher smiled lopsidedly. "Don't ya see that fuggin Croft is blind now?"

Croft leaned down and grasped Gallagher by the collar. "I don' care drunk I am, none you men got a call to talk to me that way, none of you men." He pushed Gallagher back suddenly. "I'm rememberin' just what the hell you say . . ." His voice trailed off. "I'm rememberin', wait till tomorrow." He stopped and laughed again, and then walked a little uncertainly toward his tent.

Wilson rolled the empty canteen back and forth. He burped once. "What the hell we gonna do?" he asked again.

"Damn liquor go too fast," Martinez said. He was beginning to feel very gloomy at the thought of how much money he had spent.

Wilson leaned forward. "Listen, men, Ah got an idea. Y'know

207

them Japs've got those rollin' whorehouses they bring right up to the lines."

"Where'd ya hear that?" Gallagher demanded.

"Ah heard it, that's for certain. Well, why don' we jus' sneak over tonight an' get in their tail line, and we can knock off a piece of that yellow stuff?"

Red spat. "What's the matter, ya want to see if their slits are horizontal?"

"That's Chinee," Wilson said

Gallagher leaned forward truculently and said, "Wilson, you're a nigger-lover."

Wilson laughed. "Shi-i-i-it," he drawled. He had forgotten his scheme already.

Red was thinking once more of the bodies in the draw. He felt a curious fascination as he remembered how they had looked. A wash of fear penetrated through the whirling in his mind, and he looked over his shoulder again. "Why don't we go looking for souvenirs?" he shouted furiously.

"Where?"

"There ought to be some dead Japs around here," Red said. He resisted the impulse to look behind him.

Wilson giggled. "They is, they is," he said suddenly. "Down 'bout two-three hunnerd yards from that mess sergeant's still, they was a battle. Ah 'member we passed right by it, jus' right by it."

Martinez spoke up. "Night we go up to the river, and the Japs come. That night Japs come down almost to here."

"Tha's right," Wilson said. "Ah heard they had tanks down 'bout here."

"Well, let's go lookin' then." Red muttered. "We rate a couple of souvenirs."

Wilson stood up. "If they's one goddam thing Ah gotta do when Ah get likkered up it's to start roamin' round." He stretched his arms. "Well, men, let's git goin'."

The others looked at him dumbly. They had settled into a stupor and their conversation had been random and purposeless. They had talked without thinking of what they said, and now they were be-

208

wildered by Wilson's energy. "Come on, men," he repeated.

They obeyed him because they were passive and would have obeyed anybody who told them to do something. Wilson picked up his rifle, and the others, seeing him do this, slung theirs also.

"Where the hell do we go?" Gallagher asked.

"Jus' follow me, men," Wilson said. He let out a drunken whoop.

They tailed along behind him in a rough straggling file. Wilson led them through the bivouac area. His good spirits revived again. "Show me the way to go home," he sang.

Some soldiers stared at them, and Wilson halted. "Men," he said, "they's gonna be some goddam officers lookin' at us, so goddammit let's look like soldiers."

"Eyes right," Red bawled. He felt suddenly gleeful.

They began to move with exaggerated caution, and when Gallagher stumbled once the others turned on him. "God*dammit,* Gallagher," Wilson reproved softly. He was walking jauntily, his legs just the least bit unsteady, and he began to whistle. They reached a gap in the barbed wire, and trudged through a chest-high field of kunai grass. Gallagher kept falling and cursing, and Wilson would turn around each time and hold his finger to his lips

After a hundred yards the jungle encircled them again, and they weaved through the grass parallel to it until they found a trail. Far in the distance an artillery battery was firing, and Martinez shivered. He was sweating freely from the walk and he felt very depressed. "Where goddam battlefield?" he asked.

"Jus' at the end of the trail," Wilson said. He remembered the fourth canteen of whisky, which he had hidden, and he began to giggle again. "Jus' a little while," he told them. They stumbled along the trail for a hundred and fifty yards before it debouched into a narrow road. "This's Jap road," Wilson said.

"Where's the fuggin Japs?" Gallagher asked.

"Oh, they's miles away," Wilson assured him. "This yere's where we pushed them back."

Gallagher sniffed. "I can smell them already," he announced.

"Oh, yeah," Wilson said. "I hear they's lots of them round here."

209

The road passed through a coconut grove and then extended into a field of kunai grass. Gradually, as they walked they had become aware of a familiar stench rising from the plain on either side of them. It was a smell of decay not exactly sweet but a good deal like ordure leavened with garbage and the foul odor of a swamp. The smell varied in intensity and quality; sometimes it struck their noses with the acute loathsome scent of rotting potatoes, and sometimes it was more like the lair of a skunk.

"Jesus," Red swore. He stepped around the dead body of a Japanese soldier that lay crushed on the road.

In the coconut groves at the edge of the field, the trees were stripped of leaves and their trunks appeared black or brown as if they had withered from drought. Most of them had their branches sheared away, and they stood solitary and naked like a row of pilings on a sand flat when the tide is out. There was nothing green left in the groves.

All over the landscape were the black silhouettes of burnt tanks; somehow they blended into the wreckage of trees and the circles of black charred grass so that they were camouflaged as in the child's picture-game where the faces of famous men are concealed in the leaves of trees. A litter of wreckage lay all over the field. There were the dead bodies of Japanese soldiers everywhere, and in one place on a small ridge, where the Japanese had entrenched themselves for a few hours, the artillery had torn great crumpled holes in the earth.

The men wandered through the field, which was perhaps a quarter mile long. In the grass they could see the twisted bodies of a few dead men, and they lay very far from repose, their bodies frozen in the midst of an intense contortion. They skirted around them, and continued to stroll down the road. A few yards away a destroyed Japanese half-track and an American tank had careened on their sides, leaning against each other like old houses ready to totter. They had burned together, and they looked black and crippled. The bodies of the Japanese had not been carried away, and the driver of the half-track had almost fallen out of his seat. His head was crushed from his ear to his jaw and it lay sodden on the runningboard of the vehicle as if it were a beanbag. One of his legs was thrust tensely through the shattered glass of the windshield and the other one, which had been lopped off at the thigh, lay at right angles to his head. It seemed to have a separate existence from him.

Another Japanese lay on his back a short distance away. He had a great hole in his intestines, which bunched out in a thick white cluster like the congested petals of a sea flower. The flesh of his belly was very red and his hands in their death throe had encircled the wound. He looked as if he were calling attention to it. He had an anonymous pleasant face with small snubbed features, and he seemed quite rested in death. His legs and buttocks had swollen so that they stretched his pants until they were the skin-tight trousers of a Napoleonic dandy. Somehow he looked like a doll whose stuffing had broken forth.

At an angle to him lay a third soldier, who had received a terrible wound in his chest. His thighs and torso had been burned in escaping from the half-track, and he was stretched out on his back with his legs separated and his knees raised. The singed cloth of his uniform had rotted away and it exposed his scorched genitals. They had burned down to tiny stumps but the ash of his pubic hair still remained like a tight clump of steel wool.

Wilson poked about the wreckage, and then sighed. "They done stripped 'em all of souvenirs," he said.

Gallagher swayed back and forth drunkenly. "Who did? Who the fug did? Wilson, you're a goddam liar. You stole all the souvenirs."

Wilson ignored him. "It's a damn shame's all Ah can say when a bunch of men like us is risking our ass for a whole goddam week, and they ain't even any souvenirs left." His voice trailed off bitterly. "Goddam shame," he repeated to himself.

Martinez prodded with his shoe the genitals of the charred corpse. The genitals collapsed with a small crispy sound as if he had stuck his finger into a coil of cigar ash. He felt a trace of pleasure, which was lost in the gloominess he now felt. This liquor had made him despondent and the walk had intensified this; he felt no horror nor any fear at the bodies; his own terror of death had no relation to the smells and the cruel shapes into which physical death could force a body. He could not have said why he was gloomy, but he had to fasten it upon something. He resented the money he had spent for the whisky, and for the past half hour he had been trying to calculate how long it would take him to replace that money with his pay.

Red leaned against the half-track. He was feeling dizzy and he extended his arm over the metal tread guard. His hand closed on a piece of pulpy fruit and he dropped it hastily. The fruit was red and looked like a pear, but he had never seen anything like it before. "Where the hell this come from?" he asked thickly.

"That's Jap food," Wilson said.

"Where'd they get it?"

"Ah don' know," Wilson shrugged. He kicked it aside.

A touch of fear penetrated through Red's drunkenness. For an instant he thought of Hennessey. "Well, Wilson, where the fug is the souvenirs?" he asked bitterly.

"Men, you jus' got to follow me," Wilson said.

They wandered away from the vehicles and made a little exploration off the side of the road on the ridge where the Japanese had entrenched themselves. Once there had been foxholes and dugouts pocking the entire surface of this shallow hill, but the artillery had collapsed most of these. The dirt walls were half caved in like a sand hole on the beach after the children have deserted it and people tread over its edges. There were dead Japanese lying all about this ridge, perhaps twenty or thirty men scattered in groups of two and three and four. Littered among them were thousands of small pieces of rubble, and a strong intense smell close to that of burning garbage arose from the ridge. There were rations rotting and boxes of equipment half emptied, their contents spilling out. There were mangled packs and rusted rifles and shoes and canteens and bits of rotting flesh strewn everywhere over the blasted earth. On the ridge there was not an area of five square yards which did not have some refuse. The debris was scattered everywhere in thousands of chaotic items. The Japanese had been dead for a week, and they had swollen to the dimensions of very obese men with enormous legs and bellies, and buttocks which split their clothing. They had turned green and purple and the maggots festered in their wounds and covered their feet.

Each maggot was about a half inch long and it looked like a slug except that it was the color of a fish's belly. The maggots covered the

212

dead bodies the way bees cluster over the head of a beekeeper. It was impossible to see any longer where the wounds had been, for the maggots covered every bit of ruptured flesh and crawled sluggishly over all the minor sores on the corpse. Gallagher watched drunkenly while a train of maggots filed into the gaping mouth of the dead man. Somehow he expected the maggots to make some sound, and their rapt noiseless feeding angered him. The stench was acute and flies lusted over the corpses.

"Goddam flies," he muttered. He walked around a body and picked up a small paper carton which was lying on the ground. The cardboard was sodden and fell apart in his hands; he picked out a few tiny vials which contained a dark liquid, and looked morosely at them for a few seconds. "What are these?" he asked. No one answered, and after a moment he threw them to the ground again. "What I want to know is where the fug is the souvenirs?"

Wilson was trying to remove the bolt from a rusted rifle. "Ah'm gonna get me one of them sammerigh swords one of these days," he announced. He prodded a corpse with the butt of the Japanese rifle, and made a face. "Goddam carrion, that's all we are, men, goddam carrion." A few ribs were protruding from the cadaverous chest and in the late afternoon light they had a silver sheen. The exposed flesh had turned a sickly brown-green. "Look jus' like a shoulder o' lamb," Wilson stated. He sighed again, and began to wander off down the ridge. There were a few natural caves on the reverse slope, and in one of them were a half dozen dead men piled over many boxes and crates. "Hey, men," Wilson yelled, "Ah found ya somethin'." He was proud of himself. The drunken taunts of the others had hurt his feelings. "If ol' Wilson tell ya that he get somethin', then he do it."

A truck went rumbling down the road toward the forward bivouac areas. Wilson waved childishly, and then squatted on his haunches and peered into the cave. The others had come up beside him, and they all examined the cave. "They's a bunch of foot lockers down there, men."

"They're just crates," Red said.

"Tha's what Ah mean," Wilson told him. "We empty them, an' then we got foot-lockers to take back with us."

213

Red swore. "If you want a crate you can get it back at head-quarters company."

"Aw, no," Wilson told him, "those crates we got are jus' old shoddy. These yere are built way a box should be built."

Red looked again. "I'm fugged if I'm going to tote a box all the way back."

Martinez wandered off a few yards. He had noticed a corpse whose open mouth was filled with gold teeth, and fascinated he kept turning around to look at it. He stood over the body and looked down at the teeth. There were at least six or seven which seemed to be of solid gold, and Martinez darted a quick look back at the other men, who were going into the cave.

He was filled suddenly with a lust for the gold teeth. He could hear the men thrashing about in the cave, swearing thickly to one another, and despite himself he looked down again at the gaping mouth of the cadaver. No good to him, he told himself. Tensely he was trying to estimate how much the teeth were worth. Thirty dollar, maybe, he told himself.

He turned away, and then came back. The battlefield was very silent, and he could hear nothing for a moment but the intent buzzing silence of the flies on the ridge. Down below in the valley everything stank, and the wreckage of mutilated men and vehicles was scattered everywhere. It looked like a junk yard, rust-red and black with an oc-casional patch of green grass. Martinez shook his head, Everything stink. A discarded rifle was lying at his feet, and without thinking he picked it up, and smashed the butt of it against the cadaver's mouth. It made a sound like an ax thudding into a wet rotten log. He lifted the rifle and smashed it down again. The teeth spattered loose. Some landed on the ground and a few lay scattered over the crushed jaw of the corpse. Martinez picked up four or five gold ones in a frenzy and dropped them in his pocket. He was sweating terribly, and his anxiety seemed to course through his body with the pumping of his heart. He took a few deep breaths, and gradually it subsided. He was feeling a mixture of guilt and glee, and he thought of a time in his childhood when he had stolen a few pennies from his mother's purse. "God-dam," he said. He wondered idly when he could sell the teeth. The opened battered mouth of the corpse bothered him, and he turned the body over with his foot. A school of maggots was uncovered, and he shivered. For some reason, he was very frightened, and he turned and went back to the men in the cave.

The cave was small and the air in it was dank and oppressive. The men were sweating heavily, and yet the air seemed cold. The bodies were heaped over the boxes like bags of flour, and when they would try to move one the maggots would scatter like a school of minnows. Inside was a disordered rubble of fragments, black charred objects, rusted scraps of metal, shell fragments, a few broken boxes of mortar shells, a few mounds of gray ash like the kind found in trash barrels; there was even just a little bit of a dead body, a charred shinbone jutting from a mound of dirt and ash. The stench had the intensity and delirium of ether.

"We ain't gonna get a goddam box," Red said. He was feeling sick, and his back had begun to ache inordinately from the effort it took to shift the bodies with his fingertips.

"Let's quit this mess," Gallagher said. The sunlight at the mouth of the cave seemed astringent.

"Men, you ain't gonna quit now, are ya?" Wilson pleaded. He was determined to bring back a box.

The sweat ran into Martinez's eyes. He was irritable and impatient. "We go back now, huh?" he suggested.

Wilson threw a body aside, and then stepped back with an exclamation. He had uncovered a snake, which moved its head slowly from side to side over the top of one of the boxes. The men all drew away with a murmur of fear and flattened against the opposite wall of the cave. Red pressed the safety on his gun, and drew a bead slowly on the head of the snake. His hands were wavering, and he watched the flat eyes of the snake with absorption. "Don' miss," Wilson whispered.

The sound of the shot bounded from wall to wall with the overpouring clamor of an artillery piece. The snake's head disappeared into a mash of pulp, and its body quivered frenetically for many seconds. The men watched intently, awe-struck, their ears deafened by the noise of Red's gun. "Let's get out of here," Gallagher cried.

215

They stumbled over one another in their sudden frenzy to get out. All of them had an acute panic. Wilson mopped his face and breathed deeply of the air outside the hole. "Ah guess that's one box Ah'll never get," he said casually. Actually, he was feeling very tired, and his restlessness had spent itself temporarily. "Ah guess we might as well get on back," he said.

The men descended the ridge and struck out along the road leading back to the bivouac area. They passed a gutted tank which lay moldering off the road, its treads broken and rusted, looking like the skeleton of a lizard. "Goddam snake like that soon," Martinez said.

Red grunted. He was looking at a corpse which lay almost naked on its back. It was an eloquent corpse, for there were no wounds on its body, and its hands were clenching the earth as if to ask for a last time the always futile question. The naked shoulders were hunched together in anguish, and he could easily conceive the expression of pain that should have been on the corpse's mouth. But the corpse lay there without a head, and Red ached dully as he realized the impossibility of ever seeing that man's face. There was only a bloody fragment at the terminus of the neck. The body seemed to lie in a casing of silence.

Abruptly Red realized he was sober and very weary. The other men were already many yards ahead of him on the road, but he continued to look, drawn by some emotion he could not express. Very deep inside himself he was thinking that this was a man who had once wanted things, and the thought of his own death was always a little unbelievable to him. The man had had a childhood, a youth and a young manhood, and there had been dreams and memories. Red was realizing with surprise and shock, as if he were looking at a corpse for the first time, that a man was really a very fragile thing.

The stench of the cave was still in his nostrils, and the cadaver gave him the same kind of horror that he had felt once in stepping on a coil of human feces in the middle of a lawn. There had been a strange self-sufficiency about that as there was now in the torso and limbs of this body. He realized that in a little while the fetidness of this corpse would seep into the earth and be lost, but now it was horrible in its stench. It caused him a deep pang of fear. He could still

216

recall the odor of the cave, and it combined with this to terrify him —
he passed from the first warm smell of decay into the pungent quivering core of the stink, a clear nauseous odor that shocked him with cold
fingers. It was the smell he would have expected if he had lifted a
coffin lid, and it remained in him for a long bad moment in which he
looked at the body and didn't look, thought of nothing, and found his
mind churning with the physical knowledge of life and death and his
own vulnerability.

Then it was all over and he continued to walk, looking at the
tangle of war on the left and right of the road. The smell continued
to oppress him. The way a bunch of ants would kill each other, he
thought. He trotted after the other men, and walked moodily beside
them through the coconut grove and along the trail. The liquor was
wearing off for all of them, and they were silent. Red had a headache.
He stumbled over a root, and swore, and then without any relation to
what they had been talking about, he muttered, "There damn sure
ain't anything special about a man if he can smell as bad as he does
when he's dead."

Back at 2d Battalion, Wyman had just wounded an insect. It was
a long hairy caterpillar with black and gold coloring, and he had
jabbed a twig into its body. The caterpillar began to run about in
circles and then flopped over on its back. It was struggling desperately
to right itself until Wyman held his burning cigarette near the insect's
back. The insect writhed, and lay prostrate again, its back curled into
an L and its legs thrashing helplessly in the air. It looked as if it were
trying desperately to breathe.

Ridges had watched this with displeasure, his long dumpy face
wrinkled in a scowl. "That ain't the right way to treat a bug," he said.

Wyman was absorbed in the convulsions of the insect, and the
interruption irritated him. He felt a trace of shame. "What do you
mean, Ridges? What the hell's so important about a bug?"

"Shoot," Ridges sighed, " ' tain't doin' you no harm. Jus' mindin'
its own business."

Wyman turned to Goldstein. "The preacher's gettin' all excited over a bug." He laughed sarcastically, and then said, "Killin' one of Gawd's creatures, huh?"

Goldstein shrugged. "Every man has his own viewpoint," he said gently.

Ridges lowered his head stubbornly. "Not sayin' 'tain't hard to make fun of a man if he believes in the written Word."

"You eat meat, don't ya?" Wyman demanded. He was pleased to have the better arguments, for usually he felt inferior to most of the men in the squad. "Where the hell's it say you can eat meat but you can't kill a bug?"

"Meat ain't the same. Y' don' eat a bug."

Wyman poured a little dirt over the caterpillar and watched it struggle to free itself. "I don't see you caring if you kill a Jap or two," he said.

"They're *heathen*," Ridges said.

"Excuse me," Goldstein said, "but I don't think you're quite right. I was reading an article a few months ago which said there were over a hundred thousand Christians in Japan."

Ridges shook his head. "Well, Ah wouldn' want to be killing one of them," he said.

"But you'll have to," Wyman said. "Whyn't you admit you're wrong?"

"The Lord'll keep me from shooting a Christian," Ridges said stubbornly.

"Aaaaah."

"That's what Ah believe," Ridges said. Actually, he was quite upset. The writhing of the insect had recalled to him the way the bodies of the Japanese had looked the morning after they had tried to cross the river. They had seemed the same as the animals who had died on his father's farm. He had told himself that it was because they were heathen, but now after Goldstein's statement he was confused. One hundred thousand was a vast number to him; he assumed that was at least half the people in Japan, and now he was thinking that some of the dead men he had seen in the river must have been Christians. He brooded over it for a moment or two, and then understood. It was very simple to him.

218

"You believe man got a soul?" he asked Wyman.

"I don't know. What the hell is a soul?"

Ridges chuckled. "Shoot, you ain't so smart as you think y'are. The soul's what leaves a man after he dies — that's what goes up t' heaven. That's why he looks so bad when you see him jus' lyin' in the river, it's because he ain't what he was before. That somethin' that's important, his soul, that's gone from him."

"Who the hell knows," Wyman said. He felt philosophical.

The insect was dying under the last handful of earth he had poured over it.

Wilson finished the last canteen of whisky by himself while he was on guard that night. It made him a little drunk again, and it revived his restlessness. He sat on the edge of his foxhole, and peered irritably through the barbed wire, shifting his position every few minutes. His head was lolling from side to side, and he found it difficult to keep his eyes open. There was a bush about fifteen yards beyond the barbed wire and it bothered him. It threw a shadow which extended into the jungle and made it impossible for him to see a certain section of the perimeter. The more he gazed at it, the more irritable he became. Goddam bush, he told himself, think you're gonna hide a Jap, don't ya? He shook his head. No goddam Jap's gonna sneak up on me.

He got out of the hole and walked a few steps away. His legs were unsteady, which annoyed him. He sat down in the hole again, and peered at the bush. "Whoinhell tol' ya to grow there?" he asked. When he closed his eyes he was very dizzy and his jaws felt as though they were chewing a piece of sponge. Man cain't even sleep on guard with the goddam bush, he told himself. He sighed, and then pulled the bolt of the machine gun back and forth. He sighted along the barrel and aimed it at the base of the bush. "Ah coulda tole ya not to grow there," he muttered and then pulled the trigger. The handle of the gun bucked viciously as he fired a long burst. When he had finished the bush was still standing, and in anger he fired the machine gun again.

To the men in recon, who were sleeping about ten yards back of him, the sound of the machine gun was terrifying. It tore them violently out of their sleep as if an electric charge had bored through them, ground their heads into the dirt, and then pulled them to their knees. They did not know that Wilson was firing; they thought it was a Japanese attack again, and they staggered through several terrible seconds between sleep and wakefulness while all kinds of thoughts and fears went through their heads.

Goldstein thought he was on guard and had fallen asleep. He whispered desperately several times, "I wasn't sleeping, I was only closing my eyes to fool the Japs, I was ready, I swear I was ready."

Martinez whimpered, "I give back the teeth, I promise I give back the teeth."

Wyman dreamed he was letting go of the antitank gun, and said, "It really wasn't my fault. Goldstein let it go." He felt guilt, and then was awake in the next instant, and had forgotten everything.

Red lay on his stomach, and thought it was the soldier with the bayonet who was shooting at him. "Come on, you sonofabitch, you sonofabitch," he kept muttering.

Gallager thought, They're out to get ME.

And Croft felt a paralyzing instant of fear while the Japanese charged across the river and he sat tied hand and foot by his machine gun. The second burst of fire loosed his bonds, and he roared, "COME AND GET ME!" The sweat formed on his face, and then he was crawling along the ground toward Wilson's gun. "RECON, UP, UP ON THE LINE!" he bellowed. He was still uncertain whether they were on the river or not.

Wilson fired again, and Croft realized that he was shooting and not the Japanese. In the next instant he understood that they were far from the river, and this was the 2nd Battalion bivouac. He dropped into the hole beside Wilson and jerked his arm. "What're you firing at?" It had taken until now for Croft to awaken completely.

"Ah got it," Wilson said. "Ah knocked down the sonofabitch."

"What?" Croft whispered.

"The bush." He pointed. "Yonder. Ah couldn' see through it. Was gettin' me all in a lather."

The other men in recon were crawling cautiously toward them. "You didn't hear any Japs?" Croft said.

"Hell, no," Wilson said. "Ah wouldn' use a machine gun if Ah saw a Jap, Ah'd use a rifle. Don' want me to spot the position for one lousy Jap, do ya?"

Croft was repressing a violent rage. He grasped Wilson by the shoulders and shook him although Wilson was much larger than he. "I swear, I swear," he said thickly, "you ever pull a trick like that again, Wilson, and I'll shoot you myself. I'll . . ." He broke off, shaking from his violence. "Go on back," he called to the men who were crawling up. "It was a goddam false alarm."

"Who fired?" someone whispered.

"Go on back!" Croft commanded.

He turned to Wilson again. "Of all the tricks you've ever pulled. Man, you're on my shit-list from now on." He stepped out of the hole, and walked back to his blankets. He could feel his hands still trembling.

Wilson was bewildered. He kept thinking of how merry Croft had been that afternoon, and he couldn't understand his sudden rage. What's there to get a man so fussed about? he wondered. He chuckled to himself, and then remembered how Croft had shaken him. This made him angry. Ah don' care how long Ah know him, Wilson told himself, they ain't no call for him to handle me any ol' way. Next time he do somethin' like that, Ah'll give him a belt or two. He broke off moodily, and looked out across the barbed wire. The bush had been sheared away at its roots, and he had a fine field of view. Shoulda done that long ago, he told himself. He was feeling very hurt by Croft's anger. Jus' a little ol' burst o' machine-gun fire. Abruptly, he realized that the entire bivouac probably was awake now, and men everywhere were listening tensely. Goddam, Wilson sighed, Ah get in *more* trouble when Ah get drunk . . . He began to giggle to himself.

Next morning the squad returned to the bivouac of headquarters and headquarters company. They had been away for seven days and eight nights.

The Time Machine:

RED VALSEN

THE WANDERING MINSTREL

Everything about him was bony and knobbed. He was over six feet tall without weighing one hundred and fifty pounds. In silhouette his profile consisted almost entirely of a large blob of a nose and a long low-slung jaw, a combination which made his face seem boiled and angry. He had an expression of concentrated contempt but behind it his tired eyes, a rather painful blue, were quiet, marooned by themselves in a web of wrinkles and freckles.

The horizon is always close. It never lifts beyond the hills that surround the town, never goes past the warped old wood of the miners' houses or rises above the top of the mine shafts. The pale-brown earth of the Montana hills has settled over the valley. You must understand that The Company owns everything. A long time ago they laid the track into the valley, bored the mine shafts, built the miners' frame houses, threw up the company store, and even gave them a church. Since then, the town is a trough. The wages skid out of the shafts and end up in a company hopper; what with drinking in the company saloon, buying food and clothing, and paying the rent, there is nothing left over. All the horizons end at the mine elevator.

And Red learns that early. What else is there to learn once his father is killed in a mine-shaft explosion? Some things are inflexible and one of them is that in The Company's town, the oldest single son supports the family if the father is killed. In 1925, when Red is thirteen, there are other miners' sons who are younger than him also working in the shafts. The miners shrug. He is the oldest man left in the family and that suffices.

By the time he is fourteen he is able to use a drill. Good money

222

for a kid, but down in the shafts, at the extreme end of the tunnel there isn't room to stand. Even a kid works in a crouch, his feet stumbling in the refuse of the ore that has been left from filling the last cart. It's hot, of course, and damp, and the lights from their helmets are lost quickly in the black corridors. The drill is extremely heavy and a boy has to hold the butt against his chest and clutch the handles with all his strength as the bit vibrates into the rock.

When the hole is drilled, the charge is set up, and the miners retreat around a bend in the tunnel, and explode the dynamite. The loosened ore is shoveled onto a tiny flatcar, and when it is filled they roll it away, stopping to clear the tracks of the earth that has scattered over it. Then they come back with another cart and continue to shovel. Red has ten hours a day, six days a week. In the wintertime he can see the sky on Sundays.

Puberty in the coal dust.

In the late spring evenings he sits with his girl in a little park at the end of the company street. Behind them the town ends, and the brown bare hills, deepening in the twilight, roll away into the west. Long after it is dark in the valley, they can still see the last striations of the sunset beyond the western peaks.

Beautiful scenery, the girl murmurs.

To hell with that, I'm getting out of here. Red at eighteen.

I always wonder what's on the other side of the hills, the girl says quietly.

He grinds his shoes in the grudged sparse grass of the park. I got restless feet, I'm like my old man was, he used to be full of ideas, had a bunch of books, but my mother went and sold them. That's a woman for you.

How can you go, Red? She'll be needing the money you make.

Listen, when the time comes, I'm just gonna pick up and go. A man's gotta get out where he don't owe nobody nothing. (Staring into the darkness. Already there's the deep impatience, the anger, and the other thing, the distillate of the sunset beyond the encircling hills.) You're a good kid, Agnes. (The sense of minor loss and pleasurable self-pity as he thinks of leaving her.) But I tell ya I ain't gonna end

223

up living the kind of life my old man did. I ain't gonna sweat out my guts in the mine.

You're going to do a lot of things, Red.

Sure. (He breathes the sweet-laden night air and smells the earth. The knowledge of strength, the taunt at the surrounding hills.) You know, I'll tell ya something, I don't believe in God.

You don't mean that, Red!

(Underneath the blanket his father's body had been crushed almost flat.) Yeah, that's right, I just don't believe in God.

Sometimes I don't either, Agnes says.

Yeah, I can talk to you, *you* understand.

Only you want to go away.

Well. (There is the other knowledge. Her body is young and strong and he knows the smell of her breasts, which are like powdered infant-flesh, but all the women turn to cordwood in the town.) You take that guy Joe Mackey who got Alice with a kid and left her, my own sister, but I tell ya I don't blame him. You got to see that, Agnes.

You're cruel.

Yeah, that's right. It's praise to the eighteen-year-old.

Of course you can always depend on the mines to shut down.

It's good for a week; there's hunting for jack rabbit and a ball game or two, but it loses its edge. There's more time to be in the house, and it's all bedrooms except for the kitchen. His kid brothers are always making noises, and Alice is sullen as she nurses her bastard. When he was working it was easier, but now he's with them all the time.

I'm getting out of this town, he says at last.

What? No, by God, no, his mother says. Just like his father. (A short squat woman who has never lost her Swedish accent.)

I can't take it any more, I'm gonna rot my life away, Eric's old enough to work in the mines if they ever open.

You don't go.

You're not going to tell me! he shouts. What the hell does a man get out of it, some food for his belly?

Soon Eric works in the mines. You get married. A nice Swenska.

He slaps his cup against the saucer. To hell with that, get tied down with a marriage. (Agnes. The idea is not wholly unpleasant, and he rejects it furiously.) I'm getting out of here, I ain't gonna waste my life in back of a drill, waiting for a goddam tunnel to collapse on me.

His sister comes into the kitchen. You lousy kid, you're only eighteen, where do you talk of getting away?

Stay out of this, he shouts.

I'm not going to stay out, it's my business more than ma's. That's all you men are good for, you get us in trouble and then you skip out. Well, you can't do it! she screams.

What's the matter? There'll always be some grub for ya.

Maybe I want to get out, maybe I'm sick to death of hanging around here without a man who'll marry me.

That was your lookout. You're not going to stop me, goddammit.

You're just like that louse that skipped out on me, if there's anything that's worthless it's a man who won't stick around to face the music.

(Trembling) And if I'd been Joe Mackey I'da skipped out on ya too. That was the smartest thing he ever did.

Take sides against your sister.

What the hell was in it for him, he had all the good out of you. (She slaps him. Tears of anger and guilt form in his eyes. He blinks them back, and glares at her.)

His mother sighs. You go then. It's bad thing when family fights like animals. Go.

What about the mines? (He feels himself weakening.)

Eric. She sighs again. Someday you know just how bad you be tonight, by God.

A man's got to get out. He's trapped in a hole here. (This once, it gives him no relief.)

In 1931 all the long voyages end in a hobo jungle.

But the itinerary is various:

Freight trains out of Montana through Nebraska into Iowa.

Handouts at farmhouses for a day's work.

The harvest and working in a granary.

225

Manure piles.

Sleeping in parks, being picked up for vagrancy.

When they let him out of the county workhouse he walks back to town, spends the dollar he has made for a good meal and a package of cigarettes, and catches a freight out of town that night. The moon gives a silver wash to the cornfields, and he curls up in a flatcar and watches the sky. An hour later another hobo drops into his car. He has a flask of whisky and they drink it up and finish Red's cigarettes. In the flatcar lying on his back the sky quivers in time to the clacking and jolting of the train. It's not too bad.

Jesus, tonight's Saturday night, the other bum says.

Yeah.

On Saturday night in his mining town there is always a dance in the basement of the church. The round tables have checked cloths on them, and each family sits around one table, the miners and their grown sons, the wives and daughters and grandparents, the younger kids. There are even infants slobbering drowsily at their mothers' teats.

Provincial.

Only it stinks. The miners bring a bottle with them, and fall into sullen drunks, tired men at the end of a week. By midnight they're quarreling with their wives. All through his childhood his father would be cursing at his mother while the company band — violin, guitar and piano — would be whining out a square dance or polka.

To a kid from a mining town, getting drunk in a flatcar on Saturday night is still fun. The horizon extends for a million miles over the silver cornfields.

In the hobo jungle, in the marshes outside town near the railroad tracks, a few shanties sprawl in the weeds. The roofs are made of rusted sheets of corrugated iron, and the grass inside grows through the planking. Most of the men sleep on the ground outside, and wash in the brown sluggish river that sloughs through the flat railroad bogs. Time lolls away in the sun; the flies are golden-green against the gray and orange litter of the garbage dump. There are a few women in the camp, and at night Red and a few of the other men stay with them. In the daytime, it's wandering through town, sifting the garbage cans, and trying for handouts. But most of all it's sitting in the shade watching the trains labor past, just talking.

I got it from Joe they're gonna be kicking us outa here soon. Sonsofbitches.

They's gonna be a revolution, men, I tell ya what we got to do is make a march on Washington.

Hoover'll run ya out. What are ya doin', kidding yourself, Mac?

I can see us marchin'. 'I Love a Parade, the Beat of a Drum.'

Listen, boys, I watched it myself right from the beginning, it's the fuggin Jews, it's the fuggin International Jews.

Mac, ya don't know what you're talkin' about, what we want is revolutionary action, we're being exploited. You got to wait for the dictatorship of the proletariat.

What are you, a Communist? Listen, I owned my own business, I was a big man in my town, I had money in the bank, I was all set to go but there was a conspiracy.

It's the big boys, they're scared of us, 'I'll Be Glad When You're Dead, You Rascal, You,' what do ya think those songs don' mean anything? That's the only line anybody remembers.

Red sits there drowsing. (They're full of crap. Talk is pretty cheap. The thing to do is to keep moving, and keep your mouth shut.)

You think I'm a Communist; listen, I'm a student of human nature, I'm self-educated. American aspirations, that's what those songs are, opium for the masses, catch phrases to fool a man. Listen . . . it's a passion for movement, it's to trick us into staying at home and being exploited.

Aaaah.

They're gonna move us out, men.

I'm movin' anyway, Red says. Itchy feet.

Somehow it seems as if you never do go under, there is always the providential handout, or the pair of shoes you can buy after the ones you own flap in the wind. Somehow, there is always a little job, or some meal to keep you going, or there's a new town to go to, there is even the good feeling once every month or two when you catch a

227

freight at dawn, and the land rises out of the night and you're not too hungry.

If you throw a handful of straw into a river, some of it stays afloat even in a rapids, there is always something to give you a boost. You keep going and the summer ends, the nights get chill (half a buck in your pocket and winter acoming) but there's always a railroad track heading south, there is usually a jail where they'll let you sleep the night.

And if you get through it there's Relief after a while, and even a couple of jobs. Dishwasher, short-order cook, a shingler, a farm hand, a house painter, a plumber, even a gasoline pump.

In 'thirty-five he works in a restaurant for almost a year, the best dishwasher they ever had. (The rush hour lasts from twelve to three at that end of the kitchen. The dishes come clanking down the dumbwaiter, and the tray man mops the food and grease with his hand, fingers the lipstick on the glasses to loosen it, and drops them in a rack. In the machine, the steam vibrates and sings, whips out at the other end, where the finish man pulls out the tray with tongs, and wiggles the plates with his fingertips as he flips them on a pile. You don't grab it with your bare hand, Jack.)

After work Red goes back to his furnished room (two-fifty a week, the carpeting on the stairs has thickened with age and springs underfoot like soft dusty turf) and lies down on his bed. If he's not too pooped, he gets up after a while, and drifts down to the bar around the corner. (The gray cracked asphalt, the garbage cans spilling over in the areaways, the stippled light of the neon sign, two letters are missing.)

A man always has philosophy. I'll tell ya, Red, I used to think for a time I made a mistake gettin' married. I used to get mad, you know, I'd start wondering what am I workin' for, but, aah, you get over it. You take those two kids over there feeling each other in that booth. Right now one of them can't even breathe without the other — my old lady used to be like that with me. I don't get mad, I know what the score is, those kids are gonna end up like you, like me, like everybody.

(The beer is flat and tastes like pennies.) Me, Red says, I never

228

horse around much with the women. They just want to trap ya, I seen enough of it.

Aw, it ain't that bad, there's good things about marriage and women, but it ain't what you think you're gonna get when you start off. You know a married man has worries, I'll tell ya, Red, sometimes I wish I been the places you have.

Yeah, I'll take Two-bit Annie.

In the brothel the girls wear halters and trim panties with a tropical print, an actress has made the style famous this year. They gather like burlesque queens in the living room with the ashtrays and the chipped modernistic furniture.

Okay, Pearl, let's go.

He follows her up the gray spongy carpeting of the stairs, watching the automatic waggle of her hips.

Haven't seen ya in a long time, Red.

Just two weeks.

Yeah, ya went to Roberta last time. She reproves him, Dearie.

In the cubicle, the blanket is folded at the foot of the bed, smudged with the shoes of other men. Pearl is humming. (BETTY COED HAS LIPS OF RED FOR HARVARD.) She slips his dollar under the pillow. Easy, Red, momma's had a long hard day.

The throe quivers along his back, leaves his loins charged and sickly.

How about one on the house?

Aw, now, honey, you know what Eddie would do if he found us girls givin' it away.

He dresses quickly, feeling her arm on his shoulder. I'm sorry, Red, listen, you come up next time, and I'll talk a little French to you, just between you and me, okay?

At this moment her mouth is soft, and her breasts seem swollen. He touches her nipple for a moment; counterfeit of passion, it strains against his finger. You're a good kid, Pearl.

One of the best.

The light bulb is naked, and it flares in his eyes cruelly. He inhales her powder, the sweet sweat of her armpits .

How'd you get started, Pearl?

I'll tell ya over a glass of beer someday.

Outside, the air is cold like a tart and icy apple. He feels a deep melancholy, pleasurable and extensive, but when he is in his room he cannot sleep.

I been in this town too long. (The brown bare hills deepening in the twilight. The night rolls away into the west.) WHERE IS THE BEAUTY WE LOST IN OUR YOUTH?

He gets up and looks out the window. Jesus, I feel old, twenty-three and I'm an old man. After a time he falls asleep.

In the morning the sweat eddies corrosively in his eyes, and the steam erupts from the dish racks. Rub the lipstick loose before the glasses go in.

I guess I'll be moving again. It's no good having it steady pay. But this time there is less hope in it.

A park bench is really too small for a man to sleep comfortably. If his feet dangle over the edge, the slats cut into the back of his knees, and if he draws them up, he awakens with a cramp in his thigh. For a skinny man, it's impossible to sleep on his side. The boards grate against his hipbones, and his shoulder becomes stiff. He has to lie on his back with his knees propped toward the sky, and his hands under his head; when he gets up his fingers are numb for many minutes.

Red is awakened by a jarring shock in his skull. He springs up, sees the policeman raising his nightstick to strike the soles of his shoes again.

Okay, I'm movin', take it easy.

You ought to know better than to stay here, Mac.

In the false dawn of four A.M. the milk trucks are advancing slowly down the silent streets. Red watches the horse chomp at his feed bag, and walks down toward the railroad. At an all-night hash house, across from the black iron mangle of the railroad yards, he nurses a cup of coffee and a doughnut until it is morning. For a long time he stares at the dirty floor and the white marble counter with its coffee rings, the round celluloid cake covers. Once he falls asleep with his head on the counter.

Aaah, I been doing this too long. It's no good steady, and it's no good bumming. Ya lose whatever you want when you start goin' for it.

At first it looks like his period of relative prosperity and then like the tail of the comet, but it turns out to be neither. He catches a job as a truck driver on an overnight freight route from Boston to New York, and holds it for two years. Route 1 wears a furrow in his mind. Boston to Providence to Groton to New London to New Haven to Stamford to the Bronx to the markets, and back the next night. He has a room on West 48th, near Tenth Avenue, and he can save money if he tries.

But he hates the truck. It's the coal mines in open air, it jars at his back and in a thousand, a million tiny jounces, his kidneys begin to go and his stomach is too tricky in the morning to chance breakfast. Maybe there has been one park bench too many, maybe there was too much rain in too many open places, but the truck route is no good. The last hundred miles he always drives with his teeth clenched. He drinks a lot, drifting along the bars on Ninth and Tenth Avenues, and sometimes he spends his free time in one movie house after another, the tawdry second-runs on 42nd Street.

One night in a bar he buys an ordinary seaman's card for ten bucks from a drunk who is about to go under, and he quits his job. But after a week of hanging around South Street, he gets tired of it and goes on a long drunk. After a week, when his money is gone, he sells the seaman's card for five bucks and keeps going for an afternoon on the whisky it buys.

He wakes up that night in an alley with a blood crust on his cheek. When he grimaces he can feel the crust shredding into cracks. A cop picks him up and sends him to Bellevue, where he is kept for two days, and when he gets out he panhandles for a couple of weeks.

But there is the happy ending. He catches a job finally as a dishwasher in a fancy restaurant in the East Sixties, and he gets friendly with a waitress there, ends up by living with her in a couple of furnished rooms on West 27th Street. She has an eight-year-old kid who likes Red, and they get along well for a couple of years.

Red switches to a job as night clerk in one of the flophouses on the Bowery. It's easier than dishwashing, and pays him five bucks

231

more, twenty-three a week. He holds on to it for the last two years before the war, drifting along through the liquid fetid heat of summer in the Bowery and the chill damp winters when the walls leak and the brown plaster becomes stained with gray. Long nights pass in which he thinks of nothing, listening dully to the periodic wrangling passage of the trains on the Third Avenue el, waiting for the morning so he can go home to Lois.

Several times a night he passes through the main room where forty or fifty men are sleeping uneasily on their iron cots, and he listens to the constant soft coughing and smells the harsh styptic formalin and the bodies of the old drunks, a crabbed smell, glum and soured. The hallways and the bathroom stink of disinfectant, and over the urinals there is almost always a drunk retching his liquor, holding dreamily to the porcelain near the flush lever. He closes the door and goes into the card room, where a few old men are playing pinochle around an old round table, the floor under them black with grease and cigarette ends. Red listens to their talk, mumbled and unfinished.

Maggie Kennedy was a fine figure of a woman, she said to me, now, what was it she said?

I told Tommy Muldoon he had no call to be running me in, and when I got done, he let me go I'll tell you that. They're afraid of me ever since I broke Ricchio's jaw, you know he was the precinct sergeant, back in, well, now wait a minute and I'll tell you the date, I broke his jaw with one punch back in a New Year's night eight year ago, 1924 it was, no, wait a moment back in 1933 that's closer to it.

The standing gag. Hey, you rummies, pipe down goddammit we got some paying guests in the next room. I'll run you out.

They're silent for a moment and then one of them says in his low mumbling voice, You ain't so smart, young feller, and ifen you don't shut your mouth I'll be obliged to whop you.

Come on down in the street, and I'll take you on.

Then one of them comes up to Red, and whispers to him, You better leave him alone 'cause he'll throw you down the stairs, the last night man he broke his neck.

Yeah. Red grins. I'm sorry I disturbed ya, pop, I'll be minding my manners.

232

You do that, son, and you and me won't have no trouble.

Across the street, they can hear a jukebox grinding in a barroom.

Back behind the night desk, Red turns on his radio and plays it softly. (THE LEAVES OF BROWN CAME TUMBLING DOWN.) One of the men awakens screaming. Red goes into the hall and quiets him, patting him on the shoulder and leading him back to his cot.

In the morning the bums dress hurriedly, and the big room is empty by seven. They hustle along the chill streets in the dawn, their caps pulled down to their eyes, and their old jacket collars scrounged around their necks. As if they were ashamed, they won't look at one another, and like automatons most of them line up in the alleys off Canal Street for the coffee they receive from soup kitchens. Red walks through the streets for a while before he catches the bus up to West 27th. The long night is always depressing.

He looks at his feet striding along. Nothing's worth a good goddam.

But back in their furnished room, Lois is cooking his breakfast on a hotplate, and the kid, Jackie, comes running up to him, shows him a new schoolbook. Red feels tired and happy.

Yeah, that's nice, kid, he says, patting him on the shoulder.

When Jackie has left for school, Lois sits down to eat breakfast with him. Since he has been working in the flophouse they have only their mornings together. At eleven she leaves for the restaurant.

The eggs dry enough for you, honey? she asks.

Yeah, swell.

Outside, in the new morning, some trucks are grinding by on Tenth Avenue. The traffic has an early-morning sound. Jesus, this is okay, he says aloud.

You like it, huh, Red.

Yeah.

She fingers her glass. Listen, Red, I went to see a lawyer yesterday about gettin' a divorce from Mike.

Yeah?

I can do it for a hundred dollars, a little more maybe, but should I, I mean whatthehell if nothing should come of it, maybe it'd be better not to.

233

I dunno, kid, he says to her.

Red, I ain't askin' you to get married, you know I ain't nagged you, but I gotta look ahead.

It's all there before him. The choice again, but it means admitting he's through. I dunno, Lois, that's the goddam truth. I like ya a lot and you're a good kid, there's no gettin' away from that, an' it's only fair to ya, but I gotta think about it. I ain't made for stayin' in one place, I dunno there's just somethin', it's kind've a big country.

Just be fair, Red. Ya gotta let me know one way or the other.

Only the war starts before he has made up his mind. That night all the drunks in the flophouse are excited.

I was a sergeant in the last one, I'm going to go up there and ask them to take me back.

Yeah, they'll make ya a major.

I'm going to tell you, Red, that they need me. They're gonna need every one of us.

Someone is passing around a bottle, and on an impulse Red sends one of the men down with a ten-dollar bill to buy some whisky.

Lois could use the ten, and he knows the answer then. He can marry her and stay out of the war, but he's not old yet, he's not that tired. In the war you keep on moving.

THERE'S A LONG LONG TRAIL AWINDING, one of the bums sings.

We're gonna do a lot of cleaning up, I hear they got some niggers down in Washington that's a fact, I was readin' it in the newspapers they got a nigger down there tellin' white men what to do.

War's gonna fix all that.

Aaah, balls, Red butts in, the big boys are just gonna get a little more. But he is excited. So long, Lois, no entangling alliances.

And Jackie too. A little pit of misery. But if you stop and quit moving you die.

Have a drink.

It's my liquor, Red bellows, what do ya mean, have a drink! (Laughter.)

On his last pass before he went overseas, Red wandered around San Francisco. He climbed up to the top of Telegraph Hill, and shivered in the fall winds sweeping across the summit. A tanker was heading for the Golden Gate, and he watched it, and then stared across Oakland as far as he could see into the east. (After Chicago the land was flat for a thousand miles, across Illinois and Iowa and halfway into Nebraska. On a train you could read a magazine for an afternoon, then look out the window, and the country would seem exactly the same as when you had stared out before. The foothills began as gentle rolls in the plain and after a hundred miles became isolated as hills, took almost a thousand miles to become mountains. And on the way were the steep brown hills that massed into Montana.) Maybe I should write them a letter. Or Lois.

Aaah, you don't look back.

Two ensigns with young girls in fur coats were laughing and hugging at the other end of the paved summit of Telegraph Hill. I might as well go down.

He walked through Chinatown, ended up in a burlesque house. It was a Tuesday afternoon, and the place was almost empty. The girls dragged languidly through their dances, the comedians fumbled through the skits. After the last strip and the ensemble the lights went on, and the hawkers began to sell Nestlé bars and picture books. Red sat in his seat and dozed a little. What a lousy joint.

There seemed nothing to do, and all through the movie he thought of the boat he would be traveling on soon. You keep rolling along and you never know what the hell the score is. When you're a kid they can't tell you a damn thing, and when you ain't a kid no more there's nothing new for you. You just got to keep pushing it, you don't look back.

When the picture ended and the show began again, he listened to the music for a moment and then went out. In the painful sun of late afternoon he could hear the band still playing.

WE'RE GONNA SLAP THE DIRTY LITTLE JAP.

Fug it.

8

Lieutenant (SG) Dove finished covering his bare legs with sand and groaned. "Oh, God, it's brutal," he exclaimed.

"What's brutal?" Hearn asked.

Dove wiggled his toes through the sand. "Just being out here. My God, a hot day like this. A year ago I was in Washington, and if you think there weren't some parties there. Oh, this goddam climate."

"I was in Washington about a year and a half ago," Conn said in his whisky voice.

They were off. Hearn sighed to himself, and eased himself slowly down on the sand, letting his head touch the ground, exposing his chest to the sun. Its heat was palpable, and he could feel the sun boring through his eyelids, exciting his retina into blind and angry circles of red. From the jungle a dank sulphurous breeze was exuded from time to time like the draft from an oven when the door is opened.

Hearn sat up again, folded his forearms over his hairy knees, and stared about the beach. Some of the officers who had come down with them were swimming now, and a few others were playing bridge on a blanket inside the shade of a peripheral coconut tree which leaned over the beach. About a hundred yards away on a small sand spit there was the occasional sharp ineffectual pop of a carbine as Major Dalleson threw a pebble into the air and fired at it. The water had deepened in color from its almost transparent early-morning blue to a deep violet, and the sun glittered over it like the reflections from a rainy pavement at night. About a mile to the right a lone landing craft was chugging leisurely in toward shore after having transferred a load of supplies from one of the freighters anchored out in the water.

Sunday at the beach. It was a little incredible. If you added a few striped beach umbrellas, the average quota of women and children, this would be indistinguishable from any of the more exclusive beaches at which his family had bathed one summer or another. Perhaps a sailboat should be substituted for the landing craft, and Dalleson could be fishing instead of shooting pebbles, but it was really close enough.

Completely incredible. Out of decency, perhaps, they had retreated for this beach party to the extreme tip of the peninsula, twenty-five miles from the base where the front-line troops were patrolling this Sunday morning against the Toyaku Line. Go, my children, and God bless you, the General had said in effect. And of course the guards along the road, and the detail of quartermaster troops who were bivouacked on the beach and were responsible this morning for patrolling the fringes of the jungle near where they were bathing would hate them for it, and as Cummings had said, would fear them even more.

He shouldn't have come along, Hearn decided. Yet the headquarters bivouac would have been deadly this morning with most of the officers gone. The General would want to talk to him, and it was important to stay away from the General now. Besides, he had to admit it was pleasant here. It had been a long time since he had felt the sun's heat relaxing his body, absorbing and melting his tensions.

"The natural role of twentieth-century man is anxiety," the General had said.

Then twentieth-century man was also a sunbather. Very neat. Hearn kneaded a stiffened cake of sand into powder between his fingers.

"Oh, I have to tell you this," Dove was saying now. "We had a party once at Fischler's place in the Wardman Park Hotel, Lieutenant Commander Fischler, an old sidekick of my brother's at Cornell, hell of a swell fellow and knew a lot of VIPs, that's how he got the room in the Wardman Park, but he gave this party, and in the middle of it he started wandering around pouring a couple of drops of liquor in everybody's hair. Good for dandruff, he kept saying. Oh, it was wonderful." Dove giggled remembering it.

"Yeah?" Conn said. "Yeah?"

Hearn stared at Dove. Lieutenant (sg) Dove, USNR. A Cornell man, a Deke, a perfect ass-hole. He was six feet two and weighed about a hundred and sixty pounds, with straight ash-blond hair cut close, and a clean pleasant vacuous face. He looked more like a Harvard clubman, varsity crew.

Conn fingered the red bulb of his nose, and said in his husky assured voice, "That's right, many's the good time I've had in Washington. Brigadier General Caldwell and Major General Simmons — do you know them? — old friends of mine. And there was that Navy feller, Rear Admiral Tannache, got to be good friends with him too. Damn fine man, he was a good officer." Conn surveyed his paunch, which projected in sharp curved lines just beneath his shorts, like a football inflated inside him. "We've had some wild times between us. That Caldwell is hell on wheels when it comes to women. We've had some times between us would singe your back hair."

"Oh, we had lots of that too," Dove inserted eagerly. "I couldn't go back to Washington with Jane, because there're so many girls there, if I should meet one of them with her, well, it wouldn't be so good. Jane's a hell of a swell kid, wonderful wife, but you know she takes her church seriously, and she'd be awfully upset."

Lieutenant (sg) Dove. He had been assigned to the division as an interpreter at almost the same time Hearn had come in, and with amazing, with startling naïveté he had announced very carefully to everyone that his rank was equivalent to captain in the Army, and that the responsibilities of a lieutenant sg were greater than those of a major or a lieutenant colonel in the Army. He had told the officers this in officers' mess on Motome and had been loved accordingly. Conn had not spoken to him for a week. But to the impedimenta that kept true love apart, or the poem went something like that. In any case, they were delighted with each other now. Hearn remembered Dove's saying to him once when he first came to the division, "You know, really, Hearn, you can appreciate this because you're an educated man like me, but do you know there's sort of a coarser element in the officers in the Army. The Navy's more careful." Apparently, Dove had made the sublime effort; he accepted Conn now.

They all accepted one another in time, with of course all the gossip requisite to acceptance. Dekes under the skin. Even Conn and he had made up. They hated each other, of course, but that was conveniently forgotten. A week after their quarrel he had passed Conn in the G-2 tent, and Conn had cleared his throat forcibly and said, "Looks like it's gonna be cooler today."

"Yes," Hearn had said.

"I got a lot of work today, I appreciate it cooler," Conn had added, and after that they made a point of nodding to each other. To-day on the beach he had been talking to Dove, and Conn had come over.

"Yes, sir," Conn repeated, "many's the party we've had. You talk about that whisky and dandruff gag, what was his name, Fischler, any relation to Commodore Fischler?"

"I don't think so."

"The Commodore's a good friend of mine. Anyway I remember one time when Caldwell got a woman over and by God if she didn't drink her liquor at both hatches."

"Lord, you'd think she'd burn herself to death," Dove exclaimed.

"Not her. That was her specialty. Caldwell almost bust a gut laughing. He liked his good time, Caldwell."

Dove was visibly shocked. "I can't say I've ever seen anything like that. God, isn't it disgusting, you're out in the open air like this, and the chaplain's probably giving his services now."

"Well, we really shouldn't be talking like this on Sunday," Conn agreed, "but what the hell, we're all men." He lit a cigarette, and speared the match in the sand. The crack of Dalleson's carbine sounded again, and a few shouts came from the water where some officers were having a water fight in the shallow surf. "I've made a study of parties," Conn said, "and there's just two ingredients to have a good one, enough to drink and some willing slits. Ready, willing, and able."

Hearn squinted along the sand. You could reduce it probably to four kinds of parties. There were the ones that made the newspaper society columns with the senators and the important representatives, the industrialists, the high brass, the foreign dignitaries, even his father had gone to one of them once, and been miserable no doubt. But then they all were miserable there. It was the highest flowering of an industrial capitalist culture, and a good time was segregate from the social forms, the power swappings, the highly elaborated weather talk. Everyone hated everyone else as a matter of course, for if they came to do business they found they could not, and if they came as snobs bearing gifts they were contemptuous of the men who had the power and lacked the conversational aptitudes.

239

There were the hotel parties with field officers and congenial lower-level brass, the American Legion—Washington Extension, and big small-business men with nice factories in Indiana, and call girls. A desperate boredom always lay over those things until they got drunk, and then they all had a wonderful time, and went back with refreshed loins and new Pullman tales to their desks in Washington and Indiana. Sometimes, if you could get ahold of a representative who was a regular guy he would come along, and your business would be consummated with a couple of drunken bear hugs, a sentimental cognition that everybody was a hell of a good guy, and a call girl yelling in your ear, "Break it up, honey, break it up." His father had never mentioned it, but of course he had gone to that kind of party too.

There were the parties his own friends gave, with the quiet sustained drinking and essential joylessness. All the American college intellectuals, the ones who weren't sick, with their clear logical voices, their good manners, their kindness, their tact and their miserable, dreary and lucid intelligences. They were all in government now, or they wore bars and had hush-hush jobs, and they talked of Roger who had been lost on some OSS mission, or they analyzed politics, sometimes hopefully, sometimes sadly, with a detached and helpless and intrinsically superior attitude. There was good wit, incisive but always peripheral information, and the dry dejuiced hopelessness of all of them with their rational desiccated minds and their wistful contemplation of lusts and evils they would never understand with their bodies. William Blake angels, gray and clear, hovering over horseshit.

And Dove's parties. But of course they were common to San Francisco and Chicago and Los Angeles and New York at times. The American Legion — Washington Extension, Junior Auxiliary. Only with something more. Give it credit. In a proper light with proper glasses, these parties were sometimes magical and sad, festooned with all the echoes of all the trains that had brought them there, all the advance awarenesses of the great hollow stations that would bear them away again. And they were always young, Air Corps pilots and ensigns, and good-looking girls in fur coats, and always the government secretary or two, the working girl as a carry-over from the fraternity parties when she was always the girl who could be made because in some mysterious way the women of the lower classes could be depended upon to copulate like jack rabbits. And they all knew they were going to die soon with a sentimental and unstated English attitude which was completely phony. It came from books they had never read, and movies they shouldn't have seen; it was fed by the tears of their mothers, and the knowledge quite shocking, quite unbelievable, that a lot of them did die when they went overseas. Its origins were spurious; they never could connect really the romance of their impending deaths with the banal mechanical process of flying an airplane and landing and living in the barren eventless Army camps that surrounded their airfields. But nevertheless they had discovered it was a talisman, they were going to die soon, and they wore it magically until you believed in it when you were with them. And they did magical things like pouring whisky on each other's hair, or setting mattresses afire, or grabbing hats on the fly from the heads of established businessmen. Of all the parties those were perhaps the best, but he had come to them too old.

". . . and damn if we didn't find out she had hair growing clear up her belly," Conn said, finishing a story.

Dove laughed. "If Jane knew the things I've done."

Their talk had ended by revolting him. He was becoming a prude, Hearn decided. He was disgusted and there wasn't sufficient cause for it. Slowly he extended his arms and legs, lowered himself gradually to the ground, feeling the muscle tension in his stomach. There had been an instant when he was tempted to hug Conn and Dove with his arms, and rather deliberately knock their heads together. All right, he was tough. But there had been too many thoughts like that lately, in officers' mess, the time he wanted to strike the General, or just now. It was the trouble with being a big man. He raised his head and stared across the bulk of his body, pinching the roll of fat that had started on his belly. Under the hair that covered his chest his flesh had become white. Five years more, ten at most, and he might be having to buy it from women. When a big man's body started going, it fell apart quickly.

Hearn shrugged. Then he'd end up like Conn and to hell with it.

241

He'd buy it and talk about it, and it was probably a damn sight easier than getting rid of women who had found something in him that he didn't have or he didn't care to give.

"She looked at it, and she said, 'Major' — I was a major then — 'what are they gonna do next? White ones, silver ones, gold ones, they'll probably be puttin' the American flag on 'em.'" Conn laughed and spat a little phlegm into the sand.

Why didn't they quit? Hearn rolled over on his belly, and felt the sun warming his body to its core. He'd be needing a woman soon, and short of ferrying to the next island, a couple of hundred miles away, where there were supposed to be native women, he was going to find little comfort.

"Hey," he said abruptly to Conn and Dove, "if you can't bring a whorehouse in, how about letting the women go for a while?"

"Beginning to get you down?" Conn asked with a smile.

"It's brutal," Hearn said, imitating Dove. He lit a cigarette, shaking the sand out of the pack.

Dove looked at him, tried another gambit. "Say, I was thinking before, Hearn, is your father's name William?"

"Yeah."

"We had a William Hearn who was a Deke about twenty-five years ago; could it be him?"

Hearn shook his head. "Hell, no, my father can't even read or write. All he can do is sign checks."

They laughed. "Wait a moment," Conn said, "Bill Hearn, Bill Hearn, by God, I know him, has some factories in the Middlewest, Indiana, Illinois, Minnesota?"

"That's right."

"Sure," Conn said, "*Bill* Hearn. You look like him, come to think of it. I met him when I was out of the Army in 'thirty-seven, organizing the stock for a couple of companies. We got along fine."

It was possible. His father would throw back his straight black hair, and clap Conn on the back with one of his meaty moist hands. "Hell you say, man," he could hear his father booming, "either you throw your goods on the table, and we talk a little turkey, or you can admit you're just a goddam fraud" — then the twinkle, the charm —

242

"and we can just get potted together, which is what the hell we want to do in the first place." But, no, Conn wasn't right, Conn didn't quite fit it.

"I saw his picture in the papers about a month ago. Have about ten papers sent to me regularly. I can see your old man's putting on a little weight."

"Keeping about even, I guess." He had been sick in the past three years and was down to almost the normal weight for a man his size. Conn didn't know his father. Of course not. Conn wasn't even a first sergeant in 'thirty-seven. You didn't quit the Army to organize companies when you were a staff sergeant. Abruptly Hearn realized that Conn had not whored with Generals Caldwell and Simmons in Washington, oh, possibly once he'd had a drink with them, or more likely he'd served under them as a noncom before the war but the whole thing was pathetic, and a little disgusting. Conn, the big operator. Even now the watery sagging eyes, the paunch, the mottled bulbous nose, were staring at him with sincerity. Sure he knew Bill Hearn. If they put Conn on the rack, he'd die swearing he knew him, believing he knew him.

"I'll tell you what, when you see Bill Hearn again, you tell him you saw me, or write to him, tell him that."

What had gone on in Conn's head for twenty years in the Army? Or particularly the last five when he had discovered he could swim as an officer?

Pop! went Dalleson's carbine.

"I'll tell him. Why don't you look him up? He'll be glad to see you."

"I might. I'd kinda like to see him again. They don't make them more sociable than your father."

"Sure." With a delicious effort Hearn restrained himself from saying, Maybe he can give you a job at the gate, keeping people out.

Instead he stood up. "I'm going in for a dip," he announced. He sprinted down the beach, hit the water flatly, and coasted under, feeling his mirth, his disgust, his weariness wash away in the delight of cold water against his heated flesh. When he came up he spouted some water gleefully, and began to swim. On the beach the officers were still sunning themselves, playing bridge or talking. Two of them were throwing a ball back and forth. The jungle looked almost pretty from the water.

Some artillery boomed very faintly over the horizon. Hearn ducked under again, came up slowly. The General had said once, savoring the epigram, "Corruption is the cement that keeps the Army from breaking apart." Conn? Cummings hadn't applied it that way, but Conn was still a product.

All right and so was he. What was corruption but knowing virtue and eschewing it? All very neat. And where did General Cummings fit in? That was a bigger question, that was one which couldn't be tied up in a package. In any case he was going to stay away from the General. Cummings had left him alone, and he would return the compliment. He stood up in shallow water, and shook his head to clear his ears. It was good swimming, damn good. Clean. He did a somersault underwater and then struck out with a steady stroke parallel to the shore. Conn was probably still beating his gums, still elaborating the myth that had become the man.

"Wakara, what does *umareru* mean?" Dove asked.

Lieutenant Wakara extended his slim legs, and wiggled his toes thoughtfully. "Why, it means, 'to be born,' I think."

Dove squinted along the beach, and watched Hearn swimming for a moment. "Oh, sure, *umareru* — to be born. *Umashi masu, umasho*. Those are the basic verb forms, aren't they? I remember that." He turned to Conn and said, "I don't know what I'd do without Wakara. It takes a Jap to figure out the damn language." And he clapped Wakara on the back, and added, "Hey, Tom, am I right?"

Wakara nodded slowly. He was a short thin man with a quiet sensitive face, rather dull eyes, and a thin neat mustache. "Good old Wakara," Dove said. Wakara continued to look at his legs. About a week before, he had overheard Dove saying to some officer, "You know our Jap translators are overrated. I do all the work in our unit, of course I'm in charge, but Wakara isn't much help at all. I'm always having to correct his translations."

Now Dove was massaging his bony chest with a towel he had

244

brought along. "Feels wonderful to get a sweat up in the sun," he muttered, and then turned to Wakara again. "I should have known that word, you know it's that diary we picked off that Jap major's corpse, fascinating document, did you have a look at it?"

"Not yet."

"Oh, well, it's wonderful. No military information, but the guy was a crackpot. The Japs are weird, Wakara."

"They're dopes," Wakara said shortly.

Conn lumbered into the conversation. "I have to go along with you there, Wakara. You know I was in Japan, back in 'thirty-three, and the people are illiterate. You can't teach them a damn thing."

"Gee, I didn't know you were there, Colonel," Dove said. "Do you know any of the language?"

"I never bothered to pick it up. I didn't like the people and I wanted no truck with them. I knew we were going to go to war."

"No kidding." Dove formed a little mound in the sand with his palm. "It must have been a valuable experience. Did you know the Japs were going to go to war, Wakara, when you were there?"

"No, I was too young, I was just a kid." Wakara lit a cigarette. "I didn't think so at all."

"Well, that's 'cause they're your people," Conn told him.

Pop! went Dalleson's carbine.

"I suppose so," Wakara said. He exhaled his smoke carefully. At the turn of the beach he could see an enlisted man patrolling, and he turned his head down toward his knees, hoping he would not be seen. It was a mistake to come out here. Those American soldiers wouldn't like the idea of protecting a Jap.

Conn drummed his paunch reflectively. "It's damn hot, I'm going to take a swim."

"Me too," Dove said. He stood up, rubbed some sand off his arms, and then with a perceptible pause, asked, "Want to come along, Wakara?"

"No, no, thanks, I'm not ready to go in yet." He watched them walk off. Dove was a funny man, rather typical, Wakara decided. Dove had seen him walking along the beach, and immediately he had had to call him over, ask that stupid question about *umareru*, and then

245

he didn't know what to do with him. Wakara was a little tired of being treated as a freak.

He stretched out on the sand, a little relieved that he was alone again. For a long time he stared at the jungle, which thickened, became impenetrable after thirty or forty yards. There was an effect which could be got; the jungle could be built up on a canvas out of a black-green background, but it would be a questionable technique. He certainly couldn't carry it off after not painting for two years. Wakara sighed. Perhaps it would have been better if he had stayed with his family in the relocation camps. At least he would be painting now.

Through the glare of the sun on his back, the glittering brilliance of the sand, Wakara realized that he was very depressed. What was it Dove had said about Ishimara's diary? "Fascinating document." Had Dove actually been touched by it? Wakara shrugged; it was impossible for him to understand Americans like Dove, just as it was impossible for him to understand Japanese. In limbo. Still there had been a time in Berkeley in his senior year when his paintings were getting some notice, and many of the American students were friendly with him. But of course that was all shattered by the war.

Ishimara, S., Major Infantry, Japanese Army. That was the way he had signed it, relinquishing himself again to anonymity.

"Did you have a look at it, Wakara?" Dove had asked.

Wakara grinned, staring at the sand. His own translation was in his breast pocket now. Poor Ishimara, whoever he was. The Americans had looted his corpse, and some noncom had brought the diary back. No, Wakara thought, he was too much of an American himself to understand really the kind of things that had gone on in Ishimara's head. Would an American keep a diary, write in it an hour before an attack? The poor bastard Ishimara, dumb, dumb like all the Japanese. Wakara unfolded his translation, read it over again for a moment.

The sun was red in its setting tonight, red with the blood of our soldiers who died today. Tomorrow my blood shall be in it.
This night I cannot sleep. I find myself weeping.
I have thought achingly of my childhood, and I remember the boys, my school friends, and the games we have played. I think of the year I have spent with my grandparents in the prefecture of Choshi.

246

I think, I am born and I die. I am born, I live, and I am to die, I think on this night.
I do not believe in the Emperor, His Most Exalted, I must confess it. I am going to die. I am born, I am dead.
I ask myself — WHY? I am born, I am to die. WHY? WHY? What is the meaning?

Wakara shrugged again. A thinker, a poet; there were many Japanese like him. And yet they died like anything but poets, died in mass ecstatic outbursts, communal frenzies. NAZE, NAZE DESU KA? Ishimara had written in huge trembling characters, WHY, WHY IS IT? and he had gone out and been killed in the river on the night of the big Japanese attack. He had fallen, shrieking, no doubt, a unit in an anonymous exalted mass. Who could comprehend it fully? Wakara wondered.

When he had been in Japan as a child of twelve, it had seemed the most wonderful and beautiful country he had ever seen. Everything was so small; it was a country built for the size of a twelve-year-old. Wakara knew Choshi where Ishimara had spent a year with his grandparents; perhaps he had even spoken once to Ishimara's grandparents. And in the peninsula at Choshi, in two miles, one could see everything. There were great cliffs which dropped several hundred feet into the Pacific, there were miniature wooded groves, as perfect, as tailored as emeralds, there were tiny fishing towns constructed of gray wood and rocks, there were rice paddies and mournful low foothills, and the cramped choked streets of the city of Choshi with its smells of fish tripe and human dung, the crowded bloody docks of the fishing wharves. Nothing went to waste. All the land had been manicured for a thousand years.

Wakara put out his cigarette in the sand and scratched at his thin mustache. It was all like that. No matter where you went, Japan was always beautiful, with an unreal finite beauty, like a miniature landscaped panorama constructed for a showroom or a fair. For a thousand years or more perhaps the Japanese had lived like seedy caretakers watching over precious jewels. They tilled the land, expended their lives upon it, and left nothing for themselves. Even when he was twelve years old he had known that the faces of the women were dif-

247

ferent from those of American women. And now in retrospect there was a curious detached wistfulness about the Japanese women as if they had renounced even the desire to think about joys they would never have.

Behind the beauty it was all bare, with nothing in their lives but toil and abnegation. They were abstract people, who had elaborated an abstract art, and thought in abstractions and spoke in them, devised involuted ceremonies for saying nothing at all, and lived in the most intense fear of their superiors that any people had ever had.

And a week ago a battalion of those wistful people had charged to their death with great terrifying screams. Oh, he understood, Wakara thought, why the Americans who had been in Japan hated the Japanese worst of all. Before the war they had been so wistful, so charming; the Americans had picked them up like pets, and were feeling the fury now of having a pet bite them. All the conversations, the polite evasions, the embarrassed laughs the Japanese had given them had suddenly assumed another meaning, had become malign once the war started. The Japanese to a man had been plotting against them. It was rot. Perhaps ten of the million or two million peasants who would be killed would have an idea of why they were being slaughtered. Even in the American Army the number was far greater.

But killed they would be, because the Japanese were dopes. They had been dopes for a thousand years. Wakara lit another cigarette, and sifted some sand through his fingertips.

Pop! The carbine sounded again.

Well, there was nothing he could do about it. The Americans would march in eventually and after twenty or thirty years the country would probably be the same again, and the people would live in their artistic abstract rut, and begin generating some more juice for another hysterical immolation. Two million, three million killed, it was all in the Oriental's stepped-up version of the Malthusian law. He could feel it himself, understand that better than the Americans.

Ishimara had been a fool. He didn't see things like population density; he saw it through his own shortsighted eyes, watching the sun go down with atavistic dread. The red sun and his own blood; that was what Ishimara knew. It was the sop allowed the Japanese. Deep in their own hearts, deep in the personal concretion of a diary, they could be philosophers, wistful philosophers, knowing nothing about the vehicle that moved them. Wakara spat on the sand, and then with a nervous furtive motion of his hand, he covered it over, and turned around to look at the sea.

They were dopes.

And he was alone, a wise man without a skin.

The tide was coming in, and the sand spit on which Major Dalleson had been firing his carbine was beginning to be inundated. He retreated a step or two as a wavelet pattered around his ankles, and then bent down to pick up another pebble. He had been shooting pebbles for almost an hour now, and he was beginning to weary. His large chest and belly had reddened in the sun, his body hair was slicked with perspiration, and the waist band of his cotton shorts, the only clothing he was wearing, had become quite wet. He grunted, looked at the pebbles in his hand, and selected one which he held between his forefinger and thumb. Then he slumped forward like a buffalo, his head almost parallel to the sand, the muzzle of his carbine pointing vertically downward just past his toe. He bent farther forward until his head was not more than a foot from his knees, and then he straightened abruptly, throwing the pebble into the air with his left hand and raising his carbine with his right arm. For just an instant he caught the pebble in his rear sight, a tiny speck of dust against the blue of the sky, and then he squeezed the trigger and the pebble spattered.

"Goddam," Dalleson said with satisfaction, wiping the sweat from his eyes with his heavy forearm, licking the dried salt at the corners of his mouth. That pebble made four in a row he had hit.

He selected another one, went into his motion, threw it up, and missed this time. "Well, anyway, I been hitting them about three out of five on an average," he told himself. It was all right; he hadn't lost his eye. He'd have to write a letter to his rifle club back in Allentown telling them about this.

That skeet shooting was all right. He'd have to try it when he got back. If he could hit pebbles three out of five with a carbine, they'd

249

have to blind him before he'd miss a clay plate with a shotgun. His ear ached slightly, comfortably, from the noise of firing the carbine.

Conn and Dove were sporting in the water about a hundred yards away and he waved to them. Another wavelet encircled his ankles. Or better than writing to the rifle club, he could send them a picture.

Dalleson turned around and looked over the sand at the officers playing bridge. "Hey, Leach, where the hell are you?" he bellowed.

A tall slim officer with a lean face and silver-rimmed glasses sat up in the sand. "I'm over here, Major, what do you want?"

"Did you take your camera along?" Leach nodded dubiously. "Well, bring it over, will ya?" Dalleson shouted. Leach was his assistant, a captain, in operations and training.

Dalleson grinned at him as he came over. Leach was a good fellow, agreeable, did his work all right, anxious to please. "Listen, Leach, I'd like ya to take a picture of me shooting some pebbles."

"It's going to be kind of hard, Major. This's just a little ol' box camera, and it's only got a shutter speed of one-twenty-fifth of a second."

Dalleson frowned. "Aw hell, it'll be good enough."

"Well, I'll tell you, Major, I'll be frank about it" — Leach's voice was soft with a southern accent — "I'd like to oblige you but I only have but three pictures left, and it's kinda hard to get film."

"I'll pay you for it," Dalleson offered.

"Aw, no, I wasn't thinking of that, but, well, you see — "

Dalleson interrupted him. "Come on, man, all I'm asking you for is a picture. What the hell are you gonna shoot it up of, except some of these other Joes around here?"

"All right, Major."

Dalleson beamed. "Okay, now look, Leach, what I want is for you to get out on that spit a little bit, and I want you to get me in, of course, and the jungle in back so my friends'll know where the hell it was taken, and also I want you to get that pebble when it busts in the air."

Leach looked distressed. "Major, you can't get all that in. That would include a ninety-degree arc, and the angle of lens of this camera isn't more than thirty-five degrees."

250

"Well, look, man, don't give me all those goddam facts and figures. It seems to me it ain't that goddam hard to take a little picture."

"I might be able to take you from the back with you in the foreground and tilt the camera up so it catches the pebble, but I'll tell you, Major, it's just a waste of film because that pebble isn't even gonna register. It's too small."

"Leach, it ain't that complicated. I've taken pictures. All you got to do is press a damn button. Now let's cut out all this jawing."

Obviously miserable, Leach squatted behind Dalleson and hopped around for a few seconds trying to find the proper angle. "Will you throw a practice pebble up, Major?" Leach asked. Dalleson flipped one in the air. "Let's get these dry runs over," he grumbled.

"All right, I'm ready now, Major."

Dalleson bent over, straightened, and fired at the pebble when it was at the top of the parabola. He missed, and turned around to Leach. "Let's try another one."

"All right," Leach said grudgingly.

This time Dalleson hit the pebble, but Leach had reacted too late, and he snapped the shutter after the pebble fragments were dispersed. "Goddammit, man!" Dalleson roared.

"I'm doing my best, Major."

"Well, let's not drop the ball next time." Dalleson threw away the pebbles in his hand and searched for a larger one.

"This's the last picture in the roll, Major."

"Hell, we'll make it." Dalleson wiped the sweat out of his eyes again, bent over, and stared at his knees. His heart was beating a little rapidly. "You snap it soon's you hear the carbine go off," he growled.

"Yes, sir."

Up went the pebble and his rifle pointing after it. There was a panicky instant when he couldn't locate it in his sights, and then as it started to fall he caught it over the front-leaf sight, adjusted instinctively, and felt the reassuring minor jolt of the stock, the slight kick, as he pressed the trigger.

"I got it that time, Major."

Ripples on the water were still spreading from the fragments of the pebble. "Goddam," Dalleson said again with enjoyment. "I appreciate this, Leach."

"That's okay, sir."

"Lemme pay you for it."

"Well . . ."

"I insist," Dalleson said. He slipped the magazine out of the carbine, and fired the round remaining in the chamber into the air. "Let's call it a quarter for the three pictures. I sure hope they come out good." He patted Leach on the back. "C'mon, son, let's you and me go for a swim. Hell, we deserve it."

This was *all right*.

9

RECON began working on the road again after they returned from the front. The line companies advanced their positions several times and the men in the rear heard rumors that they were close to the Toyaku Line. Actually they knew very little about what was happening in the campaign; the days repeated themselves without incident, and they were no longer able to distinguish between things which had happened a few days before. They would stand guard at night, awaken a half hour after dawn, eat breakfast, wash their mess kits, shave, and load onto trucks which drove them through the jungle to the stretch of road upon which they were working. They would return at noon, go out again after chow, and work until late afternoon when they would come back for supper, take a bath perhaps in the stream just outside the bivouac, and then go to sleep soon after dark. They had about an hour and a half of guard each night, and they were thoroughly accustomed to it; they had forgotten what it was like to sleep for eight consecutive hours. The rainy season had come on and they were always wet. After a time it was no longer a discomfort. The dampness of their clothing seemed perfectly natural to them, and it was very difficult to remember just what it had felt like to wear a dry uniform.

252

About a week after they had come back, a load of mail came to the island. They were the first letters the men had received in several weeks, and for a night it relieved the changeless pattern of their lives. One of the infrequent rations of beer was given out the same night, and the men finished their three cans quickly, and sat about without saying very much. The beer had been far too inadequate to make them drunk; it made them only moody and reflective, it opened the gate to all their memories, and left them sad, hungering for things they could not name.

On the night they got their mail, Red drank his beer with Wilson and Gallagher, and did not return to his tent until dark. He had received no letters, which did not surprise him since he had not written to anyone in over a year, but he had felt a trace of disappointment. He had never written to Lois, so he never heard from her; she didn't even know his address. But once in a while, usually on mail-call nights, he had a momentary and irrational little hope. The business with Lois was dead, but even so . . .

His depression had increased while he was with the other men. Gallagher was busy writing to his wife, leafing through the fifteen letters that had come from her in order to answer some of her questions, and Wilson had been complaining about his wife. "Ah gave that damn woman lovin' she'll never forget, and now she's always fussin' over why Ah don' send some o' my pay."

"You're gonna die in jail," Red had snorted.

By the time he returned to his own tent, he was very depressed. At the entrance he kicked aside an empty beer can and crawled into the hole. As he straightened his twisted blankets in the dark, he swore a little. "It's just like the goddam Army," he said to Wyman, "three cans of beer. They got more ways to tease a man."

Wyman turned over in his bedding, and spoke up softly. "I only drank one of my beers. Why don't you take the other two, Red?"

"Well, thanks, kid." Red hesitated. A tacit friendship had developed between them since they had been bunking together, but Wyman was making more and more overtures lately. You start buddy-buddying with 'em and they get knocked off, Red thought. More and more Wyman reminded him of Hennessey. "You better drink the beer yourself, kid," he said, "they ain't gonna give 'em out again for a while."

"Naw, I don't like beer much."

Red opened a can and passed it to Wyman. "C'mon, we'll each have one." If he had kept both of them and drunk them it might have muddled him enough to fall asleep easily. Ever since the night they had marched up to the front, Red's kidneys had been bothering him steadily, keeping him awake at night. And with insomnia there was always a re-enactment of the moment when he had waited for the Japanese soldier to stab him. But even so, two beers was a big favor, too big a one. It would give Wyman a call on him. It was better when you didn't owe anybody.

They drank silently for a few minutes. "You get lots of mail, kid?" Red asked.

"I got a batch from my mother." Wyman lit a cigarette and looked away.

"What about your girl friend, what's-her-name?"

"I don't know, I didn't get anything from her."

In the dark, Red grimaced. The whole setup should have told him. Giving away a beer, mooning by himself in the tent — he should have guessed what was wrong with Wyman and avoided a conversation. "Aw, hell, kid, she'll write you," he blurted.

Wyman fingered his blanket. "I can't figure it out, Red. I haven't got any mail from her since I been overseas. Back in the States she used to write me every day."

Red rinsed his mouth with a swallow of beer. "Aaah, it's just the Army's got the mail fugged up," he said.

"I used to think that, but I don't believe it any more. When I was in the replacement depot I didn't expect to get any, but now we've had two mail calls here, and I got a bunch of letters from my mother each time, and nothing from her."

Red fingered his nose and sighed.

"I'll tell you the truth, Red, I'd be scared to get a letter from her now. It'd probably be a Dear John."

"There's lots of women, kid. You're better off if you learn early."

254

Wyman's voice was troubled and hurt. "She ain't like that, Red. She's really a swell kid. Oh, Jeez, I don't know, there was something real different about her."

Red grunted. Wyman's emotion was embarrassing him, and he knew he would have to listen. He drank some beer, and smiled wryly. I'm paying for the goddam drink, he said to himself. Abruptly, he pictured again Wyman brooding by himself all evening, and the thought softened him. "It's kind of hard just to sit around and think," he said. By now he had stirred at best only a partial sympathy. Other men's troubles usually bored him. Everybody gets his share of bloody noses, and it's Wyman's turn now, he thought.

"How'd you meet her?" he asked.

"Aw, she was the kid sister of Larry Nesbitt, you remember he was that buddy of mine I was telling you about?"

"Yeah." Red had a vague recollection.

"Well, I always used to see her around his house, and she was just a kid, I never paid any attention to her. But then one time a couple of months before I came into the Army, I went over to his house and he wasn't in, and I noticed her. You know, she'd sort of grown up. So I asked her to go for a walk with me, and we sat in the park and talked, and . . ." Wyman broke off. "I could talk to her about a lot of things, and I don't know, we just sat there on a park bench, and I told her I wanted to be a sports writer, and she said she wanted to design dresses, and I started laughing until I realized she was serious, and we talked a long time about what we wanted to do with ourselves." He swallowed his beer.

"A lot of people were walking past us," Wyman said, "and we started playing a game, you know guessing how old they were and what they did for a living, and she would try to guess whether they were happy or not. And then we started analyzing all our friends, and we talked a lot."

Red grinned. "And then you asked her, 'What do ya think of me?'"

Wyman looked at him with surprise. "How'd you know?"

"Ah, I just guessed." Red was remembering the park at the end of the main street in the company town. For a moment, he could see

Agnes's face again, and the sound of his voice, "You know I don't believe in God." He felt wistful, and then smiled to himself. That evening had had a beauty which he had never felt in exactly the same way again. "What was it, summer time?" he asked Wyman.

"Yeah, early in the summer."

Red smiled again. It happens to all the fuggin kids, he thought, and they all think it's something special. Wyman probably had been a shy kid, and he could see him talking in the park, telling a girl things he had never been able to say to anyone else. And of course the girl would have been like him. "I know what you mean, kid," he said.

"You know she told me she loved me," Wyman said defiantly, as if he expected Red to laugh. "We were really going steady after that night."

"Wha'd your mother say?"

"Aw, she didn't like the idea, but I wasn't worried about that. I knew I could bring her around."

"Sometimes it's hard," Red said. "You don't know what you would have been running into."

Wyman shook his head. "Red, listen, this sounds stupid, but Claire really made me feel like I could be something. After a date I'd leave her, and walk around for a while by myself, and I don't know, I just *knew* I was gonna be a big guy someday. I was sure of it." He stopped for a moment, absorbed in what he had said.

Red wondered what to answer. "You know a lot of people feel that way, kid."

"Aw, it was *different* with us, Red. It was *really* something special."

Red winced. "I don't know," he muttered. "Lots of people feel like that, and then for some reason they bust up, or they go sour on each other."

"We wouldn't have busted up, Red. I'm telling ya, she loved me." He thought about this, and his face became tense. He wrapped his blanket around him and then said, "She couldn't have been lying, Red, she's not that kind of girl. She's not cheap." He was silent, and then blurted out suddenly, "You don't think she coulda been lying to me, do ya?"

256

"Naw, she wasn't," Red said. He felt a pang. "Naw, she didn't lie, but people change, you know."

"Not her," Wyman said. "It was different with us." His voice expressed the frustration he felt at being unable to put his feeling into words.

Red thought of the mother Wyman would have to support if he married his girl, and he had a quick elliptic knowledge of everything that would contain — the arguments, the worries over money, the grinding extinction of their youth until they would look like the people who walked by them in the park — it was all clear to Red. It would not be this girl for Wyman but it would be some other, and it did not matter because both girls would look the same in thirty years and Wyman would never amount to very much. He saw a future vista of Wyman's life, and rebelled. He wanted to be able to tell Wyman something more comforting than the fact that it didn't matter. But he could think of nothing, and he settled back in his blankets. His back was paining. "Aaah, you better try to sleep it off, kid," he said.

"Yeah, okay," Wyman murmured.

Like a relapsing fever, Red had again the familiar ache of age and sadness and wisdom.

Croft and Martinez had not received any mail either; they never got any.

Ridges was given a letter from his father. It was written laboriously on coarse ruled paper into which the pencil lines had cut deeply. Ridges gave it to Goldstein to read for him.

It went: Dere Son, we one and al of us miss you, the crop was harvest, and we made som little money, enuff to kepe us, Thank the Lord. Sim grew prette near haff a foot and your other brothers and sisters are kepeing him compeny, ma is felling pretty good. Old man Henry lost his 3 acres, it is a shaim, but the company will not take a no for a answer. We appreshate the monee you sent, you are a gud son, we al saye that. Your loveing father.

"That's a mighty fine letter," Ridges said when Goldstein had finished. "Pa writes a nice hand."

"It's a very nice letter," Goldstein said. He read over again the last lines of one of the letters his wife had sent him. "Danny asked about you yesterday, I've been telling him all the time that daddy is in the Army, and he hasn't forgotten you one bit. He's so cute, oh, Joey, I wish you could see him growing up, there's nothing like it. He said yesterday, 'When does Daddy come back from going boom-boom?' I didn't know whether to laugh or cry. Manny Straus promised he'd take some pictures of him . . ."

Goldstein sipped his beer and felt an awful longing.

Wilson had Gallagher reread one of the letters from Wilson's wife next morning. He laughed angrily several times as Gallagher read.

"I am not going to stand for this I hav been a gud wife to you and you no that, I hav alwaze giv you all the monie you want, and I am entitel now to one hunedird and twentie dollar everie monthe I was tawking to Wes Hopekinds down at the cowntie clerke offis and he saiy that you hav to giv me the monie the armie take care of it thair is no thing you can do abowt it. Unles you do that yurselfe Woodrow I am goeing to rite a leter to the armie I no the adres cawze Wes done tolde me how to go abowt it. I am tird of be a gud wife to you cawze you do not unnderstan . . ."

"Well, now, how do you like that ol' shit?" Wilson said. He was angry and he brooded over his answer. "You're gonna write a letter for me, tonight. Ah'm gonna tell her that she cain't get away with none of that stuff." He phrased a few sentences to himself. "Ah'm tellin' ya, y' better start actin' like a decent wife, and cut out all that fussin' an' naggin' or I damn sure ain't gonna come back to ya." He censored "damn." Wilson had an obscure prejudice against using profanity in a letter. "There's plenty of women would be glad to have me, an' you know it. Ah cain't stan' a woman who's always tryin' to take away the last cent from a man. If Ah want a little money in the Army, Ah'm gonna have it. Ah don' want no more talk about this 'lotment." Wilson felt bitter and righteous, and the act of composing had given him a heady pleasure. His mind was filled with things to tell her, and he felt a glow each time he conceived a biting phrase.

258

He sat on the edge of the hole at the tent entrance and squinted at the sun. "Y' take that other gal," he said to Gallagher, "she's awright. Ah got a letter from her Red read me last mail call we had, an' she tol' me she was jus' waitin' for me to come back to Kansas so we could git married an' then go on south. That was a woman. Use' to cook for me, mend my clo'es, starch up my shirts for Satidday inspection, an' she gave me as good lovin' as Ah've had for a long time."

Gallagher spat with disgust and envy. "What a bastard you are. If you like her so goddam much why don't you tell her you're married, and give her a break?"

Wilson looked at him as if Gallagher were stupid. "Hell, man," he protested, "why should Ah tell her? Ah never can tell how Ah'm gonna be feelin' when Ah git out of the Army. Maybe Ah'm gonna want to go to Kansas and hook up with that other woman. There's no way of sayin'. Be a damn shame ifen Ah was to tell her, an' she wasn't around when Ah got out, an' Ah wanted her." He shook his head and giggled. "The less you tell a woman the better off y'are."

Gallagher flew into a rage. "You fuggin crackers, you're a bunch of animals."

"Aw."

Gallagher smoldered. A guy like Wilson went around taking life easy and making everybody pay for him. It wasn't fair. He looked off into the jungle, righteous, envious.

After a while he calmed, and began to look over his mail again. He had had time the night before to read only the mail he had received from his wife. They were all old letters; the newest was a month old, and he had kept telling himself with surprise that he was probably a father by now. The date his wife had mentioned for the birth of his child had elapsed a few days ago but he was unable to believe it. He assumed that what she wrote about had happened on the same day that he read the letter; if she said that she was going to visit one of her girl friends on the next day, he would be thinking on the day after he read the letter that Mary was seeing her friend at this moment. His reason was always correcting him, but still she lived for him only at the exact time when he read her letters.

Now he was going through the rest of his mail. He skimmed

through a letter from his mother, and read aloud to Wilson some of the funnier passages in a letter he had got from Whitey Lydon. Then he opened a long thick envelope and extracted a newspaper from it. It was tabloid size and had only eight pages, which were badly printed. "I used to work for this," he said to Wilson.

"Ah never knew you were a reporter."

"Naw, this is political. The gang over at the party headquarters puts this out before the primaries." He looked at the date. It was printed in June. "This thing's old as hell," he said. He felt a pang of envy as he looked at the names on the masthead; one of his friends who was not in the Army had been put in charge of the advertising department. Gallagher knew what that meant. In the last primary before he entered the Army he had gone from door to door in his ward, soliciting contributions for the paper. The man who brought in the most contributions was called advertising manager, and he usually received a job on the school board in his ward. He had missed out by only a few hundred dollars, but he had been told he would certainly win the next year.

"Just my fuggin luck to get in the Army," he said resentfully. He started reading the paper. A headline caught his attention.

ANDREWS A BIGOT IN WARD 9. LET'S GET HIM OUT

It's just the old Andrews BALLY-HOO in Action, just like the last time he ran for State Leg. when his slogan was ANDREWS vs. COMMUNISM, remember? then what did he do about COMMUNISM? N-O-T-H-I-N-G as far as we can see. One of his workers at his headquarters was a vice-president of CIO and another worker was a director of the Anti-Nazi League of N.Y., remember this league that did not like Father Coughlin and wanted to boycott Catholic Franco.

Now Jimmy Andrews, Old Boy, remember the old gray mare Aint What She Used To Be, so don't start off on the wrong foot, don't kid the Public or the Veterans, make sure what you say. Help The Veteran—Don't Kid. We're all on to you, Jimmy Andrews, and the voters of Ward 9 don't want a bigot. So watch out for the Company YOU KEEP. There's no place in the party for men like YOU. We're on to that old game.

NO BIGOTS ALLOWED

NO COMMUNISTS

LET'S GET ANDREWS OUT

260

Gallagher felt a dull anger as he read. It was those kind of guys you had to watch out for, the fuggin Communists. He remembered once when he was driving a truck and the AFL had tried to organize them. He'd mentioned it down at the ward headquarters, and the organizer had never come back. There was something funny there, he'd noticed there were guys in the party who would play around with the Red Labor Outfits, men like Big Joe Durmey, and this Jim Andrews guy, and they had no call to deal with bigots, Gallagher decided. Those were the kind of guys who were always working against him; no wonder he had never got anywhere. He felt a pang of envy as he thought of Whitey Lydon. Everybody was getting ahead of him while he was stuck here. There wasn't anybody you could trust. Dog eat dog.

He folded the paper and crammed it into his pocket. Croft was calling to them and they got out of their tents, and strolled toward the truck that was to take them to the section of road upon which they were working. The sun had been up for only an hour and the morning still had a fine clear youth. It was not yet hot. Gallagher thought vaguely of early summer mornings when he set out for work, and the pavements were still cool and fresh from the summer night. He had forgotten the newspaper and was humming to himself as he climbed on the truck.

In the mail room, a pyramidal tent with two field desks, the mail clerk was sorting some of the letters that had been misaddressed. There was a stack of twenty letters for Hennessey, tied together with a thin piece of twine, and they lay for several hours on a corner of the desk. At last the mail clerk noticed them. He prided himself on remembering the name of every man in the regiment, and he was annoyed now because he could not place Hennessey.

"Was Hennessey transferred from headquarters company?" he asked his assistant.

"I don't know, name's familiar." The assistant thought a moment and then said, "Wait a minute, I remember, he was knocked off the day we came in." The assistant was pleased that he had recalled it when the mail clerk had forgotten.

"That's right," the mail clerk said hastily. "He got it right on

261

the beach, I was talking to Brown about it." He looked at the tied bundle of envelopes, sighed, and stamped on them, "Addressee Killed in Action." He was about to put the letters in one of the bags at his feet, when he noticed the return address. He skimmed through the envelopes and discovered it was the same on all of them. "Hey, look at this," he said to the assistant.

The return address on the letters was "Mom and Dad, 12 River-dale Avenue, Tacuchet, Indiana." The assistant read it to himself, and thought for a moment of a rosy-cheeked man and woman with graying hair, the Mom and Pop of a thousand billboard ads for soft drinks and mouthwashes and toothpastes. "Gee, isn't that sad," he said.

"Yeah, it sure is."

"Makes you think," the assistant said.

After the midday meal, Gallagher was sitting in his tent when Croft called him. "What is it?" Gallagher asked.

"The chaplain wants to see you," Croft said.

"What about?"

"I don't know," Croft shrugged. "Why don't you go see him? We'll be gone when you get back, so you'll have perimeter guard for the afternoon."

Gallagher walked through the bivouac and stopped at the chaplain's tent. His heart was beating quickly, and he was trying to suppress the hope he was feeling. Before they had landed on Anopopei, he had asked the chaplain if he needed another assistant, and the chaplain had promised to consider him. To Gallagher it meant getting out of combat, and he had allowed himself to dream about the possibility several times.

"Good afternoon, Father Leary," he said. "I heard you wanted to see me." His voice was polite and uncomfortable, and he was perspiring from the effort of having to watch his profanity.

"Sit down, Gallagher." Father Leary was a tall slim middle-aged man with light hair, and a caressing voice.

"What is it, Father?"

"Go ahead and smoke, son." Father Leary lit a cigarette for him. "You get much mail from home, Gallagher?"

"My wife writes to me every day, almost, Father. She's gonna be having a baby any day now."

"Yes." Father Leary was silent; he fingered his lip, and then sat down abruptly. He put his hand on Gallagher's knee. "Son, I have some pretty bad news for you."

Gallagher felt a chill. "What is it, Father?"

"You know, son, there're a lot of things which are difficult to understand. You just have to believe that it's right, and that there's a good reason for it, that God understands and sees and does what is best, even if we don't understand right away."

Gallagher was ill at ease and then abruptly frantic. All kinds of wild thoughts passed through his mind. He blurted out, "My wife didn't leave me, did she?" He felt shame as soon as he had spoken.

"No, son, but there has been a death."

"My mother?"

Father Leary shook his head. "Not your parents."

Gallagher thought his child had died in birth. He felt a quick passage of relief. That ain't so bad, went through his mind. For an instant he wondered again dumbly if Father Leary had called him in to give him the job as chaplain's assistant.

"No, son, I'm afraid it was your wife."

The words passed through Gallagher numbly. He sat there without any response, without thinking of anything at all. An insect buzzed in through the folded flaps of the tent, and he watched it. "Wha-a-a-at?" he asked.

"Your wife died in childbirth, Gallagher." Father Leary looked away. "They were able to save your child, though."

"Mary wasn't very big," Gallagher said. The word "dead" formed for him, and because it now had only one meaning to him, he saw Mary quivering and twitching like the Japanese soldier who had been killed in the draw. He began to shiver uncontrollably. "Dead," he said. The word had no sense. He sat there very numb; his thoughts had retreated into some deep secure closet of his mind and the words of the chaplain fell abstractly on the anesthetized surface of his brain. For a few seconds he felt as if he were hearing a story about someone else in which he was not very interested. Oddly, the only thing he told himself was that he had to look alert to impress the chaplain. "Ohhhhhh," he said at last.

"The information they gave me was very slight, but I'll give you the details when I hear them, son. It's terribly hard to be so far away from home, and be unable to see your beloved ones for a last time."

"Yeah, it's hard, Father," Gallagher said automatically. Like the rising of the dawn, Gallagher was slowly becoming able to distinguish the objects about him, and understand the news he had heard. His mind was telling him something bad had happened, and he thought, I hope Mary don't worry over the news. He realized suddenly that Mary would not be worrying, and before the contradiction, he retreated; he gazed dully at the wood of the chair upon which the chaplain was sitting. He felt as if he were in a church, and mechanically he looked at his hands and tried to assume a serious expression.

"Life goes on. It's not without meaning that your child was saved. If you wish, I'll inquire for you as to who will take care of her. Perhaps we can arrange a furlough for you."

Gallagher's spirits rose. He would be seeing his wife. But Mary was dead; this time his mind did not retreat quite so far. He sat there thinking of how pleasant the sunlight had been that morning as he climbed on the truck, and dumbly he understood that he wanted to go back to that moment.

"Son, you've got to have courage."

"Yes, Father." Gallagher stood up. He could not feel the soles of his feet, and when he rubbed his mouth it felt swollen and alien under his fingers. He had a moment of panic, and he thought of the snake in the cave. I bet a fuggin Yid was the doctor, he said to himself, and then forgot the thought. It left him with a pleasant glow of righteousness, however. "Well, thanks, Father," he said.

"Go to your tent, son, and lie down," Father Leary said.

"Okay, Father." Gallagher walked through the bivouac area. It was almost deserted now that the men were out on detail, and this gave him a secure feeling of isolation. He came to his tent, dropped in the hole, and stretched out on his blanket. He was feeling nothing except an extreme weariness. His head ached and he wondered idly if he should take an atabrine tablet from his jungle aid kit. Maybe I got

264

malaria, he said to himself. He remembered the expression on Mary's face in the first days of their marriage when she would set a plate down before him with food upon it. Her wrists were very slim and he could see again the golden hairs on her forearm.

"I bet a fuggin Yid was the doctor," he said aloud. The sound startled him, and he rolled over on his back. He was becoming angry as he thought about it, and once or twice he muttered, "The Yid killed her." It relieved the tension he was feeling. He felt a joyful self-pity, and he let it flow through him for several minutes. His shirt was wet, and every few seconds he would grind his teeth because the tension on his jaws pleased him.

He felt suddenly clammy, and with a rush he began really to understand that his wife was dead. He felt an awful pain and longing which mounted in his chest until he began to weep. The sounds became noticeable to him after a minute or two, and he stopped, a little terrified, for they seemed remote from him. It was as if he had a coating of insulation about all his feelings, and the insulation could be shed for only a moment or two, before his pain drew it about him again.

He began to think of the dead soldiers in the draw, only his mind pictured Mary consecutively in each of the postures their bodies had assumed. He began to shiver again, and an intense feeling of horror and nausea and fear spread through him. He clenched the blanket in his hand and muttered without realizing what he said, "I ain't gone to confession for too long." He became acutely conscious of the odor of his clothing. I stink, I need a bath, he thought. The idea began to bother him, and he thought of going down to the stream and stripping his clothing. He got out of the tent and felt too weak to walk the hundred yards, so he stopped outside Red's tent and filled a helmet from a jerrican of water. When he set the helmet on the ground it tipped and the water slopped over his feet. He took off his shirt, filled the helmet again, and poured the water over his neck. It felt cold and jarring, and he shuddered. Without thinking, he put on his shirt again, and stumbled back to his tent, where he lay without thinking anything for half an hour. The heat of the sun was oppressive on the rubber fabric of the poncho, and he became drowsy, and slept at last. In his slumber, his body would twitch from time to time.

265

The Time Machine:

A short man with a bunched wiry body that gave the impression of being gnarled and sour. His face was small and ugly, pocked with the scars of a severe acne which had left his skin lumpy, spotted with swatches of purple-red. Perhaps it was the color of his face, or it might have been the shape of his long Irish nose, which slanted resentfully to one side, but he always looked wroth. Yet he was only twenty-four.

In South Boston and Dorchester and Roxbury the gray wooden houses parade for miles in a file of drabness and desolation and waste. The streetcars jangle through a wilderness of cobblestone and sapless wood; the brick is old and powders under your fingertips if you rub it vigorously. All colors are lost in the predominating gray; the faces of the people have assumed it at last. There are no Jews or Italians or Irish — their features have blurred in an anonymous mortar which has rendered them homogeneous and dusty. It is in their speech. They all talk with the same depressing harsh arid tongue. "If I had a caah, I'd show it some caaer, I mean some caaer, I wouldn't paaark it just any-whaah."

It was founded by burghers and is ruled by bourgeois; everything flows on glabrous surfaces, everything is fine in Boston to read the newspapers, which are all the same, everything is okay in politics because the political parties are the same. Everybody belongs to the middle class, everybody down to the bums who drowse and retch on the subway that goes to Maverick Square in East Boston at two A.M. on Saturday night. Somewhere they must have protested against going into the mortar but it is all lost now.

There is a deadening regularity and a sullen vicious temper that rides underneath the surface, the glabrous surface of the Boston *Herald* and *Post* and *Traveler* and *Daily Record* and *Boston-American,* it erupts in the drunks who splatter the subways more completely than the drunks of any other city, it skitters around Scollay Square, where lust is always sordid and Sodom copulates in garbage. It even moves in the traffic, which is snarled and sullen and frenetic, and it rides the brow when the kids are beaten up in the alleyways, and the synagogues and cemeteries are fouled with language and symbol, "The fuggin kikes" and the cross or swastika. "I am distressed to hear of it," says Governor Curley, Saltonstall, Tobin.

The kids have gang fights with stones and sticks and knucklebands; in the winter the snowballs are packed with rocks. It is of course harmless, a mere tapping of the healthycompetitiveinstinct.

Hey, Gallagheh, Lefty Finkelstein's gang is gonna fight us.

Sonsofbitches, let's get them. (Fear is something alien to the gang, stored far down in his stomach.) I been layin' for him.

Get Packy and Al and Fingers, we're gonna clean up the Yids.

What time we start?

What the fug you caaeh? Ya yella?

Who's yella. I'm gonna get me my bat.

(On the way he passes a synagogue. "Ya yella?" He spits on it.) Hey, Whitey, I'm givin' it one for good luck.

Hey, Gallagheh, the kids yell . . .

Watch out for your old man when he's got a bag on.

In the house his mother winces at sounds and walks on tiptoe. His old man sits at the round table in the living-dining room, and grabs the yellow lace cover and crushes it in his big mitts. Then he spreads it out on the table again.

Goddam, sure a man has . . . Sonofabitch. Hey, PEG!

What is it, Will?

His father massages his nose and chin. Cut out the goddam mousing around, walk like a woman goddammit.

Yes, Will?

That's all goddammit, get away.

When your old man's as big a sonofabitch as Will Gallagher, you leave him alone when he's got a bag on. But you watch him so one of his mitts don't catch you on the side of the mouth.

He sits stolidly at the round table, and beats his fist down once or twice. He looks at the walls. (The brown pictures which once were green of shepherd girls in a wooded valley. They came off a calendar.) GODDAM PLACE.

The triptych on the whatnot shudders as he bangs the table.

Will, don't drink so much.

SHUT UP! Shut your stupid mouth. He lumbers to his feet and staggers to the wall. The glass over the shepherd girl splatters as he throws it to the floor. He sprawls on the shabby gray-brown sofa, looks at the gray shiny nap of the carpet where it has worn through. Work your ass off, FOR WHAT?

His wife tries to slip the bottle off the table. LEAVE IT THERE!

Will, maybe you can get something else.

Yeah . . . yeah. Have you whining I need a little this, a little that. Grocers butchers. Just let me break me back wrestling that truck around. Something ELSE. I'm stuck, I'm in a hole. GET THAT BOTTLE DOWN.

He stands up, lurches toward her, and strikes her. She slips to the floor and lies there without moving, uttering a dull passionless whimpering. (A slim woman, drab now.)

CUT OUT THE GODDAM NOISE! He looks at her dumbly, mops his nose again and rumbles toward the door. Get out of the way, Roy. At the door he stumbles, sighs, and then goes pitching down the street into the night.

Gallagher looks at his mother. He is empty, close to weeping. Here, Ma. He helps her up. She begins to cry loudly, and numbly he supports her

Ya keep your mouth shut when the old man's got a bag on, he thinks.

Later, he goes up to his room, and reads a book he drew from the library. King Arthur and His Knights of the Round Table. Boy-wise, he dreams of women in . . . lavender dresses he picks.

I ain't gonna be like the old man. (He shall defend his wife with his sword.)

268

The bright glorious passage of youth.

His teachers never remember him in high school, a sullen morose student without enthusiasm. He quits a year before graduation, out into the tag end of the depression and a job as an elevator boy. His old man is without work that year, and his mother goes out by day, cleans stucco, Spanish tile, and Colonial houses in Brookline, in Newton. At night she goes to sleep after supper, and his old man is down at the corner bar, waiting for someone to offer him an argument or a drink.

Roy starts hanging around the Democratic Club in his ward. In the small rooms at the back there are the poker games, crap games, the con talk. The big room at the entrance where the kids come in and mingle with the cigar smoke, the serge suits, the attendants.

Ladies in waiting.

And the recruiting talks. Steve Macnamara who is getting up in the party:

Sure, you guys, take a look, just take a look. A man can split a gut tryin' to go it the hard way. What's in it for ya? The only thing is politics, politics, that's what gets ya somewheah, you put in a couple of yeaahs, you show 'em you're a right guy, an' you're made, the organization'll take caah of ya. I remembeh when I was a punk like you kids, I showed 'em I was a willin' workeh, and now I'm set, you know this ain't a bad waard, it's easy to pull in the vote heah.

Yeah, Gallagher admits, yeah.

Listen, I've had my eye on you, Roy, you're okay, I can see wheah you'd have a future heah, you just got to show the boys you're a willin' workeh. I know y'are but you got to prove it to them. I'll tell ya what, the primary's comin' up in another month, and theah's a lot of leg work got to be done, givin' out the pamphlets, and havin' a couple of boys in the crowd to do a little yellin' when one of our candidates is makin' a speech, we'll tell you when.

Yeah, that's okay.

Sure, listen, theah's money to be made in this, you know you stick with the boys theah's always a lot of jobs, a lot of easy gelt, you'll be a big guy someday, I'll say I knew you when, I can see right off and I'm a student of human nature, you got to be in this racket, that you got the stuff for politics, you know, chaaarm.

269

I'll be puttin' in my nights here.

That's it, how old are ya now? Close to eighteen, by the time you're twenty you'll be making ten times what you are now . . .

On the way home, he meets a girl he has talked to once or twice, and he stops to banter with her.

I'm tired of my job, I'm gettin' a better one, he bursts out.

What?

Something big. (Suddenly he is shy.) Big, something big.

You're mysterious, Roy, cut the kiddin'. (She giggles.)

Yeah. (He can think of nothing to say.) Yeah, I'm on my way, I'm going places.

You're a caard.

Yeah. (He looks at her, lights a cigarette with elaborate nonchalance, swaggers self-consciously.) Yeah. (He looks at her again, and feels panicky.) I'll be seein' ya.

When he is twenty, he has a new job, he works in a warehouse. (Roy, you done a lotta work, Steve Macnamara has said to him, don't let anyone tell ya different, and the boys appreciate it, you're goin' places. He makes himself say, Yeah, but Whitey's on the payroll, I done as much work as him . . . Now, listen, Roy, listen, don't let anyone hear ya talkin' like that, Jesus, they'll be thinkin' you're a sorehead, you built up a name heah for yourself, you don't want to be takin' chances with it.)

One night he goes out to Cambridge to see a girl, but she has stood him up. He ends by walking through the streets, and wandering along the banks of the Charles. The goddam bitch, none of them can fool me, they all put out for the right guy, but they just don' gimme a chance, the caards are stacked against me, it's the goddam breaks I just never get them. I work my ass off at the club, and what does it get me?

He sits down on a bench, and looks at the water languidly flowing. The lights from the Harvard Houses are reflecting in it. Work your ass off, work, work, work, and who the hell gives a damn, you're just stuck, if I'd had some big dough she'da been waitin' around for me, and with her legs ready to spread too, I bet she ran off with some

270

Jewboy who's got the dough. I don't know, they always grab all the money, grab, grab, grab, you'd think that was all there was in life. Disgusting.

Two Harvard undergraduates pass, and he stiffens in momentary panic. I wonder if I can sit here. Jesus, I shouldn'ta sat down.

I just held my breath, I tell you, that extension of Markova's was the most superbly terrifying thing I have ever seen, it was, oh, simple and subtle and just tremendous, terriFYING, absolutely terrifying.

Coupla fairies, what kind of crap was that, talkin' like a bunch of women. He turns around and looks at the lights in the Harvard buildings. Somebody ought to wipe out all those mother-fuggers. He watches the automobiles speeding past on Memorial Drive. Go ahead, hit the gas, hit it, hit it, go as fast as you goddam please, and break your goddam necks. That Harvard, goddam lefty outfit, somebody ought to blow up the fuggin place, work your ass off so some of those goddam fairies can sit around and act like women, life of Riley, how do they rate it, aah, the caards are never shuffled right, I'd like to kill every one of the mother-fuggers, there ought to be a man to take care of them, somebody ought to drop a bomb.

He sits on the bench for over an hour, calms at last. The river languishes by, stippled and quivering like the play of light on a metallic cloth. Across from him, the dormitories of the business school lance their reflections into the water, and the automobiles in the distance seem tiny and alive. He feels the earth under him germinating in the spring night, the sweet assuasive air. In the sky the stars are studded in the warm intimate velvet of the night.

Jeez, it's beautiful out. A play of yearnings, lost and never articulate. Makes ya think. He sighs. Real beautiful, makes ya think. The woman with whom he could share this. I'm gonna be something.

Awe. Night like this makes you know there's a God, dumb atheists. Jeez, it's beautiful, really beautiful, it makes ya think things are gonna be okay.

He sits there, absorbed in the night. I ain't like the other guys, theah's somethin' special in me. He sighs again. Boy, to . . . to . . . He fumbles for his thought as though his hand were groping for a fish in the water. Jeez to . . .

271

Roy, you're okay with us, I don't have to tell ya that, you know that we're gonna be givin' ya somethin' special real soon, and to show what the boys think of ya, we got a little outfit you're gonna be working with for a while, it ain't tied up to us exactly [Macnamara moves his hand deprecatingly] but mentioning no names theah's a couple of the big boys kinda like the way they work against the international plot, you know the one the rich kikes got all figured out to bring us communism.

On the payroll at ten dollars a week even though he is only working nights. The office is on the top of a two-story loft, a desk and a room filled with pamphlets and magazines tied in bundles. Behind the desk there is a large banner with a cross and an interlocking C and U.

Christians United, that's the name of this here outfit, Gallagheh, *CHRISTIANS . . . UNITED,* you get it, we're out to break the goddam conspiracy, what this country needs is some blood, y'afraid of blood? the big guy behind the desk asks. He has pale-brown eyes like panes of dull glass. We gotta staart mobilizing and get ready, the International Jews is tryin' to get us to war, an' we gotta get them first, ya see the way they take away all the jobs, we let it go an' we won't have a fuggin chance, they're high up but we got our friends too.

He sells magazines on street corners (READ ABOUT THE BIG FOREIGN PLOT! GET FATHER KILIAN'S MAGAZINE AND LEARN THE TRUTH!), he goes to secret meetings, drills for an hour a week in a sporting club which uses old Springfields.

What I wanta know is when we gonna staart, I wanta see some action.

Y' got to take it easy, Gallagheh, it takes time, we gotta get everything set up and then we can come out in the open, we're gonna get this country run right, you come in with us at the bottom and you're in.

Yeah. (At night sometimes he cannot sleep, the thick lusting dreams, the quick ache in his chest.) I swear I'm gonna bust up if we don't . . . we don't get goin'.

But . . .

272

The girl friend at last, the hormones no longer distilled into vinegar.

You know, Gallagher says to Mary, you're really a swell kid, I ... I get a bang outa talkin' to ya.

This is a swell night, Roy. (Looking off across the beach, searching the lights of Boston Harbor, which flicker like star formations in an uncertain clouded sky. She picks up a handful of sand, and pours it on her shoe, the glare from the bonfire making her hair seem golden. Her slim long face, freckled and sad, seems pleasant, almost lovely.)

Ya want me to toast a hot dog?

Let's just talk, Roy.

Around them, the couples with whom they have come have deserted the fire and are giggling in the shadowed hollows of the beach. A girl screams in mock fright, and he strains at the noise; uncomfortable, he thinks he hears the liquid slapping sounds of love.

Yeah, it's been a swell night, he repeats. He wonders if he can make love to her, and becomes suddenly shy. (She ain't like that, she's the pure kind, a good religious girl.) He feels guilty with his desire.

There's lots of things I'd like to talk to you about.

Sure, Roy.

Well, you know, we been goin' out for a coupla months, you know, what do ya think of me? He flushes at the crudeness of it, at the part of his mind that hopes for a physical issue. (The giggles become louder on the beach.) I mean do ya like me?

I think you're really swell, Roy, you know you are a gentleman, you're not fresh like all the other fellows.

Oh, yeah. He is disappointed, vaguely humiliated, and yet he generates some pride. I got other things on my mind.

I know, you always seem to be thinking, you know, Roy, I never know what's going on in your head, and I'd like to know because I think you're different.

How?

Well, you're shy, I don't mean shy but you're nice.

You should heah me talkin' to the guys. (They laugh.)

Oh, I believe you're just the same with them, you wouldn't be any different. (Her hand drops abstractedly on his knee, and she jerks it away with embarrassment.) I wish you'd go to church more often.

I go pretty regularly.

Yes, but there's something bothering you, I wonder about it, you're a mystery.

Yeah? He is pleased.

Roy, you always seem so angry about something, it worries me. My father was talking about you, and he said you're in Christians United, I don't know anything about politics, but I know one of them, Jackie Evans, was a nasty kid.

Aw, he's all right, it's just something with the club, you know they were tryin' me out, but it's nothin' much.

I wouldn't want you to get in trouble.

Why?

(She looks at him, her eyes passive and calm. This time she puts her hand on his arm.) You know why, Roy.

His throat is tense and his chest aches with warmth and hunger. He shivers as he hears the girl giggling again. This is swell out here at City Point, he says. (The thick lusting dreams at night for he knows not what.) I'll tell ya, Mary, if I was goin' steady — his voice is strong with his sense of renunciation — I wouldn' be hangin' around with them so much, 'cause you know I'd be wantin' to see more of you.

You would?

He listens to the lapping of the surf. I love ya, Mary, he says suddenly, holding himself stiff and cold, troubled delicately by a passing uncertainty.

I think I do too, Roy.

Yeah. After a while he kisses her gently, then hungrily, but a corner of his mind has retreated and become cold. Oh, I love ya, kid, he says huskily, trying to cauterize the doubt. His eyes stare away.

City Point is so beautiful, she says.

In the night they cannot see the garbage that litters the beach, the seaweed and driftwood, the condoms that wallow sluggishly on the foam's edge, discarded on the shore like the minuscule loathsome animals of the sea.

274

Yeah, it's something, he says slowly.

Hey, theah, Roy, how's the old married man, how's it feel gettin'
it steady, what do ya say?

Aw, it's okay. (He shivers in the September dawn that lifts
bleakly over the gray stone pavement and the slatternly wooden
houses.) Jesus, it's cold out, I wish the goddam polls'd open.

I'm glad you're with me today, Roy, you know we think you're
all right, but we ain't seen much of ya.

Aaah, well, I quit the CU, he mumbles, and I thought maybe the
boys were you know not so glad to see me.

Well, ya shoulda told 'em, but between you an' me, the club is
gonna lay off 'em for a while, started gettin' pressure from on top,
clear out of the state I heard. It always pays to stick with the club, you
don't go wrong that way, I bet if you hadn't been with the CU you
woulda been the election captain here today, I hope there's no hahd
feelin's, Roy.

Naw. (He feels a dull resentment. Back wheah I staarted.) I bet
some of those rich kikes in the party are the ones that creamed the CU.

Might have been.

The wife wanted me to quit 'em.

How is she?

Okay. (He thinks of her sleeping now, hears the rough surprisingly male heartiness of her snoring.)

Married life gone okay with ya? What're ya doin' now?

Yeah, it's fine. I'm drivin' a truck . . . like my old man. (Mary
has bought a lace cover for the table.)

Listen, these Reds who are runnin' M'Gillis, aw, M'Gillis a
Black Irishman if there ever was one, imagine a guy givin' up his religion, well, anyway the big boys ain't worryin' about him for the
primaries, but theah's a bunch of union men in this district and Mac
says we got to make a good showing right here so they won't be build-
in' up.

We bringin' over any repeatehs? Gallagher asks.

Yeah, but I got me own little idea. (He removes several bottles of
ketchup from a paper bag, and begins to pour them on the sidewalk.)

275

What are ya doin'?

Oh, this is neat, this is gonna take the cake. That's good, get it. You stand here and give out the pamphlets for Haney, and give 'em a spiel with it, we can't miss.

Yeah, that's a good one. (Why didn't I think of it?) Your idea?

All mine, Mac was really tickled when I told him, he called up Nolan who's the saargeant for the two bulls in this poll, and they ain't gonna cause us no trouble.

Gallagher stands by the ketchup, and begins to talk as the first voters get in line for the polls. TAKE A LOOK, SEE WHAT HAPPENS. THIS IS BLOOD, THIS IS WHAT HAPPENS TO DECENT AMERICANS WHEN THEY TRY TO VOTE AGAINST A RED. THEY GET BEAT UP BY THE FOREIGNERS THAT ARE BEHIND M'GILLIS. THIS IS M'GILLIS'S WORK, BLOOD, HUMAN BLOOD.

During a lull he examines the ketchup, which seems too red. He sprinkles a little dirt on it. (Work and work and then some smart guy gets a bright idea and gets all the credit, those goddam Reds, they're causin' me all the trouble.)

HERE Y'ARE, TAKE A LOOK, he shouts as some voters approach.

Where you goin', Roy? Mary asks. Her voice has a whining nagging quality and he turns in the door, and shakes his head. I'm just goin' out. She cuts her boiled potato in half, and puts a big portion in her mouth. A few flakes of potato stick to her lip, which angers him. Don't ya ever eat anythin' but potatoes? he asks.

Roy, we have meat.

Yeah, I know. Questions tug at his mind. He wants to ask her why she never eats with him at night, but always serves him first; he wants to tell her that he doesn't like to be asked where he is going.

You're not going to be at a CU meeting, are ya? she asks.

What do you care? (Why don't you ever put a dress over that slip?)

Roy, you're going to get in trouble there, I don't like those men,

276

you're only going to hurt yourself at the club, you know now the war's on they have nothing to do with them.

There's nothing wrong with the CU. Leave me alone, goddammit.

Roy, don't swear.

He slams the door, and walks into the night. It is snowing a little, and at the street corners his shoes crunch icily through the slush. He sneezes once or twice. A man's gotta get out and have some . . . some relaxation. Y'get some ideals to fight for in the organization and a woman wants to stop ya. I'm gonna be up there someday.

In the meeting hall, the air is hot and metallic from the heaters, and the smell of wet clothing is sour. He grits a cigarette butt into powder with his foot.

All right, we're in a war, men, the speaker says, we gotta fight for the country, but we don't want to be forgettin' our private enemies. He pounds the speaker's table over which a flag with a cross is spread. There's the foreign element we got to get rid of, that are conspiring to take over the country. There are cheers from the hundred men seated in camp chairs. We gotta stick together, or we'll be havin' our women raped, and the Red Hammer of Red Jew Fascist Russia WILL BE SMASHING YOUR DOOR DOWN.

That's tellin' him, the man next to Gallagher says.

Yeah, Wat's okay. Gallagher feels a pleasurable fury forming in him.

Who takes away your jobs, who tries to sneak up on your wives and your daughters and even your mothers 'cause they wouldn't stop at nothing, who's out to get YOU and YOU 'cause you ain't a Red and a Jew, and you don' wanta bow down before a filthy goddam no-good Communist who don't respect the Lord's name, and would stop at nothing.

Let's kill them! Gallagher shrieks. He is shaking with excitement.

That's it, men, we're gonna clean up on 'em, after the war we're really gonna have an organization, I got telegrams here from our com-*pat*-riots, patriots as well as friends, and they're all stickin' with us. You're all in on the ground floor, men, and those of ya that are goin'

into the Army gotta learn to use your weapons so that afterward . . .
afterward . . . You get the idea, men. We ain't licked, we're gettin'
bigger all the time.

When the meeting is over, Gallagher drifts into a bar. The dry
throat, the painful tension in his chest. As he drinks, his rage diffuses
and he grows sullen and bitter.

They're always cheatin' ya at the last minute, he says to the man
beside him. They had come out of the meeting together.

It's a plot.

That's all it is, it's a goddam mother-fuggin plot, and they ain't
gonna break me, I'm gonna get out on top.

On the way home he slips in a puddle, and wets his pant leg up
to his hip. Fug you, he roars at the pavement. Plot, always fuggin a
guy, well, you ain't gonna get me.

He lurches into his flat, and pitches off his overcoat. His nose is
bitter. He sneezes raspingly, and swears to himself.

Mary wakes up in her chair, and looks at him. You're all wet.

That all you got to say? I'm . . . I'm . . . what the hell do you
know about it?

Roy, every time you come back you're like this.

Trying to keep a man down, all you're interested in is the goddam dough I bring back, well, I'LL GIVE YOU ALL THE DOUGH
YOU WANT.

Roy, don't talk to me like that. Her lip wavers.

Staaart crying, go ahead, staaart crying, I'm on to you.

I'm going to bed.

C'mere.

Roy, I'm not going to hold it against you, I don't know what's
the matter with you, but there's something in you I just don't understand, what do you want of me?

Lea' me alone.

Oh, Roy, you're wet, take off your pants, honey, why do you
drink, it always makes you so bitter, I've been praying for you, honest
I have.

Oh, lea' me alone. He sits by himself for a few minutes staring
at the lace doily on the table. Aaah, I don' know, I don' know.

278

What's in it for a guy?

Work tomorrow.

(He would defend the lady in the lavender dress with his sword.)

He fell asleep in the chair, and in the morning he had a cold.

10

GALLAGHER'S numbness continued. In the days that followed the news of Mary's death he worked furiously on the road, shoveling without pause in the drainage ditches, and chopping down tree after tree whenever they had to lay a corduroy. He would rarely halt in the breaks they were given every hour, and at night he would eat his supper alone and curl into his blankets, sleeping exhaustedly with his knees near his chin. Wilson would hear him shuddering in the middle of the night, and would throw his blanket over him, clucking to himself at the misery Gallagher was undergoing. Gallagher showed no sign of his grief except that he became even leaner and his eyes and eyelids were swollen as if he had been on a long drinking bout or had played poker for forty-eight hours at a stretch.

The men tried to feel sorry for him, but the event had given a variation to the monotonous sweep of their days on the road. For a short time they sustained a quiet compassion when he was near and spoke in soft voices, uncomfortable in his presence. They ended by feeling merely uncomfortable and were resentful when he sat by them, for it inhibited their speech and made them acutely uneasy. Red felt a little shame and brooded over it one night on guard, deciding there was nothing he could do about it. It's tough, but I can't change it. He looked off into the night and shrugged. To hell with it, it's Gallagher's bloody nose, not mine.

The mail began to come in almost daily, and a frightening thing happened. Gallagher continued to receive letters from his wife. The first one came a few days after Father Leary had told him about her death; it had been mailed almost a month before. Wilson collected the

279

letters for the platoon that night from the orderly room, and he debated whether to give it to Gallagher. "It's gonna make him feel mighty funny," he said to Croft.

Croft shrugged. "You can't tell. He may want it." Croft was curious to see what happened.

Wilson's voice was casual when he gave it to Gallagher. "Some mail for ya, boy." He felt embarrassed and looked away.

Gallagher's face whitened as he gazed at the letter. "That ain't for me," he muttered. "Some mistake."

"It's your letter, boy." Wilson put an arm on his shoulder, and Gallagher shook it off. "You want me to throw it away?" Wilson asked.

Gallagher looked at the date on the envelope. He shivered a little. "No, give it to me," he blurted. He walked away a few yards and ripped it open. The words were indistinguishable to him, and he could not read it. He began to tremble. Holy Mary, Joseph and Jesus, he said to himself. His eyes were able to focus on a few lines, and their meaning seeped into his mind. "I been worrying about you, Roy, you're allways so angrie about everthing, and I pray for your safety every night. I love you so much when I think of the baby, only sometimes I can't beleive that its going to come so soon. Only three weeks now, the doctor said." Gallagher folded the letter, and walked around blindly. The purple lump on his jawbone twitched dully. "Oh, Christ Saviour," he said aloud. He began to tremble again.

Gallagher could not accept Mary's death. At night, on guard, he would catch himself thinking of his return, and he would imagine what it would be like with Mary to greet him. A dull despair would settle on him, and he would say automatically, She's dead, she's dead, but he did not believe it completely. He had numbed himself.

Now, as the letters from Mary kept coming every few days, he began to believe that she was alive. If someone had asked him about his wife, he would have said, She died, but nevertheless he was thinking about her the way he always had. When she would say that the child was due in ten days, he would count off the time and pick the date that fell ten days after he read the letter. If she told him that she had visited her mother the preceding day, he would think, That was about the time yesterday we were eating chow. For months he had known of her life only through her letters and the habit was too deep for him to break now. He began to feel happy; he looked forward to her letters as he always had done, and he would think about them at night before he fell asleep.

After a few days, however, he came to a terrifying realization. The date for her confinement was approaching closer and closer, and finally there would come a last letter and she would be dead. There would be nothing more of her. He would never hear from her again. Gallagher varied between panic and disbelief; there were times when he believed completely and simply that she was alive — the interview with the chaplain was part of a dream. But sometimes, when several days went by without a letter, she became remote, and he realized that he would never see her again. Most of the time, however, the letters moved him superstitiously; he began to think that she had not died but that she was going to, unless he could find some way to prevent it. The chaplain had asked him several times if he wanted a furlough, but he was incapable of considering that; it would have made him admit the thing he did not want to believe.

In contrast to the first frenzy with which he had worked, he began to wander away from the details, and go for long walks by himself along the road. He was warned several times that some Japanese might be waiting in ambush but he was unable to worry about that. Once he walked all the way back to the bivouac area, a distance of seven miles. The men thought he was going mad; occasionally they would discuss him at night, and Croft would say, "That boy's goin' to flip his lid." They felt helpless; they had no idea of what they could say to him. Red suggested they didn't give him any more letters, but the other men were afraid to meddle. They felt the awe and absorption they would have known at watching any process which was inevitable. Gallagher no longer embarrassed them; they would study him morbidly as they might stare at a sick man who they knew had not much time to live.

The mail clerk was told about it and he went to see the chaplain, who spoke to Gallagher. But when Father Leary suggested that it might be best if he didn't receive any more of the letters, Gallagher pleaded with him, and muttered, "She's gonna die if you take the letters away." The chaplain did not understand his words, but he recognized the intensity of Gallagher's feeling. He was disturbed, and he debated with himself whether to recommend that Gallagher be sent to a hospital, but he had a horror of mental wards and a prejudice against them. Secretly he made out an application for a furlough for Gallagher, but it was refused by Base Headquarters, who notified him that the Red Cross had investigated and the child was being cared for by Mary's parents. He ended by watching Gallagher too.

And Gallagher wandered around, absorbed in things he did not talk about, and the men would see him smile occasionally at some secret knowledge he held. His eyes had become redder, and his eyelids looked raw and angry. He began to have nightmares, and Wilson was awakened one night by Gallagher moaning, "Please, God, you can't let her die, I'll be a good guy, I swear I'll be a good guy." Wilson shuddered, and clapped his hand over Gallagher's mouth. "You're havin' a nightmare, boy," he whispered.

"Okay." Gallagher was silent, and Wilson decided to say something about it to Croft the next day, but in the morning Gallagher was solemn and quiet and he worked very hard on the road. Wilson kept his mouth shut.

A day or two later the platoon was sent down to the beach on an unloading detail. Gallagher had received the final letter from his wife the preceding night and he had been trying to rouse enough courage to read it. He was moody and abstracted; he paid no attention to the conversation of the men in the truck, and soon after they came to the beach he wandered off by himself. They had been unloading crates of rations from a landing craft, and the dead weight of the box on his shoulder had irritated him dully. He dropped the load he was carrying, muttered, "Fug it," and began to walk away.

Croft shouted after him, "Where you going?"

"I don't know, I'll be back." He spoke without looking over his shoulder, and then as if to forestall any more questions, he began to jog through the sand. After he had gone a hundred yards, he felt suddenly tired, and he slowed to a walk. At a turn on the beach, he looked back disinterestedly at the men. There were several landing craft riding against the shore with their motors running, and two columns of men were filing between the supply dump and the boats. A haze was spreading over the sea almost obscuring the few freighters riding at anchor offshore. He walked around the bend, and saw a few squad tents just off the beach. The flaps were rolled and he could see several men lying on cots and talking to each other. Dully, he read the sign, "5279 Quartermaster Trucking Company." He sighed and continued to walk. Goddam quartermaster's got all the breaks, he told himself, but without any real bitterness.

He passed by the strip of beach where Hennessey had been killed. It roused a mood of pity, and he halted to sift a handful of sand through his fingers. "Young kid, didn't even know what the fuggin score was," he thought. He remembered abruptly that when they had picked Hennessey up to move him farther away from the water, his helmet had fallen off. It had landed with a dull grating sound, and it spun once with a gritty noise in the sand. Guy's dead, and that's all he gets. He began to tremble as he remembered the letter in his shirt pocket. He had taken one look at the date, and he had known it would be the last one he would ever get. Maybe she wrote another one, he thought, and kicked some sand. He sat down, looked about him with the suspicious attitude of an animal about to eat in its lair, and then ripped open the flap. The sound tore at his nerves; he was beginning to feel the finality of each of his motions now. Abruptly, he realized the irony of pitying Hennessey. "I got my own fuggin troubles," he muttered. The sheets of paper felt pitifully flimsy in his hands.

He reread the last paragraph when he had finished. "Roy, honey, this'll be the last letter I'll write for a coupel of days, the pain started just a little while ago, and Jamie went down to get Dr Newcome. I'm awful scared cawse he said I'm going to have a hard time, but dont worrie cawse everything will be alright, I know it. I wish you could be with me, you got to take awful good care of youeself cawse I would be afraide to be alone. I love you so much, honey."

He folded the letter and put it back in his pocket. He felt a dull ache, his forehead was burning. For several minutes he did not think of anything at all, and then he spat bitterly. Aaah, the fuggin women, that's all they know, love, I love you, honey, just want to hold a man down. He trembled again; he was remembering the frustrations and annoyances of his marriage for the first time in many months. All a woman wants is to get a man and then she goes to pot, to hell with it all. He was thinking of how wan Mary looked in the morning, and how the left side of her jaw would swell in sleep. Incidents, unpleasant fragments of their life churned turgidly in his brain like a pot of thick stew coming to a boil. She used to wear a tight hair net in the house, and always of course her habit of sitting around in a slip which had a frayed edge. Worst of all was something he had never quite admitted to himself; the walls of the bathroom were thin and he could hear the sounds she made. She had faded in the three years they had been married. She didn't take the right care of herself, he thought bitterly. At this moment he hated the memory of her, hated the suffering she had caused him in the past few weeks. Always that love-dove stuff, and they don't give a fug how they look. He spat again. Don't even have any . . . any manners. He meant "modesty." Gallagher thought of Mary's mother, who was fat and very dowdy and he felt an inarticulate rage at a variety of things — at the very fact that she was so immense, at the lack of money that had made him live in a tiny drab apartment, at all the breaks he had never got, because his wife in dying had caused him so much pain. Never get a goddam thing. He thought of Hennessey and his mouth tightened. Get your head blown off . . . for what, for what? He lit a cigarette, and tossed the match away, looking at where it fell in the sand. Goddam Yids, fight a war for them. He thought of Goldstein. Bunch of fug-ups, lose a goddam gun, won't even take a drink when it's free. He lurched to his feet, and began to walk again. A dull pain and hatred beat through his head.

On the beach giant kelp had washed ashore, and he walked down to the water's edge and looked at it. It was dark brown and very long, perhaps fifty feet, and its dark rubbery skin glistened like snakes, and gave him a jolt of horror. He was remembering the bodies in the cave. "What drunken bastards we were," he said. He was remorseful, or more correctly he generated remorse in himself because he felt he had done something bad. The kelp frightened him — he walked away.

After a few hundred yards, he sat down on the top of a dune which looked out to sea. A storm was coming up, and he felt suddenly cold; a great cloud perhaps thirty miles long, shaped like a flat fish and very dark, had covered most of the sky. A wind had sprung up and was lashing the sand in horizontal sheets along the beach. Gallagher sat there and waited for the rain that did not come. He was feeling pleasurably moody, he was enjoying the barrenness and brooding of the scene, the remote froth of the waves against the shore. Without quite realizing it, he began to draw a woman in the sand. She had great breasts and a narrow waist and very wide full hips. He looked at it soberly, and remembered that Mary was very ashamed of her tiny breasts. She had once said, "I wish they were big."

"Why?"

"I know you like them better that way."

He had lied. "Naw, they're just right the way they are."

An eddy of tenderness wound through him. She had been very small, and he thought of how she had seemed like a little girl to him at times, and how he had been amused at her seriousness. He laughed softly, and then abruptly, with no defenses raised, he realized that she was utterly dead and he would never see her any more. The knowledge flowed through him without resistance, like a torrent of water when a floodgate is lowered. He heard himself sob, and then was no longer conscious of the choking sounds of his anguish. He felt only a vast grief which mellowed him, dissolved the cysts of his bitterness and resentment and fear, and left him spent and weeping on the sand. The softer gentler memories of Mary were coming back to him; he recalled the sweltering liquid rhythms of their bodies against each other in heat and love, he felt dumbly the meaning of her smile when she handed him his lunch box as he went to work in the morning; he recalled the sad clinging tenderness they had felt for each other on the last night of his last furlough before he went overseas. They had gone on a moonlight excursion in Boston Harbor and he remembered with a pang how they had sat silently in the stern of the ship, holding each other's hands, and watching with a tender absorbed silence the turbulence of the wake. She was a good girl, he said to himself. He was thinking without quite phrasing it that no other person had ever understood him so fully, and he felt a secret relief as he realized that she had understood him and still loved him. This opened again the wound of all his loss, and he lay weeping bitterly for many minutes, unconscious of where he was, feeling nothing but the complete sorrow in his body. He would think of the last letter every now and then, and this would send him off into a new spasm of grief. He must have cried for almost an hour.

At last he was spent, and he felt clean and gentle. For the first time he remembered that he had a child, and he wondered what it looked like and what its sex might be. It gave him a delicate joy for an instant, and he thought, If it's a boy, I'm gonna train him early. He'll be a pro baseball player, that's where the money is. His thoughts eddied away, and his mind became rested and empty. He looked moodily at the dense jungle behind him, and wondered how far he would have to walk back. The wind was still sweeping along the beach, and his emotions became vague and shifted about like vapors. He was sad again and thought of cold and lonely things like wind on a winter beach.

It was a shame such a misfortune had to come to Gallagher, Roth thought. The men had taken an hour break from the unloading detail to eat their K rations, and Roth had gone for a stroll along the beach. He was thinking now of the way Gallagher had looked when he came back from his walk. His eyes had been very red, and Roth decided he had been crying. Still, he takes it well, Roth sighed to himself. He's an ignorant fellow, no education, he probably doesn't have so many feelings. Roth shook his head and continued to trudge through the sand. Absorbed in thought, his chin rested almost on his chest and it emphasized the misshapen humped appearance of his back.

The great rain cloud that had spread over them that morning had blown away and the sun was very hot on his green fatigue cap. He stopped, and mopped his forehead. This tropical weather is uncertain, he told himself, very unhealthy, it's miasmal. His legs and arms ached from the labor of carrying the boxes from the boat to the dump, and he sighed. I'm too old for this kind of thing. It's all right for someone like Wilson or Ridges or even Goldstein, but it's not for me. A wry smile played over his mouth. I figured that Goldstein out wrong, he said to himself, for his height he's built very well, he's a strong fellow, but he's changed, I don't know what's the matter with him. He's very gloomy all the time, he's got a chip on his shoulder. There's been something the matter with him ever since that first squad came back from the front; it's the combat, I suppose, it makes changes in a man. But when I first met him he was such a cheerful fellow, a regular Pollyanna, I figured he could get along with anyone. First impressions, it doesn't pay to follow them. Someone like Brown, he's too sure of himself, he goes on first impressions, that's why he has it in for me. Just because I stayed on guard too long one night; if I'd tried to cut off a few minutes for myself, then he'd have a case, but this way I think he just has it in for me.

Roth rubbed his nose and sighed. I could be friends with them but what do I have in common? They don't understand me and I don't understand them. To pal around you have to have a species of confidence I don't possess. If it hadn't been the depression when I got out of college . . . But what's the use of kidding myself, I'm not the aggressive type, I never would have been much of a success. You can kid yourself just so long. I can see it here in the Army, all they know is that I can't do as much manual labor as they can so they look down on me. They don't know what goes on inside my head, they don't care. What are finer thoughts to them, intellect? If they'd let me I could be a good friend to them, I'm mature. I've had experience, there're things I could tell them, but would they listen to me? Roth clicked his tongue in frustration. It's always been this way with me. Still, if I could get a job which fitted my qualifications, I could make a success of myself.

He passed by the strip of beach where the kelp had washed ashore, and curious, he went over to examine it. Giant kelp, I should know something about that, it was my major only I've forgotten it all. The thought made him bitter. What's the use of all that education, when you can't even remember it? He looked down at the kelp, and held the head of one in his hand. It looks like a snake. Such a simple organism. It's got an anchor in its tail where it fastens onto a rock, and it's got a mouth at the top, and a connection between them. What could be simpler? A basic organism, brown algae, that's what it is, if I

287

were to try it would all come back to me. Macrocystis something, that's what it was called, common name Devil's Shoelace, or is that something else? Macrocystis pyrifera, I remember we had a lecture on it. Maybe I should do something with my botany yet, it's only twelve years since I had it, I could refresh my memory and there'll be better jobs now in that. It's a fascinating subject.

He dropped the head of the kelp. That's an unusual plant, I wish I could remember more about it. All those marine plants are well worth studying, plankton, green algae, brown algae, red algae, I'm surprised at how much I remember. I'll have to write Dora and ask her if she can find my botany notebooks, maybe I should start studying it again.

He walked back, examining the seaweed and driftwood along the beach. All dead things, he thought, everything lives to die. Already I can feel it, I'm getting older, thirty-four, I'm probably through half my life already and what do I have to show for it? There's a Yiddish word for it, Goldstein would know. Still I'm not sorry I never learned any Yiddish, it's better to have modern folks the way I did.

Oh, my shoulder aches, why don't they ever leave us alone for a day? In the distance Roth could see the men, and he felt a pinch of anxiety. Oh, they're all working again. They're all going to be making cracks and what can I tell them, that I was looking at some kelp? They wouldn't understand. Why didn't I think of coming back sooner?

Wearily, timorously, Roth began to run.

"What are you . . . Si*cill?*" Polack asked Minetta. They were trudging along together through the sand. Minetta with a grunt dropped his ration box on a new pile they were starting. "No, Ven-*eetz*," he said. "My grandfather was a big shot, you know, an aristocrat near Venice." They turned around to go back to the landing craft. "How do you know that stuff?" Minetta asked Polack.

"Aaah, what do ya t'ink?" Polack said. "I lived with a bunch of dagoes. I know more about 'em than you do."

"No, you don't," Minetta said. "Listen, I wouldn't tell anybody this, 'cause you know how guys are, they'll think you're handing them a line of crap, but you can believe me, this is the truth, honest. We were really society, nobility, back in the old country. My father never did a day's work in his life, all he'd ever do was go hunting. We had a regular estate."

"Yeah."

"You think I'm kidding you. Look, look at me. You see, I don't look like an Italian, I got light-brown hair and light skin. You ought to see the rest of my family, they're all blond, I'm the black sheep. That's how you tell the aristocrats, they got light complexions. This town we come from is named after one of my ancestors, the Duke of Minetta."

Polack sat down. "What're we breaking our asses for, let's take it easy."

Minetta continued talking eagerly. "Listen, I know you don't believe me, but you ever get to New York and look me up, I'll show you some of the family medals. My father's always taking them out to show us. My aching back, he's got a whole boxful of them."

Croft passed by them, and called over his shoulder. "All right, troopers, let's quit fuggin the dog."

Polack sighed and got to his feet. "I'll tell you what, there ain't no future in this. What's it to Croft if we take it easy?"

"That guy is stripe-happy," Minetta said.

"They're all that way," Polack answered. He pronounced "that" as "dat."

Minetta nodded. "Jus' let me meet up with one of those guys after the war."

"What'll you do, buy Croft a drink?"

"You think I'm scared of him?" Minetta said. "Listen, I been in the Golden Gloves, I ain't afraid of any of these guys." Polack's grin irritated him.

"The only guy you could take is Roth," Polack said.

"Aaah, fug you, there's no use talkin' to you."

"I'm too ignorant."

They lifted two boxes from the pile in the boat, and began to walk back to the supply dump. "Boy, I can't stand this," Minetta burst out angrily. "I'm losing all my ambition."

"Aaah."

"You think I'm just a fug-off, don't you?" Minetta asked. "You ought to seen me back when I was a civilian. I knew how to dress, I had an interest in life, I was always the leader in everything I did. I could be a noncom now if I wanted to buck for stripes, suck the way Stanley does, but it ain't worth it. You got your self-respect."

"What do ya get worked up for?" Polack asked. "You know I was makin' a hundred fifty a week, and I had my own car. I was in with Lefty Rizzo, but 'in.' There wasn't a dame in the world I couldn't make, models, actresses, good-lookin' twots. And all I'd work would be twenty hours a week, no, wait it was twenty-five, about four hours a night from five to nine, six nights a week, just collectin' the receipts from the numbers and turnin' them in. You hear me bitchin' now? Listen, it's all in the turn of the cards," Polack said, "all in the turn. The way to figure it is you're layin' low now, you're takin' it easy."

Polack was about twenty-one, Minetta figured. He wondered if he was lying about the money. It always made Minetta uncomfortable to realize that he never knew what went on in Polack's head, while Polack always seemed to guess what he was thinking about. Not knowing what to answer, he attacked Polack. "Just laying low, huh? You got in the Army 'cause you wanted to?"

"How do you know I couldn'ta stayed out?"

Minetta snorted. "I know it 'cause nobody who's got a brain in their head would go in unless they had to.". He dumped his box on top of some others, and started back to the boats. "You're out on a limb when you get stuck in the Army. They ain't a damn thing you can do if somethin' happens to ya. Look at Gallagher. Poor bastard's wife dies, and he's stuck out here."

Polack grinned. "You want to know why Gallagher feels bad?"

"I know."

"No, you don't. There was a cousin of mine whose wife got killed in an accident. Jesus, you shoulda seen the way he carried on. For what? For a dame? I tried to talk to him, I said to him, 'Listen, what the hell are you lettin' go all that water for? There's lots of dames. In six mont's you'll be shackin' up again an' you won't even remember what this one looked like.' He looks at me and starts bawl-in', 'Oh, oh, oh,' and I try to tell him again. So what does he say to me?'' Polack paused.

"All right, what?"

"He says, 'Six mont's hell, what am I gonna do for tonight?' "

In spite of himself, Minetta laughed. "You expect me to believe that?"

Polack shrugged, and picked up a box. "What do I care if ya believe it. I'm tellin' ya, that's all." He began to walk. "Hey, you know what time it is?"

"Two o'clock."

Polack sighed. "Two more hours of this crap." He trudged through the sand. "Wait, I'll tell ya about this dame that wrote a book," he said.

At three o'clock the platoon took its last break of the afternoon. Stanley sprawled out on the sand beside Brown and offered him a cigarette. "Go ahead, you might as well take one, I'm supporting you on cigarettes anyway."

Brown groaned, stretching his arms. "I'm getting old. I'll tell you what, a man can't do the kind of work he's capable of out in this tropical heat."

"Why don't you just admit you're goofing off?" A change had come about in Stanley's attitude toward Brown since he had made corporal. He no longer agreed with Brown completely, and he bantered with him much more frequently. "You'll be like Roth in another week," he said.

"Up yours."

"It's all right, sergeant, I'm on to you." Stanley had not noticed the change in himself. During the first months he had been in the platoon he had been painfully alert, he had never said anything without thinking or feeling what its purpose would be, he had selected his friendships with care, and he had felt his way through the filter of Brown's likes and dislikes. Without ever analyzing it carefully, he had subtly formed Brown's attitude toward men about whom Brown originally had not much opinion. In turn Stanley found it politic to like the men of whom Brown spoke approvingly. Yet he never phrased all this to himself; he knew he had wanted to make corporal, but he never admitted it to himself. He merely obeyed the hints and the anxieties that his mind generated in relation with Brown.

Brown had understood him, had laughed at him secretly, but Brown ended by recommending him for corporal. Without realizing it, Brown had found himself dependent on Stanley, warmed by his admiration and respect, by his complete interest in everything Brown had to say. Brown had always thought, Stanley's brown-nosing me, and I'm on to him, yet when Croft had talked to him about making a corporal, Brown had been unable to think of anyone but Stanley. There were objections to all the others; he had forgotten the source of his contempt for some of the other men they were considering, but it had been originated by Stanley. To his surprise, he had found himself praising Stanley to Croft.

Afterward, as Stanley grew accustomed to giving orders, the change became apparent. His voice developed authority, he began to bully the men who displeased him, and he approached Brown with easy familiarity. Again, without ever thinking of it articulately, he knew that Brown could not help him any longer; he would remain a corporal until one of the sergeants was wounded or killed. At first he had continued to show deference to Brown, continued to agree with him, but he had become conscious of his hypocrisy, a little uncomfortable with it. Now he noticed when Brown was obviously inaccurate. He began to state his own opinions. In time he had begun to boast.

Now Stanley exhaled leisurely, and repeated, "Yep, you're getting just like Roth." Brown made no answer, and Stanley spat. "I'll tell you something about that Roth," he said. His speech had become declarative like Brown's. "He really don't mean so bad, it's just he ain't got any guts. He's the kind of guy that always ends up a failure cause he ain't willing to take chances."

"Don't kid yourself, boy," Brown told him. "They ain't many men want to take chances when it's a case of stopping a bullet."

"Naw, I don't mean that," Stanley said. "You can see the way he was in civilian life. He wanted to get ahead just like you and me, but he didn't have the guts to stick to something. He was too cautious. You got to be a smart apple if you want to live big."

"What the hell'd you ever do?" Brown asked.

"I've taken my chances, and got away with them too."

Brown laughed. "Yeah, fugged a dame when her husband was out."

Stanley spat again. It was a habit he had assimilated from Croft. "I'm going to tell you something. Just after Ruthie and me got hitched, we had a chance to buy some furniture from a guy who was movin' out of the state, and it was one hell of a buy, only he wanted cash. I didn't have it, and my old man didn't have it just then. For about three hundred bucks we could get a whole living room that must have been worth a thousand new. You know, you invite people over, it makes an impression. What do you think I did, folded my hands, and said it's a shame, and let the thing go? Hell, no, I didn't. I took the money from the garage I was working at."

"What do ya mean ya took the money?"

"Oh, it wasn't so hard, if you watched the angles. I was the book-keeper there and we were taking in a thousand dollars a day in repairs. It was a big garage. I just took the money out of the till, and I held over to the next day the Work Completed slips on three cars which had repairs totaling up to the three hundred bucks. Those cars had gone out that afternoon, and I had to hold them over in the books so the receipts for that day on work completed and paid for wouldn't show a hole. Then the next day I checked them out in the books and held over another three C's worth."

"How long did ya do it for?" Brown asked.

"For two whole weeks, how do ya like that? There was a couple of days when we only had a couple of cars being paid for, and I was sweating blood 'cause by the time I took out the three hundred there wasn't much left. Of course I carried over the receipts from the day before that I didn't credit, but there was so few cars it would have showed up kind of funny if anyone had looked at the books that day."

"Well, how'd you get out of it?" Brown asked.

"This'll kill ya. After we bought the furniture I took out a loan for three hundred with that as security, and then I just slipped the three hundred back in a couple of days, and paid off the loan in monthly payments. But I had the furniture dirt-cheap. And maybe it didn't make some good impression on people. I never woulda had it, if I didn't take the chance."

"That was pretty good," Brown admitted. He was impressed; this was a facet of Stanley about which he had been ignorant.

"It took a lot to do it, I'll tell ya," Stanley said. He was remembering the nights he had lain awake worrying during those two weeks. He had suffered from any number of fears which attacked him in the night. His manipulations had become confused and impossible in the black hours of the morning; he would go over and over in his mind the changes he had made in the books and they would seem in error to him; he would become convinced he would be discovered the next day. He would try to concentrate, and find himself repeating an addition in his mind over and over again. "Eight plus thirty-five makes . . . makes . . . eight plus thirty-five makes three and carry one . . ." His stomach had become upset, and he could hardly eat any food. There would be times when he woud lie sweating in his bed, completely conquered by despair and anxiety. He wondered that everyone did not know what he was doing.

His love-making had suffered. He had been just eighteen when he married a few weeks before, and in his inexperience he had been inept, incapable of controlling himself. His love spasms had been quick and nervous; he had wept once or twice in his wife's arms at his failure. He had married so young because he was in love, but also because he had felt cocky and confident. People always told him that he looked old for his age, and he believed in gambling, in assuming burdens because he was confident of carrying them. He had bought the furniture for the same reason and, in his anxiety over that, the demands of his marriage had been overwhelming, and his failure in one had fed on his anxiety in the other.

After he replaced the money, his love-making became a little more accomplished but he always lacked a necessary confidence in it; unconsciously he had longed for the days before his marriage when he had necked with his wife for long passionate hours. Stanley, however, showed very little of this; he never told his wife just how the furniture was bought, and in their coupling he would feign great passion until he began to believe it himself. He had passed on from the garage to an accountant's office, where he worked as a clerk while he studied accounting in night school. He learned other ways of making money, and he conceived their child deliberately. He had new money worries, and more nights when he lay motionless and perspiring in his bed trying to see the ceiling in the darkness. But in the morning he would always be confident and the chances would seem worth the taking.

"It takes a lot for a guy to do it," he said again to Brown. The memories were uncomfortable, and yet they furnished him a deep pride. "If you want to get anywhere you got to know what the score is," he said.

"Yeah, you got to know who to suck," Brown reminded him.

"That's part of it," Stanley said coldly. Brown still had a few tools he could employ against him.

Stanley gazed at the men sprawled on the beach, looking for a better answer to give Brown. He noticed Croft stalking along the edge of the beach, searching the jungle, and he watched him.

"What's Croft up to?" he asked.

"He probably saw something," Brown said. He was getting to his feet. All about them the men in the platoon were beginning to stir like cattle turning their heads toward a new sound or smell.

"Aaah, Croft is always looking for something," Stanley grunted.

"There's something doing," Brown mumbled.

Just then Croft fired a burst into the jungle and dropped to the ground. The sound of the shots was unexpectedly loud and the men in the platoon winced, fell prostrate again in the sand. A Japanese rifle fired back, and the men began to fire indiscriminately into the jungle. Stanley found himself sweating so intensely that he could not focus the sights of his rifle. He lay there with his senses blurred, flinching unconsciously every time a bullet passed. It sounded like a bee humming past, and he thought with surprise, A guy can get hurt. He remembered immediately afterward the joke about that, and began to laugh weakly. Behind him, on the beach, he heard someone scream, and then the firing halted. There was a long uneasy silence

295

among the men, and Stanley watched the air rise shimmering off the sand.

At last Croft got cautiously to his feet, and darted into the jungle. At its edge he motioned for the men nearest him to approach, and Stanley stared at the sand and hoped Croft would not notice him. There was a pause, a wait of several minutes, and then Croft and Wilson and Martinez appeared from the brush, and came strolling back toward the beach.

"We got two of them," Croft said. "I don't think they was any others or they'd have left their packs when they took off." He spat onto the sand. "Who got hit?" he asked.

"Minetta did," Goldstein said. He was leaning over him, holding a first-aid compress against Minetta's leg.

"Let's see it," Croft said. He ripped away Minetta's trouser and gazed at the wound. "Just a scratch," he said.

Minetta moaned, "If you had it, you wouldn't say that."

Croft grinned. "You're gonna live, boy." He turned around and looked at the men in the platoon, who had gathered about him. "Goddammit," he said, "let's spread out. They may be some other Japs messin' around near here." The men were talking and chattering with a nervous profuse relief. Croft looked at his watch. "We only got about forty minutes till the truck come for us. Jus' spread out on the beach and keep your eyes open. We ain't gonna do any more unloadin'."

He turned to one of the landing-craft drivers standing beside him and asked, "You men on guard here at the dump at night?"

"Yeah."

"With those Japs I guess you'll stay awake tonight." Croft lit a cigarette, and walked over to Minetta again. "You'll have to stay here, boy, until the truck comes. Jus' hold that compress there, and nothin' is gonna happen to ya."

Stanley and Brown lay on their stomachs, talking to each other and looking at the jungle. Stanley was feeling very weak. He tried to ignore his panic but he kept thinking of how safe they had felt when there had been Japanese so near to them. You never know when you're safe, he muttered to himself. He felt an intense horror which he repressed with difficulty. All his nerves seemed to have come apart. He felt he would say something absurd in a moment or so, and he turned to Brown and uttered the first thought in his mind, "Wonder how Gallagher took it?"

"What do ya mean?"

"You know, the Japs being killed, and him thinking of his wife."

"Aaah," Brown said. "He didn't even connect it."

Stanley looked at Gallagher, who was talking quietly to Wilson. "He seems to be coming around," Stanley said.

Brown shrugged. "I feel sorry for the guy, but I'll tell you what, maybe he's lucky."

"You don't mean that."

"When you get rid of a woman, you never know when you're well off. I don't know Gallagher's wife, but he's not a big guy, he probably wasn't able to give her too much loving. Hell, they'll cheat on ya even when you do give 'em something to remember, so I wouldn't be too surprised if she had her little fling, especially in the first months when she knew the kid was coming and she wasn't taking any chances if she fooled around with anybody."

"That's all you ever think about," Stanley muttered. He hated Brown for a moment. Brown's contempt for women stroked the jealousy, the fear that Stanley usually was able to control. For a moment or two, he was half convinced his wife was cuckolding him, and though he flung off the idea, he sat there troubled and nervous.

"I'll tell ya something *I* think about," Brown said. "Just what happened right now. You're sitting around talkin' and *wham* something starts. You never know what's gonna hit ya. Y'think Minetta ain't scared now? He's learnin' what it's all about. Listen, I'll tell ya, they ain't gonna be a moment until I get back and touch my foot on the ground in the States before I stop believin' that I never know when I'm gonna get it. You stay over awhile and you're due, that's all."

Stanley felt a nameless anxiety rising in him. Dimly, he knew that part of it came from fearing death, really fearing it for the first time, but he knew that it also swelled out of everything he had been thinking about before the skirmish had begun. It fed upon his jealousy and his indifferent love-making, it came from the nights at home when he had been sleepless and frantic. For some reason he found it painful suddenly to think about Gallagher and the abrupt way in which his wife had died. You look out for everything, he thought, and you still get hit from behind. It's a trap. Stanley felt a deep malaise. He stared about him, listening to some artillery fire in the distance, and the anxiety increased, became almost painful for a moment. He was sweating, close to whimpering. The heat of the day, the glare of the sand, and the nervous fatigue from the action, had combined to drain him of any strength. He was weak and terrified, and he didn't understand. Outside of a few uneventful patrols, he had experienced no combat. Yet now he was feeling an intense loathing and fear at the thought of having any more. He wondered how he could lead men in combat when he was so terrified himself, and yet he knew that he had to get another stripe, and then another, that he would force himself to move up. There was something wrong, basically upset in himself at that moment, and he muttered to Brown, "Goddam heat makes a man weak." He sat there, sweating damply. A vague oppressive horror bothered him.

"You think you know all the angles, but you never do," Brown said. "Like before with that garage deal, you were lucky. You think we knew there were Japs? I'll tell ya, Stanley, it was the same with you there. How the hell did you know when something was gonna pop? It's the same with my old game, selling. There's tricks, there's ways to grab the big money, but you're never sure."

"Yeah," Stanley said. He was not really listening. Stanley was feeling a diffused rebellion at the things that made him worried and envious, made him always ferret for some advantage. He did not know what caused it in himself, but without putting it into words he was brooding that there would be many nights through all the rest of his life when he would lie sweating and restive, prey to all the latest torments of his mind.

THE CAMPAIGN had gone sour. After the week of successful advances that followed the failure of the Japanese attack across the river, Cummings had paused for a few days to strengthen his lines and complete his road net. It had been planned as a temporary halt before breaching the Toyaku Line, but the layoff was fatal. When Cummings started again, his tactics were as well conceived as they had ever been, his staff performances as thorough, his patrols as carefully planned, but nothing happened. The front had been given its first chance to solidify, and like a weary animal it had done even more; it had fallen asleep, it had hibernated. A deep and unshakable lethargy settled over the front-line troops.

In the two weeks that followed the rest period, after a series of intensive patrols and strong local attacks, his lines had advanced a total of four hundred yards in a few sectors, and had captured a total of three Japanese outposts. Companies went out on combat patrols, engaged in desultory fire fights, and then retreated back to their bivouacs. The few times an important piece of terrain was taken, the men had relinquished it at the first serious counterattack. As a sure sign of the reluctant temper of the troops, the best line officers were becoming casualties now, and Cummings knew the type of engagement that signified. An attack would be made on some strong point, and the men would lag behind, the co-ordination would be poor, and it would end with a few men, a few good officers and noncoms, engaging a superior force while their support evaporated.

Cummings made several trips to the front and found the men had bedded down. The bivouacs had been improved, there were drainage pits and overhead covers on the foxholes, and in a few companies duckwalks had been laid in the mud. The men would not have done this if they expected to move. It represented security and permanence, and it introduced a very dangerous change in their attitudes. Once they halted and stayed in one place long enough for it to assume familiar connotations, it was immeasurably harder to get them to fight again. They were dogs in their own kennel now, Cummings decided, and they would bark sullenly at orders.

Each day that elapsed without any fundamental change on the front would only increase their apathy, and yet Cummings knew that he was temporarily powerless. After intense preparation, he had mounted a large attack with good artillery plotting, some Air Corps bomber support which had been granted only after much pleading, had thrown his tanks into it, his reserve troops, and after a day the attack had ground down to nothing; the troops had halted before the most insignificant resistance, had gained in one small sector perhaps a quarter mile. When they had done and the losses been counted, the minor alterations in his front line established, he had all of the Toyaku Line still before him, unbreached, unthreatened. It was humiliating.

Indeed, it was terrifying. The communications from corps and army were growing progressively impatient. Soon, like a traffic jam, that pressure would be backed up all the way to Washington, and Cummings could imagine without difficulty the conversations that must be going on in certain rooms of the Pentagon. "Well, what's happening here, what's this, Anopopei, what's holding it up, whose division, Cummings, Cummings, well, get the man out of there, get someone else."

He had known it was dangerous to rest the troops for a week, but it was a gamble he had had to take while he finished the road, and it had boomeranged. The shock cut deeply into the General's confidence. The process at most times was unbelievable to him, and he was suffering the amazement and terror of a driver who finds his machine directing itself, starting and halting when *it* desires. He had heard of this, military lore was filled with such horror tales, but he had never imagined it would happen to him. It was incredible. For five weeks the troops had functioned like an extension of his own body. And now, apparently without cause, or at least through causes too intangible for him to discover, he had lost his sensitive control. No matter how he molded them now the men always collapsed into a sodden resistant mass like dishrags, too soft, too wet to hold any shape which might be given them. At night he would lie sleepless on his cot, suffering an almost unbearable frustration; there were times when he

300

was burning with the impotence of his rage. One night he had lain for hours like an epileptic emerging from a coma, his hands clasping and unclasping endlessly, his eyes staring fixedly at the dim outlines of the ridgepole of his tent. The power, the intensity of the urges within himself, inexpressible, balked, seemed to course through his limbs, beating in senseless fury against the confines of his body. There was everything he wanted to control, everything, and he could not direct even six thousand men. Even a single man had been able to balk him.

He had made furious efforts for a time, launched that attack, had kept the troops patrolling constantly, but deep inside himself, unadmitted, he was becoming frightened. A new attack on which he had had Major Dalleson and the G-3 staff working for days had been called off several times already. Always there had been good superficial reasons — a large shipment of supplies was due from a few Liberty ships in a day or two, or else he felt it more advisable to capture first some minor features of land which might seriously impede the attack. But actually he was afraid; failure now would be fatal. He had expended too much on that first attack, and if this one foundered, weeks and possibly months would accrue before a third major drive could be initiated. By that time he would be replaced.

His mind had become dangerously lassitudinous, and his body had been troubled for some time by a painful diarrhea. In an effort to scour his ailment he had had officers' mess suffer the most rigid inspections, but despite the new standards of cleanliness his diarrhea continued. It was acutely difficult now to conceal his annoyance with the most insignificant details, and it was affecting everything about him. Hot wet days sloughed past, and the officers in headquarters snapped at each other, had petty quarrels and cursed the unremitting heat and rain. Nothing seemed to move in all the cramped choked spaces of the jungle, and it developed an attitude in which no one expected anything to move. The division was going subtly and inevitably to pot, and he felt powerless to alter it.

Hearn suffered the results in all their immediacy. Without the disturbing and fascinating intimacy the General had granted him in his first weeks as an aide, the job had become reduced quickly to its onerous humiliating routine. A change had come about in their relationship, quietly achieved, but its end product left him in a formal and obviously subordinate status. The General no longer confided in him, no longer lectured him, and the duties of his job, which had been treated between them until now as a tacit joke, had become demanding and loathsome. As the campaign floundered along day after day, the General became stricter about the discipline in his headquarters, and Hearn suffered the brunt of it. Each morning Cummings made a point of inspecting his tent, and almost every time he delivered a criticism of the way Hearn had supervised the orderly. It was always a quiet rebuke, uttered slyly, with a sidewise glance at Hearn, but it was disturbing and finally harassing.

And there were other tasks, silly pointless ones which assumed a galling character after they had continued long enough. One time, almost two weeks after they had had their last long conversation on the night of the chess game, the General had stared at him blankly for a few seconds, and then had said, "Hearn, I think I'd like to have some fresh flowers in my tent each morning."

"Fresh flowers, sir?"

And the General had given his mocking grin. "Yes, it seems to me there're enough of them in the jungle. Suppose you just tell Clellan to collect a few each morning. Good God, man, it's a simple enough affair."

Simple enough, but it added a further tension between Clellan and himself, which Hearn detested. Despite himself, he paid greater attention to the way Clellan made up the General's tent each morning, and it became a humiliating duel between them. To his own surprise, Hearn discovered that the General was making him vulnerable; he was beginning to care that the tent was made up correctly. Each morning now he approached the General's tent with distaste, figuratively squared his shoulders, and then went in to continue his feud with Clellan.

Clellan had started it. A tall slim Southerner with a complete and insolent poise, a facility for never questioning himself, he had resented any of Hearn's suggestions from the very beginning. Hearn had ig-

302

nored him at first, amused a little by the proprietary concern with which Clellan regarded his work, but Hearn knew by now that he was contributing a little to the feud himself.

One morning they almost quarreled. Hearn entered the tent as Clellan was finishing his work, and he examined it while Clellan stood at the General's cot, his hands by his sides. Hearn prodded the bed, which was made very neatly, the extra blanket folded squarely at the foot, the pillow centered at the head with its ends tucked in. "Good job on that bed, Clellan," Hearn said.

"You think so, Lieutenant?" Clellan didn't move.

Hearn turned away and inspected the flaps of the fly-tent. They were tied neatly and evenly, and when he yanked at one of the tie cords the knot did not slip. He strode about the outside of the tent, examining the stakes. They were all in line, all slanted at the same angle — since there had been a heavy rain the night before, Hearn knew that Clellan had already straightened them. He walked back inside the tent, and looked at the board floor, which had been swept and washed. Clellan stared sullenly at Hearn's feet. "You're tracking it up, Lieutenant," he said.

Hearn stared at the muddy marks his shoes had left. "I'm sorry, Clellan," he said.

"It's a lot of work, Lieutenant."

Hearn's temper flared. "Clellan, you don't work so hard."

"Cain't say as any of us do," Clellan drawled.

Well, what the hell! All right, he had deserved that answer. Hearn turned away again, examined the map board. The cover was draped smoothly over it, and the red and blue pencils at its base had been sharpened and separated into their compartments. He walked about, opening the General's foot locker to see that his clothing was stacked tidily, sat down before the General's desk to open the drawers and inspect the insides. Searching for dust, he trailed his fingers under the ledge. Hearn grunted with distaste and stood up to inspect the rain ditch that ran around the tent. Clellan had already removed the silt from the night's rain, and the ditch was clean with new soil. Hearn stepped inside.

"Clellan," he said

"Yes?"

"Everything seems okay today except the flowers. You can change them."

"I'll tell you, Lieutenant," Clellan said flatly, "it don't seem to me as if the General cares much about having flowers."

Hearn shook his head. "Get them anyway."

Clellan remained still. "Yestiday, General said to me, 'Clellan, whose idea is those damn flowers anyway?' I told him I didn't know, but I said I 'spected it was yours."

"The General said that?" Hearn was amused and then furious. The sonofabitch! He lit a cigarette, and exhaled it slowly. "Suppose you change the flowers, Clellan. I happen to be the one who hears the complaints."

"Lieutenant, I pass the General maybe ten times a day. I reckon he'd say something to me if he figgered I wasn't doin' it right."

"You'll just have to take my word for it, Clellan."

Clellan pursed his lips, flushed a little. He was obviously angry. "Lieutenant, you just want to remember that the General's a man, he's no better than you or me, and there's no sense in being afraid of him."

That was about enough. He'd be damned if he'd stand around arguing with Clellan. Hearn started to walk out of the tent. "Just get those flowers, Clellan," he said coldly before he stepped out.

Disgusting, humiliating. Hearn stared morosely at the raw cropped earth of the bivouac as he walked over to officers' mess for breakfast. That sort of thing could go on for a year or two, a daily and nasty piece of business to be taken each morning on an empty stomach. Clellan of course would love it. Every retort Clellan could get away with would be just so much grist to his self-esteem, and any time he would be rebuked he could generate the satisfying hatred of the underdog. There were angles to being an enlisted man. Hearn kicked a pebble with his foot.

Lo, the poor officers! Hearn grinned at himself, and waved to Mantelli, who was also approaching officers' mess.

Mantelli cut over to him, and clapped him on the back. "Keep away from poppa today."

"What's the matter?"

"Last night we got a Lonely Hearts from corps. They told Cummings to get his ass in gear. Jesus! He'll be having me leading headquarters company in a charge." Mantelli took out his cigar and extended it forward like a spear.

"All you're good for is charging a chow line."

"Ain't it the truth. I got a desk job, flat feet, Hollandia, Stateside, Pentagon, I wear eyeglasses, I cough . . . listen."

Hearn shoved him playfully. "Do you want a word with the General?"

"Sure, get me in USO." They walked in together to chow.

After breakfast Hearn reported to the General's tent. Cummings was sitting at his desk studying an Air Corps engineer report. "They won't have the airfield ready for two months. They switched a priority on me."

"That's too bad, sir."

"Naturally I'm expected to win the damn campaign without it." The General griped abstractedly as if unaware of the identity of the man before him. "This is the only division in action at the moment which doesn't have any dependable air support." The General wiped his mouth carefully, looked at Hearn. "I thought the tent was pretty good this morning."

"Thank you, sir." Hearn was annoyed with the pleasure this gave him.

Cummings extracted a pair of eyeglasses from a drawer in the desk, wiped them slowly, and put them on. This was one of the few times Hearn had seen him wearing eyeglasses, and they made him look older somehow. After a moment Cummings took them off and held them in his hand.

"You junior officers getting all your liquor supplies?"

"Why, yes, I believe we are."

"Mm." Cummings clasped his hands.

Now, what was this all about? Hearn wondered. "Why do you ask?" he said at last.

But the General didn't answer. "I'm taking a trip up to Second Battalion this morning. Will you tell Richman to have the jeep ready for me in about ten minutes?"

305

"Am I coming along, sir?"

"Eh, no. You see Horton. I want you to go out to the beach, and pick up some extra supplies for officers' mess."

"Yes, sir." A little puzzled, Hearn went down to the motor pool, gave the order to Richman, the General's driver, and then saw Major Horton, who gave him a list of supplies to be purchased from a Liberty ship out in the harbor.

Hearn collected a detail of three men from the first sergeant of headquarters company, requisitioned a weapons carrier, and drove down to the beach. Already the morning had become hot, and the sun, obscured by overcast, refracted from the jungle and heated the moist dank air. Occasionally on the trip along the road, the sound of some artillery would eddy back to them, heavy and depressed like a heat storm on a summer night. Hearn was sweating by the time they reached the end of the peninsula.

After a few minutes' wait, he was able to requisition a landing craft, and they rode out over the water to where the freighters were anchored. A mile or two away over the sullen torpid water, Anopopei was almost obscured by haze, and the sun, a smudged yellow, burned a fierce gap through the sluggish vault of the clouds. Even on the water it was extremely hot.

The landing craft cut off its motors, and drifted in against the side of the freighter. When it bumped against the side, Hearn caught the ladder and climbed up to the deck. Above him on the rail were a number of seamen staring at him, and the blank look on their faces, critical and slightly disdainful, irritated him. He stared down through the rungs of the ship ladder at the landing craft, which had backed off toward the loading crane at the bow of the ship. Hearn found himself sweating again from the minor exertion of climbing the ladder.

"Who's in charge of ship's stores?" he asked one of the seamen at the rail.

The sailor looked at him, and then without speaking jerked a thumb in the direction of a hatch. Hearn walked past him, pushed open the heavy hatch door, and started down a ladder. The heat smote him with an unexpected shock; he had forgotten how unbearable a ship's hold could become.

306

And of course it stank. He felt like an insect crawling through the entrails of a horse. "Damn," he muttered in disgust. As usual the ship smelled of stale cooking — fat mixed with something as nauseous as the curds from a grease trap. Abstractedly, he rubbed his finger against a bulkhead and drew it away wet. All over the ship the bulkheads sweated a film of oil and water.

He stepped warily along the passageway, narrow and lighted poorly, the metal floor plates obstructed by an occasional pile of equipment sloppily covered with a small tarpaulin. Once he skidded and almost fell on some oil slick. "Goddam filthy place," he swore. He was enraged, inordinately angry, and it seemed without cause. Hearn paused, wiping his forehead roughly with his sleeve. What the hell's the matter with me?

"Are you junior officers getting your liquor supplies?" the General had asked, and something had leaped in him at that moment, left his nerves raw and displaced since then. What had the General meant?

After a moment or two he pushed down the corridor again. The ship's stores office was in a medium-sized cabin off the passageway. It was cluttered with odd ration crates, bits of wood from broken boxes, a pile of papers which had overflowed from a wastebasket, and a large worn desk pushed into one corner.

"Are you Kerrigan?" Hearn asked the officer sitting at the desk.

"That's right, sonny, what can I do for you?" Kerrigan had a lean, rather battered face with a few teeth missing.

Hearn stared at him a moment, his anger pulsing again. "Let's cut out all this 'sonny' crap." He was rather startled by his own rage.

"Anything you say, Lieutenant."

Hearn controlled himself with an effort. "I've got a landing barge over the side. Here's the requisition for the supplies I want. I'd like to get out of here without taking up too much of your time or mine."

Kerrigan went through the slip. "This's for officers' mess, eh, Lieutenant?" He ticked off the items aloud. "Five cases of whisky, a carton of salad oil, carton of mayonnaise" — Kerrigan pronounced it "myonize" with an amused brogue — "two crates of boned canned chicken, a box o' condiments, a dozen bottles of Worcestershire, a

307

dozen bottles of chili, a crate of ketchup . . ." He looked up. "It's a small list. Restrained tastes y' have. I surmise tomorra you'll be sendin' out a barge to pick up a coupla jars of mustard." He sighed. "Pick and choose, pick and choose." He drew his pencil through most of the items. "I can give y' the whisky. For the rest of it, we're not runnin' a stop-and-shop."

"If you'll notice the requisition is signed by Horton for the General."

Kerrigan lit a cigarette. "When the General runs this ship, I'll start to sweat before him." He stared gleefully at Hearn. "One of Horton's men, a captain something or other, picked up the supplies for Division Headquarters yesterday. We're not special caterers to officers' mess, you know. Ye'll draw your supplies in bulk and break 'em down on the beach."

Hearn restrained his temper. "These are purchases. I have funds from officers' mess to pay for them."

"But I'm not obliged to give them to you. And I damn sure won't. If y' want Spam, that I can give you, and not a penny out of your pocket. But for these little extras, I suggest that you wait till a Navy ship appears again. I don't have any truck with this selling of myonize." He scribbled something on the requisition. "If ye'll take this down into hold number two, ye'll get your whisky. If I didn't have to give you that, I wouldn't."

"Well, thank you, Kerrigan."

"Any time, Lieutenant, any time."

Hearn paced down the corridor, his eyes glittering. The ship rolled on a swell and he lurched into a bulkhead, smacking his hand painfully against the metal to break the impact. Then he halted, wiped the perspiration from his forehead and mouth again.

He'd be damned if he'd go back without the supplies. Kerrigan's smile angered him again, and with an effort he forced himself to grin. This was getting out of hand; Kerrigan after all had had style, was amusing. There were other ways to get the supplies, and he'd get them. He wasn't going to face the General and have to give explanations.

He came to hold No. 2 and descended the ladder to the refrigerator vaults. To the man on duty, he handed the requisition.

308

"Just five cases of whisky, huh?"

Hearn massaged his chin. A jungle sore had formed near the cleft and it smarted. "How about getting the rest of that, Jack?" he said abruptly.

"Can't. Kerrigan crossed it off."

"It's worth ten pounds to you if you give me that stuff."

The seaman was a small man with a worried face. "I can't get away with that. What if Kerrigan sees me loading it on?"

"He's in his office doing some work. He won't be out."

"I can't take the chance, Lieutenant. It would show up in inventory."

Hearn scratched his head. He could feel a heat rash forming on his back. "Look, let's get in the refrigerator vault. I want to cool off." They opened one of the huge doors, and stood inside talking, surrounded by turkeys and hams on hooks and crates of Coca-Cola. One of the turkeys had some meat exposed, and Hearn picked off a few slivers of white flesh and ate them as he spoke. "You know damn well it isn't going to show up in inventory," Hearn improvised. "I've worked with things like this, Jack. You can't account for food."

"I don't know, Lieutenant."

"You mean to tell me Kerrigan's never been down here to pick up a little food for himself?"

"Well, it's a risky business giving it to you."

"How about twelve pounds?"

The seaman deliberated. "Maybe for fifteen?"

He had him now. "Twelve's my price," Hearn barked. "I'm not bargaining."

"All right, I'll take a chance."

"Good boy." Hearn pulled off another piece of turkey and ate it with relish. "You get the crates separated, and I'll find my men and have them bring it up."

"All right, Lieutenant, but let's do it fast, okay?"

Hearn went on top, leaned over the rail, and shouted to the three-man detail on his landing barge to come aboard. After they had climbed the scramble net, Hearn led them below to the hold, and they each picked up a carton and carried it to the deck. After three trips everything had been brought up, the whisky, the canned chicken, and all the condiments, and in a few minutes it was loaded in the crane net and lowered into the barge. Hearn paid the seaman his twelve pounds. "Come on, men, let's get going," he shouted. Now that it was over, he was worried that Kerrigan might appear on deck and discover his transaction. They clambered down into the barge, and Hearn dragged a tarpaulin over the supplies.

As they were about to back off, he saw Kerrigan looking down at them from the rail. "If ye don't mind, Lieutenant," Kerrigan bawled, "I'd like to have a look at what ye're taking away."

Hearn grinned. "Start the motors," he called to the helmsman, and then looked up blankly at Kerrigan. "Too late, man," he shouted. But the motors coughed, sputtered and died. And Kerrigan, seeing this, began to climb over the side.

"*Start those motors,*" Hearn shouted furiously. He glared at the helmsman. "*Get going!*"

The motor sputtered again, caught momentarily, lapsed, and then steadied. From the stern the propeller wake became steady. Kerrigan was halfway down the scramble net. "All right, let's go!" Hearn shouted.

The barge backed off slowly, leaving Kerrigan stranded foolishly in the middle of the net. A few of the seamen looking over the side laughed at him as he started to climb back to the deck. "So long, Kerrigan!" Hearn shouted. He was gleeful. "Goddam, man," he said to the helmsman, "that was a hell of a time to have the motors go back on you." The landing craft was bouncing steadily as it overtook the waves riding toward shore. "I'm sorry, Lieutenant."

"Okay." He felt relaxed, extremely relaxed, in comparison to the tension he had sustained when they were loading the food, and with surprise he noticed how wet his clothing had become. Some spray was washing over the forward ramp, and Hearn stood in the supply well, and let it patter down upon him. Overhead, the sun was breaking through the clouds, the overcast retreating wispily before it like paper curling away from a flame. He mopped his forehead once more, felt his collar gathered like a sodden rope around his neck.

Well, twelve pounds was not bad. Hearn grinned. Kerrigan

310

would have charged him at least fifteen pounds for those supplies, perhaps twenty. That seaman had been an ass, and the General was an ass too. Cummings had expected him to come back with only the whisky. Of course. Yesterday Horton had been talking about a purser. "That sonofabitch won't co-operate at all," Horton had said. And the purser was Kerrigan.

The General had sent him out on a special detail to buy some extras for officers' mess when clearly it was a job for one of the officers in Horton's section. Somehow he had sensed the General's motive, he must have, otherwise why would he have gone to the trouble of bribing the seaman or become so angry when Kerrigan had given him lip? So the General was having an effect on him. Hearn sat down on the tarpaulin covering the supplies, took off his shirt, swabbed his wet body with it, and then, holding it dourly in his hand, he lit a cigarette.

After the boat landed, Hearn had the supplies transferred to a weapons carrier, and rode back with his detail. He reached the bivouac before noon, and dropped in at the General's tent to report, savoring the idea of disappointing Cummings, but the General was not there. Hearn sat down on a foot locker, and surveyed the tent distastefully. Nothing in it had been altered since early morning when Clellan had worked on it, and in the sunlight that glanced through the open flaps the tent was rectangular and unfriendly with all the corners squared, and no sign that anyone ever lived in it. The floor was spotless, the blankets were drawn tautly over the General's mattress, the desk was uncluttered. Hearn sighed, felt a vague uneasiness stirring in him. Ever since that *particular* night.

The General was putting the screws on him. The things Cummings gave him to do could be done easily enough, but there was always a special brand of humiliation in them. The General knew him in some ways better than he knew himself, Hearn realized. If he had a job he would do it, even if it meant being a bastard about it, but each time he was a bastard it was a little easier to be one the next time. Cute enough. That business with Kerrigan this morning was taking on another aspect. When you looked at it coldly it amounted to bribing a man, sneaking out some supplies and sweating until you got away.

311

On another level it was the sort of deal his father might have pulled. "Every man has his price, there's more ways than one to skin a cat." Oh, there were enough platitudes to cover it, but the General was showing him that he wasn't superior to the platitudes either. It had been the recreation tent all over again with fifty, perhaps a hundred variations.

"You forget, Robert, there's such a thing as papal dispensation." All right, now there was no dispensation. He was merely a second lieutenant, squeezed by all the pressures above and beneath him, no more capable than any of the other officers of maintaining his own course with a little dignity, a little restraint. After it went on long enough the reactions would become automatic, fear-inspired. Somehow you never did win when you were with the General. Even on that night of the chess game it was he who had felt sick, not Cummings; it was he who had lain on his cot and dredged his memory for all the silt and cankers.

"Are you junior officers getting your liquor supplies?" What the hell had he meant by that? On an impulse Hearn opened the General's liquor closet, and examined the opened bottles. Almost every night Cummings could be counted on to drink an inch or two of Scotch, and with a curious niggardliness he would mark the level of the bottle with a pencil before he put it away. Hearn had noticed this with amusement, found it an interesting little quirk in all the contradictions of the General.

But today the liquor level on his bottle of Scotch was at least two and a half inches below the last pencil mark. Cummings had seen that this morning, had rebuked him for drinking it. "Are you junior officers getting your liquor supplies?" Only, that was absurd. Cummings would know better than that.

It could have been Clellan. *Possibly.* But it was unlikely Clellan would jeopardize a sinecure like general's orderly merely for a drink. And besides, Clellan was shrewd enough to mark the liquor level himself if he wanted to take a nip.

Suddenly, Hearn had an image of Cummings sitting in his tent the night before, about to go to bed, examining thoughtfully the label of his whisky bottle. He might even pick up his pencil, deliberate a

312

moment or two, and then he would leave the bottle unmarked, return it to the closet. What had his face looked like at that moment?

This, now, was not funny. Not after the recreation tent and the flowers and Kerrigan. Until this little episode, he could consider the General's antics as pranks that spewed out of twisted and intense hungers. It had been in a way like the probing banter between friends. But *this* was vicious. And frightening, a little. With all his concerns, with all the pressures upon him, Cummings had had time to concoct these schemes, release a little of the greater frustration he was feeling.

And that basically was what their relationship had always been, Hearn understood at this moment. He had been the pet, the dog, to the master, coddled and curried, thrown sweetmeats until he had had the presumption to bite the master once. And since then he had been tormented with the particular absorbed sadism that most men could generate only toward an animal. He was a diversion for the General, and he resented it deeply with a cold speechless anger that came to some extent from the knowledge that he had acquiesced in the dog-role, had even had the dog's dreams, carefully submerged, of some-day equaling the master. And Cummings had probably understood even that, had been amused.

He remembered a story Cummings had told him about an employee in the War Department who had been discharged after some Communist documents had been planted in his desk.

"I'm surprised it worked," Hearn had said. "You say everybody knew the man was harmless."

"Those things always work, Robert. You can't begin to imagine how effective the Big Lie is. Your average man never dares suspect that the men in power have all the nasty impulses he has, except they're more effective about carrying them out. Besides, there's never a man who can swear to his own innocence. We're all guilty, that's the truth. This particular fellow began to wonder if perhaps he had belonged to the party. Why do you think Hitler was able to stay un-molested so long? The diplomat mentality at its poorest just couldn't believe that he wasn't playing the old game with some new wrinkles. It took an outside observer like you or me to see that he was the inter-preter of twentieth-century man."

Certainly Cummings would have been perfectly capable of plant-
ing those documents if he had thought it necessary. Just as he had
finagled the whisky label. And he was not going to become a chess
piece for the General to direct. No doubt Cummings saw him now as
a diversion.

Hearn stared around the tent. It would be a pleasure to wait for
the General and tell him that he had brought back the supplies successfully, but it was a tainted pleasure and Cummings would be quite
aware of it. "Had to extend yourself a bit, didn't you, Robert?" he
might say. Hearn lit a cigarette, and walked over to the wastebasket
to drop the match.

There it was, that instinctive reaction, *don't drop a match on the
General's floor*. He paused. There was a limit to how far he could let
the General prod him.

The clean floor. If you looked at it clearly without the aura of
military mumbo-jumbo, it became absurd, perverted, a revolting idea.

He dropped the match near the General's foot locker, and then
with his heart beating stupidly, he threw his cigarette carefully onto
the middle of the General's spotless floor, ground his heel down brutally upon it, and stood looking at it with amazement and a troubled
pride.

Let Cummings see that. Let him.

In the G-1 tent the air had become stifling by midday. Major
Binner wiped his steel-rimmed glasses, coughed dolefully, and removed a trickle of sweat from the corner of his neat temple. "This is
a serious thing, Sergeant," he said quietly.

"Yes, sir, I know."

Major Binner glanced at the General for a moment. Then he
drummed on his desk and looked at the enlisted man who was standing at attention before him. A few steps away, near one of the corner
poles, Cummings paced a small circle back and forth.

"If you give us the facts, Sergeant Lanning, it will have a very
important bearing on your court-martial," Binner said.

"Major, I don't know what to tell you," Lanning protested. He
was a short rather stocky man with blond hair and pale-blue eyes.

"The facts will be sufficient," Binner drawled in his sad voice.

"Well, we went out on patrol, and since we'd gone to the same place the day before yesterday, I just couldn't see any point to it."

"Was that for you to judge?"

"No, sir, it wasn't, but I could see the men weren't too happy, and when we got out about halfway I just set my squad down in a little draw, and waited an hour, and then I came on back and gave my report."

"And the report was completely false," Binner intoned. "You said you had been to a place to which . . . *in which* you hadn't even been within a mile of."

In the midst of his anger, Cummings felt a mild contempt at the way Binner had mangled the sentence.

"Yes, sir, that's true," Sergeant Lanning said.

"You got the idea in precisely that manner, it just occurred to you, so to speak?"

Cummings restrained himself from interrupting the questioning to speed it up.

"I don't understand, Major?" Lanning asked.

"How many other times have you dropped the ball on patrol?" Binner asked sadly.

"This was the first time, sir."

"What other sergeants in your company or battalion have been giving false and misleading patrol reports?"

"None, sir, I never heard of any."

The General walked up to him abruptly, and glared at him. "Lanning, do you ever want to go back to the States or do you want to rot over here in a prison camp?"

"Sir," Lanning stammered, "I've been with the outfit for three years, and . . ."

"I don't care if you've been with us for *twenty* years. What other sergeants have been giving false patrol reports?"

"I don't know any, sir."

"Have you got a sweetheart?"

"I'm married, sir."

"Do you want to see your wife again?"

315

Lanning reddened. "She left me about a year ago, sir. I got a Dear John."

The General's shoes made a dry scraping sound as he turned away. "Major, you can bring this man up for court-martial tomorrow." He paused in the doorway. "Lanning, I warn you, you'd better tell the truth. I want the name of every noncom in your company who's been doing this."

"There weren't any I know of, sir."

Cummings stalked out and walked across the bivouac, his knees weak with impotent anger. The cheek of Lanning, "There weren't any I know of, sir." The entire front was made up of noncoms like him, and the chances were that three-quarters of the reports they gave were false; probably even the line officers were faking their patrols. And the worst of it was that he could do nothing about it. If he was to bring Lanning up before a general court-martial, the sentence would be reviewed, and it would be common knowledge throughout the South Pacific that his men had become unreliable. Even if Lanning told him who the other noncoms were, he could take no action. The men who would replace them would probably be even worse. But he'd be damned if he'd send Lanning back to his company without any punishment. Let him wither on the stalk. They could wait until the campaign was over to bring him up to trial (if it ever ended) and in the meantime there could be any number of interrogations, any number of promises that he would be tried the next day or the day after. The General walked along, spurred by an angry satisfaction which fed itself. If that didn't break Lanning, there were other ways. But the men were going to learn if he had to rub their noses in the dirt that the line of their least discomfort lay in winning the campaign. They liked their bivouacs, did they? Well, there were methods of fixing that. Tomorrow there could be a general troop movement to one side or another, adjustments of a few hundred yards with new foxholes to be dug, new barbed wire to be laid, new tents to be put up. And if they started laying duckwalks again, and improving their latrines, there could be still another movement. It was the American's capacity for real estate improvement; build yourself a house, grow fat in it, and die.

316

The discipline had to be tightened all through the division. If men were dicking off on patrols, then there were malingerers in the hospital. He'd have to send a memo down to Portable Surgical to crack down on all the doubtful cases. There was entirely too much coddling going on in the outfit, and there were too many men resisting his authority, thwarting him. Oh, they'd be happier with a new general in command, a butcher who would waste their lives to no purpose. Well, if they didn't perk up, they'd be having their butcher soon. There were always enough military hacks around.

In a fury he came back to his tent, sat down at his desk, and found himself doodling with a pencil. He threw it down and stared with a febrile loathing at the map board by his cot. By now, it was a taunt to him.

But something was wrong with the tent. Something was changed since Clellan had fixed it this morning. He turned around, gazed about the room with a feeling of inordinate anxiety.

"God!" It came out as something between a grunt and a choked exclamation. A deep pang of pain and fear lanced through his chest. On the middle of his floor was the match and the cigarette butt, mashed into the duckboards in a tangled ugly excrement of black ash, soiled paper, and brown tobacco.

There was a note for him, too, on the desk, which he had not noticed:

Sir,
  Waited for you but you didn't show up.
  I brought back the supplies you indicated.
                                          Hearn.

Then it was Hearn who had soiled his floor. Of course. Cummings walked over to the match and cigarette butt, picked them up with intense distaste and dropped them in a wastebasket. There was a little black ash left, which he scattered with his foot. Despite himself he felt obliged to keep sniffing his fingers although he loathed the odor of a dead cigarette.

Deep in his bowels something had reacted and a twinge of diar-

317

rhea made him perspire. He reached over, picked up his field telephone, cranked it once, and murmured into the receiver, "Find Hearn and send him over to my tent." Then he rubbed vigorously at the flesh on the left side of his face, which seemed to have grown numb.

"To do *that*." His rage was just beginning to function; a furious uncontrolled anger tightened his mouth, set his heart beating over-rapidly, and tingled in the tips of his fingers. Almost unbearable. He walked over to his refrigerator and poured himself a glass of water, which he drank with short distraught swallows. For an instant, deep beneath the currents of his rage, there was another feeling, an odd compound of disgust and fear perhaps, and something else, a curious troubled excitement, a momentary submission as if he had been a young girl undressing before the eyes of a roomful of strange men. But his rage choked this off, expanded inside him until it clotted all the conduits of his emotion, and left him trembling with an unendurable wrath. If he had been holding an animal in his hands at that instant he would have strangled it.

And with it was another sort of fear, overt and aware; what Hearn had done was equivalent to a soldier's laying hands on his person. To Cummings it was a symbol of the independence of his troops, their resistance to him. The fear, the respect his soldiers held for him now was a rational one, an admission of his power to punish them, and that was not enough. The other kind of fear was lacking, the unreasoning one in which his powers were immense and it was effectively a variety of sacrilege to thwart him. The cigarette butt on the floor was a threat, a denial of him, as fully as Lanning's defection, or a Japanese attack on his lines, and he had to meet it directly and ruthlessly. The longer you tarried with resistance the greater it became. It had to be destroyed.

"You want to see me, sir?" It was Hearn entering his tent.

Cummings turned around slowly, and looked at him. "Yes, sit down, I want to talk to you." His voice had been cold and even. With Hearn before him, his anger became incisive, controllable, an instrument of his actions. With great deliberation he lit a cigarette, his hands steady now, and exhaled it leisurely. "It's been a long time since we've had a little talk, Robert."

318

"Yes, sir, it has been."

Not since the night of the chess game. And they were both aware of it. Cummings surveyed Hearn with loathing. Hearn was an embodiment of the one mistake, the one *indulgence* he had ever permitted himself, and it had been intolerable to be with him since then. "My wife is a bitch, Robert." Cummings writhed at the memory, revolted with himself for that temporary weakness. At that time . . .

There was Hearn before him now, sprawled in the camp chair, his large body not nearly so relaxed as it seemed, his sullen mouth, his cold eyes staring back at him. For a while he had thought there was something in Hearn, a brilliance to match his own, an aptitude for power, the particular hunger that had meaning, but he had been wrong. Hearn was a vacuum with surface reactions, surface irritations. No doubt he had mashed the cigarette on an impulse.

"I'm going to give you a lecture, Robert." Until now Cummings had had no idea of how he would proceed. He had trusted his instincts to direct him. And this was the way. Put it on the intellectual frame, let Hearn slip into it, be unaware that there was going to be an end product today.

Hearn lit a cigarette. "Yes, sir?" He was still holding the match in his hand, and they both looked at it. There was a quite perceptible pause while Hearn fingered it, and then leaned forward to drop it in an ashtray.

"You're remarkably neat," Cummings said sourly.

Hearn's eyes lifted, searched his for an instant, wary, judging his answer. "Family upbringing," he said shortly.

"You know, it seems to me there are things, Robert, you could have learned from your father."

"I didn't know you knew him," Hearn said quietly.

"I'm familiar with the type." Cummings stretched. Now the other question while Hearn was unready for it. "Have you ever wondered, Robert, why we're fighting this war?"

"Do you want a serious answer, sir?"

"Yes."

Hearn kneaded his thighs with his large hands. "I don't know, I'm not sure. With all the contradictions, I suppose there's an objective right on our side. That is, in Europe. Over here, as far as I'm concerned, it's an imperialist tossup. Either we louse up Asia or Japan does. And I imagine our methods will be a little less drastic."

"Is that your contribution?"

"I don't pretend to read history in advance. I'll be able to give you the real answer in a century probably." He shrugged. "I'm surprised that you want my opinion, General." His eyes had become lazy again, studiedly indifferent. Hearn had poise. That was undeniable.

"It seems to me, Robert, you can do a little better than that."

"All right, I can. There's an osmosis in war, call it what you will, but the victors always tend to assume the . . . the, eh, trappings of the loser. We might easily go Fascist after we win, and then the answer's really a problem." He puffed at his cigarette. "I don't go in for the long views. For want of a better idea I just assume it's a bad thing when millions of people are killed because one joker has to get some things out of his system."

"Not that you *really* care, Robert."

"Probably not. But until you show me some other idea to replace it, I'll hold to this one."

Cummings grinned at him. His anger had subsided to a cold effective resolve. Hearn was fumbling now, he had noticed that in him. Whenever Hearn had to search his ideas he was obviously uncomfortable, obviously trying to avoid the other conclusions.

Hearn seemed absorbed for just a moment. "We're moving toward greater organization, and I don't see how the left can win that battle in America. There're times when I think it's Gandhi who's right."

Cummings laughed out loud. "You know you couldn't have picked a more unperceptive man. Passive resistance, eh. You'd be good in that role. You and Clellan and Gandhi."

Hearn sat up a little straighter in his chair. The noon sun, harsh now that the overcast had blown away, glinted cruelly over the bivouac, threw into bold relief the shadows under the flaps of the tent. About a hundred yards away, on a downhill slope through the sparse foliage, Cummings watched the chow line, two hundred and fifty men long, trudge slowly forward.

320

"It seems to me," Hearn said, "Clellan's more in your line. And while we're on that you might tell him that the flowers are your idea."

Cummings laughed again. That had taken effect then. He opened his eyes widely, conscious of the effect their bald white surfaces would give, and then he slapped his thigh in a facsimile of mirth. "Are you getting enough liquor, Robert?" Of course, that was why he had crushed the cigarette on the floor.

Hearn made no answer, but his jaws quivered just perceptibly.

Cummings sat back, enjoying himself. "We're wandering a little far afield. I was going to explain the war to you."

"Yes, if you would." Hearn's sharp voice, slightly unpleasant, was exhibiting the least bit of irritation.

"I like to call it a process of historical energy. There are countries which have latent powers, latent resources, they are full of potential energy, so to speak. And there are great concepts which can unlock that, express it. As kinetic energy a country is organization, co-ordinated effort, your epithet, fascism." He moved his chair slightly. "Historically the purpose of this war is to translate America's potential into kinetic energy. The concept of fascism, far sounder than communism if you consider it, for it's grounded firmly in men's actual natures, merely started in the wrong country, in a country which did not have enough intrinsic potential power to develop completely. In Germany with that basic frustration of limited physical means there were bound to be excesses. But the dream, the concept was sound enough." Cummings wiped his mouth. "As you put it, Robert, not too badly, there's a process of osmosis. America is going to absorb that dream, it's in the business of doing it now. When you've created power, materials, armies, they don't wither of their own accord. Our vacuum as a nation is filled with released power, and I can tell you that we're out of the backwaters of history now."

"We've become destiny, eh?" Hearn said.

"Precisely. The currents that have been released are not going to subside. You shy away from it, but it's equivalent to turning your back on the world. I tell you I've made a study of this. For the past century the entire historical process has been working toward greater and greater consolidation of power. Physical power for this century, an extension of our universe, and a political power, a political organization to make it possible. Your men of power in America, I can tell you, are becoming conscious of their real aims for the first time in our history. Watch. After the war our foreign policy is going to be far more naked, far less hypocritical than it has ever been. We're no longer going to cover our eyes with our left hand while our right is extending an imperialist paw."

Hearn shrugged. "You think it's going to come about as easily as that? Without resistance?"

"With much less resistance than you think. In college the one axiom you seem to have carried away is that everyone is sick, everyone is corrupt. And it's reasonably true. Only the innocent are healthy, and the innocent man is a vanishing breed. I tell you nearly all of humanity is dead, merely waiting to be disinterred."

"And the special few?"

"Just what do you think man's deepest urge is?"

Hearn grinned, his eyes probing Cummings. "A good piece of ass probably."

The answer grated, made Cummings's flesh tingle. He had been absorbed in the argument, temporarily indifferent to Hearn, concerned only with unfolding his thesis, and the obscenity stirred little swirls of apprehension in him. His anger returned again.

For the moment, however, he ignored Hearn. "I doubt it."

Hearn shrugged once more, his silence unpleasantly eloquent.

There was something unapproachable and unattainable about Hearn which had always piqued him, always irritated him subtly. The empty pit where there should be a man. And at the moment he desired, with an urgency that clamped his jaws together, to arouse some emotion in Hearn. Women would have wanted to excite some love from him, but for himself — to see Hearn afraid, filled with shame if only for an instant.

Cummings went on talking, his voice quiet and expressionless. "The average man always sees himself in relation to other men as either inferior or superior. Women play no part in it. They're an index, a yardstick among other gauges, by which to measure superiority."

"Did you arrive at that all by yourself, sir? It's an impressive analysis."

Hearn's sarcasm riled him again. "I'm quite aware, Robert, that you've worked out the ABC's of something like that, but you don't carry it any further. You stop there, go back to your starting point, and take off again. The truth of it is that from man's very inception there has been one great vision, blurred first by the exigencies and cruelties of nature, and then, as nature began to be conquered, by the second great cloak — economic fear and economic striving. That particular vision has been muddied and diverted, but we're coming to a time when our techniques will enable us to achieve it." He exhaled his smoke slowly. "There's that popular misconception of man as something between a brute and an angel. Actually man is in transit between brute and God."

"Man's deepest urge is omnipotence?"

"Yes. It's not religion, that's obvious, it's not love, it's not spirituality, those are all sops along the way, benefits we devise for ourselves when the limitations of our existence turn us away from the other dream. To achieve God. When we come kicking into the world, we *are* God, the universe is the limit of our senses. And when we get older, when we discover that the universe is not us, it's the deepest trauma of our existence."

Hearn fingered his collar. "I'd say *your* deepest urge is omnipotence, that's all."

"And yours too, whether you'll admit it or not."

Hearn's sharp voice softened a little with irony. "What moral precepts am I supposed to draw from all this?"

Cummings's tension altered. There had been a deep satisfaction in expounding this, a pleasure apart from all the other concerns of this discussion with Hearn. "I've been trying to impress you, Robert, that the only morality of the future is a power morality, and a man who cannot find his adjustment to it is doomed. There's one thing about power. It can flow only from the top down. When there are little surges of resistance at the middle levels, it merely calls for more power to be directed downward, to burn it out."

Hearn was looking at his hands. "We're not in the future yet."

323

"You can consider the Army, Robert, as a preview of the future."

Hearn looked at his watch. "It's time to go to chow." Outside the tent the earth was almost white in the glare of the overhead sun.

"You'll go to chow when I release you."

"Yes, sir." Hearn scraped his foot slowly against the floor, stared at him quietly, a little doubtfully.

"You threw that cigarette on my floor today, didn't you?"

Hearn smiled. "I figured that was going to be the point of all this talk."

"It was simple enough for you, wasn't it? You resented some of my actions, and you indulged a childish tantrum. But it's the kind of thing I don't care to permit." The General held his half-smoked cigarette in his hand, and waved it slightly as he spoke. "If I were to throw this down on the floor, would you pick it up?"

"I think I'd tell you to go to hell."

"I wonder. I've indulged you too long. You really can't believe I'm serious, can you? Supposed you understood that if you didn't pick it up, I would court-martial you, and you might have five years in a prison stockade."

"I wonder if you have the power for that?"

"I do. It would cause me a lot of difficulty, your court-martial would be reviewed, and after the war there might be a *bit* of a stink, it might even hurt me personally, but I would be upheld. I would have to be upheld. Even if you won eventually, you would be in prison for a year or two at least while it was all being decided."

"Don't you think that's a bit steep?"

"It's tremendously steep, it has to be. There was the old myth of divine intervention. You blasphemed, and a lightning bolt struck you. That was a little steep too. If punishment is at all proportionate to the offense, then power becomes watered. The only way you generate the proper attitude of awe and obedience is through immense and disproportionate power. With this in mind, how do you think you would react?"

Hearn was kneading his thighs again. "I resent this. It's an unfair proposition. You're settling a difference between us by . . ."

324

"You remember when I gave that lecture about the man with the gun?"

"Yes."

"It's not an accident that I have this power. Nor is it that you're in a situation like this. If you'd been more aware, you wouldn't have thrown down that cigarette. Indeed, you wouldn't have if I were a blustering profane General of the conventional variety. You don't quite believe I'm serious, that's all."

"Perhaps I don't."

Cummings tossed his cigarette at Hearn's feet. "All right, Robert, suppose you pick it up," he said quietly.

There was a long pause. Under his breastbone, Cummings could feel his heart grinding painfully. "I hope, Robert, that you pick it up. For your sake." Once more he stared into Hearn's eye.

And slowly Hearn was realizing that he meant it. It was apparent in his expression. A series of emotions, subtle and conflicting, flowed behind the surface of his face. "If you want to play games," he said. For the first time Cummings could remember, his voice was unsteady. After a moment or two, Hearn bent down, picked up the cigarette, and dropped it in an ashtray. Cummings forced himself to face the hatred in Hearn's eyes. He was feeling an immense relief.

"If you want to, you can go to chow now."

"General, I'd like a transfer to another division." Hearn was lighting another cigarette, his hands not completely steady.

"Suppose I don't care to arrange it?" Cummings was calm, almost cheerful. He leaned back in his chair, and tapped his foot slowly. "Frankly, I don't particularly care to have you around as my aide any longer. You aren't ready to appreciate this lesson yet. I think I'm going to send you to the salt mines. Suppose after lunch you report over to Dalleson's section, and work under him for a while."

"Yes, sir." Hearn's face had become expressionless again. He started toward the exit of the tent, and then paused. "General?"

"Yes?" Now that it was over, Cummings wished that Hearn would leave. The victory was losing its edge, and minor regrets, delicate little reservations, were cloying him.

325

"Short of bringing in every man in the outfit, all six thousand of them, and letting them pick up your cigarettes, how are you going to impress them?"

This was the thing that had sullied his pleasure. Cummings realized it now. There was still the other problem, the large one. "I'll manage that, Lieutenant. I think you'd better worry about your own concerns."

After Hearn had gone, Cummings looked at his hands. "When there are little surges of resistance, it merely calls for more power to be directed downward." And that hadn't worked with the line troops. Hearn he had been able to crush, any single man he could manage, but the sum of them was different still, resisted him still. He exhaled his breath, feeling a little weary. There was going to be a way, he would find it. There had been a time when Hearn had resisted him too.

And his elation, suppressed until now, stimulated him, eased to some extent the sores and frustrations of the past few weeks.

Hearn returned to his own tent, and missed lunch. For almost an hour he lay face down on his cot, burning with shame and self-disgust and an impossible impotent anger. He was suffering an excruciating humiliation which mocked him in its very intensity. He had known from the moment the General had sent for him that there would be trouble, and he had entered with the confidence that he wouldn't yield.

And yet he had been afraid of Cummings, indeed afraid of him from the moment he had come into the tent. Everything in him had demanded that he refuse to pick up the cigarette and he had done it with a sick numbed suspension of his will.

"The only thing to do is to get by on style." He had said that once, lived by it in the absence of anything else, and it had been a working guide, almost satisfactory until now. The only thing that had been important was to let no one in any ultimate issue ever violate your integrity, and this had been an ultimate issue. Hearn felt as if an immense cyst of suppuration and purulence had burst inside him, and was infecting his blood stream now, washing through all the conduits of his body in a sudden violent flux of change. He would have to react or die, effectively, and for one of the few times in his life he was quite uncertain of his own ability. It was impossible; he would have to do something, and he had no idea what to do. The moment was intolerable, the midday heat fierce and airless inside the tent, but he lay motionless, his large chin jammed into the canvas of his cot, his eyes closed, as if he were contemplating all the processes, all the things he had learned and unlearned in his life, and which were free now, sloshing about inside him with the vehemence and the agony of anything that has been suppressed for too long.

"I never thought I would crawfish to him."

That was the shock, that was the thing so awful to realize.

The Time Machine:

ROBERT HEARN

THE ADDLED WOMB

A big man with a shock of black hair and a small sharp voice, a heavy immobile face. His brown eyes, imperturbable, stared out coldly above the short blunted and slightly hooked arc of his nose. His wide thin mouth was unexpressive, a top ledge to the solid mass of his chin. He liked very few people and most men sensed it uneasily after talking to him for a few minutes.

In the center is the city, lashing at one's senses.

For a thousand, two thousand miles the roads and the earth have led up to it. The mountains have snubbed down to hills, lapsed into plains, rolled on majestically in leisurely convolutions and regroupings. No one ever really comprehends it, the vast table of America, and the pin points, the accretions, the big city and the iron trails leading to it.

The nexus.

(All the frenetic schemings, the cigar smoke, the coke smoke, the carbolic and retch of the el, the frightened passion for movement of an ant nest suddenly jarred, the vast hurried grabbing plans of thousands of men whose importance is confined to a street, a café, and there is no other sense than one of the present. History is remembered with a shrug; its superlatives do not match ours.

The immense ego of city people.

How do you conceive your own death, your own unimportance in all that man-created immensity, through all the marble vaults and brick ridges and the furnaces that lead to the market place? You always believe somehow that the world will end with your death. It is all more intense, more violent, more rutted than life anywhere else.)

And in the humus around the mushroom stem grow the suburbs.

Since we added that last wing, we got twenty-two rooms now, Lord knows what the hell we're gonna do with 'em, Bill Hearn shouts. But Ina you can't tell her a goddam thing, she figures she needs it, and we got it.

Now, Bill, Ina says. (A pretty woman who looks younger, slimmer, than the mother of a twelve-year-old son. No beauty, however. There is the thin aseptic mouth, the slightly bucked teeth, the midwestern woman's denial of juice.)

Well, I'm as regular as an old shoe, Bill Hearn says. There ain't any pretense about me, and if I come off an old scratch farm, I ain't a bit ashamed of it. The way I see it a man needs a parlor or a living room, a coupla bedrooms, a kitchen, maybe a rumpus room downstairs, and y' got enough, agree with me, Mrs. Judd?

(Mrs. Judd is plumper, softer, more vacant-looking.) I suppose so, Mr. Hearn. Mr. Judd and I are mighty pleased with our place in Alden Park Manor, an apartment's so easy to keep.

Nice place, Germantown. We have to visit the Judds there, Ina.

Any time, I'll show you the sights, Mr. Judd says. There is silence, and they eat self-consciously, muting the noise of their tableware. Lovely view out there, Mrs. Judd comments.

It's the only place you can get away from the heat in Chicago, Ina says. We're so backward to New York, you think they would have had a roof garden on a hotel here before this. It's so hot for May. I can't wait until we get out to Charlevoix. Pronounced: Choliveoil.

Michigan, that's a green state, Bill Hearn says. There is silence again, and Mrs. Judd turns to Robert Hearn and says, you're such a big boy for twelve, Bobby, I thought you were a little more.

No, ma'am, only twelve. He ducks his head uncomfortably as the waiter places the roast duck before him.

Don't mind Bobby, he's just kind of shy, Bill Hearn booms, he certainly ain't a chip off my old block. Pushing his scanty black hair over the bald spot on his head, his little red nose a button in the round sweating jowls of his face.

When we were out to Hollywood, Mrs. Hearn says, we got taken over the Paramount lot by some assistant director fellow, Jew, but he was sort of nice. He was telling us all about the stars.

329

Is it true Mona Vaginus is a tramp? Mrs. Judd asks.

(Looking at Bobby, and whispering.) Oh, an awful tramp, the things she's supposed to do. But she hasn't got much of a future anyway now that those talkie pictures are the only ones being made.

This ain't the place to talk business, Mr. Judd of Budd (Hearn laughs), I guess you hear that all the time, Judd of Budd, but the truth is you're in business to do business, and a curiosity enough, I'm out for the same thing, so it's just a case of our compromising on the price, but there's one thing this Thompson machine is on the way out and if the reformers come in it's going to be a case of playing ball with 'em, or else havin' to put perfume in the factory toilet bowls and such stuff for all the Polack element that don't know a washcloth from their underwear, so I gotta be careful about my commitments. I been plannin' for a bust 'cause we got an overexpanded economy, an' your prices over at Budd ain't makin' it any easier for me.

Mr. Judd and I are planning to go to Paris. The petits-fours and the melting ice are set before them.

I'll tell ya, tomorrow do you want to ride in with me to see those auto races at Indianapolis? Bill Hearn asks.

Poor Robert, he's falling asleep, Ina says, nudging him with her elbow.

My it's hot, Mrs. Judd says.

Ina reaches up and turns on the bed lamp. Bill, how could you have asked the Judds where Mount Holyoke was? If you don't know something don't ask so many questions about it.

So what if their daughter does go there? I ain't afraid of the damn Judds, I want to tell you something, Ina, that society stuff don't impress me 'cause the truth of it is it's the money that counts, and we ain't got a daughter to worry about, and as far as Robert goes with all the books he reads he ain't gonna be much on the social end anyway, not so long as you're never around the goddam house, and he's got a nigger cook for a mother.

Bill, I wish you wouldn't talk that way.

Well, you can't change a sow's ear, Ina. I got my business and you got your social engagements, and each of us oughta be happy.

330

Only it seems to me you could give a little time to Robert, that kid's a big kid, and he's healthy, only he's like a cold fish, and there's just no life in him.

He's going to camp this summer, and we're starting him at Country Day in the fall.

The truth is we shoulda had another kid, or a bunch of them.

Let's not go into that, Bill. Ina is settling down under the covers.

No, not from your end anyway, I swear, Ina.

Bill!

Now, fellows, the counselor says, if you're a good fellow you co-operate and if you're square and honest you do your part of your duties. Who was it that left his bed undone this morning?

No answer. It was you, Hearn, wasn't it?

Yes.

The counselor sighs. Fellows, I'm going to give this tent a demerit because of Robert.

Well, I don't see why you have to make a bed when you just got to take it apart at night. The kids snicker.

What's the matter, Hearn, are you filthy, how were you brought up if you don't make a bed? And why didn't you come out like a man and say you were guilty?

Aw, leave me alone.

Another demerit, the counselor says. Fellows, it's up to you to make Robert behave.

Only he wins back the demerits at the team boxing matches that afternoon. He shuffles in clumsily against the other kid, his arms tired from the heavy gloves, and swings his fists desperately.

His father has come up to see him for the day. Sock it to him, give it to him, Robert, in the head, in the stomach, give it to him.

The other kid jolts him in the face, and he pauses for a moment, drops his gloves, and dabs at his outraged nose. Another punch makes his ear ring. *Don't let up, Bobby,* his father shouts. A missed punch travels around his head, the forearm scraping the skin on his face. He is ready to cry.

In the belly, Robert.

331

He swings out feverishly, flailing his arms. The other kid walks into a punch, sits down surprised, and then gets up slowly. Robert keeps swinging at him, hitting him, and the kid goes down again, and the referee stops the fight. Bobby Hearn on a TKO, he shouts, gives four points to the Blues. The kids yell, and Bill Hearn is putting a bear hug around him as he climbs out of the ropes set up on the grass. Oh, you gave it to him, Bobby, I told you to give it to him in the belly, that was the way to fight, kid, goddam, I got to hand it to you, you're not afraid to step in and mix it.

He wiggles out of the hug. Leave me alone, Pop, let me go, and he runs away over the grass to his tent, trying not to cry.

There are the summers in Charlevoix, the expanding house in the Chicago suburb, the world of long green lawns, and quiet beaches, and croquet courses and tennis courts; there are all the intimate and extensive details of wealth, the things he takes for granted, and understands, separates only later. There is also six years at Fieldmont Country Day, more of the fellows and demerits, the occasional sermon, the individual regular-fellow ethic borrowed from more exclusive eastern prep schools.

You do not lie	You do not cheat
You do not swear	You do not screw

And you go to church.

Always of course with the booming voice, the meaty palm of Bill Hearn in the background, combined somehow — never believably — with dancing lessons on Saturday mornings, and the persistent avid aspirations of Ina Hearn. Bobby, why don't you take Elizabeth Perkins to your Junior Dance?
Deep in the womb which covers me,
Green as grass from house to house . . .
Only that idea comes later.

The week after he graduates from Fieldmont Country Day, he goes on a drinking bout with a few contemporaries, fellow graduates, to a shack out in the woods, owned by one of their fathers. A two-story shack with a built-in bar.

At night they sit around in one of the upstairs bedrooms, passing the bottle after swigging at it gingerly.

If my old man knew.

To hell with your old man. They are all shocked, but it was Carsons who spoke, and his father committed suicide in 1930. Carsons can be forgiven.

Here's good-bye to Fieldmont, good old FCD, we had a lot of time there.

That's no lie.

The Dean wasn't bad but I never could figure him out, and you remember what a good-looking wife he had.

Here's to the wife, I heard she left him last year for a month.

Oh, no. The bottle goes on its second and third circuit.

All in all we had a good time there, only I'm glad to be out, I sure wish I was going with you fellows to Yale.

In a corner the football captain of the previous season is bending Hearn's ear. I wish I could be back for this next fall, what a team we're going to have with those juniors, you mark my words, Haskell is going to be All-American in four years, and while we're on the subject, Bob, I would like to give you just a little word of advice 'cause I've kept my eye on you for a long time now, and you don't try hard enough, you don't pull, you could've made the team 'cause you're big and you got natural ability but you didn't want to, and it's a shame because you ought to pull harder.

Stick your head in a bucket of ice.

Hearn's drunk, the captain yells.

Look at old Hearn off in the corner again. I bet he busted up with Adelaide.

She's a keen girl, but she necks around an awful lot, I bet Lantry used to worry about it before he went off to Princeton.

Aw, brothers don't care, that's my theory. I've got a sister, and she doesn't fool around, but I wouldn't care if she did.

You're only saying that 'cause she doesn't, I mean if she did, oh, that liquor is going around in my head. Who's drunk?

Yippeeee! It is Hearn standing in the middle of the floor with his head tilted back, gasping at the spout of the bottle. I'm a sonofabitch, what I say is all you men put your cards on the table.

Man, is he potted.

Go ahead, dare me to jump out the window, watch me pull my oar. Sweating, his face red with sudden anger, he pushes one of them away, opens the window and teeters on the sill. I'm gonna jump.

Stop him.

Yippeeeeeee! And he is gone, leapt out into the night. There's a thud, a crash of some bushes, and they rush horrified to the window. How are you, Hearn, are you all right, where are you, Hearn?

Fieldmont, Fieldmont über alles, Hearn roars back at them, lying on the ground in darkness, laughing, too drunk to have hurt himself.

What an odd egg Hearn is, they say. Remember last year when he got potted?

The last summer before college is a succession of golden days, and shining beaches, the magic of electric lights on summer evenings, and the dance band at the summer bathing club, AN AIRLINE TICKET TO ROMANTIC PLACES, and the touch and smell of young girls, lipstick odor, powder odor, and the svelte lean scent of leather on the seats of convertibles. The sky always has stars, always has moonlight gilding the black trees. On the highways the headlights lance a silver tunnel through the foliage overhead.

And he has a girl friend, a great catch, the young beauty at this summer colony. Miss Sally Tendecker of Lake Shore Drive, and the inescapable connotations to come of Christmas holidays, and fur coats, perfume, and college dances in the hue-titled rooms of the big hotels.

Bob, you drive faster than anybody I know, you're going to kill yourself one of these days.

Uh-huh. He's slow at speech with women yet, absorbed for the instant in negotiating the turn. His Buick swings out wide to the left, resists, struggles against going to the right, and then straightens from the turn. There had been panic for a second, and then relief, exultation as he goes streaming down the straightaway.

I declare you're a wild man, Bob Hearn.

334

I don't know.

What goes on in your head, Bob?

He parks the car off the highway, turns to her with a sudden abrupt outpouring of speech. I don't know, Sally, sometimes I think . . . but that isn't true, I just get all worked up, and I stew around, and I don't want to do anything, I'm going to Harvard just 'cause my father said something about Yale, and I don't know, there's things, there's something else, I can't put my finger on it, I don't want to be pushed, I don't know.

She laughs. Oh, you're a crazy boy, Bob, I guess that's why all we girls love you.

You love me?

Just listen to him talk. Why, of course I do, Bobby. Across from him on the leather seat cushions, her perfume is a little too strong, a little too mature for a girl of seventeen. And he senses the truth beneath her banter, moves over to kiss her with his heart beating. Only back of it is the forecast of dates at all the holidays, of college weekends, and the identification with this summer resort, and the green lawns in the suburbs, and the conversations with his father's friends, the big wedding.

You know I can't plan on anything if I'm going to be a doctor, because you know eight years, ten years, it's a long time.

Bob Hearn, you're conceited. What do you think I care? You're too conceited, that's all.

Now, son, now that you're going away to college, there's some things I want to be talking to you about, we don't get much of a chance to say much to each other but, what the hell, we're pretty good buddies I always like to think, and now that you're going to college, just remember that you can always depend on me. There's gonna be some women, what the hell, you wouldn't be my son if there weren't, not since I been married of course — a patent lie which both of them ignore — but if you get in any trouble you can always depend on me, what the hell, my old man used to tell me you get in any trouble with any of the mill girls, you just let me know — the embarrassing ambiguity of the grandfather who has been sometimes a farmer, some-

335

times a factory owner — so that goes for you too, Bob, and remember it's always easier, always more natural to buy a woman off than to get in any alliances with her, so you just let me know, letter marked personal is okay.

All right.

And as for being a doctor, well, that's okay, we got lots of friends here, we can set you up in a decent practice, buy into some old quack who's ready to retire.

I want to do research.

Research. Listen, Bobbo, there isn't a man you know, not one of our acquaintances who can't buy and sell a carload of research men, that's just some damn fool idea you picked up somewhere, and you're gonna change your mind, I can tell you that right now. The way I really look at it, your mother and me, is that you'll end up in the business, which is where you belong anyway.

No.

Well, I ain't gonna argue with you, you're just a damn fool kid anyway, you'll change your mind.

He flounders through the first weeks of freshman year, walks in bewilderment through the Yard. Everyone knows so much more than he does here — there is an instinctive resistance to them — the left-handed remnant of the humus around the mushroom stem — everyone talks flippantly of things he had thought about in the privacy of his own room, his own head.

His roommate cozens him, product of another midwestern city, another Country Day school. You know when Ralph Chestley comes around, isn't he a swell fellow, you ought to get to meet him, Delphic, which is pretty damn good, better than we'll ever get I can tell you, but of course we've got that thing against us, if I knew then what I know now, I would have come east to Exeter or Andover, although they're not nearly good enough that's what I've been learning, but if we can get to meet the right fellows, we ought to make Speakers anyway, that's not so hard, and we can certainly make Hasty Pudding, but to get into a Final Club that's the trick, although I've heard they're getting more democratic lately.

336

I haven't thought about it.

Well, you ought to, you've got to go at it carefully.

His first self-assertion. To hell with it.

Well, now look, Hearn, we get along pretty well, so don't cream it for me, I mean a fellow's chances can be hurt by his roommate, so don't do anything excessive, you know what I mean.

For the first year Hearn has little chance to do anything excessive. The skids are not greased that smoothly. He bogs down, sees his roommate seldom, spends nearly all his afternoons in lab and his nights studying. He makes himself a schedule which charts everything down to the fifteen minutes he can allow himself to read the comic pages on Sunday morning, and the movie he can see on Saturday night. He drifts through the long afternoons, copying the changes on the thermometer in his flask, and marking beside it the variations in the hydrometer. There is a nerve in the head of the frog which he is always severing. On the fourth attempt he nibbles successfully with his scalpel at the desiccated preserved flesh of the frog head until the nerve glistens thinly, freed like a tenuous wire of spittle. In his triumph, he feels depressed. Do I really want to do this?

In the lecture rooms, despite himself, he drowses through class. The voice of the assistant professor with the steel-rimmed glasses and the bony scientist's face laps fuzzily at his ear. His eyes close.

Gentlemen, I would like you to consider the phenomenon of the kelp. Nereocystis lütkeana, macrocystis pyrifera, pelagophycus porra, he writes on the blackboard. They are a very distinctive form of marine life, consider this: they have no roots, no leaves, they receive no light from the sun. Under the water the giant kelp form veritable jungles of plant life where they live without movement, absorbing their nutrition from the ocean medium.

The bourgeois of the plant species, the student next to him murmurs, and Hearn is awake, startled by the chord of recognition, of excitement. He has almost phrased it himself.

It is only in storms, the professor says, that they are washed ashore; normally we must think of them as living in the dense tangle of marine jungles, stationary, absorbed in their own nutriment. These

337

species had to remain behind when other aquatic plants moved onto land. Their brown color, which is an advantage in the murky underseas jungles, would be fatal in the intense illumination of land. The professor holds up a withered brown frond with a ropelike stalk. Pass it around, men.

A student holds up his hand. Sir, what is their main use?

Oh, they have been used many ways. Essentially they are fertilizer. Potash deposits can be extracted.

But the moments like that come too seldom. He is empty and hungering for knowledge, the vessel that must be filled.

Slowly he gets around, meets a few people, starts going to places. In the spring of his freshman year he goes out of curiosity to a meeting of the Harvard Dramatic Club. The president is ambitious and the discussion of plans is elaborate.

It's completely absurd when you stop to think of it. It's absolutely ridiculous having us bat out these silly musical jangles, we've got to broaden our scope.

I know a Radcliffe girl who's studied Stanislavsky, someone drawls. If we had a decent program we could get her in, and have some decent training in the method.

Oh, lovely, let's do Chekhov.

A slim youth with horn-rimmed glasses is on his feet, demanding to be heard. If we're going to shed the chrysalis, then I demand, I just demand that we do *The Ascent of F-6*. It's just kicking around, and it's not even being put on. I mean it's ridiculous when you stop to think of it, what a barrel of kudos it'll mean to us.

I can't agree with you about Auden and Isherwood, Ted, someone answers.

A dark-haired student, heavy set, with a deep important voice, is talking. I think we ought to do Odets, he's the only playwright in America who's doing anything serious, at least he has his feet in the frustrations and aspirations of the common people.

Boooooh, someone yells.

O'Neill or Eliot are the only ones.

Eliot doesn't belong in the same bed with O'Neill. (Laughter)

They argue for an hour and Hearn listens to the names. A few are familiar to him, Ibsen and Shaw and Galsworthy, but he has never heard of Strindberg, Hauptmann, Marlowe, Lope De Vega, Webster, Pirandello. The names go on, and he tells himself desperately that he must read.

He makes a start in the late spring of his first year, rediscovers the volume of Housman that nourished him in prep school, but to it he adds poets like Rilke and Blake and Stephen Spender. By the time he goes home for the summer he has switched his major to English, and he deserts the beach many afternoons, the Sally Tendeckers and her replacements, spends the nights writing short stories.

They are poor enough, but there is a temporary focus of excitement, a qualified success. When he returns to Harvard, he makes one of the literary magazines in the fall competitions, glares drunkenly into the spotlight at the initiation, and comes off without making too big a fool of himself.

The changes come slowly at first, then quickly. He reads everything, spends a lot of time at Fogg, goes to the symphony on Friday afternoons, absorbs the pleasant connotative smell of old furniture and old prints and the malty odor of empty beer cans in the aged rooms of the magazine. In the spring he wanders through the burgeoning streets of Cambridge, strolls along the Charles, or stands talking outside his house entry while the evening comes, and there is all the magic of freedom.

Several times he goes out on drunks to Scollay Square with a friend or two. It is a self-conscious business with old clothing, an undeviating tour of all the bars and dives.

Practice for finding the sawdust saloons on Third Avenue.

If there is puke on the floor, they are delighted; they are fraternity men dancing with movie stars. But the moods all change. After they become drunk, there is the pleasurable sadness of late spring evenings, the cognition of all hope and longing arrayed against the casual ugly attrition of time. A good mood.

God, look at these people, Hearn says, talk of your animal existences.

What do you expect, his friend says, they're the by-product of an acquisitive society, refuse, that's all, the fester in Spengler's world-city.

Jansen, you're a phony, what do you know about an acquisitive society, there's things I could tell you, it's different, you're a phony, that's all.

So are you, we're all phonies. Parasites. Hothouse flowers. The thing is to get out and join the movement.

What's the matter, Hearn asks, you going political on me?

I'm not political, that's bullshit, everything's bullshit. He waves his arm sweepingly.

Hearn, cupping his chin in his hand. You know when nothing else is left I'm going to become a fairy, not a goddam little nance, you understand, but a nice upright pillar of the community, live on green lawns. Bisexual. Never a dull moment, man or woman, it's all the same to you, exciting.

Jansen's head lolls. Join the Navy.

No, thanks. None of your machine-made copulations for me. You know the trouble with Americans is they don't know how to screw, there's no art in our lives, every intellectual has a Babbitt in the closet. Oh, I like that one, I like it. Can it for me, will you, Jansen?

We're all neurotic.

Sure.

For a little while it is all quite glorious. They are wise and aware and sick and the world outside is corrupt and they are the only ones who know it. Weltschmertzen, mahogany melancholies, and Weltanschauungen are the only currency.

But it does not always work. I'm a phony, Hearn says, and there are times when it goes beyond the flippancy, the easy depression, the almost gratifying self-disgust. Sometimes there are things which can be done about it.

He broods about this through the summer, has a fight with his father.

I'll tell you, Robert, I don't know where you picked up all this union idea guff, but if you think they ain't a bunch of gangsters, if you think my men weren't better off depending on me, when Jesus

340

Christ I've helped them out of many a scrape, and Christmas bonuses, why don't you stay out of this, you don't know what the hell you're talking about.

I resent that, but you never could understand what paternalism is.

Maybe I don't being as it's a big word, but it seems to me it's easy enough to bite the hand that feeds ya.

Well, you don't have to worry about that any more.

Now, hold on.

But after a further series of supplications and quarrels, he goes back to school early, gets a job washing dishes in the Georgian, and keeps it once classes have started. There are movements toward reconciliation; Ina comes out to Boston for the first time in three years, and a grudged truce is achieved. He writes home from time to time, but he will not take any money, and junior year is a grind of selling college subscriptions and pressing and laundering contracts to freshmen, odd jobs on weekends, and waiting on tables in the house as a substitute for dishwashing. He likes none of it particularly, but there are new processes discovered, new sources of strength. He never really debates the idea of taking money from his parents any longer.

And he feels himself growing older through the year, tougher, wonders at it and picks up no answers. Maybe I have my father's stubbornness. The closest things, the dominant patterns are usually unanswerable. He has lived in a vacuum for eighteen years, cloyed by the representative and unique longings of any youth; he has come into the shattering new world of college and spent two years absorbing, sloughing off shells, putting out feelers. And inside himself a process, never fully understood, had taken place. A casual fight with his father that has expanded into a rebellion, apparently out of proportion, but it is the sum, he knows, of everything, even of things he has forgotten.

The old friends are still there, still appreciated, but their charm is lessened. In the daily grind of waiting on tables, doing library work, tutoring clubmen, a certain impatience has developed. Words and words, and there are other realities now, a schedule to hold to from necessity. He spends little time at the magazine, frets in some of his classes.

The number seven has a deep significance to Mann. Hans Castorp spends seven years on the mountain, and if you will remember the first seven days are given great emphasis. Most of the major characters have seven letters in their name, Castorp, Clavdia, Joachim, even Settembrini fulfills it in that the Latin root of his name stands for seven.

The scribbling of notes, the pious acceptance. Sir, Hearn asks, what's the importance of that? I mean frankly I found the novel a pompous bore, and I think this seven business is a perfect example of German didacticness, expanding a whim into all kinds of critical claptrap, virtuosity perhaps, but it leaves me unmoved.

His speech causes a minor stir in the class, a polite discussion which the lecturer sums up gently before continuing, but it is a significant impatience for Hearn. He would not have said that the preceding year.

There is even a political honeymoon for a month. He reads some Marx and Lenin, joins the John Reed Society, and argues stubbornly all the time with the members.

I don't see how you can say that about the syndicalists, they've done some damn good work in Spain, and if there can't be a greater co-operation of the elements involved . . .

Hearn, you don't appreciate the issues involved. There is a history of deep political antagonism between the syndicalists and ourselves, and there has never been a time when it was historically more inappropriate to divert the masses with an unattainable and uncoordinated utopia. If you would take the trouble to study the revolution, you would realize that the anarchists have a record of sensuality and political debauch in times of stress, and tend to assume a feudal discipline with terrorist leaders. Why don't you study the career of Batko Makhno in 1919? Do you realize even Kropotkin was so repelled by the anarchist excesses that he took no stand in the revolution?

Should we lose the war in Spain, then?

What if it is won by the wrong elements on our side who will be unaffiliated with Russia? How long do you assume they would last with the Fascist pressures present in Europe today?

That's a little too farsighted for me. He stares around the dormitory room, at the seven members spread out over the couch, the floor, and the two worn chairs. It seems to me you just do the thing that seems best at the moment, and worry about the rest of it later.

That's bourgeois morality, Hearn, harmless enough in the middle classes outside of its capacity for inertia, but the representatives of morality in a capitalist state employ the same morality toward other ends.

Later, after the meeting, the president talks to him over a beer in McBride's, his serious owlish face rather sad. Hearn, I welcomed you as a member, I must admit, I've searched myself and I understand it's a remnant of bourgeois aspirations, you come from a class which I envy still to the extent that I'm not wholly educated, but I'm going to have to ask you to leave, because you're not at the stage in your development where we can teach you anything.

I'm a bourgeois intellectual, huh, Al.

There's great truth in that, Robert. You've reacted against the lies of the system, but it's a nebulous rebellion. You want perfection, you're a bourgeois idealist, and therefore you're undependable.

Isn't this distrust of the bourgeois intellectual a little old-hat?

No, Robert. It's founded on Marx's perception, and the experience of the past century proves his wisdom. If a man moves to the party because of spiritual or intellectual reasons, he's bound to move away again once the particular psychological climate that moved him there in the first place is changed. It's the man who comes to the party because economic inequities humiliate him every day of his life who makes a good Communist. You're independent of economic considerations, and so you're without fear, without the proper understanding.

I guess I will get out, Al. We're friends then, though.

Certainly. They shake rather self-consciously and leave each other. *I've searched myself and I understand it's a remnant of bourgeois aspirations.* What a meatball, Hearn thinks. He is amused, a little contemptuous. As he passes a store front, he stares at himself for a moment, regarding his dark hair and hooked blunted nose. I look more like a Jew-boy than a midwestern scion. Now if I'd had blond hair, Al really would have searched himself.

343

But there are other elements. *You want perfection.* Perhaps, or was it something else, something less definable?

His senior year he branches out, plays house football with a surprising and furious satisfaction. One play he never quite forgets. A ball carrier on the opposing team breaks through a hole in the line, is checked momentarily, and is standing there stock upright, helpless, when Hearn tackles him. He has charged with all his strength and the player is taken off the field with a wrenched knee while Hearn patters after him.

You all right, Ronnie?

Yeah, fine. Good tackle, Hearn.

I'm sorry. Only he knows he isn't. There has been an instant of complete startling gratification when he knew the ball carrier was helpless, waiting to be hit. There is not even any cynical pleasure in making the All-House football team.

And other fields too. He attains a grudged notoriety by seducing a DeWolfe Street deb. He even ties up with some of the men he has met through his freshman roommate, now in Speakers, receives after four years a belated invitation to one of the Brattle Hall dances.

The stags line up against the wall, chat cursorily with one another, and cut in to dance with either a girl they know or the girl of a man they know. Hearn smokes a cigarette or two, quite bored, and then cuts in on a little blonde girl dancing with a tall blond clubman.

The gesture toward conversation:

And your name is Betty Carreton, eh, where do you go to school?

Oh, to Miss Lucy's.

I see. And then the barbarity he cannot forswear. And does Miss Lucy tell you girls how to keep it until marriage?

What did you say?

More and more often this inexplicable humor. Somewhere in the cavernous and undoubtedly rotten tissues of the collective brain of Al, of Jansen, of the magazine men, the college literary critics, in the aesthetes' salons, in the modern living rooms on the quiet back streets of Cambridge, there would be the unadmitted hunger to be bored and superior at a Brattle Hall dance, either that or go to Spain.

344

He thinks it out one night. He can be genuinely indifferent to the Brattle Hall thing because it is the Class AA minor league affair which all his training on the green lawns, at the dancing school, or riding at night in convertibles on the highways back of Cholive-oil, has satisfied. It is for the others, the salon men, to be tortured and attracted by the extra quotient of wealth, the elaboration of social fences.

And about Spain he knows he is never serious. That war is in its last spring, and there is nothing in himself he wants to satisfy by going there, no over-all understanding or compassion which he cares to satisfy. The graduation and class week is upon him, and he is cool and friendly to his parents, bored with them too.

What are you gonna do, Bob, don't you want any help? Bill Hearn asks.

No, I'm going to head for New York, Ellison's father promised me a job there.

This is quite a place, Bob, Bill Hearn says.

Yes, a funny four years. And inside himself he is straining. *Go away, leave me alone. All of you.* Only he has learned not to say that out loud any longer.

For his thesis he has been given a magna: *A Study of the Cosmic Urge in Herman Melville.*

He functions easily through the next two years, sees himself consciously, amusedly as The Young Man in New York. He is first a reader and then a junior editor at Ellison and Co.: Harvard, New York Extension, as he terms it, and a room and kitchenette in the East Sixties. Oh, I'm just a literary con man, he will say.

I can't tell you how I've slaved over the thing, the lady historical novelist says to him. I was so worried about the motivations of Julia, such an *elusive* bitch, but I think I achieved the effect I hungered for in her, the one who worries me, however, is Randall Clandeborn.

Yes, Miss Helledell, two more of the same, waiter. He lights a cigarette, revolving slowly in the leather arc of their round booth. You were saying, Miss Helledell?

Do you think Randall comes across?

345

Randall Clandeborn, mmm. (Now which one was he?) Ay, yes, I think he's successful on the whole, but perhaps you need a little sharper definition on him. We can discuss that when we get back to the office. (After the drinks he will have a headache.) To be frank, Miss Helledell, I'm not really worried about your characters, I know they'll come across.

Do you think so, Mr. Hearn? Your opinion means an awful lot to me.

Oh, yes, it's a very successful job.

And George Andrew Johannesson, how is he?

Well, to tell you the truth, Miss Helledell, I should prefer to discuss it when we've got the manuscript between us. I remember the characters perfectly but I'm awfully bad on names. It's one of my faults for which you'll have to forgive me.

And there is always the game of mentally plucking, one by one, all the feathers in her hat.

Or the young serious novelist, not quite good enough, he has decided.

Well, now, Mr. Godfrey, I think you've got a damn good book there and it's a damn shame that publishing exigencies being what they are, this is not quite the season, perhaps in thirty-six, it would have been a classic if it had come out in the twenties, George, for example, liked it a hell of a lot.

Yeah, I understand, but still it seems to me you could take a chance, after all, that crap you put out, I understand, bread and butter, but a serious book is a publisher's only excuse for being.

Sure, it's a damn shame. Sipping his drink mournfully. You know if you intend to do another book we're awfully interested in it.

The weekends in the summer:

You have to talk to Carnes, what a delicious humor. I don't mean he's quaint or anything like that, he's a man in his own right of course that's perfectly apparent, but as a gardener he's a find. Even the natives consider him one apart, with that Lancashire accent of his — If i' twere rainin' soup, there Ay'd be stahndin' with a fork in me hand,' his hostess says, putting down her drink.

346

And across the porch the gossip is easily overheard. I can't tell you what a bitch she is, the woman is *incredible*. When she went out on tour she hand-picked her leading man, purely by the genital heft, so to speak, and when he started fooling around with poor little Judy, damn if Beroma didn't give a party to which she invited *everyone* but little Judy and the corpus delicti.

In the office in the middle of the afternoon: He's coming up today, Hearn, he would, we're all invited. Ellison has suggested that our attendance is requested.

Oh, Gawd.

Get up near him when he's had five or six. He says the most amazing things. And talk to his wife, the new one, she's fantastic.

In a bar with a Harvard contemporary:

Hearn, you have no idea what it's like working on *Space*. That man! He's hideous, he's a Fascist. The writers he's got up there, the talent, all grubbing away, afraid to leave 'cause it's two hundred a week, and they don't know what they can do on their own. I tell you my stomach turns every time I see them grind out the particular brand of swill at which he's so tricky. Jabbing out a cigarette. What are you in this racket for?

I'm playing it for the laughs.

Sure you're not trying to be a writer from the wrong end?

No, I'm not writer, I don't have a deep enough itch.

Jesus, there's a million who have. I don't know anybody who's worth a goddam.

Who does?

Get potted, get screwed, and get up in the morning, somehow.

Sure.

And the women:

Hearn, she says, in her deep husky voice, you're a shell, you're nothing but a goddam shell. After you've had fifty thousand of us up here, you'll probably cut it off and hang it up to dry. You learned an acceptable wiggle somewhere along the line and you think that's all you need to get by. You've got a faeces complex, haven't you, you can't stand being touched. You get me so goddam mad, a million miles away, aren't you, nothing ever hits you. Nothing's worth touching.

Oh, the girl says quietly in her childish breathless voice, you're really good, there's such goodness in you, but you're wrong, you see, because true compassion is evil, when I was in the hospital there were a few minutes when I loved a doctor, and then I didn't care about him any more, and when I was in the shock treatment I kept thinking contact was evil, and it's only freedom that's worth while, it's why you don't want me because you're free and good.

Her voice is reedy, well modulated. Oh, well, darling, what could I do, it was perfectly preposterous, all those silly apprentices just *loathing* my guts, all of them perfectly convinced of course they could do the thing better than I could, and my God you should have seen some of the interpretations they had, they were just *bound* to make trouble, and they creamed everything, everything, between Eddie and me, I could have had the ingénue in Sing at Breakfast, I don't know why I hang around with you, I'm just wasting my time.

Still there are moments. Different women, different nights, when he lies in embrace, steeped in a woman's flesh until the brew is intolerably joyous. There are love harvestings, sometimes months in a row when there is one woman, one affair, and a proud secret knowledge of each other's loins, admirable matings, sensitive and various, lewd or fierce or dallying gently, sometimes sweet and innocent like young lovers.

Only it never lasts.

I can't tell you why, he says one night to a friend. It's just every time I start an affair, I know how it's going to end. The end of everything is in the beginnings for me. It's going through the motions.

If you saw my analyst . . .

The hell with that. If I'm afraid of having my dick cut off or something like that I don't care to know it. That's not a cure, it's a humiliation, it's a deus ex machina. I find out what's wrong and bango I'm happy and go back to Chicago and spawn children and terrorize ten thousand people in whatever factory my father decides to give me. Listen, if you're cured, everything you've gone through, everything you've learned is pointless.

348

And if you don't go you're just going to get sicker.

Only I don't feel sick. I just feel blank . . . superior, I don't give a damn, I'm just waiting around.

Perhaps. He doesn't know the answer himself, hardly cares. For months there is very little in his head beyond the surface reactions, the amusement and the boredom.

When the war in Europe starts, he decides to get into the Canadian Air Force but his night vision is not quite good enough. He has been thinking in terms of leaving New York, and he finds he cannot bear to remain in it. There are nights when he goes off by himself, and wanders through Brooklyn or the Bronx, taking buses or elevated trains to the end of the route, exploring along the quiet streets. More often he walks through the slums at night, savoring the particular melancholy of watching an old woman sitting on her concrete stoop, her dull eyes reflecting on the sixty, seventy years of houses like this and streets like this, the flat sad echo of children's voices rebounding from the unyielding asphalt.

It swells into movement again, and through a friend he gets a job as an organizer for a union in an upstate city. There is a month of organizer's school, and then a winter of working in a factory, signing men up. And again the break. For after the majority is achieved and the union recognized, the leaders make a decision not to strike.

Hearn, you don't understand, you can't afford to give a condemnation, you're just a dilettante in labor, and things that seem simple to you aren't.

Well, what's the use of building up the union if we're not going to strike? This way it's just dues out of the pay envelopes.

Listen, I know this outfit we're up against. If we strike they'll drop their recognition, fire the lot of us, and pull in a bunch of scabs, this's a mill town, don't forget.

And we'll throw them right up against the NLRB.

Sure, and after eight months there'll be a decision in our favor, and what the hell are the men going to do in the meantime?

Then why have started the union, and given the men all that bullshit? Because of higher politics?

You don't know enough about it to judge. The CIO would have

been in here next year, Starkley's outfit, Red all the way through. You've got to build fences, you're being a kid about it, you want everything simple, do this and get that, well, I'll tell you it won't work that way, you got to build a fence around those boys.

The editorship is out, and this too, and the others, he realizes. A dilettante skipping around sewers. Everything is crapped up, everything is phony, everything curdles when you touch it. It has not been the experience itself. There was the other thing, unfocused, the yearning for what?

On an impulse he goes back to Chicago for a few weeks with his parents.

Now, Bob, there's no use kidding around, you been out working and know what the goddam score is, you might as well come in with me, what with these war contracts with Europe, and the armies we're building I can use you, I'm getting so goddam big I don't even know all the damn factories I got a finger in, and it's gonna be getting bigger and bigger. I tell you it's different from the way it used to be when I was a kid, everything's tied up now, you know, it sorta gets out of hand, I get a funny feeling when I think of how big the whole works is, it's all consolidated, I can tell you. You're my son, and you're just like me, the only reason you been dicking around is there ain't anything big enough for you to get your teeth in.

Maybe. And he wonders, feels the stirrings of the deeper urge. I want to think about it.

Everything is lousy, so at least why not do it in a big way?

He meets Sally Tendecker Randolph at a party, talks to her in a corner.

On, sure, Bob, I'm domesticated now. Two children, and Don (a prep-school classmate) is putting on weight, you won't recognize him. It brings back memories looking at you.

After the preliminaries they have a casual affair and he drifts around on the outskirts of her group for a month, and then two. (The few weeks have elongated.)

An odd setup. They are nearly all married with one or two children and governesses and the children are sometimes seen at bedtime. There is a migratory party almost every night from house to house along Lake Shore Drive, and the wives and husbands are always mixed, always drunk. It is all done in a random, rather irritable kind of lust, and the petting is more frequent than the cuckolding.

And once a week or so there is usually a nice public quarrel, or a drunken bathos which grates his spine.

Now look, old man, Don Randolph says to him, you and Sally used to be great friends, maybe you are still by God I don't know (the drunken accusing stare) but the truth is Sally and I love each other, a great passion, I've been fooling around and I'm a dog, woman in our office, and Alec Johnson's wife, Beverly, you were there you saw us coming back in the car, stopped off at her house, oh God, wonderful, but I'm a dog, no moral fiber, and I'm . . . I'm . . . (starting to weep) Wonderful children, Sally's a bitch to them. He stands up, lumbers along the dance floor to separate Sally from her partner.

Stop drinking.

Go away, Don dear.

The Randolphs are at it again, someone giggles. And the thing lurches in his head, and Hearn discovers he is drunk.

You remember me, Bob, Sally says, you know what capabilities I have, what talent. I tell you there's nothing can stop me, but Don's impossible, he'd like to keep me in a rut, and my Lord he's perverted, the things I could tell you about him, and sullen, we went a month and a half one time without touching each other, and you know really he's no good in the business, my father much as told me that, it's just tied down with children and nothing really, you know nothing really I mean definite I can get my teeth into, if I were a man, and I have to make an appointment to get braces for Dorothy's teeth, and I'm always worried about cancer, you can't imagine what a deep worry that is for a woman, somehow I just don't keep up with things, once there was an Air Corps lieutenant, young but really very nice, very sweet, oh, but so naïve, you can't imagine how old I feel, I envy you, Bob, if I were a man.

He knows this thing will not take either, the Lake Shore and conventions and entertaining men who bore him, the rigidity of an office, and eluding his mother's matches, transforming the *impulse* into carloads and contacts, the campaign contributions and representatives, senators, who are amenable, the Pullman cars, and the tennis courts, the absorption in golf, the particular hotels, and the odor of liquor and carpeting in a suite. Behind it there is the primal satisfaction, but he has learned too many other things on the way.

New York again, and a job doing copy for a radio network, but this is a stopgap and he knows it. Rather abstractedly, without any deep feeling, he does a lot of work for Bundles for Britain, and follows the newspaper headlines of the advance on Moscow, thinks not very seriously of joining the Party. At night sometimes he throws off his covers and lies naked on his bed feeling the late fall air eddy through the window, listening with a somber ache to the harbor sounds that float in on the fog. A month before Pearl Harbor he enlists in the Army.

On the troop transport, which slips under the Golden Gate Bridge and heads out into the Pacific on a chill winter twilight two years later, he stands on deck and stares at San Francisco, fading away like dying logs in a fireplace. After a time he can see only the gaunt dark line of land still separating the water from the deepening night. The waves splash coldly against the hull.

The new phase. In the old one he has looked and looked and butted his head against the wall of his own making.

He ducks into a hatchway and lights a cigarette. There is the phrase "I'm seeking for something" but it gives the process an importance it doesn't really possess, he thinks. You never do find out what makes you tick, and after a while it's unimportant.

Somewhere in America now were the cities, and the refuse sitting on the steps, the electric lights and the obeisance to them.

(All the frenetic schemings, the cigar smoke, the coke smoke, the passion for movement like an ant nest suddenly jarred. How do you conceive your own death in all the marble vaults, the brick ridges and the furnaces that lead to the market place?)

It was disappearing now, the water washing almost completely over the land, the long vast night of the Pacific settling overhead. And there was the yearning toward the land that disappeared.

352

Not love, not hate necessarily, but an emotion when he had expected none at all.

Always there was the power that leaped at you, invited you.

Hearn sighed, went out to the rail again. And all the bright young people of his youth had butted their heads, smashed against things until they got weaker and the things still stood.

A bunch of dispossessed . . . from the raucous stricken bosom of America.

12

MINETTA was sent to the Division Clearing Hospital after he had been wounded. It was very small. Eight squad tents, each with a capacity of twelve men, had been set up in a clearing near the shore. The tents were aligned in two rows of four, and around each tent a four-foot wall of sandbags had been erected. That was the extent of the hospital with the exception of a few extra tents at one end of the clearing which contained the field kitchen, the doctor's quarters, and the enlisted men working there.

It was always quiet at the hospital. By midafternoon the air was heavy and the inside of the tents had become unbearably hot from the intense sun. Most of the patients drowsed uncomfortably murmuring in their sleep or groaning from their wounds. There was really very little to do. A few of the convalescents might play cards or read a magazine or at most take a shower in the center of the clearing where a gasoline drum filled with water had been fastened to the top of a platform made of coconut logs. There were also the three meals a day, and the morning round of the doctor.

Minetta enjoyed himself at first. The wound he had received was hardly more than a scratch; it had laid open a few inches of his thigh, but the bullet had not been embedded and the bleeding had been moderate. He was able to walk with a slight limp an hour after he had been wounded. At the hospital he had been given a cot and some blankets, and he lay in bed comfortably and read magazines until dark. A doctor gave him a cursory examination, dressed his cut with sulfa powder, and left him alone until the next morning. Minetta felt weak and comfortable. He was suffering to a slight extent from shock, just enough to make him lassitudinous, but it kept him from thinking about the surprise and pain he had felt when the bullet had struck him. It was the first night in six weeks he had been able to sleep without being awakened for guard and the cot felt soft and luxurious in comparison to bedding on the ground. He awakened alert and cheerful. He played checkers with one of the men in his tent until the doctor came. There were only a few patients, and Minetta had a pleasant vague memory of talking to them the night before in the darkness. This is okay, Minetta decided. He hoped they would keep him in the hospital for a month, or perhaps evacuate him to another island. He began to tell himself that his wound was very serious.

The doctor, however, glanced at his leg for a moment, replaced the dressing and told him, "You'll be able to leave by tomorrow."

The information gave Minetta a pang. "You think so, sir?" he managed to say eagerly. He shifted his position on the cot, feigning some difficulty, and added, "Yeah, I'd like to get back to my buddies."

"Well, you just take it easy," the doctor said, "and we'll see tomorrow morning." He jotted down something in his notebook, and went on to the next cot. The sonofabitch, Minetta told himself, I can hardly walk. As if to prove it, his leg began to ache a trifle, and he thought with bitterness, They don't care if you live or die here. All they want is to get you back where you can stop a bullet. He became sullen, and drowsed through the afternoon. They didn't even take stitches, he said once to himself.

It began to rain toward evening, and he felt comfortable and secure beneath the tent. Boy, am I glad I don't have to be on guard tonight, he told himself. He listened to the downpour on the tent, and thought with pleasurable pity of the men in the platoon who would be awakened in their damp blankets to sit shivering in the muddy machine-gun hole while the rain penetrated their clothing. "Not for me," he said.

But then he remembered what the doctor had said. It would be raining again tomorrow; it rained every day. He would be back working on the road or the beach, standing guard at night, perhaps going out on a patrol soon where he might be killed instead of wounded. He thought of how he had been caught on the beach, and he felt an acute surprise. It didn't seem possible that something as small as a bullet could have hurt him. The sounds of the firing, the emotions he had felt were returning to him, and he shuddered a little. It seemed unreal, the way a man's face may sometimes seem unreal if he gazes at it too long in the mirror. Minetta drew his blanket over his shoulder. They ain't getting me back tomorrow, he assured himself.

In the morning, before the doctor came, Minetta took off his bandages and examined his wound. It was almost healed; the lips of the cut had come together and were filled with new pink flesh. They would certainly discharge him today. Minetta looked about him. The other men were occupied or sleeping, and with a quick motion he ripped open the gash again. It began to bleed, and he wrapped up the bandages with trembling fingers, feeling a guilty glee. Under the blanket he would rub his wound every few minutes to start the bleeding again. He felt a nervous impatience, waiting for the doctor to come. His thigh felt warm and sticky under the bandages, and Minetta turned to the man in the next cot. "My leg's bleeding," he said. "Those wounds are funny things."

"Yeah."

When the doctor examined him, Minetta was silent. "I see your wound's opened."

"Yes, sir."

The doctor looked at the bandage. "You haven't been touching it, have you?" he asked.

"I don't think so, doc. Just started bleeding." He's on to me, Minetta decided. "Naw, it's okay, I'll be able to get back to my platoon today, won't I?" he pleaded.

"You better wait another day, son. It shouldn't have opened that way." The doctor began dressing it again. "Let the bandage alone this time," he said.

"Yeah, why, sure, sir." He watched the doctor move on. Minetta was depressed. It's the last time I can pull that gag, he told himself.

He was restless all day, trying to think of some way he could

355

remain in the hospital. He became dejected every time he realized that he would have to go back to the platoon. He thought of the endless days ahead with the work and the combat and the unending repetition. I ain't even got a buddy in the platoon. You can't trust Polack. He thought of Brown and Stanley, whom he hated, Croft, of whom he was afraid. They got a goddam clique, he told himself. He thought of the war, which would stretch on forever. After this island there's gonna be another one and then another one . . . Aaah, there's no future in the whole goddam thing. He slept a little and awoke even more miserable. I can't take this, he said to himself. If I'd been lucky I woulda got a real bad wound, and I'd be on a plane to the States now. Minetta brooded over this. Once he had boasted to Polack that if he ever got into a hospital, he'd never come back to the platoon. "Just let me get in, and I'll work it," he had said.

There had to be a way. Minetta discarded one wild idea after another. He thought of jamming a bayonet into his wound, or of falling off a truck when he went back to headquarters company. He twisted on his cot, and felt pity for himself. He heard a soldier groaning slightly on one of the cots, and this irritated him. He told himself, That guy's gonna flip his lid if he don't shut up.

The idea went through his mind without his phrasing it, and he sat up in excitement, panicky with the fear he might forget it. Oh, that's it, that's it, he said to himself. He became frightened as he thought of how hard it would be. Have I got the guts? he asked himself. He lay motionless, trying to remember what he had heard about soldiers who had got out for that reason. Jesus, a Section Eight, he said to himself. He recalled a soldier in his training platoon, a thin nervous man who had begun to weep on the rifle range when he fired his gun. The soldier had been taken to the hospital, and he heard weeks later that he had been discharged. Oh, man, Minetta said to himself. He felt happy for a moment as if he were actually out of the service. I'm as smart as any of these guys, I can work it. Nervous shock, that's the story, nervous shock. I got wounded, didn't I? You'd think the Army would discharge a guy after he got wounded, but all they do is patch him up and send him back. Cannon fodder, that's all they care about us. Minetta felt righteous.

356

His mood ebbed, and he became frightened again. I wish I could talk to Polack, he'd know how to work it. Minetta looked at his hands. I'm as good a man as Polack. I can be out while he's still talking about it. He held his forehead. They'll only keep me here a couple of days, and then they'll send me to another hospital where they keep the loonies. If I get there, I'll be able to copy them. Abruptly, he was depressed again. That doc is watching me, I'm gonna have a tough time of it. Minetta hobbled over to a table in the center of the tent, and picked up a magazine. If I get out, he told himself, I could write Polack a letter and say, "Who's crazy now?" Minetta began to giggle as he thought of Polack's face when he read that. It's just a question of guts, he said to himself.

He lay down and remained without moving for half an hour, holding the magazine over his face. The sun had heated the tent until it felt like a steam room, and Minetta was weak and miserable. A tension increased inside him, and suddenly, without allowing himself to think, he stood up and shrieked, "Fug yez all."

"Take it easy," a soldier said from a nearby cot.

Minetta threw his magazine at him, and screamed, "There's a Jap outside the fuggin tent, there's a Jap right over there, right over there." He looked about wildly, and shouted, "Where's a gun, gimme a gun." He was shaking with excitement. He picked up his rifle, and pointed it through the door of the tent. "There's the Jap, there he is," he screamed, and fired the rifle. He heard it numbly, a little amazed at his audacity. I ought to be an actor, went through his mind. He waited, expecting the soldiers to grab him, but no one moved. They were watching him warily, frozen with astonishment and fear on their cots. "Get rid of your guns, men, they're attacking," he said, and threw his gun to the ground. He kicked it once, and then went over to his cot, which he picked up and hurled down again. He threw himself in the dirt and began to scream. A soldier fell on top of him, and Minetta struggled for a moment and then relaxed. He could hear men shouting, and the sounds of footsteps running toward him. I did it, I bet, he told himself. He began to tremble, and allowed some spittle to form on his lips. That'll work. He had a picture of a madman he had seen once in a movie who had foamed at the mouth.

357

Someone picked him up roughly, and sat him on a cot. It was the doctor who had dressed his wound. "What's this man's name?" the doctor asked.

"Minetta," somebody said.

"All right," the doctor began, "let's cut this out, Minetta. You're not going to get away with it."

"Fug you, you wouldn't get the Jap," Minetta screamed.

The doctor shook him. "Minetta, *you're talking to an officer in the U. S. Army.* If you don't answer civilly, I'll have you court-martialed."

Minetta was terrified for a moment. I'm in, but *in,* he said to himself. It was the last line of an obscene joke, and he began to laugh a little hysterically. The sound of his mirth encouraged him, and he increased it wildly. They can't do a thing to me if I play it right, he thought numbly, and he stopped laughing suddenly, and said, "Fug you, you sonofabitch Jap." In the silence he heard a soldier say, "He's nuts, all right," and then someone answering him, "Did ya see him point that gun? Jeez, I thought he was gonna kill us all."

The doctor grew thoughtful. "You're acting, Minetta, I'm on to you," he said suddenly.

"You're a Jap." Minetta dribbled some spittle over his lower lip. He giggled once. I got him by the balls, he told himself.

"Give him a sedative," the doctor said to an orderly standing beside him, "and move him over to Number Seven."

Minetta gazed vacantly at the dirt floor. That was the tent that contained the serious patients, he had heard. He began to spit on the ground. "You Jap," he shouted after the doctor. He stiffened as the orderly grasped him and then relaxed and began to giggle meaning-lessly. He made no motion when the hypodermic needle went into his arm. I'm gonna make this, he told himself.

"Okay, Jack, follow me," the orderly said. Minetta stood up and walked across the clearing. He was wondering what he should do next. He caught up to the orderly and whispered to him, "You're a fuggin Jap, but I won't tell no one if you give me five bucks."

"Come on, Jack," the orderly said wearily.

Minetta shambled behind him. When they came to tent No. 7,

358

he stopped and began to shriek again. "I ain't gone in. There's a fuggin Jap in there who's gonna kill me. I ain't going in."

The orderly seized his arm in a wrestler's grip, and pushed him inside the tent. "Lemme go! Lemme go! Lemme go!" Minetta yelled. They stopped before a cot, and the orderly told him to lie down. Minetta sat on the cot and started to undo his shoes. I better take it easy for a while, he told himself. The sedative was beginning to work. He lay back and closed his eyes. For a moment he realized what he had done, and he had an excited lost feeling in the pit of his chest. He swallowed several times. His mind was boiling with mirth and fear and pride. All I got to do is keep it up. They'll have me out of here in a day or two.

He fell asleep in a few minutes and didn't wake until morning. It took him several minutes to remember the events of the previous day, and he began to feel frightened again. For a moment he debated whether to act normal and try to pass it off, but when he thought of returning to the platoon . . . No! Jesus, no! He'd stick it out. Minetta sat up and looked about the tent. There were three men in it, and two of them had their heads wound in bandages; the third man lay on his back without moving, his eyes staring vacantly at the ridgepole. He's Section Eight, Minetta told himself with a shiver, and then became amused as he realized the irony. But a moment later he was frightened again; probably that was the way a crazy man acted, he didn't move and he didn't say anything. Maybe he had put it on too thick the day before. Minetta was worrying. He decided that he would act in a similar way. It's a helluva lot easier on the vocal cords, he told himself.

The doctor passed through at nine o'clock, and Minetta lay on his back without moving, babbling a few words from time to time. The doctor took a glance at him, dressed his leg without speaking, and then moved on. Minetta felt a mixture of relief and resentment. They don't care if you die, he said to himself again. He closed his eyes and began to think. The morning passed quite easily; he was feeling cheerful and confident, and when he recalled the doctor's visit he decided it was a good sign the doctor had paid no attention. They gave up on me; they're gonna send me to another island soon.

359

He began to dream of what it would be like returning home. He thought of the ribbons he would be wearing, and he pictured himself walking through the streets in his neighborhood, talking to the people he met. "How was it, rough?" they would ask. "Naw, naw, it wasn't so bad," he would say. "You can't kid me, it must have been pretty bad." He would shake his head. "I can't complain, I had it easy." Minetta laughed to himself. They would be going around saying, "That Steve Minetta is a pretty good kid, you got to hand it to him. Think of all he went through, and look how modest he is."

That was the thing, Minetta decided, you had to get back first. He could see himself at all the parties; what a hit he'd make. The girls would be looking for men, and he was gonna play hard to get. Rosie'll come across this time, he said to himself. He was going to take it easy when he got back; a guy was a sucker to take a job where he worked his balls off. What did work ever do for a guy?

Lying motionless for so many hours, he began to be bothered by sexual fantasies. The tent was becoming hot from the sun again, and he lay in a pleasurable welter of heat and sweat. He progressed through long seduction scenes, creating them in detail, remembering with little shudders of passion how firm the ripple of flesh above Rosie's waist had felt. Rosie's a good kid, he said to himself, I'm gonna marry her one of these days. He remembered her perfume, and the shiny exciting line of her eyelashes. She put vaseline under them, he decided, but it's all right when a girl knows all the tricks. He was beginning to think of the women he had had at different Army posts, and his fantasies transferred to them; he began to count the women with whom he had coupled. Fourteen, that's pretty good for a guy my age, there ain't many who can beat me. He drifted off into sexual reverie again, but it was becoming painful. They're all easy to get; all you got to do is shoot 'em a little line, tell 'em you love 'em. A dame's a sucker who gives it to a guy. He began to think of Rosie again, and he became angry. She's cheating on me; that letter where she said she wasn't dancing with anybody till I get back is a crock of . . . I know her, she likes to dance too much. If she lies on something like that, she probably lies on everything. He became jealous, and to vent his frustration he shrieked suddenly. "Get

360

that Jap!" It was such an easy thing to do. He shrieked again.

The orderly got up from his chair, approached him, and put a hypodermic in his arm. "I thought you were quieting down, Jack," he said.

"The Jap," Minetta screamed.

"Yeah, yeah, yeah." The orderly turned away and sat down again. Minetta fell asleep in a short while, and didn't awaken until morning.

He felt doped the next day. He had a headache, and his limbs were numb. The doctor passed by without even looking at him, and Minetta was enraged. The goddam officers, they think the whole Army is just set up for them to have a good time. He had a deep resentment. I'm as good as anybody else; why should some sonofabitch give me orders? He twisted uncomfortably on his cot. It's a conspiracy. He felt a vague bitterness at everything. The whole world's a trick; if you're not on top you just get the shitty end of the stick. Everybody's against you. He thought of how Croft had looked at his wound and laughed. He don't give a damn about anybody, he'd just as soon see us dead. Something of the pain and shock and bewilderment he had felt when the bullet had struck him was returning to him now. He was really afraid for the first time. I ain't goin' back to that. They'll shoot me first. He moved his lips. You never know when you're safe. That's no way to live. He brooded through the afternoon. In two days he had gone from mirth to boredom to resentment, and he was becoming a little desperate. I'm a good man, he told himself, I'm noncom material if they'd give me a chance, but not Croft. He likes to look at a guy and size him up right away. He kicked his blanket away. What should I work and break my ass for? I could do the job but there's no future in it. They got a good case if they think I'm going to work for nothing. He thought of the time in training when he had led the platoon in drill. There wasn't a soldier who could beat me, he thought, but you lose your ambition. I'm becoming a bum now. I know too much, that's my trouble. It ain't worth working for, 'cause the Army never gives you a break anyway. He became sad at this, and thought with a wistful pleasure of how his life had been ruined. I know what the score is, I'm too smart to waste my time trying for anything. When I get out of the Army I won't know what to do with myself. I won't be able to work, I'll be a failure. All I'll want is to go around tail-chasing. He turned over on his face. What the hell else is there in life? He sighed. It's like Polack says, the only thing to do is to get yourself a racket. This gave him a vindictive pleasure, and he imagined himself in prison, a killer, while tears of pity came into his eyes. He turned over again nervously. I got to get out of here. How long they gonna keep me without even looking at me or paying any attention? They gotta move me outa here soon or I'll really flip my lid. The stupidity of the Army amused him. They're gonna lose a soldier that way, just 'cause they don't give him any care.

He fell asleep, and was awakened in the middle of the night by the sound of voices and the noise of orderlies moving patients into the tent. Occasionally he could see the red skeletal outline of a hand covering a flashlight, and once or twice a midgeon of light cast an eerie shadow across a patient's face. What's going on? Minetta wondered. He could hear a man groaning, and the sound formed goose flesh on his scalp. The doctor came in, and talked for a little while with one of the orderlies. "Watch the drain on that thoracic, and give him a hypo, twice the usual amount, if he's too restless."

"Yes, sir."

That's all they know, Minetta thought, hypo, hypo, I could be a sawbones myself. He was watching the scene through half-opened eyes, and he listened cautiously to the conversation between the two patients whose heads were bandaged. It was the first time he had heard them speak. "Hey, orderly," one of them was asking, "what's up?"

The orderly came over to them, and talked for a little while. "I hear there was a lot of patrolling today, and these guys just came from Battalion Aid."

"You know if E Company was in it?"

"Ask the General," the medic said.

"I'm glad I wasn't in it," one of the patients muttered.

"You ain't just a bird-turding, Jack," the orderly said.

Minetta turned over. What a way to get waked up, he thought. There was a patient at the far end of the tent who was weeping with

362

loud thick sounds that seemed to writhe out of his chest and throat. Minetta closed his eyes. What a setup, he thought disgustedly. His annoyance was suppressing a great deal of fear; he had become conscious suddenly of the thrumming of the jungle night outside the tent, and he had the childish horror that comes from waking suddenly in the darkness. "Jesus," he muttered. With the exception of the minor exertions that had been required to use the bed pan under the cot and to eat the food that had been set before him, he had been completely inactive for two and a half days, and it made him extremely restless. I can't take this, he said to himself. The patient who had been weeping had begun to scream now, and the sounds had such terror that Minetta ground his teeth and held the blanket over his ears. "NEEEE-YOWWWWWWW, NEEEEEEE-YOWW-WWWRR," the patient wailed, imitating the sound of a mortar, and then he screamed again, "God, you got to save me, *you got to save me!*"

There was a long silence afterward with no sound at all in the black tent, and then one of the patients muttered, "Another psycho."

"What the hell are we in the loony ward for?"

Minetta shivered. That nut could kill me when I'm asleep. His thigh, which was almost healed, began to throb. I gotta stay awake. He pitched restlessly, listening to the crickets and the animals in the brush beyond the tent. A few shots were fired far in the distance, and he began to shudder again. I will be nuts by morning, he thought, and began to giggle to himself. His stomach felt empty; he was hungry. What did I get into this for? he wondered.

One of the new patients began groaning, and lapsed at last into a bubbly cough. That guy sounds bad, Minetta thought. Death. It seemed at the moment almost tangible. He became afraid to breathe, as if the air were polluted. In the darkness things seemed to be moving about him. What a night, he said to himself. His heart was beating quickly. Oh, Jeez, lemme just get out of here.

His stomach was tense and nervous; he retched emptily once or twice. I ain't gonna get any sleep, that's a cinch. Jealousy began to torment him. Minetta went through a long fantasy in which Rosie made love to another man; it began with her going alone to dance at

363

Roseland; and it ended inevitably, sickly, in his mind; he felt a chill sweat forming on his shoulders and the backs of his thighs. He began to worry about his family. They ain't gonna hear from me for a couple of months. How the hell will I write them a letter? They'll think I'm dead. He felt a pang as he thought of his mother's anxiety. Jeez, the way she'd fuss over me when I got a cold. Italian mothers and Jewish mothers, they're always that way. He tried to repress the concern his mother was causing him, and began to think of Rosie again. If she don't hear from me, she'll be fooling around with someone else. He became bitter. Aaah, fug her, I've had dames who give me a better time than her. There's lots of others. He thought of the exciting shiny luster of her eyes, and felt a comfortable grief and self-pity. He longed for her.

The man who had combat fatigue screamed again, and Minetta sat up shuddering. I gotta get some sleep, I can't take this. He began to shout out. "There's the Jap, I see him, *I see him,* I'm going to kill him!" He got off his cot and began to wander about the dirt floor of the tent. The earth was cold and damp against his bare feet. He trembled genuinely.

The orderly got up from his chair and sighed. "Oh, man, what a ward." He picked up a hypodermic from the table beside him and approached Minetta. "Lie down, Jack."

"Fug you." He let himself be marched back to his cot.

He held his breath while the needle jabbed into his muscle, and then exhaled. "Oh, what a time," he groaned.

The man who had the chest wound was making the bubbling coughing sounds again, but to Minetta they sounded remote. He relaxed, feeling comfortable and warm, thinking about the sedative. That stuff is good . . . I'll become a dope addict . . . aah, anyway to get out . . . He fell asleep.

In the morning he awoke to find that one of the patients was dead. The blanket was drawn up over the dead man's head and his feet made a stiff peak which traced an icy caress along Minetta's spine. He looked at the body and turned away. There was an envelope of intense silence about it. There's something different about a guy when he's dead, Minetta thought. He felt an acute curiosity about the man's face under the blanket; he wondered what it looked like. If there had been no one in the tent, he might have walked over and lifted the blanket. That's the guy with the hole in his chest, he told himself. He was afraid again. How do they expect a guy to stay here, after some poor Joe died right next to you? A touch of horror welled in him; he felt a little sick. The sedative had left him with an acute headache, and his stomach was raw, his limbs ached. Oh, Jeez, I got to get out of here.

Two orderlies came in, placed the dead man on a stretcher, and carried him out of the tent. None of the patients said anything, but Minetta found himself still looking at the vacant cot. I can't take another night like last one. A sour fluid retched from his stomach into his mouth, and he swallowed it automatically. Oh, murder.

When his breakfast came, he was unable to touch it. He sat there musing; he knew he could not bear another day in the hospital. He wished he were back with the platoon. Anything to get out of here.

The doctor came, and Minetta watched him quietly while he stripped the bandages from his leg. The cut was entirely healed except for the line of pink new flesh; the doctor smeared a red antiseptic over it, and did not replace the bandages. Minetta's heart was beating rapidly. His head felt hollow and quivering.

The sound of his voice surprised him. "Hey, doc, when am I gonna get out?"

"What's that?"

"I don't know, I woke up this morning. Where am I?" Minetta smiled with bewilderment. "I remember I was in another tent with my leg, and now I'm here. What's the score?"

The doctor looked at him quietly. Minetta forced himself to stare back; in spite of every effort, he ended by grinning weakly.

"What's your name?" the doctor asked.

"Minetta." He gave his serial number. "Can I get out today, doc?"

"Yes."

Minetta felt a mixture of relief and disappointment. At that moment he wished for a second that he had remained quiet.

"Oh, and, Minetta, after you get dressed, I want to talk to you."

The doctor turned, and then said over his shoulder, "Don't skip out. That's an order, I want to talk to you."

"Yes, sir." Minetta shrugged. What's up? he wondered. He was feeling a little glee now as he thought of how easily he had managed it. All you got to do is think fast and you can get away with anything. He put on his clothing, which had been wrapped in a ball at the head of the cot, and slipped into his shoes. The sun was not yet too hot, and he felt cheerful. That wasn't for me, he thought, I can't go this staying on your back all the time. He looked at the cot where the soldier had died, and shrugged to overcome a quiver of anxiety. A guy's lucky to get out. He remembered abruptly the patrolling that had taken place yesterday, and was depressed. I hope they don't send the platoon on something. He wondered if he had made a mistake.

After he dressed, he felt hungry, and he went over to the hospital's mess tent and talked to the first cook. "You wouldn't send a guy back to the lines without a breakfast in his belly, would ya?" he asked.

"Awright, awright, take something, then." Minetta wolfed down the rubbery remains of the scrambled powdered eggs, and drank a little of the lukewarm coffee still remaining in a ten-gallon boiler. The chlorine in it was very strong, and he made a wry face. Might as well drink iodine, he thought.

He clapped the cook on the back. "Thanks, bud," he said, "I wish they cooked as good as this in our outfit."

"Yeah."

Minetta collected his rifle and helmet from the hospital supply sergeant and strolled over to the doctor's tent. "You wanted to see me, doc?" he asked.

"Yes." Minetta sat down on a folding chair.

"Stand up!" the doctor said. He looked coldly at Minetta.

"Sir?"

"Minetta, the Army's got no use for men like you. That gag you pulled was pretty low."

"I don't know what you're talking about, sir." Minetta's voice had a meek irony.

"Don't give me any of your lip," the doctor snapped. "I'd have

366

you court-martialed if it didn't take too long, and if it wasn't just what you wanted anyway."

Minetta was silent. He could feel his face reddening, and he stood there tense and enraged; he wished he could kill the doctor.

"Answer me!"

"YES, SIR!"

"You pull that trick again, and I'll see to it personally that you get ten years for it. I'm sending a note to your CO to put you on company duty for a week."

Minetta tried to look disdainful. He swallowed once, and then said, "Why're you discriminating against me, sir?"

"Shut your mouth."

Minetta glared at him. "That all you want, doc?" he asked at last.

"Get out of here. If you come back, you better have a hole through your belly."

Minetta stalked out sullenly. He was quivering with rage. Goddam fuggin officers, he said to himself. They're all the same. He stumbled over a root, and stamped the ground angrily. Just let me get ahold of him after the war. I'll show that sonofabitch. He walked out to the road that ran past the edge of the hospital clearing, and waited for a truck to come by from the beach. He spat once or twice. That dumb bastard probably couldn't make a living before the war. Some doctor. Shame passed through him. I'm mad enough to cry, he thought.

After a few minutes a truck ground by and stopped for him. He climbed into the back, sat on top of a load of small-arms ammunition boxes, and fretted. A guy gets hurt and how do they treat him? Like a dog. They don't give a damn about us. Here I was willing to go back on my own accord, and he treated me as if I was a criminal. Aaah, fug 'em, they're all a bunch of bastards. He pushed his helmet off his forehead. I'm damned if I'll try any more. I'm out for myself. If they want to treat me that way, okay. The thought gave him some relief. Okay, then, he said at last.

He stared at the jungle which slid thickly past on either side of the truck. Okay. He lit a cigarette. *Okay.*

Red saw Minetta at midday chow when the platoon came in from working on the road. After he filed through the chow line, he sat down beside Minetta, and laid his mess gear on the ground. With a grunt he eased his back against a tree. "Just got back, huh?" he nodded to Minetta.

"Yeah, this morning."

"They kept you pretty long for just a scratch," Red said.

"Yeah." Minetta was silent for a moment and then added, "Well, you know how it is, hard to get in, hard to get out." He swallowed a mouthful of Vienna sausage. "I had a pretty soft time there."

Red piddled the dehydrated mashed potatoes and canned string beans with his spoon. It was the only eating utensil he owned; months ago he had thrown away his knife and fork. "They treated you pretty good, huh?" He was annoyed with his own curiosity.

"Damn good," Minetta said. He swallowed some coffee. "Well, I had a run-in with a doctor there, the sonofabitch. I lost my temper and told him where to get off, so I'm on company duty now, but outside of that it was okay."

"Yeah," Red said. They continued eating in silence.

Red was uncomfortable. For weeks his kidneys had been growing more painful, and that morning on the road he had strained himself badly in lifting a pick. A severe pain had seized him at the top of his swing, and he had ground his teeth, his fingers trembling. After a minute or so he had been forced to quit, and his back had throbbed for the rest of the morning with a dull constant ache. When the trucks had come, he had hoisted himself with great difficulty over the tail gate. "You're gettin' old, Red," Wyman had piped.

"Yeah." The jarring of the truck over the bumps had aggravated his pain, and he had been silent. The artillery was firing constantly and the men talked about an attack supposed to start soon. They're gonna be sendin' us out again, Red had thought, I better get fixed up. For a moment he had allowed himself to think, Maybe the hospital, and then he had repressed the thought with disgust. I never run out on anything, and I won't now. But he had kept looking uneasily over his shoulder. I ain't over that week yet, he had told himself.

"They treat you pretty fair, huh?" Red asked Minetta again.

Minetta set down his coffee, looked at Red warily. "Yeah, okay."

Red lit a cigarette, and then hoisted himself awkwardly to his feet. As he washed his mess gear in the hot water cans he debated whether to go on sick call. It seemed shameful to him somehow.

He compromised at last by stopping off at Wilson's tent. "Look, boy, I think I'm gonna go on sick call. You wanta come along?"

"Ah don' know. Never did know a doctor did a man any good."

"I thought you were sick."

"Ah am. Ah'll tell ya, Red, mah insides are shot plumb to hell. Ah cain't even take a leak any more without it burnin'."

"You need some monkey glands."

Wilson giggled. "Yeah, somepin the matter with me."

"What the hell, we might as well go," Red suggested.

"Aw, listen, Red, if they cain't see it, you ain't got it. All those sonsofbitches know is to give ya a short-arm or an asp'rin. Besides Ah hate to goof-off on the road. Ah may be a sonofabitch some ways but no man can say Ah don' do mah share of the work."

Red lit a cigarette, closing his eyes and suppressing a grimace as his back knotted suddenly. When the spasm had passed he muttered, "Come on, we rate a day off."

Wilson sighed. "Awright, but Ah feel a little low about it."

They walked over to the orderly room tent, and gave their names to the company clerk. Then they walked across the bivouac to the regimental-aid tent. Some men were standing around inside, waiting to be examined. There were two cots at one end of the tent and a half dozen men were sitting on them, and painting the fungus sores on their bare feet with a red antiseptic. An enlisted man was examining the men.

"It's a slow goddam line," Wilson complained.

"All lines are slow," Red said. "They got everything down to a system. Wait in line, wait in line, I tell you they ain't anything worth doing because of the lines."

"Ah suspec' when we get back we'll be waitin' in line for a woman."

They talked idly as the line moved forward. When Red reached the medic, he was tongue-tied for an instant. He remembered the old migrants, their limbs warped by rheumatism and arthritis and syphilis. Their eyes had become vacant, and they were usually drunk. Once they had snuffled up to him, and begged for a pill.

Now it was reversed, and for a second he could not speak. The medic was looking with boredom at him.

"It's my back," Red muttered in embarrassment at last.

"Well, take off your shirt, I can't see through your clothing," the medic snapped.

This broke the spell for Red. "If I took it off you wouldn't know any more," he flared. "It's my kidneys."

The medic sighed. "You guys can figure out more ways. Go over there to the doctor." Red noticed a shorter line, and walked over to it without answering. He was tense with anger. I don't have to take that crap, he told himself.

Wilson joined him in a moment. "They don' know nothin'. Jus' shuffle ya from man to man."

Red was about to be examined when an officer walked into the tent and greeted the doctor. "Come on over," the doctor called to him. They talked for a few minutes as Red listened. "I picked up a head cold," the officer said. "It's this hellish climate. Can you give me something to snap out of it, and I don't want any of your bloody aspirin." The doctor laughed. "I've got something for you, Ed; we got a little of it in the last shipment. Not nearly enough to go around, but you're welcome to it."

Red turned to Wilson and snorted. "If *we* came in with a cold, they'd give us a t.s. slip." He spoke loudly enough for the officers to hear, and the doctor looked at him coldly. Red glared back.

The officer left, and the doctor stared at Red. "What's the matter with you?"

"Nephritis."

"Let me do the diagnosing if you don't mind."

"I know what it is," Red said, "I been told by a doctor in the States."

"All you men seem to know just what your trouble is." The doctor asked him for the symptoms and listened inattentively. "All right, so you have nephritis, what am I supposed to do?"

370

"That's what I came here for."

The doctor looked at the ridgepole with an expression of disgust. "You wouldn't mind going to the hospital, I suppose."

"I just want to get fixed up." The doctor's words made him uneasy. Was that why he was here?

"We got a report from the hospital today to watch out for malingerers. How do I know you're not faking the symptoms?"

"There's some tests you can give me, ain't there?"

"If there wasn't a war on." He reached under his table, and handed Red a package of wound tablets. "Drink these with a lot of water, and if you're faking the whole thing, just throw them away." Red became pale. "Next man," the doctor said.

Red turned and strode out of the tent. "That's the last goddam time I ever fool around with those fuggin medics." He was quivering with rage. "If you're faking . . ." He thought of the places he had slept, the park benches, and frigid hallways in the middle of the winter. Aaah, fug 'em.

Red remembered a soldier who had died in the States because he had not been admitted to the hospital. He had gone through training for three days with a fever because the post hospital had a rule that no men could be taken into the hospital unless their temperature was over 102. The soldier had died a few hours after he came into the hospital on the fourth day; he had had galloping pneumonia.

Sure, they got it all figured out, Red thought. If they get ya to hate 'em enough you'll crack a nut before you'll go to 'em, and that way they keep ya on the line. Of course a guy dies every now and then, but what the hell's another guy to the Army? Those quacks get their orders to be sonsofbitches from the top. He felt a bitter righteous pleasure in the knowledge. You'd think we weren't men.

But immediately afterward he knew that his anger also stemmed from fear. Five years ago I woulda told that doctor off. It was one of the old jokers, and it was even worse in the Army. A man had to take crap even if it was just by keeping his mouth shut. You don't last a month if you do everything you want, he told himself. And yet nothing was worth doing if you let yourself be pushed around. There was no way to figure that one out.

He was startled by Wilson's voice. "C'mon, Red, let's go."

"Oh." They began to walk together.

Wilson was silent, and his broad high forehead was puckered in a frown. "Red, Ah wish we hadn't gone on that sick call."

"Yeah."

"Ah gotta have an op-per-ration."

"You going to the hospital?"

Wilson shook his head. "Naw, that doc said it can wait till the campaign's over. Ain't no hurry."

"What's the matter with ya?"

"Damn if Ah know," Wilson said. "That guy in there said Ah'm all shot to hell inside. Peter trouble." He whistled for a moment, and then added, "Mah old man died from an op-per-ration an' Ah don' like none of it."

"Aaah," Red said, "it ain't too bad, or they'd be doin' it now."

"Ah jus' cain't figger it out, Red. You know Ah had a dose five times and Ah cured it every single time. Buddy of mine told me about this thing, it's called pirdon or pridion or somepin like that, and Ah jus' took it, an' it fixed me up fine, but that doc says it didn't."

"He don' know what the score is."

"Aw, he's a sonofabitch, all right, but the thing is, Red, Ah'm all shot to hell inside. Ah cain't take a leak easy, and mah back hurts, and Ah gets the cramps sometimes." Wilson snapped his fingers deprecatingly. "It's a hell of a note, Red. You take somethin' like lovin', it's so nice and warm and you get to feelin' like jelly, an' then it ends up ru'nin' your insides. Ah cain't understand it, Ah tell ya Ah think that man is wrong. Ah'm sick counta somepin else. Lovin' ain't goin' to hurt a man."

"It can," Red said.

"Well, there's somepin all fugged up, that's all Ah can say. It jus' don' make sense for a good thin' like that to end up hurtin' ya." He sighed. "Red, Ah swear the whole thing is confusin' as hell." They walked back to their tents.

The Time Machine:

WOODROW WILSON

THE INVINCIBLE

He was a big man about thirty with a fine mane of golden-brown hair and a healthy ruddy spacious face whose large features were formed cleanly. Incongruously, he wore a pair of round silver-rimmed glasses which gave him at first glance a studious or, at least, a methodical appearance. "With all the gals Ah've had, Ah'll never forget that little old piece," he said, wiping the back of his hand against his high sculptured forehead, sliding it up over his golden pompadour.

Clichés like lazy decadence, death and disease, monotony and violence, well up in your mind. The main street has assumed its tawdry prosperity with discomfort; it is hot and packed with people and the stores are small and dirty. Languid and feverish, the girls walk by on thin legs, with painted faces, staring at the movie houses with gaudy placards, picking at the sore on their chin, squinting with their pale insolent eyes as the sun glares on the dirty asphalt and models the dust-filled pores of the trampled papers underfoot.

A hundred yards away the back streets are green and lovely, and the foliage of the trees meets overhead. The houses are old and pleasant; you cross a bridge and look down on a tiny stream winding and twisting gently over some soft rounded rocks; there are the sounds of things growing and the soughing of the leaves in the swollen torpid May breeze. A little farther on, there is always the small rotting mansion with its broken shutters, its peeling columns, and the dull black-gray of its walls like a tooth after the nerve has been killed. The mansion alters the loveliness of the streets, limns it with darker mortal lines.

373

The grass enclosure in the center of the town square is deserted, and the statue of General Jackson stands on its pedestal and looks with calculation at the cannon balls pyramided in cement, the old cannon whose breech is missing. Behind him the Negro quarter stretches out along the sandy roads into the farm lands.

There, in the black ghetto, the shacks and two-room shanties sag on their stilts, the wood dry and splintered and dead, the rats and roaches scurrying across the sapless planks. Everything withers in the heat.

Toward the end, almost out in the country, the poor whites live in similar huts, hoping to graduate to the other side of town where the shoe clerks and the bank tellers and the mill foremen live in cubical houses along rigid streets where the trees are not old enough to cover the sky.

Over it all hangs the torpid sullen breeze of May, stifling in the late spring.

Some people feel only the heat. Woodrow Wilson, almost sixteen, sprawls on a log along the sandy road, and drowses in the sun. His loins are warm and a lazy delight drifts along his body. In a couple hours Ah'll go see Sally Ann. Warm smells, the image of teat and female pubes, tickle his nose with passion. Ah, man, Ah wish this here evenin' was over. A man'll melt in the sun thinkin' about nookie. He sighs, moves his legs leisurely.

Guess Pa's sleepin' it off.

Behind him, on the slanting warped porch above the stilts, his father sleeps in a rusty swinging couch, his undershirt gathering soddenly about his chest.

Ain't anyone can drink like Pa. He giggles to himself. 'Cept me, come a year or two. Goddam, ain't anythin' a man wants to do but lie in the sun.

Two colored boys walk by, leading a mule by the halter. He rouses himself.

Hey, you niggers, what's that mule's name?

The boys look up frightened and one of them rubs his foot in the dust. Josephine, he mumbles.

374

Okay, boy. He chuckles easily to himself. Man, Ah'm glad Ah don' have to work today. He yawns. Hope Sally Ann don' find out Ah ain't nineteen. She like me anyway, she's a good little ole gal.

A colored girl about eighteen walks past him, her bare feet swirling tiny clouds of dust before her. Under her sweater she wears no brassière, and her pendulant breasts look very full and soft. She has a round sensual face.

He stares at her, and moves his legs again. Goddam. Her strong hips roll slowly, and he watches her stroll away with pleasure.

One of these days Ah'm gonna try somethin' like that.

He sighs again easily, and yawns. The sun feels almost unbearably delicious on his loins. Ah guess it jus' don't take much to keep a man happy.

He closes his eyes. They's jus' an awful lot of fun a man can have.

In the bicycle shop it is dark, and the benches are stained with grease. He turns the bicycle about, scanning the hand brakes. He has never seen anything but a coaster brake until now and he is confused. Ah guess Ah'll ask Wiley how to fix these little buggers; he turns toward his boss and then halts. Might as well work it out for mahself, he decides.

He squints in the gloom, traces the tension of the brakes along the connecting rod, pushes the metal pad against the metal of the wheel. After a search, he finds a loose nut where the connecting wire fails to bind, and he tightens it. The brakes work now.

That's a smart man invented that, he says to himself. He is about to put the bike away when he decides to take it apart. Ah'm gonna learn all the little doodads in that brake.

An hour later, after he has stripped it and reassembled it, he grins happily. They ain't nothin' like a piece of machinery. He feels a deep content as he traces in his mind the wires and nuts and levers that make up the hand brake.

All that machinery is simple, you jus' got to work it out for yourself. He whistles a little, pleased with himself. Ah bet in a coupla years they won't be anythin' Ah cain't fix.

But in a couple of years he is working in a hotel. The bicycle shop shuts down in the depression, and the only job he can get is as a bellhop working for tips in the fifty-room hotel at the end of the main street. He makes a little money and there are always women and liquor to be had. On night duty there seldom is a time when he can't find a girl in the hotel to spend a few hours with.

One of his buddies has an old Ford, and on weekends when he's off he goes tearing around the sandy roads with him, a gallon jug between them rattling over the loose rubber pads near the gear shift. Sometimes they take a couple of girls with them, and many Sundays they wake up in a strange room, not knowing what happened.

One Sunday he wakes up married. (Turning in bed drowsily, slipping his arm about the round belly beside him. The sheets are over his head and he looks at the warm skin and the deep black hair of the triangle. He places his finger in her navel.) C'mon, wake up. He is trying to remember her name.

Mornin', Woodrow. She has a heavy strong face, and she yawns evenly and turns to him. Mornin', hubby.

Hubby? He shakes his head and slowly assembles the events of the past night. You two sure you want to get married? the j.p. had said. He begins to laugh. Goddam! He is trying to think of where he met her.

Where's ol' Slim?

He'n Clara are in the nex' room.

Ol' Slim's married too? That's right, he is. Wilson begins to laugh again. He is beginning to remember their making love, and he feels a spasm of heat. Slowly he caresses her. You're pretty good, honey, as I remember.

You're a fine man, Woodrow, she says huskily.

Yea-a-ah. For a moment, he is thinking. (Guess Ah had to git married, sometime. Ah can move out from Pa's, and git that house over on Tolliver Street, an' we can set up.) He looks at her again, gazes at her body. (Knew what Ah was doin' even if Ah was drunk.) He giggles. Married, goddam, let's give us a kiss, honey.

The day after his first child is born, he talks to his wife in the hospital.

376

Alice, honey, Ah want ya to gimme some money.

What for, Woodrow, you know why Ah been keeping the money, same thing's gonna happen as last time, Woodrow, we need that money, we got the kid to pay for, bein' in a hospital.

He nods. Alice, a man wants to git drunk once in a while, Ah been workin' goddam hard at the garage, and Ah feel like havin' me a little time, Ah couldn' be more hones' with ya.

She looks at him suspiciously. You ain't gonna be layin' up with no woman.

Ah'm sick an' tired of that, Alice, ifen you don' trust your own husband, you're pretty bad off, Ah'm kinda hurt you talk like that.

She signs a check for ten dollars, scrawling her name laboriously. He knows she's proud of the checkbook. You write mighty fine, he says.

Come back tomorrow mornin', honey?

Sure.

On the street, after he has cashed the check, he stops for a drink. Ah don' know, a woman's the goddamnedest animal God eveh made, he announces. You marry 'em an' they're one thing, and damn ifen they don't turn out plumb opposite. You marry a girl that's cherry and she turns out a whore, an' you marry a whore and damn if she don't cook and sew and keep her legs clos' for everyone but you, and goddam ifen by the time she's done she don' keep 'em closed for you too. (Laughter.) Ah tell ya Ah'm gonna be a free man for a couple of days.

He wanders down the road, and hitches a ride on an automobile through the shrub lands. After he has been let off, he hefts his gallon of corn to his shoulder and trudges down a trail through the stunted pines. At a farm cabin he stops and kicks the door open. Clara, honey.

Woodrow — ya got here, huh?

Yeah, figgered Ah'd see ya awhile. Ol' Slim oughta know better than to be away for a week, job or no job.

Thought he was a friend of yours.

Sure, but his wife's prettier. (They laugh.) Commere, honey, let's have a drink. He strips his shirt, and holds her on his lap. It is intensely hot in the cabin and he strains against her. Ah'm gonna tell

377

ya somethin', they was a little old whore Ah had back a while ago that Ah took twelve times in a night, and the way Ah'm fixin' now, what with the honey in mah insides, Ah'm gonna beat that with you.

Better not drink too much, Woodrow, it'll keep ya down.

Nothin' keeps me down, Ah'm a man likes his lovin'. He tilts the jug to his mouth, and bridles his neck pleasurably as a trickle of liquid slips over his ear to be lost in the golden hairs on his chest.

Woodrow, Ah think you're pretty goddam mean, they ain't nothin' so low as a man'll lie to his wife, and spend all their money while she's in the hospital with his baby. (Alice's voice is whining.)

Ah ain't gonna say nothin', Alice, but let's cut out this talk, Ah'm a good husband to ya mos' of the time, an' they ain't no call for ya to talk to me like that, Ah jus' wanted a little fun and Ah took it and ya better quit messin' with me.

Woodrow, Ah'm a good wife to ya, Ah been faithful as a woman can be since the day we was married, an' you got a child now an' you gotta settle down, how do ya think Ah felt when Ah found out you wrote out another check in mah name, an' jus' took out all the money we had.

Ah figgered you'd be glad to see me havin' a decent time, but all a woman wants is for ya to stay right close by her.

An' then you had to pick up a disease from that no-good bitch.

Now, you quit messin' with me, Ah got some pyridin or whatever the hell it is, and it's fixin' me up jus' right, Ah've fix mahself up with it plenty of times.

A man can die from that.

You jus' talk nonsense. (He feels a tremolo of fear, which he represses quickly.) On'y kind of man that ever gets sick is the kind that jus' sticks in a corner. You have your funnin' an' it keeps ya all right. (He sighs and pats her on the arm.) Now, come on, honey, let's quit your fussin', you know Ah love ya, an' Ah can be awful sweet to ya at times.

He sighs again to himself. (Ifen you could just do what ya wanted, a man'd never get in no trouble. This way Ah gotta lie, an' fool around, an' walk fifty yards to the south ifen Ah want to walk ten to the no'th.)

He walks down the main street with his oldest girl, who is now six. Now, what y'lookin' at, May?

Daddy, Ah'm jus' lookin'.

Okay, honey.

He watches her stare at a doll in the store window. At its feet is a price tag for $4.59. What's the matter, ya want that doll?

Yes, Daddy.

She is his favorite, and he sighs. Honey, you're gonna make your daddy broke. He feels in his pocket and holds the five-dollar bill; it has to last him for the rest of the week and it's Wednesday now. All right, let's go in, honey.

Daddy, Momma gonna be mad at you for buyin' me it?

Naw, honey, Daddy'll take care of Mommy. He laughs internally. (What a smart little bugger she is.) He pats her affectionately on her tiny rump. (Some man's gonna be lucky one of these days.) Come on in, May.

As they walk home, he thinks of the quarrel Alice will start over the doll. (Aw, shoot, Ah don' give a damn. She starts messin' up, an' Ah'll jus' throw a little ol' fit, and she'll quit right fast. Jus' git 'em afraid, that's only way a woman understands.) Come on, May.

He walks back along the street with her, nodding and calling to his friends. (Ah jus' don' understand how screwin' makes a kid, one thing's one thing, and t'other's t'other. It's jus' too damn confusin' when you set down and try to start thinkin' things out, wonderin' what you're gonna do next. Hell, ya jus' let it happen to ya and you go along all right that way.)

The child's steps lag, and he picks her up. Come on, honey, you hold the doll and Ah'll hold you, and we'll git along okay.

(All a man got to do is take it easy an' he'll enjoy himself.) Feeling pleased and content, he continued home. When Alice started complaining about the price of the doll, he threw his little ole fit, and poured himself a drink.

13

CUMMINGS put in a busy week after Hearn was transferred to Dalleson's section. The final and major assault on the Toyaku Line, which Cummings had been postponing for almost a month, had become virtually a necessity. The character of the messages he had been receiving from Corps and Army permitted no further delay and Cummings had his informants in higher echelons as well; he knew he would have to produce some success in the next week or two. His staff had developed the attack plan through its final variations and details, and the assault was scheduled to start in three days.

But Cummings was unhappy with it. The force he could muster would be relatively powerful for the few thousand men involved, but it was a frontal attack and there was no reason to assume it would be any more successful than the attack that had preceded it and failed. The men would advance, and halt probably to a crawl at the first serious resistance. There would be no compulsion for them to keep moving.

Cummings had been toying with another plan for several weeks, but it depended on receiving some naval support, and that was always doubtful. He sent out a few cautious feelers and received some contradictory answers which had left him undecided; the secondary plan had been sidetracked in his mind before the need to produce something tangible and effective. But it was this other plan that intrigued him, and at a conference of his staff officers one morning he decided to draw up an additional set of plans which would incorporate the naval support.

This other plan was simple but powerful. The extreme right flank of the Toyaku Line was anchored on the water's edge a mile or two behind the point where the peninsula joined the island. Six miles to the rear of that was a small cove called Botoi Bay. The General's new plan was to land about a thousand men at Botoi and have them drive inland on a diagonal to take the center of the Toyaku Line from the rear. At the same time his frontal attack, reduced in strength, of course, would drive forward to meet the invading troops. That invasion could work if the landing was successful.

380

Only that was the doubtful part of it. The General had enough landing craft assigned him for ferrying supplies from freighters off the island to be able to transport his invasion troops in one wave if necessary, but Botoi Bay was almost out of range of his artillery, and air reconnaissance had shown that fifty or perhaps even a hundred Japanese troops were entrenched in bunkers and pillboxes on that stretch of beach. Artillery couldn't drive them out nor dive bombers. It would take at least one destroyer and preferably two firing at point-blank range, perhaps a thousand yards offshore. If he were to send a battalion in without naval support a bloody and disastrous massacre would occur.

And the beach at Botoi Bay was the only place where he could land troops for at least fifty miles down the coast. Past Botoi some of the densest jungle forests on Anopopei grew virtually into the water, and nearer his own front line were bluffs too steep to be scaled by invasion troops. There was no alternative. To take the Toyaku Line from the rear they would need the Navy.

The thing that appealed to Cummings about this flanking invasion was what he called its "psychological soundness." The men who would land at Botoi would be in the enemy rear without any safe way to retreat, and their only security would be to drive ahead and meet their own troops. They would *have* to advance. And, conversely, the troops attacking frontally would do so with more enthusiasm. Cummings had found from experience that men fought better when they believed their share of an assignment was the easy part. They would be pleased they missed the invasion, and even more important, they would believe that the resistance before them would be softer, less decisive, because of the movement in the rear.

After the battle plan for the frontal assault had been completed, and it was merely a question of waiting a few days until all the supplies had been brought up to the front, Cummings called a special conference of his staff officers, outlined the new plan to them, and gave orders that it should be developed as a corollary of the major attack, to be used as opportunity granted. At the same time he sent a request through channels for three destroyers. Then he put his staff to work.

After a hurried lunch, Major Dalleson returned to his G-3 tent, and began to draw up the plans for the Botoi invasion. He sat himself down before his desk, opened his collar, sharpened a few pencils with slow absorbed motions, his heavy lower lip dangling pensively and moistly, and then he selected a blank piece of paper and wrote "Operation Coda" in large block letters at the top of his sheet. He sighed pleasurably and lit a cigar, diverted momentarily by the word "coda," which was unfamiliar to him. "Code, it means probably," he muttered to himself, and then forgot about it. Slowly, laboriously, he forced himself to concentrate on the work before him. It was a problem for which he was quite suited.

A more imaginative man would have loathed the assignment, for it consisted essentially of composing long lists of men and equipment and creating a timetable. It demanded the same kind of patience that is needed to construct a crossword puzzle. But Dalleson relished the first portion of the work before him because he knew he could do it, and there were other kinds of work about which he was not so certain. This was the type of job that could be managed by following the procedures to be found in one Field Manual or another, and Dalleson had the kind of satisfaction a tone-deaf person might know in recognizing a piece of music.

Dalleson began by estimating the number of trucks that would be necessary to move the invasion troops from their front line positions down to the beach. Since the frontal attack would undoubtedly be in progress then, it was impossible to decide now which troops could be used. That would depend on the future situation, but it had to be one of the four rifle battalions on the island, and Dalleson separated it into four isolated problems, allotting a different number of trucks for each possibility. There would be trucks needed for the land attack, and the assignment of them could be handled by G-4. Dalleson looked up and scowled, staring at the clerks and officers in his tent.

"Hey, Hearn," he shouted.

"Yes?"

"Bring this over to Hobart, and tell him to work out where we can draw the trucks from."

Hearn nodded, took the piece of paper Dalleson handed him,

and strolled out of the tent, whistling to himself. Dalleson watched him with a puzzled and slightly belligerent expression. Hearn irritated him slightly. He could not express it, but he was a little uncomfortable with him, a little uncertain. He always had the feeling that Hearn was laughing at him, and he had nothing concrete to fasten it upon. Dalleson had been a little surprised when the General had transferred Hearn, but it had been none of his affair, and he had assigned Hearn to supervising the draftsmen in their map overlays, and forgot about him almost entirely. Hearn had done his work well enough, quietly enough, and with over a dozen men in the tent almost all the time, Dalleson had paid little attention to Him. Or at least at first. Lately it seemed as if Hearn had introduced a new humor. There was a kind of sour snickering at the more boring and meaningless procedures now, and once Dalleson had overheard Hearn saying, "Sure, old Blood and Guts puts the outfit to bed. He doesn't have any children, and dogs don't take to him, so what do you expect?" There had been a burst of laughter which stopped abruptly when they saw he had overheard, and since then Dalleson had had the idea that Hearn had been talking about him.

Dalleson mopped his forehead, turned back to his desk, and began to work on the embarkation and debarkation timetables for the invasion battalion. As he progressed he chewed his cigar with relish, pausing every now and then to probe his mouth with one of his large fingers whenever some tobacco leaves had lodged in his teeth. From time to time, out of habit, he would look up and stare about the tent to check whether the maps were in place and all the men were working at their desks. When the phone would ring, he would pause, waiting for someone to answer, shaking his head blackly if it took too long. His own desk was set at an angle to one of the corner uprights, and whenever he wished he could have a fair view of the bivouac. A little wind had sprung up, and it quivered faintly the trodden grass under his feet, cooled all the red spacious areas of his face.

The Major had been one of many children in a poor family, and he considered himself lucky to have finished high school. Until he had joined the Army in 1933 he had been bogged down by a series of missed opportunities and plain bad luck. His ability for hard sustained

383

work and complete loyalty had been relatively unnoticed because as a young man he had been shy and taciturn. But in the Army he had made a perfect soldier. By the time he became a noncom he brought a painstaking thoroughness to all the details he supervised, and his further promotions came quickly. But if the war had not started, Dalleson would probably have remained a first sergeant until retirement.

The influx of draftees made him an officer, and he moved quickly from second lieutenant to first lieutenant to captain. In training he had commanded his company well; they had good discipline, they turned out well for inspections, and their marching was precise. Above all, it was said that they had pride in their outfit. Dalleson always harped on this, and his speeches on the company street had been a source of much mockery. "You're the best fuggin soldiers in the best goddam company of the best goddam battalion of the best goddam regiment . . ." and so forth, but behind their mockery the soldiers realized his sincerity. He had a way with a cliché. It was only natural he should have been promoted to major.

Only it was as a major that Dalleson's troubles had begun. He found that he seldom had any direct contact with enlisted men, he had to deal almost exclusively with officers, and it left him somewhat beached. For the truth was that he was uncomfortable with officers; even as a captain he had considered himself three-quarters an enlisted man, and he missed the days when his easy profanity was appreciated by the men. As a major he had to watch his manners, and he never was quite certain what to do. He felt himself at last — secretly, without admitting it to himself — miscast for the job. He was a little overwhelmed by the high rank of the men with whom he collaborated; he was depressed at times by the responsibilities of his work.

The fact that he was the G-3 had contributed to his discomfort. The G-3 of a division is in charge of operations and training on the division commander's staff, and to be completely effective he must be brilliant and thorough, quick and yet capable of a great deal of detail work. In another division Dalleson probably would not have lasted, but General Cummings had always taken a more direct interest in operations than the average division commander; there were very few plans he did not initiate, practically no military actions no matter how small which he did not personally approve. In such a situation, the Major's stint of blacking in the shadows in the General's drawings did not demand all the talents of a G-3. The Major had been able to survive; indeed, he had the example of his predecessor, a lieutenant-colonel, who had been masterfully suited for the job, but had been transferred precisely because of that — he had begun to assume some of the functions the General preferred to keep for himself.

The Major floundered through his work, or more exactly, he sweated through it, for what he could not supply in brilliance he was determined to produce in hard work. In time he mastered the daily procedures, the mechanisms of Army planning, the forms he had to fill out, but he was always uneasy. He feared the slowness of his mind, the unconscionable time it took him to make a decision when he had no paper before him and time was pressing. Nights like the one he had spent with the General when the Japanese attacked tormented him if he allowed himself to think of it. He knew that he could not have disposed his troops with even a fraction of the ease and dispatch with which the General had managed it over the field telephone, and he wondered how he would have managed if the General had left it to him. He was always afraid that a situation would develop in which he would have to call upon the more dazzling aptitudes that his position demanded, and which he did not have. He would have preferred any other job but that of G-3.

Yet the Major never thought of asking for a transfer; nothing could have been more repugnant to him. He had always possessed an intense loyalty to his commander if he felt the man was a good officer, and no one had ever impressed him more than the General. It was inconceivable to Major Dalleson that he should desert the General unless he was ordered to; he would, if the bivouac had been overrun by Japanese troops, probably have died defending the General in his tent. It was the only romantic attitude in his heavy mind and body. And besides this, the Major had his ambition to sustain him. It was, of course, a very backward ambition; the Major had no more hope of becoming a general than a rich merchant in the Middle Ages might have dreamed of becoming king. The Major wanted to make lieutenant-colonel, or even conceivably colonel before the war ended, and in his position as G-3 he was entitled to that. His reasoning was simple; he had every intention of remaining in the Army after the war and he judged that if he rose as high as lieutenant-colonel the chances were very good that in the postwar Army he would be demoted no lower than captain. Out of all the ranks it was the one he preferred the most next to top sergeant, and he felt a little wistfully that it would not be very correct for him to become an enlisted man again. So, unhappily, he continued to wrestle with his job as the chief of operations.

Now as he completed the timetables he turned with reluctance to the march orders that would be necessary to remove a battalion from the line and divert them to the beach. In itself it was not too complicated a process, but since he didn't know which battalion would be removed, he had to draw up four sets of withdrawal orders and work out the subsidiary movements of the troops who would have to fill the gap in each case. It kept him busy through most of the afternoon, for, although he assigned part of it to Leach and his other assistant, it was necessary to check their work, and the Major was very thorough, very slow.

He finished that at last, and sketched a tentative march order for the invasion battalion once it had landed at Botoi. Here there was no precedent for him to follow — the General had sketched the outline of the attack, but he had been a little vague. From experience, Dalleson knew he would have to submit something and the General would proceed to rip it apart and give him the movement in detail. He hoped to avoid this but he knew there was little likelihood of it, and so, sweating profusely in the heat of the tent, he indicated a route of combat march along one of the main trails, and estimated the time it should take for each portion of it. This was unplotted terrain of his mind as well, and he halted many times, wiped his forehead, and tried unsuccessfully to conceal his anxiety from himself. The steady murmur of voices in the tent, the steady bustle of men moving from desk to desk, or the draftsmen humming over their work, irritated him. Once or twice he looked up, glared balefully at whoever was talking, and then returned to his work with an audible grunt.

The telephone rang frequently and despite himself Dalleson began to listen to the conversations. Once for several minutes, Hearn chatted with some other officer over the phone, and Dalleson finally threw down his pencil and shouted, "Goddammit, why don't you men all shut up and get to work?" It was obviously directed toward Hearn, who murmured something into the receiver and hung up after staring thoughtfully at Dalleson.

"Did you give those papers to Hobart?" he asked Hearn.

"Yes."

"What the hell you been doing since then?"

Hearn grinned and lit a cigarette. "Nothing in particular, Major." There was a subdued titter from a few of the clerks in the tent.

Dalleson stood up, surprised to find himself suddenly in a rage, "I don't want any of your goddam lip, Hearn." This made it worse. It was bad to reprimand an officer in front of enlisted men. "Go over and help Leach."

For several seconds Hearn stood motionless, and then he nodded, sauntered carelessly over to Leach's desk, and sat down beside him. Dalleson had trouble in getting back to work. In the weeks that had elapsed since the division had stalled on the line, Dalleson had expressed his concern by driving his men. He would worry frequently that his subordinates were slacking off and the work was becoming sloppy. To correct that, he was after his clerks all the time to make them retype papers in which there was one error or even one erasure, and he consistently bullied his junior officers to produce more work. It was basically a superstition. Dalleson believed that if he could make his own small unit function perfectly the rest of the division would follow his example. Part of the discomfort Hearn had caused him until now had come from Dalleson's conviction that Hearn cared very little about the work. It was a dangerous business. "One man can louse up an outfit," was one of Dalleson's axioms, and Hearn was a threat. It was the first time he could ever remember a subordinate telling him that he had been doing nothing. When that started happening . . . Dalleson fretted through the rest of the afternoon, outlined the march order very uncertainly, and an hour before evening chow had finished enough of the battle plan to present it to the General.

He went over to Cummings's tent, gave it to him, and stood by uncomfortably, waiting for comments. Cummings studied it carefully,

387

looking up from time to time to voice a criticism. "I see you've got four different withdrawal orders, and four assembly areas."

"Yes, sir."

"I don't think that'll be necessary, Major. We'll pick one assembly point back of Second Battalion, and whichever outfit we use for the invasion will go there. It won't be more than a five-mile march at the very most, no matter which one we take."

"Yes, sir." Dalleson busied himself scribbling notes on a little pad.

"I think you'd better allow 108 minutes instead of 104 for the trip with the LCMs."

"Yes, sir."

And so on. Cummings gave his objections, and Dalleson continued to mark them in his note-pad. Cummings watched him with a little contempt. Dalleson's got a mind like a switchboard, he told himself. If your plug will fit one of his mental holes, he can furnish the necessary answer, but otherwise he's lost.

Cummings sighed, lit a cigarette. "We've got to co-ordinate the staff work on this more thoroughly. Will you tell Hobart and Conn I'll want them with you in the morning first thing?"

"Yes, sir," Dalleson rumbled.

The General scratched his upper lip. That would have been Hearn's job if he were still orderly. Cummings had been doing without an aide. He exhaled his cigarette. "By the way, Major," Cummings asked. "How's Hearn getting along with you?" Cummings yawned casually, but he was tense. With Hearn out of his daily view, certain regrets, certain urges, were tempting him once more. But he repressed them. What a touchy business that thing with Hearn could have been, Cummings thought. Hearn couldn't come back. That was out.

Dalleson knitted his heavy forehead. "Hearn's all right, sir. He's got too goddam much lip, but I can knock that out of him."

Thinking about it now, Cummings was a little disappointed. In the few times he had caught a glimpse of Hearn in officers' mess, his face had been as expressionless, as sullen as ever. It was not likely that Hearn would ever show what he was thinking, but still . . . The punishment had lost its effect, become submerged already in the daily

388

routine of small events. The General felt an urge to . . . to extend the humiliation he had inflicted upon Hearn. The picture of their last conversation was not so deeply satisfying to him now. Somehow he had let Hearn off too easy.

"I've been thinking of transferring him again," Cummings said quietly. "How would you feel about it?"

Dalleson was confused. He had no objections to losing Hearn, it appealed to him, but he was puzzled by the General's attitude. Cummings had never told him anything about Hearn, and Dalleson still assumed Hearn was one of the General's favorites. He couldn't understand the motive behind Cummings's question. "I don't feel very much about it one way or another, sir," he said at last.

"Well, it's worth bearing in mind. I have my doubts that Hearn can make a good staff man." If Dalleson were indifferent to Hearn, then it meant little keeping him there.

"He's about average," Dalleson said carefully.

"What about a line outfit?" Cummings said casually. "Do you have any ideas about where we might put him?"

This confused Dalleson more. It was very odd for a general officer to be at all concerned with where a lieutenant was sent. "Well, sir, Baker Company of the 458th is short an officer, 'cause the patrol reports of one of their platoons is always signed by a sergeant, and then there's F Company needs two officers, and I think Charley Company of the 459th needs an officer."

None of this appealed particularly to Cummings. "Is there anyone else?"

"There's the I and R platoon of headquarters company here, but they don't really need an officer."

"Why?"

"Their platoon sergeant's one of the best men in the 458th, sir. I've been meaning to talk to you about him, I was thinking after the campaign he oughta be made an officer. Croft is his name. He's a good man."

Cummings considered what Dalleson would call a good soldier. The man's a virtual illiterate probably, he thought, with a lot of common sense and no nerves at all. He fingered his mouth again. In I and

R he could still keep an eye on Hearn. "Well, I'll think about it. There's no hurry," he said to Dalleson.

After Dalleson had gone, Cummings slumped in his chair and sat without moving, thinking for a long time.

There was still that *thing* with Hearn. The particular set of desires that had culminated in his order to pick up the cigarette had not been appeased, not really. And before him still was the question of getting some Navy support.

Abruptly, Cummings was depressed again.

That night Hearn was on duty for a few hours in the G-3 tent. The side flaps were unrolled, the double entrance was raised, and the corners were covered over to make a blackout tent. And as always, it was painfully humid inside. Hearn and the clerk on duty with him sat drowsing in their chairs, their shirts opened, their eyes turned away from the glare of the Coleman lanterns, the perspiration coursing down their faces. It was a convenient time to think, for with the exception of the hourly telephone reports from the front there was no work to do, and the bare tables, the empty desks, and the draped mapboards surrounded them, induced the proper mood of somnolence and absorption. Sporadically, like a muted burst of thunder, they could hear the harassing fire of the artillery sounding in the night.

Hearn stretched, looked at his watch. "What time do you get relieved, Stacey?" he asked.

"Two A.M., Lieutenant."

Hearn was on until three. He sighed, stretched his arms, and slumped down in his chair. There was a magazine in his lap, but he had scanned through it, and a little bored, he tossed it onto a table. After a moment or two, he took a letter from his breast pocket, and read it again slowly. It was from a college friend.

Here in Washington you can see all the patterns. The reactionaries are frightened. Despite what they want to believe they know this has become a people's war, and the currents of world revolution are in the air. It's a people's movement and they're bringing all the old tools of repression to try to stop it. After the war there's going to be a witch-hunt, but it'll fail and the basic will of the people toward communal freedom will be expressed. You've no idea how frightened the reactionaries are. It's the last-ditch fight for them.

And there was more in the same tenor. Hearn finished the letter and shrugged. Bailey had always been an optimist. A sound Marxian optimist.

Only that was all bullshit. There would be the witch-hunt after the war all right, but it would hardly be a frightened witch-hunt. What was it Cummings had said? America's energy had become kinetic and it would not be reversed. Cummings wasn't frightened, not in that sense. The terrifying thing in listening to him was his calm and unshakable certainty. The Right was ready for a struggle, but without anxiety this time, with no absorbed and stricken ear listening to the inevitable footstep of history. This time they were the optimists, this time they were on the offensive. There was the thing Cummings had never said, but it was implied tacitly in all his arguments. History was in the grasp of the Right, and after the war their political campaigns would be intense. One big push, one big offensive, and history was theirs for this century, perhaps the next one. The League of Omnipotent Men.

It wasn't that simple, of course, nothing ever was, but still there were powerful men in America, on the march and aroused, some of them perhaps even conscious in their particular dream. And the tools were all ready to hand, the men like his father, the ones who would function in instinctive accord, not knowing, not even caring where the road led them. It could be narrowed probably to a dozen, two dozen men, not even in communication with each other, not even all on the same level of awareness.

But it was much more than that. You could kill the dozen men, and there would be another dozen to replace them, and another and another. Out of all the vast pressures and crosscurrents of history was evolving the archetype of twentieth-century man. The *particular* man who would direct it, make certain that "the natural role . . . was anxiety." The techniques had outraced the psyche. "The majority of men must be subservient to the machine and it's not a business they instinctively enjoy." And in the marginal area, the gap, were the peculiar tensions that birthed the dream.

Hearn flipped over the letter a little distastefully. "Man had to destroy God in order to achieve Him, equal Him." Cummings again. Or had Cummings said it? There were times when the demarcation between their minds was blurred for him. Cummings could have said it. Effectively, it was Cummings's idea. He folded the letter and put it away again.

Where did all this leave him? All right, just where? There had been a time, many times when it would have appealed, more than appealed, to whatever impulse there had been in him to . . . to do what Cummings was capable of doing. That was it. Divorced of all the environmental trappings, all the confusing and misleading attitudes he had absorbed, he was basically like Cummings. Without "the wife is a bitch" kind of urges, but even there, could he label it for certain? Cummings had been right. They were both the same, and it had produced first the intimacy, the attraction they had felt toward each other, and then the hatred.

It was between them still as far as he was concerned. Every time he saw Cummings, if even for an instant, there was the same clutch of fear and hatred inside him, the same painful evocation of that moment when he had stooped to pick up the cigarette. It was still humiliating, still informative. He had never realized the extent of his own vanity, the hatred it was capable of generating when wounded. Certainly, he had never hated anyone the way Cummings affected him now. The week he had spent in G-3 under Dalleson had been lived at half-throttle; he had absorbed the procedures, done his work automatically, and had smoldered inside with an almost unbearable frustration. Lately, he had begun to step out; this afternoon he had been flip with Dalleson, and that was an indication of something else, something not so pleasing. If he remained here he was likely to dissipate himself in a series of insignificant rebellions that would end only in further humiliation. The thing to do was to move out, be transferred, but Cummings would not let him. And the rage he had kept tightly throttled all week was surging again. If only he could go up to Cummings and ask for a front-line platoon, but that would be fatal. Cummings would give him anything but that.

The phone rang, and Hearn picked it up. The voice at the other end spluttered at him. "This is Paragon Red, negative report from 0030 to 0130."

"Okay." Hearn hung up, and stared at the message he had scribbled on a pad. It was a completely automatic report which was phoned in every hour from every battalion. On an ordinary night fifty such reports would come in. He picked up his pencil, about to mark it in the Journal, when Dalleson stepped into the tent. Stacey, the clerk, who had been drowsing over his magazine, straightened up. Dalleson's hair had been quickly combed, and his heavy face was reddened from sleep; he looked inquiringly about the tent, his eyes blinking from the light. "Everything okay?" he asked.

"Yes," Hearn said. He realized suddenly that Dalleson had awakened worrying about the campaign and it amused him.

"I heard the phone ringing," Dalleson said.

"It was Paragon Red, negative report, that's all."

"Did you record it yet?"

"No, sir."

"Well, then do it, man." Dalleson yawned.

Hearn had recorded few reports in the Journal and he looked at the preceding one to check on the form. Then he copied it.

Dalleson walked toward him, and examined the Journal, fingering the spring clip on the beaverboard. "Let's do it more neatly next time."

He'd be damned if Dalleson would lecture him like a child "I'll do my best, Major," he murmured sarcastically.

Dalleson ran his thick index finger under the notation. "What time is this report for?" he asked abruptly.

"0030 to 0130."

"Then whyinhell can't you put it down like that? Goddammit, man, you've got it for 2330 to 0030. Can't you even read? Don't you know what the hell time it is?"

He had even copied the time on the preceding report. "Sorry," Hearn muttered, furious with himself for the error.

"What else you gonna do with this report?"

"Damn if I know. This isn't the work I've been doing."

"Well, now, I'll tell you," Dalleson said with relish. "If you'll

393

get the cobwebs off your brain you'll know that this is a Combat Report, so after you mark it in the Journal and on the map, you put it in the file for my Periodic Report, and when I'm done with it, which'll be tomorrow, you empty the file of the previous day, and put it in the Historical File, and you have one of the clerks make a copy and put it in the Journal File. Nothing too hard about that for a man with a college education, is there, Hearn?"

Hearn shrugged. "Since the report doesn't say anything, why go to all that bother?" He grinned, enjoying the opportunity to lash back. "It doesn't make much sense to me."

Dalleson was enraged. He glowered at Hearn, his jowls darkening, his mouth pressed thin by the powerful clamps of his jaws. A first trickle of sweat slid past his eye and outlined his cheek. "It doesn't make sense to you, eh," he repeated, "it doesn't make sense to you." Like a shot-put hurler hopping on one foot to increase his momentum, Dalleson turned to Stacey and said, "It doesn't make sense to Lieutenant Hearn." Stacey tittered uncomfortably, while Dalleson balanced on an infuriated sarcasm. "Well, now, I'll tell you, Lieutenant, maybe there's a lot of things that don't make sense, maybe it don't make sense for me to be a soldier," he sneered, "maybe it ain't natural for you to be an officer, maybe it don't make sense," he said, repeating the original phrase "Maybe I'd rather be anything else than a soldier, maybe, Lieutenant, I'd rather be a . . . a . . . " Dalleson searched for a sufficiently damning word, and then clenching his fist powerfully he shouted, "Maybe it would be more natural for me to be a *poet.*"

Hearn had been growing increasingly pale as the tirade continued. He was incapable of speech for a moment in his anger. And behind it was a bewildered amazement at the force of Dalleson's reaction. If you knocked out Army procedure, Dalleson was a man carrying packages with his suspenders about to rip loose. Hearn swallowed, gripped the edge of the table. "Take it easy, if you please, Major," Hearn muttered.

"What was that?"

But they were interrupted by Cummings's entering the tent. "I was looking for you, Major, I had an idea you might be here." Cummings's voice was odd, extremely precise and clear, but without any feeling at all. Dalleson stepped back and straightened instinctively as though coming to attention. "What is it, sir?" And Hearn was angered at himself for the relief he felt at the interruption.

Cummings fingered his chin slowly. "I received a message from one of my friends at GHQ." He spoke abstractedly as if he were not concerned with it. "It just came from message center."

The explanation was not necessary, and it was odd for Cummings to repeat himself. Hearn stared at him. The General was upset, he realized. Until now Hearn had been standing rigid, his flesh sweating in painful recognition of the General's presence, his heart pumping. It was painful to be near Cummings.

The General smiled, and lit a cigarette. "How're you getting along, Stacey?" he asked the clerk.

"Fine, thank you, sir." That was one of Cummings's tricks. He always remembered the names of enlisted men he had spoken to once or twice.

"I'll tell you, Major," Cummings's voice was still impersonal, "I'm afraid your work on Operation Coda was done for nothing."

"No Navy, sir?"

"I'm afraid not. My little friend says there's not much chance of it." Cummings shrugged. "We'll launch Operation Plunger as planned. There'll be just one little exception. I think we ought to take the outpost opposite I Company first. I want you to draw up an order tonight for Taylor to start a push in the morning."

"Yes, sir."

"Let's take a look at it." He turned toward Hearn. "Lieutenant, will you hand me that map, please."

"Sir?" Hearn started.

"I said hand me the map." Cummings turned toward Dalleson again.

"This one?"

"What other one is there?" Cummings snapped.

The map was fastened to a large drawing board with an overlay of celluloid tacked to it. While it was not heavy, it was awkward because of its size, and Hearn, unable to see the floor, had to move cautiously.

It had been unnecessary to move it, he realized abruptly. Cummings could easily have walked over, indeed Cummings knew the map by heart.

"Hurry, man," Cummings barked.

For the moment Hearn was standing over him, everything became magnified. He could see each of Cummings's features, the ruddy skin moist from the heat of the tent, the great bald eyes staring at him with indifference and contempt.

Cummings extended his arm. "Well, give it to me, man, stop holding it." His hand reached for it.

Hearn let go of the board prematurely, perhaps he even hurled it down. The distinction was unimportant, for he knew he wanted Cummings to drop it. And he succeeded. The map-board struck the General's wrist with a thump. Then it toppled over.

As it fell it struck the General across the shins.

The board bounced once across the floor, and the map and overlay ripped off. Hearn stared at Cummings, feeling something between terror and triumph. He heard his voice issuing coolly, a trifle ironically. "I'm *sorry*, sir."

The pain was acute. To Cummings at that instant, after the effort of maintaining his poise, it was unbearable. To his horror, he felt tears forming in his eyes, and he shut his eyelids, trying desperately to blink them back. "*Dammit*, man," he roared, "WHY DON'T YOU WATCH IT?" It was the first time any of them had ever heard Cummings shout, and Stacey quivered.

The shout relieved him, however, and he was able to resist the temptation to rub his shinbone. The ache was subsiding into a dull throb. But Cummings felt himself close to exhaustion, and a spasm of diarrhea cramped him. To ease it, he leaned forward in his chair. "Do you want to repair the overlay, Hearn?"

"Yes, sir."

Dalleson and Stacey were scrabbling on the floor picking up the portions of the map that had torn in the fall. Hearn looked at Cum-

396

mings, his eyes expressionless, and then stooped down for the overlay.

"Does it hurt, sir?" His voice was flatly solicitous.

"It's all right, thank you."

In the tent, the heat had become even more oppressive. Cummings felt a little faint. "After you get the map fixed, will you take care of that movement, Major," he said.

"Yes, sir," Dalleson said from the floor.

Cummings stepped outside, leaning against the corner pole for a few seconds. The night air was almost cold against his wet clothing. He looked about and then kneaded his shin tenderly before limping across the bivouac.

He had extinguished the Coleman lantern in his own tent before leaving, and he lay down on his cot in the darkness, and stared at the dim outlines of the tent. Like a cat his eyes reflected some light, and a man entering the tent would have been able to discern them in the darkness before he could see anything else. His shin was throbbing powerfully now, and his stomach felt a little upset. The crack of the map-board against his legs had unseated all the disorders that the tension and absorption of the past two months had spawned. His flesh crawled as if he had a scabies, and his body was laved with an unreasonable sweat. He was familiar with the process, called it "coming apart at the seams," and it had happened to him at Motome, and at specific times in the past. It was a demand his body exacted of him and with a passive, almost a submissive acceptance, Cummings would let it have its course, allowed his mind to follow in its wake for a miserable hour or two, and then always he would recover from it in a night's sleep, feel refreshed and puissant by the following morning.

This time he took a mild sedative, and fell asleep in less than an hour. When he awakened it was still dark, but he felt restless, and his mind was extremely active. The shin was still sore, and after massaging it for a minute or two in the dark he lit the Coleman lantern by his cot, and examined the bruise gingerly.

It had been no accident. Hearn had dropped the board purposely, or at the very least it had been only a partial accident, Cummings was certain. And in reassurance his heart began to thump

397

powerfully. Perhaps he had even wanted it to happen; there had been a certain alertness to Hearn, an awareness of him, when he had told him to bring over the map-board. Cummings shook his head. It was unprofitable to plumb that sort of thing. He understood himself and it was best to let it go at that. Although he had awakened only a few minutes previously, his mind was painfully clear, and beneath the threshold of speech he was containing anxiety.

He would transfer Hearn. It would be dangerous to keep him under his thumb. There would be further episodes, further rebellions, and it might come to a court-martial, which was always messy, always unpleasant. That time with the cigarette butt, he would have carried it through, as he would now if anything developed, but the appeal could be nasty for him. They would never override him in higher echelons, but it could be a black mark.

Hearn would have to go. Cummings was feeling a mingled triumph and frustration. He could move Hearn where he wanted, and yet there was still an area of rebellion he had not been able to override completely. That was the burr. He squinted his eyes against the glare of the lantern, turned it down a trifle, and then kneaded his thigh with one of his hands, realizing with annoyance it was one of Hearn's gestures.

Where should he send him? It was not terribly important; that reconnaissance platoon Dalleson had mentioned would do well enough. And it would keep Hearn in headquarters. He would have an idea of what was happening to Hearn. In any case he could take care of that in the morning. When he saw Dalleson about the I Company outpost, he could maneuver it so that the decision seemed to come from Dalleson. It would be better that way, less apparent.

Cummings lay down again, his hands clasped under his head, staring once more at the ridgepole. As if it were mocking him, he could see the map of Anopopei superimposed on the canvas, and he twisted over uncomfortably, feeling again the frustration and anger he had suffered when he received the message that he would probably get no Navy support. His hopes had been too great. Now he could not divert his mind from the idea of invading Botoi Bay. There might be another maneuver, there should be one, and yet his mind kept pic-

398

turing the pincers of a frontal assault and an invasion from the rear. He wondered if he should chance it without naval support, but it would be a massacre, the rubber boats again. He could do it only if Botoi were undefended beach.

There was the nucleus of an idea in that. If he could level the beach defenses first with one force, and then send in his landing craft . . . Perhaps a small detachment could capture the beach at night, and in the morning the others could land. But that was far too risky. A night invasion — he had no troops who were skilled enough for that.

A striking force to take Botoi, that could be his substitute for the Navy. But how to do it? It would be impossible to send a company through from his own lines, it would take a break-through for that. Perhaps he could land troops twenty miles behind the Japanese lines and have them advance along the coast. But the jungle was too thick. There were places where they would have to leave the shore and there was an impenetrable forest along the coast behind Botoi. If he could . . .

An idea had formed, not even articulated, and he held it numbly, conscious at first only that he had an idea. He got out of bed, and trod over the duckboards in his bare feet to examine some aerial photographs in his desk. Could a company do it?

It was quite possible. He could send a company in assault boats completely around the island, have them land on the unexplored southern shore, which was separated from Toyaku and his troops by the Watamai mountain range. They could strike out directly across the middle of the island, go through the pass adjacent to Mount Anaka and descend into the Japanese rear, where they could attack the beach at Botoi Bay and hold it until he could land a battalion. It would be a plausible attack, for the beach defenses at Botoi were pointed toward the sea; like almost all Japanese positions, there was little maneuverability in the fire lanes.

He rubbed his chin. The timing will be a bitch on that. But what a conception it was. There was an unorthodoxy, a daring about it, which appealed to him greatly. Cummings did not concern himself with that, however. As in all such moments when he was considering new plans, his mind had become practical and direct. Quickly, he was estimating the distances. It was twenty-five miles across the island to the Japanese side of the pass, and from there it was seven miles to Botoi Bay. Without any delaying incidents a company could do it in three days, two if they were to push themselves. He studied the aerial maps. The terrain was formidable, of course, but not impassable on the other side of the island. There was a fringe of jungle not more than a few miles wide at the water's edge, and then a relatively open march over hills and kunai grass until they would reach the mountains and the pass. It could be done. The problem was to find a route through the jungle in the Japanese rear once they were through the pass. If he were to send a company out they would almost certainly blunder into an ambush.

Cummings sat back in his chair and mused. He would need reconnaissance first. It would be too expensive, too risky, to tie up a company for a week when the thing might be impossible. A patrol of a few men, a squad or two, would be the better idea. They could go out, break a route, reconnoiter the trails in the Japanese rear, and then return over the way they had come to be picked up by the boats. If they got back without trouble, he could send out a company and pull off the plan. Cummings stared at the lamp for a few seconds. The first reconnaissance patrol would take five days, at most six, and on their return he could dispatch a company that could reach Botoi in three days. For safety's sake, he could allow ten days altogether, or eleven actually since he couldn't start it until tomorrow night. His attack would begin in two days, and by the time he would be ready to launch the Botoi Bay invasion it would be nine days old. With luck some penetration might be made by them, but it was unlikely the frontal assault would be that successful. As it was, the timing might be very opportune. He lit a cigarette. The thing had its appeal.

Whom could he send out on the first patrol? He thought at once of recon, and then deliberated, searching his memory for what he knew of them. They had been in the rubber boats but there were only a few of those men left, and since then they had been relatively inactive. The night the Japanese had attacked across the river they had acquitted themselves well, very well. There was that platoon leader Croft whom Dalleson had mentioned. Best of all, they were a small platoon, and he could send them all out. If he were to split a larger platoon, the men who would have to go would be bitter at their bad luck in being selected.

With a little shock he realized that Hearn was to be assigned to recon tomorrow. It wasn't a particularly good idea to send out an officer who would be unfamiliar with his platoon, but he couldn't leave the success of a patrol like this to a noncom. And Hearn was intelligent with the physical requirements necessary for such an extended mission — at this instant Cummings considered Hearn coldly, as though he were totting up the merits and demerits of a horse. Hearn could manage it; he probably had a flair for command.

A reaction was setting in. This new plan had a great many risks, almost too many to depend on it. For a few moments Cummings considered dropping it. But the initial investment was cheap enough. A dozen or fifteen men and if it went badly for them nothing was lost. In the meantime, the Navy was not irretrievably lost. He could make a trip perhaps to GHQ once the attack was launched, and see if he couldn't promote those destroyers.

He walked back to his bed and lay down. In his pajamas the tent was suddenly cold, and he shivered, feeling a muffled anticipation and elation. He might as well try it. Hearn could be sent out.

If he were ever successful with this. For an instant he allowed himself to dwell on the kudos such a victory would be worth. He turned out the lantern and rested on his cot, looking again into the darkness. Somewhere in the distance artillery was firing.

He knew he would not fall asleep again before morning. Once he could feel his shin throbbing again, and he laughed out loud, almost startled by the sound of his voice in the empty tent and the night. This had not been casual. It was a process which had developed in his mind along subterranean routes, directed, coming to fruition when it was necessary. Some of his actions toward Hearn were fitting together now. You could always find a pattern if you looked for it.

"Still, I'm serious about this patrol."

Or was he? It seemed both brilliant and impractical at the same instant, and the confusion, the complexity of his attitudes toward it left him excited and troubled, close to laughter again.

He yawned instead. This patrol was a good augury. He had been barren of ideas for too long, and he had a certainty now that there would be many others to follow in the next week. Whatever strait-jacket there had been about his movements lately would be sloughed off . . . as he had sloughed off Hearn. In the final analysis there was only necessity and one's own reactions to it.

The Time Machine:

GENERAL CUMMINGS

A PECULIARLY AMERICAN STATEMENT

At first glance he did not look unlike other general officers. A little over medium height, well fleshed, with a rather handsome sun-tanned face and graying hair, but there were differences. His expression when he smiled was very close to the ruddy complacent and hard appearance of any number of American senators and businessmen, but the tough good-guy aura never quite remained. There was a certain vacancy in his face . . . there was the appearance and yet it was not there. Hearn always felt as if the smiling face were numb.

The town has existed for a long time in this part of the Mid-west, more than seventy years by 1910, but it has not been a city very long. "Why, not so long ago," they will say, "I can remember when this here town was nothin' much more than a post office and the school house, the Old Presbyterian church and the Main Hotel. Old Ike Cummings had the general store then, and for a while we had a feller barbered hair, but he didn't last long, moved on some'er else. And then," with a slow evaluating wink, "they was a town whoor used to do business in the county."

And of course when Cyrus Cummings (named after the older McCormick) went to New York on those banking trips, he didn't waste his time. "I tell you," the people will say, "they had to bring that factory here. Cy Cummings didn't give his help to McKinley for nothing back in 'ninety-six; he's a Yankee trader. He might not a had much of a bank in those days but when he called in all the farmer debts the week before election this here became a McKinley county. Cy is even smarter than old Ike, an' you remember when Ike had the general store nobody traded him a horse with a canker." And the old man on the vanishing cracker barrel fluffs some spittle into his corded

403

stale handkerchief. "Course," with a grin, "I ain't sayin' that anyone in town loves Cy more than is proper, but the town . . ." (with another grin) "I mean, the city, sure as hell owes him a lot, be it in gratitude or hard dollar bills."

The town is set in the middle of the great American plain. There are a few knolls or rills bordering it, one of the insignificant accidents of land in the long flat face of the Midwest, and you can find quite a few trees on the lee side of the railroad tracks. The streets are broad and the elm and oak bloom in summer, soften the harsh crabbed outlines of the Queen Anne houses, throw interesting shadows into the angles of the gable windows and truncated dormer roofs. Center Street has only a few buildings left with false façades, and there are lots of stores now, so many farmers in town on Saturday afternoons that they are beginning to pave it with cobblestones so the horses won't bog in the mud.

For the richest man in town, Cy Cummings's house is not too different. The Cummingses built it thirty years ago at a time when it stood all alone on the edge of town and you walked to your thighs in mud to reach it in early fall and spring. But the town has encompassed it now and there is not much Cy Cummings can do in the way of improvements.

The worst of the changes you can blame on his wife. The folks who know them say it's her fault, a fancy eastern woman with Culture. Cy's a hard man, but he isn't a fancy one, and that new front door with all the windowpanes on the bias is something French. She's mentioned the name at church meeting, Newvelle something. And Cy Cummings has even turned High Episcopal for her, was instrumental in getting the 'Piscopal church built.

Odd family, people will tell you, funny kids.

In the parlor with the portraits on the wall, the brown murky landscapes in golden scalloped frames, the dark draperies, the brown furniture, the fireplace — in the parlor the family is sitting around.

That feller Debs is making trouble again, Cy Cummings says. (A sharp-featured face with a partially bald head, silver-rimmed glasses.)

404

Yes, dear? The wife turns to her sewing, embroiders another golden stitch on the buttocks of the Cupid in the center of the doily. (A pretty woman, flutters a little, with the long dress, the impressive bosom of the period.) Well, why does he make trouble?

Aaahr, Cy snorts, the basic disgust for a woman's remark.

Hang 'em, Ike Cummings says, with the old man's quaver. In the war (the Civil War) we use to take 'em up, set 'em on a mare, and spank her rump, and watch them kick their heels a little.

Cy rustles his paper. Don't need to hang 'em. He looks at his hands, laughs dourly. Edward go to sleep yet?

She looks up, answers quickly, nervously, I think so, that is he said he was. He and Matthew said they were going to sleep. (Matthew Arnold Cummings is the younger one.)

I'll take a look.

In the boys' bedroom, Matthew is asleep, and Edward, age seven, is sitting in a corner, sewing snips of thread into a scrap of cloth.

The father steps toward him, throws his shadow across the boy's face. What are you doing, boy?

The child looks up petrified. Sewin'. Ma said it was okay.

Give it to me. And the scraps, the thread, are hurled into the wastebasket. Come up, 'Lizabeth.

He hears the argument raging about him, conducted in hoarse passionate whispers as a sop to his sleeping brother. I won't have him actin' like a goddam woman, you're to stop feedin' him all these books, all this womanish . . . claptrap. (The baseball bat and glove are gathering dust in the attic.)

But I didn't . . . I didn't tell him a thing.

You didn't tell him to sew?

Please, Cyrus, let him alone. The slap reddens his cheek from the ear to the mouth. The boy sits on the floor, the tears dropping on his lap.

And you're to act like a man from now on, do you understand?

Only when they have gone, too many things twist in his comprehension. The mother had given him the thread, told him to do it quietly.

405

The sermon ends in church. We are all children of the Lord Jesus and God, instruments of His compassion, committed unto earth to enact the instruments of His goodness, to sow the seeds of brotherhood and good works.

A fine sermon, the mother says.

Yeahp.

Was he right? Edward asks.

Certainly, Cyrus says, only you got to take it with a grain of caution. Life's a hard thing and nobody gives you nothing. You do it alone. Every man's hand is against you, that's what you also find out.

Then he was wrong, Father.

I didn't say that. He's right and I'm right, and it's just in religion you act one way, and in business, which is a lesser thing, well, you go about things in another way. It's still Christian.

The mother caresses his shoulder. It was a wonderful sermon, Edward.

Nearly everybody in this town hates me, Cyrus says. They hate you too, Edward, you might as well learn it early, ain't nothing they hate like a success, and you're sure gonna be one, if they don't like you they can still lick your boots.

The mother and the son pack up the paints and easel, start back in the chilly spring afternoon from their jaunt outside the town, sketching the meager hills on the plain.

Have a good time, Eddie dear? Her voice has a new trill in it now, a new warmth when they they are alone.

Loved it, Ma.

When I was a little girl, I always used to dream I'd have a little boy and I'd go out with him and paint, just like this. Come on, I'll teach you a funny song while we go back.

What is Boston like? he asks.

Oh, it's a big city, it's dirty, coooold, everybody's always dressed up.

Like Pa?

She laughs doubtfully. Yes, like Pa. Now, don't you say anything to him about what we did this afternoon. . . . Was it wrong?

406

No, now you just march right on home with me, and don't say a word to him, it's a secret.

He hates her suddenly, and is quiet, moody, as they walk back to the town. That night he tells his father, listens with a kind of delicious glee and fright to the quarrel that follows.

I'm going to tell you that that boy is all your fault, you indulge him, you bring out the worst in him, you never could get over leaving Boston, now, could you, we're really not fine enough out here for you.

Cyrus, please.

I'll be damned, I'm going to send him to military school, he's old enough to shift for himself, at nine years old a boy has to start thinking how to act like a man.

Ike Cummings nods. Military school's all right, that boy likes to listen to things about the war.

What is partially behind it all is the conversation Cyrus has had with the town doctor. The fabulous beard, the hard shrewd eyes have twinkled at him, got a little of their own back. Well, now, Mr. Cummings, there ain't a damn thing can be done now, it's over my head, if he were a little older I'd say take the boy over to Sally's and let him git some jism in his system.

The basic good-bye at the age of ten, the railroad train, the farewell to the muddy roads at the periphery of town, the gaunt family houses, the smell of his father's bank, and the laundry on the lines.

Good-bye, Son, and do all right for yourself, do you hear?

He has accepted the father's decision without any feeling, but now he shudders almost imperceptibly at the hand on his shoulder.

Good-bye, Ma. She is weeping, and he feels a mild contempt, an almost lost compassion.

Good-bye, and he goes, plummets into the monastery and becomes lost in the routine of the school, in polishing his buttons and making his bed.

There are changes in him. He has never been friendly with other boys, but now he is cold rather than shy. The water colors, the books like *Little Lord Fauntleroy* and *Ivanhoe* and *Oliver Twist* are far less important; he never misses them. Through the years there he gets the

407

best marks in his class, becomes a minor athlete, No. 3 man on the tennis team. Like his father, he is respected if he is not loved.

And the crushes of course: he stands by his bunk at Saturday morning inspection, rigidly upright, clicking his heels as the colonel headmaster comes by. The suite of officer-teachers pass, and he waits numbly for the cadet colonel, a tall dark-haired youth.

Cummings, the cadet colonel says.

Yes, sir.

Your web belt has verdigris in the eyelets.

Yes, sir. And he watches him go, shuttling between anguish and a troubled excitement because he has been noticed. A subterranean phenomenon, for he takes no part in the special activities pertinent to a boys' private school, is almost conspicuous by his avoidance.

Nine years of it, the ascetic barracks, and the communal sleeping, the uniform-fears, the equipment-fears, the marching-tensions, and the meaningless vacations. He sees his parents for six weeks each summer, finds them strange, feels distant toward his brother. Mrs. Cyrus Cummings bores him now with her nostalgia.

Remember, Eddie, when we went out to the hill and painted?

Yes, Mother.

He graduates as cadet colonel.

At home he makes a little stir in his uniform. The people know he is going to West Point, and he is pointed out to the young girls, to whom he is polite and indifferent. He is handsome now, not too tall, but his build is respectable, and his face has an intelligent scrubbed look.

Cyrus talks to him. Well, Son, you're ready for West Point, eh?

Yes, sir, I expect so.

Mmm. Glad you went to military school?

Tried to do the best I could, sir.

Cyrus nods. West Point pleases him. He has decided long ago that little Matthew Arnold can carry on the bank, and this strange stiff son in the uniform is best away from home. Good idea sending you there, Cyrus says.

Why . . . His mind is blank, but a powerful anxiety stirs along his spine. His palms are always wet when he talks to his father. Why,

408

yes, sir (knowing somehow that this is what Cyrus wants to hear). Yes, sir. I hope to do well at the Point, sir.

You will if you're a son of mine. (Laughing heartily in the con-summation-of-business-deal heartiness, he claps him on the back.)

Again . . . Yes, sir. And he withdraws, the basic reaction.

He meets the girl he is to marry in the summer after his second year at West Point. He has not been home in two years because there have been no vacations long enough for him to make the trip, but he has not missed the town. When this vacation comes he goes to Boston to visit his mother's relatives.

The city delights him; the manners of his relatives come as a revelation after the crude probing speech of the town. He is very polite at first, very reticent, aware that until he learns the blunders he must not make he cannot talk freely. But there are stirrings. He walks the streets of Beacon Hill, ascending eagerly along the narrow sidewalks to the State House where he stands motionless, watching the light-play on the Charles, a half mile below him. The brass knock-ers, the dull black knockers intrigue him; he stares at all the narrow doors, touches his hat to the old ladies in black who smile pleasantly, a trifle doubtfully, at his cadet's uniform.

This is what I like.

I'm very fond of Boston, he says a few weeks later to his cousin Margaret. They have become confidants.

Are you? she says. It's getting a little seedy. Father said there are always less and less places where one may go. (Her face is delicately long, pleasantly cold. Despite the length of her nose it turns up at the tip.)

Oh, well, the Irish, he miffs, but he is vaguely uncomfortable in saying it, conscious that his answer is trite.

Uncle Andrew is always complaining that they've taken the gov-ernment away from us. I heard him say the other night that it's like France now, he was there, you know, the only careers left are in the service (State department) or in uniform, and even there the elements are undependable. (Conscious of an error, she adds quickly) He's very fond of you.

409

I'm glad.

You know, it's odd, Margaret says, only a few years ago Uncle Andrew was very intolerant about the whole thing. I'll tell you a secret. (She laughs, puts her arm through his.) He always preferred the Navy. He says they have better manners.

Oh. (For a moment he feels lost. All their politeness, their acceptance of him as a relative is seen from the other side of the door. There is the brief moment when he tries to reverse all the things he remembers their saying, examines them from the new approach.)

That doesn't mean anything, Margaret says, we're all such frauds. It's a terrible thing to say, but you know whatever we have in the family is what we accept. I was terribly shocked when I first realized that.

Then I'm all right, he says lightly.

Oh, no, you won't do at all. (She laughs first, and he joins in a little hesitantly.) You're just our second cousin from the West. That isn't done. (Her long face seems merry for a moment.) Seriously, it's just that we've known only Navy up till now. Tom Hopkinson and Thatcher Lloyd, I think you met him at Dennis, well, they're all Navy, and Uncle Andrew knows their fathers so well. But he likes you. I think he had a crush on your mother.

Well, that makes it better. (They laugh again, sit down on a bench and throw pebbles into the Charles River basin.)

You're awfully vivacious, Margaret.

Oh, I'm a fraud too. If you knew me you'd say I was awfully moody.

I bet I wouldn't.

Oh, I wept, you know I completely wept when Minot and I lost our boat class race two years ago. It was just silly. Father wanted us to win it, and I was terrified what he would say. You can't move around here at all, nothing one can do, there's always a reason why it isn't *advisable*. (For an instant her voice is almost bitter.) You're not like us at all, you're serious, you're important. (Her voice lilts again.) Father told me you were second from the top in your class. That's bad manners.

Would the middle third be respectable?

410

Not for you. You're going to be a general.

I don't believe it. (His voice in these weeks in Boston has assumed the proper tone, become a little higher, a little more lazy. He cannot express the excitement, perhaps the exaltation Boston gives him. Everyone is so perfect here.)

You're just doodling me, he says. (A leprous phrase of the Midwest, he realizes too late, and is unbalanced for a moment.)

Oh, no, I'm convinced you're going to be a great man.

I like you, Margaret.

You should after I praised you like that. (She giggles once more, says ingenuously) I suppose I want you to like me.

At the end of summer when he is leaving she hugs him, whispers in his ear, I wish we were definitely engaged so you could kiss me.

So do I. But it is the first time he has thought of her as a woman to be loved, and he is a little shocked, a little empty. On the train going back, she has lost her disturbing individuality already, remains as the pleasant focus of her family and Boston behind them. He feels an unfamiliar, a satisfying identity with his classmates when he talks about his girl. It's important to have one, he decides.

He is always learning things, understanding already that his mind must work on many levels. There is the thing he thinks of as the truth, the objective situation which his mind must unravel; there is the "deep layer," as he calls it, the mattress resting on the cloud, and he does not care to plumb for the legs; there is, and it is very important, the level where he must do and say things for their effect upon the men with whom he lives and works.

He learns the last dramatically in the hour on Military History and Tactics. (The brown scrubbed room, the blackboards at the front, the benches where the cadets sit in the unquestioned symmetry of ancient patterns, the squares of a chessboard.)

Sir (he gets permission to speak), is it fair to say that Lee was the better general than Grant? I know that their tactics don't compare, but Grant had the knowledge of strategy. What good are tactics, sir, if the . . . the larger mechanics of men and supplies are not

411

developed properly, because the tactics are just the part of the whole? In this conception wasn't Grant the greater man because he tried to take into account the intangibles. He wasn't much good at the buck-and-wing but he could think up the rest of the show. (The classroom roars.)

It has been a triple error. He has been contradictory, rebellious and facetious.

Cummings, you'll make your points in the future more concisely. Yes, sir.

You happen to be wrong. You men will find out that experience is worth a great deal more than theory. It is impossible to account for all your strategy, those things have a way of balancing out as happened at Richmond, as is happening now in the trench warfare in Europe. Tactics is always the determinant. (He writes it on the blackboard.)

And, Cummings . . .

Sir?

Since you will be fortunate if you command a battalion by the end of twenty years, you'll do a sight better to concern yourself with the strategic problems of a platoon (there is muffled laughter at his sarcasm) than with those of an Army. (Seeing the approval in his eyes, the class releases its laughter, singeing Cummings's flesh.)

He hears about it for weeks. Hey, Cummings, how many hours will you need to take Richmond?

They're sending you over, Ed, I hear, as adviser to the French. With the proper concepts the Hindenburg Line may be breached.

He learns so many things from this, understands, besides all else, that he is not liked, will not be liked, and he can't make mistakes, cannot expose himself to the pack. He will have to wait. But he is hurt, cannot restrain himself from writing about it to Margaret. And his contempt thrives in recompense; there is a world of manners about which these men know nothing.

In *The Howitzer,* when he graduates, they have printed "The Strategist" under his record, and then to soften it, for it jars with the mellow sentimental glow of yearbooks, they have added a little ambiguously, "Handsome Is as Handsome Does."

412

He goes out to an abridged furlough with Margaret, the announcement of their engagement, and the rapid shuttle on the transport to the war in Europe.

In the planning section of GHQ he lives in the remaining wing of a château, occupies the bare whitewashed room that had once belonged to a chambermaid, but he does not know this. The war has caught him up agreeably, altered the deadening routine of forms, the detail work of outlining troop movements. The sound of the artillery is always an enrichment to his work, the bare gnashed ground outside speaks of the importance of his figures.

There is even one night when the entire war stands out for him on the edge of a knife blade, a time when everything balances in his mind.

He goes out with his colonel, an enlisted chauffeur, and two other officers on an inspection of the front. It is picnic style with sandwiches packed away and a hot thermos of coffee. The canned rations are brought along, but there is not likely to be an opportunity of using them. They motor along the back roads to the front, jouncing slowly over the potholes and shellholes, splashing ponderously through the mud. For an hour they move along a vast desolated plain, the drab afternoon sky lighted only by the bursts of artillery, the crude evil flickering of the flares like heat lightning on a sultry evening in summer. A mile from the trenches they come to a low ridge-line barely obscuring the horizon and they halt, march slowly along a communication trench which is filled with a half foot of water from the morning's rain. As they approach the secondary trenches the communication ditch begins to zigzag and becomes deeper. Every hundred yards Cummings steps up on the parapet, and peers cautiously into the gloom of No Man's Land.

In the reserve trenches they halt, and take up their position in a concrete dugout, listening respectfully to the conversation between their colonel and the Regimental Commander of that sector of the line. He too has come up for the attack. An hour before dark the artillery begins a creeping barrage which moves closer and closer to the enemy trenches, finally centers on them for a bombardment which lasts fifteen minutes. German artillery is answering, and every few

413

minutes a misdirected shell swooshes down near their observation post. The trench mortars have begun to fire and the volume of sound increases, floods everything, until they are shouting at each other.

It's time, there they go, someone bellows.

Cummings puts up his field glasses, looks out the slit in the concrete wall. In the twilight, covered with mud, the men look like silver shadows on a wan silver plain. It is raining again, and they waver forward between a walk and a run, falling on their faces, tottering backward, sliding on their bellies in the leaden-colored muck. The German lines are aroused and furious, return the fire cruelly. Light and sound erupt from them viciously, become so immense that his senses are overwhelmed, finally perceive them only as a background for the advance of the infantry across the plain.

The men move slowly now, leaning forward as if striding into the wind. He is fascinated by the sluggishness of it all, the lethargy with which they advance and fall. There seems no pattern to the attack, no volition to the men; they advance in every direction like floating leaves in a pool disturbed by a stone, and yet there is a cumulative movement forward. The ants in the final sense all go in one direction.

Through the field glasses he watches one soldier run forward, plunge his head toward the mud, stand up and run again. It is like watching a crowd from a high window or separating a puppy from the rest of the wriggling brood in a pet-store window. There is an oddness, an unreality, in realizing that the group is made up of units.

The soldier falls, quivers in the mud, and he switches his glasses to another.

They're at the German trenches, someone shouts.

He looks up hastily, sees a few men jumping over the parapet, their bayonets forward like pole vaulters approaching the bar. They seem to move so leisurely, so few men follow them that he is puzzled. Where are the rest he is about to say when there is a shout from the Regimental Commander. They took it, they're good boys, they took it. He is holding the phone in his hand, shouting orders quickly.

The German artillery is beginning to fall on the newly taken trenches, and columns of men advance slowly through the dusk over

414

the quiet field, circling around the dead men, and filing into the German trenches. It is almost dark, and the sky has assumed a rosy wash in the east where a house is burning. He cannot see through his field glasses any longer, and he puts them down, stares across the field with a silent wonder. It looks primal, unfamiliar, the way he has imagined the surface of the moon might look. In the craters the water glistens, slides away in long rippling shadows from the bodies of the men who have fallen.

What'd you think of it? The Colonel nudges him.

Oh, it was . . . But he cannot find the words. It has been too immense, too shattering. The long dry battles of the textbooks come alive for him, mass themselves in his mind. He can only think of the man who has ordered the attack, and he pictures him with wonder. What . . . courage. The responsibility. (For want of a richer word he picks up the military expression.)

There were all those men, and there had been someone above them, ordering them, changing perhaps forever the fiber of their lives. In the darkness he looks blankly at the field, tantalized by the largest vision that has ever entered his soul.

There were things one could do.

To command all that. He is choked with the intensity of his emotion, the rage, the exaltation, the undefined and mighty hunger.

He returns a captain (temporary), is promoted and demoted in the same order, made first lieutenant (permanent). There is his marriage with Margaret against the subtle opposition of her parents, the brief honeymoon, and they settle down at an Army post, drift in the pleasantly vacant circle of parties and Saturday night dances at the officers' club.

Their lovemaking is fantastic for a time:

He must subdue her, absorb her, rip her apart and consume her.

This motif is concealed for a month or two, clouded over by their mutual inexperience, by the strangeness, the unfamiliarity, but it must come out eventually. And for a half year, almost a year, they have love passages of intense fury, enraged and powerful, which leave him sobbing from exhaustion and frustration on her breast.

Do you love me, are you mine, love me.

Yes yes.

I'll take you apart, I'll eat you, oh, I'll make you mine, I'll make you mine, you bitch.

And surprising profanity, words he is startled to hear himself speak.

Margaret is kindled by it, exalted for a time, sees it as passion, glows and becomes rounded, but only for a time. After a year it is completely naked, apparent to her, that he is alone, that he fights out battles with himself upon her body, and something withers in her. There is all the authority she has left, the family and the Boston streets and the history hanging upon them, and she has left it, to be caught in a more terrifying authority, a greater demand.

This is all of course beneath words, would be unbearable if it were ever said, but their marriage re-forms, assumes a light and hypocritical companionship with a void at the center, and very little lovemaking now, painfully isolated when it occurs. He retreats from her, licks his wounds, and twists in the circle beyond which he cannot break. Their social life becomes far more important.

She busies herself with running her house, keeping a list of the delicate debits and credits of entertainment and visiting. It always takes them two hours to figure out the list for their monthly party.

Once they spend a week wondering if they can invite the General to their house, discuss the elaborate arguments on either side. They conclude it would be in bad taste, might hurt them even if he came, but a few nights later Captain Cummings wrestles with the problem again, wakes up at dawn and knows it is a chance he must take.

They plan it very carefully, picking a weekend when the General has no obligations and it seems as if none will develop. From the General's house orderly, Margaret finds out which foods he likes; at a post dance she talks to the General's wife for twenty minutes, discovers an acquaintance of her father's whom the General knows.

They send out the invitations and the General accepts. There is the nervous preceding week, the tension at the party. The General walks in, stands about at the buffet table, picking not without zeal at the smoked turkey, the shrimp for which she has sent to Boston.

It is finally a success and the General smiles at Cummings mistily, pleased with his eighth Scotch, the puffed and tufted furniture (he had been expecting maple), the sharp sweet bite of the shrimp sauce through the fur of drinking. When he says good-bye he pats Cummings on the shoulder, pinches Margaret's cheek. The tension collapses, the junior officers and their wives begin to sing. But they are too exhausted and the party ends early.

That night when they congratulate each other Cummings is satisfied.

But Margaret ruins it; she has a facility for ruining things now. You know, honestly, Edward, I wonder what the point to it all was, you can't get promoted any faster, and the old fart (she has taken to swearing mildly) will be dead by the time it's a question of recommending you for general's rank.

You have to start your reputation early, he says quickly. He has accepted all these mores, forced himself dutifully into them, but he does not like them to be questioned.

Oh, what a perfectly vague thing to say. You know I'm feeling now as if we were silly to have invited him. It would have been much more fun without him.

Fun? (This hits at the core of him, leaves him actually weak with anger.) *There are more important things than fun.* He feels as if he has closed a door behind him.

You're in danger of becoming a bore.

Let it go, he almost shouts, and she subsides before his rage. But there it is between them, stated again.

I don't know what gets into you, he mutters.

There are other movements, other directions. For a time he moves through the drinking circles of the officers' club, plays poker, and indulges in a few side affairs. But it is a repetition of Margaret with humiliating endings, and in another year or two he keeps to himself, devotes himself to running his outfits.

In that he has talent. He absorbs the problem completely, thinks

417

at night in bed of how best to treat the different men, how to command them most effectively. In the daytime he spends nearly all his time with the company, supervising labor details, conducting continual inspections. His companies are always the best managed on the post; his company street is easily the cleanest and neatest.

On Saturday mornings a squad from each platoon is put to work cutting the weeds from under the barracks.

He has all the patent brass polishers tested, selects the best, and has an order posted that the men can use only that brand.

In the daily latrine inspections he is always one step ahead of the men; one morning he gets down on his hands and knees, lifts the drain plate, and gigs the platoon because there is grease in the pipe.

When he inspects he brings a needle, probes the cracks on the stairs for dust.

In the gymkhana which the post holds every summer his company teams always win. He has them practicing from the first of February.

The company mess floor is scrubbed with boiling water after every meal.

He is always ahead of the men. One big Saturday inspection when a visiting general is expected, he instructs his first sergeant to have the men grease the soles of their extra shoes, which are exhibited at the foot of their bed.

He has been known to strip a rifle on the parade ground and examine the rear of the hammer spring for dirt.

There is always a standing gag in his company that the Old Man is thinking of having the men take off their shoes before they enter the barracks.

The field officers are agreed that Captain Cummings is the best junior officer on the post.

On a visit to her family in Boston, Margaret is questioned.

You're not planning any children yet?

No, I don't think so, she laughs. I'm afraid to. Edward would probably have him scrubbing the bassinette.

Don't you think seven years now is a long time?

418

Oh, it is, I suppose. I really don't know.

It's not a good idea to wait too long.

Margaret sighs. Men are very odd, positively odd. You always think they're one thing and they turn out to be another.

Her aunt purses her thin mouth. I've always felt, Margaret, that you'd have done better to have married someone we know.

That's an awfully stuffy idea. Edward is going to be a great general. All we need is a war, and I'll feel just like Josephine.

(The shrewd look.) There's no need to be flippant, Margaret. I had expected that marriage in all this time might have made you more . . . womanly. It isn't wise to marry someone about whom you know nothing, and I've always suspected that you married Edward for precisely that reason. (The significant pause.) Ruth, Thatcher's wife, is carrying a third child.

(Margaret is angry.) I wonder if I shall be as dirty as you when I'm as old.

I'm afraid you'll always be *pungent,* my dear.

At the officers' dance on Saturday night, Margaret gets drunk a little more frequently. There are times when an indiscretion is not too far away.

Captain, I see you're all alone, one of the officers' ladies remarks.

Yes, I'm afraid I'm a little too old-fashioned. The war and . . . (Her husband has been commissioned after 1918.) One of my more recurrent regrets is that I never learned to dance well. (His manner, which is to set him off from other professional officers, is beginning in these years.)

Your wife does.

Yes. (At the other end of the officers' club, Margaret is the center of a circle of men. She is laughing loudly now, her hand on the sleeve of a second lieutenant's blouse.) He stares across at her with loathing and disgust.

From Webster's: *hatred,* n., strong aversion or detestation; settled ill will or malevolence.

A thread in most marriages, growing dominant in Cummings's. The cold form of it. No quarrels. No invective.

419

He is all application now, all study. At night, in the parlor of the succession of post houses in which they live, he reads five or six nights a week. There is all the education he has missed, and he takes giant strides in recouping it. There is philosophy first, and then political science, sociology, psychology, history, even literature and art. He absorbs it all with the fantastic powers of memory and assimilation he can exhibit at times, absorbs it and immediately transmutes it into something else, satisfies the dominant warp of his mind.

It comes out a little in the infrequent intellectual discussions he can find on an Army post. I find Freud rather stimulating, he says. The idea is that man is a worthless bastard, and the only problem is how best to control him.

In 1931 Spengler is particularly congenial. To his company he makes short cautious talks.

I don't have to tell you men how bad things are. Some of you are in the Army for just that reason. But I want to point out that we may have an important function. If you read the papers you see where troops are being called out everywhere. There may be a great many changes, and your duty in such a case will be to obey the orders of the government as they come down through me.

The plans, not quite defined, never put to paper, dissolve at last. By 1934 Major Cummings is far more interested in foreign news.

I tell you that Hitler is not a flash in the pan, he will argue. He has the germ of an idea, and moreover you've got to give him political credit. He plays on the German people with consummate skill. That Siegfried business is fundamental to them.

In 1935 Cummings is remembered for making some innovations at the Infantry School in Fort Benning.

In '36 he is considered the most promising field officer of the year at the War College in Washington. And he makes a little ripple in Washington society, becomes friendly with a few congressmen, meets the most important hostess in town. For a while he is in danger of becoming Military Adviser to Washington Society.

But always he is branching out. The confusions, the cross-

420

impulses are concealed now, buried under the concentration with which he works. On a thirty-day leave in the summer of '37 he pays a visit to his brother-in-law, who is vacationing in Maine. They have become very friendly during Cummings's tour of duty in Washington.

On one of the afternoons in a sailboat:

You know, I've always disagreed with the family, Edward. Through no fault of your own they've never entirely approved of you. I think their backward attitude is a little distressing, but of course you understand it.

I think I do, Minot. (There is this other network of emotions and ambitions which recurs now and then. The ineffable perfection of Boston, which had beckoned him, leaves him always curiously satisfied yet troubled. He has traded on Boston in Washington, he knows cynically, aware of himself, but there is still the attraction and the uncertainty.) His speech sounds florid in his ears. Margaret has been mighty fine about it all.

Wonderful woman, that sister of mine.

Yes.

I think it a shame I didn't know you very well years ago. You really would have fitted into the department. I've watched you develop, Edward; I think, when the occasion demands, you have as much perception and tact, you grasp the core of a situation as quickly as any man I know. It's a pity it's too late now.

I think sometimes I might have been good at it, Cummings agrees. But you know I'll be lieutenant colonel in a year or two, and after that I'm free of seniority. It might be a little impolitic to brag, but I should make colonel within a year after.

Mmm. You don't speak French, do you?

A fair amount. I learned some over there in '17, and I've kept up with it since.

The brother-in-law fingers his chin. You know, Edward, I suppose it's one of the laws of government, but there are always many points of view in a department. I'll tell you, I've been wondering if you couldn't be sent on a little joust to France, in your capacity as an officer of course. Nothing official.

What about, Minot?

Oh, it's nebulous. A few talks here and there. An element in the department is attempting to change our Spain policy. I don't think they're going to succeed but it would be disastrous if they should, be tantamount to handing Gibraltar to the Russians. What worries me is France. So long as they stay on the fence I don't think there's a chance of our trying anything by ourselves.

I'm to keep them on the fence?

Nothing so big as that. I've got some assurances, some financial contracts which might put a little pressure in the proper places. The thing to remember is that everyone in France can be bought, none of them has clean hands.

I wonder if I could get away.

We're sending a military mission to France and Italy. I can work it through the War Department. I'll have quite a briefing to give you, but that should give you no trouble.

I'm very interested, Cummings says. The problems of manipulation . . . He trails off, not finishing the sentence.

The water slaps past, resolves itself again behind the stern, quietly, softly, like a cat grooming its fur. Beyond the catboat the sunlight is scattered over the bay, tinkling upon the water.

We might as well put back, the brother-in-law says.

The shore line is wooded, olive-green, a pristine cove.

I never get over this, he says to Cummings. I still expect to see Indians in the forest. Pure country, Maine.

The office is smaller than he has expected, more leathery, somehow more greasy. The map of France is covered with pencil smudges, and a corner is folded over like a dog-eared book.

I must apologize for this place, the man says. (His accent is negligible, a certain preciseness of speech perhaps.) When you first suggested the nature of our business I thought it perhaps best to meet here, not that there should be anything clandestine, but you would attract attention at the Bourse. There are spies everywhere.

I understand. It's been difficult to see you. The party we know suggested Monsieur de Vernay, but I think he is a little too far away to judge.

You state there are credits?

More than enough. I must emphasize that this is not official. There is a tacit agreement . . .

Tacit? Tacit?

An understanding with Leeway Chemical that they will invest in such French firms as *he* thinks advisable. There is no *chou* involved. (He wonders if the slang is correct.) A legitimate business arrangement, but the profits I think are large enough to benefit Sallevoisseux Frères, and enable you to conduct any *adjustments* which might be necessary.

On s'arrangera.

I would have to know some further details of course on the processes you will employ.

Ah, Major Cummings, I can assure you of the vote of twenty-five members of the Chamber of Deputies.

I think it would be best if it didn't come to a vote. There are other ways.

I do not believe I may disclose my routes of access.

(The core of the situation.) Monsieur Sallevoisseux, a man of your . . . vision can see certainly that an enterprise of the magnitude which Leeway Chemical is proposing would demand something more concrete on your part. The decision to set up a subsidiary in France has been taken for some years; it is a question of who will get it. I have with me, subject to the necessary financial guarantees on your part, the power to consolidate with Sallevoisseux Frères. If you cannot give me more definite assurances I will be obliged unfortunately to deal in other channels which I am investigating at present.

I should regret that, Major Cummings.

I should regret it myself.

Sallevoisseux twists in the chair, stares out the high narrow window at the cobblestones in the street below. The horns of the French automobiles sound high-pitched to Cummings.

There are routes. For example — I will give the assurances, the documents, the introductions afterward — for example, I have friends in Les Cagoulards who can influence certain firms, not Chemical, by virtue of some tasks they have performed for them in the past. These firms in turn could if necessary control the decision of a bloc of seventy-five deputies. (He raises his hand.) I know you prefer it does not come to a vote, but no man may control that for you. I can free the vote of any uncertainty. Many of these deputies can influence members of the Ministry.

He pauses. These politics are complicated.

I understand them.

There are several Radical Socialists high-placed in the Foreign Department whom I may influence. I know from a service that there is information to be bought about them. They will be amiable. There are journalists by the dozen, several men in the Bank of France whose *dossiers intimes* I possess. A block of Socialists is controlled by a labor leader with whom I have an understanding. These routes, all indirect, mount up, create a necessary dispersion. You must realize I am not working alone. I can assure you that nothing will be done for eighteen months; beyond that history is involved, and no man may divert it indefinitely.

They talk for several hours, work out the first terms of the agreement.

As he leaves, Cummings smiles. What we're doing is really in the long run what is best for France and America.

Sallevoisseux smiles also. Of course, Major Cummings. A peculiarly American statement, do you know?

You'll show me the dossiers you possess at hand. Tomorrow, is that right?

D'accord!

A month later, his part in the assignment completed, Cummings moves down to Rome. A telegram reaches him from his brother-in-law.

Preliminary dispositions satisfactory. Very well done. Congratulations.

He talks to an Italian colonel as part of the military mission.

I would like you to see, Signor Maggiore, our work on the problems of dysentery in the successful African campaign. We have discovered a new series of sanitary measures 73% more effective in avoid-

424

ing the dreadful, the malign propensities of such a disease.

The summer heat is stifling. Despite the lecture by the Italian Colonel he suffers from diarrhea, and is plagued by a severe cold. He spends a miserable week in bed, abysmally tired. A letter follows from his brother-in-law.

I think it's a shame to ruin the understandable elation you must be feeling now after such a neat job in Paris, but there's something I really ought to tell you. Margaret, you know, has been down in Washington with me for the past two weeks, and to put it as kindly as possible, she has been acting very odd. There's a certain abandonment about her which is not proper to her age; I must confess I find it hard to believe she is my sister at times. If it were not for you, I would have told her to leave my house. I'm really awfully disturbed to ruin what must be a vacation in Rome, but I think if you can it might not be a bad idea to be thinking of coming back. Do see Monsignor Truffenio and give him my regards.

This time it is a tired hatred. I just hope she keeps it quiet he swears to himself. He has a nightmare that evening, waking up on a fever-ridden bed. He thinks of his father for the first time in a year or two, remembers his death a few years ago and relives a little of the anxiety it had caused him. After midnight he gets up on an impulse and walks the streets, ending up in an alley where he becomes drunk in a bar.

There is a little man pawing him. Signor Maggiore you come home with me now?

He staggers along dimly aware of what he wants, but he does not find it. In another alley the little man and a confederate jump him, strip his pockets, and leave him to awaken in the harsh glare, the quick stench of the sun on a garbage-filled alley in Rome. He makes it back to his hotel without too many people seeing him, changes his clothes, takes a bath, and goes to bed for over a day. He feels as if he is breaking apart.

I must confess, your Reverence, that I have admired the Church for many years. In the immensity of your conception lies your greatness.

The Cardinal bows his head. I am pleased to give you an audience, my son. You have done good work already. I have heard of your labors in Paris against the Antichrist.

I labored for my country. (In this setting the words cause him no embarrassment.)

There is a nobler labor.

I am aware of it, your Reverence . . . There are times when I feel a great weariness.

You may be preparing for an important change.

Sometimes I think so. I've always looked upon your Church with admiration.

He walks through the great courtyard of the Vatican, stares for a long time at the dome of St. Peter's. The ceremony he has just heard has moved him, sent music lapping through his brain.

Maybe I should turn.

But on the boat going back he thinks of other things, reads with quiet satisfaction in the newspaper he has brought on board that Lee-way Chemical is opening negotiations with Sallevoisseux Frères.

Man, I'll be glad to get back from frog-land and the wops, one of the officers who has been on the mission says to him.

Yes.

That Italy's a backward country even if they say Musso did a lot for it. You can still keep it. The Catholic countries are the ones who are always backward.

I suppose so.

He thinks clearly for a few minutes. The thing that happened in the Rome alley is a danger sign, and he will have to be very careful from now on. It must never come out again. The Church business is understandable in its light, a highly impractical move at this juncture. *I'll be a colonel soon. I can't risk it turning.*

Cummings sighs. I've learned a lot.

Yeah, me too.

Cummings looks at the water. Slowly his eyes raise, include the horizon. Lieutenant colonel . . . colonel . . . brigadier . . . major general . . . lieutenant general . . . general?

If there's a war soon it'll help.

426

But afterward. The politicos were even more important. After the war . . .

He must not commit himself politically yet. There would be too many turns. It might be Stalin, it might be Hitler. But the eventual line to power in America would always be anticommunism.

He must keep his eyes open, Cummings decided.

Chorus:

WHAT IS A MILLION-DOLLAR WOUND?

The latrine, early morning. It is a six-holer off in the bushes at one end of the bivouac, and is without a tarpaulin. At either end is a stick with a roll of paper on it, and a tin can covering it.

GALLAGHER: Some fuggin mornings like this I wish I'd catch a bullet.

WILSON: Only goddam trouble with that is you can't pick the spot.

STANLEY: You know if you could, the Army wouldn't be keeping me long.

GALLAGHER: Aaah, there ain't a goddam place you can get a million-dollar wound that it don't hurt.

STANLEY: Sometimes I think I'd lose a leg, and call it quits.

WILSON: Only trouble with losing a goddam leg is you're h'isted on to a woman, and there's her husban' in the door, and how in the hell you gonna run? (Laughter)

MARTINEZ: Lose arm maybe.

STANLEY: Jeez, that's way worse, I don't think I'd even take that. I mean how the hell can you get a job without an arm or, Jesus, without both arms?

GALLAGHER: Aaah, the fuggin government'll support ya.

WILSON: But then you cain't jack-off if you got a mind to.

GALLAGHER: (Disgustedly) Haw.

MARTINEZ: Get wound, okay, means should get killed, only wounded. Goddam nigger luck.

STANLEY: Yeah, that's what they say. (Pause.) The million-dollar wound for somebody like Ridges would be to lose his head. (Laughter)

428

GALLAGHER: For that Roth and Goldstein, you could shoot 'em in the nuts and they wouldn't even know the difference.

STANLEY: Oh, Jesus, don't even talk about that. I get the shivers.

GALLAGHER: The Aarmy got the fuggin percentages on their side, you can't even get a wound and get out where it's worth it.

STANLEY: I'd take a foot anytime. I'd sign the papers for it now.

MARTINEZ: Me too. Not so hard. Toglio, elbow shot up, he get out.

WILSON: Goddam, ain't that somethin! Ah tell you, men, Ah don' even 'member what that chickenshit Toglio looks like any more. But Ah'll *never* forget he got out on a busted elbow.

(They continue talking)

PART THREE

Plant and Phantom

"Even the wisest among you is only a disharmony and hybrid of plant and phantom. But do I bid you become phantoms or plants?"

— NIETZSCHE

1

RECON set out on the patrol the next afternoon. They boarded their assault boat several hours before dusk, and in a short time their landing craft rounded the peninsula and wallowed out toward the western tip of Anopopei. The swell was heavy. Although their pilot held them always within a mile of shore, the boat rolled and pitched, continually shipping water which sprayed over the forward ramp and sloshed along the deck. The boat was small, identical to the one in which they had landed on invasion day, and it was poorly equipped to circuit half the island. The men huddled on their cots, covered themselves with their ponchos, and prepared for a miserable trip.

Lieutenant Hearn stood for a time on the pilot's hatch at the stern, staring down into the troop well. He was a little weary; only an hour or two after Dalleson had told him he was to be assigned to recon he had been given the instructions for the patrol, and the rest of the day had been spent in checking the men's equipment, in drawing rations, and in absorbing the maps and orders Dalleson had furnished him. He had acted automatically, efficiently, postponing until later his surprise and pleasure at being transferred from Cummings's staff.

He lit a cigarette and gazed down again at the men clustered in the rectangular box of the troop well. All thirteen were squeezed into an area not more than thirty feet long or eight feet wide, together with their equipment, their packs, rifles, their cartridge belts and canteens, and the Army cots they had spread out on the floor of the boat. He had attempted earlier that day to procure an assault craft which had bunks built in along the walls but it had been impossible. Now the cots filled most of the available space. The men squatted on them, their feet drawn up to keep them free of the water that washed along the deck. Under their ponchos they winced whenever some spray would arch over the front ramp.

Hearn examined their faces. He had made it his business to learn their names immediately, but that was hardly equivalent to knowing anything about them, and it was obviously important that he should form some quick idea of them as individuals. He had talked to a few casually, joked with them, but it was not a process he enjoyed particularly, and he knew his own aptitudes were poorly suited. He could learn more from observation. The only trouble was that observation was necessarily slow, and by tomorrow morning they would land on the beach, begin their patrol. Then every bit of knowledge about them would be important.

As Hearn watched their faces, he was aware of a vague discomfort. It was the kind of physical readiness, the slight guilt, the slight shame, perhaps, that he had felt in walking through a slum neighborhood, conscious of the hostility of the people who watched him pass. Certainly whenever one of the men stared at him, it was a little difficult not to look away. Most of them had hard faces; their eyes were blank with something cold and removed in their expression. As a group they had a forbidding and rigid quality as though they no longer held an excess bit of weight nor a surplus emotion. Their skins had turned sallow, almost yellow, and their faces, their arms and legs, were pocked with many jungle sores. Nearly all of them had shaved before they started out, and yet their faces were unkempt their clothing sloppy.

He looked at Croft, who had put on a clean fatigue uniform. He was squatting on his cot, sharpening his trench knife against a little whetstone he had withdrawn from his pocket. Hearn knew Croft perhaps best of all, or more exactly he had spent the most time with him that morning discussing the patrol, but actually he did not know

434

him at all. Croft had listened to him, had nodded, spat occasionally to the side, and answered him when necessary with a few bare words, uttered in a low toneless murmur. Croft obviously handled the platoon well, he was tough and capable, and Hearn was reasonably certain that Croft resented him. It would be a difficult relationship to handle, for Croft knew more than he did yet, and unless he was careful the platoon would soon realize it. Almost with fascination, Hearn watched Croft working on his trench knife. He brooded over it, his cold gaunt face examining his hands as he drew the blade back and forth against the stone. There was something frozen about him, something congealed in the set of his tight mouth, the concentration of his eyes. Croft was tough, all right, Hearn told himself.

The boat was turning now, angling against the swells. Hearn grasped a strut more firmly as it jarred against a wave.

There was Sergeant Brown, whom he knew slightly; he was the one who looked like a boy with his snubbed nose and freckles and light-brown hair. The Typical American Soldier — the agreeable composite hatched out of the tobacco smoke and hangovers of the advertising conferences. Brown looked like all the smiling soldiers in the advertisements, a trifle smaller, perhaps, plumper, more bitter than was permissible. Brown had an odd face actually, Hearn decided. Up close there were jungle sores on Brown's skin, and his eyes had become dull and remote, his skin had begun to wrinkle. He looked surprisingly old.

But, then, all the veterans did. It was simple to pick them out. There was Gallagher, who probably had always looked that way, but still he had been in the platoon for some time. And there was Martinez, who seemed more fragile, more sensitive than the others. His fine features had been nervous, his eyes had blinked as he talked to Hearn that morning. He was the one you would pick instantly to crack up, and yet he was probably a good man. A Mexican had to be to become a good noncom.

There was Wilson, and the one they called Red. Hearn watched Valsen. That one had a craggy face with a rough boiled look about it which emphasized the blueness of his eyes. His laugh had a hoarse sarcastic edge as if everything disgusted him exactly the way he had known it would disgust him. Valsen was the one who was probably worth talking to, and yet he would be unapproachable.

Collectively, they lent something to each other, seemed harder and meaner than they would if isolated. As they lay on their cots, their faces seemed the only things alive in the troop well. Their fatigues were old, faded to a pale green, and the boat walls had rusted brown. There was no color, no movement in anything but the of their faces. Hearn threw his cigarette away.

On his left was the island, not more than half a mile across the water. The beach was narrow at this point and the coconut trees grew almost to the water's edge; behind them grew the brush, a dense tangle of roots and vines and plants, of trees and foliage. Inland there were hills, set heavily on the earth, their ridge-lines lost in the forests that covered them. Their lines were ugly, broken and scraggly, with bald patches of rock like the hide of a bison when it is shedding in summer. Hearn felt the weight and resistance of that land. If the terrain was similar at the place where they landed tomorrow, it would be hell working through it. Abruptly, the idea of the patrol seemed a little fantastic to him.

For a moment he became aware again of the steady grind of the assault craft's motors. Cummings had sent him out on this, and therefore he could distrust the mission of the patrol, distrust Cummings's motives in initiating it. It seemed a little inconceivable that Cummings should have made the mistake of transferring him; certainly the General must have known that this was what he preferred.

Was it remotely possible that the decision to transfer him had come from Dalleson? Hearn doubted it. With ease he could imagine the scene in which Cummings had given the idea to Dalleson. And the patrol was quite likely an extension of the General's motives in assigning him to recon.

But that seemed a little extravagant. He had discovered the hatred Cummings was capable of bearing, but he could not imagine Cummings expending a platoon for a week in order to work out a minor vengeance. There were other and easier ways; besides, Cummings was too much of a military craftsman to be wasteful. Consciously, he must

436

have considered the patrol as an effective maneuver. What bothered Hearn was that the General might not be aware of his own motives.

Certainly, it seemed a little unbelievable that they could march for thirty or forty miles through unexplored jungle and hills, go through a mountain pass, scout the Japanese rear and return; the more carefully he considered it the more difficult it became. He was inexperienced, of course, and the mission might actually be easier to accomplish than he estimated, but at best it was a doubtful business.

It softened the edge of his satisfaction at being given a platoon. Whatever Cummings's reasons, there was no assignment Hearn preferred more. He foresaw the annoyances, the dangers, the inevitable disillusionments, but at least this was a positive action. For the first time in many months there were a few things he wanted again, simply and honestly. If he could manage it, if it turned out the way he wanted, he could establish some kind of liaison with the men. A good platoon.

It rather surprised him. It was a little too naïve, too ideal an attitude for himself. The moment it was established in another frame it became ridiculous. A good platoon . . . to do what, to work a little better in an institution he despised, whose ligaments Cummings had exposed to him? Or perhaps because it was his platoon, his baby? The private property concept. And he could detect elements of that in himself. Paternalism! The truth was, he grinned, he wasn't ready for Cummings's brand-new society in which everything was issued and never owned.

In any case he would discover his own motives later. Now he knew intuitively that it was better for himself. He had liked most of the men in the platoon, quickly and instinctively, and quite astonishing to himself, he had wanted them to like him. He had even made efforts, given little hints that he was a good guy, employing the tricks he had unconsciously absorbed from certain officers, his own father. There was a particular kind of buddying you could get away with when you dealt with Americans; it was close but not dangerously so, and you never let it get out of hand. That was a technique you could perform and still be a bastard essentially, but he wanted to go a little further than that.

What was at the core of it? To prove Cummings was wrong? Hearn wondered for a moment, then let it go. To hell with the introspection. It never paid to think until you knew a lot, and he had been in the platoon for too short a time to decide anything.

Directly beneath him, lying on adjacent cots, Red and Wilson were talking. On an impulse, he climbed down into the troop well.

He nodded to Wilson. "How're your GIs coming along?" he asked. About an hour ago, amid the laughter of the men, Wilson had climbed up on the side wall of the boat, and squatted over the edge.

"Aw, they ain't too bad, Lootenant," Wilson sighed. "Ah jus' hope to hell Ah git over 'em by tomorrow."

Valsen snorted. "You ain't got nothing a gallon of paregoric ain't gonna cure."

Wilson shook his head, his genial face reflective suddenly, a little worried, the expression at odds with his bland features. "Ah jus' hope that damn fool doctor is wrong and Ah don' have to have no op-per-ration."

"What's the matter with you?" Hearn asked.

"Aw, mah insides are jus' shot to hell, Lootenant. Ah got a lot of pus in 'em, an' that doctor said he'd have to cut it out." Wilson shook his head. "Ah just cain't figger it," he sighed. "Ah had a dose many a time but it don' take nothin' to get rid of the clap."

The boat slapped and pounded as it passed through a series of swells, and Wilson bit his mouth from a sudden pang.

Red lit a cigarette. "For Crisake if you believe a fuggin sawbones . . ." He stood up for a moment and spat over the side wall, watching his spittle be sucked away instantly in the foam of the wake. "All a doctor ever has is a pill and a pat on the back, and you stick them in the Army and all they got left is the pill."

Hearn laughed. "Talking from experience, Valsen?"

But Red didn't answer, and Wilson after a moment sighed again. "Ah wish to hell they didn't send us out just today. Ifen we gotta do somethin' Ah don' give a damn, put me on a detail, send me out on this, it don' matter, but Ah jus' hate to be sick like this."

"Hell, you'll pull out of it," Hearn said easily.

438

"Ah hope so, Lootenant." Wilson nodded. "Ah'm no fug-off an' any of the men'll tell you Ah'd rather work than jus' lay around an' get all hot an' bothered, but lately with this misery it makes me feel like Ah ain't worth a good goddam, Ah jus' cain't seem to do what Ah use' to do." He shook one of his long broad fingers at Hearn, who watched the sunlight glint on the blond-red hairs at his wrist. "Maybe this las' week Ah been havin' to goof-off a little, an' Croft's been on my ass the whole time. It's a helluva note when a buddy you been with in the same platoon for two years figgers you're goofin'-off on him."

Red snorted. "Take it easy, Wilson, and I'll tell that goddam engineer to take it easy with this boat over the bumps." Their pilot was a man from an engineer company. "I'll tell him to set you down easy." Red's voice was sarcastic with a touch of disgust.

Hearn realized that Valsen hadn't said a word directly to him since he had begun talking to them. And why was Wilson telling him all this? As an alibi? But Hearn didn't think so. All the time Wilson had been talking his voice had been a little abstracted as though explaining something to himself. Wilson was unconscious of him, and Valsen seemed to resent him.

Well, then, the hell with it. He wouldn't force himself on them. He stretched, yawned a little, and said, "Take it easy, men."

"Yeah, Lootenant," Wilson murmured.

Red made no answer. His face, still sullen and irritable, stared coldly at him as Hearn climbed up again on the pilot hatch.

Croft had finished sharpening his trench knife, and while Hearn and Wilson were still talking, he worked his way forward to the shelter of the front ramp. Stanley, seeing an opportunity, joined him. It was almost comfortable talking there, for although the floor was wet, the bow was raised slightly. The spray that lashed into the boat was washed toward the stern, leaving no puddles.

Stanley was busy talking. "I think it was a goddam shame the way they stuck an officer in on us. There isn't anybody can handle the platoon better than you, and they shoulda commissioned you before sticking in some ninety-day wonder."

Croft shrugged. Hearn's transfer had been a shock to him, deeper than he cared to admit. He had been in command of the platoon for so long it was a little difficult for him to realize that he had a superior. Even in the day Hearn had been with them Croft had been forced to remind himself many times before giving an order that he was no longer in charge.

Hearn was his foe. Without even stating it to himself, the attitude was implicit in everything Croft did. Automatically he considered it Hearn's fault that the transfer had been made, and resented him instinctively for it. But it was more confused than that. He could not acknowledge his own animosity, for he had been grounded in Army orders for too long. To resent an order, to be unwilling to carry it out, was immoral to Croft. Besides, he could do nothing about it. "If you can't do nothin' keep your mouth shut," was one of his few maxims.

He didn't answer Stanley, but still he was pleased.

"I kinda think I know human nature," Stanley said, "and I damn sure can tell you that I'd rather have you running this patrol than some looey they hand us on a platter."

Croft spat. Stanley was pretty sharp, he told himself. Of course he was a brown-nose, but if a man was all right outside of that, he wouldn't hold it against him. "Mebbe," he admitted.

"Now, you take this patrol, it's going to be a rough one. We need somebody who knows the score."

"What do you think of the patrol?" Croft asked softly. He ducked as some spray washed over them.

Stanley guessed that Croft would be pleased if he accepted the patrol without resentment. But he knew he would have to answer cautiously. If he was enthusiastic, Croft would distrust him, for none of the other men were eager. Stanley fingered his mustache, which was still thin and uneven despite the care he gave it. "I don't know, somebody's got to do it, and it might as well be us. To tell you the truth, Sam," he ventured, "this may sound like bullshit coming from me, but I ain't sorry we caught it. You get tired of hanging around, you want to do something."

Croft fingered his chin. "That's what you think, huh?"

"Well, I wouldn't tell it to everybody, but, yes, that's what I do think."

"Uh-huh." Half purposefully, Stanley had stroked one of Croft's basic passions. After a month of labor details and unimportant security patrols, Croft's senses had become raw waiting for activity. Any big patrol would have appealed to him. But this one . . . the conception of it was more impressive to him. Although he did not show it, he was impatient; the chore was to get through the hours on board this boat. All afternoon he had been debating possible routes, reviewing the terrain in his mind. There had been only an aerial map of the back country, but he had memorized that.

And once again he felt an unpleasant shock, reminded himself that the platoon and the patrol would not be directed by him.

"Yeah, it's all right," Croft said. "I'll tell you, that General Cummings is a smart man to have figgered it all out."

Stanley nodded. "All the guys bitch all the time about how they could do it better, but he's got a hard job."

"Reckon so," Croft said. He stared away for a moment, and then nudged Stanley. "Look." He was watching Wilson talk to Hearn, and he felt a trace of jealousy.

Unconsciously, Stanley copied Croft's speech. "Do you reckon old Wilson is sucking?"

Croft laughed quietly and coldly. "Goddam, I don't know, he's been dicking-off lately."

"I wonder if he's really sick," Stanley said doubtfully.

Croft shook his head. "You cain't trust Wilson any further'n you can throw him."

"That's the way *I* had him tabbed." Stanley felt good. Brown was always saying that nobody could get along with Croft, but he didn't know how to work it. Croft was okay, you just had to approach him on the right tack. It was all right when you could buddy with the noncoms over you.

Yet Stanley had been very tense all the while he had been talking to Croft. In his first weeks in the platoon he had acted similarly toward Brown, but now that tension was switched to Croft. Stanley never said anything to him without some purpose. It was an automatic process, however. He never thought consciously, It's a good idea to agree with Croft. At the moment he believed what he was saying; his mind worked more quickly, more effectively than his speech, so that sometimes Stanley was almost surprised at his own words. "Yeah, Wilson's an odd guy," he muttered.

"Uh-huh."

Yet for a moment Stanley was depressed. Perhaps he had started to buddy with Croft too late. What good was it to him now that the Lieutenant had come into the platoon? One of the reasons he resented Hearn was that he had hoped Croft would be commissioned, and there might have been a chance for him to fill the vacancy. He could not visualize either Martinez or Brown as platoon sergeant. Actually, this ambition was vague precisely because he did not want to halt there. Stanley had no single goal; his dreams were always vague.

Indeed, as they talked, Croft and Stanley were sensing a similarity between themselves, and it drew them together. Croft felt a mild affection for him. This Stanley kid ain't too bad, he told himself.

The deck under their feet shuddered as the boat slapped against a few waves. The sun was almost down, and the sky overhead was clouding over. It was the least bit chill, and they drew closer to light cigarettes.

Gallagher had worked his way up to the bow. He stood quietly beside them, his thin knotted body shivering a little. They listened to the water sloshing about the bottom of the boat. "One minute you're hot, and then you're cold," Gallagher muttered.

Stanley smiled at him. He felt it necessary to be tactful with Gallagher since his wife had died and it irked him. Basically, he had only contempt for Gallagher and annoyance, for Gallagher made him uncomfortable. "How're you feeling, boy?" Stanley said, however.

"All right." But Gallagher was depressed. The grayness of the sky made him mournful; he had been exceptionally sensitive to the moods of the weather since Mary's death, and often now he languished in a gentle melancholy close to easy tears. He felt little volition, and surprisingly little bitterness; the façade of anger remained, even erupted occasionally in a spate of profanity, but Red and Wilson and one or two of the others had recognized the change. "Yeah, I'm

442

all right," he muttered again. Stanley's sympathy irritated him, for he sensed it to be false; Gallagher was more perceptive now.

He wondered why he had come up beside them, and thought of moving back to his cot, but it was warmer here. The bow lurched and bumped under his feet and he grunted. "How long are they gonna keep us here like goddam sardines?" he growled.

Croft and Stanley, after a pause, were talking about the patrol again, and Gallagher listened with resentment. "You know what the mother-fugger'll be like?" he blurted. "We'll be lucky to get out of there with our goddam heads on." He felt a quick remorse which was mixed with fear. I got to cut out that swearing, he told himself. In the past week and a half since the last letter had come, Gallagher had been making attempts to reform. His profanity was sinful, he believed, and he was afraid of more retribution.

The talk about the patrol frightened him, and his remorse at swearing added to this. Once again Gallagher saw himself lying dead in a field, and it loosed a nervous flush along his back which prickled painfully. He could see the dead Japanese soldier whom Croft had killed, still lying in the green draw.

Stanley ignored him. "What do you figure on doin' if we can't get through the pass?" It was important to know all these things, he told himself; he might end up in command of the platoon. You could never tell what kind of accidents there might be. Skillfully suspended, he conceived the accidents occurring in a vacuum, forcing his mind away from the idea of who might be killed.

"I'll give you a bit of advice," Croft said. The words felt strange in his mouth; he almost never gave advice. "In the Army, if you can't do somethin' one way you damn sure better do it another."

"Then what'll you do, go over the mountain?"

"I ain't in command. The Lieutenant is."

Stanley made a face. "Aww." He felt young when he was with Croft, but he did not try to conceal it. Without reasoning why, he assumed Croft would like him better if he weren't too cocky.

"But if the platoon was mine, that's the way I'd do it," Croft added.

Gallagher heard them dully, not quite listening. Their talk about the patrol offended him; always superstitious, his mind was charged with taboos, and he felt it dangerous to talk about combat. He was still depressed, and he saw the patrol ahead in a gloomy vista of fatigue and danger and misery. His feelings boiled over into self-pity, and some tears formed in his eyes. To repress them, he spoke angrily to Stanley. "You think you're going to see something? You'll be lucky if you don't get your head blown off." He almost swore and caught himself.

This time they could not ignore him. For an instant Stanley remembered the casual, almost ridiculous way Minetta had been wounded, and he was tormented by the emotions he had felt then. His confidence was eroded. "You talk an awful lot," he said to Gallagher.

"You know what you can do about it."

Stanley stepped toward him, and then halted. Gallagher was much smaller than he, so there would be no glory in fighting him. Moreover, Stanley saw it vaguely as fighting a cripple. "Listen, Gallagher, I can break you in two," he said. He didn't realize it but this was what Red had said to him the morning they landed on the beach.

"Aaaaah." Gallagher made no motion, however. He was afraid of Stanley.

Croft watched them indifferently. He too had been bothered by Gallagher's speech. He had never forgotten the Japanese charge across the river, and occasionally he would dream of a great wave of water about to fall on him while he lay helpless beneath it. He never connected the dream to the night attack, but intuitively he felt the dream signified some weakness in himself. Gallagher had disturbed him, and he thought consciously of his own death for a moment. That's a damn fool thing to kick around in your head, he said to himself. But he could not shake it immediately. Croft always saw order in death. Whenever a man in the platoon or company had been killed he would feel a grim and quiet satisfaction as though the death was inevitably just. What bothered him now was the idea that the wheels might be grinding for him. Croft had none of the particular blend of pessimism and fatalism that Red and Brown felt. Croft did not believe that the longer he was in combat the poorer his chances became. Croft be-

444

lieved a man was destined to be killed or not killed, and automatically he had always considered himself exempt. But now he was not so assured. He had a sense of foreboding for an instant.

The abortive fight over, they stood silently behind the ramp, feeling the lethargic sullen power of the ocean beneath the thin metal of the deck. Red had joined them, and they stood quiet, hunched against the spray, shivering from time to time. Stanley and Croft began talking again about the patrol, and Red listened with dull resentment. His back was aching, which made him irritable. The slapping and pounding of the assault boat, the constraint of the cots and men in their tiny space, even the sound of Stanley's voice, were offensive.

"You know," Stanley was confiding to Croft, "I'm not saying I'm happy about the patrol, but still it's going to be an experience, you know. You can't be a lower kind of noncom than I am, but still you got duties, and you need experience to carry it out right." His speech had a modest tone, too modest for Red, who snorted scornfully.

"Jus' keep your eyes open," Croft said. "Most of the men in the platoon walk around like a bunch of goddam sheep lookin' at the ground."

Red sighed to himself. Stanley's ambition made him contemptuous, but there was an uneasy basis to his scorn which he partially understood. He was the least bit envious. The contradiction ended by depressing him. Aaah, he thought, every man jack eats his heart out, and what does it get him? He could see Stanley rising higher and higher in the months to come, and yet he would never be happy. Any of us'll be lucky if we don't get a bullet in our gut. He felt his skin tightening across his back, and despite himself he turned around to look at the bare metal wall of the bow ramp. Since the day when he had lain helpless on the ground waiting for the Japanese soldier to kill him he had been feeling a recurring anxiety. Often in the night he would awaken with a start, and turn around in his blankets, trembling unreasonably.

What the hell do I want to be a noncom for? he asked himself. You get a guy killed in your squad and you never stop thinking about it. I don't want to take no orders from nobody, and I don't want nobody to give 'em to me. He looked at Hearn standing in the rear of

445

the boat, and felt a dull anger working in his throat. The goddam officers. Red snorted. A bunch of college kids who think it's like going to a football game. That bastard is glad to be going out on this. Deep within him a passionate hatred was brewing for everyone in the Army who endangered his life. What the hell is it to the General if we get knocked off? Just an experiment that got fugged-up. Guinea pigs.

Stanley amused him, roused his irony. His emotions finally boiled into speech. "Hey, Stanley, you think they'll give you a Silver Star?"

Stanley looked at him, tensing instantly. "Fug you, Red."

"Just wait, sonny," Red said. He guffawed loudly and turned to Gallagher. "They'll give him the Purple Ass-hole."

"Listen, Red," Stanley said, trying to edge some menace into his voice. He knew that Croft was watching him.

"Aaah," Red snorted. He didn't want to fight at all. His back, even when it did not ache, left him weak and lethargic. He realized abruptly that he and Stanley had changed in the few months they had been on Anopopei; Stanley looked fatter and sleeker, more self-assured. He was still growing. Red felt the tired leanness of his own body. Because of all this, because of his doubt, his pride made him go on. "You're biting off more than you can take, Stanley."

"What's the matter, you ganging up with Gallagher?"

Gallagher was frightened again, unwilling to be involved. In the past weeks he had drawn in upon himself, become passive. His occasional bursts of rage left him apathetic. Yet he could not withdraw now; Red was one of his best buddies. "Red don't need to gang up with me," he muttered.

"You guys think you're pretty tough 'cause you been around a little longer than me."

"Maybe," Gallagher said.

Stanley knew he had to tell Red off if he was to hold Croft's respect. But he felt incapable of it. Red's taunt about combat had lacerated his confidence again; abruptly he was forced to face the knowledge that he was terrified at the thought of it. He took a deep breath. "This ain't the time, Red, but wait'll we get back."

"Yeah, send me a letter."

Stanley's mouth tightened but he could think of no answer. He

446

looked at Croft, whose face was impassive. "I just wish you guys were in my squad," he said to Red and Gallagher. They guffawed at this.

Croft was annoyed. He had wavered between his desire to see a fight and his knowledge that it would be a bad thing for the platoon. Now he was contemptuous of Stanley; a noncom had to know how to keep a man in his place, and it had been bungled. Croft hawked a little spittle over the side wall of the boat. "What's the matter, everybody worked up already?" he said coldly. Aimless talk irritated him.

They were all quiet again. The tension between them had collapsed like a piece of moist paper shredding of its own weight. All of them except Croft were secretly relieved. But the patrol to come draped them in a shroud of gloom. Each retreated into silence and his private fears. Like an augury the night was coming closer.

Far in the distance they could see Mount Anaka rising above the island. It arched coldly and remotely from the jungle beneath it, lofting itself massively into the low-hanging clouds of the sky. In the early drab twilight it looked like an immense old gray elephant erecting himself somberly on his front legs, his haunches lost in the green bedding of his lair. The mountain seemed wise and powerful, and terrifying in its size. Gallagher stared at it in absorption, caught by a sense of beauty he could not express. The idea, the vision he always held of something finer and neater and more beautiful than the moil in which he lived trembled now, pitched almost to a climax of words. There was an instant in which he might have said a little of what he was feeling, but it passed and he was left with a troubled joy, an echo of rapture. He licked his lips, mourning his wife again.

Croft was moved as deeply, as fundamentally as caissons resettling in the river mud. The mountain attracted him, taunted and inflamed him with its size. He had never seen it so clearly before. Mired in the jungle, the cliffs of Watamai Range had obscured the mountain. He stared at it now, examined its ridges, feeling an instinctive desire to climb the mountain and stand on its peak, to know that all its mighty weight was beneath his feet. His emotions were intense; he knew awe and hunger and the peculiar unique ecstasy he had felt after Hennessey was dead, or when he had killed the Japanese prisoner. He gazed at it, almost hating the mountain, unconscious at first of the

447

men about him. "That mountain's mighty old," he said at last.

And Red felt only gloom, and a vague harassment. Croft's words bothered him subtly. He examined the mountain with little emotion, almost indifference. But when he looked away he was bothered by the fear all of the men in the platoon had felt at one time or another that day. Like the others, Red was wondering if this patrol would be the one where his luck ran out.

Goldstein and Martinez were talking about America. By chance they had chosen cots next to each other, and they spent the afternoon lying on them, their ponchos drawn over their bodies. Goldstein was feeling rather happy. He had never been particularly close to Martinez before, but they had been chatting for several hours and their confidences were becoming intimate. Goldstein was always satisfied if he could be friendly with someone; his ingenuous nature was always trusting. One of the main reasons for this wretchedness in the platoon was that his friendships never seemed to last. Men with whom he would have long amiable conversations would wound him or disregard him the next day, and he never understood it. To Goldstein, men were friends or they weren't friends; he could not comprehend any variations or disloyalties. He was unhappy because he felt continually betrayed.

Yet he never became completely disheartened. Essentially he was an active man, a positive man. If his feelings were bruised, if another friend had proved himself undependable, Goldstein would nurse his pains, but almost always he would recover and sally out again. The succession of rebuffs he had suffered in the platoon had made him more wily, more cautious in what he said and did. But still, Goldstein was too affectionate to possess any real defenses; at the first positive hint of friendship he was ready to forget all his grievances and respond with warmth and simplicity. Now he felt he knew Martinez. If he had phrased his opinion he would have said to himself, Martinez is a very fine fellow. He's a little quiet but he's a nice guy. Very democratic for a sergeant.

"You know in America," Martinez was saying, "lots of opportunity."

448

"Oh, there is," Goldstein nodded sagely. "I know I've got plans for setting up my own business, because I've considered it a lot, and a man has to strike out for himself if he wants to get ahead. There's a lot to be said for steady wages and security, but I'd rather be my own boss."

Martinez nodded. "Lots of money in your own business, huh?"

"Sometimes."

Martinez considered this. Money! A little perspiration formed on his palms. He thought for a moment of a man named Ysidro Juaninez, a brothelkeeper who had always fascinated him when he was a child. He shivered as he remembered the way Ysidro would hold a thick sheaf of dollar bills in his hand. "After the war maybe I get out of the Army."

"You certainly ought to," Goldstein said. "I mean you're an intelligent fellow and you're dependable."

Martinez sighed. "Still . . ." He did not know how to say it. He was always embarrassed at mentioning the fact that he was a Mexican. He thought it was bad manners as if he were blaming the man he told it to, implying that it was his fault there were no good jobs for him. Besides, there was always the irrational hope he might be taken for a pure Spaniard.

"Still, I'm no educated," he said.

Goldstein shook his head in commiseration. "That's an obstacle, it's true. I've always wanted a college education, and I feel its absence. But for business a good head can carry you through. I really believe in being honest and sincere in business; all the really big men got where they are through decency."

Martinez nodded. He wondered how big a room a very rich man needed to hold his money. Images of rich clothing, of shoeshines and hand-painted ties, a succession of tall blonde women with hard cold grace and brittle charm languished in his head. "A rich man do anything he damn well feel like it," Martinez said with admiration.

"Well, if I were rich I'd like to be charitable. And . . . what I want is to be well off, and have a nice house, some security . . . Do you know New York?"

"No."

449

"Anyway there's a suburb I'd like to live in," Goldstein said, nodding his head. "It's really a fine place, and nice people in it, cultured, refined. I wouldn't like my son to grow up the way I did."

Martinez nodded sagely. He never possessed any definite convictions or ambitions, and he always felt humble when he talked to a man who had sharp complete plans. "America's a good country," he said sincerely. He had a glow of righteous patriotism for a moment; half-remembered was his image of a schoolroom and the children singing "My Country 'Tis of Thee." For the first time in many years he thought of being an aviator, and felt a confused desire. "I learn to read good in school," he said. "The teacher thought I was smart."

"I'm sure she did," Goldstein said with conviction.

The water was less rough, and the spray had become infrequent. Martinez looked about the boat, listened for a moment to the random sounds of conversation, and shrugged again "Long trip," he said.

Gallagher had come back to his cot, which was adjacent to Martinez's, and he lay down without saying anything. Goldstein was uncomfortable; he had not spoken to Gallagher for over a month. "It's a wonder none of the men are seasick," Goldstein said at last. "These boats aren't good for traveling."

"Roth, Wyman, they're sick," Martinez said.

Goldstein shrugged proudly. "I don't mind it. I'm used to being on boats. A friend of mine had a sailboat on Long Island, and in the summer I used to go out with him a lot. I enjoyed it thoroughly." He thought of the Sound and the pale dunes that surrounded it. "It was beautiful there. You know you can't beat America for beautiful country."

"You can say that again, brother," Gallagher snorted suddenly.

It was just his way of talking, Goldstein decided. He didn't mean any harm. "Did you ever go out on boats, Gallagher?" he asked mildly.

Gallagher raised himself on an elbow. "Aaah, I went canoeing once in a while out on the Charles, past West Roxbury. Used to go with my wife." He said it first, and then thought about it. His face altered for an instant, assumed a numb stricken cast.

"Oh, I'm sorry," Goldstein breathed.

"That's all right." Gallagher felt some irritation at getting sym

450

pathy from a Jew. "Forget it," he added, a little meaninglessly. But he was becoming tender again, dissolving in a bath of self-pity and pleasant gentle sorrow. "Look," he said abruptly, "you got a kid, ain't ya?"

Goldstein nodded. "Oh, yes," he answered eagerly. "My boy is three years old now. Wait, I'll show you a picture of him." With some effort, he rolled over on the cot and withdrew his wallet from his back pocket. "This isn't a good picture of him," Goldstein apologized, "he's really one of the handsomest children you could imagine. We've got a big picture at home of him that we had a professional photographer take, and honestly you couldn't beat it. It could win a prize."

Gallagher stared at the picture. "Yeah . . . yeah, he's a cute kid, all right." He was a little bewildered, uncomfortable with the praise that welled clumsily out of his mouth. He looked at the picture again, seeing it really for the first time, and he sighed. In the one letter he had written home since Mary died he had asked for a picture of his child. He had been waiting with increasing impatience for it ever since, and it had become an important need in his life. He would idle away many dull inactive hours daydreaming about his child, wondering what it looked like. Although he had not been told, he assumed it was a boy. "That's a real cute kid," he said in a rough voice. He fingered the side of the cot for a moment. Surmounting his embarrassment, he blurted, "Hey, what is it like, havin' a kid?"

Goldstein debated for a moment, as if to give the definitive answer. "Oh, it's a lot of . . . of joy." He had been about to say *"nochis."* "But there's a lot of heartaches in it too. You worry about them a lot, and of course there are the economic difficulties."

"Yeah." Gallagher nodded his head in agreement.

Goldstein went on talking. He had some constraint, for Gallagher was the man he had hated most in the platoon. The warmth and friendliness he felt toward him now were perplexing. Goldstein was self-conscious when he saw himself as a Jew talking to a Gentile; then every action, every word, was dictated to a great extent by his desire to make a good impression. Although he was gratified when people liked him, part of his satisfaction came from the idea that they

451

were liking a Jew. And so he tried to say only the things that would please Gallagher.

Yet in talking about his family, Goldstein experienced once more an automatic sense of loss and longing. Wistful images of the beatitudes of married life drifted in his head. He remembered a night when his wife and he had giggled together in the darkness and listened to the quaint pompous snoring of their baby. "Children are what makes life worth while," he said sincerely.

Martinez realized with a start that he was a father too. He remembered Rosalie's pregnancy for the first time in years. He shrugged. Seven years now? Eight years? He had lost count. Goddam, he said to himself. Once he had been free of the girl he had remembered her only as a source of trouble and worry.

The fact that he had begotten a child made him vain. Goddam, I'm okay, he said to himself. He felt like laughing. Martinez make a kid and run away. It gave him a malicious glee, as though he were a child tormenting a dog. What the hell she do with it? Knock her up. Goddam! His vanity swelled like a bloated belly. He mused with naïve delight about his potency, his attraction for women. That the child was illegitimate increased his self-esteem; somehow it made his role more extravagant, of greater magnitude.

He felt a tolerant, almost condescending affection for Goldstein. Before this afternoon he had been a little afraid of him and quite uneasy. They had had an argument one day and Goldstein had disagreed with him. Whenever that happened, Martinez would react inevitably like a frightened schoolboy reprimanded by his teacher. There had never been a time when he was comfortable as a sergeant. But now he had been bathed in Goldstein's affection; he no longer felt Goldstein had despised him that day. Goldstein, he is okay, Martinez said to himself.

He became conscious of the vibration of the boat, its slow pitching advance through the swells. It was almost dark now, and he yawned and curled his body down farther beneath the poncho. He was slightly hungry. Lazily, he debated whether to open a ration or merely to lie still. He thought of the patrol, and the quick fear it roused made

452

him alert again. Oh. He expelled his breath. No think about it, no think about it, he repeated to himself.

He became conscious abruptly that Gallagher and Goldstein were no longer talking. He looked up, and saw nearly all the men in the boat standing on their cots or chinning themselves on the starboard bulkhead. "What're they lookin' at?" Gallagher asked.

"It's the sunset, I think," Goldstein said.

"Sunset?" Martinez gazed at the sky above him. It was almost black, clotted with ugly leaden rain clouds. "Where the sunset?" He stood up on his cot, straddling his feet on the side poles, and stared into the west.

The sunset was magnificent with the intensity and brilliance that can be found only in the tropics. The entire sky was black with the impending rain except for a narrow ribbon along the horizon. The sun had already disappeared, but its reflection was compressed, channeled into a band of color where the sky met the water. The sunset made an arc along the water like the cove of a harbor, but a strange and illusory harbor, washed in a vivid spectrum of crimson and golden yellows and canary greens. There was a string of tiny clouds shaped like miniature plump sausages and they had become a royal stippled purple. After a time, the men had the impression they were staring at a fabulous island which could have existed only in their imagination. Each detail glowed, became quiveringly real. There was a beach whose sands were polished and golden, and on the false shore a grove of trees had turned a magnificent lavender-blue in the dusk. The beach was separate from everything they had ever known; it possessed every outcropping of rock, every curve of sand dune on a barren and gelid shore, but this beach was alive and quivering with warmth. Above the purple foliage the land rose in pink and violet dales, shading finally into the overcast above the harbor. The water before them, illumined by the sunset, had become the deep clear blue of the sky on a summer evening.

It was a sensual isle, a Biblical land of ruby wines and golden sands and indigo trees. The men stared and stared. The island hovered before them like an Oriental monarch's conception of heaven, and they responded to it with an acute and terrible longing. It was a vision of all the beauty for which they had ever yearned, all the ecstasy they had ever sought. For a few minutes it dissolved the long dreary passage of the mute months in the jungle, without hope, without pride. If they had been alone they might have stretched out their arms to it.

It could not last. Slowly, inevitably, the beach began to dissolve in the encompassing night. The golden sands grew faint, became gray-green, and darkened. The island sank into the water, and the tide of night washed over the rose and lavender hills. After a little while, there was only the gray-black ocean, the darkened sky, and the evil churning of the gray-white wake. Bits of phosphorescence swirled in the foam. The black dead ocean looked like a mirror of the night; it was cold, implicit with dread and death. The men felt it absorb them in a silent pervasive terror. They turned back to their cots, settled down for the night, and shuddered for a long while in their blankets.

It began to rain. The boat churned and pushed through the darkness, wallowing only a hundred yards offshore. Over them all hung the quick fearful anticipation of the patrol ahead. The water washed mournfully against the sides of the boat.

2

THE PLATOON landed early the next morning on the back shore of Anopopei. The rain had halted during the night, and in the dawn the air was fresh and cool, the sunlight pleasant on the beach. The men lolled about on the sand for a few minutes, watching the assault craft back off from shore and start on its return journey. In five minutes the boat was a half mile away, but it seemed like much less, an easy swim across the bright glittering tropic water. The men stared at it wistfully, envying the pilots who by nightfall would return to a safe bivouac and hot food. That's the job to have, Minetta was thinking.

The morning still possessed the new shining quality of a minted coin. The men were thrilled only slightly by the idea that they were on an unexplored shore. The jungle behind them looked essentially familiar; the beach, covered with fine delicate shells, was barren and isolated and would shimmer later in the heat, but now it seemed like every beach upon which they had ever landed. They sprawled about, smoking and laughing, waiting for the patrol to begin, perfectly content for the sun to dry their clothes.

Hearn was feeling a little tense. In a few minutes they would begin a march over forty miles of strange country, the last ten through the Japanese rear. He turned to Croft and pointed again at the aerial map they had spread out between them on the sand. "It seems to me, Sergeant, the best way is to work up that river" — he pointed to the mouth of a stream which debouched from the jungle a few hundred yards farther down the beach — "as far as we can, and then cut trail till we reach the kunai grass."

"Ain't no other way to do it far as I see," Croft said. Hearn was right, which annoyed him slightly. He rubbed his chin. "It's gonna take a lot more time than you figure, Lootenant."

"Perhaps." Croft made him the least bit uneasy. He knew a lot, that was obvious, but you would have to ask him before he supplied any answers. Damn Southerner. He was like Clellan. Hearn flicked the map with his fingers. Already, he could feel the sand warming under his feet. "It's only two miles through the jungle."

Croft nodded dourly. "You can't trust an aerial map. That little ol' stream might take us where we want to go, but you can't depend on it." He spat into the sand. "Only damn thing to do is start out, and see jus' what happens."

"That's right," Hearn said, making his voice sharp. "Let's get started."

Croft looked at the men. "Okay, troopers, let's get goin'."

The men slung their packs again and wiggled their arms to settle the burden and ease the bite of the pack straps across their shoulders. In a minute or two they formed a straggling column and began to shuffle through the sand. When they reached the mouth of the stream, Hearn halted them. "Give them an idea of what we're doin'," he said to Croft.

Croft shrugged, then spoke for a minute. "We're gonna head up this here river far as we can go, and you might just as well expect to

455

get your asses wet. So if y'got any bitching to do, you might as well do it now." He hitched his pack a little higher on his shoulders. "They ain't supposed to be any Japs down this far, but that don' mean you're to walk like a bunch of goddam sheep looking at the ground. Let's try to keep our eyes open." He stared at them, examining each of their faces in turn, deriving a mild pleasure from the way most of them dropped their eyes. He paused for a moment, licking his tongue as if wondering whether there was something more to say. "Anything y'want to tell them, Lootenant?"

Hearn fingered his carbine strap. "Yes, as a matter of fact there is." He squinted into the sun. "Men," he said casually, "I don't know any of you, and you don't know me. Maybe you don't want to know me." A few men snickered, and he grinned suddenly at them. "Anyway, I'm your baby, I've landed in your lap, and you've got me for better or worse. Personally, I think we're going to get along. I'll try to be fair, but you've got to remember that along about the time your tails are dragging and I give an order to move on, you're going to hate my guts. Okay, fine, but just don't forget that I'll be as bushed as any of you, and I'll be hating myself more." They laughed, and for a moment he had the orator's knowledge that they belonged to him. The satisfaction was strong, almost surprising in its force. Bill Hearn's son, sure enough, he thought. "All right, let's set out."

Croft led the way, annoyed at Hearn's speech. It was wrong; a platoon leader didn't buddy. Hearn was going to screw them up with that kind of talk. Croft always despised a platoon leader who made efforts to have his men like him; he considered it womanish and impractical. Goddam platoon'll go to hell, he told himself.

The river seemed deep in its middle, but along the banks a band of shallow water, perhaps fifteen yards wide, pebbled and rippled over the stones. The platoon set out in a single column of fourteen men. Overhead the jungle soon met in an archway, and by the time they passed the first bend in the stream it had become a tunnel whose walls were composed of foliage and whose roadbed was covered with slime. The sunlight filtered through a vast intricate web of leaves and fronds and vines and trees, until it absorbed the color of the jungle and became at last a green shimmering wash of velvet. The light

456

eddied and shifted as though refracting through the intricate vaults of a cathedral; all about they were surrounded by the jungle, dark and murmurous. They were engulfed in sounds and smells, absorbed in the fatty compacted marrows of the jungle. The moist ferny odors, the rot and ordure, the wet pungent smell of growing things, filled their senses and loosed a stifled horror, close to nausea. "Goddam, it stinks," Red muttered. They had lived in the jungle for so long that they had forgotten its odor, but in the night, on the water, their nostrils had cleared; they had forgotten the oppression, the intense clammy weight of the air.

"Smells like a nigger woman," Wilson announced.

Brown guffawed nervously. "When the hell'd you ever have a nigger?" But he was troubled for a moment; the acute stench of fertility and decay loosed a fragile expectation.

The stream wound its burrow into the jungle. Already they had forgotten how the mouth appeared in sunlight. Their ears were filled with the quick frenetic rustling of insects and animals, the thin screeching rage of mosquitoes and the raucous babbling of monkeys and parakeets. They sweated terribly; although they had marched only a few hundred yards, the languid air gave them no nourishment, and black stains of moisture spread on their uniforms wherever the pack straps made contact. In the early morning, the jungle was exuding its fog drip; about their legs the waist-high mists skittered apart for the passage of their bodies, and closed again sluggishly, leisurely, like a slug revolving in its cell. For the men at the point of the column every step demanded an inordinate effort of will. They shivered with revulsion, halted often to catch their breath. The jungle dripped wetly about them everywhere; the groves of bamboo trees grew down to the river edge, their lacy delicate foliage lost in the welter of vines and trees. The brush mounted on the tree trunks, grew over their heads; the black river silt embedded itself in the roots of the bushes and between the pebbles under their feet. The water trickled over the stream bank tinkling pleasantly, but it was lost in the harsh uprooted cries of the jungle birds, the thrumming of the insects.

Slowly, inevitably, the men felt the water soak through the greased waterproofing of their shoes, slosh up to their knees whenever they had to wade through a deeper portion of the stream. Their packs became heavy, their arms grew numb and their backs began to ache. Most of the men were carrying thirty pounds of rations and bedding, and with their two canteens of water, their ten clips of ammunition, their two or three grenades, their rifles and machetes, each of them had distributed almost sixty pounds of equipment over his body, the weight of a very heavy suitcase. Most of them became tired in walking the first few hundred yards; by the time they had gone perhaps half a mile they were weary and their breath was short; the weaker ones were beginning to have the sour flat taste of fatigue. The density of the jungle, the miasmal mists, the liquid rustlings, the badgering of the insects lost their first revulsion and terror. They were no longer so conscious of the foreboding wilderness before them; the vague unnamed stimulations and terrors of exploring this tunnel through the jungle became weaker, sank at last into the monotonous grinding demands of the march. Despite Croft's lecture, they began to walk with their heads down, looking at their feet.

The river narrowed, and the ribbon of shallow water contracted to a strip along the bank, no wider than a footpath. They were beginning to climb. Already the stream had dropped from a few minor waterfalls, had churned over a short stretch of tumbled rocks. The pebbles underfoot slowly were replaced by river sand and then by mud. The men marched closer to the bank, and at last the foliage began to whip at them, obstructing their way. They proceeded much more slowly now.

Around a turn they halted and surveyed the stretch ahead. The foliage grew into the water at this point, and Croft, after considering the problem, waded out to the center of the stream. Five yards from the shore he halted. The water was close to his waist, swirling powerfully about him. "We're gonna have to hold to the bank, Lootenant," he decided. He began to fight his way along the edge of the stream, holding to the foliage, the water covering his thighs. Laboriously the men followed him, strung out along the bank. They proceeded for the next few hundred yards by grasping the nearest bushes, yanking and tugging themselves up the stream against the current. Their rifles kept slipping off their shoulders, almost dipping into the water, and

458

their feet sunk loathsomely in the river mud. Their shirts, from perspiration, became as wet as their trousers. Besides their fatigue and the dank moist air, they were sweating from anxiety. The stream had a force and a persistence which seemed alive; they felt something of the frenzy they would have known if an animal had been snarling at their feet. Their hands began to bleed from the thorns and the paper-edged leaves, and their packs hung heavy.

They moved like this until the stream widened again, became shallower. Here the current was not so rapid, and they made better progress sloughing through the knee-deep water. After a few more turns, they came upon a broad flat rock about which the river curved, and Hearn called a break.

The men flopped down, lying silent and motionless for several minutes. Hearn was a little worried; he could feel his heart beating with the clamor of early fatigue, and his hands trembled a little. Flat on his back, he peered over his chest at the quick rise and fall of his stomach. I'm in bad condition, he told himself. It was true. The next couple of days, particularly this first day, was going to be rough; he hadn't had any exercise in too long. But that would pick up; he knew his strength.

And he was getting used to the tension of being point. Somehow it was harder to be the first man. Any number of times he had halted, wincing at an unsuspected noise or shuddering when some insect darted across his path. There had been a few huge spiders with bodies as big as walnuts, a leg spread as wide as his extended fingers. Those things got you; he had noticed that they bothered Martinez and Brown as well as himself. There was a special kind of fear when the ground was unexplored; each step farther into the jungle was difficult.

Croft hadn't shown too much discomfort. That Croft was a *boy*, all right. If he wasn't careful Croft would keep effective command of the platoon. The trouble was that Croft knew more, and it was silly to disagree with him; until now the march had demanded a woodsman.

Hearn sat up and stared about him. The men were still sprawled on the rock, resting quiet. A few of them were talking or scaling pebbles into the water, and Valsen was carefully stripping the leaves from a tree which overhung the rock. Hearn looked at his watch. Five minutes had gone by since the break had begun, and another ten minutes would not hurt. He might as well give them a decent break. He stretched and rinsed his mouth out with some water from his canteen, chatted for a minute or two with Minetta and Goldstein.

Once he had regained his wind, Brown began to talk to Martinez.

Brown was depressed; the jungle ulcers on his feet had begun to itch and smart, and he knew they would become more painful as the patrol continued. Idly, quite hopelessly, he was thinking how pleasant it would be if he could lie in the sun with his feet bare, allowing the heat to dry his sores.

"This is gonna be a rough sonofabitch," he sighed.

Martinez nodded. "Five days out, long time."

Brown lowered his voice. "What the hell do you think of this new looey?"

"Okay." Martinez shrugged. "Nice guy." He felt cautious about answering. The men knew he buddied with Croft, and he felt they would guess his hostility to Hearn. With Croft everything had been okay. "Too friendly, maybe," Martinez suggested. "Platoon leader should be tough guy."

"This guy looks like he can be a mean sonofabitch," Brown said. He was undecided about Hearn. Brown didn't like Croft particularly, and he sensed that Croft was contemptuous of him, but at least the situation was stable. With a new lieutenant, he'd have to be careful, always do his best, and even then he might not please him. "He seems like a good guy though," Brown said mildly. There was something else bothering him. He lit a cigarette and exhaled cautiously, his lungs still raw from the exertion of the march. The cigarette tasted unpleasant, but he continued to smoke it. "You know, I swear, Japbait," he blurted, "the times like this when you're on a patrol I wish I was a private. Those guys think we got it easy, especially all the replacements, they think being a noncom is a snap where you get all the breaks." He fingered one of the sores on his chin. "What the hell, they don't know the kind of responsibilities we got. You take someone like Stanley, he ain't seen a damn thing hardly so he's ambitious, he

460

wants to get ahead. I'll tell you, Japbait, I was pretty goddam proud when I made sergeant, but I don't know if I'd take it if I had to do it over again."

Martinez shrugged. He was feeling slyly amused. "It's hard," he offered.

"You're fuggin ay, it's hard." Brown plucked a leaf from a branch which overhung the rock, and chewed reflectively on it. "You know you can take just so much, and then your nerves start goin' to pot. I'll tell ya, I can talk to you, 'cause you know just what the hell the score is, but if you had to do it all over again would you take sergeant?"

"Who know?" But Martinez had no doubts; he would have taken it. For a moment he saw again the three chevrons he had worn on his dress olive-drabs and felt a characteristic uneasy pride.

"You know what scares me, Japbait? I'll tell ya, my nerves are gone. Sometimes I'm afraid I'll just go to pieces and I won't be able to do a goddam thing. You know what I mean?" Brown had worried about this many times. He gained some satisfaction in admitting it, excusing himself ahead of time so that the onus would be less if his failure was realized. He scaled a stone into the river, watching the ripples.

Martinez had a quiet contempt for Brown. It pleased him that Brown was frightened. Japbait frightened, okay, he told himself, but Japbait . . . he don't give in.

"The worst of it," Brown said, "is not if you get knocked off, hell, then you don't know anything. But what if one of the guys in your squad stops a bullet and it's your fault. Jesus, you never get it out of your head then. I'll tell ya, remember that patrol back on Motome when MacPherson got knocked off? I couldn'ta done a thing out it, but how the hell do ya think I felt leavin' him like that, takin' off and leavin' him behind?" Brown flipped his cigarette away nervously. "It ain't all it's cracked up to be, being a sergeant. When I first got in the Army I wanted to get ahead, but sometimes I get to wondering. What the hell does it get ya?" He mused on this and then sighed. "I don't know, I suppose human nature bein' what it is I wouldn'ta been satisfied just being a private. It means something to make sergeant." This statement always gave him pleasure. "It shows you got something a little special. I'll tell ya, I feel my responsibilities. I ain't goin' to back down. No matter what the hell I get into, I know damn well I'm gonna keep trying because that's what I'm being paid for." He felt a little sentimental. "It shows they got trust in you if you make sergeant, and I'm not going to let anybody down, I'm not that kind of guy. I think there'd be nothing lower."

"Gotta stick," Martinez agreed.

"That's just it. What the hell kind of guy would I be to take all the government's money, and then goof-off? Naw, I mean it, Jap-bait, we come from a pretty good part of the country, and I'd hate like hell to go back and show my face to the neighbors if I wasn't proud of myself. Personally since I'm from Kansas I like it better than Texas but just the same we come from two of the best goddam states in the country. You never need to be ashamed, Martinez, when you tell somebody you're a Texan."

"Yes." Martinez was warmed by the name. He liked to think of himself as a Texan, but he had never dared to use the title. Somewhere, deep in his mind, a fear had clotted; there was the memory of all the tall white men with the slow voices and the cold eyes. He was afraid of the look they might assume if he were to say, Martinez is a Texan. Now his pleasure was chilled, and he felt uneasy. I'm better noncom than Brown, he assured himself, but he was still uncomfortable. Brown had a kind of assurance which Martinez had never known; something in him always withered when he talked to such men. Martinez had the suppressed malice, the contempt, and the anxiety of a servant who knows he is superior to his master.

"Good part of the country," he agreed. He was moody and had no desire to talk to Brown any longer. After a minute or two, he mumbled something and went over to Croft.

Brown turned around and looked about him. Polack had been sprawled a few feet away from them during the conversation. His eyes were closed now, and Brown gave him a little nudge. "You sleeping, Polack?"

"Uh?" Polack sat up and yawned. "Yeah, I t'ink I dropped off." Actually he had been wide awake, had been listening to them. He

462

always obtained a subtle gratification from eavesdropping; while he seldom expected to receive any immediate profit, Polack usually found it amusing. "That's the only way to get a line on a guy," he had said once to Minetta. Now he yawned again. "Naw, I been gettin' some shut-eye. What, are we hittin' the trail again?"

"Coupla minutes, I guess," Brown said. He had sensed Martinez's scorn, and it left him uncomfortable, anxious to regain his poise. He stretched out beside Polack and offered him a cigarette.

"Naaah, I'm savin' me wind," Polack told him. "We got a long way to go."

"That's no lie," Brown agreed. "You know, I been trying to keep my squad out of patrols, but maybe it wasn't such a good idea. You're out of condition now." He was not conscious of exaggerating. At the moment Brown believed himself, and mused with self-approbation how he protected his squad.

"It was okay, keepin' us out. We appreciate it," Polack said. To himself, he thought, What a crock of shit! Brown entertained him. There's always that kind of guy, Polack thought. Act like a prick to get the stripes, and then when he's got them he starts worrying whether you think he's a right Joe or not. He held his long pointed chin in his hand, brushed his mop of blond straight hair off his forehead. "That's a fac'," Polack said. "You t'ink the boys in your squad don't appreciate the deals you get us. We know you're okay."

Brown was pleased despite his doubts of Polack's sincerity. "I'll tell you, I'll be frank with you," he said. "You been in the platoon a couple months and I've had my eye on you. You're a pretty smart apple, Polack, and you know to keep your mouth shut."

Polack shrugged. "I'm all right."

"You take the job I've got. I gotta keep you men happy. You may not know it, but that's even in the manual, right there in black and white. I figure if I look out for my men they'll look out for me."

"Sure, we're right behind ya." The way Polack looked at it, you were a goddam fool if you didn't say what your boss wanted you to say.

Brown was fumbling for something. "There's lots of ways a noncom can be a sonofabitch, but I'd rather treat my men right."

463

What the hell does he want out of me? Polack thought. "It's the only way to be," he said.

"Yeah, but a lot of noncoms don't know that. The responsibility can get you down. You don't know the kind of worries there are. I'm not saying I don't want to have 'em, 'cause the truth of the matter is you gotta plug if you wanta get ahead. There's no short cuts."

"Naah." Polack scratched himself.

"You take Stanley. He's too smart for his own good. You know he pulled a pretty slick deal in a garage he was at." Brown told Polack the story, and finished by saying, "That's smart enough, but you just get in trouble that way. You got to stick to something and take the headaches as they come."

"Sure." Polack decided he'd underrated Stanley. It was something worth knowing about him. Stanley had more on the ball than Brown. Jesus, Polack thought, this guy Brown is gonna end up runnin' a gasoline station, and t'inkin' he's a big operator. Stanley had the right idea. You did something that was maybe a little too cozy, but if you kept your tongue in your head you got out okay.

"All right, men," the Lieutenant was calling.

Polack stood up with a grimace. If that lieutenant had anything but rocks in his head, he decided, he'd go back to the beach, and let us toast marshmallows until the boat comes. But all he said was, "I been needing a little exercise." Brown laughed.

The river remained shallow and unobstructed for another few hundred yards. As they walked, Brown and Polack talked idly. "I used to have a lot of ideas when I was a kid," Brown said, "you know, kids and marriage and the rest of it, but you get a little smarter, you see where they ain't many women you can trust."

It's a guy like Brown that lets a dame throw a horse collar on him, Polack thought. All she had to do was yes him when he was talkin' and he thought she had everything.

"No," Brown said, "you get older and you lose a lot of that. You know there ain't too many things you can trust." He got a bitter pleasure from saying this. "The only damn thing that's worth it is money, I'll tell you. In selling you can see the kind of time a big boy

464

can have. I remember some of those hotel parties. Man! the dames at that, the times you'd have."

"You could have a good time," Polack agreed. He remembered a party that his numbers boss, Lefty Rizzo, had given. Polack closed his eyes for an instant, and felt a faint trickle of passion. That blonde, she had known her business. "Yeah."

"If I ever get out of the Army," Brown said, "I'm headin' for the bucks. I'm tired of kickin' around."

"They ain't found anyt'ing better than that yet."

Brown looked at Polack, shuffling through the water beside him. Polack wasn't a bad kid, he thought. Just a little skinny guy who never had any education. The chances were he'd never get anywhere. "What do you figure on doin', Polack?" Brown asked.

Polack recognized the condescension. "I'll get along," he said shortly. Like the flick of a lash, he remembered his family and grimaced. What a dumb Polack his old man had been. Poor all his life. Aaah, it makes you tough, he decided. A guy like Brown could shoot his mouth off, but when you knew the way to make a pile you kept quiet. In Chicago you could do it; that was a *town*. Women and lots of noise, lots of big operators. "They can keep this goddam jungle," he said. The water was a little deeper and he felt it tickling against the back of his knees. If he hadn't got in the Army he'd probably be workin' right under Kabriskie now. "A-a-ah," Polack said.

And Brown was dejected. He did not know why, but the oppression of the air, the resistance of the current, had exhausted him already. He felt an unreasonable catch of fear. "Boy, I hate these goddam packs," he said.

The river was mounting a series of minor cascades. Coming around a turn the men were almost spilled by the force of the current over a rapids. The water was shockingly cold, and the men scrambled for the bank and held onto the wall of foliage that grew to the river's edge. "C'mon, let's keep goin'," Croft shouted. The bank was almost five feet high, which made it difficult to advance. The men moved along with their bodies parallel to the wet clay walls of the bank,

465

their eyes on a level with the jungle floor. They extended their arms, caught a root, and pulled themselves toward it, their chests scraping against the bank, their feet drudging through the water. Their hands and faces became scratched, their fatigue uniforms covered with mud. For perhaps ten minutes they progressed in this way.

The river leveled again, and they advanced in file a few feet from the bank, toiling slowly through the river mud. At times aware of the intricate liquid rustlings of the brush, the screams of the birds and animals, the murmuring of the river, they were usually conscious only of their own parched sobs. They were becoming very tired. The weaker men in the platoon had lost the first sensitive control of their limbs and wavered in the current or floundered in one place for many seconds at a time, buckling to their knees from the weight of their packs.

They came to another rapids which was too rocky, too swift, to be crossed on foot. Croft and Hearn discussed it for a minute, and then Croft clambered up the bank with Brown, hacked his way a few feet into the brush, and cut some thick vines which he tied together with large square knots. He started to tie one end about his waist. "I'm gonna take it across, Lootenant," he said.

Hearn shook his head. Croft, effectively had been leading the patrol until now, but this was something he could do himself. "I'll take a whack at it, Sergeant."

Croft shrugged.

Hearn fastened the vine about his belt, and stepped out into the rapids. He was planning to carry the vine upstream, across to the other bank, where it could provide a life rope for the platoon. But it was much more difficult than he had expected. Hearn had left his pack and carbine with Croft, yet even unfettered the crossing was exceptionally demanding. He waded through the rapids, stumbling from rock to rock, slipping to his knees many times. Once he went under completely, rammed his shoulder against one of the stones, and came up gasping for air, faint from the pain. It took him almost three minutes to move fifty yards and when he reached the other bank he was exhausted. For thirty seconds he remained motionless, panting and coughing from the water he had swallowed. Then he stood up,

466

lashed the vine about a tree, while Brown tied the other end to the roots of a sturdy bush.

Croft was the first one across, carrying Hearn's pack and carbine besides his own. Slowly, one by one, the men struggled across the river, holding to the vine. Some of them lopped their pack straps about it, and pulled themselves along hand over hand, their legs thrashing in the surf of the rapids or floundering anxiously to fend themselves off the rocks. The water would have reached only to their thighs if they had been able to stand upright, but all of them were drenched by the time they reached the other bank. They collected in a little eddy ahead of the rapids, and sat in the water panting, enervated for the moment.

"Jesus," one of them would mutter from time to time. The force of the rapids had been terrifying. Each of them as he had negotiated the line had expected secretly that he would be drowned.

After a rest of ten minutes they began to march again. There were no more rapids for a time but the river was flowing down a chain of stone ledges, and every ten or fifteen yards they would have to climb a waist-high shelf, tread forward cautiously along a rock platform over which a few inches of water was flowing, and then scramble up to the next ledge. Almost all of them wet their guns at one time or another, and their grenades, wedged by the spoon handle into their cartridge belts, kept spilling out into the water. Every few seconds one of them would swear dully.

The river became narrower. In some places the banks were not more than five yards apart, and the jungle overhead grew so close to the water that it brushed against their faces. They continued on for a quarter of a mile, squatting under the foliage and bellying over the ledges. Crossing the rapids had drained them, and most of the men were too weary to lift their legs. When they came to a new shelf of rock, they flopped their bodies over the edge and slid their legs up behind them with the motions of salmon laboring upstream for the spawning season. The river was dividing into its tributaries; every hundred yards a rill or tiny brook would trickle out of the jungle, and Croft would halt, examine it for a moment, and then move on again. After his solo across the rapids, Hearn had been content to let Croft manage the platoon again for a time. He plodded behind with the others, still unable to regain his wind.

They came to a junction where the stream divided in two. Croft deliberated. In the jungle, unable to see the sun, it was impossible for anyone but Martinez or him to know in what direction they were traveling. Croft had noticed earlier that the larger trees leaned toward the northwest; he had checked it with his compass, and decided they had been wrenched that way in a hurricane when they were young. He accepted it as a reliable guide, and all that morning as they had moved up the river he had been noting the direction in which they marched. He guessed that they must be very close to the end of the jungle; they had walked more than three miles, and the river generally had moved toward the hills. But here it was impossible to determine which stream to follow; both veered off at an angle, and it was conceivable they might meander for miles through the jungle, parallel to the open hills. He and Martinez talked about it, and Martinez selected a tall tree off the stream and began to climb it.

He clambered up by grasping the vines that circled about it, using the nodes of the trunk for his footholds. When he reached the highest fork, he crawled out on a limb, edging himself forward cautiously. High up, he halted and surveyed the terrain. The jungle spread beneath him in a green velvet nap. He could no longer see the river, but not more than half a mile away the jungle ended abruptly, and a progression of bare yellow hills mounted toward the distant slopes of Mount Anaka. Martinez drew out his compass, and determined the direction. He was feeling the satisfaction of doing a job at which he knew he was proficient.

He climbed down, and talked to Croft and the Lieutenant. "We follow this one," he said, pointing to one of the tributaries, "maybe two-three hundred yard, then we cut trail. No river in the hill right there." He pointed toward the open country he had seen.

"Okay, Japbait." Croft was pleased. The information had not surprised him.

The platoon began marching again. The stream Martinez had chosen was very narrow, and the jungle closed over it almost completely. After a hundred yards they were forced to slough through the water on their hands and knees, ducking their heads to avoid the leaves and brambles that drooped into the stream. It became shortly no wider than a footpath and began shredding into many tiny runs of water which seeped from the rocks of the forest. Before they had gone a quarter of a mile, Croft decided to cut trail. The stream took a bend back toward the ocean, and it would be worthless to follow it any longer.

"I'm gonna divide up the platoon for cutting trail," he told Hearn, "but I'm gonna leave us out of it, 'cause we'll have enough to do."

Hearn was panting. He had no idea of what was customary on something like this, and he was too fatigued to care much. "Anything you say, Sergeant." Afterward he was a little worried. When you were with Croft, it was too easy to let him handle all the decisions.

Croft took a sight with his compass in the direction he wanted to travel, and found a tree, in the brush about fifty yards away, which would be a good target. He gathered the platoon around him, and divided them into three teams of four. "We're gonna cut trail," he told them. "To start you can aim about ten yards to the left of that tree. Each team is gonna work about five minutes, and then get spelled ten. They ain't any reason why we gotta be all day doin' this, so let's not be fuggin-off. You can take ten before you start, and then, Brown, you begin it with your men."

They had to slash a route through a quarter mile of dense brush, through vines and bushes and bamboo groves, around trees, and into the thickest brambles. It was slow, tedious work. Two men labored side by side, hacking with their machetes at the net of foliage, trampling underfoot what they could. They progressed at a rate of about two yards a minute, working quickly through a thinner patch of brush only to halt and chop inch by inch at a tangle of bamboo. It had taken them three hours to advance up the river, and by noon, after two more hours of hacking a trail, they had added only a couple of hundred yards. But they did not mind it; each man had to work only two or three minutes in a quarter hour, and they were shedding their fatigue. When they were not working they lay on the trail resting and joking. The fact that they had gone so far cheered them; they

469

assumed instinctively the open hills would present no problems. After toiling through the muck and water of the stream, after being convinced so many times they would never reach its end, they were proud and pleased to have managed it, and for the first time some of them were optimistic about the success of the patrol.

Roth and Minetta were wretched, however. Minetta was in poor condition from his week in the hospital, and Roth had never been very strong. The long march up the river had fagged them brutally; overtired, the rest periods did them little good and laboring on the trail was torture. After thirty seconds, after three or four slashes with his machete, Roth was unable to raise his arm. The machete felt heavy as an ax. He lifted it with both hands, dropped it feebly on the branch or vine before him. Every half minute, the knife slipped out of his sweating nerveless fingers and went clattering to the ground.

Minetta's fingers had begun to blister and the handle of the machete rasped against his palm, rubbed sweat into all the sores on his hand. He would attack a bush violently and clumsily, forcing himself into a rage at its stubbornness, and then he would halt, winded, cursing between his sobs at the dank pappy mesh of verdure before him. He and Roth worked side by side, cramped together in the narrow aisle of the trail. In their exhaustion they often blundered against each other, and Minetta would swear with irritation. They disliked each other as intensely as they hated the jungle, the patrol, and Croft. Minetta brooded because Croft was not working; it became the crux of his bitterness. "It's easy enough for that goddam Croft to tell us what to do, but he ain't doin' it. I don't see him working his ass off," Minetta muttered. "If I was a platoon sergeant, I wouldn't treat the guys like that. I'd be right with them, working."

Ridges and Goldstein were standing about five yards behind them. The four men made up one of the teams, and theoretically they were supposed to divide their five-minute shift. But after an hour or two, Goldstein and Ridges were working for three minutes and then four minutes. Watching Minetta and Roth hack with their machetes, Ridges was indignant. "Shoot," he would reprove them, "ain't you city fellers ever learned to use a little ol' knife like that?"

Breathless, enraged, they would make no answer, and this would annoy Ridges more. He had a lively discernment of injustice toward other men and toward himself, and thought it was decidedly unfair for Goldstein and him to work more than the other pair. "Ah done the same work you done," he would complain, "Ah went up the same river you did, an' they ain't no reason 'tall why Gol'stein and me gotta be doin' all yore work."

"Blow it out," Minetta shouted back.

Croft had come up behind them. "What's the matter with you men?" he demanded.

"Ain't nothin'," Ridges said after a pause. He gave his horsy guffaw. "Shoot, we jus' been talkin'." Although he was displeased with Minetta and Roth, he did not think of complaining to Croft. They were all part of the same team, and Ridges considered it heinous to complain about a man with whom he was working. "Ain't nothin' wrong," he repeated.

"Listen, Minetta," Croft said with scorn, "if you an' Roth ain't the meanest wo'thless shiftless pair of bastards I ever had. You men better get your finger out of your ass." His voice, cold and perfectly enunciated, switched them like a birch branch.

Minetta, if harried enough, was capable of surprising courage. He threw down his machete, and turned on Croft. "I don't see you working. It's pretty goddam easy . . ." He lost all idea of what he wanted to say, and repeated, "I don't see you working."

Smart New York kid, Croft said to himself. He looked at him furiously for an instant. "Next river we come to, you can carry the Lieutenant's goddam pack across, and *you* won't have to work." He was enraged with himself for even answering, and he turned away for a moment. He had excluded himself from the labor of cutting trail because he had considered it necessary as platoon sergeant to reserve a little extra strength. Hearn had surprised him in crossing the rapids; when he had followed along the vine, he knew what an effort it had taken. And that had alerted him, worried him secretly. Croft knew he still controlled the platoon, but once Hearn gained some experience he was likely to take over the patrol.

Croft really did not admit all this to himself. With his Army

471

sense, he knew his resentment of Hearn was dangerous, and he also knew his motives on many little actions would not bear examination. He rarely questioned his reasons for doing anything, but now he sensed he could not search himself, and it made him furious. He strode up to Minetta and stared at him with rage. "Goddammit, man, you gonna keep bitchin'?"

Minetta was afraid to answer. He stared back as long as he dared and then dropped his eyes. "Aaah, c'mon," he said to Roth. They picked up their machetes and continued to slash out the trail. Croft watched them for a few seconds and then turned and walked away, filing down the newly fashioned path to the platoon.

Roth felt he was to blame for the incident. He had again the corrosive sense of failure that always dogged him. I'm no good at anything, he bleated to himself. He made a stroke with the machete and the impact snapped it out of his hand. "Ohh." Drearily, he bent down to pick it up.

"You might just as well quit now," Ridges told him. He picked up one of the machetes they dropped, and began to work shoulder to shoulder with Goldstein. As Ridges slashed at the brush with stolid patient motions, his broad short body became less awkward, assumed a strong fluent grace. From the rear he looked like an animal fashioning its nest. He had a simple pride in his strength. As his powerful muscles tensed and relaxed, as the sweat laced his back, he was completely happy, absorbed in the toil, the smells of his body.

Goldstein also found the work acceptable, took the same pleasure in the sure motions of his limbs, but his satisfaction was not so pure. It was cloyed with a prejudice Goldstein had against manual labor. That's the only kind of job I ever find, he told himself wistfully. He had sold newspapers, worked in a warehouse, become a welder, and it had always bothered him that he had never had an occupation where he could keep his hands clean. The prejudice was very deep, brewed out of all the memories and maxims of his childhood. He wavered between warmth and disdain at working well with Ridges. It's all right for Ridges, Goldstein told himself, he's a farmer, but I'd like something better. He had a mild self-pity at his fate. If I could have had an education, culture, I could have done something better with myself.

472

He was still fretting when they were relieved by the next team. He trudged back along the trail to where he had left his rifle and pack and settled down into his melancholy. Ach, so many things I could have done. Apparently without cause, a deep and limitless sorrow welled in his chest. He pitied himself, but his pity grew larger, swelled to include everybody in his compassion. Ai! it's hard, it's hard, he thought. He could not have said why he made this statement; it seemed a truth he had absorbed in his bones.

The mood did not surprise Goldstein; he was accustomed to it, enjoyed it. He would be cheerful for days, liking everyone, pleased with whatever task was assigned, and then suddenly, almost inexplicably, for the causes already seemed minor, he would wallow in a self-induced gloom.

Now he bathed himself in despondency. Oh, what does it all mean? What are we born for, why do we work? You're born and then you die, is that all there is to it? He shook his head. Look at the Levine family. They had such a promising son, he had a scholarship to Columbia, and then he got killed in an automobile accident. Why? What for? They worked so hard to let him go to school. He had known the Levine family only casually but he felt like weeping. Why should it be? Other sorrows possessed him, minor ones, major ones, in a suite of random undisciplined waves. He remembered when his family was very poor and his mother had lost a pair of gloves which she treasured. Ai! he sighed again. It's a hard business. He had drawn apart from the platoon, from the patrol ahead. Even Croft, what will he get out of it all? You're born and then you die. The knowledge somehow made him feel superior. He shook his head once more.

Minetta was sitting beside him. "What's the matter with you?" he asked sharply, his sympathy guarded for Goldstein had been Ridges's partner.

"Oh, I don't know." Goldstein sighed, "I was just thinking."

Minetta nodded. "Yeah." He stared down the corridor they had hewn out of the jungle. It extended in a reasonably straight line for almost a hundred yards before bending around a tree, and all along it the men in the platoon were sprawled on the ground or sitting on their packs. Behind him he could hear the steady chopping and macing of

473

the machetes. The sound depressed him, and he shifted his position, feeling the dampness of the earth against his buttocks. "That's all you can ever do in the Army, sit and think," Minetta said.

Goldstein shrugged. "Sometimes it's not so good. I'm the type of man it's better for me when I don't think so much."

"Yeah, the same for me." Minetta realized Goldstein had forgotten how poorly he and Roth had worked, and it made Minetta like him. He ain't one of these other guys holdin' a grudge. That made Minetta think of his argument with Croft. The anger that had sustained him in his quarrel was gone and he could think only of the consequences. "That sonofabitch Croft," he said. To avoid facing them, he was generating his indignation again.

"Croft!" Goldstein said with loathing. He looked about warily for a moment. "I thought when we got that lieutenant, things would be different, you know he seemed like a nice fellow." Goldstein realized suddenly how much hope he had fabricated because Croft was no longer in command.

"Aaah, he don't do a fuggin thing," Minetta said. "Listen, I wouldn't trust an officer. They work hand in glove with guys like Croft."

"Only, he should take over," Goldstein said. "If you leave it to somebody like Croft, we're just dirt to him."

"He's got it in for us," Minetta told him. He had a spasm of doubtful pride. "I ain't afraid of him, I told him what I thought, you saw that."

"I should have done it." Goldstein was upset. Why couldn't he tell people what he thought of them? "I'm too easygoing," he said aloud.

"Yeah, you are," Minetta said. "You can't let those guys run right over ya. You got to tell 'em where to get off. When I was in the hospital there was a doctor tried to give me a pushing around. I told him off." Minetta believed himself.

"It's a good way to be."

"Sure." Minetta was pleased. The aching in his arms had dulled, and a weary gentle relief was spreading through his body. Goldstein was all right, a thinker, Minetta told himself. "You know I've fooled

474

around a lot, dances and kidding around with the girls, you know. Back home I'm the life of the party, you ought to see me. Only I ain't really like that, 'cause when I'd be goin' out with Rosie, for instance, we'd have a lot of serious talks. My aching back, the things we'd talk about. That's what I really am," Minetta decided. "I go a lot for stuff like philosophy." It was the first time he had ever thought of himself in such a way and the classification pleased him. "Most of these guys when they get back are gonna do just what they were doin' before, just screwing around. But we're different, you know that?"

Goldstein's love of discussion roused him from his melancholy. "I'll tell you something I've often debated with myself, is it worth it?" The sad lines that extended from his nose to the corners of his mouth became deeper, more reflective, as he spoke. "You know maybe we'd be happier if we didn't think so much, maybe it's better to live and let live."

"That's something I've wondered about too," Minetta said. His thoughts, ambiguous, indefinite, troubled him. He felt himself on the edge of something profound. "Sometimes I get to thinking, you know, what's it all about? There was a guy who died in the hospital in the middle of the night. Sometimes I start thinking about him."

"Oh, that's terrible," Goldstein said. "He died just like that with nobody near him." He made a clucking sound of sympathy, and surprisingly, abruptly, a few tears mounted in his eyes.

Minetta looked at him in amazement. "Jesus, what's the matter?"

"I don't know, it's just so sad. He probably had a wife, parents."

Minetta nodded. "It's a funny thing about you Jews. You know you feel sorrier for yourself and sorrier for everybody else than most people do."

Roth, who had been lying beside them, quite silent until now, roused himself. "I'd like to take exception to that." The generalization made him apprehensive, as if a drunk were mouthing abuse at him

"What do ya mean?" Minetta snapped. Roth irritated him reminded him that in a few minutes they would be turning back to work. It loosed the covert fear that Croft would be watching them. "Who the hell invited you, Roth?"

"I think your statement had no foundation." The rebuff keyed

Roth to defiance. A twenty-year-old kid, he said to himself, even they think they know it all. He shook his head, and said in his slow pompous voice, "It's a big question. A statement like that . . ." He waved his hand slowly in contempt.

Minetta had been pleased with his observation; Roth's interference fed his malice. "Who do you think is right, Goldstein? Me or the undertaker over there?"

Despite himself, Goldstein laughed. He had some compassion for Roth when he was not near him, but Roth was always so slow, so solemn, in everything he said. It was annoying to wait for him to finish a sentence. Besides, Minetta's analysis had not displeased Goldstein. "I don't know, I thought there was a lot of sense in what you said."

Roth smiled sourly. He was used to it, he told himself. Everybody always sided against him. Earlier, when they were working, he had resented the way Goldstein was so efficient. In some manner he had felt it to be a betrayal. That Goldstein agreed with Minetta now, caused him no surprise. "Absolutely without foundation," he repeated.

"Is that all you can say?" Minetta sneered. "Ab-so-lute-ly without foun-da-tion," he mimicked.

"All right, then, consider me." Roth ignored his sarcasm. "I'm a Jew, but I'm not religious. I probably am less well informed about it than you are, Minetta. Who are you to say what I feel? I have never detected any similarities in Jews. I consider myself an American."

Goldstein shrugged. "Are you ashamed?" he asked softly.

Roth expelled his breath with annoyance. "That's a species of question I don't like." His heart was thumping powerfully from the tension he felt at arguing into their blank unsympathetic faces. A strong, apparently irrational, anxiety moistened the palms of his hands. "Is that the only answer you can think of?" he snapped. His voice tapered shrilly.

Aaah, the guineas and Jews are all the same, Minetta told himself. Always getting worked up over nothing. It made him feel superior to the argument.

"Listen, Roth," Goldstein said. "Why do you think Croft and Brown don't like you? It's not because of you, it's because of your religion, because of something that you say has nothing to do with

476

you." Yet he was uncertain. Roth disturbed him; he was always a little chagrined that Roth was Jewish, for he felt he would give a bad impression to Gentiles.

Roth had a pang because Croft and Brown didn't like him. He knew it, and yet it hurt somehow, hearing it put into words. "I wouldn't say that," he protested. "It's got nothing to do with religion." He was completely confused. It would be comforting if he could believe his religion was the cause of their antipathy, but other problems issued from it, other portents of future failure. He wanted to close his arms over his head, tuck up his knees, and shut out the clamant bickering about him, the incessant hacking of the machetes, the murmur of conversation, and the necessity to keep straining and exerting himself through one pain-racked hour after another. The jungle was protective suddenly, a buffer against all the demands that would be made. He longed to lose himself in it, become separate from the men. "I don't know," he said. It seemed important to stop arguing.

They fell silent, lay again on their packs, relapsing into their private thoughts. Minetta's weariness colored his reverie, made him sad. He thought of Italy, which he had visited with his parents when he was a child. Very few memories remained; he could recall the town in which his father was born and a little of the city of Naples, but the rest had become clouded.

In his father's village the houses tumbled down a hillside in a network of tiny alleyways and dusty courtyards. At the foot of the hill a little mountain stream lashed over the rocks and raced along vigorously into the valley below. The women would carry their laundry down in baskets in the morning, and wash the family clothing on the flat rocks of the bank, kneading and slapping and scrubbing with the ancient absorbed motions of peasant women at work. The boys in the town would fetch water every afternoon from the same stream and carry it up the hill, moving slowly, their small brown legs cording with labor as they toiled up the footpath to the town.

Those were about the only details he could remember, but they stirred him. He seldom thought of the town, and he had forgotten almost all the Italian he once knew how to speak, but when he was

477

moody or reflective he would remember things like the heat of the sun between the walls of the alleyways, or the acrid fermy odors of the dung on the fields.

Now, for the first time in many months, he brooded about the war in Italy and wondered if the town had been destroyed in bombardments. It seemed almost impossible to him; the little houses of rock and plaster must remain forever. And yet . . . He was very depressed. He had seldom thought of returning to that village, but now, transiently, it was what he wanted most to do. Jesus, that place all ruined, he thought. It made him very sad. For a few seconds his mind held in montage all the wrecked towns, the corpses on the road, the perpetual muted thunder of artillery over the horizon; it even contained a place for this patrol on an island in another ocean. Everything's being smashed all over the world. The magnitude of the idea was too great; his mind veered away, careened back giddily to the rock on which he was sitting, absorbed itself once more in the wretchedness and fatigue of his body. Aaah, it's all so big you get lost in it. There's always some goon on top of ya. Despite himself, he pictured his village destroyed, the cold shattered walls standing like the upraised arms of dead soldiers. It shocked him, made him feel guilty as though he were imagining the death of his parents, and he tried to shut out the fantasy. He was enraged at the waste. Again it seemed impossible that the women should not be washing laundry on the rocks. He shook his head. Aaah, that fuggin Mussolini. But he was confused; his father had always told him Mussolini had brought prosperity, and he had accepted it. He could remember the arguments between his uncles and his father. They were so goddam poor they needed a guy who could run things, he told himself now. He remembered one of his father's cousins who had been a big shot in Rome, and had marched with Mussolini's army in 1922. All through his childhood, Minetta had heard tales of those days. "All a the young men, the patriotists, they fight with Mussolini in 'twenty-two," his father had told him, and he had dreamed of marching with them too, of being a hero.

Everything was mixed up. His mind could see no farther than his eyes. He was hemmed by the dense palpable mesh of the jungle.

"Aaah, that fuggin Mussolini," he said again, as if to relieve himself

Goldstein was stirring beside him. "Come on, it's our turn again."

Minetta lurched to his feet. "Why the hell don't they give us a decent break? Jesus Christ, we just sat down." He glared at Ridges, who was shouldering his way along the narrow ragged swath of the trail; nothing was left of his reverie but the resentment and fatigue that had initiated it.

"C'mon, M'netta," Ridges called back. "We got work to do." Without waiting for an answer, he plowed ahead to relieve the crew that had been laboring. Ridges was angry and perplexed. He had spent the rest period debating whether he would have time to clean his rifle, and he had decided he could never do the job properly in ten minutes. It annoyed him. The rifle was wet and muddy, and would rust if he couldn't take care of it soon. Shoot, Ridges said to himself, a man never has time to do one thing, when they ain't cussin' for him to do somethin' else. He felt pleasantly spiteful at the stupidity of the Army, and yet guilty too. He was taking poor care of a valuable piece of property, which bothered his sense of honesty. The gov'ment give me that M-one 'cause they figgered Ah'd watch over it, an' Ah ain't doin' it. The rifle must be worth a hundred dollars, Ridges thought, and that was a vast sum to him. Ah gotta clean it, but what ifen they don't gimme time? It was too much for him to resolve. He sighed, picked up his machete, and began to work. In a few seconds Goldstein had joined him.

The platoon reached the end of the jungle after five hours of cutting trail. The jungle was bordered by another stream, and on the other side yellow hills covered only with kunai grass or an occasional grove of shrubbery rolled away toward the north. The sunlight was brilliant, reflected with an incredible glare from all the bare hills and the clear blazing arch of the sky. The men, accustomed to the gloom of the jungle, blinked their eyes, were uncertain, a little afraid of the vast open spaces before them. It was all so bare, so painful.

All that space!

The Time Machine:

JOEY GOLDSTEIN

THE COVE OF BROOKLYN

*A sturdy man about twenty-seven, perhaps, with blond straight
hair and eager blue eyes. His nose is sharp, and there are deep sad
lines which extend from his nose to the corners of his mouth. If it
were not for this, he would look very young. His speech is quick and
sincere and a little breathless as if afraid he will not be permitted to
finish.*

The candy store is small and dirty as are all the stores on the
cobblestoned street. When it drizzles the cobblestones wash bare and
gleaming on top, and the manhole covers puff forth their shapeless
gouts of mist. The night fogs cloak the muggings, the gangs who
wander raucously through the darkness, the prostitutes, and the
lovers mating in the dark bedrooms with the sweating stained wall-
paper of brown. The walls of the street fester in summer, are clammy
in winter; there is an aged odor in this part of the city, a compact of
food scraps, of shredded dung balls in the cracks of the cobblestones,
of tar, smoke, the sour damp scent of city people, and the smell of
coal stoves and gas stoves in the cold-water flats. All of them blend
and lose identity.

In the daytime, the peddlers stand at the curb and hawk their
fruit and vegetables. Middle-aged women in black shapeless coats
pluck at the food with shrewd grudging fingers, probing it to the
marrow. Cautiously, the women step out from the sidewalk to avoid
the water in the gutters, stare with temptation at the fish heads that
the owner of the fish store has just cast into the street. The blood
gives a sheen to the cobblestone at first, fades, becomes pink, and
then is lost in the sewer water. Only the smell of fish remains to-

480

gether with the dung balls, the tar, the rich uncertain odors of the smoked meats in the delicatessen windows.

The candy store is at the end of the street, a tiny place with grease in the ledges of the window, and rust replacing the paint. The front window slides open doubtfully to make a counter where people can buy things from the street, but the window is cracked and dust settles on the candy. Inside there is a narrow marble counter and an aisle about two feet wide for the customers who stand on the eroded oil-cloth. In the summer it is sticky, and the pitch comes off on one's shoes. On the counter are two glass jars with metal covers and a bent ladling spoon containing essence of cherry, essence of orange. (Coca-Cola is not yet in vogue.) Between them is a tan moist cube of halvah on a block of wood. The flies are sluggish, and one has to prod them before they fly away.

There is no way to keep the place clean. Mrs. Goldstein, Joey's mother, is an industrious woman, and every morning and night she sweeps out the place, washes the counter, dusts the candy, and scrubs the floor, but the grime is too ancient, it has bedded into the deepest crevices of the store, the house next door, the street beyond, it has spread into the pores and cells of everything alive and unalive. The store cannot remain clean, and every week it is a little dirtier, a little more suppurated with the caries of the street.

The old man Moshe Sefardnick sits in the rear of the place on a camp stool. There is never any work for him to do and indeed he is too old for it, too bewildered. The old man has never been able to understand America. It is too large, too fast, the ordered suppressed castes of centuries wither here; people are always in flux. His neighbors become wealthier, move away from the East Side to Brooklyn, to the Bronx, to the upper West Side; some of them lose their little businesses, drift farther down the street to another hovel, or migrate to the country. He has been a peddler himself; in the spring before the first World War, he has carried his goods on his back, tramped the dirt roads through small New Jersey towns, selling scissors and thread and needles. But he has never understood it and now in his sixties he is prematurely senile, an old man relegated to the back of a tiny candy store, drifting in Talmudic halls of thought. (If a man hath a worm on his brain, it may be removed by laying a cabbage leaf near the orifice onto which the worm will crawl.)

His grandson, Joey, now seven, comes home from school weeping, a bruise on his face. Ma, they beat me up, they beat me up, they called me sheenie.

Who did, who was it?

It was the Italian kids, a whole gang, they beat me up.

The sounds move in the old man's mind, alter his thought stream. The Italians. He shrugs. An undependable people; in the Inquisition they let the Jews in at Genoa, but at Naples . . . Naples.

He shrugs, watches the mother wash the blood away, fit a patch of adhesive to the cut. Oh, mein Joey.

The old man laughs to himself, the delicate filtered laughter of a pessimist who is reassured that things have turned out badly. Nu, this America is not so different. The old man sees the goy faces staring at the victims.

Joey, he calls in a harsh cracked voice.

What is it, zaydee?

The goyim, what did they call you?

Sheenie

The grandfather shrugs again. Another name. For a moment an ancient buried anger moves him. He stares at the unformed features of the boy, the bright blond hair. In America even the Juden look like goyim. Blond hair. The old man rouses himself to speech, talks in Yiddish. They beat you because you're a Jew, he says. Do you know what a Jew is?

Yes.

The grandfather feels a spasm of warmth for his grandchild. So handsome. So good. He is an old man and he will die soon, and the child is too young to understand him. There is so much wisdom he could give.

It's a difficult question, the meaning of a Jew. It's not a race, he says, it's not even a religion any more, maybe it will never be a nation. Dimly, he knows he has lost the child already, but he continues talking, musing aloud.

482

What is it, then? Yehudah Halevy said Israel is the heart of all nations. What attacks the body attacks the heart. And the heart is also the conscience, which suffers for the sins of the nations. He shrugs once more, does not differentiate between saying aloud what he thinks or merely moving his lips. It's an interesting problem, but personally I think a Jew is a Jew because he suffers. Olla Juden suffer.

Why?

So we will deserve the Messiah? The old man no longer knows. It makes us better and worse than the goyim, he thinks.

But the child must always be given an answer. He rouses himself, concentrates and says without certainty, It is so we will last. He speaks again, wholly lucid for a moment. We are a harried people, beset by oppressors. We must always journey from disaster to disaster, and it makes us stronger and weaker than other men, makes us love and hate the other Juden more than other men. We have suffered so much that we know how to endure. We will always endure.

The boy understands almost nothing of this, but he has heard the words and they engrave a memory which perhaps he will exhume later. He looks at his grandfather, at the wrinkled corded hands and the anger, the febrile intelligence, in his pale old-man's eyes. Suffer. It is the only word Joey Goldstein absorbs. Already he has forgotten most of the shame and fear of his beating. He fingers the plaster on his temple, wonders if he can go out to play.

The poor are the great voyagers. There are always new businesses, new jobs, new places to live, new expectations evolving into old familiar failures.

There is the candy store in the East Side, which fails, and another which fails, and still another. There are movements: to the Bronx, back to Manhattan, to candy stores in Brooklyn. The grandfather dies, and the mother is alone with Joey, settles at last in a candy store in Brownsville with the same front window that slides open painfully, the same dust on the candy.

By the time he is eight and nine and ten, Joey is up at five in the morning, sells the papers, the cigarettes, to the men going to work, leaves at seven-thirty himself for school, and is back in the candy store again until it is almost time for bed. And his mother is in the store almost all day long.

The years pass slowly in the work-vacuum, the lonely life. He is an odd boy, so adult, the relatives tell his mother. And he is eager to please, a fine salesman on the honest side, but there are no potentialities for the big operator, the con man. It is all work, and the peculiar intimate union between his mother and himself of people who work together for many years.

He has ambitions. During the time he is in high school there are impossible dreams about college, of being an engineer or a scientist. In his little spare time he reads technical books, dreams of leaving the candy store. But of course when he does it is to work in a warehouse as a shipping clerk while his mother employs a kid to do the work he has done formerly.

And there are no contacts. His speech is different, quite different from that of the men with whom he works, the few boys he knows on the block. There is virtually nothing of the hoarse rough compassionate accent of Brooklyn. It is like his mother's speech, slightly formal, almost with an accent, a loving use of bigger words than are really necessary. And when at night he sits on one of the stoops and talks to the youths with whom he grew up, whom he has watched play stick ball and touch football on the streets for many years, there is a difference between them and him.

Look at the knockers on her, Murray says.

A dish, Benny says.

Joey smiles uncomfortably, sits among the dozen other youths on the stoop, watches the foliage of the Brooklyn trees rustle in contented bourgeois rhythms over his head.

She got a rich father, Riesel says.

Marry her.

And two steps farther down, they are arguing about batting averages. Whadeya mean? I know, ya wanta bet on it? Listen, that was the day I woulda made sixteen bucks if Brooklyn won. I had Hack Wilson picked for two for five to bring him up to .281 and Brooklyn to win, and he did three for four only they dropped it to the Cubs 7-2 and I lost. Whadeya handing me ya want to bet on it?

484

Goldstein's cheek muscles are tired from the stupid outsider grin.

Murray nudges him. How come you didn't go with us to the Giant doubleheader?

Oh, I don't know, somehow I never can concern myself properly with baseball.

Another girl wiggles by in the Brooklyn gloaming, and Riesel, the card, stalks after her, moving like an ape. Wheeeeeeh, he whistles, and her heels tap in the coquettish mating sounds of the bird flying away for only this night.

What bumpers on her.

You don't belong to the Panthers, do you, Joey? says the girl sitting next to him at the party.

No, but I'm familiar with them all, nice fellows, he says. In this year, his nineteenth, out of high school, he is cultivating a blond mustache which will not take.

I heard Larry is getting married.

And Evelyn too, Joey says.

Yeah, to a lawyer.

In the middle of the cellar, in the cleared place, they are dancing sharpy style, their backsides out, their shoulders moving insolently. IS IN THE STAR DUST OF A SONG.

You dance, Joey?

No. A momentary anger toward all the others. They have time to dance, time to become lawyers, time to become smooth. But it passes, is uncharacteristic, and he is merely uncomfortable again.

Excuse me, Lucille, he says to the hostess, but I have to go now, got to get up early, convey my fondest apologies to your mother.

And back inside his house at the socially rejected hour of ten-thirty, he sits with his mother, drinks a glass of hot tea on the eroded white porcelain table, is obviously moody.

What's the matter, Joey?

Nothing. And it is unbearable that she knows. Tomorrow I got a lot of work, he says.

At the shoe factory they should appreciate you more, all the work you do.

He tilts the carton off the floor, gets his knee back of it, and zooms it up over his head, lofting it onto the top of the seven-foot pile. Beside him the new man is wrestling it up clumsily.

Here, let me show you, Joey says. You have to combat the inertia of it, get it in momentum. It's very important to know how to lift these things or you get a rupture, all kinds of physical breakdowns. I've made a study of this. His powerful back muscles contract only slightly as he flips up another carton. You'll get the hang of it, he says cheerfully. There are lots of things in this kind of work you have to study about.

A lonely deal. Sad things, like leafing through the annual catalogues sent out by MIT, Sheffield School of Engineering, NYU, and so on.

But there is a party at last, a girl to whom he can talk, a pretty dark-haired little girl with a soft shy voice and an attractive mole on her chin of which she is self-conscious. A year or two younger than he, just out of high school, and she wants to be an actress or a poetess. She makes him listen to the symphonies of Tchaikovsky (the Fifth is her favorite) and she is reading *Look Homeward, Angel,* works as a salesgirl in a woman's store.

Oh, it's not a bad job, I suppose, she says, but it's . . . the girls are not really high class, it's nothing special I could write a letter about. I'd like to do something else.

Oh, I would too, so much, he says.

You ought to, Joey, you're a finer-type person, I can see we're the only thinkers. (They laugh, suddenly and magically intimate.)

Soon they are having long conversations on the stuffed rigid cushions of a maroon sofa in the parlor of her house. They discuss marriage versus a career for her, academically, abstractly; of course it concerns neither of them. They are the thinkers, regarding life. And in the complicated, relished, introspective web of young lovers, or more exactly, young petters, they progress along the oldest channel in the world and the most deceptive, for they are certain it is unique to them. Even as they are calling themselves engaged, they are losing the details of their subtle involved pledging of a troth.

486

They are moved and warmed by intimacies between them, by long husky conversations in the parlor, in inexpensive restaurants, by the murmurs, the holding of hands in the dark velvet caverns of movie houses. They forget most of the things that have advanced them into love, feel now only the effect of them. And of course their conversation alters, new themes are bruited. Shy sensitive girls may end up as poetesses or they may turn bitter and drink alone in bars, but nice shy sensitive Jewish girls usually marry and have children, gain two pounds a year, and worry more about refurbishing hats and trying a new casserole than about the meaning of life. After their engagement, Natalie talks over their prospects.

Oh, honey, you know I don't want to nag you, but we can't get married on the money you're making; after all, you wouldn't want me to live in a cold-water flat. A woman wants to fix up things and have a nice home, it's awfully important, Joey.

I understand what you mean, he answers, but, Natalie honey, it's not such an easy thing, there's been a lot of talk about a recession, and you can't tell, it might be a depression coming again.

Joey, it's not like you to talk like that, what I like about you is you're so strong and optimistic.

No, you make me that way. He sits there quite silent. You know, I'll tell you, I do have an idea, I've been thinking of going into welding, it's a new field but not so new that it isn't established. Of course I think that plastics or television is the thing to come, but it's undependable yet, and I don't have the education for that, I have to face it.

That sounds all right, Joey. She considers. It's not such a snooty profession, but maybe in a couple of years you'll be able to own a store.

A shop.

A shop, *shop,* that isn't anything to be ashamed of. You'd be a . . . a businessman then.

They discuss it, decide he must go to night school for a year until he is trained. The thought makes him moody. I won't be able to see you so much, maybe only a couple of nights a week, I'm wondering if that's such a healthy thing.

Oh, Joey, you don't understand me, when my mind is made

487

up it's made up, I can wait, you don't have to worry about me. She laughs softly, warmly.

He begins a very hard year, working for forty-four hours in the warehouse, eating his quick supper, and striving to remain alert in the classrooms and workshops at night. He gets home at twelve, goes to bed, and drags himself up to meet the next morning. On Tuesday and Thursday nights he sees Natalie after class, staying up till two and three in the morning to the displeasure of her parents and the nagging of his mother.

They have fights over this.

Joey, I've got nothing against the girl, she's probably a very nice girl, but you're not ready to get married, for the girl's sake I don't want you to get married. She wouldn't want to live in a place not so nice.

But that's what you don't understand, that's where you underestimate her, she knows what we'll have to face, it isn't as if we're going into it blindfolded.

You're children.

Look, Mama, I'm twenty-one, I've been a good son to you, haven't I, I've worked hard, I'm entitled to a little pleasure, a little happiness.

Joey, you talk as if I begrudge it to you, of course you've been a good son. I want you to have all the joys in the world, but you're ruining your health, you're staying out late, and you're going to be taking on too much responsibility. Oh (tears form in her eyes), it's only your happiness I want, you should understand that. When the time comes I'll be happy for you to be married, and I only hope you should get a wife who deserves you.

But I don't even deserve Natalie.

Nonsense! Nothing is too good for you.

Mama, you got to face it. *I'm going to get married.*

She shrugs. Nu, you've got a half year yet, and then you got to find a job with this welding. I only want you should keep an open mind on the question, and when the time comes we'll see.

But my mind's made up. It's no longer an issue. I swear, Mama, you make me so upset.

488

She becomes silent, and they eat for a few minutes without speaking, both troubled, both absorbed with new arguments they are loath to use for fear of beginning it again. At last she sighs and looks at him.

Joey, you shouldn't say anything of what I said about Natalie, I've got nothing against her, you know that. Cautious, half convinced, she is beginning to hedge the bet.

He graduates from welding school, gets a job for twenty-five dollars, and they get married. The wedding presents come to almost four hundred dollars, enough for a bedroom set from a department store, and a couch and two chairs for the living room. They extend their furniture with a few pictures, an inaccurate calendar scene of cows in a pasture at sunset, a cheap reproduction of "The Blue Door" and a Maxfield Parrish from an advertisement. On an end table, Natalie puts their wedding pictures, joined like book covers in a double frame. His mother gives them a whatnot and a collection of tiny painted cups and saucers with plump nude angels chasing around the circumference. They settle down in their three-room flat, and are very happy, very warm and absorbed in each other. By the end of the first year he is making thirty-five a week, and they are moving through the regular ordained orbit of friends and relatives. Joey becomes adept at bridge. Their marital storms are infrequent and quickly lost, the memories of them buried in the avalanche of pleasant and monotonous trivia that makes up their life.

Once or twice there is some tension between them. Joey, they decide, is very virile and the knowledge that she wants him less often than he needs her is bitter and sometimes ugly. This is not to say that their matings always fail or that they even talk or brood about it a good deal. But still he is a little balked at times. He cannot understand her unpredictable coldness; during their engagement she had been so passionate in her petting.

After the boy is born there are other concerns. He is making forty dollars a week, and working as a soda jerk in the corner drug store on weekends. He is tired, often worried; her delivery is a Caesarean, and they go into debt to pay the doctor. Her scar troubles him;

despite himself he looks at it with distaste and she notices that. She is completely involved with the child, content to stay at home for week after week. In the long evenings, he wants her very often and contains himself, sleeping irritably. One night their coupling ends in a quarrel.

He has a bad habit in the middle. Always, despite his injunctions, he must ask, are you warm? Her smile is so noncommittal; he is vaguely angered.

A little, she will say.

He slows himself, rests his head on her shoulder, relaxing, breathing deeply. Then he moves again.

How are you now? Are you close, Natalie?

Her smile again. I'm all right, Joey. Don't worry about me.

He glides through the passage of several neutral minutes, his mind far away, imagining another child. They had the last one after discussing it and agreeing that they wanted a baby, but now he cannot afford another one, and he is wondering if her diaphragm has been set properly. He thinks he can feel it, which worries him. Abruptly, he is conscious of the pressure in his loins, the perspiration on his back, and he halts roughly, relaxing again.

How close are you?

Don't worry about me, Joey.

He is angry suddenly. *Tell me, how close are you?*

Oh, darling, I won't be able to tonight, it's not important, go ahead, don't mind me, it's not important.

The bickering offends both of them, makes them cold. He dreads his tasteless isolated throe, knows suddenly that he cannot do it, cannot lie afterwards on his bed depressed with failure.

For once he swears. To hell with it. And he leaves her on the bed, and walks over to the window, staring at the drab parchment of the shade. He is trembling, partially from cold.

She comes up beside him, nuzzling her body against his to warm him. The caress is tentative, uncertain, and it offends him. He feels her maternalness. Go away, I don't want a . . . a mother, he blurts, feeling doubt and then dread at the awfulness of what he has said.

Her mouth forms in the blank smile, wrinkles suddenly into

490

weeping. She cries on the bed like a little girl. He realizes abruptly after two and a half years of marriage that when she forms that smile she is close to hysteria and terror and perhaps even loathing. The knowledge freezes in his chest.

After a moment he flops down beside her, cushions her head, and tries to comfort her weeping, his numb hand moving over her forehead and face.

In the morning none of it seems so awful, and by the end of a week he has nearly forgotten it. But on his side it marks the end or almost the end of one expectation from marriage, and for Natalie it means she must pretend excitement in order to avoid hurting him. Their marriage settles again like a foundation seeking bedrock. For them, that species of failure is not acute, not really dangerous. They ensconce themselves in their child, in adding and replacing furniture, in discussing insurance and finally buying some. There are the problems of his work, his slow advances, the personalities of the men in the shop. He takes to bowling with a few of them, and Natalie joins the sisterhood at the local temple, induces them finally to give courses in the dance. The rabbi is a young man, quite liked because he is modern. On Wednesday nights they have a baby sitter, and listen to his lectures on bestsellers in the social room.

They expand, put on weight, and give money to charitable organizations to help refugees. They are sincere and friendly and happy, and nearly everyone likes them. As their son grows older, begins to talk, there are any number of pleasures they draw from him. They are content and the habits of marriage lap about them like a warm bath. They never feel great joy but they are rarely depressed, and nothing immediate is ever excessive or cruel.

The war comes and Joey doubles his salary with overtime and promotion. He is up before the draft board twice and is deferred each time, but in 1943 when they start drafting the fathers he does not try for an exemption because he is a war worker. There is a sense of guilt in all the familiar landscape of his home, there is the discomfort of walking the street in civilian clothes. More, he has convictions, reads *PM* from time to time, although he will say that it upsets him

491

too much. He reasons it all out with Natalie, is drafted against the protests of his boss.

In the draft-board office on the early morning when he reports for induction he talks to a father like himself, a portly fellow with a mustache.

Oh, no, I told my wife to stay at home, Joey says, I figured it would be too upsetting for her.

I had an awful time, the other fellow says, settling everything, it was a crime what I had to take for my store.

In a few minutes they discover they know a few people in common. Oh, yes, the new friend says, Manny Silver, nice fellow, we got along fine up at Grossinger's two years ago, but he travels in a crowd a little too fast for me. Nice wife, but she'd better watch her weight, I remember when they were married they were inseparable for a while, but of course you got to get out, meet people, it's bad for married people to stay alone together all the time.

Farewell to all this.

It has been lonely at times, empty, but still it has been a harbor. There are all the friends, all the people you understand immediately, and in the Army, in the bare alien worlds of the barracks and the bivouacs, Goldstein fumbles for a new answer, a new security. And in his misery the old habits wither away like bark in winter, and he is left without a garment. His mind searches, plumbs all the cells of his brain, and comes out with the concretion, the heritage, smudged for so long in the neutral lapping cradle of Brooklyn streets.

(We are a harried people, beset by oppressors . . . we must always journey from disaster to disaster . . . not wanted and in a strange land.)

We are born to suffer. And although he strains with the sinews of his heart and mind back toward his home, his cove, his legs are beginning to steady, his thighs to set.

Goldstein is turning his face to the wind.

3

THE PLATOON forded the stream and assembled on the other side. Behind them, the jungle gave virtually no hint of the trail they had cut. In the last twenty yards, glimpsing the hills, the men had hacked away very little shrubbery, had crawled through the periphery of the brush on their stomachs. Now if a Japanese patrol should come by it was unlikely the new trail would be discovered.

Hearn spoke to them. "It's three o'clock, men. We've got a lot of ground to cover. I want to make at least ten miles before dark." There was some muttering in the platoon. "What, are you jokers bitching already?" Hearn said.

"Have a heart, Lieutenant," Minetta called out.

"If we don't make it today, we'll just have to do it tomorrow," Hearn said. He found himself slightly annoyed. "Anything you care to tell them, Sergeant?"

"Yes, sir." Croft stared at them, fingering the sodden collar of his fatigue shirt. "I want all you men to remember where the trail is. You can line it up by those three rocks over there, or by that little ol' tree that's bent in half, an' if for any reason one of you troopers gets lost, you wanta remember what these hills look like, so's when you head south and reach the stream, you'll know whether to turn right or left." He paused and readjusted a grenade in his belt. "From now on we're gonna be in open country, an' you gotta keep patrol discipline. I don't want any goddam yelling or messing around, and you damn sure better keep your eyes open. When we cross a ridge-line we do it fast and low. If you're gonna walk like a bunch of sheep you'll be ambushed . . ." He fingered his chin. "I don' know if we're gonna make ten miles or two 'cause you can't tell ahead of time, but we're damn sure gonna do it right, I don't care what distance." There was a low murmur from the men, and Hearn flushed slightly. Croft had virtually contradicted him.

"All right, men, let's go," he said sharply. They started off in a long loose column, plodding forward wearily. The tropical sun glared on them, reflected from every blade of grass, and dazzled their eyes.

The heat made them sweat profusely; their uniforms, which had been wet first by the spray of the boat, had been unable to dry for almost twenty-four hours, and the cloth stuck dankly to their bodies. The sweat ran into their eyes and smarted, the sun burned on their fatigue caps, the high kunai grass lashed against their faces, and the unending hills absorbed their sinews. Their hearts would pound as they toiled up a hill, and they would sob with exertion, their faces burning with fever. An intense pendant silence had settled over the hills, become ominous at last in its depth and pervasiveness. The men had not thought about the Japanese at all while they were in the jungle; the denseness of the brush, the cruelty of the river, had absorbed all their attention. The last thing they had considered was an ambush.

But now in the great open quiet of the hills they felt a constraint and fear even through their fatigue. The hills stared down on them when they were in a valley, and in crossing a ridge-line the contrast rendered them naked, as though they could be seen for miles. The country was beautiful; the hills were tinted a canary yellow, and spread about them in an unending run of broad smooth curves, but the men did not appreciate the beauty. They had the isolation, the insignificance of insects traversing an endless beach.

They walked for a mile across a deep flat valley, and the sun blazed on them. The kunai grass grew to terrifying heights. On the plain each blade of grass was an inch wide and many feet high. Sometimes they would trudge for a hundred yards through grass that was over their heads. It roused a new kind of terror in them, drove them on more quickly than was bearable. They felt as though they blundered through a forest, but the forest was not solid. It weaved and swayed, rustled against their limbs, was soft and yielding, and therefore nauseous. They were afraid to let the man in front move too far away, for they could not see more than two or three yards, and so they dogged at each other's heels, the grass whipping nastily into their faces. Every now and then a cloud of gnats would be disturbed and flicker tantalizingly about them, goading their flesh with a dozen tiny bites. There were many spiders in the field, and the webs kept trickling across their faces and hands, lashing them forward in a minor frenzy. Pollen and bits of grass teased their exposed skin.

Martinez led the way like an arrow shot across the field. Most of the time the grass was too tall for him to see, but he directed himself by the sun, never pausing for a moment. It took them only twenty minutes to cross the valley, and then after a short break they trudged over the hills again. Here, the tall grass was welcome, for they grasped tufts of it to aid their ascent, and slowed their fall by clutching it on the downslopes of the hills. The sun continued to beat on them.

Their first fear of being observed by enemy troops had ebbed in the physical demands of the march, but a new and subtler terror began to obsess them. The land extended so far, was so completely silent, that they became acutely conscious of its unexplored weight, its somnolent brooding resistance. They remembered a rumor that natives had once lived in this portion of the island, and had died decades ago in a plague of scrub typhus, the survivors moving to another island. Until now they had never thought about the natives except to miss their labor, but in the vast buzzing silence of the sun and the hills the men forced themselves onward in nervous spasms, halting and starting, their limbs quivering with exertion. Martinez led them at a cruel pace as if pursued. Even more than the others, he was awed by the thought of the men who had lived on this island and died. It seemed sacrilegious to him to move through this empty land disturbing the long untrampled earth.

Croft experienced it in a different way. The land was foreign to him, and spawned a deep instinctive excitement at the thought that no one had trod this earth for many years. He had always known land well; he knew by heart every rock outcropping on every hill for miles about his father's ranch, and this country, unexplored, appealed to him deeply. Each new vista that the summit of a hill might furnish him was gratifying. It was all his, all terrain which he could patrol with the platoon.

And then he remembered Hearn, and shook his head. Croft was like a high-spirited horse, unused to the bit, reminded he was no longer free by an occasional harsh pressure on his jaws. He turned around and spoke to Red, who was behind him. "Pass this back. Tell them to snap it up."

The order passed through the column, and the men moved forward even more quickly. As they progressed farther away from the jungle their fear mounted, each hill behind them an added obstacle to their return. The platoon propelled itself with a nervous dread. They marched for three hours with only a few halts, lashed by the silence, forcing themselves onward in a tacit accord. At dusk, when they halted for their night's bivouac, the strongest men in the platoon were drained and overtired, and the weaker ones were close to collapse. Roth lay on the ground for half an hour without moving, his hands and legs twitching uncontrollably. Wyman lay hunched over, retching emptily. They had continued for the last two hours only through their fear of being left behind; their nerves had charged them temporarily with a spurious energy, and now that they had halted they felt too weak, their fingers were too numb, to undo the buckles on their packs and withdraw their blankets for the night.

None of the men talked. Grouped together in a rough circle against the coming night, those who could stomached their rations, drank their water, and spread out their bedding. They had bivouacked in a hollow near the crest of a hill, and before it was dark Hearn and Croft hiked through a small orbit from the bivouac to determine the best place to post a guard. Thirty yards above the men, at the top of the hill, they looked out at the terrain they would have to cross the next day. For the first time since they had entered the jungle, they were able to see Mount Anaka again. It was closer than they had ever seen it before, although the peak must have been twenty miles away. But past the valley beneath them, the yellow hills extended only a short distance before altering into darker tans and browns and the gray-blue of rock. In the evening a haze was spreading over the hills, obscuring the pass to the west of Mount Anaka through which they must travel. Even the mountain was growing indistinct. It was colored a deep lavender-blue, its mass dissolving, becoming transparent in the late twilight. Only the ridge-lines remained distinct. Above the peak a few delicate clouds perched tenebrously, their forms lost in mist.

Croft put up his field glasses and stared through them. The mountain looked like a rocky coast and the murky sky seemed to be an

496

ocean shattering its foam upon the shore. The movement of the clouds across the peak seemed like mist spray. Through the glasses, the image became more and more intense, holding Croft in absorption. The mountain and the cloud and the sky were purer, more intense, in their gelid silent struggle than any ocean and any shore he had ever seen. The rocks gathered themselves in the darkness, huddled together against the fury of the water. The contest seemed an infinite distance away, and he felt a thrill of anticipation at the thought that by the following night they might be on the peak. Again, he felt a crude ecstasy. He could not have given the reason, but the mountain tormented him, beckoned him, held an answer to something he wanted. It was so pure, so austere.

He realized with anger and frustration that they would not climb the mountain. If the next day went without incident, they would advance through the pass by nightfall, and he would never have a chance to attempt the mountain. He was balked as he handed the glasses to the Lieutenant.

Hearn was very weary. He had survived the march without incident, had even felt capable of marching farther, but his body demanded rest. He was gloomy, and as he stared through the glasses the mountain troubled him, roused his awe and then his fear. It was too immense, too powerful. He suffered a faint sharp thrill as he watched the mist eddy about the peak. He imagined the ocean actually driving against a rockbound coast, and despite himself strained his ears as though he could hear the sound of such a titanic struggle.

Far in the distance, past the horizon, was something which did sound like surf, or perhaps like rolling muted thunder.

"Listen!" He touched Croft's arm.

The two of them lay rapt and attentive, their bodies prone at the crest of the hill. Again he could hear the thunder coming faintly, dully, through the falling night.

"That's artillery, Lootenant. It's coming from the other side of the mountain. I guess they's an attack goin' on."

"You're right." They were silent again, and Hearn handed Croft the field glasses. "You want to look again?" he asked.

"Don't mind if I do." Croft put up the glasses to his eyes again.

497

Hearn stared at him. There was an expression on Croft's face. He could not name it, but it sent a momentary shudder along his spine. The face was consecrated for that instant, the thin lips parted, the nostrils flared. For an instant he felt as if he had peered into Croft, looked down into an abyss. He turned away, gazed at his hands. You couldn't trust Croft. Somehow there was reassurance in stating it so banally. He looked out for a last time at the clouds and the mountain. This time it disturbed him more. The rocks were very great, and the darkening sky flowed over it in wave after wave of swirling mist. It was the kind of shore upon which huge ships would founder, smash apart, and sink in a few minutes.

Croft returned the glasses, and he put them back in the case. "Come on, we have to settle the guard before it's too dark," Hearn said.

Turning, they slid down the hill to the men in the hollow beneath them.

498

Chorus:

In the hollow that night, lying side by side.

BROWN: Listen, you know, before we left, I heard a rumor that the rotation quota is coming in next week, and headquarters company this time is gonna have ten men.

RED: (Snorting) Yeah, they'll clean out the orderlies.

MINETTA: How do you like that, though, here we are goin' out shorthanded, and they got a dozen orderlies back there for those lousy officers.

POLACK: You wouldn't take a job being orderly?

MINETTA: You're fuggin ay I wouldn't, I got my self-respect.

BROWN: But I'm not kidding, Red, maybe you and me'll be in it.

RED: How many did they have last month?

MARTINEZ: One man, month before two men.

RED: Yeah, one man out of a company. We got a hundred men in headquarters got eighteen months in. Listen, Brown, cheer up, all you got to do is wait a hundred months.

MINETTA: Aaah, it's a screwing.

BROWN: What do you care, Minetta? I swear, you ain't been overseas long enough to get a tan.

MINETTA: If you guys don't get out of here, I never will when my eighteen months come up. Just like a prison sentence, Jesus.

BROWN: (Thoughtfully) You know, that's always when you get it. Remember Shaughnessy in P and D? Supposed to go home on rotation, got his orders and everything, and they send him out on a security patrol and he gets it.

RED: Sure, that's why they picked him. Listen, boy, forget about it, you ain't gonna get out of the Army, ain't any of us gonna get out.

499

POLACK: You wanta know something, if I had eighteen months, I could work that rotation. You just gotta start sucking Mantelli, or that fat fug first sergeant, and you win a little money in poker, slip them twenty-thirty pounds, and say, 'Here, for a cigar, for a rotation cigar, get it!' There's ways.

BROWN: By God, Red, Polack could be right, you remember when they picked Sanders, who the hell was he, not a goddam thing to recommend him except that he had his nose up Mantelli for the last year.

RED: I'll tell you what, don't try it, Brown. You start sucking Mantelli and he'll get to like you so much he couldn't bear to let you go.

MINETTA: I mean what kind of deal is this? Just like the goddam Army, give you something with one hand and take it away with the other, they just make you eat your heart out.

POLACK: You're getting wise to yourself.

BROWN: (Sighing) Aah, it makes you sick. (Turning over in his blankets) Good night.

RED: (Lying on his back, gazing at the pacific stars) That rotation ain't a plan to get men home, it's a plan how not to get them home.

MINETTA: Yeah, good night.

(Assorted speeches) Good night . . . good night.

(The men sleep surrounded by the hills and the whispering silence of the night.)

4

THE PLATOON passed an uneasy night in the hollow. The men were too tired to sleep well, and shivered in their blankets. When it came each man's turn for guard, he would stumble up to the crest of the hill and stare over the grass into the valley below. Everything was cold and silver in the moonlight, and the hills had become gaunt. The sleeping men in the hollow beneath him were removed and distant. Each man on guard felt alone, terribly alone, as though looking out on the valleys and craters of the moon. Nothing moved, and yet nothing was still. The wind was wistful and reflective; the grass rustled, advanced and retreated in shimmering rustling waves. The night was intensely silent and pendant.

In the dawn they folded their blankets, made their packs, and ate a K ration, chewing slowly, and without relish, the cold tinned ham and eggs and the square graham crackers. Their muscles were stiff from the previous day's march, and their clothing was damp with yesterday's perspiration. The older men were wishing that the sun was higher; there seemed no warmth left in their bodies. Red's kidneys were aching again, Roth's right shoulder was rheumatic, and Wilson had a spasm of diarrhea after he ate. They all felt dull, without volition; they scarcely thought of the march ahead.

Croft and Hearn had gone to the top of the hill again, and were discussing the morning's march. In the early morning, the valley was still hazy with mist and the mountain and pass were obscured. They squinted into the north, looking at the Watamai Range. It extended as far as they could see like a cloud bank in the haze, rising precipitously to its peak at Mount Anaka, and dropping abruptly, shudderingly, into the pass at its left, before mounting again.

"Damn sure seems like the Japs would be watching that pass," Croft commented.

Hearn shrugged. "They probably have enough to do without that, it's pretty far behind their lines."

The haze was dissolving, and Croft squinted through the field glasses into the distance. "I wouldn't say, Lootenant. That pass is narrow enough for a platoon to hold it till hell freezes over." He spat. "Course we got to find that out." The sun was beginning to outline the contours of the hills. The shadows in the hollows and draws were considerably lighter.

"There's not a damn thing else we can do," Hearn murmured. Already he could sense the antipathy between Croft and himself. "With any luck we'll be able to bivouac behind the Jap lines tonight, and then tomorrow we can scout the Jap rear."

Croft was doubtful. His instincts, his experience, told him that

501

the pass would be dangerous, probably futile, and yet there was no alternative. They could climb Mount Anaka, but Hearn would never hear of that. He spat again. "Ain't nothin' else to do, I suppose." But he felt disturbed. The more he looked at the mountain . . .

"Let's start," Hearn said.

They went down again to the men in the hollow, put on their packs, and began to march. Hearn alternated with Brown and Croft in leading the platoon, while Martinez acted as point and scouted ahead, almost always thirty or forty yards in front of them. The grass was slick from the night's dew, and the men slipped frequently as they moved downhill, panted hoarsely as they toiled up an ascending slope. Hearn, however, was feeling good. His body had reacted from the preceding day's march and was stronger now, the waste burned out of him. He had awakened with stiff muscles and a sore shoulder, but rested and cheerful. This morning his legs were firm, and he sensed greater reserves of endurance. As they crossed the first ridge-line, he hefted his pack higher on his broad shoulders, and turned up his face to the sun for an instant. Everything smelled fine, and the grass had the sweet fresh odor of early morning. "Okay, men, let's hit it," he called to them cheerfully as they passed by. He had dropped back from the point, and he moved from man to man, slowing his stride or increasing it in order to keep pace with them.

"How's it going today, Wyman, you feel any better?"

Wyman nodded. "Yes, sir. I'm sorry I pooped out yesterday."

"Hell, we all were bushed, it'll be better today." He clapped Wyman on the shoulder and dropped back to Ridges.

"Lot of country, heh, boy?"

"Yeah, Lootenant, always enough country." Ridges grinned.

He walked for a while beside Wilson, kidding him. "Still fertilizing the ground, boy?"

"Yeah, Ah lost mah petcock, ain't nothin' to hold it in now."

Hearn nudged him in the ribs. "Next break we're gonna cut a plug for you."

It was easy, it was swell. He hardly knew why he was doing it, but it gave him a great deal of pleasure. He had suspended all judgments, scarcely cared now about the patrol. They would probably be successful today, and by tomorrow night they would be ready to start back. In a few days the patrol would be over, and they would be in bivouac.

He thought of Cummings, an felt a sour hatred, had no desire suddenly for the patrol to end. His mood was spoiled momentarily. Whatever they accomplished would be for Cummings's benefit.

To hell with it. If you ever traced anything out to the end, you found yourself in trouble. The trick was to keep putting one foot in front of the other. "Okay, men, let's keep moving," he said quietly, as they filed past him on a slope. "That's it, hit it."

And there were other problems. There was Croft. As never before he would have to keep his eyes open, absorb things, learn in a few days the lessons Croft had acquired over months and years. Now he was in command only through the most delicate of balances. In a sense Croft could kick it over whenever he wanted to. Last night on the hilltop . . . Croft had the wrong kind of command, a frightening command.

He continued talking to the men as they marched, but the sun was hotter, and everyone was tired again, a little irritable. His own approach was less spontaneous now.

"How's it going, Polack?"

"No kicks." Polack kept walking silently.

There was a resistance they had toward him. They were cautious, perhaps distrustful. He was an officer, and instinctively they would be wary. But there was more to it, he felt. Croft had been with them so long, had controlled the platoon so completely, that probably they could not believe Croft was no longer the platoon leader. They were afraid to respond to him, afraid Croft would remember whenever he resumed his command. The thing was to make them understand that he would be with the platoon permanently. But that would take time. If only he had had a week with them in bivouac, a few minor patrols before this. Hearn shrugged again, wiped some sweat from his forehead. The sun was fierce once more.

And the hills were always rising. All morning the platoon plodded through the tall grass, climbing slowly, trudging through valleys, laboring awkwardly around the slopes of the hills. Their fatigue started again, their breath grew short, and their faces burned from the sun and the exertion. Now, no one was talking, and they progressed sullenly in file.

The sun clouded over, and it began to rain. This was pleasant at first, for the rain was cool and stirred a breeze along the top of the grass, but soon the ground turned soft and their shoes fouled with mud. By degrees they became completely wet again. Their heads drooping, their rifle muzzles pointed toward the ground to avoid the rain, the file of men looked like a row of wilted flowers. Everything about them sagged.

The terrain had altered, become rockier. The hills were steeper now, and some of them were covered with a waist-high brush of low thickets and flat-leafed plants. For the first time since they had left the jungle they passed a grove of trees. The rain halted, and the sun began to burn again, directly overhead. It was noon. The platoon halted in a tiny grove, and the men stripped their packs, and ate another ration. Wilson fingered his crackers distastefully, mouthed down a square of cheese. "Ah heard this binds a man up," he said to Red.

"Hell, it must be good for something."

Wilson laughed, but he was confused. All morning his diarrhea had plagued him, his back and groin had ached. He could not understand why his body had deserted him so. He had always prided himself on being able to do as much as any other man, and now he had to drag along at the tail of the column, pulling himself over even the smallest hills by tugging at the kunai grass. He had been doubled up with cramps, had sweated terribly, his pack abusing his shoulders like a block of concrete.

Wilson sighed. "Ah swear, Red, Ah'm jus' shot to hell inside. When Ah get back Ah'm gonna have that op-per-ration. Ah ain't good for a fuggin thing without it."

"Yeah."

"Ah mean it, Red, Ah'm jus' holdin' back the whole platoon."

Red guffawed. "You think we're in a hurry?"

"Naw, but Ah cain't help frettin' over it. What ifen we fall into somethin' when we're goin' through the pass. Man' Ah've plumb forgot what a tight ass-hole feels like."

504

Red laughed. "Aaah, you just take it easy, boy." He was unwilling to involve himself with Wilson's trouble. Nothin' I can do, he told himself. They went on eating slowly.

In a few minutes Hearn gave the order to move again, and the platoon filed out of the grove, and trudged forward in the sun. Although the rain had halted, the hills were mucky, and steam arose from them. The men marched with drooping bodies, the line of hills extending endlessly before them. Slowly, strung out in a file almost a hundred yards long, they weaved through the grass, absorbed in the varied aches and sores of their bodies. Their feet were burning, and their thighs quivered with fatigue. About them the hills shimmered in the noon heat, and a boundless nodding silence had settled over everything. The whirring of the insects was steady and not unpleasant. To Croft and Ridges, even to Wilson, it brewed vague warm images of farm lands in summer heat, quiet and bountiful, stirring only in the fragile traceries a butterfly might make against the sky. They drifted through a train of memories, idly, as if they were sauntering down a country road, seeing again the fertile roll of the fields, smelling in the musty damp germination of this earth after the rain the ancient redolent odors of plowed land and sweating horses.

The sunlight, the heat, was everywhere, dazzling.

For an hour they marched uphill almost constantly, and then halted at a stream to fill their canteens. They rested for fifteen minutes and went on again. Their clothing had been wet at least a dozen times, from the ocean spray, from the river, their sweat, from sleeping on the ground, and each time it dried it left its stains. Their shirts were streaked with white lines of salt, and under their armpits, beneath their belts, the cloth was beginning to rot. They were chafed and blistered and sunburned; already some of them were limping on sore feet, but all these discomforts were minor, almost unnoticed in the leaden stupor of marching, the fever they suffered from the sun. Their fatigue had racked them, exploited all the fragile vaults of their bodies, the leaden apathy of their muscles. They had tasted so many times the sour acrid bile of labor, had strained their overworked legs over so many hills, that at last they were feeling the anesthesia of exhaustion. They kept moving without any thought of where they

505

went, dully, stupidly, waving and floundering from side to side. The weight of their packs was crushing, but they considered them as a part of their bodies, a boulder lodged in their backs.

The bushes and thickets grew higher, reached almost to their chests. The brambles kept catching in their rifles, and hooking onto their clothing. They thrashed forward, plunging through the brush until halted by the barbs clinging to their clothing, and then stopped, picked the barbs loose, and swooped forward again. The men thought of nothing but the hundred feet of ground in front of them; they almost never looked upward to the crest of the hill they were climbing.

In the early afternoon, they took a long break in the shadow of some rocks. The time passed sluggishly in the chirping of the crickets, the languid flights of the insects. The men, wretchedly tired, began to sleep. Hearn had no desire to move, but the break was too prolonged. He stood up slowly, hitched on his pack, and called out, "Come on, men. On your feet." There was no response, which furnished him with a sharp irritation. They would have obeyed Croft quickly. "Come on, let's get going, men. We can't sit around on our butts all day." His voice was taut and impersonal, and the soldiers rose out of the grass slowly and sullenly. He could hear them muttering, was aware of a glum crabbed resistance.

His nerves were more keyed than he had realized. "Quit the bitching and let's go," he heard himself piping. He was damn tired of them, he realized suddenly.

"That sonofabitch," one of them muttered.

It shocked him, and generated resentment. He repressed it, however. What they were doing was understandable enough. In the fatigue of the march, they had to have someone to blame, and no matter what he did they would hate him sooner or later. His approach would end by confusing and annoying them. Croft they would obey, for Croft satisfied their desire for hatred, encouraged it, was superior to it, and in turn exacted obedience. The realization depressed him. "We've still got a long way to go," he told them more quietly.

They continued to plod on. They were much closer to Mount Anaka now. Every time they crossed a ridge-line they could see the towering cliff walls bordering the pass, could distinguish even the individual trees in the forests on its middle slopes. The country, even the air, had changed. It was cooler here, but the air was perceptibly thinner, and burned faintly in their lungs.

They reached the approach to the pass by three o'clock. Croft climbed the crest of the last hill, crouched behind a bush, and examined the land before them. Beneath the hill, a valley extended for perhaps a quarter of a mile, an island of tall grass surrounded by the mountain range in front, and by hills to the left and right. Beyond the valley the pass wound through the range in a twisting rocky gorge between sheer walls of stone. The floor of the defile was hidden in foliage, and might conceal any number of men.

He stared at the few knolls set in the opening of the pass, searching the jungle that circled about its foot. He had a quiet satisfaction that he had come so far. A damn lot of land we crossed, he told himself. Through the silence which hung over the hills, he could hear the muffled rumble of artillery on the other side of the mountains, the sporadic grumble of a battle.

Martinez had come up beside him. "All right, Japbait," he whispered, "let's keep to the hills around the edge of this valley. If they's anyone sitting at the entrance to the pass, they'll see us if we go through the field." Martinez nodded, crouched over the top of the hill, and turned to the right to circle the valley. Croft waved his arm to the rest of the platoon to follow, and started down the hill.

They moved very slowly, keeping close to the tall grass. Martinez would advance only thirty yards at a time, and then halt, before moving forward again. Something of his caution was transferred to the men. Without anything being said, they all were wary. They roused themselves from their fatigue, alerted their dulled senses, even restored to some extent a necessary delicate control of their limbs. They were careful where they placed their feet, and they lifted their legs at each step, and set them down firmly, trying to make no noise. They were all acutely conscious of the silence in the valley, and started at unexpected rustles, halted every time an insect began its chirping. Their tension increased. They expected something to happen, and their mouths became dry, their heartbeats pounded high in their chests.

507

It was only a few hundred yards from the place where Croft had studied the valley to the approaches of the pass, but the route Martinez took was more than half a mile. It took them a long time to circle around, perhaps half an hour, and their alertness diminished. The men in the rear of the column had to wait minutes at a time, and then jog forward on the half-run to keep up with the rest of the platoon. It was trying, it was exhausting, and it grated on them. Their fatigue became alive again, and throbbed in their backs, in the exhausted hamstrings of their thighs. They would stand in a partial crouch, waiting for the signal to move ahead, their packs resting cruelly on their shoulders. The sweat would run into their eyes, and their eyes would tear. They lost the fine edge of their tension, became surly. A few of them began to grumble, and in one of the longer halts Wilson stopped to relieve himself. They began to move while he was still occupied and the column was confused. The men in the rear whispered up the file to halt the leaders, and for a minute or so men were moving back and forth and whispering to each other. When Wilson was ready, they advanced again, but discipline was broken. Although none of the men talked aloud, the sum of their whispers, their decreased caution in walking, added up to a detectable murmur of sound. Occasionally Croft would give a hand signal to be silent, but it did not have enough effect.

They reached the cliffs at the base of Mount Anaka, and bore to the left again, darting toward the pass from rock to rock. They reached a place where there was no defilade; an open field, a cove of the larger valley extended for a hundred yards to the first saddle in the pass. There was nothing to do but walk across it. Hearn and Croft squatted behind a ledge and discussed their strategy.

"We got to divvy up into the two squads, Lootenant, and have one of them go across the field while the other covers."

"I guess that's it," Hearn nodded. It was oddly, incongruously pleasant, to be sitting on the rock ledge, absorbing the warmth of the sun on his body. He took a deep breath. "That's what we'll do. When the first squad reaches the pass, the other one can come on up."

"Yeah." Croft massaged his chin, examining the Lieutenant's face. "I'll take the squad, huh, Lootenant?"

No! This was where he had to step in. "I'm going to take it, Sergeant. You cover me."

"Well . . . all right, Lootenant." He paused a moment. "You better take Martinez's squad. Most of the older men are in it."

Hearn nodded. He thought he had detected a trace of surprise and disappointment in Croft's expression and it pleased him. But immediately afterward he was annoyed with himself. He was getting childish.

He motioned to Martinez and held up one finger to indicate he wanted the first squad. After a minute or two, the men formed about him. Hearn could feel some tension in his throat, and when he spoke his voice was hoarse, a whisper. "We're going to move into that grove, and the second squad will cover us. I don't have to tell you to keep your eyes open." He fingered his throat, feeling as though he had forgotten something. "Keep at least five yards apart." Some of the men nodded in agreement.

Hearn stood up, climbed over the ledge, and began to walk across the open field toward the foliage that covered the entrance to the pass. Behind him and to his left and right, he could hear the footsteps of the squad. Automatically he held his rifle at his side, both hands gripping the stock. The field was a hundred yards long, and perhaps thirty yards wide, bordered by the cliffs on one side and the valley of tall grass on the other. It sloped downward slightly over a run of scattered small rocks. The sun beat on it fiercely, refracting brightly from the stones and the barrels of their rifles. The silence was intense again, laving itself in layers of somnolence.

Hearn could feel the impact of each step on the sore bruised ball of his foot, but it seemed to exist at a great distance from his body; he knew remotely that his hands were slippery on the gun. The tension banked itself in his chest only to flare forth at any unexpected sound, anyone kicking a stone or scuffling his feet. He swallowed, looked behind him for a moment at the squad of men. His senses were exceptionally alert. Behind everything, he had a suppressed joy and excitement.

Some of the foliage in the grove seemed to move. He halted abruptly, and stared across the fifty yards which separated them. Seeing nothing, he waved his hand forward again, and they continued to advance.

BEE-YOWWWWW!

The shot ricocheted off a rock and went singing into the distance. Suddenly, terrifyingly, the grove crackled with gunfire, and the men in the field withered before it like a wheat prairie in a squall. Hearn dropped to the ground behind a rock, looked behind him to see the rest of the men crawling for cover, squirming and cursing and shouting at each other. The rifle fire continued, steady and vicious, mounting in crescendo with the parched snapping sound of wood in a forest fire. The bullets chirruped by in the soft buzzing sound of insects on the wing, or glanced off a rock and went screaming through the air with the tortured howl of metal ripping apart. BEE-YOWWWWWW! BEEE-YOWWWWWWW! TEE-YOOOOO-OOOONG! The men in the field flopped behind their rocks, quivered, helpless, afraid to raise their heads. Behind them, back of the rock ledge, after a pause, Croft and his squad had begun to fire into the grove at the other end of the field. The walls of the cliff refracted the sound, bounced it back into the valley, where it rushed about in disorder, the echoes overlapping like conflicting ripples in a brook. A wash of sound beat over the men, almost deafening them.

Hearn lay prone behind a rock, his limbs twitching, sweat running into his eyes. He stared for long seconds at the granite veins and tissues of the rock before him, looking with numb absorption, without volition. Everything in him had come undone. The impulse to cover his head and wait passively for the fight to terminate was very powerful. He heard a sound trickle out of his lips, was dumbly surprised to know he had made it. With everything, with the surprising and unmanning fear was a passionate disgust with himself. He couldn't quite believe it. He had never been in combat before, but to act like this . . .

BEE-YOWWWWWW! Rock fragments and powder settled on his neck, itched slightly. The gunfire was spiteful, malevolent. It seemed directed at him, and he winced unconsciously every time a bullet passed. All the water in his body had rushed to the surface. Perspiration dripped steadily, automatically, from his chin, the tip of his nose, from his brow into his eyes. The skirmish was only fifteen or twenty seconds old, and he was completely wet. A steel band wrenched at his clavicle, choked his throat. His heart pounded like a fist beating against a wall. For ten seconds he concentrated only on knitting his sphincter, roused to a pitch of revulsion by the thought of soiling himself. "NO! NO!" The bullets whirred past with an ineffable delicate sound.

He had to get them out of here! But his arms cushioned his head, and he flinched each time a bullet ricocheted off a rock. Back of him he heard the men bawling to each other, shouting words back and forth incoherently. Why this fear? He had to shake it. What had happened to him? This was unbelievable. Before him for an instant, in shame and fear, was the touch of Cummings's cigarette as he had stooped to pick it up. He felt as though he could hear everything, the scattered men breathing hoarsely behind their rocks, the Japanese in the grove calling to each other, even the rustling of the grass and the tense humming sounds of the crickets in the valley. Behind him, Croft's squad was still firing. He ducked behind the rock, scrounging his body as a volley of Japanese fire ricocheted off it. The stone and dust stung the back of his neck.

Why didn't Croft do something? And abruptly he realized that he had been waiting here for Croft to take over, waiting for the sharp voice of command that would lead him out of this. It roused a vivid rage. He slid his carbine around the side of the rock, started to squeeze the trigger.

But the gun wouldn't fire; the safety catch was still on. This mistake infuriated him. Not quite conscious of what he was doing, he stood up, pressed the safety and fired a volley of three or four shots into the grove.

"GET BACK, GET BACK," he roared. "COME ON, GET UP, GET UP! . . . BACK!" Numbly he heard himself shouting, his voice shrill and furious. "COME ON, GET UP AND RUN!" There were bullets whipping past him, but standing on his feet they seemed insignificant. "GET BACK TO THE OTHER SQUAD!" he roared again, running from rock to rock, his voice bellowing like something apart from himself. He turned and fired again, five shots as quickly as he could squeeze them off, and waited dumb, motionless. "GET UP AND FIRE. GIVE THEM A VOLLEY!"

A few of the men in the squad stood up and fired. Awed, confused, the grove was silent for a few seconds. "COME ON, RUN!"

The men straggled to their feet, looked mutely at him, and began to race toward the ledge from which they had started. They faced the grove, fired a few shots, and ran back for twenty yards, stopped to fire again, retreating pell-mell, sobbing like animals in anger and fear. The Japanese in the grove were firing once more, but they paid no attention. All of them were frantic. In motion, they wanted only one thing — to reach the safety of the ledge.

One by one, gasping, panting angrily, they climbed the last shelf of rock and dropped behind its bank, their bodies pungent with sweat. Hearn was one of the last. He rolled over on the ground, came to his knees. Brown and Stanley and Roth, Minetta and Polack were still firing, and Croft helped him to stand. They crouched behind the rock. "We all get back?" Hearn panted.

Croft looked about quickly. "Looks like all of us." He spat. "C'mon, Lootenant, we got to get out of here, they'll be circling around soon."

"Everybody here?" Red shouted. He had a long abrasion on his cheek, powdered with embedded dirt. His sweat etched through it like tears on a dirty face. The men were clambering behind the shelter of the rock, shouting angrily and nervously at each other.

"IS THERE ANYBODY THE FUG MISSING?" Gallagher shouted.

"Everybody's here," someone yelled back.

The grove at the other end of the field was silent. Only an occasional shot chirruped over their heads.

"Let's get out of here."

Croft peered over the top of the shelf, searched the field for an instant and saw nothing. He ducked down as a few shots chased after him. "Want to go, Lootenant?"

Hearn was unable to concentrate for a moment. He was still caught in the ferment that had aroused him. He could not quite believe they were back to a temporary safety; all his energies were

512

balked. He wanted to drive them for another hundred yards and another, bawling out his commands, bellowing his rage. He rubbed his head. It was impossible for him to think. He was churning. "All right, let's go," he blurted. There was an emotion in it somewhere, as sweet as anything he had ever known.

The platoon jogged away from the shelf, keeping close to the cliffs of Mount Anaka. They walked quickly, almost running, the men at the rear crowding up to the men ahead of them. There was a low hill they had to cross which put them in view of the grove for a few seconds, but it was several hundred yards away. They drew only a few scattered shots as they darted quickly, one by one, over the summit. For twenty minutes they kept walking and running, going farther and farther to the east, parallel to the base of the mountain. They were more than a mile away, separated by many small hills from the entrance to the pass, before they halted. Hearn, following Croft's example, selected a draw near the summit of a knoll, and posted four men at the approaches. The others flung themselves down, panting breathlessly.

They had been in the draw for ten minutes before they discovered Wilson was missing.

5

WHEN THE PLATOON fell into the ambush, Wilson took cover behind a rock near the tall grass. He had lain there, exhausted, feeling nothing, content to let the skirmish pass above him. When Hearn commanded the retreat, he had stood up obediently, had run back a few steps, and turned to fire at the Japs.

The bullet hit him in the stomach with the force of a blow to the solar plexus. It turned him around, sent him reeling a few feet, and then pitched him into the tall grass. He lay there a little startled, his first emotion anger. "Who the fug hit me?" he muttered. He rubbed his belly, planning to get up and rush the man who had punched him, but his hand came away wet with blood. Wilson shook his head, hearing the sound of rifle fire again, the shouts of the men in recon from the other side of the rock ledge, only thirty yards away. "Everybody here?" he heard somebody shout.

"Yeah, yeah, I'm here," he mumbled. He thought he had spoken loudly, but it was no more than a whisper. He rolled on his belly, suddenly afraid. Goddam, them Japs hit me. He shook his head. His glasses had been lost when he fell in the grass, and he squinted. He could see the field only a yard or two from where he lay and its emptiness pleased him. Goddam, Ah'm jus' pooped, that's the motherfuggin truth. He relaxed for a minute or so, his mind swirling languidly toward unconsciousness. Dimly, he could hear the platoon leaving, but he hardly thought about it. Everything was relaxed and peaceful, except for the dull throbbing in his stomach.

Abruptly, he realized the firing had stopped. Ah gotta git back in the weeds where the Japs won' find me. He tried to rise but he felt too weak. Slowly, grunting from the effort, he crawled a few yards farther back into the tall grass, and relaxed again, content because he could no longer see the field. His dizziness, his well-being sifted through his body. Feels like Ah'm likkered up. He shook his head in bewilderment. He remembered sitting in a bar once, pleasantly drunk, his hand around the hips of the woman beside him in the booth. He was going home with her in a few minutes, and a tingle of passion flushed through him at the thought. "That's right, honey," he heard himself say, looking at the roots of the kunai grass before his nose.

Ah'm gonna die, Wilson told himself. A cold charge of fear awakened his body, and he whimpered for a moment. He pictured the bullet tearing through his body, ripping apart the flesh inside, and he felt nausea. A little bile welled out of his mouth. "All that poison inside me is gonna be messin' aroun' now, jus' killin' me." But he drifted away again, settled into the warm lapping content of his drowsiness and weakness. He was no longer afraid of dying. That bullet's gonna clean up mah insides. All the pus'll be comin' out now, an' Ah'll be okay. This cheered him. Pappy said his granpappy used to have an ole nigger woman bleed him wheneveh he had the fever. Tha's jus' what Ah'm doin' now. He looked mistily at the ground. The blood was sopping against his shirt front, which made

514

him slightly uncomfortable. He held his hand over it, smiling faintly.

His eyes stared at the ground two inches away. Time hung still, unmoving about him. He felt the heat of the sun on his back; he dropped, submerged, in the chattering rhythms of the insect life about him, and the square foot of earth he could see became magnified until every grain stood out perfect and complete. The ground was no longer brown; it was a checkerboard of individual crystals, of red and white and yellow and black; his sense of dimension vanished. He thought he was looking from an airplane at several fields and a patch of wood, and the tall grass blurred a few inches from the ground, became nebulous and shifting like cloud vapors. The roots were surprisingly white with thick scaly bark stippled with brown like birch trees. Everything he saw was proportioned to the size of a forest, but a new forest, one he had never seen before, and quite odd.

A few ants meandered past his nose, turned about to look up at him, and then waddled on. They seemed the size of cows, or the way cows would look from the top of a high hill. He watched them pass out of his line of vision.

Goddam, they're cute little buggers, he thought weakly. His head settled on his forearm, and the wood darkened before his eyes, turned upside down as he fainted.

He awoke, he drifted out of unconsciousness perhaps ten minutes later. And lay there motionless, wavering between wakefulness and sleep. Each of his senses seemed to have sprung free of the other; he would stare emptily at the ground, or close his eyes and breathe, only his ears alert, or his head would roll on the ground, his nose twitching over the faint bouquet of earth, the pungent spice smell of the grass roots, or over the dry decay of mold.

But something was wrong. He raised his head, listened, and heard some men talking softly in the field ten yards away. He stared through the tall grass, unable to see clearly. He thought it was someone in the platoon perhaps, and he worked his throat to speak, and then stiffened.

There were Japanese in the field, or at least he heard men talking in a strange guttural, pitched in odd tones, rather breathless. If them Japs get me . . . He felt a choking horror. Tag ends of all

515

the stories of Jap torture flicked his brain. Sonofabitch, they'll cut mah nuts off. He felt his breath escaping through his nose, slowly, with compression, stirring the hairs in the nostril. He could hear them puttering around, their words slicing abruptly against his ears.

"Doko?"

"Tabun koko."

They were thrashing the grass, moving around again. He heard them coming nearer. Absurdly, he began to repeat a jingle to himself. "Doko koko cola, doko koko cola." He buried his face in the earth, mashing his nose against the ground. Every muscle in his face was working to keep from making a sound. Ah gotta git my rifle. But he had left his gun a yard or two away when he crawled deeper into the grass. If he moved to get it, they would hear him.

He tried to decide, and in his weakness he felt like weeping. It was all too much for him, and he burrowed his face into the ground and tried to hold his breath. The Japanese were laughing.

Wilson remembered the bodies he had disturbed in the cave, and he began to argue silently as if he had already been captured. Shoot, Ah was jus' lookin' for a little souvenir, you men understan' that, they wa'n' no harm done. You can do the same to mah buddies, Ah don' give a damn. A man's dead, he's dead, don' do him no harm. They were swishing the grass only five yards away. He thought for an instant of making a rush for his gun, but he had forgotten in which direction he had crawled. Already the grass had straightened, leaving no swath. Oh, goddam. He tensed his body, squeezed his nose against the earth. His wound was throbbing again, and beneath his eyelids a suite of concentric circles, colored blue and gold and red, bored into his mind. If Ah jus' get out of this.

The Japanese had sat down, were talking. Once, one of them lay back in the grass, and the rustle traveled to his ears. He tried to swallow, but something gagged in his throat; he was afraid of retching and lay with his mouth open, spittle dribbling over his lip. He could smell himself, the sharp bite of his fear and the sour flat odor of the blood like stale milk. His mind carried him for an instant back to the room where his child, May, had been born. He smelled her

516

baby scent, of milk and powder and urine, which blended back into his own stench. He was afraid the Japs would smell him.

"Yuki masu," one of them said.

He could hear them stand up, laugh a little again, and then walk away. His ears were ringing, his head had begun to throb. He gritted his fists, forced his face against the ground once more to stifle his blubbering. All of his body felt weaker, more spent, than he had ever known it. Even his mouth trembled. Sonofabitch. He was growing faint, and he tried to rouse himself, but it was hopeless.

Wilson didn't awake for half an hour. He came to slowly, floating back to consciousness uncertainly, his mind quite dull. For a long time he lay still, his hand under his belly to catch the trickling of the blood. Where the hell is ever'body? he wondered. He had realized for the first time that he was completely alone. Jus' take off an' leave a man. He remembered the Japs who had been talking a few feet from him, but he could no longer hear them. A residue of his fear returned. For a few minutes he remained motionless again, not believing that the Japanese had departed.

He wondered where the platoon had gone, and was bitter because they had deserted him. Ah been a damn good buddy to a lot of them men, and they jus' took off an' lef' me. It's a hell of a way to do. If it been one of them, I damn sure woulda stuck with him. He sighed, and shook his head. The injustice seemed remote, a little abstract.

Wilson yawped onto the grass. The odor was faintly unpleasant, and he drew his head away, and crawled off a few feet. His bitterness, abruptly, became acute. Ah done so damn much for them men, an' they never did 'preciate it. That time Ah got the liquor for 'em, ol' Red thought Ah was cheatin' him. He sighed. What the hell kind of way was that not to trust a buddy? Thinkin' Ah cheated him. He shook his head. An' then when Ah jus' shot that little ol' bush away, an' Croft grabbed me like that. He's jus' a itty-bitty fellow, Ah coulda broken him in half if he didn't take me by surprise. But that was a hell of a way to act jus' 'cause Ah was pissin' around a little. His thoughts ambled along, drawing a righteous contentment from all the times the men had misunderstood him. Ah give Gol'stein a drink, or at least Ah wanted to but he was so damn chickenshit about it, he wouldn't even take it. And then Gallagher callin' me a dumb cracker, and po' white trash. He didn't have to do that, Ah was damn nice to him when his wife died, but none of them 'preciate anythin', they jus' take off an' save they own ass, and to hell with anybody else. He felt very weak. Croft didn't have to ride me since Ah got sick, Ah cain't he'p it if mah insides are shot plumb to hell. He sighed again, the grass blurring before his eyes. Jus' took off an' left me alone, don' give a damn what happens to me. He thought of all the distance they had covered, and wondered if he could crawl back. He dredged himself over the ground for a few feet, halting in pain. His mind hovered about the realization that he was badly wounded, marooned miles and miles from anywhere, alone in a barren wilderness. But he could not grasp it, sinking back again into a partial stupor from the effort it had cost him to crawl. He heard someone groan, then groan again, and realized with surprise that he was making the sounds. Goddam.

The sun was burning on his back, laving his body with a pleasant heat. Slowly he could feel himself sinking into the earth, its warmth spreading about, supporting him. All the grass and the roots and the ground smelled of sunlight, and his mind eddied back through the images of plowed earth and steaming horses, back to the afternoon when he had sat on a stone by the side of the road, and watched the colored girl walk by, her breasts jouncing against her cotton frock. He tried to remember the name of the girl he was going to see that night, and began giggling. Wonder if she knows Ah'm sixteen? His wound had roused a warm and blunted nausea in his belly, almost like the bubbling of passion in his groin, and he floated along, not quite anchored to either the road beside the house where he had been born or to the valley of grass in which he lay. Vague lusts chased themselves through his head. The tall grass, nebulous and waving, seemed as high as a forest to him; he could not remember if he was in the jungle or not, and his nose amplified the odors here, blended them into his memory of the rich fetor of the jungle. Goddam, just to smell a woman again.

518

The blood was trickling faster over his fingers, and he sweated, thinking of liquid things, lost in a welter of lovemaking, recalling acutely the feel of a woman's belly and hips, her mouth. The sun was very bright, very satisfactory. Plays hell on a man when he don' get his ass regular. Ah bet that's why mah insides turned back on me, an' got full of pus. His reverie was shattered by the thought. Ah don' want no op-per-ration, they gonna kill me with it. When Ah git back, Ah'll tell 'em, Ah won' take no truck, Ah'll jus' tell 'em that all the pus jus' bled out of me, an' mah insides are fixed up. He began to giggle weakly. Goddam, when that ol' wound closes, Ah'm gonna have two belly buttons, one right under t'other. Wonder what t' hell Alice'll say when she sees it?"

The sun passed behind a cloud and he felt cold and shivered. His senses cleared again for a minute or two and he was frightened and miserable. They cain' jus' lea' me alone here, the men gotta come back for me. The grass was rustling in the wind, and he listened to it mournfully, hovering near a knowledge he did not want to confront. Ah gotta hold on. He roused himself, managed to stand up in the grass for a moment, caught sight of the hills and the cliffs of Mount Anaka, and then pitched forward, sweating coldly. Ah'm a man, he told himself, Ah cain't go to pieces. Ah never took no crap from no one, an' Ah ain't gonna start now. If a man's chicken, he ain't worth a goddam.

But his limbs were cold, and he shuddered continually. The sun had come out but it gave him no warmth. He heard the sound of groaning again, and then once again; he writhed from a sudden convulsion. That was me made that noise. The pain returned, hammered at his entrails. "Goddam sonofabitch," he bawled out suddenly. He felt a passionate rage at the pain, heard himself coughing blood over his fingertips. It seemed like someone else's blood, and he was surprised how warm it felt. "Ah jus' gotta hold on to myself," he mumbled, as he lost consciousness again.

Everything had gone wrong. The entrance to the pass was closed, and even at this moment probably the Japanese were relaying a message to their headquarters. All the secrecy of the patrol was lost.

519

Croft almost bellowed with rage when he learned Wilson had been left behind. He sat down on a rock, his thin mouth white and furious, and smacked his fist into his palm several times, his eyes glaring.

"That big dumb bastard," he muttered to himself. His first impulse was to leave him. But they had to go back for Wilson; that was one of the rules, and he knew there was no other decision possible. Already he was debating what had happened to him, considering which men he could take back with him for the search.

He talked to Hearn. "I ought to take just a few men with me, Lootenant. Any more ain't gonna be no help, and just that much more chance of some other trooper getting hit."

Hearn nodded. His big body sagged, and his cold eyes were wary, a little reflective. He ought to go back himself, for it was a mistake to let Croft take the initiative, but he knew Croft's experience would be more effective. Besides, there had been other reactions, things about himself which he distrusted. He had been angry too when he had heard Wilson was lost, and his first impulse had been to leave him.

There were so many desires in him at the moment, conflicting, ambiguous, things he had never quite felt before. He had to stop and think it out. "All right, take anybody you want." He lit a cigarette, and stared at his leggings, dismissing Croft.

Around them, the men were pacing moodily through the hollow, agitated, a little hysterical from the suddenness of the ambush and the discovery that Wilson had been lost. They snapped at each other irritably.

Brown and Red were having an argument. "You bastards weren't in the field, you were sitting there behind that goddam rock. Couldn't you even keep your fuggin heads up high enough to see if anybody got hit?" Red swore.

"What the hell are you talkin' about, Red? If it hadn't been for us covering you guys, you all woulda been knocked off."

"Aaah, balls, you yellow bastards, ducking down behind that rock."

"Fug you, Red."

Red slapped his forehead. "Jesus Christ, Wilson, of all the guys to be lost."

Gallagher wandered back and forth, smacking his hand against his forehead. "How the fug did we lose him?" he demanded. "Where is he?"

"Sit down, Gallagher," Stanley shouted.

"Blow it out."

"All you men can just shut your mouth," Croft snapped. "Pack of goddam women." He stood up and looked at them. "I'm gonna take a few men back to find Wilson. Who wants to go?" Red nodded, and Gallagher nodded his head in agreement.

The others were silent for a perceptible second or two. "Shoot, Ah might as well go," Ridges announced.

"I want one more man."

"I'll go," Brown said.

"I ain't taking any noncoms. The Lootenant'll be needing ya."

He looked around, staring at them. I shouldn't take any chances, Goldstein told himself. What'll Natalie do if something happens to me? But he felt a sense of guilt when everyone remained silent. "I'll go too," he said abruptly.

"All right. We'll jus' leave our packs in case we got to move fast."

They picked up their rifles, and filed out of the hollow, heading back toward the field where they had been ambushed. They moved silently, strung out in a long column, each man ten yards apart. The sun was moving toward the west, and it glared in their eyes. They were a little reluctant now.

They followed in reverse the route of their retreat, moving quickly without any attempt at concealment except when they crossed a ridge. The country was dotted with groves of bushes and trees, but they gave them only a cursory examination. Croft was certain Wilson had been wounded in the ambush, and hadn't left the field.

It took them less than half an hour to reach the ledge, and they advanced toward it stealthily, crouching close to the ground. There seemed no one about, no sound at all. Croft bellied forward over the rock slab, raised his head slowly, and searched the field. He could see nothing, and in the grove at the other end of the field, nothing seemed to be stirring.

"Goddam, goddam sonofabitching belly."

The men stiffened at the sound. Someone was moaning only ten or twenty yards away. "Goddam, ohhhhhhhh."

Croft stared into the grass. "Ohhhh, that mother-fuggin . . ." The voice trailed off in a babble of curses.

He slid down from the ledge, and joined the others, who waited for him nervously, their rifles unslung. "I think it's Wilson. Come on." He worked over to the left, slid up the broad flat slab of the ledge again, and dropped from it into the grass. In a few seconds he found Wilson, turned him over gently. "He's hit, all right." Croft stared at him with a mild pity, mixed with a trace of disgust. If a man gets wounded, it's his own goddam fault, Croft thought.

They knelt in the grass around him, careful to keep their heads low. Wilson had become unconscious again. "How're we going to get him back?" Goldstein asked in a whisper.

"Let me worry about that," Croft murmured coldly. He was concerned with something else for the moment. Wilson had been groaning loudly, and if the Japs were still in the grove they must have heard him. It was inconceivable that they wouldn't have come out to kill him, and therefore the only answer was that they had retreated. Their fire had been too sporadic, too small in volume, to have come from more than a squad of men. Undoubtedly it had been only an outpost with orders to retreat if any patrols were sighted.

Then the entrance to the pass was no longer guarded. He wondered if he should leave Wilson, and take the others with him on a reconnaissance. But it seemed pointless; there would certainly be more Japs deeper in the pass, and they would never get through. Their only chance was to go over the mountain. He stared up at it again, and the sight roused a delicate shiver of anticipation.

There was Wilson to be taken care of. It angered him. And he had to face something else. When the ambush had started, he had been paralyzed for a few seconds. It had not been fear, he had merely been unable to move. In remembering this he felt a little balked, al-

522

most teased, as if he had missed an opportunity. To do what . . . ? He was uncertain, but the emotion was similar to the one he felt now because he could not reconnoiter the pass. There had been a gap before he fired, and in that . . . Something he had wanted. I fugged up, he told himself bitterly, not quite certain of what he meant.

And here was Wilson. Properly, it would take six men to carry him back to the beach. Croft felt like swearing.

"All right, let's drag him through the grass until we get to the ledge and then we can carry him." He grasped Wilson by the shirt, and began tugging him along the ground, Red and Gallagher helping. They reached the ledge in less than a minute, and passed Wilson over it. On the other side of the shelf they set him down, and Croft began to fashion an emergency stretcher. He removed his shirt, buttoned it, and slipped his rifle through one sleeve, and Wilson's rifle through the other. The barrels protruded at the waist, and the stocks projected through the cuffs of the sleeves. With his belt he bound Wilson's wrists together, and wrapped him in a blanket from his discarded pack.

When the stretcher was completed it was about three feet long, the length of the shirt. They put it under Wilson's back, slid his bound arms over Ridges's neck, and Ridges then grasped the rifle stocks at the rear. Red and Goldstein each supported one of the muzzles at Wilson's thigh, and Gallagher stood at the front, holding Wilson's ankles. Croft guarded them.

"Let's get out of here," Gallagher muttered. "The damn place is spooky."

They listened uneasily to the silence, staring at the rock precipices.

They looked at Wilson, watched the slow pulse of his bleeding. His face had become blanched, almost white. He looked unfamiliar. They could not believe it was Wilson. It was just an unconscious wounded man.

Red had a vague sadness for a moment. He liked Wilson, and Wilson had been full of hell, but he couldn't feel very much. He was too tired, and he wanted to get out of this place. "We oughta put a goddam compress on him."

"Yeah."

They set Wilson down again. Red opened his first-aid packet, and took out the flat cardboard box that held the bandage. He peeled it open with stiff fingers, set the aseptic surface against Wilson's wound, and bound it about him lightly. "Should I give him wound tablets?"

"Not with a belly wound," Croft said.

"Think he's gonna last?" Ridges asked hoarsely.

Croft shrugged. "He's a big ox."

"You can't kill ol' Wilson," Red muttered. Gallagher looked away. "Come on, let's get going."

They started out, progressing slowly and carefully over the hills back to the hollow where they had left the rest of the platoon. It was hard labor, and they took frequent rests, alternating the guard for the litter-bearers.

Wilson gained consciousness slowly, muttering incoherently for minutes at a time. He seemed awake for almost a minute, but he recognized none of them.

"Doko koko cola," he muttered several times, giggling feebly.

They stopped, wiped the blood from his mouth, and then set out again. It took them more than an hour to reach the platoon, and they were very tired when they got there. They laid Wilson down, slipped him off the stretcher, and flopped on the ground to rest. The other men gathered about them nervously, asking questions, mildly jubilant that Wilson had been found, but they were too weary to talk much. Croft began to swear. "Goddam it, you men, stop standing around with your finger in your ass." They looked at him in bewilderment.

"Minetta and Polack and Wyman and . . . Roth, git over there in that grove, and cut two poles about six feet long, and about two inches in diameter, and bring back a couple of struts about eighteen inches wide?"

"What for?" Minetta asked.

"What the hell do you think it's for? For a stretcher. Now git goin', you men."

Muttering, they picked up a couple of machetes, and filed out of the hollow to the grove. In a minute or so, the platoon could hear them hacking away at the trees. Croft spat disgustedly. "Them men are enough to frost your nuts." There was a restless titter. Wilson, unconscious now, lay in the center of the hollow, very still. Despite themselves, they all kept looking at him.

Hearn had joined Croft, and after talking for a moment or two, they called Brown and Stanley and Martinez over to them. It was about four o'clock in the afternoon, and the sun was still hot. Croft, afraid of becoming sunburned, pulled the rifles out of his shirt sleeves, flapped it a few times, and put it on. He grimaced at the bloodstains on it, and then began to talk. "The Lootenant thinks that all the non-coms ought to talk this over now." He mentioned this flatly as if to convey that the idea had not come from him. "We're gonna send some men back with Wilson, an' I think we ought to figure out who we don't want."

"How many you sending with him, Lootenant?" Brown asked.

Hearn hadn't thought about that until now. How many would it be? He shrugged, trying to remember the number of men specified in the manual. "Oh, I think six will about do it," he said.

Croft shook his head, made an abrupt decision. "We ain't gonna be able to spare six, Lootenant, we'll have to make it four."

Brown whistled. "It's gonna be a sonofabitch with four men."

"Yeah, four men, not so good," Martinez said sarcastically. He knew he would not be chosen as one of the litter-bearers, and this once it made him bitter. His nerves were still taut from the ambush. He knew Brown would maneuver himself into going back with Wilson, while he would have to go ahead with the platoon.

Hearn interrupted. "You're right, Sergeant, we can spare only four litter-bearers." His voice was easy, forceful, as if he had been commanding them for a long time. "We never can tell when some other man jack is going to get hit, and we'll need bearers for him."

This was the wrong thing to say. They all looked glum, and their mouths tightened. "Goddammit," Brown blurted out, "we been pretty lucky up to now this campaign. Outside of Hennessey and Toglio . . . why in the hell did it have to be Wilson?"

Martinez rubbed his fingertips, staring at the ground. He slapped at an insect on his neck. "His number up."

525

"We might be able to get him back okay," Brown said. "You're gonna send a noncom with the litter-bearers, aren't you, Lootenant?"

Hearn didn't know the procedure, but there was no point in admitting it. "I think we can spare one of you noncoms."

Brown wanted to be picked. He had concealed it from the others, but nevertheless he had gone to pieces behind the ledge. "I guess it's Martinez's turn to go back," he said, however, not without guile, for he knew Croft would want Martinez with him. Yet on another level Brown was trying to be fair.

"I need Japbait," Croft said shortly. "I guess it'll be you, Brown." Hearn nodded.

"Any way you want it." Brown rubbed his hand over his cropped brown hair, fingered a jungle ulcer on his chin. He felt vaguely guilty. "Who'll I take?"

Croft reflected. "How 'bout Ridges and Goldstein, Lootenant?"

"You know the men better than I."

"Well, they ain't much fuggin good, but they're strong enough, an' if you push 'em, Brown, they ain't gonna goof-off on ya. They were awright when we carried Wilson back from where he got hit." Croft looked at them. He remembered that Stanley and Red and Gallagher had almost got into a fight on the boat. Stanley had crawfished, and he wouldn't be much use now. Still, he was a smart kid, Croft thought, probably smarter than Brown.

"Who else?"

"I figure you need a good man since you got a coupla fug-ups. How about takin' Stanley?"

"Sure."

Stanley was not certain what he wanted. He was relieved to be heading back for the beach, to be out of the patrol, but still he felt cheated. If he stayed with the platoon, there would be better chances later with Croft and the Lieutenant. He didn't want any more combat, not like that ambush certainly, but still . . . It was Brown's fault, he told himself. "If you think I oughta go, I'll go, Sam, but I kinda feel as if I ought to stay with the platoon."

"Naw, you go with Brown." Any answer would have left Stanley unsatisfied. It was like spinning a coin to decide your decision,

526

and wishing the coin had landed on the other side. He was silent.

Hearn scratched his armpit. What a goddam mess! He chewed on some grass, spat it out quietly. When they had brought Wilson back, he had been . . . all right, he had been annoyed. That was the first emotion, the honest one. If they hadn't found him the patrol would be relatively simple, and now they were shorthanded. It was a hell of a thing for a platoon leader to feel. He had to face some things; this patrol meant more to him than it should. And everything was loused up, he didn't know what they were going to do now. He had to get away by himself, think it out.

"Where the hell are those men with the poles for the stretcher?" Croft asked irritably. He was depressed for once, almost a little frightened. Their talk was finished and they stood about uncomfortably. A few feet away, Wilson was moaning deliriously, shivering under his blanket. His face was very white, and his full red mouth had turned a leaden pink, pinched at the corners. Croft spat. Wilson was one of the old men, and it hurt more, stirred him more, than if they had lost one of the replacements. There were so few of the old men left — Brown, and his nerves were shot; Martinez; Red, who was sick; and Gallagher, who wasn't much use now. There were all the men who had been lost when the rubber boats were ambushed, the few others who had been wounded or killed in the months on Motome. And now Wilson. It made Croft wonder if his turn was coming due. His mind would never release the memory of the night when he had shuddered in his foxhole, waiting for the Japanese to cross the river. His senses were raw, a little inflamed. He remembered with a thick lusting anger in his throat how he had killed the prisoner in the draw. Just let me get ahold of a Jap. He felt balked on this patrol, infuriated; his rage extended to include everything. He stared up at Mount Anaka as if measuring an opponent. At that moment he hated the mountain too, considered it a personal affront.

A hundred yards away, he could see the stretcher detail straggling back toward the hollow, the poles they had cut balanced on their shoulders. Lazy sonsofbitches. He restrained himself from calling out to them.

Brown watched their approach dourly. In a half hour he would be setting out with his litter-bearers, and they would toil a mile or more, perhaps, and then bivouac for the night, alone in this wilderness with only a wounded man for company. He wondered if he knew the way back, felt completely unsure of himself. What if the Japs sent out patrols? Brown felt bitter. There was no way out of it. It seemed like a plot against them all. They were betrayed, that's all. He could not have said who betrayed them, but the idea fed his bitterness, was fragilely pleasant.

In the grove while they were cutting the stretcher poles, Roth found a bird. It was a tiny thing, smaller than a sparrow, with soft dun-colored feathers and a crippled wing, and it hopped about slowly, chirping piteously, as if very tired. "Oh, look at that," Roth said.

"What?" Minetta asked.

"That bird." Roth dropped his machete and approached it warily, clucking with his tongue. The bird made a little beeping sound, ducking its head to one side like a shy girl. "Ah, look at that, it's hurt," Roth said. He extended his hand, and when the bird didn't move, he grasped it. "Aw, what's the matter," he said to it softly, lisping a little as if talking to an infant or a dog. The bird strained in his hand, tried to flutter away, and then subsided, its tiny eyes examining his fingers fearfully.

"Hey, let's see it," Polack demanded.

"Leave it alone, it's frightened," Roth whined. He turned away to hide it from the others, holding it a few inches from his face. He made little kissing sounds. "What's the matter, baby?"

"Aaah, for Christ's sake," Minetta muttered. "Come on, let's go back." They had finished trimming the poles, and he and Polack each picked up one of them, while Wyman gathered the two crosspieces and the machetes. They strolled back toward the hollow, Roth following with the bird.

"What the hell took you men so long?" Croft snapped.

"We did it fast as we could, Sergeant," Wyman said meekly.

Croft snorted. "All right, come on, let's make the stretcher." He took Wilson's blanket, spread it out smoothly on top of his poncho, and then laid the poles along each side, parallel and about four feet

528

apart. He flipped the blanket and poncho over each pole, and then they began rolling it up like a scroll, tightening it as much as possible. The struts were notched at each end, and when the poles were about twenty inches apart, he slipped the struts in place, one at each end, about six inches from the tips. Then he took his belt and Wilson's and lashed them in a loop about each strut to make it secure. When he had done he picked up the stretcher and dropped it again. It held together, but he was not satisfied. "Give me the belt to your pants," he told them. He worked busily for a few minutes and when he had done, the stretcher was a rectangle formed by the two poles and the two struts, with the blanket and poncho substituting for a canvas. Underneath them, the belts were fastened diagonally like stays to keep the stretcher poles from shearing. "I think that oughta hold," he muttered. He frowned and looked up to see most of the platoon gathered in a circle about Roth.

Roth was completely absorbed in the bird. Each time it would open its tiny beak and try to bite his finger, he would feel a protective pang. Its jaws were so weak. Its entire body would flutter and vibrate from the effort, and yet there was hardly any pressure at all on his finger. In his hand, its body was warm with a delicate musky odor, reminiscent of face powder. Despite himself he would bring the bird up to his nose and sniff it, touching his lips against its soft feathers. Its eyes were so bright and alert. Roth had fallen in love with the bird immediately. It was lovely. And all the frustrated affection he had stored for months seemed to pour out toward the bird. He fondled it, breathed its bouquet, examined its injured wing, filled with tenderness toward it. He felt exactly the same joy he knew when his child had plucked at the hairs on his chest. And back of it, not quite conscious, he was also enjoying the interest of the men who had crowded around him to look. For once he was the focus of attention.

He could not have picked a worse time to antagonize Croft.

Croft was sweating from the labor of making the stretcher; when he finished, all the difficulties of the patrol were nagging at him again. And deep within him his rage was alive again, flaring. Everything was wrong, and Roth played with a bird, while nearly half the platoon stood about watching.

His anger was too vivid for him to think. He strode across the hollow, and stopped before the group around Roth.

"Jus' what the hell you men think you're doin'?" he asked in a low strained voice.

They all looked up, instantly wary. "Nothin'," one of them muttered.

"Roth!"

"Yes, Sergeant?" His voice quavered.

"Give me that bird."

Roth passed it to him, and Croft held it for a moment. He could feel the bird's heart beating like a pulse against his palm. Its tiny eyes darted about frantically, and Croft's anger worked into his fingertips. It would be the simplest thing to crush it in his hand; it was no bigger than a stone and yet it was alive. Strange impulses pressed through his nerves, along his muscles, like water forcing itself through fissures in a rock mass. He wavered between compassion for the bird and the thick lusting tension in his throat. He didn't know whether to smooth its soft feathers or mash it in his fingers, and the impulse, confused and powerful, shimmered in his brain like a card on edge about to fall.

"Can I have it back, Sergeant?" Roth pleaded.

The sound of his voice, already defeated, worked a spasm through Croft's fingers. He heard a little numbly the choked squeal of the bird, the sudden collapsing of its bones. It thrashed powerlessly against his palm, and the action aroused him to nausea and rage again. He felt himself hurling the bird away over the other side of the hollow, more than a hundred feet. His breath expelled itself powerfully; without realizing it, he had not inhaled for many seconds. The reaction left his knees trembling.

For a long instant no one said anything.

And then the reaction lashed about him. Ridges stood up in a fury, advanced toward Croft. His voice was thick with wrath. "What you doin' . . . why'd you do that to the bird? What do ya mean . . .?" In his excitement, he stammered.

Goldstein, shocked, genuinely horrified, was glaring at him. "How can you do such a thing? What harm was that bird doing you?

530

Why did you do it? It's like . . . like . . ." He searched for the most heinous crime. "It's like killing a baby."

Croft, unconsciously, retreated a step or two. He was startled momentarily into passiveness by the force of their response. "Git back, Ridges," he mumbled.

The vibration of his voice in his throat stirred him, revived his anger. "I'm tellin' you men to shut up. *That's an order!*" he shouted.

The revolt halted, hovered uncertainly. Ridges had been complaisant all his life, was unaccustomed to rebellion. But this . . . Only his fear of authority kept him from leaping at Croft.

And Goldstein saw a court-martial and disgrace and his child starving. He halted too. "Ohhh," he exclaimed meaninglessly, choked with frustration.

Red moved more slowly, more deliberately. The hostility between him and Croft had to come to an issue sooner or later; he knew it, and he also knew without ever admitting it that he was afraid of Croft. He didn't say all this to himself; what he felt was anger and the understanding that this was a propitious time. "What's the matter, Croft, you throwing orders around to save your ass?" he bellowed.

"I've had enough, Red."

They glared at each other. "You bit off a little too much this time."

Croft knew it. Yet, a man's a damn fool if he don't follow something through, he told himself. "Anything you're gonna do about it, Red?"

This was very fundamental for Valsen. Croft had to be halted sometime, he told himself, or he'd run over them completely. Back of his anger and his apprehension, he felt a certain necessity. "Yeah, there is."

They continued to watch each other for perhaps a second, but the second was broken into many units of alertness, of decisions made and broken to launch the first blow. And then Hearn interrupted them, pushed them apart roughly. "Break it up, are you men crazy?" Not more than five seconds had elapsed since Croft had killed the bird, and he had crossed from the other side of the hollow. "What's happened here, what's going on?"

They moved apart slowly, sullenly. "Not a damn thing, Lootenant," Red said. To himself, he thought, I'll be fugged if I need a goddam looey to help me. He was feeling proud and relieved, and yet in another sense he was uneasy that the outcome was postponed.

"Who started all this?" Hearn was demanding.

Ridges spoke up, "He didn't have no call to kill that little ol' bird. He jus' stopped up and took it outen Roth's hand, and jus' killed it."

"Is that true?"

Croft was uncertain how to answer. Hearn's voice angered him. He spat to the side.

Hearn hesitated, staring at Croft. Then he grinned, slightly conscious of how much he was enjoying this moment. "All right, let's cut this out," he told them. "If you have to fight, don't fight with non-coms." Their eyes had turned bitter. For a moment Hearn sensed the impulses that had made Croft kill the bird. He turned to him, staring down into the emotionless glitter of Croft's eyes. "You happen to be wrong, Sergeant. Suppose you apologize to Roth." Someone tittered.

Croft looked at him in disbelief. He took several deep breaths. "Come on, Sergeant, apologize."

If Croft had been holding a rifle in his hand, he might have shot Hearn at this instant. That would have been automatic. But to deliberate, and then disobey him was in another category. He knew he had to comply. If he didn't, the platoon would fall apart. For two years he had molded it, for two years his discipline had not relaxed, and one breach like this might destroy everything he had done. It was the nearest thing to a moral code in him. Without looking at Hearn, he paced over to Roth and stared at him, the corner of his mouth twitching. "I'm sorry," he blurted, the unaccustomed words dropped leadenly from his tongue. He felt as if his flesh were crawling with vermin.

"All right, that chalks it off," Hearn said. He had some idea of how he had provoked Croft, and was amused by it faintly. Except that . . . Cummings had probably felt the same way when he had obeyed the order to pick up the cigarette butt. Abruptly, Hearn was disgusted with himself.

532

"Let's have all the platoon here, except the guards," he called out.

The rest of the men shuffled over. "We've decided to send Sergeant Brown and Corporal Stanley and Goldstein and Ridges back with Wilson. You want to make any changes, Sergeant?"

Croft stared at Valsen. He was unable to think; he worked at the idea as if wrestling with pillows. It would be better to get rid of Valsen now, and yet he couldn't. By coincidence, two of the other men who had opposed him were going on the litter detail. If he sent Red, the men would think he was afraid of him. This was such a new attitude for Croft, so contrary to all his thinking in the past that he was confused. All he knew was that someone must pay for his humiliation. "Naw, no changes," he blurted again. He was surprised at the difficulty with which he spoke.

"Well, then you men can start out right now," Hearn said. "The rest of us will . . ." He halted. What were they going to do? "We're going to stay here overnight. You can use the rest, I suppose. Tomorrow we'll find a way through the pass."

Brown spoke up. "Lootenant, couldn't I have another four men for, say, the first hour and a half march with Wilson? We can cover more ground that way, so by tomorrow when we start out again we'll be away from the Japs."

Hearn deliberated. "All right, but I want them back by dark." He looked around him, picked Polack and Minetta and Gallagher at random and then Wyman. "The rest of us will take up guard posts till they get back."

He drew Brown aside, talked to him for a few minutes. "You know the way to the trail we cut through the jungle?"

Brown nodded.

"All right, follow it through to the beach, and then wait there for us. It'll take you about two days, or maybe a little more. We should return in three or at most four days. If the boat comes before we do, and Wilson is . . . is still alive, then go back right away, and have them send another boat out for us."

"Okay, sir."

Brown assembled the litter-bearers, had Wilson placed on the stretcher, and began to move off.

533

There were only five men left in the hollow, the Lieutenant and Croft, Red and Roth and Martinez. They settled down, each alone on a knoll bordering their hollow, searching the valleys and hill-lines about them. They watched the litter-bearers progressing over the hills to the south, alternating their two teams every few minutes. In half an hour they were out of sight, and nothing remained but the hills, the mute mountain walls, and the late afternoon sky washing already into the golden hues of sunset. To the west, perhaps a mile away, there were Japanese bivouacked in the pass, and in front of them, high up, out of sight, was the top ridgeline of Mount Anaka. Each of them brooded, alone with his thoughts.

By nightfall, Brown and Stanley, Ridges and Goldstein were left with Wilson. The extra litter-bearers had turned back an hour before dark, and Brown, after progressing a half mile farther, had decided to halt for the night. They settled in a tiny grove just below the saddle of two small hills, spread out their blankets in a circle around Wilson, and lay talking drowsily. Darkness came, and in the wood it was very dark. Agreeably tired, it was pleasant to curl into their bedding.

The night wind was cool, rustling the leaves in the trees. It suggested rain, and the men mused idly of summer nights when they had sat on their porches at sundown, watching the rain clouds gather, feeling at ease because they were under cover. The idea set off a long stream of wistful recollections, of summer and the sounds of dance music on Saturday nights, the rapt air and the smell of foliage. It made them feel rich and mellow. They thought of things they had forgotten for months: the excitement of driving a car on a country road, the headlights painting a golden cylinder through the leaves; the tenderness and heat of love on a breathless night. They burrowed more deeply into their blankets.

Wilson was becoming conscious again. He floated upward from one cloud of pain to another, groaning and mumbling unintelligibly. His belly ached terribly, and he made feeble efforts to draw his knees up to his chest. It felt as if someone were binding his ankles, and he wrenched himself into wakefulness, the sweat pocking his face.

534

"Leggo of them, leggo of them, y' goddam sonofabitch, lea' my legs alone."

He swore very loudly, and the men started from their reveries. Brown leaned over him, daubing the moistened end of his handkerchief over Wilson's lips. "Take it easy, Wilson," he said softly. "You got to keep quiet, boy, or you'll be stirrin' up the Japs."

"Leggo, goddammit!" Wilson bawled. The shout exhausted him and he fell back on the stretcher. Dimly he felt himself bleeding again, and he drifted along the impressions it aroused, uncertain if he was swimming or if he had wet his pants. "Went and pissed in them," he mumbled, waiting for the hand to slap him. "Woodrow Wilson, you're a little ol' slob," some woman's voice was saying. He giggled, shying away from the blow. "Aw, Mommy, didn't mean to." He yelled the words, pleading, twitching on the stretcher as if avoiding a cuff.

"Wilson, you got to keep quiet." Brown massaged his temples. "Just relax, boy, we're gonna take care of ya."

"Yeah . . . yeah." Wilson dribbled a little blood out of his mouth and lay motionless, feeling it dry on his chin. "Rainin'?"

"Naw. Listen, boy, you got to keep quiet on account of the Japs."

"Uh-huh." But the words corroded his stupor, and left him afraid. He was sinking again in the tall grass of the field, waiting for the Japanese to find him, and he began to blubber softly without realizing it, as if his weeping came from an excreta of his nerves. Ah gotta hold on. Only he could feel the blood pulsing out of his belly, trickling, searching for new stream beds along the muscular ravines of his groin to end at last in a pool between his thighs. Ah'm gonna die. He knew it; as if he had sight in his belly he formed an image of roiled and twisted flesh, curling about itself, writhing. It kept squeezing the blood out.

"Looks like a pussy," he heard himself murmuring, only the words sounded with a roar.

"Wilson, you got to shut up."

The fear lapsed, became a vague disquiet, lulled by Brown's hand. This time, Wilson really whispered. "One damn thing Ah cain't figger out. Two in bed and wake up three, two in bed an' wake up three." He repeated it like a jingle. "What t'hell's one got to do with t'other; you jus' do your screwin' an' it comes out a kid." He wrinkled his face, partially from pain, and then relaxed again, sinking into the sensual fetid memories of a woman over him. Then the image blurred, and his vision faded into a series of concentric circles boring into his head with the delirium of ether. Ah gotta hold on. When they done op-per-rated on ya, an' ya got a hole in ya, y' cain't go to sleep. Pappy went to sleep an' he woke up dead. His mind swirled, plumbing back into his core, considering himself objectively as a man who was going to die. He fought against it, terrified, not really believing it, like a man who looks in a mirror and speaks, and cannot believe that the face he has seen really belongs to himself. He careened from one unexplored cavern into another, believing at last that he had heard his daughter saying, "Pappy went to sleep an' he woke up dead."

"No!" Wilson shouted. "Where'd you git that idea, May?"

"That's a cute girl you got," Brown said. "That her name, May?"

Wilson heard him, made the long journey back. "Who's that?"

"Brown. What's May look like?"

"She's a goddam little hellion," Wilson said. "Smartest little bugger you'd ever want to see." Remotely, he felt his face twisting into a smile. "Ah tell ya, she can jus' twist me 'round, an' she knows it. She's one hell of a little girl."

The pain in his belly became acute again, and he lay there panting, absorbed only in the racking demands of his body like a woman in childbirth. "Ohhhh," he groaned thickly.

"You got any other kids?" Brown asked quickly. He massaged Wilson's forehead with slow tender motions as if he were soothing a child.

But Wilson did not hear him. He was concerned only with his pain, and he fought against it numbly, almost hysterically, like a man grappling in the dark, pitching with his opponent down an endless flight of stairs. Protesting, whimpering from the pain, he reeled into unconsciousness, his mind seeming to revolve over and over beneath his closed eyelids.

Brown continued to massage Wilson's forehead. In the darkness,

Wilson's face seemed connected to him, an extension of his fingers. He swallowed once. An odd complex of emotions was working in Brown. Wilson's cries of pain, his shouts, had alerted Brown, made him worry about enemy patrols. It shattered the security of the grove, and reproduced the isolation of their position, the vast empty stretches of the hills around their little wood. He flinched unconsciously every time he heard an unexpected sound. But it was more than fear; he was keyed very high, and every quiver, every painful gesture of Wilson's body traveled intimately through Brown's fingers, through his arms, deep into his mind and heart. Without realizing it, he winced when Wilson winced. It was as if his brain had been washed clean of all the fatigue poisons of experience, the protecting calluses, the caustic salts, the cankers of memory. He was at once more vulnerable and less bitter. Something in the limitless darkness of the night, the tenuous protection of the grove, and the self-absorbed suffering of the wounded man beside him had combined to leave him naked, alone, a raw nerve responding to every wind and murmur that filtered into the wood from the bare gloomy hills in the blackness about them.

"Just take it easy, boy," he whispered.

All the lost things, the passions and ambitions of his childhood, the hopes that had curdled and turned to bile, swashed through him. Wilson's talk of his child loosed an old desire in Brown; for perhaps the first time since he had been married he wished he was a father, and the tenderness he felt for Wilson had little to do with the amused condescension with which he usually considered him; Wilson was not wholly real to him at this moment. He existed in this brief duration of Brown's mood as the body, the flesh, of Brown's longings. He was Brown's child, but he was also a concretion of all Brown's miseries and disappointments. For a few minutes he was more vital to Brown than any other man or woman had ever been.

Only it could not last. It was as if Brown had awakened in the middle of the night, helpless in the energies his mind had released in sleep. In the transit to awareness, to wakefulness, he would be helpless for a time, tumbling in the wake of his dream, separated from all the experience, all the trivia that made his life recognizable and bearably blunted to himself. He would be uncovered, lost in the plain of

537

darkness, containing within himself not only all of his history and all of the present in the ebbs and pulses of his body, but he would be the common denominator of all men and the animals behind them, waking blindly in the primordial forests. He was at that moment the man he might have been for good or for bad.

But inevitably he climbs out of the sea, grasps in his vision the familiar bedposts, the paler rectangle of the window, smells the flat commonplace odors of his body, and the pit of anxiety and aliveness shrinks to its normal place, is almost forgotten. He begins to brood about his concerns for the coming day.

So Brown thought about his wife, remembered her at first with longing and a flood of long-compressed love, and saw her face over his, her breasts nuzzling richly against his neck. But the unfamiliarity, the nakedness of his feeling was leaving him. He heard Goldstein and Ridges talking, felt the moistness of Wilson's forehead, and he was cast again into the worries and problems of the two days ahead. Seeing the bedpost, his heart clamped on the memory of his wife like a dog crunching a bone, and he pushed her away, immersed again in bitterness. Fooling around with anything that wears pants.

He began to brood about the difficulties of carrying Wilson back. There was a strong residual fatigue in his body from the first two days of the patrol, and the hills ahead would be demanding, exhausting, now that their relief had returned to the platoon. He had a sharp preview of the next day's march. With only four of them to bear the litter, they would be working all the time without relief, and after fifteen minutes in the morning they would be cruelly tired, dragging on painfully, having to halt for rest every few minutes. Wilson weighed two hundred pounds, and when their packs were lashed to the stretcher, it would be easily three hundred pounds. Seventy-five pounds to a man. He shook his head. Through experience he knew how exhaustion broke him down, dissolved his will, and muddied his mind. He was the leader of this detail, and it was his duty to get them through, but he felt unsure of himself.

The aftermath of all this — his sympathy for Wilson, the purge he had felt, and then the return of his bitterness — left him very honest with himself for a few minutes. He knew that he had wanted this detail because he was afraid of going on with the platoon, and he had to succeed here. A noncom ain't worth a goddam when he loses his nerve if he lets himself show it, Brown told himself. But it was more than that. Somehow he could slide through the months, perhaps the years ahead. They were in combat only a small part of the time really, and even then nothing might happen; his fear might not be noticed, nobody might be hurt because of it. If he did the rest of his work well enough it would be all right. After the Motome campaign was over, I was a hell of a lot better than Martinez for drilling and training, he thought.

What he realized partially was that he was afraid of breaking up completely, of being inefficient even in garrison. I gotta get ahold of myself or I'll be losing my stripes. For a moment he wanted this; it seemed as if life would be so much easier if he had no worries and no responsibility; he rebelled against the tiresome demands of watching labor details to make sure the job was done well. He had begun to feel an increasing tension whenever an officer or Croft examined the work his squad had been doing.

But he knew that he could never give up his sergeancy. I'm one man in ten, he told himself, they picked me 'cause I stood out. It was his bulwark against everything, his doubts of himself, the infidelities of his wife. He couldn't let go of that. And yet, he had added a further torment. He was bothered often by a secret guilt. If he wasn't good enough, he should be busted, and he was trying to conceal it. I gotta get Wilson back, he swore to himself. Something of the compassion he had felt for Wilson returned to him. There he is and he can't do a damn thing, he depends on me and I'm supposed to be able to do the job. The whole thing was very clear. It left him frightened, and he massaged Wilson's forehead gently, looking off into the darkness.

Goldstein and Stanley were talking, and Brown turned to them. "Keep it down. We don't want to get him stirred up again."

"Yeah," Stanley agreed softly, without rancor at the reprimand. He and Goldstein had been talking about their children, eagerly, companionably, welded by the darkness.

"You know," Stanley went on, "we're really missing the best

539

part of them. Here they are growing up, getting to understand things, and we're not even there."

"It's hard," Goldstein agreed. "When I left, Davy could hardly talk, and now my wife tells me he carries on a conversation on the telephone just like an adult. It's a little difficult to believe it."

Stanley clucked his tongue. "Sure. I'm telling you, we're missing the best part of them. When they get older, it'll probably never be the same. I remember when I started growing up, there wasn't a thing my old man could tell me. What a damn fool I was." He said this modestly, almost sincerely. Stanley had discovered that people liked him when he made confessions like that.

"We're all like that," Goldstein agreed. "I should think it's a process of growing up. But when you get older you see things more clearly."

Stanley was silent for a minute. "You know I don't care what they say, you can't beat it, being married." His body was stiff, and he turned over carefully in his blanket. "Marriage can't be beat."

Goldstein nodded in the dark. "It's very different from the way you think it's going to be, but personally I'd be a lost soul without Natalie. It steadies you down, makes you realize your responsibilities."

"Yeah." Stanley pawed the ground for a moment with his hand. "Being overseas is no way to have a marriage, though."

"Oh, no, of course not."

This was not quite the answer Stanley had wanted. He deliberated a moment, seeking a way to phrase it. "Do you ever get . . . well, you know, jealous?" He spoke very softly so that Brown could not hear them.

"Jealous? No, I can't say I ever do," Goldstein said with finality. He had an inkling of what was bothering Stanley, and automatically he tried to soothe him. "Listen," he said, "I've never had the pleasure of meeting your wife, but you don't have to worry about her. These fellows that are always talking about women that way, they don't know any better. They've fooled around so much . . ." Goldstein had a perception. "Listen, if you ever notice, it's always the ones who go around with a lot of, well, loose women who get so jealous. It's because they don't trust themselves."

540

"I guess so." But this didn't satisfy Stanley. "I don't know, I guess it's just being stuck out here in the Pacific with nothing to do."

"Certainly. Listen, you've got nothing to worry about. Your wife loves you, doesn't she? Well, that's all you got to think about. A decent woman who loves a man doesn't do anything she shouldn't do."

"After all, she's got a kid," Stanley agreed. "A mother wouldn't tool around." His wife seemed very abstract to him at the moment. He thought of her as "she," as "x." Still he was relieved by what Goldstein had said. "She's young, but you know she made a good wife, she was serious. And it was . . . cute the way she took up responsibilities." He chuckled, deciding instinctively to salve all the sore spots of his mind. "You know we had a lot of trouble on our marriage night. Of course we worked it out later but things weren't so good that first night."

"Oh, everybody has that problem."

"Sure. Listen, I'll tell ya, all these guys who are always braggin', even a guy like Wilson here." He lowered his voice. "Listen, you can't tell me they didn't have the same troubles."

"Absolutely. It's always hard to get adjusted."

He liked Goldstein. The amalgam of the night, the rustling of the leaves in the wood, worked subtly on him, opening the door to all his uncertainties. "Look," he said abruptly, "what do you think of me?" He was still young enough to make this question the climax of any confidential talk.

"Oh." Goldstein always answered a question like this by telling people what they wanted to hear. He was not being consciously dishonest; he always generated warmth for the person who asked him even if he had never been a friend. "Mmm, I'd say that you're an intelligent fellow with your feet on the ground. And you're kind of ambitious, which is a good thing. I'd say you'll probably go places." And until this moment he had never quite liked Stanley for exactly these reasons, although he had not admitted it to himself. Goldstein had a formal respect for success. But once Stanley had exposed his weaknesses, Goldstein was ready to make virtues of all his other qualities. "You're mature for your age, very mature," Goldstein finished.

"Well, I've always tried to do more things than I had to." Stanley fingered his long straight nose, scratched at his mustache, which had become scraggly in the past two days. "I was president of our junior class in high school," he said deprecatingly. "I don't mean that that's anything to beat my meat about, but it taught me how to get along with people."

"It must have been a valuable experience," Goldstein said wistfully.

"You know," Stanley confided, "a lot of the guys in the platoon are pissed off at me 'cause I came in after them and made corporal. They think I brown-nosed and there ain't a goddam bit of truth in that. I just kept my eyes open, and did what I was told to do, but I'll tell ya it's a damn sight harder job than you realize. These guys who been around in the platoon for a long time, they think they own it, when all they do is fug-off on the details, and just try to make it hard for you. They give me a pain in the ass." His voice became husky with admission. "I know I got a tough job, and I don't say I haven't made mistakes, but I'm learning, and I want to try hard. I take it seriously. Could anyone ask for more than that?"

"No, they couldn't," Goldstein agreed.

"I tell you, I've watched you, Goldstein, and you're a good man. I've seen the way you work on details, and no noncom could ask for more. I don't want you to think it ain't appreciated." Indefinably, Stanley felt superior to Goldstein once more; his voice, warm, pliable, had the faintest touch of condescension. He was the noncom talking to the rookie. Effectively, he had forgotten that two minutes before he had waited tensely for Goldstein to say that he liked him.

Goldstein was pleased, and yet his satisfaction was cloyed. That's what it's like in the Army, he told himself. The opinion of a youngster is so important.

Wilson was moaning again. They stopped talking and turned about in their blankets, propped on their elbows to listen. Brown, with a sigh, had sat up, and was trying to soothe him. "What's the matter, boy, what's the matter?" he asked softly, as if trying to comfort a puppy.

"Ohh, mah belly is killin' me. Sonofabitch."

542

Brown wiped away his perspiration. "Who's this talking to you, Wilson?"

"That's you, Brown, ain't it?"

"Yeah." He felt relieved. Wilson must be better. It was the first time he had recognized him. "How're you feelin', Wilson?"

"Ah'm okay, but Ah cain't see a damn thing."

"It's dark out."

Wilson began to giggle weakly. "Ah thought that hole in mah belly made me blind." He worked his mouth dryly, and in the darkness it sounded like the tense choking murmurs of a woman in grief. "It's a sonofabitch." He seemed to roll on the stretcher. "Where the hell am I?"

"We're takin' you back to the beach, Stanley and Goldstein and Ridges and me."

Wilson digested this slowly. "Ah'm out of the patrol, huh?"

"Yeah, all of us, boy."

He giggled again. "Ah bet Croft was mad as a goosed bee. Sonofabitch, they're gonna op-per-rate on me now, an' cut out all that pus, ain't they, Brown?"

"Yeah, they'll fix you up."

"By the time Ah git done, Ah'll have two belly-buttons, one right on top of t'other. Goddam that's gonna make me a hell of an attraction to the women." He tried to laugh, and began to cough softly. "On'y thing beat that would be two peters."

"You old bastard."

Wilson shivered. "Ah can taste blood in mah mouth. Is that good?"

"Can't hurt ya," Brown lied. "Just comes out both ends."

"Ain't that a sonofabitch though, man who's been around's long as me in the platoon gettin' hit in a lousy shit-storm like that." He lay back reflecting. "Ah wish to hell that hole in mah belly would stop actin' up."

"It'll be all right."

"Listen, they was Japs after me in that field, jus' a couple of yards away from me. They was talkin', jus' jabberin' away, doky cola kinda it sounded like. But they was right after me." He began to tremble.

He's off again, Brown thought. "You feeling cold, boy?"

At the suggestion, Wilson shuddered. Slowly, as he had been talking, his body had been losing its fever, becoming increasingly chill and damp. Now he shivered with cold.

"You want another blanket?" Brown asked.

"Yeah, can you gimme that?"

Brown stepped away from him, moved over to where the others were talking. "Anybody got two blankets?" he asked.

None of them answered immediately. "I have just one," Goldstein said, "but I can sleep in my poncho." Ridges was slumbering. "I'll sleep in my poncho too," Stanley offered.

"The two of you bunk together with a blanket and a poncho, and I'll take one from each of you." Brown returned to Wilson, covered him with his own blanket, and the blanket and poncho the others had donated. "You feel better, boy?"

Wilson's shuddering was becoming less frequent. "Feels good," he murmured.

"Sure."

Neither of them said anything for a moment or two, and then Wilson began talking once more. "Ah want you to know Ah 'preciate what you men are doin'." A spasm of gratefulness welled in him, and tears formed in his eyes. "You're pretty goddam good men, an' they ain't a damn thing good enough for ya. The on'y thing worth a damn is when a man's got good buddies, an' you men are really stickin' to me. Ah swear, Brown, we maybe got a little pissed off at each other from time to time, but they ain't a thing Ah won' do for ya when Ah git fixed up. Ah always knew you was a buddy."

"Aw, shit."

"No, a man wants, wants . . ." In his eagerness he began to stutter. "Ah 'preciate it, an' Ah jus' want you to know that Ah'm always gonna be your buddy. You're gonna be able to know that they's one man, Wilson, who'll never have a bad thing to say about ya."

"Better take it easy, boy," Brown said. Wilson's voice was rising.

"Ah'm gone to sleep, but don' think Ah don' 'preciate it." He was beginning to ramble again.

After a few minutes he became silent.

544

Brown stared into the darkness. Once more he swore to himself.

I gotta get him back. More than anything else it was a plea to whatever powers had formed him.

The Time Machine:

WILLIAM BROWN

NO APPLE PIE TODAY

About medium size, a trifle fat, with a young boyish face, a snub nose, freckles, and reddish-brown hair. But wrinkles had formed about his eyes and there were jungle ulcers on his chin. At second glance he was easily twenty-eight years old.

The neighbors always like Willie Brown, he is such an honest boy, he has such an average pleasant face, you can see it in all the stores, in the framed pictures on the desks of all the banks and offices in the country.

Nice-looking boy you have there, they always say to his father, James Brown.

Fine boy, but you ought to see my daughter, she's the bee-yootey.

Willie Brown is very popular. The mothers of his friends always take to him, the teachers always make him a pet.

But he has a knack for squaring it. Aw, that old crow, he says of the teacher, I wouldn't spit on her. (Proceeding to spit on the dusty baked sod of the schoolyard.) I don' know why in tee hell she don' lea' me alone.

And his family is nice. Good stock. The father works for the railroad in Tulsa but he is an office man even if he has started in the yards. And they have their own house in the suburbs, a decent plot of ground behind it. Jim Brown is dependable, always improving his house a little bit, fixing the plumbing or planing the sill of a door that jams.

Isn't the kind of man who runs into debt.

Ella and me try to hold to one of those budgets, he says deprecatingly. If we find we're gone a little over, we jus' cut down on the

546

liquor for the week. (Half-apologetically) I kinda look on liquor as a luxury, especially now when you gotta break a law to get it, and you're never sure when it'll leave you blind.

Keeps up with things too. The *Saturday Evening Post* and *Collier's* and back in the early twenties a charter subscriber to *Reader's Digest*. It all comes in handy for small talk when you're visiting, and the only dishonesty people have ever noticed him in is that he has a habit of talking about the articles without crediting the source.

Do you know thirty million people smoked cigarettes in 1928? he'll say.

The Literary Digest keeps him informed on politics. I voted for Herbert Hoover in the last election, he admits pleasantly, even though I've been a Democrat as long as I can remember. But I think I'll vote Democrat in the next. The way I look at it, one party's in power for a while and then you give the other a turn.

And Mrs. Brown nods her head. I allow Jim to show me the way for those political things. She does not add the business about keeping up her home, but you can guess. Nice people, nice family, church on Sundays of course. Mrs. Brown's only violent opinion is on the New Morality. I don't know, people aren't Godfearing any more. Women drinking in bars, doing God knows what else, it isn't right, isn't Christian at all.

Mr. Brown nods tolerantly. He has a few reservations, but after all women somehow just are more religious, really religious, than men, he will say in a confidential talk.

Naturally they're very proud of their children, and they'll tell you with amusement how Patty is teaching William to dance now that he's in high school.

We were worried about sending them to the State University what with the depression and all, but I think we can see our way clear now. Mr. Brown, she'll add, always has wanted them to go, especially since he missed it.

The brother and sister *are* good friends. In the sun parlor where the maple sofa is flanked by the vase (which had been a flower pot until the rubber plant died) and the radio, the girl makes him lead her.

547

Now, look, Willie-boy, it's easy. You just don' have to be afraid of holdin' me.

Who's afraid of holdin' ya?

You're not such a roughneck, she says from the vantage of senior year in high school. You're gonna be dating soon.

Yeah, he exclaims with disgust. But he feels her small pert breasts against his chest. He is almost as tall as her. Who's gonna date?

You are.

They shuffle along the smooth red stone of the floor. Hey, Patty, when Tom Elkins comes around to see you, lemme talk to him. I wanna know if he thinks I'll be big enough to get on the football team in a coupla years.

Tom Elkins, that ol' fool.

(It's sacrilege.) He looks at her in disgust. What's the matter with Tom Elkins?

It's all right, Willie, you'll make the team.

He never does get quite big enough, but by his junior year he is the head of the cheer leaders, and he has talked his father into buying him a used car.

You don't understand, Pop, I really need the car. A guy's gotta get around. Like last Friday when I had to get all the crew together to practice for the Wadsworth game, I wasted all the afternoon just running around.

Are you sure, Son, it won't be a wanton extravagance?

I really need it, Pop. I'll even work summers to pay you back.

It's not a question of that, although I think you oughter to keep you from getting spoiled. I tell you what, I'll just talk it over with Mother.

The victory is his and he grins. Far back in his head, quite beneath the surface of his sincerity in this conversation, is the memory of many others. (The youths talking in the locker room after gym period, the profound discussions in the cellars converted to clubrooms.)

Folklore: If you want to make a girl, you got to have a car.

His senior year is fun. He is a member of SG (Student Government) and he manages the School Dance. There are all the dates on Saturday night at the Crown Theatre and once or twice in the roadhouse out of town. There are the parties on Friday night at the girls' houses. He even goes steady for a part of the year.

And always the cheer leading. He squats, does knee-bends in the white flannel pants, the rough white sweater not quite warm enough in the fall winds. Before him the one thousand kids are yelling, the girls in their green plaid skirts jumping up and down, their knees red from the cold.

Let's give a Cardley for the team, he shouts, running up and down with the megaphone. There is the pause, the respectful hush while he extends one arm, swings it over his head, and brings it down.

CARDLEY HIGH . . . CARDLEY HIGH.

HIIIIIIIIII SCORE   HIIIIIIII SCHOOOOOL

YAAAAAAAAY TEAM!

And the kids are yelling, watching him as he does a cartwheel, comes up clapping his hands, his body turned toward the playing field in an attitude of devotion, of pleading. It's all his. One thousand kids awaiting on him.

One of the glory moments that you pull out later.

In the lag between basketball season and baseball, he takes his car apart, installs a muffler (he is tired of the sound of the exhaust) greases the gear housing, and paints the chassis a pale green.

There are important conversations with his father.

We have to be thinking seriously of what you want to do, Willie.

I've kinda set my mind on engineering, Pop. (This is no surprise. They've talked of it many times, but this occasion there's the tacit understanding that it's Serious.)

Well, now, I'm glad to hear that, Willie. I don't want to say I've ever tried to form your opinion for you, but I couldn't ask for anything better.

I really like machinery.

I've noticed that, Son. (The pause) It's aeronautical engineering that interests you?

I think it's gonna be the field.

549

It is, Son, I think it's a good choice. That's an up-and-coming business. His father claps him on the shoulder. I want to mention one thing though, Willie. I noticed you been getting a little cocky, nothing to speak about, and you keep your manners with us, but it's not a good policy, Son. It's perfectly all right to know that you can do something better'n the next man, but it isn't good sense to let the other man know it.

Never thought of it that way. He shakes his head. Listen, Pop, it's nothin' serious, but I'll watch it from now on. (An insight) Really learned something from you there.

The father chuckles, quite pleased. Sure, Willie, the old man can still tell you a thing or two.

You're a swell guy, Pop. The whole thing is warm between them. He feels himself coming of age, the equal ready to talk to his father as a friend.

That summer he works at the Crown Theatre as an usher. It's a pleasant job. He knows at least half the people who come there, and he can talk to them for a few minutes before he shows them a seat. (It's a good idea to be friends with everybody; you never can tell when you'll want a favor from a man.)

Indeed, the only dull times are in the afternoons when hardly anyone is there. Usually there's a few girls to talk to, but since he has broken up with his senior year sweetheart he is not interested. I don't want any wedding bells, he always wisecracks.

One day, however, he meets Beverly. (The slim dark-eyed, dark-haired girl on the left with the exciting red mouth she has penciled over her lips.) How'd you like the picture, Gloria? he asks the other one.

I thought it was a mighty sorry picture.

Yeah, it's awful. Hello. (To Beverly.)

Hello, Willie.

He smiles blankly. How do you know me?

Oh, I was the year behind you in school. I remember you from the cheer leaders.

The introductions, the bright talk. Bridling pleasantly. So you knew me, huh?

Everybody knows you, Willie.

Yeah, ain't it tough? They laugh.

Before she leaves, he has made a date.

The hot summer nights, the languor of the trees, the leaven in the earth. After the dates they ride in his car to a park at the crest of a hill on the highway outside the suburb. Inside the car they roll and squirm, bang their knees and their backs against the gearshift, the steering wheel, the knobs for the windows.

Aw come on, baby, I won't do a thing if you won't let me but come on.

No, I can't, I better not.

God, I love you, Beverly.

I do too, Willie. (The car radio is playing when it rains it rains . Pennies from Heaven. Her hair has a clean root smell, and her nipple is delicately fragrant against his mouth. He feels her writhing in his grasp, sobbing-panting.)

Oh, kid.

I can't, Willie, I love you so much please I can't.

I wish we were married.

Oh, do I. (Nuzzling his hair with her mouth) Ohhh.

The analyses: You made her yet, Willie?

I got to third base last night, I'll make her yet. Oh, what a dame.

What'd she do?

She moaned. Jeez, I go for her. I made her moan.

Aaah, if they won't put out.

Folklore: If she won't lay she's frigid; if she does she's a whore.

I'll make her yet. Don't forget she's cherry. (Way back is a sneaking guilt — I love you, Beverly.)

Talking serious: You know I dreamt about you last night, Willie.

Me too. You know that movie we saw the other day, *Captain Blood*, I thought Olivia de Haviland looked like you. (Identification with the square of canvas in the dark cavern. His love is perfect like theirs.)

You're sweet. (Ineffable attraction of the girl playing mother. The red bow of her lips.) If you weren't so sweet I wouldn't . . . go so far. You don't have a bad opinion of me?

No. (Teasing.) I'd have a better one if . . . you know.

Uh-uh, momma knows best. (Silence, her head on his shoulder.) I feel funny when I start thinking of us.

Me too.

Do you suppose everybody is like us? I wonder if Madge pets the way I do, she always giggles when I try to pump her. (Augury of the practical woman) Something fishy there. (The maiden again) Don't you feel funny when you start thinking about things?

Yeah, it's all very . . . funny. (But said profoundly.)

I feel much older since I've known you, Willie.

I know what you mean. Gee, it's swell talking to you. (She has so many virtues; she feels so soft, and her mouth excites him so, and she's a good dancer, looks swell in a bathing suit, and besides that she's intelligent. He can talk to her. No one else had it like this. He glows with the intoxicating esteem of first love.) Oh, Beverly.

At the State University he is accepted in a good frat, is disappointed vaguely because initiations are forbidden. (He sees himself as a senior conducting it.) But it is fine. He learns to smoke a pipe, is introduced to the rewards of college life. Brother Brown as a pledgee in good standing of Tau Tau Epsilon we will preside over the circumsional rites. In the vernacular you will lose your cherry.

The brothel is expensive, catering to the college. He has heard of it before, is drunk enough to acquit himself without fear. Afterward in the college quadrangle he sings. Once in a While . . . Wheeeee-hooooooooh. Once in a while, get it, Father Perkins.

Quiet.

You're a good sonofabitch. (A new theme.)

He never means to slip, he has the best intentions in the world, but somehow drafting, freshman trig, freshman physics, etc., etc., is a little less vital than he has imagined. He tries to study, but there are better things. A man wants to get out after spending the whole after-noon in a lab.

The glamour of getting plastered on beers in the local tavern, the long deep conversation. I got a girl, Bert, I tell you she can't be beat. She's beautiful, look at her picture. It's a goddam shame the helling around I do, cheating on her and writing lovey-dovey letters.

Hell, boy, she ain't missin' any bets either.

Now, don't say that, or I'm gonna take offense. She's pretty god-dam pure.

All right, all right, just take it from my point of view. What she don't know won't hurt her.

He considers this, begins to giggle. I gotta tell ya the truth, that's the way I feel about it. Have a beer.

I wish I could tell you boys (slightly drunk) just what the hell this is all gonna mean to us years from now. We're storin' up memo-ries, and that's a fact. They ain't, all right I said ain't even if I am in college, but shit I'm just plain folks, they ain't a one of you I'll ever forget, that's the goddam Lesbian truth.

What the hell you talkin' about, Brown?

Damn if I know. (Laughter.) Tee hell with the physics test to-morrow. I just got helling in my blood.

Amen.

In June, after he has flunked out, it is hard to face his father, but he comes back with resolutions.

Listen, Pop, I know I've been an awful disappointment to you, and it's a damn shame after all your sacrifices, but I just don't think I'm cut out for that kind of work. I ain't gonna make any apologies about my intelligence 'cause I still think it's as good as anyone's my age, but I'm the kind of a fellow who needs something he can get his teeth into better. I believe I'm cut out for selling or something like that. I like to be around people.

(The long sigh) Maybe, maybe. No use cryin' over spilt milk is what I say. I'll talk to some of my friends.

He gets a job with a farm-machinery company, is making fifty dollars a week before his first year is out. He introduces Beverly to his folks, takes her to see Patty, who is now married.

Do you think she liked me? Beverly asks.

Sure she did.

They're married in the summer, and settle down in a six-room house. He's up to seventy-five dollars, but they're always a little in debt; liquor runs to twenty or twenty-five dollars a week counting what it costs them to go out.

Still, they don't have a bad time. The wedding night is a shambles but he recovers quickly, and after a decent interval their lovemaking is rich and various. They have a secret catalogue:

Lovemaking on the stairs.

Beverly's profanity in heat.

Experimenting with costumes.

——————————. (He will not give it a name because he has heard it in places he would not mention to her. She will not because she's not supposed to know it.)

And of course there are the other things that seem to have no relation. Eating meals together until it gets boring.

Hearing each other tell the same stories to different people.

His habit of picking his nose.

Her habit of adjusting her stockings on the street.

The sound he makes when he spits into a handkerchief.

The way she gets sullen after an evening of doing nothing.

There are mild pleasures too: Discussing the people they meet.

Relating the gossip about their friends.

Dancing together. (Merely because they are good dancers. A random phenomenon.)

Telling her his business worries.

There are neutral things: Riding in their automobile.

Her bridge and mah-jongg club.

His clubs: The Rotary, the High School Alumni Association, the Junior Chamber of Commerce.

Going to church.

The radio

554

The movies.

At times when he is restless he has a bad habit of spending an evening with his bachelor friends.

Bachelor Folklore: The only thing I got against marriage is people are just too uninteresting to be forced to spend their lives together.

Brown: You don't know what you're sayin'. Wait'll it's there for you, nice and steady, an' not worryin' about gettin' caught. The thing to do with women is to try it . . .

Folklore (dirty jokes): Sacrebleu, the ninety-eighth way

The middle of the night: Now, go 'way, leave me alone, Willie, I thought we agreed to lay off for a couple of days.

Who did?

You. You said we were getting too used to it.

Forget what I said.

Ohhhh. (Exasperation and submission.) You're just an old hound dog, that's all you are. Always wanting to put it in something. (The alloy of tenderness and irritation, unique to marriage.)

There are external shocks. His sister, Patty, gets a divorce, and he hears talk, merely the faintest suggestions, but he is worried. He asks her, subtly he thinks, but she flares at him.

What do you mean, Willie, Brad coulda had the divorce instead of me?

I don't mean anything, I'm just asking you.

Listen, Willie-boy, you don't have to be looking at me thataway. I am what I am, that's all, you understand?

The shock enters, burrows deeply, and explodes sporadically for months to follow. There are times in the middle of the day when he halts in the middle of a report, catches himself looking at his pencil. *You're not such a roughneck,* Patty says, slim and crisp and virginal, the older sister — half mother.

Memory as the flagellant. I don't understand it a goddam bit. What the hell makes them change that way, why can't a woman stay decent?

You'll never be like that, will you, Beverly? he says that night.

Aw, no, honey, how can you even think it?

They are very close for the moment, and his troubles spill out. Honestly, Bev, keeping up with everything makes me go so goddam fast; I get so I just want to take a breath, you know what I mean. A man's own sister, it puts quite a stir in you.

In the barrooms, in the smoking cars, in the locker room at the golf club they are talking about Patty Brown.

I swear, Bev, I ever catch you in anything like that, I'll kill you, so help me I'll kill you.

Honey? You can trust me. But she is thrilled by the sudden burst of his passion.

I feel a hell of a lot older, Bev.

On the eighteenth he lines up the putt, estimates the roll of the green. It is a five-foot shot and he should make it, but he knows suddenly that he's going to fail. The handle of the putter thonks dully against his palms as the ball rolls short a foot.

Missed again, son, Mr. Cranborn says.

Just not my day, I guess. We might as well get back to the locker room. His palms still hold a numb uncertain feeling. They stroll back slowly. You come to Louisville, son, and it'll be a pleasure to take you out to my club, Mr. Cranborn says.

I might take you up on it, sir.

As they shower, Mr. Cranborn is singing *"When you wore a tulip and I wore a . . ."*

What're we doin' tonight, son?

We'll just do the town, Mr. Cranborn; you don't have to worry, I'll show you around.

I've heard a good deal about this town.

Yes, sir, well, most of it's true. (The lewd cackle from the adjacent shower.)

In the night club they talk business. Every time he leans back he can feel the potted palm against his hair so that he finds himself leaning forward breathing the smoke from Mr. Cranborn's cigar. Well, you got to see, sir, that we're entitled to a little profit, I mean after

556

all that's what makes the wheels of business go round, and you wouldn't want us to be working for you for nothing with our product any more than you'd want to work for someone else. That'd hardly be business, now, would it? The fifth drink is almost empty, and his jaws clamp spongily. The cigarette is a little remote from his lips. (I gotta slow down on the drinking.)

A good point, son, a good point, but there's also the question of making something cheaper than the next feller, and that's business too, competition. You're out for yourself, and I'm out for myself, and that's the way things work.

Yes, sir, I see what you mean. For a moment the whole thing is in danger of revolving and revolving in his head, and he thinks of flailing out, breathing some air. Let's look at it from this angle.

Who's that little blonde girl in the show, Brown? Know her?

(He doesn't.) Well, yes, sir, but frankly you wouldn't be wanting to know her. She's gone to the well a little too often and, well, frankly there's doctors involved. I know a place though, sir, decent respectable.

In the lobby the hat-check girl can hear him phoning. He leans against the wall in danger of supporting himself with his face against the phone. The line is busy, and for an instant he wants to cry.

Hello, Eloise? he asks. The woman's voice crackles at him from the other end.

It's more fun being out with the gang from the office on a tear.

I tell ya I never saw anything like it, picking up a half dollar like that, why, she just picked it right off the edge of the table. I suppose if it wasn't the place where I saw it you'd have to go to Paris or a nigger whorehouse anyway.

It takes all kinds to make a world.

Yeh, that's about the way I look at it, there's a lot of things go on in people's heads you don't know nothing about

What do you figure goes on in the Chief's head?

Uh-uh, we ain't talking shop tonight, that's understood. Come on, let's start a round going.

They drink up, exhaust the circle of rounds owed.

557

I'm going to tell you men something, Brown says, a lot of people think we might have a soft job selling, but the God's honest truth of it is that we work hard as any man jack, am I right?

None harder.

Exactly. Now when I was up at the university before I flunked out, I flunked out I want you to know 'cause I think a man's a goddam fool if he's got false pride, I don't believe in making out you're exactly what you ain't. I'm as ordinary as an old shoe and I'll admit it to anyone who asks me.

Brown, you're a good old sonofabitch.

Well, now, I'm glad to hear you say that, Jennings, because I know you mean it, and it means a lot. A man works his fool ass off and he wants to have some friends, people he knows will trust him and like him, 'cause if he ain't got that what's the point to his working?

That's exactly it.

I'm pretty fortunate, I'll say that to any man in his face, but of course I've had my troubles, who the hell hasn't, but we're not here to cry about that tonight, now, are we? I want to tell you men, I got a beautiful wife, now, that's the truth.

One of the gang guffaws. Brown, I got a beautiful wife too, but I swear after you been married two years a woman might just as well look like a coon dog for all the good it does you.

I can't quite agree, Freeman, but there's a point to what you say. He feels his words dribbling out of his mouth, lost in the babel of glasses and conversation.

Come on, let's be goin' over to Eloise's.

And the inevitable coming back.

Freeman, you said something a while ago that kinda put a stir in me, but I want to tell you I got a beautiful wife, and there's no one could improve on her a bit. I think it's a goddam shame the way we go around screwing God knows what, and then goin' back to our wives, it's a helluva note I want to tell you that. When I think of her and then what I do I'm pretty goddam ashamed of myself.

It's a hell of a note.

Exactly. You'd think we have some sense, but the damn truth of it is we just go around screwing and drinking and . . .

558

And having a hell of a good time.

Having a hell of a good time, Brown finishes. That's exactly what I was gonna say, Jennings, but you beat me to it. He stumbles, sits down on the pavement.

Helluva note.

He wakes up in his bed with Beverly undressing him. I know what you're gonna say, honey, he mumbles, but I got my troubles, you just keep pushing something through, trying to make ends meet, trying to produce 'cause that's what you gotta pay off on, and it takes a long time, it's, it's a hard life, as the preacher says.

And in the morning, massaging his headache, examining an estimate, he wonders what Beverly did last night.

(The sly winks, the droll expressions of anguish among the men who had gone out the night before. At ten in the lavatory, Freeman joins him.)

Oh, what a bag I got on.

I feel rocky today, Brown says. What the hell we do it for?

Got to get out of the rut, I guess.

Yeah. *Oh, man!*

6

THIS SAME night, on the other side of the mountain range, Cummings was making a tour of his positions. The attack had been progressing favorably for a day and a half, and his line companies had advanced from a quarter to a half mile. The division was moving again, more successfully than he had expected, and the long wet month of inactivity and stagnation seemed to have ended. F Company had made contact with the Toyaku Line, and according to the last report Cummings had received that afternoon, a reinforced platoon from E Company had captured a Japanese bivouac on F Company's flank. For the next few days the attack would teeter from enemy counterattacks, but if they held, and he was going to see that they held, the Toyaku Line might be breached within two weeks.

Secretly, he was a little surprised at the advance. He had prepared the attack for over a month, hoarded his supplies, revised his battle plans from day to day through all the eventless weeks that had followed the aborted Japanese attack across the river. He had done everything a commander could do, and yet he had been gloomy. The memory of the bivouacs at the front with their covered foxholes and duckwalks through the mud had depressed him more than once; it spoke with such finality of the men sitting down to rest permanently, implacably.

He knew now he was wrong. The lessons learned from every campaign were different, and he had absorbed an obscure but basic axiom. If the men settled down long enough they became restless, ennuied to the point of courage again by the drab repetition of their days. It's a mistake to relieve a company which has not been advancing, he told himself. Just let them sit in the mud long enough, and they'll attack through their own volition. It was fortuitous that his battle orders had been launched at a time when the men were eager to move ahead again, but deep in his mind he knew he had been lucky. He had misjudged their morale completely.

If I had a few company commanders who were perceptive, the whole process would be simpler, more responsive, and yet it's too much to ask sensitivity of a CO besides all the other things he has to have. No, it's my fault, I should have seen it in spite of them. Perhaps for this reason the early success of the attack gave him little elation. He was pleased, naturally enough, because his greatest burden had been removed. The pressure from Corps had relaxed, and the fear that for a time had colored everything — that he would be relieved of his command in the middle of the campaign — had retreated now, and would expire if the advance continued favorably. Still he had substituted one dissatisfaction for another. Cummings was bothered by a suspicion, very faint, not quite stated, that he had no more to do with the success of the attack than a man who presses a button and waits for the elevator. It muddied the edges of his satisfaction, angered him subtly. The odds were that the attack would bog down sooner or later in any case, and when he left tomorrow for Army, this present success was going to hurt his chances of getting naval support for the

Botoi Bay operation. In effect he would have to commit himself, claim that the campaign could be won only by that side invasion, and there would be the ticklish business of having to undercut, disparage the advances he had made already.

Nevertheless, things had changed. Reynolds had sent him a confidential memo that Army might not frown completely on the Botoi idea now, and when he saw them he could maneuver it. That type of favor was manageable.

In the meantime he had been playing the fraud with himself, he knew. All day as he had sat in the operations tent, reading the reports that had come in, he had been a little annoyed. He had felt like a politician on election night, he thought, who was watching the party candidate win and feeling chagrined because he had tried to nominate another man. The damn thing was unimaginative, stale, any commander could have mounted it as successfully, and it would be galling to admit that Army was right.

But of course they weren't. There was going to be trouble ahead, and they refused to accept it. For a moment Cummings thought of the reconnaissance patrol he had sent to the other side of the mountain, and he shrugged. If that came off, if they brought back a report of some value, if indeed he could manage to send a company over their route, and pull off the Botoi Bay invasion that way, it would be fine, impressive. But there were too many chances against it. The best thing was to dismiss Hearn's patrol from his calculations until it returned.

Despite all his internal objections he had been busy, he had given all his attention to the advance, concentrated on all the reports that came in. It had been exhausting, demanding work, and by nightfall he was tired, needed some diversion. Almost always when the division was in action he found it stimulating to tour the front daily, but at night now it would be impossible for him to inspect the infantry positions. He decided instead to visit his artillery bivouacs.

Cummings phoned for his jeep and driver, and about eight P.M. he set out on the road. The moon was almost full. He relaxed in the front seat of the jeep, and watched the play of the headlights against the jungle foliage. They were far enough behind the lines to avoid blacking out, and the General smoked idly, feeling the wind wash

561

pleasantly against his face. He felt drained, yet still tense; the passing sentient traces of the ride, the sound of the motor, the jouncing against the seat cushions, the smell of his cigarette, lulled him, caressed his nerves like a warm lapping bath. He began to feel cheerful and pleasantly empty.

After a fifteen-minute ride, they reached a battery of 105s off the side of the road. On an impulse he told his driver to turn in, and the jeep jounced over a crude culvert made by aligning empty gasoline drums in a ditch and covering them with earth. The wheels sloughed through the mud of the motor pool, and they came to a halt on a stretch of relatively dry earth. The guard at the entrance had phoned the Captain, who came up to the jeep to meet the General.

"Sir?"

Cummings nodded. "Just looking around. How's the battery coming?"

"Fine, sir.'

"Service Battery was supposed to bring up two hundred rounds about an hour ago. You get them?"

"Yes, sir." The Captain paused. "Have your touch on everything, don't you, sir?"

This pleased Cummings. "Have you told the men how successful the battalion concentration was this afternoon?" he asked.

"I did say something about it, sir."

"You can't emphasize it enough. When the men have completed a good fire mission, it's smart to tell them so. It's good for the men to have a sense of participation."

"Yes, sir."

The General strode away from the jeep with the Captain tagging at his side. "Your routine orders are for harassing fire every fifteen minutes, is that correct?"

"Since last night, sir."

"How're you resting your cannoneers?"

The Captain smiled deprecatingly. "I've cut the gun crews in half, sir, and each half-squad is on for an hour, firing four missions. That way the men miss only an extra hour's sleep."

"I think that's a pretty good setup," the General agreed. They

562

crossed a small clearing which contained the battery mess tent and the orderly room tent. In the moonlight the tents were silver, and their roofs sloped upward precipitously to give them the appearance of miniature cathedrals. They passed through, and walked along a footpath which cut for fifty feet through a patch of brush. On the other side the four howitzers were extended in a short battery front, not more than fifty yards separating the two flank pieces, their muzzles pointing above the jungle in the direction of the Japanese lines. The moonlight played over them in random mottled patches, tracing over the barrel and trails the stippled outline of the leaves above. Behind the guns five squad tents were dispersed irregularly in the brush, almost blending into the deep shadows of the jungle. This was virtually the entire battery: the motor pool, the supply and mess, the howitzers, and the tents. The General surveyed it, scrutinized the few cannoneers who sprawled between the trails of one of the 105s, and had a mild nostalgia. For a moment or two he was weary, felt an unimportant passing regret that he could not be a cannoneer himself with only his belly to be filled, and nothing more odious to consider than the labor of digging a gun emplacement. A curious uncharacteristic mood mounted in him, and furnished a new kind of self-pity, a gentle indulgent one.

In the squad tent he could hear an occasional burst of laughter, a few raucous jeers.

Always, he had had to be alone, he had chosen it that way, and he would not renege now, nor did he want to. The best things, the things worth doing in the last analysis, had to be done alone. The moments like these, the passing doubts, were the temptations that caught you if you were not careful. Cummings stared at the vast dark bulk of Mount Anaka, visible in the darkness as a deeper shadow, a greater mass than the sky above it. It was the axis of the island, its keystone.

There's an affinity, he told himself. If one wanted to get mystical about it, the mountain and he understood each other. Both of them, from necessity, were bleak and alone, commanding the heights. Tonight, Hearn might have negotiated the pass, be traveling under the shadow of Anaka itself. He felt an odd pang, composed of anger and expectation, not quite certain whether he wanted Hearn to succeed.

The problem of what he must do with him eventually was still not settled, could not be unless Hearn did not come back. And again he was uncertain what he felt, was mildly troubled.

The Captain disturbed his reverie. "We're going to fire in a minute, sir. Would you like to watch?"

The General started. "Yes." He strolled beside the Captain to the artillery piece about which the cannoneers were grouped. As they approached, the men finished adjusting the piece, and one of them loaded the long slim shell into the breech. They became silent, stiffened, as Cummings approached, standing about awkwardly, their hands behind their backs, uncertain whether to come completely to attention. "At ease, men," Cummings said.

"All set, DiVecchio?" one of them asked.

"Yeah."

The General looked at DiVecchio, a short squat man with his sleeves rolled up, and a tangle of black hair covering his forehead. City-runt, the General thought with a mixture of condescension and contempt.

One of them giggled roughly out of embarrassment and constraint. They were all conscious of him, terribly conscious, he realized, like youths outside a cigarette store, ill at ease because a woman was talking to them. If I had just walked by, they would have muttered, perhaps even jeered at me. It gave him an odd sharp pleasure almost thrilling.

"I think *I'll* fire the gun, Captain," he said.

The cannoneers stared at him. One of them was humming to himself. "You men mind if I fire the gun?" the General asked pleasantly.

"Huh?" DiVecchio asked. "Naw, why no, sir."

The General walked over to the position of No. 1 man outside the trails by the elevating mechanism, and grasped the lanyard. It was a foot-length of cord with a knob at the end. "How many seconds, Captain?"

"Fire in five seconds, sir." The Captain had looked at his watch nervously.

The knob of the lanyard hefted pleasantly in the General's palm.

564

He stared at the complicated obscured mechanism of the breech and the carriage springs, his mind hovering delicately between anxiety and excitement. Automatically he had posed his body in a relaxed confident posture; it was instinctive with him to appear unconcerned whenever he was doing something unfamiliar. The mass of the gun, however, troubled him; he had not fired an artillery piece since West Point, and he was remembering not the noise nor the concussion, but a time in World War I when he had been under an artillery barrage for two hours. It had been the most powerful single fear of his life, and an echo of it now was rebounding through his mind. Just before he fired he could see it all, the sharp detumescent roar of the gun, the long soaring plunge of the shell through the night sky, its downward whistle, and the moments of complete and primordial terror for the Japanese at the other end when it landed. An odd ecstasy stirred his limbs for a moment, was gone before he was quite aware of it.

The General pulled the lanyard.

The muzzle blast deafened him momentarily, left him shaken and numb by its unaccustomed force. He felt rather than saw the great twenty-foot flambeau of flame that discharged from the muzzle, heard dumbly the long billowing murmurs of the discharge through the dark closeted aisles of the jungle. The balloon tires, the trails were still vibrating gently from the recoil.

It had all taken a fraction of a second. Even the backward blast of wind had passed him, roiled his hair and closed his eyes before he was conscious of it. The General was recovering his sense-impressions by degrees, clutching at them in the wake of the explosion like a man chasing his hat in a gale. He took a breath, smiled, heard himself say in an even voice, "I wouldn't like to be at the other end." He noticed the cannoneers, the Captain, after he spoke. He had said it because a part of his mind always considered the objective situation; consciously he had been unaware of the men about him as he talked. He strode away slowly, drawing the Captain with him.

"Artillery is a bit more impressive at night," he murmured. His poise was addled slightly. He would not have said this to a stranger if he were still not absorbed in the impact of firing the howitzer.

565

"I know what you mean, sir. I always get a kick out of firing the battery at night."

Then it was all right. Cummings realized he had almost made a slip. "Your battery seems in good order, Captain."

"Thank you, sir."

But he was not listening. The General was paying attention to the silent rhapsodic swoop of the shell, was following it in his mind's eye. How long did it take? Perhaps half a minute? His ears were alerted for the sound of its explosion.

"I never quite get over it, sir. It must be bloody hell at the other end."

Cummings was listening to the dull muted tones of the explosion, miles away in the jungle. He saw in his mind the bright destroying bouquet of flame, the screams and the rent iron singing through the air. I wonder if it killed anyone? he thought. He realized the tenseness with which he had been waiting for the shell to land by the weak absorptive relief that washed through his body. All his senses felt gratified, exhausted. The war, or rather, *war,* was odd, he told himself a little inanely. But he knew what it meant. It was all covered with tedium and routine, regulations and procedure, and yet there was a naked quivering heart to it which involved you deeply when you were thrust into it. All the deep dark urges of man, the sacrifices on the hilltop, and the churning lusts of the night and sleep, weren't all of them contained in the shattering screaming burst of a shell, the man-made thunder and light? He did not think these things coherently, but traces of them, their emotional equivalents, pictures and sensations, moved him into a state of acute sensitivity. He felt cleaned in an acid bath, and all of him, even his fingertips, was prepared to grasp the knowledge behind all this. He dwelt pleasurably in many-webbed layers of complexity. The troops out in the jungle were disposed from the patterns in his mind, and yet at this moment he was living on many levels at once; in firing the gun he was a part of himself. All the roaring complex of odors and sounds and sights, multiplied and re-multiplied by all the guns of the division, was contained in a few cells of his head, the faintest crease of his brain. All of it, all the violence, the dark co-ordination had sprung from his mind. In the night, at that

566

moment, he felt such power that it was beyond joy; he was calm and sober.

Later, returning to his headquarters in the jeep, he was in an excellent mood. His body was still keyed, still the least bit feverish, but the excitement it caused him went beyond restlessness, and charged his brain to intense activity. Yet it was random casual thought; he amused himself the way a child would sport in a toy store if given complete freedom to touch everything and cast it away when tired. Cummings was not unconscious of the process. Any new physical action always aroused him, infused his perceptions.

When he reached his tent, he looked cursorily at the few dispatches that had collected in his absence. He had no taste at this moment for going through them, for performing the detailed labors of digesting and committing to memory the important portions. For an instant he stepped outside his tent and breathed the night air again. The bivouac had become silent, almost ghostly, and the moonlight illumined the mists in the clearing, covered the foliage with a tenuous silver netting. In his mood everything familiar seemed unreal. How alien the earth is at night, he sighed.

In the tent, he hesitated a moment, and then unlocked a small green filing cabinet on the side of his desk, removing from it a heavy notebook bound in black like a law ledger. It was a journal in which he had jotted down his private ideas for many years. There had been a time when he had told them to Margaret, but after the first year or two of their marriage, when they had turned away from each other, the importance of the journal had increased, and in the years that had followed he had filled many ledgers, sealed them, and stored them away.

Yet when he wrote in it, the journal always had a touch of the clandestine as though he were a boy locking himself with guilty anticipation in the bathroom. On a higher level, many of his feelings were the same — almost unconsciously he would prepare an excuse in case he was discovered. "If you'll wait a moment, Major [or Colonel or Lieutenant], I'm just jotting some memorandum."

Now he turned to the first blank page in his journal, held his pencil, and thought for a moment or two. Any number of new ideas and impressions had evolved on the trip back from the battery, and he waited, knowing his mind would produce them again. Once more he experienced the smooth ovoid surface of the lanyard handle. Like holding the beast at the end of a string, he thought.

The image set off a round of ideas. He inscribed the date at the head of the page, rolled his pencil once between his fingertips, and began to write.

> It's a not entirely unproductive conceit to consider weapons as being something more than machines, as having personalities, perhaps, likenesses to the human. The artillery tonight started it all in my mind, but how much it is like a generative process except that its end is so different.

The imagery was a little unfamiliar to him; he noted the sexual symbols with some distaste, thought of DiVecchio.

> The howitzer like a queen bee I suppose being nurtured by the common drones. The phallus-shell that rides through a shining vagina of steel, soars through the sky, and then ignites into the earth. The earth as the poet's image of womb-mother, I suppose.
>
> Even the language for artillery commands, the obviously coarse connotations. Perhaps it satisfies an unconscious satisfaction in us serving the Death-Mother. *Spread trails, level your bubbles, lay the piece.* I recall that training class I inspected, the amusement of the trainees at that terminology, and the junior officer saying, "If you can't put the shell in that big hole, I don't know what you'll do when you get older." Perhaps it's a notion worth analyzing. Any psychoanalytical work on it?
>
> But there are other weapons too. These booby traps in Europe that the Germans use, or even our own experience at Hill 318 on Motome. Dangerous things like a plague of vermin, squat black ugly little things, undermining the men with nausea and horror until the act of straightening a picture might make one weep — from anticipation of the explosion or the fear that a few dark roaches might dart across the wall from the space one has uncovered.
>
> The tank and truck like the heavy ponderous animals of the

jungle, buck and rhinoceri, the machine gun as the chattering gossip snarling many lives at once? Or the rifle, the quiet personal arm, the extension of a man's power. Can't we relate all of them?

And for the obverse, in battle, men are closer to machines than humans. A plausible acceptable thesis. Battle is an organization of thousands of man-machines who dart with governing habits across a field, sweat like a radiator in the sun, shiver and become stiff like a piece of metal in the rain. We are not so discrete from the machine any longer, I detect it in my thinking. We are no longer adding apples and horses. A machine is worth so many men; the Navy has judged it even more finely than we. The nations whose leaders strive for Godhead apotheosize the machine. I wonder if this applies to me.

He sat back and lit a cigarette. The mantle in the Coleman lantern was beginning to buzz, and he sat up to adjust it, remembering for an instant Hearn's expression as he had sat before him asking for a transfer. The General shrugged, sat back again, staring at his desk. In transcribing his thought to paper it seemed somehow less profound, more contrived, and he was dissatisfied vaguely. He might have written no more, but the image of Lieutenant Hearn upset him, almost uncovered a trap door of his mind. He pushed back the picture resolutely, drew a line under his last sentence, and began to write about something else.

I was considering a little earlier a rather fascinating curve whose connotations are quite various. The asymmetrical parabola, the one which looks like this —

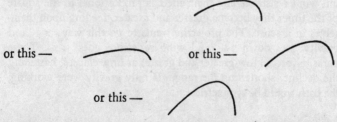

or this —   or this —

            or this —

Re: Spengler's plant form for all cultures (youth, growth, maturity, old age, or bud, bloom, wilt, decay). But the above curve is the form line of all cultures. An epoch always seems to reach its zenith at a point past the middle of its orbit in time. The fall is always more rapid than the rise. And isn't that the curve of tragedy; I should think it a sound aesthetic principle that the growth of a character should take longer to accomplish than his disaster.

But from another approach that form is the flank curve of a man or woman's breast.

Cummings halted, feeling an unaccustomed nervous play of needles along his back. The comparison disturbed him, and the first few sentences he wrote after this had little meaning to him.

. . . of a man or woman's breast, the fundamental curve of love, I suppose. It is the curve of all human powers (disregarding the plateau of learning, the checks upon decline) and it seems to be the curve of sexual excitement and discharge, which is after all the physical core of life.

What is this curve? *It is the fundamental path of any projectile,* of a ball, a stone, an arrow (Nietzsche's arrow of longing) or of an artillery shell. It is the curve of the death missile as well as an abstraction of the life-love impulse; it demonstrates the form of existence, and life and death are merely different points of observation on the same trajectory. The life viewpoint is what we see and feel astride the shell; it is the present, seeing, feeling, sensing. The death viewpoint sees the shell as a whole, knows its inexorable end, the point toward which it has been destined by inevitable physical laws from the moment of its primary impulse when it was catapulted into the air.

To carry this a step further, there are two forces constraining the projectile to its path. If not for them, the missile would forever rise on the same straight line. ↗ These forces are gravity and wind resistance and their effect is proportional to the square of the time; they become greater and greater, feeding upon themselves in a sense. The projectile wants to go this way ↗ and gravity goes down ↓ and wind resistance goes ← . These parasite forces grow greater and greater as time elapses, hastening the decline, shortening the range. If only gravity were working, the path would be symmetrical

⌒

it is the wind resistance that produces the tragic curve

⌒

570

In the larger meanings of the curve, gravity would occupy the place of mortality (what goes up must come down) and wind resistance would be the resistance of the medium . . . the mass inertia or the inertia of the masses through which the vision, the upward leap of a culture is blunted, slowed, brought to its early doom.

The General halted, looked blankly at his journal. One of the last phrases kept repeating in his mind with a cloying regularity. "The mass inertia or the inertia of the masses, the mass inertia or the . . ." He was disgusted abruptly.

I'm playing with words. All that he had written seemed meaningless, a conceit. He was filled with a powerful spasm of distaste for what he had written, and slowly with a heavy pressure of his pencil he drew a line through each of his sentences. In the middle of the page his pencil broke, and he flung it down and strode outside the tent, breathing a little quickly.

It had all been too pat, too simple. There was order but he could not reduce it to the form of a single curve. Things eluded him.

He stared about the silent bivouac, looked up at the stars of the Pacific sky, heard the rustle of the coconut trees. Alone, he felt his senses expanding again, lost the intimate knowledge of the size of his body. A deep boundless ambition leaped in him again, and if his habits had not been so deep he might have lifted his arms to the sky. Not since he had been a young man had he hungered so for knowledge. It was all there if only he could grasp it. To mold . . . mold the curve.

An artillery piece fired, shattering the loom of the night.
Cummings listened to its echoes and shuddered.

7

IN THE TWILIGHT the cliffs of Mount Anaka were glowing with reds and golds, reflecting back into the hills and fields at the base. In their bivouac what was left of the platoon was settling for the night. The four extra men who had gone along with Brown's detail for the first hour had returned now and were adjusting their blankets. Gallagher was on guard in the knoll that overlooked the hollow; the rest of the men were eating their ration or clumping a few yards into the grass to relieve themselves.

Wyman was brushing his teeth very carefully, sprinkling a few drops of water from his canteen onto the bristles and then massaging his gums thoughtfully.

"Hey, Wyman," Polack called, "turn on the radio for me, will ya?"

"Naah, I'm tired of listening to it," Minetta said.

Wyman flushed. "Listen, you guys, I'm still civilized," he piped. "If I want to brush my teeth I can."

"Not even his best friends will tell him," Minetta wisecracked.

"Aaah, go fug yourself, I'm sick of ya."

Croft stirred in his blankets, propped himself on an elbow. "Listen, you men, you can just shut up. You want to stir up a whole pack of Japs?"

What answer could there be? "Awright," one of them muttered.

Roth had heard them. Squatting in the grass, he peered over his shoulder fearfully. Behind him was nothing but the vast darkening sweep of the hills. He had to hurry up. The paper was in the ration carton, but even as he fumbled for it a new spasm caught him, and he grunted, held his thighs as the process worked its way through him.

"Jesus," he heard one of the men whisper, "who the hell's crapping, an elephant?"

To Roth's nausea and weakness was added embarrassment. He picked up the pad of tissues, finished, and drew up his pants. He was so weak. He lay down on his poncho and pulled a blanket over him. Why did this have to start now? he asked himself. For the first two days his bowels had been tight and heavy, but that was preferable to this. It's the nervous reaction from the bird, he told himself. Diarrhea is caused by nerves as much as by food. As if to prove his statement, his belly knotted, passed through a few moments of anguish. I'm going to have to go again during the night, he told himself. But it would be impossible. If he started moving in the darkness, the man on guard might shoot him. He would have to do it right next to his blankets. Roth's eyes teared with frustration and annoyance. It was unfair. He felt a deep bitterness at the Army for not having taken into account such situations. Ohhh. He held his breath, yoked his sphincter, while the perspiration ran into his eyes. There was an instant of panic when he was certain he would soil himself. These riffraff in the platoon had an expression, "to keep a tight ass-hole." What did they know of it? It's the only way they judge anybody, he told himself.

"When the shit hits the fan that's when you keep a . . ." This afternoon, all right, he had done it; he hadn't even thought about that.

But in remembering the skirmish at the entrance to the pass, he felt a helpless anxiety. He had ducked behind the ledge, and even when Croft was yelling at them to fire, he hadn't done anything at all. He wondered if Croft had noticed, and hoped he had been too busy. He'll really have it in for me if he did.

And Wilson. Roth pressed his face against the damp rubbery texture of the poncho. He had not thought about Wilson at all until now — even when they had brought him back to the hollow and had prepared the stretcher, he had been playing with the bird. He had seen him but he hadn't wanted to look at him. Only now, Wilson was so clear to him. His face had been white, and his uniform was covered with blood. It was horrible. Roth was shocked, a little sick, as he remembered how very red the blood had been. I thought it was darker somehow . . . arterial . . . venous . . . ? Oh, what does it matter?

Wilson had always been so alive, and he wasn't a bad fellow. He was very friendly. It was impossible. One moment, and then . . . So badly wounded; he had looked dead when they brought him in. It was difficult to conceive, Roth thought, and then shuddered uncontrollably. What if the bullet had hit me? Roth saw the blood rippling brilliantly out of a deep hole in his body. Ooh, the wound was like a mouth, it was horrible looking. To add to his misery his stomach began to churn, and he lay on his chest, retching feebly.

Oh, this was awful, he had to get his mind off it.

He looked at the man lying beside him. It was almost entirely dark, and he could barely make out his features.

"Red?" he whispered softly.

"Yeah?"

He caught himself from saying, "Are you awake?" Instead, he propped himself on an elbow. "You feel like talking?" he asked.

"I don't give a damn, I can't sleep anyway."

"It's overfatigue that causes it; we've been going too fast."

Red spat. "If you want to bitch, tell it to Croft."

"No, I think you misunderstood me." He was silent for a moment, and then could hold it no longer. "That was terrible what happened to Wilson."

Red started. He had been brooding about it ever since he had got into his bedding. "Aaah, you can't kill that old sonofabitch Wilson."

"You think so?" Roth was relieved. "Only there was so much blood over him."

"What the fug did ya expect to see — milk?" Roth irritated him; anyone, everyone would have irritated him tonight. Wilson was one of the old men in the platoon. Why the hell did it have to be him? Red thought. The old anxiety, the basic one was working. He liked Wilson; Wilson was perhaps his best friend in the platoon, but that didn't count; he allowed himself to like no one so well that it would hurt if he was lost. But Wilson had been in the platoon as long as himself. It was different when a replacement was knocked off, just as it meant much less when a man from another platoon was killed. That didn't affect you, that didn't touch your safety. If Wilson was gone, his turn was next. "Listen, that big sonofabitch had to stop a bullet sometime. How the hell can you miss him?"

"Only it happened so suddenly."

Red snorted. "When it's your turn I'll send you a telegram."

"You shouldn't say that even in kidding."

"Aaaah." Red shuddered unaccountably. The moon was coming out, limning the slabs of the cliffs with silver. Lying on his back, he could see up the great slopes of the mountain almost to its peak. Nothing seemed right at this moment. He could even believe it might be bad luck to say such a thing to Roth. "Forget it," he said more softly.

"Oh, that's all right, no offense. I can understand how you're

wrought up. I can't even stop thinking about it myself. It's unbelievable. One moment a man's perfectly all right and then . . . I don't
understand it."

"You want to talk about something else?"

"I'm sorry." Roth halted. His wonder, the horror that supported it, was still unappeased. It was so easy for a man to be killed;
what he could not shake was his surprise. He twisted over on his back
to relieve the constraint on his stomach. He took a breath. "Oh, I'm
knocked out."

"Who isn't?"

"How does Croft keep going?"

"That sonofabitch likes it."

Roth's mind cowered as he thought of him. The episode with
the bird had come back to him, and he blurted, "Do you think Croft
is going to have a prejudice against me?"

"For the bird? I dunno, Roth, it's better not to waste your time
trying to figure him out."

"I wanted to tell you, Red, that . . ." Roth paused. His exhaustion, the enfeeblement of his diarrhea, all the aches and bruises, the
terror Wilson had caused him, all of it was working on him abruptly.
The fact that several men, that this man beside him, had come to his
aid after Croft had killed the bird overwhelmed him with self-pity
and gratitude and warmth. "I appreciate extensively what you did today about the bird." His voice caught.

"Aaah, forget it."

"No, I . . . I want to tell you that I appreciate it." To his utter
dismay, he found himself weeping.

"Jesus Christ." Red was touched for an instant, and he almost
extended his arm to clap Roth on the back. But he aborted the motion. Roth was like the mongrel dogs with shaggy moth-eaten hides
that had always gathered in the rubbish dumps or clustered around the
flophouses when the swill was thrown out. If you gave them a scrap
of food or a pat on the head, they would follow you for days, staring
at you with watery eyes of gratitude.

He wanted to be kind to Roth now, but if he did Roth would be
coming to him all the time, donating his confidences, making a touch

for sentiment. Roth would latch on to anyone who was friendly to him. He couldn't afford it; Roth was the kind of man who would stop a bullet soon.

And more than this; he didn't want to. There was something nasty, unclean, about the emotion Roth was showing. Red always curdled before emotion. "For Christ's sakes, man, cut it out," he snapped. "I don't give a goddam about you and your bird."

Roth stopped as if he had been slapped across the face. For a moment in his weeping he had been expecting the warm arms of his mother. They were gone now; everything was gone. He was alone. It gave him a bitter pleasure, as if in having plumbed this last rejection he knew at last that there was no further humiliation he could receive. The foundation stones of his despair were at least stones. Red could not see the bitter smile Roth assumed instinctively. "You can forget about it," Roth said, turning over on his side away from Red, staring through the tears in his eyes at the cold gaunt reaches of the mountain. His throat was hot when he swallowed. At least now there was nothing left to desire, he told himself. Even his boy would grow up to mock him and his wife would become more and more of a nag. No one appreciated him.

Red stared at Roth's back, still tempted to reach out to him. The small hunched shoulders, the stiffness with which Roth held himself worked as a reproof; Red was troubled and felt a little guilty. Why did I even help him with the goddam bird? he asked himself. Now it's gonna be between me and Croft. He sighed with fatigue. Sooner or later it had to come out between them. I ain't afraid anyway, Red told himself.

Wasn't he? He wondered, and then edged away from the question. He was weary and Roth's appeal had moved him despite himself. As often happened when he was very tired, his mind had become clear and he felt as if he understood everything, but at times like this the knowledge was always wistful, burdened with the exhaustion of living. He thought of Wilson, saw him very clearly for a moment as he had looked in the assault boat months before when they had invaded the island. "C'mon in, y'old billygoat, the water's nice an' cold," Wilson had shouted to him.

"Up yours," or it had been something like that he had answered, but what difference did it make? Wilson was a mile or two away, perhaps dead by now, where the hell did it all come out?

Aaah, everybody loses. Red almost said this aloud. It was true. He knew it, they all knew it, every one of them. He sighed again. They knew it, and yet they still were soft, still didn't get used to the idea.

Even if we do get back we'll get a fuggin. What did it matter if they ever got out of the Army? It would be the same thing on the outside. Nothing ever turns out the way you want it. And yet they weren't really tough, they still believed it would all be perfect in the end, they separated all the golden grains in the sand and looked at them, only at them — with a magnifying glass. He did it himself, and he had nothing to look forward to but a succession of barren little towns and rented rooms, of nights spent listening to men talk in barrooms. What would there be outside of a whore and some tremors in his groin?

Maybe I ought to get married, he thought, and snickered immediately afterward. What was the use? He had had his chance, and turned it down, he could have had Lois, and he skipped out on her. When you're like me you're scared to admit you're getting old. That was it, nice and simple. You started out with something, something they all had, and it was just pissed away. For an instant he remembered Lois getting up in the middle of the night to look at Jackie, and then coming back to bed, shuddering against him until her body warmed. His throat choked on it for an instant and he forced it back. He had nothing to give a woman, nothing to give anybody. What do you tell them, that it's all bloody noses? Even a wounded animal went away alone to die.

In affirmation, his kidneys were aching again.

Still he could see a time when these years he was living now would seem different, when he could laugh at the men he'd known in the platoon and remember the way the jungle and the hills sometimes looked in the dawn. He might even want the kind of tension there was in stalking a man. It was stupid. He hated this. He hated it more than anything he had ever done and yet if he lived he knew

577

that in the end it might turn mellow. The magnifying glass on the gold grains.

He grimaced. You always get caught. He had been caught himself once; with all he knew he had still got burned. He had believed a newspaper. The newspapers were written for guys like Toglio to believe in, and sure enough Toglio had got a million-dollar wound, and would go home, and make speeches for bond drives, believing every word of it. "Shall the GIs have died in vain?" He remembered an argument he had with Toglio about a clipping of an editorial one of the men received from his mother. "Did the GIs die in vain?"

He snorted. Who didn't know the answer? Of course they died in vain, any GI knew the score. The war just t.s. to them who had to fight it.

"Red, you're too cynical," Toglio had told him.

"Yeah, fighting a war to fix something works about as good as going to a whorehouse to get rid of a clap."

He stared up at the moon now. Maybe it did count for something. He didn't know, and there was no way he'd ever find out, no way any of them ever would. Aaah, just chalk it off, it's down the drain and who gives a goddam.

He wouldn't live long enough to find out anyway, he thought.

Hearn couldn't sleep either. He was extremely restless, and an odd febrile fatigue had settled in his legs. For almost an hour he turned over continually in his blanket, staring at the mountain, the moon above them, the hills, the ground before his face. Since the ambush, he had been feeling something, not exactly definable, but close to anxiety and unrest, and it had been driving him. It was almost painful to remain still. After a while he stood up, and walked through the hollow. The guard on the hilltop saw him and raised his rifle. He whistled softly, and then said, "Who is it — Minetta? This is the Lieutenant."

He climbed up the slope and sat down beside Minetta. Before them in the moonlight the grass swayed in silver waves over a valley and the hills looked like stone.

"What's up, Lootenant?" Minetta asked.

"Not a damn thing, just stretching my legs." They talked in whispers.

"Jesus, it's a bitch being on guard after that ambush."

"Yeah." Hearn massaged his legs, trying to soothe them.

"What're we doing tomorrow, Lootenant?"

Well, what were they doing? This was what he had to face. "What do you think, Minetta?"

"I think we ought to turn around and go back. The damn pass is closed, ain't it?" Minetta's voice, even muted, was indignant as if he had been thinking about this for a long time.

Hearn shrugged. "I don't know, maybe we will." He sat up there with Minetta for a few minutes more, and then went down into the hollow again, slipped under his blanket. It was as simple as that. Minetta had said it. Why didn't they turn around and go back, since the pass was closed?

All right, why?

The answer was simple enough. He didn't want to turn around and call the patrol off. Because . . . because . . . The motives this time would be shoddy enough. Hearn put his hands under his head and stared up at the sky.

The patrol no longer had the chance of a snowball in hell. Even if the pass were open now, the Japs would know where they were, guess their mission easily enough. If they ever got into the Japanese rear, it would be almost impossible to remain unobserved. Looking back on it now, the patrol had never had a chance of succeeding. This was one time Cummings had dropped the ball.

And he didn't want to go back, because it meant approaching Cummings with empty hands, excuses and failure. It was the supplies off the Liberty ship all over again. Kerrigan and Croft. That had been the thing that had been back of his actions the first two days; a liaison with the platoon — that was ridiculous. He had wanted to get along with them because it would increase the chances for the patrol's success. The truth was that he didn't give a damn about them if he plumbed himself. Through the fatigue, the exertion, the tug of war with Croft, the real motive had been to get a little of his own back from Cummings.

Was it revenge? Only it became even dirtier than that. For at the heart of it was not revenge but vindication. He wanted Cummings to approve of him again. Hearn turned over on his stomach.

Leadership!

It was as filthy as everything else. And he enjoyed it now. After the ambush, after the unique excitement, call it the unique ecstasy, of leading the men out of the field, he had been replaying those few minutes over and over again in his head, wishing it could happen again. Beyond Cummings, deeper now, was his own desire to lead the platoon. It had grown, ignited suddenly, become one of the most satisfying things he had ever done. He could understand Croft's staring at the mountain through the field glasses, or killing the bird. When he searched himself he was just another Croft.

That was it. All his life he had flirted with situations, jobs, where he could move men, and always, as if he had sensed the extent of the impulse within himself, he had moved away, dropped things when they were about to develop, cast off women because deep within him he needed control and not mating.

Cummings had once said, "You know, Robert, there really are only two kinds of liberals and radicals. There are the ones who are afraid of the world and want it changed to benefit themselves, the Jew liberalism sort of thing. And then there are the young people who don't understand their own desires. They want to remake the world, but they never admit they want to remake it in their own image."

It had been there all the time, partially realized, always submerged. It had a jingle to it.

Not a phony but a Faust.

Clear enough, and what was he going to do about it? Knowing this, he had no right to go on with the patrol; objectively he was playing with the lives of the nine men left, and he didn't deserve the responsibility. If there was anything worth while left in him, he would turn back in the morning.

There was the inner smirk. *He ought to, but he wouldn't.*

The shock, the self-disgust that followed this was surprising, almost pleasing in its intensity. He was almost horrified with this sick anguished knowledge of himself.

580

He *had* to turn back now.

Once more he got out of his blanket, and strode through the hollow to where Croft was sleeping. He knelt, about to shake him, when Croft turned toward him. "What you want, Lootenant?"

"You awake?"

"Yeah."

"I've decided to go back in the morning." Once he told Croft, he could not renege on himself.

The moonlight outlined the side of Croft's face, which was motionless. Perhaps his jaw muscle quivered. For several seconds he was quiet, and then he repeated, "Go back in the morning?" His legs were out of the blanket now.

"Yes."

"Don't you think we ought to look around a bit more?" Croft was stalling for time. He had been drowsing when Hearn came up, and the decision hurt him powerfully. His chest felt numb.

"What's the point to looking around?" Hearn asked.

Croft shook his head. There was the core of an idea, but he could not seize it. His mind, even his muscles, were tense, seeking for some handhold, some advantage. If Hearn had touched him at that instant, Croft would have shuddered. "We oughtn't to give up right away, Lootenant." His voice was husky. Slowly as he realized the situation, his hatred for Hearn was working again. He felt the same frustration that he had experienced when Hearn commanded him to apologize to Roth, or when he had gone to recover Wilson and had realized the entrance to the pass was empty.

The shadow of the idea passed through his mind again. He heard himself speaking with some surprise. "Lootenant, those Japs scooted after the ambush."

"How do you know?"

Croft told him about Wilson. "We could make it through now."

Hearn shook his head. "I doubt it."

"Ain't you even gonna give it a chance?" He was trying to understand Hearn's motive, and he realized dimly that Hearn was not turning back because he was afraid. The intuition frightened him, for if it were true, Hearn would be less likely to change his mind.

"I'm not going to take the platoon through the pass after what happened today."

"Well, why don't you send out one man tonight, let him make a reconnaissance? Goddam, that's the least we can do."

Hearn shook his head again.

"Or we could climb the mountain."

Hearn scratched his chin. "The men couldn't do it," he said finally.

Croft tried one last gambit. "Lootenant, if we could make this patrol okay, it might tie up the campaign, you never can tell."

The final factor in the equation. It was becoming too complicated. For there was a nub of truth in that, Hearn realized. If the patrol did succeed, it would be one of those tiny plus contributions to the war, one of the intangibles he had talked about a long time ago to the General. "How do you measure if it's better that the war end sooner and so many men go home, or if they all stay over here and go to pot?"

If the campaign ended soon, it would be concretely good for the men in the division. It was with that line of thought that he had decided to give up the patrol, help the men in the platoon. It was too complex to work out at this instant. There was only the necessity of answering Croft, who squatted inflexibly beside him like a sullen piece of metal, bending only slightly.

"All right, we'll send out one man tonight through the pass; if he runs into anything, we turn back." Was that rationalization? Really, was he only fooling himself, looking for another excuse to continue with the patrol?

"You want to go, Lootenant?" Croft's voice mocked him slightly.

He couldn't go, however. If he was knocked off, that would suit Croft perfectly. "I don't think I'm suited for it," he said coldly.

Croft was reasoning the same way. If he himself went and was killed, the platoon would certainly turn back. "I think Martinez is about the best man for it."

Hearn nodded. "All right, send him out. In the morning we'll make a decision. And tell him to wake me when he gets back." Hearn looked at his watch. "I'm about due for guard now. Tell him to check

582

with me before he sets out so I'll know it's him moving around."

Croft looked about the hollow and picked out Martinez's blankets in the moonlight. He stared at Hearn for an instant, and then strode over to Martinez and awakened him. The Lieutenant was climbing up the hill to relieve the guard.

Croft told Martinez what his mission would be, and then in a low voice he added, "If you see any Japs bivouacking, try to work around them and keep on going."

"Yeah, understand." Martinez was tying his shoes.

"Just take a trench knife."

"Okay, I be back in three hour maybe. Tell guard," Martinez whispered.

Croft held his shoulder for a second. Martinez was shivering very slightly. "Are you okay, boy?" he asked.

"Yeah, okay."

"Well, now listen," Croft said. "When you get back, don't say anything to anybody till you see me. If the Lootenant is up, you just say to him nothing happened, do you understand?" Croft's mouth was numb, and he felt the powerful anxiety of disobeying an order. More than that, there was something else, unexpressed as yet. He exhaled his breath painfully.

Martinez nodded, clenching and opening his fists to restore the sensitivity to his fingers. "I go now," he said, standing up.

"You're a good boy, Japbait." It was eerie, whispering in the darkness. The bodies lying about them seemed dead.

Martinez wrapped his rifle in his blanket to keep it dry, left it lying on his pack. "Okay, Sam." His voice quivered just slightly.

"Okay, Japbait." Croft watched him talk for a few seconds to Hearn, and then move out of the hollow, dip into the kunai grass and bear off to the left, parallel to the great cliffs of the mountain. Croft rubbed his forearm reflectively and went back to his blanket, lay down, knowing he would not sleep until Martinez had returned.

There it was before him again. You made a decision and backtracked on it and none of the problems was changed. Hearn shrugged wryly. If Martinez came back and reported no Japs in the pass, they would be moving forward in the morning. He scratched his armpit tenderly, staring down at the valley and the empty mournful hills about him. The wind soughed through the draws, drifted over the kunai grass, and whistled along the crests of the knolls, making a small murmur in its circuit like surf breaking a long distance away.

It was a mistake, and he had played a curious deception with himself. It had been more than yielding to Croft, he had yielded to himself again, made it so complicated that he could never untangle the rationalization from what was valid. Tricks and tricks, more ways than one to skin a cat, and he had allowed it, knew that he would go forward in the morning if Martinez brought back a report of no Jap activity.

When they finally got back to their bivouac, if they ever did, he could turn in his commission. That was the thing he could do, that would be honest, true to himself. Hearn rubbed his armpit again, sensing a reluctance. He didn't want to give up his commission, and that of course was part of the mechanism. You sweated through OCS, joked about the bars, were always contemptuous of them, and in time they grew to have an existence of their own, colored more than half your attitudes. After enough time went by it was like amputating an arm.

He knew what would happen. He would be an enlisted man, a private, and the other enlisted men in whatever unit he would be assigned to would find out sooner or later that he had been an officer, and they would hate him for it, resent him, resent even the fact that he had resigned a commission, for it would mock their own ambitions conscious and unconscious. If he did this, it would be with open eyes; there would be nothing cleaner at the end of it, certainly nothing more pleasant. It would be lousy and painful, and probably the only discovery would be that he could fit into a fear ladder as well as anyone else.

But there it was. He had been running away from fear, from vulnerability, from the admission that he was a man also and could be humbled. There was a saying, "It is better to be the hunted than the hunter," and that had a meaning for him now, a value.

Mockingly, he could hear what Cummings would say to that.

584

"A nice sentiment, Robert, one of the nice lies for today, just like the lie about a rich man not going to heaven." And Cummings would laugh and say, "You know, Robert, it's only the rich who *do* go to heaven."

Well, the hell with Cummings. He had said that enough times in resentment, grudgingly, perhaps helplessly, but Cummings didn't know all the answers. If you granted him that man was a sonofabitch, then everything he said after that followed perfectly. The logic was inexorable.

But the history wasn't. All right, all the great dreams had blunted and turned practical and corrupt, and the good things had often been done through bad motives, but still it had not all been bad, there had also been victories where there should have been defeats. The world, by all the logics, should have turned Fascist and it hadn't yet.

For a moment there were a few sounds in the valley beneath him, and he picked up his rifle and stared into the shadows of the grass. It became quiet again. For some reason he was left depressed.

It was a skinny enough hope, and all the pressures, all the machines, were squeezing men a little more; with every weapon the odds became a little more out of whack. Morality against bombs. Even the techniques of revolution were changed, were accomplished with armies against armies now, or not at all.

If the world turned Fascist, if Cummings had his century, there was a little thing he could do. There was always terrorism. But a neat terrorism with nothing sloppy about it, no machine guns, no grenades, no bombs, nothing messy, no indiscriminate killing. Merely the knife and the garrote, a few trained men, and a list of fifty bastards to be knocked off, and then another fifty.

A plan for concerted action, comrades. He grinned sourly. There would always be another fifty, that wasn't the idea. It had no use. It was just something to keep you occupied, keep you happy. Tonight we strike at Generalissimo Cummings.

Aaah, horseshit.

There were no answers you could find, but perhaps there were epochs in history which had no answers. Rely on the blunder factor. Sit back and wait for the Fascists to louse it up.

Only that wasn't enough, you couldn't do that. For whatever reason, you had to keep resisting. You had to do things like giving up a commission.

Hearn and Quixote. Bourgeois liberals.

Still, when he got back he would do that little thing. If he looked for the reasons they were probably lousy, but it was even lousier to lead men for obviously bad motives. It meant leaving the platoon to Croft, but if he stayed he would become another Croft.

When things got really bad, maybe the political differences on the Left would be shelved.

Drought season for anarchists.

Martinez moved along for a few hundred yards through the tall grass, keeping well within the shadow of the cliffs. As he advanced, he awakened slowly, flexing his arms and pinching the back of his neck. He had been partially asleep while he had talked to Croft, or at least nothing that was said had any significance to him. He had understood the directions, the mission, he had known that Croft was telling him to do something and instinctively he obeyed, but he had not thought about the connotations. It had not seemed particularly dangerous or odd to be going out by himself at night into country he had never seen before.

Now of course as his mind cleared it was becoming apparent to him. Damn fool thing? he wondered, and then dismissed it. If Croft had told him it was necessary, then obviously it was. His senses became alerted, his nerve ends poised. He moved forward with an effortless silent motion, placing his heel first on the ground, and then bringing his toes down gently, his body weaving through the grass to diminish the rustling. A man twenty yards away could not have been certain that anyone was approaching. And yet with this he did not go slowly; through experience, his feet seemed to paw the ground, avoiding stones or twigs, settling confidently, noiselessly. He was functioning more like an animal now than a man.

He was frightened, but effectively so; he had no panic, and it left him intensely aware of everything he could see or feel. On the ship, in the assault boat that landed on Anopopei, a dozen times since,

586

he had been close to hysteria, worth nothing at all, but that variety of fear had nothing to do with this. If he had had to endure one more artillery shelling he might have collapsed; his terror always expanded in a situation where he could do nothing to affect it, but now he was by himself, doing the thing he could perform better than any man he knew, and it supported him. All the successful reassuring connotations of other scouting missions he had made in the past year were stored beneath the surface of his thoughts.

Martinez best man in recon, he said to himself with pride. Croft had told him this once, and he had never forgotten it.

In twenty minutes he had reached the rock shelf where they had been ambushed. He squatted in the woods behind it and examined the ledge for several minutes before advancing again. And then behind the ledge he watched the field and the grove where the Japanese had fired at them. In the moonlight the field was a wan silver and the grove an impenetrable black-green far deeper than the blanched transparent shadows that surrounded it. Behind him and to his right he could feel the huge body of the mountain glowing oddly in the darkness like a vast monument illumined by spotlights.

For perhaps five minutes he peered at the field and the grove, thinking of nothing at all, his eyes and ears the only part of him wholly alive. The tension with which he watched, the taut pressure in his chest was pleasurable, complete in itself, like a man in the first stages of drunkenness when he is content to feel only the symptoms of his intoxication. Martinez was holding his breath but he was unaware of it.

Nothing moved at all. He heard no sounds besides the whispering of the grass. Slowly, almost leisurely, he slipped over the ledge and squatted in the field searching for a shadow in which he might hide. But there was no approach to the grove where he would not have to pass through the moonlight. Martinez debated for an instant, and then sprang to his feet, stood in complete view of the grove for a startling, terrifying second and then dropped to the ground again. No one fired. He would have taken them by surprise. The chances were likely that if there was anyone in the grove they would have been startled enough to fire upon him.

Quietly, he stood up again and loped quickly across half the distance of the field, dropping behind a rock with a twisting sprawling motion. No answer, no fire. He ran another thirty yards, halted behind another rock. The borders of the grove were less than fifty feet away. He listened to his own breathing, watched the moonlight trace an oval of shadow beyond the rock. All his senses told him that there was no one in the grove, but it was too dangerous to trust them. He stood up for a full second, and then dropped down again. If they hadn't fired by now . . . He felt fatalistic about it. There was no way to cross an open field in the moonlight without being seen.

Martinez glided across the rest of the distance separating him from the grove. Once inside the trees, he paused again, flattened himself against a trunk. Nothing was moving. He waited until his eyes became acclimated to the darkness and then he crept forward from tree to tree, separating the brush with his hands in his passage. After fifteen yards he came to a path and stopped, peering to left and right. Then he paced along it to the border of the grove again, halting before a small emplacement, into which he knelt. There had been a machine gun there several days before — he reasoned this by the fact that the holes for the studs of the tripod were no damper than the surface of the emplacement. Besides, the machine gun had pointed toward the rock ledge; the Japanese would have used it that afternoon in the ambush if it had still been there.

Slowly, cautiously, he examined the periphery of the grove. The Japanese had left, and by the number of empty ration cartons, the size of their latrine trench, he estimated that they must have made up a full platoon. Recon had run into much less than that; it could mean only that most of their platoon had been withdrawn a day or two before, and the men who had attacked them were a rear guard, who had retreated up the pass shortly afterward.

Why?

As if to answer him, he could hear faintly the sound of the artillery. It had been firing frequently all that day. Japs go back to help stop attack. This seemed reasonable, and yet he was perplexed. Somewhere farther up the pass there might or might not be some Japanese. Martinez shivered, holding the damp rotting cardboard wrapper of a ration in his hand. Somewhere. He had a vague rather frightening vision of soldiers moving in the darkness, stumbling from place to place. He would go groping into that. He shook his head like an animal bridling at an unexpected sensation. The silence and darkness of the grove were wearing upon him, eroding his courage. He had to move on.

Martinez wiped his forehead. He was sweating and he realized with surprise that his shirt was quite wet and very chill. His tension had subsided for a moment or two, and it made him aware of his fatigue and the nervous shock of being awakened an hour or two after he had fallen asleep. The hamstrings of his thighs felt taut, quivered a little. He sighed. But he did not consider at all the idea of turning back.

Carefully he followed the trail through the grove toward the pass. It extended for several hundred yards through brush and forest not quite thick enough to be jungle. Once his face brushed against a long flat leaf and a few insects darted in fright across his cheek. He flicked them off, his fingers moist with anxiety. But one of the insects held on to his fingers, and then began to slide up his forearm. Martinez flung it off, stood shivering in the darkness. For a few seconds everything was in balance; his will to move forward was frustrated by the irrational terror the insects had caused, the more concrete knowledge of the Japanese there must be ahead, and most of all by the increasing deadening weight of all this strange earth he must explore at night. He breathed deeply several times, moving his weight forward to his toes and then rocking back on his heels again. A dull sluggish breeze stirred the leaves slightly, caressed his face with a momentary breath of coolness. He could feel the perspiration coursing down his face in separate extended streams like the lines formed by tears.

Gotta go. He said this automatically but it released new currents of will. The resistance he had created inside himself mounted against it and then collapsed. He took a step forward, then another, and the effect was broken. He moved on down the crude footpath the Japanese had worn in the grove, debouched after a minute or two into a clearing beyond the forest. He was in the pass now.

589

The cliffs of Mount Anaka had taken a turn to the right, were parallel again to his route. On the other side, to his left, were some steep, almost precipitous hills which rose abruptly into the Watamai Range. The channel through the mountains was about two hundred yards wide, an ascending avenue lined by tall buildings. It was uneven with rolls and dips, great boulders and slattern mounds of earth, pocked here and there in the rock crevices with spates of foliage like the weeds that grow from the cracks in concrete. The moonlight was clearing the invisible peak of Mount Anaka, lancing downward into the pass and dappling the rocks and knolls with shadows. It was all very bare, very cold; Martinez felt a thousand miles from the stifling velvet night of the jungle. He moved out from the protection of the grove, advanced a few hundred feet and knelt in the shadow of a boulder. Behind him, near the horizon, he could see the Southern Cross, and instinctively he noted its direction. The pass ran due north.

Slowly, reluctantly, he moved up through the defile, proceeding cautiously along the rocky littered floor of the pass. After a few hundred yards the pass bore to the left and then to the right again, narrowing considerably. In places the shadow of the mountain covered the corridor almost completely. He progressed at an uneven pace, loping forward almost recklessly for many yards at a time and then pausing fearfully for seconds which elapsed into minutes while he lashed himself to advance again. Every insect, every tiny animal he roused in its burrow startled him, unmanned him with the noise of its movement. He played a continual deception with himself, deciding to go on only to the next bend in the pass, and when he had reached it and the ground traversed had been harmless, he would pick another objective and proceed on to it. In this way he covered perhaps a little over a mile in less than an hour, climbing upward almost all the time. He began to wonder how long the pass might be; despite his experience he was teasing himself with the old trick of imagining that each crest before him was the final one and beyond would be the jungle, the rear of the Japanese lines, and the sea.

As time passed without incident, as more and more of the pass was set behind him, he grew more confident, more impatient. His halts became less frequent, the distance he would traverse each time became greater. At one point the pass was overgrown with tall kunai grass for a quarter of a mile, and he plodded through it confidently, knowing he could not be observed.

Until now there had been no place where the Japanese could have established an outpost, and his caution, the elaborate observation he made, had been more from terror, more from the unassailable silence of the mountain and the pass, than from any suspicion of an enemy site. But the terrain was changing. The foliage had become thicker and covered more area; in several places it was extensive enough to conceal a small bivouac. He scouted them cursorily, entering the little groves in the shadow, moving in a few yards, and then waiting for several minutes to see if he could hear the inevitable sounds of men sleeping. When nothing moved but the leaves and birds and animals, he would stalk out and continue his advance up the pass.

At a turn it narrowed again; the opposing cliff walls were not more than fifty yards apart here, and in several places along the route the defile was blocked by a patch of jungle. It took him many minutes to pass through each grove and the strain of passing through the brush without making noise was great. He reached a section which was comparatively open again and moved forward with a sense of release.

But at another turn he saw before him a tiny valley limited by the cliffs on either side and plugged by a small wood which grew completely across the gap. In the daylight it would have a fine field of view. It was the best position he had seen for an outpost, and he was certain, immediately and instinctively, that the Japanese had retreated to here. He felt it with a start of his limbs, an acceleration of his heart. Martinez examined the grove from the lee of a rock, staring across the moonlight, his face pinched and tense. There was a band of deep shadow at his right where the cliffs filleted into the base of the pass, and smoothly, not allowing himself to think about it, he glided around the rock, and crept along in the darkness on his hands and knees, keeping his face low. With fascination he found himself watching the ragged borderline between the moonlight and shadow, and unaccountably he felt himself moving toward the light once or twice. It seemed alive, with an existence as acute as his; his throat was tight, almost swelling, and he watched the shimmer of the moonlight with a dumb absorption. The grove came nearer, was twenty yards away from him, now ten. He paused at the edge of it, and examined its periphery for a machine-gun emplacement or a foxhole. In the darkness he could see nothing but the dark bulk of the trees.

Once more Martinez entered a grove and stood waiting for sounds. He could not hear anything at first, and he advanced a cautious step, parting the brush with his hands, and then moved forward another and another. His foot trod on a patch of worn earth, explored it with fright. He knelt and patted the earth, fingered the small leaves of a bush at his side. The ground was trampled, and the bush had been beaten to one side.

He was on a newly formed trail.

To corroborate it, a man coughed in his sleep not five yards away. Martinez stiffened, almost jumped as though he had touched something hot. The flesh on his face became stretched and taut. He could not have uttered a sound at that moment.

Automatically he took a step backward, and heard someone else turning over in his blankets. He did not dare to move for fear of swiping a branch and arousing them. For at least a minute he was wholly paralyzed. He felt it impossible to turn back. He could not have explained it; his fear of retreating from the grove was great but it was not so intense as his terror at the thought of moving forward. And yet he could not go back. A part of his mind played with incredible rapidity the scene where he would tell Croft.

"Japbait no fuggin good."

But there was something wrong with moving ahead. He could not perceive it clearly, his head felt as if it were churning through oil, but there was a reason. He could not think it out. With loathing, with a suppressed hysteria of his flesh as if he were trodding barefoot over a field of bloated maggots, he extended his leg, and then the other one, pacing forward with separate violent demands on his mind. In a minute he advanced not more than ten feet, the perspiration smarting his eyes. He felt as if he could detect each droplet starting out of his pores, joining with the others to wash down the damp river bed of the lines in his face and body.

One thing he realized intuitively. The Japanese would have

592

tramped out only two trails by now. One would be perpendicular to the pass, a yard or two behind the border of the grove, facing the valley. The other would lead through the grove to the other side, joining the first one in a T. He was on the head of the T now, and would have to progress along it until he reached the stem. He could never go through the brush; even the slight noises he made would be heard, and there was always the chance of blundering into something.

He crept along, on his hands and knees again. The seconds passed like individual units, almost as if he heard a clock ticking. He could have sobbed every time he heard a man mutter in his sleep. They were all around him! He seemed to exist in several parts now; there was the sore remote protest of his palms and kneecap, the choking swollen torment of his throat, and the unbearable awareness of his brain. He was very close to the final swooning relaxation a man feels when he is being beaten unconscious and no longer cares whether he can get up. Very far away he could hear the murmuring of the jungle in the night.

At a curve in the trail he halted, peered around, and almost screamed. A man was sitting at a machine gun about three feet away.

Martinez's head darted back. He lay on the ground waiting for the soldier to pivot the machine gun, fire at him. But nothing happened. He peered around again and realized the Jap had not seen him, was sitting at a slight angle to him. Behind the machine gunner was the stem of the T. He would have to get past him, and it was impossible.

Now, Martinez knew what had been wrong. Of course. They would have a guard posted along the trail. Why hadn't he thought of it? *El juicio.* With all his fright was another fear to be examined later; like the murderer remembering all the obvious things he had forgotten while he committed his crime, Martinez felt a dull dread leavened into his terror. What else, *por Dios,* what else? He peered again at the machine gunner, watching him with an absorbed fascination. If he desired he could reach out and touch him. The soldier was a young man, almost a boy, with blank young features, dull half-closed eyes, and a thin mouth. In the moonlight that sifted through the borders of the grove he looked half asleep.

593

Martinez had a sense of unreality. What was to keep him from touching him, from greeting him? They were men. The entire structure of the war wavered in his brain for a moment, almost tottered, and then was restored by a returning wash of fear. If he touched him he would be killed. But it seemed unbelievable.

He could not go back now. It was impossible to turn his body around without making some small sound, enough in any case to alert the machine gunner. And it was impossible to pass him; the trail skirted the lip of the machine-gun emplacement. He would have to kill him. Even at the thought Martinez's overpitched senses rebelled. He lay there shuddering, conscious suddenly of how weak, how tired, he felt. There seemed no strength, no capacity for effort left in his limbs. He was reduced to peering through the foliage at the moonlight on the soldier's face.

He had to hurry. At any moment the machine gunner might stand up and go to awaken the next man for his turn at guard, and he would be discovered. He had to kill him right away.

And again there seemed something wrong in his calculations. He felt that if only he could shake his head or flex his limbs this would become clear to him, but now he was caught. Martinez reached back for his trench knife, slipped it softly out of the scabbard. The handle felt uncomfortable in his palm, alien; although he had used it a hundred times for other purposes, opening cans or cutting something, he did not know how to hold it now. The blade kept reflecting a sliver of moonlight, and he held it under his forearm at last, staring with terrified stricken eyes at the soldier in the gun hole. Already he felt as if he knew him well; each of his slow leisurely motions traced a familiar route in Martinez's mind — as the Jap picked at his nose delicately a grin was wrenched from Martinez's mouth. He was not even aware of it except for the fatigue in his cheek muscles.

I go kill him, he commanded himself, but nothing happened. He remained lying on the ground with the knife concealed beneath his arm, the damp earth of the trail chilling his body slowly. At alternate instants he felt in fever and then cold. The moment had become unreal to him again, and he had the qualified controlled terror that he knew in his nightmares. It was not real, and he shuddered once more, thinking of turning back. Slowly — it took him over a minute — he got to his hands and knees, brought one foot under him, and swayed there, no more certain of attacking or retreating than a coin on edge about to fall. He became conscious of the knife in his hand again.

"Never trust a goddam Mex when he's got a knife."

It spilled into his mind, a long-concealed fragment from a conversation he had heard between two Texans, and he felt a choked resentment. Goddam lie, and then it was lost in the realization of what he had to do. He swallowed. He had never felt so numb in all his life. Behind it all was a confused bitterness toward the knife, an almost paralyzing fear, and the moonlight tantalizing him. He searched for a pebble, found one, and before he was quite willing his fingers had flipped it away to the other side of the machine-gun emplacement.

The Jap soldier turned at the sound, put his back to him. Martinez took a step forward silently, halted, and then lashed his free forearm around the soldier's neck. Dumbly, almost leisurely, he placed the point of his knife in the angle between the man's throat and shoulder, and pushed it in with all his force.

The Jap thrashed in his arms like an unwilling animal being picked up by its master, and Martinez felt only a detached irritation. Why was he making so much trouble? The knife would not go in far enough, and he tugged at it until it was loose, and then plunged it down again. The soldier writhed for a moment in his arms, and then collapsed.

With him went all of Martinez's strength. He looked stupidly at him, reached down for the knife, and tried to pull it free, but his fingers were trembling. He felt blood dribbling over his palm, and he started, wiping his hand on his trousers. Had anyone heard them? Martinez's ears were recalling the noise of their struggle as if it had been an explosion he had seen from some distance away whose report he was waiting for now.

Was anyone moving? He could hear nothing, and realized that they had made very little sound.

And then he felt the reaction. The dead sentry was loathsome to him, something to be avoided; he had the mixture of relief and revulsion a man feels after chasing a cockroach across a wall and finally squashing him. It affected him exactly that way and not much more intensely. He shuddered because of the drying blood on his hands, but he would have shuddered as much from the roach's pulp. Abruptly, the only important thing was to move on, and he darted down the stem trail, almost running.

He came out into an open stretch of pass again, moved up it for a few hundred yards, and then skirted a few small groves. He had lost the concentration he needed to scout properly and he blundered along, the fine surface of his observation gone. The floor of the pass was still ascending at a lower, less precipitous parallel to the slope of the mountain. It seemed never to end, and although he knew he had traveled only a few miles, it seemed much more.

He reached another clearing with a wood along the left side of it, and he knelt in the shadow once more and looked at it dully. Suddenly, he shivered. He had realized the error he had made in killing the guard. The man who was supposed to go next on guard might sleep through the night, but there was an even better chance he would awaken; Martinez could never sleep soundly until his turn of guard was over for the night. Once they discovered the man he had killed, they would all be awake for the rest of the night. He could never get out.

Martinez felt like weeping. The longer he remained here the more dangerous it would become. And besides, if he had made a mistake like that, how many others were there he might have made? He was close to hysteria again. He had to go back and yet . . . He was sergeant, United States sergeant.

Without this sense of loyalty he would have broken up months before. Martinez wiped his face and started forward. The weird idea of continuing until he had traversed the pass and the Japanese rear, scouted the defenses of Botoi Bay, came to him. For a moment his mind held a montage of glory; Martinez being decorated, Martinez standing before the General, Martinez's picture in the Mexican newspaper in San Antonio, but it slipped away, was rejected before the obvious impossibilities of it. He had no rations, no water, not even a knife any longer.

At that moment in the grove to his left he saw a long bar of

596

moonlight behind a bush which projected from the grove. He dropped to one knee, examined it, and then heard the delicate sound of a man flooping some spittle to the ground. There was another Japanese bivouac.

He could get by it. The shadow along the cliff wall was very deep here, and if he was cautious they would never spy him. But this time his legs were too weak, his will too flaccid. He couldn't endure another few minutes like the ones next to the machine gunner.

But he should go on. Martinez rubbed his nose like a child before insuperable difficulties. All the fatigue of the past two days, the nervous strain of this night, were bothering him now. Goddam, how far he want me go? he thought resentfully. He turned around, edged back into the grove from which he had come, and began to descend the pass. He was conscious now of the time that had elapsed since he had stabbed the sentry, and it made him increasingly anxious. There was a chance, if the guard was discovered, that they would send patrols out, but it was not likely at night, and besides he was lost if the guard had been discovered. He made virtually no attempt at concealment in the stretches of the pass where he had found no Japanese before. The only important thing was to get back soon.

He came to the rear of the grove with the T trail, and paused outside it, listening. He could hear nothing for a few seconds, and, impatient, he entered and crept up along the stem. The dead man was lying undisturbed by the machine gun. Martinez looked past him, started to tiptoe around him, and noticed a wrist watch on his arm. He paused, stared at it for two full seconds while he debated whether to remove it. He turned to go and then moved back again and knelt beside him. The hand was still warm. He fumbled with the catch, and dropped the hand in a sudden discharge of disgust and terror. No. He couldn't bear the thought of remaining in the grove any longer.

Instead of turning left at the trail and following it out of the grove into the shadow, he stepped past the machine gun into the clearing, and crept from rock to rock until he reached the protection of the cliff. He stared back a last time at the grove and then continued on down the pass.

As he moved along he was bothered by a double sense of disap-

597

pointment and frustration. He had turned back before he had to, and this bothered him. Instinctively, he was wondering how to change the story so that he would satisfy Croft. But more directly, more painfully, he was thinking with regret how easy it would have been to have taken the wrist watch. Now that he was out of the grove, he was disgusted with himself for having been afraid to linger. He thought of the things he could have done. Besides the watch he could have retrieved the knife (he had forgotten about it when he looked at the soldier) or he could have jammed the machine gun by putting a handful of dirt in the bolt. He thought with amusement of how their faces would have looked, and realized with a shock how terrified they would be when they discovered the dead man.

He smiled. Goddam, good ol' Martinez, hoping that Croft would say the same thing.

In less than an hour he reached the platoon again, and gave his account to Croft. The only change he made was to say that there was no way to slip by the second bivouac.

Croft nodded. "You had to kill that Jap, huh?"

"Yes."

Croft shook his head. "Wish you hadn't. That'll stir 'em up from here to Jap headquarters." He thought for a moment, and said pensively, "I don't know, you never can say what's gonna come out."

Martinez sighed. "Goddam, no think of that." He was too tired now to feel any deep regret, but as he lay down on his bedding he wondered how many more mistakes he would discover in the next few days. "Goddam, tired," he said to rouse Croft's sympathy.

"Yeah, I guess you had a rough go." Croft laid his hand on Martinez's shoulder, gripped it fiercely. "Don't say a damn word to the Lootenant. You went clear through the pass without seeing a damn thing, y' understand?"

Martinez was puzzled. "Okay, you say so."

"That's it, you're a good boy, Japbait."

Martinez smiled lazily. In three minutes he was asleep.

8

HEARN woke up feeling quite rested the next morning. He twisted around in his blankets and watched the sun rising over the eastern hills, which were becoming distinct now, seeming to rise like rocks from water. Everywhere the dawn mists were settling in the hollows and valleys, and he felt as if he could see a great distance, almost to the eastern end of the island a hundred miles away.

About him the others also were awakening; Croft and the men were rolling their blankets, and one or two of them were returning from the weeds. Hearn sat up, stretched his toes inside his shoes, and debated idly for a minute or two whether to change his socks. He had taken another pair, which now also were soiled, and he shrugged and then decided it was not worth the trouble. Instead, he began putting on his leggings.

Red was muttering near him. "When is the goddam Army gonna learn another way to make leggings?" He was struggling with a lace which had shrunk during the night.

"I've heard they've got a high shoe coming in soon like a paratrooper's boot. It'll do away with leggings."

Red rubbed his chin. He had not shaved since the patrol had begun and his beard was blond and rather splotchy. "We'll never see any of them," Red told him, "the fuggin quartermaster'll keep 'em all."

"Well . . ." Hearn grinned. The crabapple. Of all the men in the platoon, Red was the one worth buddying with, the wise one. Only you couldn't approach him.

On an impulse, Hearn said, "Listen, Valsen . . ."

"Yeah?"

"We're short a corporal; two, now that Stanley's with Wilson. You want to be acting jack for the rest of the patrol? And we can make it permanent when we get back." It was a good choice. Red was popular with the men, could certainly handle the thing.

But he felt slightly embarrassed by the expressionless cast Red's face assumed. "Are you ordering me, Lootenant?" Red's voice was flat, a little harsh.

Now, what had set him off? "No, of course not."

Red scratched his arm slowly. He felt suddenly and disproportionately enraged, even noticed it himself by the indirect worry it caused him for an instant.

"I don't want no favors," he muttered.

"I'm not offering you any."

He hated this lieutenant, this big guy with the phony grin who was always trying to buddy. Why didn't he leave him alone?

For an instant he was tempted, knew he was tempted, by the outrageous pang in his chest. If he took something like that, the whole thing fell apart. They got you in the trap and then you worried about doing the job right and started fighting with the men and sucking the officers. Working with Croft.

"You better pick another sucker, Lootenant."

Hearn was furious for an instant. "All right, forget it," he muttered. They hated him, they had to hate him, and it was the thing he had to accept until the patrol was over. He stared back at Red, his anger ebbing as he took in all of Red's gaunt body, his emaciated tired face with the battered red skin.

Croft passed by and called out to the men, "Don't forget to fill up your canteens, troopers, before we take off." A few of them headed toward a little brook on the other side of the knoll.

Hearn looked around, saw Martinez stirring in his blankets. He had forgotten all about him, didn't even know the information he had brought back. "Croft!" he shouted.

"Yes, Lootenant?" Croft was opening a breakfast ration, and now he threw away the cardboard wrapper he had been holding in his hand, and strode over toward him.

"Why didn't you wake me up when Martinez came back last night?"

"Couldn't do anythin' about it till the morning," Croft drawled.

"Yeah, well, in the future you can let me decide that." He returned Croft's stare, looked into his impenetrable blue eyes. "What did Martinez see?"

Croft slit the top off the inner waxed carton of the ration and spilled out the contents. His back tingled with a nervous flush as he spoke. "The pass is empty as far as he went. He thinks those Japs hit us yesterday were the only ones in the pass, and they just left it open now." He had wanted to postpone telling Hearn this as long as possible, had even hoped irrationally that it would not be necessary. The nervous needles pricked his flesh again. Carefully suspended from his thoughts was the idea behind this. He looked at the ground as he talked. When he finished, he turned to look at the guard on the hill crest above them. "Keep your eyes open, Wyman," he called softly. "Goddammit, man, you oughta had enough sleep."

There was something fishy about this. "It sounds weird that they'd leave the pass empty," Hearn murmured.

"Yeah." Croft had finished opening the small tin of ham and eggs, and was dishing it neatly into his mouth with his spoon. "Might be." He stared at his feet again. "Maybe we ought to try the mountain, Lootenant."

Hearn stared up at Mount Anaka. This morning, yes, it wasn't without its attraction. They could do that. But he shook his head firmly. "It's impossible." It would be crazy to lead the men up it, not even knowing if they could descend the other side.

Croft stared at him impassively. Since the patrol had begun, Croft's gaunt face had become even leaner, the lines in his square small chin more accentuated. He looked tired. He had brought a razor with him, but he had not shaved yet this morning, and it made his face seem smaller. "It ain't impossible, Lootenant. I've been looking at that mountain since yesterday morning and they's a break in the cliffs about five miles to the east of the pass. We start out now and we can climb that damn thing in a day."

There had been that look on Croft's face when they stared at it through the field glasses. Hearn shook his head again. "We'll try it through the pass." Undoubtedly they were the only two men who would want to try the mountain.

Croft felt a curious mixture of satisfaction and fear. The thing was committed. "All right," he said, his lips numb against his teeth. He stood up and motioned the men to gather around him. "We're gonna go through the pass," he told them.

There was a sullen murmur from the platoon.

"All right, you men, you can jus' cut it out. We're goin' that way, and maybe today you'll keep your eyes open." Martinez stared at him and Croft shrugged meaninglessly.

"What the fug good does it do if we got to fight our way through the goddam Japs?" Gallagher asked.

"You can quit your bitching, Gallagher." Croft surveyed them all. "We're gonna get moving in five minutes so you all better get your ass in gear."

Hearn held up his hand. "Hold on, men, there's something I want to tell you. We sent Martinez out last night, and he reconnoitered the pass, and it was empty. The chances are it's still empty." Their eyes disbelieved him. "I'll give you my word for one thing. If we run into anything, any ambushes, any Japs in the pass, we're turning right around and going back to the beach. Is that fair enough?"

"Yeah," a few of them said.

"Okay, then let's get ready."

In a few minutes they started out. Hearn buckled his pack and hefted it to his shoulders. It was seven rations lighter now than it had been when they started, and it felt almost comfortable. The sun was beginning to give some warmth, which made him cheerful. As they moved along out of the hollow he felt good; it was a new morning and it was impossible not to feel hopeful. The dejection, the decisions of the previous night seemed unimportant. He was enjoying this, but if he was, so much the better.

Quite naturally he assumed the point and led the platoon toward the pass.

A half hour later, Lieutenant Hearn was killed by a machine-gun bullet which passed through his chest.

At the ledge that faced the first grove he had stood up casually, had been about to motion the others to follow him, when the Jap machine gun fired. He toppled back among the men gathered behind the shelf.

The shock was acute. For ten or twenty seconds the men in the platoon did nothing, squeezed themselves into the defilade of the

602

rock, their arms covering their heads, while the Japanese rifles, the machine gun lashed above them.

Croft reacted first, poked his rifle through a gap in the rocks and fired rapidly at the grove, listening dumbly to the flat pinging sound of his empty clip as it popped out of his rifle. Beside him, Red and Polack had recovered enough to stand up and fire back. Croft felt a deep release; at that moment his body was light. "Come on, men, get some fire back," he bawled. His mind was working quickly. There were only a few men in the grove, probably not even a squad, or they would have waited for the whole platoon to show itself. This way, they wanted to frighten them off.

Well, that was all right. He wasn't going to hang around here. Croft stared for a moment at the Lieutenant. Hearn was lying on his back, the blood spurting softly from his wound, covering his face and body slowly and inevitably. Croft felt a sense of relief again. No longer was there that confusion, that momentary internal pause before he gave an order.

The skirmish continued for a few minutes, and the rifles and machine gun were silent in the grove. Croft ducked down again behind the shelf. A little frantically, the men were crawling away from the ledge.

"Hold it," he called out. "Let's get out of here the right way. Gallagher! Roth! You stay here with me, keep up some fire. The rest of you get around that knoll. Martinez, you take them" — he pointed to the hillock behind them — "when you get there, open up on the grove, and we'll pull out and join you." He stood up for a moment, squeezed off a few rounds from a new clip, and then ducked again as the Jap machine gun answered. "All right, now get going!"

They crawled away, and several minutes later Croft heard them firing behind him. "Come on," he whispered to Gallagher and Roth. They started off, sliding on their bellies for the first fifty feet and then running from a crouched position. Roth caught a glimpse of Hearn as he crawled by, and for an instant his legs went weak and he gasped rather emptily. "Oh." It passed through him in a bout of faintness, and then he began crawling and then running. "Terrible," he muttered.

Croft joined the others behind the hill. "All right, men, let's haul ass. We're gonna head right along next to the cliffs, and we ain't gonna hang around for no one." He took the lead in the column and they moved out rapidly, jogging for several hundred yards at a time before slowing to a walk, and then after a few paces beginning to trot again. In an hour they moved five miles over the hills and through the tall grass, never pausing, never slowing down for the stragglers.

Roth forgot quickly about the Lieutenant, as did the others. The shock of the second ambush was blunted in the rigors of their retreat. They thought of nothing but the breathless clamor in their chests, the trembling of their overworked legs. When Croft finally called a halt they flopped on the ground numbly, not even caring if the Japs were pursuing them. At that moment if they had been attacked they would probably have lain there dumb.

Croft alone was standing. He spoke slowly, his chest heaving, but his speech distinct. "We're gonna take a little break." He stared disdainfully at them, noting the stupor with which they listened to him. "Since you men are all so goddam pooped, I'll stand guard." Most of them had hardly heard him, and those who did gathered no sense from his words. They just lay there passively.

Slowly they recuperated, their breath becoming normal, their legs regaining some strength. But still the ambush and the march had drained them. The morning sun was high enough by now to be unpleasantly hot and they sweltered, lying on their bellies and watching the perspiration drip from their faces onto their forearms. Minetta retched up the dry sour lumps of his breakfast ration.

As they recovered, the Lieutenant's death bothered them only slightly. It had been too abrupt, too disconnected for them to feel very much, and now that he was gone they found it difficult to believe he had ever been with the platoon. Wyman crawled over to Red and lay down beside him, plucking idly at a few tufts of grass. Occasionally he would bite on one and then spit it out.

"That was funny," he said at last. It was pleasant to be lying there, knowing that in an hour they would turn back. A small filtrate of the terror he had felt in the ambush worked through him for a moment.

"Yeah," Red muttered. And now the Lieutenant. He could see Hearn scowling when he had refused the offer to be a noncom. His mind skated on the brittlest ice, and he had a vague sense of oppression as if there was something he could not afford to face, something that was going to come up again.

"The Lootenant was a good guy," Wyman blurted suddenly. The words shocked him deeply. For the first time he bridged the distance between his few contacts with Hearn and the last glimpse he had had of him, the bloody meaningless corpse. "A good guy," he repeated doubtfully, feeling his way around the edge of the terror this caused.

"They ain't a fuggin one of those officers is worth a goddam," Red swore. His exhausted limbs twitched nervously from his anger.

"Oh, I don't know, there's all kinds of guys . . ." Wyman protested gently. He was still trying to bridge the sound of the Lieutenant's voice with the color of his blood.

"I wouldn't spit on the best one of them," Minetta said furiously. A mild superstition about not saying anything bad about the dead troubled him, but he repressed it defiantly. "I ain't afraid of saying what I think. They're all bastards." Under his high forehead, Minetta's eyes looked large, excited. "If it took him being knocked off for us to go back, then I'll settle for that." They had sent him out, they didn't give a goddam, but who could he fight against? "Aaaah." He lit a cigarette, puffed cautiously at it, for the smoke roiled his stomach.

"Who says we're going back?" Polack asked.

"That looey did," Wyman said.

Red snorted. "Yeah, the Looey." He rolled over on his stomach.

Polack picked his nose. "Y'wanta bet we ain't knocking off?" There was something screwy about the whole setup, screwy as hell. That Croft, what a baby. A hood. It was the kind of guy you needed, a sonofabitch.

"Aw," Wyman said vaguely. For an instant he thought of the girl who had stopped writing letters to him. He didn't even care if she was alive or dead now. What did it matter? He stared up at the mountain, and hoped they would turn back. Had Croft said anything about it?

As if to answer him, Croft sauntered toward them from his guard post. "All right, you men, let's get movin'."

"We going back, Sergeant?" Wyman asked.

"Don't gimme any of your goddam lip, Wyman, we're gonna try the mountain." A low shocked chorus, grumbling and resentful, answered him. "Any one of you men got something to say about it?"

"Why the hell don't we go back, Croft?" Red asked.

"'Cause that ain't what they sent us out to do." Croft hovered about an intense rage. He would not be balked now. For an instant he was tempted to raise his rifle and blast it at Valsen's head. He felt himself compressing his jaws. "Come on, you men, you want the Japs to be waitin' for ya again?"

Gallagher glared at him. "That lootenant said we're goin' back."

"I'm in charge of this platoon now." He stared at them, besting them with his eyes. One by one they stood up, hoisted their packs sullenly. They were a little numb. This was a shock which left them passive. "Aah, fug him," Croft heard one of them mutter, and he grinned to himself, lashed them with his tongue. "You bunch of women!"

They were all standing now, all ready. "Let's go," he said quietly. The platoon moved out slowly in the midmorning sun. After a few hundred yards they were tired again, and plodded along encased in a stupor. They had never really believed the patrol would end so easily. Croft led them on a route parallel to the cliffs of the mountain and toward the east. After twenty minutes they came to the first rent in the great bluffs of the mountain's base. A deep ravine slanted upward for several hundred feet to the first ridge, its red clay walls refracting brightly the heat of the sun. Without a word Croft turned toward it and the platoon began to climb the mountain. There were eight men left now.

"You know that Croft," Polack said to Wyman, "he's an idealist, that's what the fug he is." The big word pleased him for a moment and then was lost in the labor of scrambling up the burning clay floor of the ravine. Something screwy. He'd have to pump Martinez.

Wyman could see the Lieutenant again. A process which had been working in him since the ambush came to a focus. Before he could think, for he was very afraid of Polack's derision, he mumbled, "Listen, Polack, you think there's a God?"

Polack grinned, worked his hands under his pack straps to ease the chafing. "If there is, he sure is a sonofabitch."

"Oh, don't say that."

Painfully, the platoon continued to ascend the ravine.

The Time Machine:

POLACK CZIENWICZ

GIMME A GIMMICK AND I'LL MOVE THE WORLD

The lewd mobile mouth, the three upper teeth missing on the left side of his face . . . perhaps twenty-one years old, but his eyes were shrewd, bawdy, and when he laughed his skin was wizened and tough like the skin of a middle-aged man. With his hooked broken nose, his long pointed jaw, which slanted back to his receded gums, Minetta thought he looked like a cartoon of Uncle Sam. Yet he felt uncomfortable with him; secretly he was afraid to match his knowledge against Polack's.

The lock on the downstairs door is broken of course, and the mailboxes have been looted long ago; the hinges that remain are rusting off. It smells like a urinal in the hallway; the dirty tile of the entrance has absorbed the odors of the leaking pipes, the cabbage and garlic, the grease traps in the plumbing, which no longer work. On your way up the stairs you must lean toward the wall, for the banister is broken and yaws over undependably like the carcass of a ship rotting on the sands. In the gray angles where the walls meet the floor you can watch the mice ambling through the dust, the pure and erratic motion of the cockroaches out for a stroll.

The air shaft that connects the bathrooms from floor to floor is filling up with trash and an occasional discharge of garbage. When it reaches the second story the janitor will set fire to it.

Improvised incinerator.

The house is exactly like every other one on the block and the square mile surrounding it.

Casimir ("Polack") Czienwicz, age of nine, wakes up in the morning and scratches his head, sits up on the pile of quilting spread out upon the floor, and looks at the stove in the center of the room, which has gone out. There are three other children besides himself sleeping there, and he rolls over, pretends he is still asleep. Soon his sister Mary will be waking, moving about and dressing, and he wants to watch her.

Outside the wind is begging against the windowpanes, slinking between the cracks to slide freely along the floor.

Jesus, it's cold, he mutters to his brother sleeping beside him.

She up yet? (The brother is eleven.)

Soon. He holds his finger against his lips.

Mary rises shivering, pokes at the stove abstractedly, and pulls her cotton slip down about her shoulders, letting the nightgown fall as the slip travels down her body. The two boys catch a glimpse of bare flesh, giggle quietly in their beds.

What are you looking at, Steve? she shouts.

Haw, I saw ya, I saw ya.

You didn't.

I did.

He has put out his hand to stop Steve too late. Casimir shakes his head in disgust, mature disgust. Wha'd ya go and do that for, now ya ruined it.

Aaah, shut up.

You dope, Steve.

Steve takes a poke at him, but Casimir has ducked, is darting about the room, avoiding him. Stop it, Steve Mary screams.

Cut it out, cut it out, Polack yells

The father, a huge heavy man, has come in from the other room, wearing only his pants. You kids stop it, he shouts in Polish. Seeing Steve he cuffs him. Don't look at the girl.

Casimir did it first.

I di'n't, I di'n't.

Leave Casimir alone. He cuffs Steve again, his hands still smelling from the cattle blood in the stockyards.

I'll get ya, Steve whispers later.

Awwww. But Casimir grins to himself. He knows Steve will forget, and if he doesn't there will be a way to escape. There always is.

In the classroom everybody is shouting.

Who put gum on the seats, who put the gum on?

Miss Marsden looks ready to cry. Quiet, children, quiet please. John, you and Louis can start cleaning it up.

Why do we have to, teacher, we didn't put the gum on?

I'll help, teacher, Casimir says.

All right, Casimir, that's a good boy.

The little girls are snuffling their noses, looking about with interest now and indignation. Casimir did it, they whisper, Casimir did it.

Miss Marsden hears them at last. Did you do it, Casimir?

Me, teacher, why would I do it?

Come up here, Casimir.

He walks up to her desk, leans against her arm when she puts it about him. Looking at the class and winking as he lays his head on her shoulder. (Snickering.)

Now, Casimir, don't do that.

Don't do what, teacher?

Did you put the gum on the seats? Tell me the truth, I won't punish you.

No, teacher.

There isn't any gum on Casimir's seat, Miss Marsden, Alice Rafferty says.

Why isn't there any? she asks him.

I dunno, teacher, maybe the kid who did it was scared of me.

Who did it, Casimir?

Oh, I dunno, teacher. Do ya want me to help clean the seats?

Casimir, you should try to be a good boy.

Yes, Miss Marsden. He walks back to his seat and on the pretense of helping the other boys, he whispers to the girls.

In the summer the kids stay out late at night, play hide-and-seek in the empty lots, bathe in the hydrants, which have been turned on for them. There's always some excitement in summer. A house is burning down, or they can go up on the rooftops and peek at the big kids fooling around with the girls. If it's hot enough they can sneak

610

into the movies 'cause the exit doors are left open for ventilation.

Once or twice they have real good luck.

Hey, Polack, there's a drunk asleep in the alley behind Salvatore's house.

He heeled?

How do I know? the other kid curses.

Aaah, c'mon.

They tiptoe up the alley, debouch into a deserted lot behind the tenements. The drunk is snoring.

Gaw ahead, Polack.

Whadeya mean gaw ahead, how we gonna split?

You can split it.

He creeps up to the drunk, feels about his body slowly for a wallet. The drunk interrupts his snoring, clutches Polack's wrist.

Leggo a me, ya goddam . . . Fumbling, his free hand finds a stone on the ground, picks it up and cracks it against the drunk's head. The hand tightens on his arm and he smashes down again.

Where is it, where is it, c'mon hurry up.

Polack fumbles through the pockets, pulls out some change. Okay, let's go.

The two boys sneak out of the alley, divide the money in front of a street light.

Sixty cents for me, a quarter for you.

Whadeya mean? I found him.

Whadeya mean? I took all the chances, Polack says, whadeya t'ink dat don't count for nuttin'.

Aaah.

Go crap in your hat. Whistling, he walks away, begins to laugh shakily as he thinks of how he struck the drunk. But in the morning the man is gone, and Polack feels relieved. Aaah, ya can't hurt a rummy, he thinks to himself, a bit of knowledge from the older boys.

His father dies when he is ten, and after the funeral his mother tries to send him to work in the stockyards. But after a month the truant officer is around, and Polack is sent to an orphanage when his mother can think of nothing else.

611

There are all the new lessons not really unfamiliar to be learned. It is even more important never to get caught now; it hurts too much when you are.

Hold out your hand, Casimir.

Why, Sister? Wha'd I do?

Hold it out. The clapper comes down with surprising force on his palm, and he jumps. Holy Jeez.

For swearing, Casimir, you have to be punished again. And once more the black-clad arm rises, strikes his palm.

The kids are laughing at him as he walks back to his seat. Through his tears of pain he manages a dubious grin. Nuttin' to it, he whispers, but his fingers are swelling, and he nurses his hand through the morning.

Pfeiffer, the gym teacher, is the guy you gotta watch out for most of all. When they march in to eat, everybody has to be quiet for three minutes while prayers are said. Pfeiffer snoops around behind the benches, watching you to see if you whisper.

Polack darts his eyes to either side; nobody seems around. What da hell we eat tonight?

Thrump! His head stings through the layers of concussion which revolve dizzily in his skull.

All right, Polack, when I say quiet I mean it.

He stares numbly at his plate waiting for the pain to subside; it's very hard to keep himself from rubbing his head.

Afterward: Jesus, dat guy Pfeiffer's got eyes in back of his head.

And there are angles. Lefty Rizzo, the big kid, fourteen, runs the joint when Pfeiffer or one of the Sisters or Fathers ain't around. You gotta pal up wit' him, or you don't get anywhere.

What can I do for ya, Lefty? (Polack at the age of ten.)

Lefty is talkin' to his lieutenants. Beat it, Polack.

Aaah, what for? Wha'd I do to you?

Beat it.

He walks through the dormitory, scanning the fifty beds, the half-opened lockers.

612

In one of them is an apple, four pennies, and a little crucifix. He cops the cross, saunters back to Lefty's bunk.

Hey, Lefty, I got somethin' for ya.

What the hell I want with that?

Give it to Sister Catherine, a present.

Lefty considers this. Yeah . . . yeah. Where'd you get it?

I hooked it from Callahan's bunk. He ain't gonna yell though, y' just tell him to shat up.

I coulda hooked it myself.

I saved ya da trouble.

Lefty laughs, and Polack is made.

There are obligations, however. Lefty likes to smoke, and he can get away with a half-pack after lights out without getting caught. Every other night, the cigarette detail goes out for Lefty.

The four kids sneak out to the wall of the orphanage in the evening, and two of them are hoisted over. They drop to the pavement outside, walk for two blocks to the shopping street and loiter beside the newspaper rack of the candy store.

Polack walks inside to the cigarette counter.

Whadeya want, kiddo? the candy store man says.

Uh, I want . . . He looks out the doorway. Mister, that kid's stealing your papers! And the confederate tears down the street with the owner starting after him. Polack grabs a couple of packs, thumbs his nose at the owner's wife, who is screaming at him, and runs away in the opposite direction.

Ten minutes later they rendezvous outside the wall of the orphanage. One of them boosts the other up to the ledge and then scrabbles after him, holding to his arm. They sneak through the empty corridors, give Lefty his cigarettes, and are in bed a half hour after they have left.

Nuttin' to it, Polack whispers to the kid next to him.

One time Lefty gets caught smoking. For the real bad offenses there is a special punishment. Sister Agnes lines the boys up in a file, and makes Lefty straddle a bench with his can up in the air. Each of the kids is supposed to walk by and give him a clout on the butt.

Only, they are all afraid to, and one after another walks by giving him only a pat. Sister Agnes is furious. You're supposed to hit Francis, she cries. I'm going to punish everyone who doesn't.

The next kid gives Lefty a mild thump, and Sister Agnes makes him hold out his palm while she hits him with the ruler she is holding. Each of the kids in turn taps Lefty and holds out his palm for the blow.

Sister Agnes gets very upset. Her gown rustles with anger. Hit Francis! she cries again.

But no one will. The kids file along, take their crack on the hand, and gather in a circle to watch. Lefty is laughing. When they are all done, Sister Agnes stands still, and it is obvious she is debating whether to make them do it over again. But she is defeated, and very coldly she tells the boys to march to class.

Polack has learned a powerful lesson. He expands with admiration for Lefty. He does not know the words yet, but he shakes his head.

Boy, Lefty is okay.

Two years later, Polack's mother brings him back to her house. One of the older sisters is married, and two of his brothers are working. Before he leaves, Lefty gives him the secret handshake.

You're okay, kid, I'm gettin' out next year an' I'll look ya up.

Back to his street and the new sports fitting his age. Hitching rides on trolleys is commonplace, stealing from stores is a source of income. The real sport is holding onto the tailgate of a fast freight truck and highballing it fifteen miles out of town. His mother makes him get a job working as delivery boy in a butcher store, and he does that for a couple of years.

It has its moments.

When he is thirteen one of the women to whom he delivers meat seduces him.

Oh, hello, she says, opening the door, you're Mrs. . . . Mrs. . . .

Mrs. Czienwicz's son, lady.

Yeah, I know your mother.

614

Where you want the meat, lady?

Over there. He puts it down, looks at her. I guess that's all.

Sit down, you must be tired.

Naah, I got a lot of orders.

Sit down.

He stares at her. Yeah, all right, maybe I will.

Afterward, he feels as if his education is completed. He has known for a long time that there is no man you can trust, but women have not concerned him. Now he is positive that women too are as unreliable as the altering sands of mutual advantage.

In leaving . . . Well, so long . . .

You can call me Gertrude. She giggles.

He has not thought of her as possessing a name. Even now she is Mrs. Something, a door at which he drops meat.

So long, Gertie. I'll be seeing ya.

It is only hours later that the advantages, the beauties, the absorptive recollections of this act he has known by name for so long catch up with him. The next day he drops in to see her, is there often for the rest of the summer.

His years elapse, and he grows older, even wiser within the rigid gamut of his wisdom, but he hardly alters. He goes from job to job, becoming a butcher, working in the stockyards, even chauffeuring a car for some people who live on the North Side, but he exhausts the possibilities of the jobs very soon, knows their limitations almost before he has begun.

In 1941, when he is eighteen, he sees Lefty Rizzo again at a ball game, and they sit down together. Lefty is putting on weight already, looks prosperous. With his mustache he looks eight years older than twenty-two.

Ay, Polack, what the hell you been doin' with yourself?

Playin' the percentages.

Lefty laughs. Still the same old Polack, boy, are you a card. Why the hell ain't ya been around to see me? I coulda fixed ya up with something.

Never got around to it, that's a fact. (But it is more than this.

615

His code, never formulated, has been at work. When a pal has hit it, y' don't touch him unless he asks ya.)

Well, I can use ya.

Whah Novikoff, ya lousy Russian. Let's see ya hit somethin' besides air. Polack sits down after shouting, cocks his feet up on the seat in front of him. What was that ya said?

I can use ya.

Polack makes a face, purses his lips. Maybe we can do business, he says in dialect.

He buys a car, using for the down payment his savings from the first two months' work. He drives around at night after supper going to the candy stores and barbershops to collect the numbers receipts. When he is done he rides over to Lefty's house and drops the receipts and cash, goes back to the new furnished apartment he has rented for himself. For this he gets a hundred dollars a week.

One night something a little different occurs.

Hey, Al, how ya doin'? He stops at the cigar counter, picks out a two-for-35-cents brand. (Rolling it in his mouth) Whadeya say?

Al, a middle-aged man, comes out to him with a bag of change. Hey, Polack, there's a guy here wants his payoff. His number came in.

Polack shrugs. Why don' ya tell the lucky gentleman that Fred'll be around tomorrow with the money?

I told him, he don't believe me. There he is. (A thin seedy guy with a red pointed nose.)

What's the story, Jack? Polack says.

Now, listen, I don't want to make any trouble, mister, I ain't lookin' for a fight, but my number came through, I just want to get my money.

Well, now hold on, Jackson, let's take a breat'. He winks at the owner. You don' wanta be gettin' your balls in an uproar.

Listen, mister, all I want is the money. 572 it paid off, didn't it? Look here's the ticket. (A couple of kids who have come in for candy are watching, and Polack grasps him by the arm.)

Let's get in here and we'll talk it over. (He slams the door behind them.) Okay, ya won, Jack, and tomorrow the payoff comes. We got one guy to collect and one guy to pay off. It's a big outfit, Jackson, we got more than your ticket to worry about.

How do I know anybody's gonna come around?

How much ya put down?

Three cents.

You're gettin' twenty-one bucks, huh? Wha' do ya t'ink, you're gonna bankrupp us? He laughs. You'll get your money, Jack.

(The hand on his forearm.) I'd like it tonight, mister, I'm dying for a drink.

Polack sighs. Look, Jack, here's a buck. Tomorrow when ya get paid y' can give it to Fred.

The man takes it, stares at it dubiously. You're levelin' with me, mister.

Yeah, Jack, yeah. (He shrugs off the arm, goes out through the store to his car.) As he drives to the next place, he shakes his head. A deep contempt brews in him.

Small potatoes. Dumb bastard wins twenty-one bucks, an' he t'inks we're gonna stay up nights to get out o' payin' him. Jesus. It's a pretty small grifter who fugs around for twenty-one bucks.

Hello, Momma, how're ya doin', how's Casimir's sweetheart?

His mother stares suspiciously through the slit in the door, then opens it widely as she recognizes him.

I haven't seen you in a month, Son, she says in Polish.

Coupla weeks, a mont', what difference it make? I'm around, ain't I? Here's some candy for ya. (At the doubtful look on her face, he frowns.) Ain't ya got your teet' fixed yet?

She shrugs. I bought a little something else.

For Crisake, Ma, when the hell ya gonna do it?

I bought some material for dresses.

Mary again, huh?

An unmarried girl needs clothes.

Aaaah. (Mary has come in, nods coolly at him.) What ya been doin', useless?

617

Dry up, Casimir.

He hitches his suspenders. Why the hell don' ya get married an' give Ma a break?

'Cause all the men are like you, out for the same thing.

She wants to become a nun, his mother says.

A nun, holy cow. He stares at her appraisingly. A *nun!*

Stevie thinks maybe she ought to.

He looks objectively at her narrow sallow face, the yellowing skin under the eyes. Yeah, maybe she ought to at that. Again he is stirred with contempt, and beneath it a vague compassion. Ya know, Momma, I'm a lucky guy.

You're a crook, Mary says.

Keep still, the mother says. All right, Son, if you're lucky, it's good.

Aaah. (He's annoyed at himself. It's a bad idea to say you're lucky.) Gaw ahead, become a nun . . . How's Steve?

He works so hard. His Mikey, the little one, was sick.

I'll see him one of these days.

You children should stick together. (Two of them are dead, the others married except for Mary and Casimir.)

Yah. He has given her money for the apartment: the scattered lace doilies, the new upholstered chair, the candlesticks on the bureau are his contribution. But the place is unutterably drab. Aaaah, it's disgustin'.

What, Casimir?

Nothin', Momma, I gotta go now.

You just came.

Yah, I know. Here, here's some money. Will ya get your teet' fixed for Crisake?

Good-bye, Casimir. (It's Mary.)

Yah, good-bye, kiddo. He looks at her again. A nun, huh? Okay. Good luck to ya, kiddo.

Thank you, Casimir.

Sure, here's a little something for you too. G'wan take it. He presses it into her hand, skips out the door and down the stairs. Some kids are trying to jimmy the hub plate off his car and he scatters them.

618

Thirty bucks left. It's not much to last for three days, and he's been losing lately in the poker games at Lefty's.

Polack shrugs. Win, lose, it's all in the cards.

He bounces the little brunette off his knee, saunters over to Lefty and the hood from Kabriskie's outfit. The four-piece band hired for the party is playing softly, and some drinks have been spilled already on the end tables.

What can I do for ya, Lefty?

I want ya to meet Wally Boletti. They nod, talk for a little while.

You're a good man, Polack, Lefty says.

One of the best.

Kabriskie's lookin' for somebody to run the girls over in the south end of his section.

That's it, huh?

Yeah.

He mulls it for a moment. (It's more money of course, a lot more, and he can use it, but . . .) It's a touchy setup, he mutters. (A little switch in the political end, a double-cross by some outfit, and he'll be the target.)

How old are ya, Polack?

Twenty-four, he lies.

Damn young, Wally says.

I want to t'ink the damn thing over, Polack says. It is the first time he has been unable to make a decision in his life.

No hurry, but no sayin' it's gonna be open next week.

I'll take the chance.

Only, the next day while he is still debating a letter comes from his draft board. He swears dully. There's a guy over on Madison Street who pricks eardrums, and he gives him a ring.

But on the way over, Polack changes his mind.

Aaaah, t' hell wit' it, the percentages are runnin' out. He turns around and drives back calmly. Beneath his mind a wonder is working.

It's a big thing, he mumbles.

619

Only, that's not it. Polack has never heard of a *deus ex machina,* and it's a new idea to him.

You figger all the angles and then somethin' new comes up. He grins to himself. There ain't anyplace I ain't gonna get along.

His wonder is smothered. Even when the new angles come, there's always a gimmick if ya go looking hard enough for it.

BEEEEEEEEEEEP. He bangs down his horn, whips past a truck.

9

A FEW HOURS later at noontime, miles away, the litter-bearers were struggling with Wilson. They had carried him all morning under the burnished metallic heat of a tropical sun, their strength and their will coursing out of their bodies with their perspiration. Already they moved stupidly, the sweat blinding their eyes, their tongues clapped against their dry and enraged palates, their legs quivering constantly. The heat rose from everything, shimmered over the grass, swirled about them with the languid resistance of water or oil. Their faces felt swathed in velvet, and the air they breathed was superheated, without refreshment, a combustible mixture which seemed to explode in their chests. They shambled along, their heads lolling, sobbing loudly with rending sounds which lacerated their throats. After hours of this they were men walking through flame.

They carted Wilson as if they were wrestling with a stone, struggling forward with agony for fifty yards or a hundred or even two hundred, with the hasty scrambling motions of laborers moving a piano, and then they would set him down, and remain swaying on their feet, their shoulders heaving for the air they could not find under the leaden arch of the sky. In a minute, afraid to rest, feeling anchored to him, they would pick up the litter and labor forward for another short increment over the endless green and yellow hills. On the up-slopes they would bog down, remain holding him for seconds, their legs incapable of climbing any farther, and then they would strain upward again, advance a few more feet, and stand watching each other.

620

And in the places where they went downhill their thighs would quiver with the effort it took to brake themselves from dropping into a full run, and the muscles in their calves and around their shins would knot painfully, tempting them to stumble and lie motionless in the grass without moving for the rest of the day.

Wilson was conscious and in pain. Every time they jolted him he would groan, and he was continually thrashing about on the litter, disturbing the balance and making them stumble. From time to time he would curse at them, and they writhed under it. His screams and shouts flicked through the layers of heat that played over them, goaded them on for a few additional yards.

"Goddammit, you men, Ah been watchin' ya, why in the hell cain't you treat a wounded man proper, jus' shakin' me up an' knockin' all the pus around inside, Stanley, you been doin' it jus' to give me the misery, Ah think it's a pretty low mean old thing jus' treatin' a buddy like this . . ." His voice would become thin, querulous. Every now and then he would scream from a sudden bump.

"Goddammit. Lea' me alone men." From pain, from the heat, he would blubber like a child. "Ah wouldn' do to you like you been doin' to me." He would lie back, his mouth open, his breath stirring in the arid cave of his throat like steam vibrating out of the spout of a kettle. "Aw, men, take it easy, sonofabitch, men, take it easy."

"We're doin' what we can," Brown would croak.

"You men are actin' pretty piss-poor. Wilson ain't gonna forget. *Goddammit*, men."

And they would labor for another hundred yards, set him down, and gaze stupidly at each other.

Wilson's wound was throbbing painfully. The muscles in his stomach were sore and exhausted from fighting against the pain, and a dry fever had settled in his body. Under the sun all his limbs had become leaden and aching, his chest and throat congested, completely dry. Each jolt of the stretcher shocked him like a blow. He felt the exhaustion of having fought against a man much bigger, much stronger than himself for many hours. He teetered often on the edge of unconsciousness, but always he would be jarred back into his pain by a sudden wrench of the litter. It brought him close to weeping. For minutes at a time he would lie stiff on the stretcher waiting for the next jolt, his teeth clenched in preparation. And when it came, the blow would travel through all the slumbering agonies of his wound, rasping his inflamed nerves. The pain would seem motivated by the litter-bearers and he hated them with the same rage that a man feels for a moment at a piece of furniture when he has barked his leg against it. "You sonofabitch, Brown."

"Shut up, Wilson." Brown shambled forward, almost reeling, his fingers slowly separating on the litter handle. When he would feel the stretcher about to rip out of his hand, he would shout, "Drop him," and kneel beside Wilson trying to regain his breath, massaging one hand with the numb fingers of the other. "Take it easy, Wilson, we're doin' what we can," he would gasp.

"You sonofabitch, Brown, you been shakin' me on purpose."

Brown wanted to cry or to strike him across the face. The jungle sores on his feet had come open and were bleeding inside his shoes, smarting unbearably whenever he halted and became conscious of them. He did not want to go on, but he could see the other litter-bearers staring at him. "Come on, men," he muttered.

They advanced like this for several hours, toiling under the brow of the midday sun. Slowly, inevitably, their will and their resolution were dissolved. They struggled forward through a glare of heat, bound to each other in an unwilling union of exhaustion and rage. Each time one of them stumbled the others hated him, for the load was suddenly increased on their arms, and Wilson's growls of pain bored through their apathy, startled them like a whiplash. They plumbed one level of misery after another. For minutes at a time their vision would blank out almost completely in a flood of nausea. The ground before them would darken, and they would taste their heartbeat in the acrid bile that filled their mouths. They toiled forward numbly, unquestioningly, suffering more than Wilson. Any one of them would have been pleased to have shifted positions with him.

At one o'clock Brown halted them. His feet had been numb for minutes at a time, and he was close to collapse. They left Wilson lying in the sun while they sprawled beside him, their faces close to the earth, drawing great gasping bursts of air. All about them the hills

622

shimmered in the early afternoon heat, refracting their glare from one slope to another without relief. There seemed no breeze at all. Wilson would mumble and rant from time to time but they paid no attention to him. The rest period gave them no relief; all the submerged effects of their exhaustion were being exhumed now, bothered them directly. They retched, languished through long flaccid minutes when they seemed close to unconsciousness, and suffered from recurring spasms of shivering when there seemed no heat left in their bodies.

After a long while, perhaps an hour, Brown sat up, swallowed a few salt tablets and drank almost half his canteen of water. The salt rumbled uncomfortably in his stomach, but he felt some relief. When he stood up to walk over to Wilson, his legs moved without familiarity, weakly, like a man who is out of bed after a long illness. "How're you feelin', boy?" he asked.

Wilson stared at him. With a groping motion his fingers had fluttered up to his forehead, removed the dampened cloth. "You men better leave me, Brown," he croaked feebly. In the past hour, lying on the stretcher, he had slid between consciousness and delirium, and now he was very tired, very spent. To Wilson there was no point in moving on any farther. He was perfectly content at the moment to remain here; he did not think at all of what would happen to him. He knew only that he didn't want to be carried again, could not bear the agony of being jolted on the stretcher.

Brown was tempted, so tempted that he did not dare to believe Wilson. "What are you talking about, boy?"

"Lea' me, men, jus' lea' me." Weaks tears came into Wilson's eyes. Remotely, almost as if it did not concern him, he shook his head. "I'm holdin' ya back, men, jus' lea' me behind." It was all confused in his mind again; he thought they were on a patrol and he was lagging back because of his sickness. "When a man gotta be crappin' all the time, it jus' slows ya up."

Stanley had come up beside Brown. "What does he want us to do, leave him?"

"Yeah."

"Think we ought to?"

Brown generated some rage. "Goddammit, Stanley, what the

hell's the matter with you?" Again Brown was tempted. A deep lassitude had filled his body; he had no desire to move on. "Come on, men, let's go," he bawled. He saw Ridges lying asleep a few feet away and it enraged him. "Come on, Ridges, will you quit dickin'-off?"

Ridges woke up slowly, almost leisurely. "Jus' restin', that's all," he complained mildly. "If a man wants to get some rest . . ." He trailed it off, hooked on his belt and walked over to the litter. "Well, *Ah'm* ready."

They moved on again, but the rest period had been bad for them. They had lost the urgency, the tension, that had driven them forward when everything else was gone. Now after marching a few hundred yards they were almost as tired as they had been when they halted, and the heat of the sun made them dizzy and weak. Wilson began to moan quite steadily.

This tormented them. Their bodies felt powerless and clumsy; each time he groaned they winced with guilt and empathy, and the torments of his wound seemed to pass through the handles of the stretcher up into their arms. They bickered constantly for the first half mile while they still had wind to speak. Everything they did grated on everybody else, and they snapped at each other continually.

"Dammit, Goldstein, why don't you watch it?" Stanley would shout after a sudden jar.

"Watch it yourself."

"Why don't you men quit the fussin' and do some work?" Ridges would mutter.

"Aaah, blow it out," Stanley would shout.

And Brown would interfere. "Stanley, you're talkin' too damn much. Why'n't you do some goddam work?"

They struggled on, enraged at each other. Wilson began to babble again, and they listened to him dully. "Men, why don' you all lea' me, a man who cain't hold up his end ain't worth a goddam. Ah'm jus' holdin' you back. Jus' lea' me, men, that's all Ah ask. Ol' Wilson'll get along, y' don' have to worry about him. Jus' lea' me, men."

"*Jus' lea' me, men.*"

It tickled in their shoulders, washed down to their fingertips,

624

which seemed to loosen on the litter handles. "What the hell you talkin' about, Wilson?" Brown panted. Each of them was fighting his private battle.

Goldstein stumbled, and Wilson shouted at him. "Goldstein, you're a no-good bastard, you done that on purpose, Ah been watchin' ya, and you're no good." The name twisted in Wilson's head; he remembered the handle at his right foot being called Goldstein, and when the litter had dipped in that direction, he had bawled out the name. But now it clicked. "Goldstein's no fuggin good, a man who won't take a drink." He giggled weakly, a little blood welling stickily from the parched hollow of his throat. "Goddam, ol' Croft never knew Ah got a free bottle off him."

Goldstein shook his head angrily, moved forward sullenly, his eyes on the ground. They never forget, the goyim, they never forget, he kept repeating to himself. He felt leagued against all of them. What did this Wilson appreciate of what they were doing for him?

And Wilson lay back again, listening to the fast taut sounds of their sobbing. They were working for him. He understood it abruptly, held the idea for an instant and then lost it, but the emotion it stirred remained with him. "Man, Ah think a lot of you all for what you're doin', but you don't have to stick with ol' Wilson. Jus' lea' me, that's all." And when there was no answer he became fretful. "Goddammit, men, Ah said you can lea' me." He whined like a feverish child.

Goldstein wanted to drop the litter handle. He said we should stop, Goldstein said to himself. But immediately afterward he was moved by Wilson's speech. In the heat and the blunting exhaustion of the march he could not think clearly, and thoughts jerked through him like muscular reactions. We can't leave him, he told himself; he's a generous fellow, and then Goldstein thought of nothing at all but the increasing torment in his arm, the muscle pains that extended across his back down into his straining legs.

Wilson rubbed his tongue against the dry edge of his teeth. "Oh, men, Ah'm thirsty," he chanted. He twisted on the litter, holding up his head toward the leaden glaring sky, his throat poised on the edge of a delicious bliss. Any moment they would give him some water and the torture of his tongue and palate would be assuaged. "Men, gimme a drink," Wilson muttered. "Le's have some water."

They hardly heard him. He had been babbling for water all day, and they had been paying no attention. He dropped his head back, rolled his thickened tongue in the arid cavity of his mouth. "Le's have some water," he bleated. Once more he waited patiently, fought against the vertigo that seemed to revolve him in circles on the litter. "Goddammit, men, y' gonna gimme some water."

"Take it easy, Wilson," Brown muttered.

"*Water,* goddammit."

Stanley halted, his legs quivering, and they set him down. "Give him some water for God's sakes," Stanley shouted.

"You can't give him water with a stomach wound," Goldstein protested.

"What do you know about it?"

"You can't give him water," Goldstein said. "It'll kill him."

"Water's out," Brown panted.

"Aaah, you guys gimme a pain in the ass," Stanley bawled.

"A little water ain't gonna hurt Wilson," Ridges muttered. He felt a touch of surprise and scorn. "Man dies ifen he don't get water." To himself he thought, What are they fussin' so much about?

"Brown, I always thought you were chickenshit. Not even giving a wounded man some water." Stanley reeled in the sunlight. "An old buddy like Wilson an' you won't even give him any water 'cause some doctor starts talking about it." There was a terror back of his speech which he could not quite face. Even in his exhaustion he knew there was something wrong, dangerously wrong, in giving Wilson a drink, but he avoided that, rousing in himself an emotion of certain righteousness. "Try to relieve a man of a little suffering and what the hell do ya get for it? Goddammit, Brown, what the hell do ya want to do, torture him?" He felt himself driven by an excitement, a necessity. "Give him a drink, what will it cost ya?"

"It would be murder," Goldstein said.

"Aw, shut up, ya dumb Jew bastard." Stanley spoke with fury.

"You can't say that to me," Goldstein piped. He was quivering with anger now too, but back of it was the shattering realization that Stanley had been so friendly the night before. You can't trust any of them, he thought numbly with a certain bitter pleasure. At least this time, he was certain.

Brown interfered. "Let's cut it out, men, let's get movin' again." Before they could say any more, he bent down at one of the litter handles, and motioned the others to take up their positions. Once again they staggered forward into the blare and dazzle of the afternoon sun.

"Gimme some water," Wilson whined.

Once more Stanley halted. "Let's give him some, get him out of his misery."

"Shut up, Stanley!" Brown waved his free arm loosely. "Keep going and cut out all this talk." Stanley glared at him. With his exhaustion he was feeling an intense hatred for Brown.

Wilson's thoughts rolled back into his pain. He drifted along, not conscious for a while of the jarring of the litter, not even thinking directly of anything about him. Sensations washed through to him through the filter of his delirium. He could feel his wound throbbing, and in his mind he saw a horn boring into his stomach, pausing and then boring forward again. "Ahhhrr." He heard himself groan without feeling his voice stir in his throat. He was so hot. For minutes he floated on the stretcher, his tongue exploring the roots of his teeth for moisture. He was convinced that his legs and feet were on fire, and he twitched them experimentally, rubbing them together as if to extinguish the blaze. "Put it out, put it out," he mumbled from time to time.

A new pain caught him, familiar and demanding. He felt a cramp in his lower belly, and the sweat stirred on his forehead, mounted into individual droplets. He fought against it with a childish fear of punishment and then relapsed into the heat and pleasure of voiding, the good strain on his bowels. For a moment he was lying again with his back upon the broken fence outside his father's house, the southern sun imparting a lazy sensuality in his loins. "Hey, nigger, what's that mule's name?" he mumbled, and then giggled weakly, content and drained. For a moment his hand clutched the litter, and he watched the colored girl walking by, twisted his head. The woman beside him was caressing his stomach. "Woodrow, do ya always spit before ya piss?"

627

"Jus' for good luck," he mumbled aloud, trying now on the litter to empty his bladder. But another pain, sharp and grinding, tore through his loins. He remembered, or at least his groin muscles recalled the difficulty, knotting in resistance. It shattered the images, left him aware and troubled and perplexed, conscious for the first time of the way he had soiled himself. He had a picture of his loins putrefacted and a deep misery passed through him. Why in the hell did it have to happen to me? What's it got to do with what Ah been doin'? And he lifted up his head and mumbled again, "Brown, you think that wound's gonna git all the pus outa me?"

But no one answered, and he fell back again, brooding over his illness. A chain of unpleasant memories bothered him, and he became conscious again of the discomforts of the stretcher, the effort it cost him to remain lying on his back for so many hours. He made a feeble attempt to turn over, but it was too painful. He felt as if somebody were leaning against his stomach.

"Git off, men," he shouted.

And then he remembered the weight. On the night so many weeks before when the Japanese had tried to cross the river he had felt that same pressure in his chest and stomach as he had waited behind the machine gun.

"We-you-coming-to-get." They had shouted that at Croft and him, and he shuddered now, bringing his hands up before his face. "We got to stop 'em, men, they're comin' now," he moaned, pitching on the litter. "Banzaaiiiigh, aaiiiiiiiigh!" he shouted, the sounds gurgling in his throat. *"Come on, recon, up, git up here!"*

The litter-bearers halted and set him down. "What's he yellin' about?" Brown asked.

"I cain't see 'em, I jus' cain't see 'em. Where the hell's the flares?" Wilson bawled. He was grasping a machine-gun handle in his left palm, his forefinger extended to the trigger. "Who the hell's at the other gun? I cain't remember."

Ridges shook his head. "He's talkin' 'bout that Jap attack on the river."

Something of Wilson's panic transferred to the other men. Goldstein and Ridges, who had been on the river, stared at Wilson un-

628

easily. The vast barren stretches of the hills about them seemed a little foreboding now.

"I hope we don't run into any Japanese," Goldstein said.

"They ain't a chance," Brown told him. He mopped the sweat out of his eyes, stared weakly into the distance. "Nobody around," he panted, but a feeling of weakness, of desperation welled in him. If they were to fall into an ambush now . . . He felt like crying again. There were too many things asked of him, and he was so enfeebled. A vortex of nausea resolved itself in his stomach, and he retched emptily, obtaining a mild relief from the coldness of his sweat. He couldn't let go. Brown heard himself saying, "We gotta move on, men."

Underneath the moistened handkerchief, Wilson could barely see. The cotton was colored olive drab, and it glared under the sun with yellow and black colors that seemed to beat into his brain. He felt as if he were choking a little for air. Once more his arms thrashed up toward his head. "Goddammit," Wilson cried, "let's move those Japs, men, if we gonna get a goddam souvenir." He struggled again on the stretcher. "Who put that bag on my head? Red, that's a lousy trick to play on a buddy. I cain't see in this fuggin cave, move that Jap off my head."

The handkerchief slipped down over his nose and Wilson blinked into the sun and closed his eyes once more. "Watch out, that snake!" he shouted suddenly, his body cringing. "Red, you got to shoot it careful, take a good bead, take a good bead." He mumbled something, and then his body relaxed. "Ah tell you, a dead man look jus' like a shoulder o' lamb been lying around too long."

Brown replaced the handkerchief, and Wilson struggled beneath it. "Ah cain't breathe. Goddammit, they're shootin' at us, you know how to swim, Taylor, goddammit lemme get behind the boat!"

Brown shuddered. Wilson was talking about the Motome invasion. Once more Brown was choking in the salt water, knowing the final resigned terror that came with accepting death. In his exhaustion, he felt for a moment as if he were swallowing the water again, feeling the same numb surprise at realizing that he could not control himself from gulping; the water had washed down his throat with a momentum and will of its own.

629

That was the cause of it all, he thought now bitterly. The memory always loosed such panic and weakness in him. He had learned then that he was helpless in the shattering gyre of the war, and he could never shake the recollection. Doggedly, through his exhaustion, he told himself that he had to bring Wilson back, but he did not believe it now at all.

Through the afternoon the litter-bearers continued on their march. About two o'clock it began to rain, and the ground quickly became muddy. The rain at first was a relief; they welcomed it on their blazing flesh, wriggled their toes in the slosh that permeated their boots. The wetness of their clothing was pleasurable. They enjoyed being cold for a few minutes. But as the rain continued the ground became too soft, and their uniforms cleaved uncomfortably to their bodies. Their feet began to slip in the mud, their shoes became weighted with muck and stuck in the ground with each step. They were too fagged to notice the difference immediately, their bodies had quickly resumed the stupor of the march, but by half an hour they had slowed down almost to a halt. Their legs had lost almost all puissance; for minutes they would stand virtually in place, unable to co-ordinate their thighs and feet to move forward. On the hills they would climb upward only a foot or two at a time and halt, staring stupidly at each other, their chests panting, their feet sinking deeper into the mud. Every fifty yards they would lay Wilson down, pause for a minute or two, and then trudge forward.

The sun came out again, inflamed the wet kunai grass and dried the earth whose moisture rose in sluggish clouds of mist. The men gasped, took deep useless breaths of the leaden wet air, and shambled forward grunting and sobbing, their arms slowly and inevitably bending toward the ground. They would start off carrying Wilson at waist level but by the time they set him down thirty or forty yards ahead his weight had bent them over until the litter was skimming the ground. The grass interfered with them, tripping at their feet, and meshing against their bodies, flicking into their faces. They labored forward in desperation and rage, advancing until their anger lapsed and then there was nothing left to force them on.

About three o'clock they stopped for another long break underneath an isolated tree. For half an hour no one said anything, but even through their prostration other emotions were working. Brown lay on his stomach staring at his hands, which were cruelly blistered and spotted with dried blood from a variety of old sores and cuts which had opened again. He knew abruptly that he was through; he could stand up, even march perhaps another mile of intolerable agony, but he was going to collapse. His entire body was racked; he had been retching emptily ever since they had halted, and his vision was uncertain. Every minute or two a wave of faintness would glide through him, darkening his sight and pocking his back with an icy perspiration. All his extremities were quivering, and his hands shook too much for him to light a cigarette. He hated himself for his weakness and he hated Goldstein and Ridges because they were less exhausted than he, and he loathed Stanley and hoped Stanley was weaker than he. His bitterness resolved into self-pity for a moment — he was angry at Croft for sending them out with only four men. Croft must have known it would be impossible.

Stanley was coughing thickly into his hands, which he held against his face. Brown looked at him, and found a focus for his resentment. He felt Stanley had betrayed him. He had made Stanley corporal, and Stanley had turned against him. Perhaps if they had had another man instead of Stanley they might have proceeded better.

"What's the matter, Stanley," he blurted out, "you ready to quit?"

"Aaah, fug you, Brown." Stanley was furious. Brown had taken this detail because he was afraid of continuing with the patrol, and he had brought him into it. What they had gone through was far worse than anything the rest of the platoon would meet. If he had stayed with them he would have done better, and Croft might have noticed him. "You think you're okay, don't you?" he asked Brown. "Listen, I know why you took this goddam litter."

"Why?" Brown listened with a numb stricken anticipation.

"It's because you were too fuggin yellow to keep up with the patrol. A sergeant taking a litter detail, Jesus."

Brown heard him almost with satisfaction. This was the worst thing he could imagine, it was the moment he had been dreading for so long, and it did not seem so horrible. "Stanley, you're just as yellow as I am, we're in the same goddam boat." He searched for something with which to hurt him, and came up with it. "You're worrying too much about your wife, Stanley."

"Aaah, shut your . . ." But it had caught him. In his weakness he was convinced now that his wife was unfaithful, and he passed through a cruel montage of her infidelities in an interval of a few seconds. It loosed a whole web of insecurities, and he felt like weeping. It was unfair that he should be left so much alone.

Brown pushed his palms against the ground, lifted himself dully. "Come on, let's get going." He felt dizzy on his feet, and his hands had the spongy powerless sensation of a man awakening in the morning, unable to grasp anything.

They all got up very slowly, fastened their belts, knelt beside the litter and started forward again, After they had gone a hundred yards, Stanley knew he was not going to continue. He had always resented Wilson mildly because Wilson had more combat than he, but now he did not think of Wilson at all. He just knew that he was going to quit; he had gone through too much, and what did it count for?

They set Wilson down for a short rest and Stanley reeled away and then fell to the ground. He closed his eyes deliberately, pretending he had fainted. The others gathered about him, looked at him without feeling.

"Shoot, le's jus' put him up on top of Wilson," Ridges said, "an' anyone else we jus' put on top o' that. I'll take y' all back." He guffawed wearily. Stanley had mocked him so often that he felt a mild revenge now. But immediately he was ashamed. Pride goeth before a fall, he told himself soberly. He listened to Stanley's rapt sobbing with a distant amusement. It reminded him of a mule which had collapsed once after plowing in a summer sun, and he felt the same mixture of amusement and pity.

"What the hell we gonna do?" Brown panted.

Wilson looked up abruptly. He seemed quite conscious for the moment, and his broad fleshy face looked incredibly tired and gaunt. "Jus' lea' me, men," he said weakly. "Ol' Wilson is through."

Brown and Goldstein were enticed. "We can't leave ya," Brown said.

632

"Jus' stop, men, and the hell with it."

"I dunno," Brown said.

Goldstein shook his head abruptly. "We have to carry him back," he said. He could not have explained why, but he had remembered abruptly the moment when the gun slid down the embankment.

Brown stared again at Stanley. "We can't go on and leave him here."

Ridges was disgusted. "If y' start a job, then y' finish it. We ain't gonna set here on account of one man."

Goldstein saw the solution abruptly. "Brown, why don't you stay with Stanley?" Goldstein was very tired, not too far from prostration himself, but it was impossible for him to quit. Brown was almost as sick as Stanley. It was the only answer, and yet Goldstein resented it. I always have to be nicer than the next fellow, he thought.

"How'll you know the way back?" Brown asked. He had to be honest now, face all the objections. In his defeat it was very important for him to maintain a last tatter of dignity.

"Ah know the way," Ridges grunted.

"Well, then, I'll stay," Brown said. "Somebody's gotta take care of Stanley." He shook him for a moment, but Stanley's moaning continued. "He's through for the day."

"Listen, I'll tell you what," Goldstein said, "after Stanley gets up you can catch us, and give some help. That'll be fine, huh?"

"Okay, leave it that way," Brown said. Both of them knew that would not happen.

"Let's be movin'," Ridges said. He and Goldstein got at opposite ends of the stretcher, lifted it painfully and staggered off. After twenty yards they set it down again, stripped off all but one pack and one rifle. "You bring that stuff in, all right, Brown?" Goldstein asked. Brown nodded.

They labored off again, advancing at a painfully slow pace. Even stripped of equipment, the litter with Wilson on it weighed more than two hundred pounds. It took them almost an hour to cross a low ridge a half mile away.

When they were out of sight, Brown took off his shoes and massaged the blisters and sores on his feet. They had almost ten miles to go. Brown sighed, and slowly kneaded his big toe. I oughta turn in my stripes, he thought.

But he knew he wouldn't. It'll just go on and on until I get busted. He looked at Stanley, who was still lying on the ground. Aaah, the two of us are just alike. He'll be havin' my worries soon.

10

CROFT had an instinctive knowledge of land, sensed the stresses and torsions that had first erupted it, the abrasions of wind and water. The platoon had long ceased to question any direction he took; they knew he would be right as infallibly as sun after darkness or fatigue after a long march. They never even thought about it any more.

Croft himself did not know the reason. He would never have been able to explain what prompted him when he was circling a bluff to decide on an upper or lower ramp when both spiraled up the walls of a cliff. He knew only that the one he had not chosen would end in a sheer fall. The lower might narrow into nothing, or the upper ramp lose itself in an isolated knoll or outcropping. A geologist with years of study and field experience might have chosen as well, but it would have taken him longer; there would have been a pause while the man raced through his jargon, weighed the factors, estimated the intangibles, correlated all the graphs of growth and decay, expansion and decrease, and then the geologist would have been uncertain. There were, too many elements, after all.

Croft felt the nature of rock and earth, knew as well as he knew the flexing of his muscles how in an age of tempest the boulders had strained and surged until the earth had shaped itself. He had always a feeling of that birth-storm when he looked at land; he almost always knew how a hill would look on the other side. It was the variety of knowledge that felt intuitively the nearness of water no matter how foreign the swatch of earth over which he was traveling.

The aptitude might have been innate, or perhaps it was developed in all the years he had worked on land driving cattle, all the patrols

634

he had led, all the thousand occasions when it had been important for him to know which route to take. In any case, he led the platoon up the mountain without hesitation, scrambling upward from ridge to ridge, branching from defile to defile, halting against his desire to wait for the others to catch up with him and regain their wind. Each halt annoyed him. Despite all the exertion of the preceding days, he was restless and impatient now, driven forward by a demanding tension in himself. He had the mountain in his teeth as completely and excitedly as a hound which has picked up the scent. He was continually eager to press on to the next rise, anxious to see what was beyond. The sheer mass of the mountain inflamed him.

He had brought the platoon up the first clay gully in the cliffs, and at the top he had paused for a moment and then filed off to the right to climb a steeply rounded slope of kunai grass which abutted a rock wall thirty feet high. He bore back to the left again, and found a series of slabs up which they could climb. Above that was a tumble of rocks which issued into a sharp ridge-line zigzagging toward the middle slopes of the mountain. He led the platoon along it, bounding forward through the tall grass, pausing only at the places where the ridge grew dangerously narrow.

The ridge was pocked with boulders, and dropped almost vertically on one side to the cliffs beneath. In the kunai grass there were places where the footing was very uncertain; the men could not see below their knees and they felt their way forward slowly, holding onto the tall stalks with both hands, their rifles crossed over their packs. They climbed along it steadily like this for half an hour, and then took a break. Little more than an hour had elapsed since Croft had led them up the first gully, and the sun was still in the east, but they were tired. They accepted the break eagerly, sprawling in a line along the narrow top of the ridge.

Wyman had been panting heavily for the last twenty minutes of the march, and he lay quietly on his back, waiting for the spring to return to his legs.

"How're you feeling?" Roth asked.

"I'm pooped." Wyman shook his head. They would be continuing like this all day, and he knew with the experience he had gained on this patrol that he would not be able to make it. "I'm going to lighten my pack," he told Roth.

But everything in it was essential. Wyman deliberated whether to throw away his rations or his blanket. They had taken twenty-one K rations with them and only seven had been eaten so far. But if they crossed the mountain and scouted through the Jap rear they would be gone at least a week. He couldn't take the chance. Wyman withdrew his blanket from the pack, and tossed it a few yards away.

"Whose blanket is that?" Croft had seen it, and was walking toward them.

"Mine, Sergeant," Wyman admitted.

"Go fetch it and stick it in your pack."

"I really don't need it," Wyman said softly.

Croft glared at him. Now that Hearn was gone, the discipline was his, and it was not going to be threatened. With Hearn, sloppy habits had developed which he must cauterize. Besides, waste always offended him. "Go get it, boy, I'm telling you."

Wyman sighed, stood up, and retrieved the blanket. As he was folding it, Croft softened a trifle. He was pleased at how quickly Wyman had obeyed him. "Listen, you're gonna need that blanket. You wake up with a cold ass tonight, and you're gonna be feeling damn glad you got it then."

"Yeah." Wyman couldn't arouse any enthusiasm. He was thinking how much the blanket weighed.

"How do you feel, Roth?" Croft asked.

"I'm all right, Sergeant."

"I don't want ya to be dickin'-off today."

"No." But Roth was furious. As he watched Croft saunter away and talk to a few of the other men, he tugged at some grass with his fingers, pulling it out angrily. "Doesn't even give a fellow a chance," he whispered to Wyman.

"Oh, gee, I wish the Lootenant . . ." Wyman felt a sudden depression. Other things were becoming clear now too; before, with Hearn, there had been a chance. "What a lousy break."

Roth nodded. You'd think he'd give the underdog a break, but Croft was like a wolf. "If I had the platoon," he said in his slow pompous voice, "I'd give the men a break, I'd try to be decent, appeal to better nature."

"Yeah, I would too," Wyman commiserated.

"I dunno." Roth sighed. Once he had been in a spot like that. His first job after two years without one during the depression had been for a real estate agent. He had made the collections. It was a job he had never liked, and he had had to take a lot of abuse from tenants who resented him. But once he had been sent out to an apartment where there was an old couple who were in arrears for several months' rent. Their story had been sad, like all the stories he was hearing then — they had lost their savings in a bank crash. Roth had been tempted to give them another month, but he did not dare to return to his office. He had taken no collections that day. And so to hide his sympathy he had become harsh with them, and had threatened eviction. They had pleaded and he had found himself enjoying his role, elaborating the terrors of being dispossessed. "I don't care where you get the money," he had said at last. "Just get it."

Now, as he thought of it, he felt some anxiety for a moment, wished he had been kinder as if that would allay his own fate. Nah, he thought, that's superstitious. It hasn't got anything to do with this. He wondered if Croft perhaps felt the same way when he was cruel, but that was ridiculous. It's something in the past, forget it, he told himself. But he was afraid.

And Wyman was thinking of a football game he had played once on a sandlot. It had been the team on his block against the team from another one, and he had been playing tackle. In the second half his legs had given out and he had a humiliating memory of the opposing runners cutting through his position almost at will while he had dragged himself unwillingly through each play. He had wanted to quit and there were no substitutes. They had lost by several touchdowns but there had been a kid on his team who had never given up. Almost every play that kid had been in on the tackles, yelling encouragement, getting angrier and angrier at every advance the other team made.

He just wasn't like that, Wyman decided. He wasn't the hero type, and he realized it with a suddenness and a completeness which would have crushed him months before. Now it only made him wistful. He would never understand men like Croft; he only wanted to keep out of the way of them. But still, what made them tick? he wondered. What were they always going for?

"I hate this damn mountain," he said to Roth.

"Likewise." Roth sighed again. The mountain was so open, so high. Even when he lay on his back he could not see the top of it. It just reared above him, ridge beyond ridge, and higher up it seemed made entirely of rock. He had hated the jungle, had started with terror every time an insect crawled over him or a bird chattered suddenly in the brush. He had never been able to see anything, and it had been rife with so many foul odors which choked his nostrils. There had seemed no room to breathe, and yet now he wished he was back in the jungle. It was so secure in contrast to these naked ridges, these gaunt alien vaults of stone and sky. They would keep going up and up and there was no safety in it. The jungle was filled with all kinds of dangers but they did not seem so severe now; at least he was used to them. But here, one misstep and it would be death. It was better to live in a cellar than to walk a tightrope. Roth plucked angrily at the grass again. Why didn't Croft turn back? What could he hope to gain?

Martinez's body ached. He was feeling a reaction from the previous night, and all morning as they had worked up the mountain he had plodded along, wretched with anxiety, his limbs trembling, his body wet with perspiration. His mind had played a few necessary tricks on him; the connection between his reconnaissance and Hearn's death was happily smudged, or at least on the surface, but ever since the second ambush he had been feeling the apprehension of a man in a dream who knows he is guilty, is waiting for his punishment, and cannot remember his crime.

Toiling up the first slopes of the mountain, Martinez brooded about the Japanese soldier he had killed. He could see his face clearly, far more vividly now in the cruel dazzle of the morning sun than he had the night before, and in his memory he traced over every motion the Jap had made. Once again Martinez could feel the blood trickling over his fingers, leaving them sticky. He examined his hand, and with a pang of horror discovered a dried black thread of blood in the web-

638

bing between two of his fingers. He grunted with disgust and the excessive fear one feels in crushing an insect. Ahrr. And immediately afterward he could see the Jap picking his nose.

He was to blame.

For what? They were on the mountain now, and if he didn't . . . if he hadn't . . . No kill Jap, go back to beach, he told himself. But that made no sense either, and his anxiety prickled along his back. He gave up the effort to think and trudged along in the middle of the platoon, finding no release in the exertion of the ascent. The more tired he felt the tauter his nerves became. His limbs had the heavy painful sensitivity of a man in fever.

In the break he flopped down beside Polack and Gallagher. There was something he wanted to talk to them about, but he was not quite sure what it could be.

Polack was grinning at him. "Whadeya say, scout?"

"Oh, nothing," he said in a low voice. He never knew what to answer to "Whadeya say?" and it always made him uneasy.

"They ought to give ya the day off," Polack said.

"Yah." He had been a poor scout the night before, he had done everything wrong. If he hadn't killed the Jap — that was the keystone of all his mistakes. He could not have named them, but he was convinced that he had made many mistakes.

"Nothin' happened, huh?" Gallagher asked.

Martinez shrugged, saw Polack looking at the dried blood on his hand. It would look like dirt, but he found himself saying, "Japs in the pass, I kill one." He felt relieved.

"Huh?" Polack said, "what's the score? That looey told us the pass was empty."

Martinez shrugged again. "Damn fool. He argue with Croft, say pass empty, after I come back, see Japs. Croft tell him Martinez good man, know what he see but Looey he don't want to listen, stubborn damn fool."

Gallagher spat. "Ya had to knock off a Jap and he didn't believe it?"

Martinez nodded, believing this was the truth now. "I listen them talk, man damn fool, I don't say nothing, Croft tell him." The entire

639

sequence was confused in his mind. He could not have sworn to it, but at that moment he felt he remembered Croft and Hearn arguing, Hearn saying that they must go through the pass and Croft disagreeing. "Croft tell me keep my mouth shut when he talk to Hearn, know Hearn damn fool."

Gallagher shook his head unbelievingly. "What a dumb stubborn fug that looey was. Well, he got it."

"Yeah, he got it," Polack said. This was all mixed up. If a guy is told there's Japs in the pass, and he decides just like that there ain't any . . . That was a little bit too dumb. Polack didn't know. He felt an annoying frustration as if there were something under his finger, something he could point to. He felt unaccountably angry.

"So ya had to knock off a Jap," Gallagher said with a grudged admiration.

Martinez nodded. He had murdered a man, and if he were to die now, be killed on the mountain or on the other side of it, he would be lost with a mortal sin. "Yes, I kill him," he said, feeling even now a trace of sustaining pride. "Sneak up back of him and *cahoootz* . . ." He made a ripping sound. "And the Jap is . . ." Martinez snapped his fingers.

Polack laughed. "Takes moxie, you know. You're okay, Japbait."

He ducked his head shyly accepting the praise. He was hovering between merriment and depression when he remembered the gold teeth he had smashed out of the corpse's jaw on the battlefield, and he was marooned suddenly in a blanket of misery and fear. That sin he had not confessed and now this one too. His first emotion was bitterness. It seemed unfair that there should be no chaplain nearby who could save him. For just a moment Martinez thought of sneaking away from the platoon and heading back across the hills to the beach, where he could return safely and be confessed. But immediately afterward he knew it was impossible.

And he realized why he had dropped down beside Polack and Gallagher. They were Catholics and they could understand this. He was so deeply absorbed in his mood that he assumed instinctively they were feeling the same way. "You know," he said, "we get hit, pop off, no priest."

640

The words lashed Gallagher like a wet towel. "Yeah, yeah, that's right," he mumbled, caught up suddenly in a train of fear and unpleasant anticipation. He pictured automatically the postures of all the men in the platoon who had been wounded or killed, capped it off by seeing himself bleeding on the ground. The mountain yawed shiveringly above them, and Gallagher was filled with dread. He wondered for a moment if Mary had received absolution, was convinced she hadn't, and felt a little resentful toward her. Her sin would be visited on him. But that was dissipated immediately in remorse at thinking unkindly of someone who was dead. At this instant he was not thinking of her as his dead wife.

The stupor, the stoicism with which he had protected himself on the patrol so far was rapidly dissolving. He hated Martinez at this second for having said what he did. He had never quite allowed himself to state this fear before on the patrol. "Just like the fuggin Army," he said furiously, and again he felt guilty for having used an obscenity.

"What're you gettin' your balls in an uproar?" Polack asked.

"No priest," Martinez said eagerly. Polack had spoken with such assurance that Martinez was certain he had some answer, some escape from the aisles of the catechism.

"You think it ain't important?" Gallagher asked.

"Listen, you want to know somethin'?" Polack said. "You don't got to worry about that stuff. It's all a lousy racket."

They were appalled. Gallagher peeked instinctively over his shoulder at the mountain. Both he and Martinez wished they were not sitting with Polack. "What are you, a fuggin atheist?" This time the profanity did not matter. Gallagher was thinking that it was true the Italians and Polacks always made the worst Catholics.

"You believe that crap?" Polack asked. "Listen, I been t'rough the mill, I know what the score is. It's just a goddam good racket for makin' money."

Martinez tried not to listen.

Polack was riding his anger. A long-repressed hostility was coming out, and with it a sustaining bravado, for he also was afraid. He felt as if he were taunting a guy like Lefty Rizzo. "You're a Mex, and

you're Irish, you get some benefits outa the goddam thing. The Polacks they don't get a damn thing. You ever hear of a Polack cardinal
in America? Naw. I oughta know, I got a sister a nun." He thought
of her for an instant, was bothered again by the sensation of something
he could not understand. He looked at Martinez. What was the score?
"I'm goddamned if they tie the can to me," he said, not quite sure
what he meant, to what he referred. He was terribly angry. "If you
know what the hell's goin' on, you're a sucker if you just sit around
and let 'em do it to ya," he said furiously.

"You don't know what you're talking about," Gallagher muttered.

"Come on, men, get your packs on." It was Croft again. Polack
looked around, startled, shook his head as Croft left. "Yeah, up the
mountain, c'mon, c'mon," he jeered. His hands were trembling a little
with rage.

Their conversation was truncated there, but each of them was
troubled as they marched.

For the rest of the morning, the platoon clambered up the ridge.
It seemed endless. They passed along rocky ledges, up knife-edged
slopes of kunai grass so steep that they climbed by clutching at the
roots as though they were ascending a ladder. They passed through a
forest which straddled the ridge and sheered down to the floor of the
gullies beneath them. They went farther and farther up until their
limbs were trembling and their packs felt like hundred-pound bags of
flour. And each time they came to a minor peak they were certain the
crest of the mountain was near, and all they saw instead was another
half mile of tortuous ridge which abutted still another crest. Croft
warned them. Several times during the morning, he stopped and said,
"You men might jus' as well realize right now that the goddam
mountain's pretty big, an' you ain't gettin' to the top in a hurry." They
listened to him, but they could not believe him. It was too painful to
climb without the supporting notion that their labors would be over
soon.

At noon they reached the end of the ridge and had a shock. It
dropped for several hundred feet of precipitous rocks into a valley of
stone set in the middle of the mountain, and beyond it the center of

Mount Anaka rose far above them, ascending as high as they could see in tier upon tier of forest and clay and jungle and rock, rising vertiginously for what seemed like thousands and thousands of feet. They could not even glimpse the peak; it was lost in a coronet of clouds.

"Jesus, have we got to climb *that?*" one of the men panted.

Croft stared uneasily at them. It was too obviously an expression of the way they all felt. He was tired himself, almost as tired as he had been, and he knew he would have to drive them every yard upward. "We're gonna eat a ration here, and then we're gonna go on. You men understand that?"

There was a subdued muttering again. He sat down on a boulder and stared in the direction from which they had come. Miles away he could see the yellow hills where they had been ambushed, and where someplace now Brown and his litter detail must be traveling. Far off he could see the fringe of jungle that bordered the island and beyond it the sea from which they had come. It was all wilderness; there seemed no one, nothing alive in any of it. The war on the other side of the mountain was remote at this moment.

Behind him Mount Anaka bored into his back as if it were a human thing. He turned around and stared at it soberly, feeling again the crude inarticulate thrill it always gave him. He was going to climb it; he swore it to himself.

But all around him he could feel the pressure of the men. He knew that none of them liked him, and he hardly cared, but now they hated him and he could feel it as almost a leaden oppression in the air.

And they had to get up. If they failed, then the thing he had done with Hearn was wrong, and he had been bucking the Army, simply disobeying an order. Croft was troubled. He would have to carry the platoon virtually on his back and it was going to be very difficult. He spat, and slit the end off a cardboard K ration. As with everything else, he did this neatly, expertly.

Late into the afternoon Ridges and Goldstein struggled along with Wilson. They moved at a torturously slow pace, toting him forward for ten yards or at most fifteen before they set him down. An ant traveling in a straight line would have gone literally as fast. They did not think of quitting or continuing, they hardly ever listened to Wilson's ramblings, there was nothing in all the heat and effort but the dumb imperative to carry him on. They did not talk, they were exhausted beyond speech, they only shambled forward like blind men crossing a strange and terrifying street. Their fatigue had cut through so many levels, had blunted finally so many of their senses that they were reduced to the lowest common denominator of their existence. Carrying him was the only reality they knew.

And so for hours they labored forward, ready to collapse at any moment, but somehow never quite falling unconscious. Toward the end they had only a dumb wonder that they could abuse their bodies so mightily and have them still function.

Wilson fell into a fever and drifted along in a heavy swell of fog. The jolting of the litter became dull and leaden, almost pleasant. The few words he heard, the hoarse panting communications between Ridges and Goldstein, the sound of his own voice, indeed all sensations entered his head quite separately like doors opening into individual closets. His senses were exceptionally vivid, he felt every spasm of their muscles in the tremors of the litter, and obversely the pains of his wound seemed remote, something that came to him outside the envelope of his body. But one thing had deserted him. He had no will. He was completely passive, blissfully tired, and it took him minutes to decide to ask for anything, or to bring his hand up to his forehead to chase an insect. And when he did, his fingers remained motionless on his face for almost as long before he dropped his arm again. He was almost happy.

He rambled on about anything that came into his mind, talking for minutes at a time, his voice rasping weakly or rising to a shout without any control. And the men carrying him listened without understanding the meaning of his words or even caring.

"They was woman in Kansas when Ah was out at Riley, she used to take me up and live wi' me jus' as if Ah was her husband. Ah never even stayed in the goddam barracks, Ah jus' use' to tell 'em mah wife was in town. That woman use' to cook for me and mend mah uniforms and starch 'em nice as you please, they wa'n't a damn thing she wouldn' do for me." He smiled dreamily. "Ah gotta picture of her Ah'd like to show ya if you jus' wait a minute." His hand would fumble at his pocket, then forget about it. "Figgered Ah wasn't married and Ah never set her right, Ah figgered Ah might even shack up with her after the waw, and what was the goddam sense of jus' losin' a good woman, Ah never could see the point to that. Ah jus' tole her Ah was a collidge gradjit, and she believe' me. Goddam women'll believe any damn thing ifen you just keep layin' 'em regular." He sighed, coughed feebly, a little blood inching once more out of his mouth. It stirred a few ripples of fear in him, and he shook his head. He was weary and yet he couldn't give up. "They get me back damn doctors'll fix me up good as new." He shook his head. The bullet had whanged into his flesh with incredible force and he had bled at intervals for a day and a half, had been shocked and jolted on the litter, had undergone the torments of his wound. But it never occurred to him to quit. There were so many things he wanted to do.

"Ah tell you men Ah ain't sayin' screwin' a nigger is right thing to do, but Ah git a little tempted ever' now and then. They was a nigger gal use' to pass mah pappy's house almost ev' day, an' Ah can still see way her ass wiggle."

He roused himself almost on his elbow, looked at Ridges evenly for a moment.

"Eveh screw any nigger stuff?" he asked him.

Ridges stopped, set the stretcher down. For once he had heard Wilson. "You can shut up that kine of talk," he told him. His breath came in heavy sobs and he stared at Wilson vacantly as if he could not focus his eyes. "Nuff of that," he blurted out. Even in his exhaustion he was profoundly shocked. "Ought know better talk like that," he panted.

"Ridges, you're jus' chickenshit," Wilson said.

Ridges shook his head like a bull. All his life there had been any number of things he could not do. Making love to a Negro was a luxury as well as a sin to him; it was one of the excessive things you could not do and survive. "Shut up, Wilson."

But Wilson was far away already. The warmth in his body, the pleasantly heavy lassitude of his limbs tricked him. He thought it was sexual anticipation, and a thick foundationless lust rose in his throat.

645

He closed his eyes, recalling a moonlit night and the creekbank of the river outside his town. He chuckled weakly, some phlegm burbling into his throat. He swallowed it again. He felt his cheeks puckering, and he lapsed into a gentle weeping which issued easily out of him. He noticed it with surprise.

Suddenly he was aware of his mouth again, felt his tongue lolling in his throat. "Gimme some water, huh, men?" There was no answer and he said again patiently. "Jus' a little drink, huh, men?"

They would not answer him, and he was angry. *"Goddammit,* men, gimme a little water."

"Hold off," Ridges said hoarsely.

"Men, Ah do anythin' for ya, y' gimme a little water."

Ridges set him down. Wilson's cries rasped against his senses. It was the only thing that could arouse him by now.

"You men are just sonsofbitches."

"You cain't have it," Ridges said. He could see no harm in it, which made it harder for him to refuse, but he was also bitter at Wilson. We done without, neveh made any fuss, he told himself. "Wilson, you cain't have it." His voice was final and Wilson lapsed into reverie again.

They picked up the stretcher and tugged forward a few yards, laid it down again. The sun was drifting toward the western horizon and it grew cooler, but they paid little attention. Wilson was a burden they had to carry; it would go on and on and they could never let him go. They did not understand this, but comprehension was lurking behind their fatigue. They only knew that they must move on, and they did. All afternoon until it was dark Ridges and Goldstein staggered forward their few inches at a time, and slowly the inches added up. By the time they had stopped for the night, covered Wilson with one of their two blankets and bundled up together beside each other to sleep in stupor, they had advanced Wilson five miles from the place where they had left Brown and Stanley. Already the jungle was not too far away. Although they did not say it, they had glimpsed it from the top of the last hill they had crossed. Tomorrow they might be sleeping on the beach, waiting for the boat to bring them back.

11

Major Dalleson was in a quandary. The General had left that morning — the third morning of the patrol — for Army Headquarters in an attempt to get a destroyer for the invasion of Botoi Bay, and Dalleson effectively had been left in command. Colonel Newton, the CO of the 460th, and Lieutenant Colonel Conn technically ranked Dalleson, but in the General's absence Dalleson was in charge of operations, and now he had a tough problem before him.

The attack had been grinding ahead for five days, had bogged down only yesterday. They had expected it, for the advance had been ahead of schedule, and it was probable the Japanese would increase their resistance. In consideration of this, Cummings had told him to mark time. "Things are going to be quiet, Dalleson. I suspect there'll be an attack or two from the Japs but nothing to worry about. Just keep up your pressure on the front as a whole. If I can wangle a destroyer or two, we'll be able to knock off the campaign in a week."

Simple enough instructions, but things were not turning out that way. An hour after the General's plane had taken off, Dalleson received a bewildering patrol report. A squad from E Company had patrolled a thousand yards into the jungle beyond their latest positions and found a Japanese bivouac deserted. Unless the co-ordinates they reported were completely incorrect, that bivouac should have been nearly in the rear of the Toyaku Line.

At first Dalleson didn't believe the report. There was the memory of Sergeant Lanning and the false reports he had given, the indications that any number of squad and platoon leaders were not fulfilling their missions. But still it seemed unlikely. If a man was going to falsify a report, he was more likely to say he had encountered resistance and turned back.

The Major scratched his nose. It was eleven o'clock and the morning sun had been baking long enough on the operations tent to make the air inside unbearably hot, leavened with the dry unpleasant smell of heated canvas. The Major was sweating, and the portion he could see of the bivouac clearing through the furled side walls of the tent shimmered in the heat and blared back in his eyes. He was thirsty and debated emptily for a few minutes whether to send one of the enlisted clerks to officers' mess for an iced beer from the refrigerator. But it seemed too much trouble. This was the kind of day when he would have preferred to do nothing except sit before his desk and wait for reports to be forwarded to him. A few feet away two officers were discussing the possibility of getting away in a jeep for the afternoon to go swimming on the beach. The Major burped. His stomach was bothering him, as it did on all particularly hot days, and he fanned himself slowly, vaguely irritable.

"There's a rumor, utterly unfounded, of course," one of the lieutenants drawled, "that we're getting some Red Cross girls after the campaign."

"We'll have to fix up a part of the beach, have lockers built. It might end up quite nicely, you know."

"We'll be moving out again. Infantry always gets the worst of it." That lieutenant lit a cigarette. "But, God, I wish the campaign was over."

"What for? We'll just have to write the history when it is. That's always the worst time."

Dalleson sighed again. Their talk about the end of the campaign depressed him. What was he going to do about that patrol report? He felt a gentle tug at his bowels. It would not be unpleasant sitting here, contemplating going to the latrine, if he had nothing to worry about. In the distance an artillery battery had fired, sending a moody echo through the sultry morning air. The Major picked up the field telephone on his desk and cranked it twice. "Give me Potential Red Easy," he grunted at the operator.

He asked for the Commanding Officer of E Company. "Listen, Windmill, this is Lanyard," he said. He was using the code names.

"What do you want, Lanyard?"

"I got a patrol report this morning from you. Number 318, you know the one I mean?"

"Yes."

"Is the goddam thing true? And let's have it, Windmill. If one

648

of your boys made it up and you cover for him, I'll have your ass over a barrel."

"No, it's true. I checked on it myself, I talked to the squad leader. He swears he didn't goof-off."

"All right, I'm going to proceed on the —" the Major looked for the word he had heard so often — "on the assumption that it's okay. And Heaven help ya if it isn't."

The Major mopped his face again. Why did the General have to be away on this of all days? He had a subdued resentment that Cummings had not foreseen it. He should get something in motion right away but he was confused. Instead, he decided to go to the latrine.

Sitting on the boards, feeling the sun bake sentiently on his exposed belly, the Major tried to think. But other things distracted him. The latrine stench was extremely powerful on this hot morning and he noticed it, made a decision to have a detail dig a new officers' latrine that afternoon. His red face sweated profusely in the open sun. This time they would have a canopy built over it. He stared morosely at the bamboo enclosure.

Well, what the hell could he do but send a platoon up to occupy that empty bivouac? If they were able to do it without difficulty, he would start worrying then about what to do next. A fragile breeze stirred against his face and he thought with longing of the beach and the pleasantly chill ocean water, the palm trees silhouetted against the shore. Somewhere in the jungle miles away from him something was happening to the Japanese. Maybe their G-3 was sitting on the can now too. The Major grinned.

But something was wrong with them. The Jap corpses lately looked skinnier. All these islands were supposed to be blockaded, not getting any supplies, but of course you could never depend on the Navy to tell the truth on that. The Major was weary. Why did he have to make these decisions? He lost track of the minutes listening to the rapt absorptive buzzing of the flies under the latrine boards. One or two whipped against his naked flanks and he grunted with displeasure. They damn sure needed a new latrine.

He lifted himself, did a makeshift job with the sodden paper which had become drenched in the night's rain. There ought to be some better way of making a cover for it than to use a No. 10 tin can. The Major tried to think of some other way to keep the paper dry. What a lazy day it was.

He got up and stopped off at officers' mess to get a can of iced beer. "How're you doin', Major?" one of the cooks asked.

"Awright." He rubbed his chin. Something was bothering him. "Oh, yeah, listen, O'Brien, I been gettin' the GIs again. You keeping your pots clean?"

"You ought to know, Major."

He grunted again, looked about under the tent at the empty wooden tables, the benches flanking them. The gray metal officers' dishes were already laid out. "You oughtn't to make the setting too early," the Major said. "It just lets the flies horse around on them."

"All right, sir."

"Okay, do something about it." He waited until O'Brien started collecting the plates, and then walked across the bivouac to the operations tent. He saw a few enlisted men lying in their pup tents, and it irritated him. He was wondering which platoon they were in when he remembered the report. He moved toward the operations tent, picked up the phone, and ordered Windmill to send a platoon fully equipped up to the deserted Jap bivouac. "And lay some wire right with them. I want a report in half an hour."

"They won't get there till then."

"That's all right. The moment they occupy it, you let me know."

Time dragged by under the heated canvas. The Major was desperately uneasy, hoping secretly that the platoon had to turn back. But still if they were able to move in, what then? He called up the commander of the reserve battalion from the 460th and told him to alert a company for movement within an hour.

"I'll have to take them off the road."

"Take them off," the Major growled. He swore quietly. If it all came to nothing, the work of a company of men would be lost on the road for a half day. And yet there was nothing else he could do. Because if the platoon could occupy the center of the Toyaku Line he would have to exploit it. The Major was working on axioms now.

Windmill phoned him forty-five minutes later and told him that the platoon had advanced without incident and was holding the Japanese ground. Dalleson picked his nose with his thick forefinger, trying to see across the jungle through the foliage heated by the intense morning sun.

"Okay, move up the rest of your company except for a squad, and you can leave the kitchen behind. You got rations?"

"Yes. But what about my rear and flanks? We're going to be stuck a thousand yards ahead of Charley and Fox."

"I'm taking care of that. You just move up, you can get them all there in an hour."

After he had hung up, the Major groaned to himself. Now everything would have to be moved around. The reserve company he had alerted from the 460th would have to fill in the flanks and rear of the salient and would be spread thin. Why had the Japs left? Was it a trap?

The Major remembered a heavy artillery barrage the night before on that empty Jap position. It was possible the CO of that Jap company had pulled out without letting anybody know. There were cases where the Japs did that which he had heard about, but it seemed a little unbelievable.

If it was true he'd have to get some men through that breach before Toyaku discovered it. The troops were supposed to have this day quiet, but if he ever got his men through he'd have to begin a frontal attack again, and he'd have to work fast if any results were to come of it before nightfall. It meant he had to alert the entire reserve battalion now, start some of them moving right now because there weren't trucks enough to bring them all up at once. The Major plucked abstractedly at the wet cloth under his armpits. The whole day would be wasted on the road now. Nothing would be done there. And he'd have to use every truck in the division to bring up new rations, more ammunition than had been planned for today. The transportation would be wicked. He had a flare of hatred for the squad leader who had started all the trouble this morning.

He called up Hobart, and told him to make a transportation schedule, and then he went over to the G-2 tent, and talked to Conn, explained what had happened.

"Bygod, you're letting yourself in for a noose," Conn told him.

651

"What the hell can I do? You're intelligence, why is that bivouac empty?"

Conn shrugged. "The goddam Japs are settin' a trap."

Dalleson walked back to his own tent, abysmally depressed. It would be a trap, but still he had to go into it. He groaned again. Hobart's men were trying to make up a transportation schedule to supply the new positions of the line companies; Conn's section was going back over old intelligence reports. There was something messy somewhere. Well, he'd have to blunder through on luck, send most of the ordnance to the new hole in the front, hope the other sectors would have enough to get by.

Dalleson alerted the reserve battalion, ordered the first movement of their troops. It would be time for lunch soon and he would have to miss it. His belly knotted into cramps from the iced beer. He thought with distaste of the tinned cheese in the blue K ration. He would have to eat that instead to bind him up.

"Any paregoric in the tent?" he bawled.

"No, sir."

He turned to one of the clerks and sent him to the aid tent. The heat dripped languidly about his body.

The phone rang. It was Windmill reporting he had moved his company up. A few minutes later the CO of the initial reserve company phoned that his men were digging in on the flanks.

Now he would have to send the battalion through. Dalleson had a headache What would they do? He had had some precedent for everything up until now, but this was a vacuum. The main Japanese supply depot was about a mile and a half behind E Company's new positions, and maybe he should try to capture that. Or he could roll up the flank. But the Major could not imagine that. The hole was a hole on paper. He had visited all the positions, he knew what the bivouacs looked like, but he had never understood exactly what went on. There were spaces between the companies. The front was not a solid line — it was a string of dots separated from each other. Now he had some men behind the Japanese dots and he would have more later, but what would they do? How did you go about rolling up a flank? He had a picture for a moment of the troops moving sullenly along a jungle trail swearing at the heat, but he could not connect that to the figures on the map.

An insect crawled sluggishly over his desk and he flicked it off. Just what in the Sam Hill was he going to do? By tonight everything would be a shambles. Nobody would know where anybody else was, and they'd never get all the wire laid straight. The radios would probably be out from static or some lousy hill. They always were when you needed them. Until now this thing had been kept within bounds but he would have to bring in Mooney, the signal officer, and G-4 was already tied up with transportation. Intelligence would have to stay up all night with him. Oh, it was a mess. Of all the days to have to put in a session of work like this. If it came to nothing he'd never hear the end of it.

The Major felt like laughing. He had the involuntary stupid merriment of a man who has pitched a pebble down a hill and watched it magnify itself into an avalanche. Why couldn't the General be here?

As a corollary of all this he could feel the added activity about him. Everyone was working in the operations tent, and he could see men moving back and forth through the bivouac all obviously on errands. Far away, he could hear the rumble of a convoy of trucks disturbing the languid tropical air. He had set all this in motion. He could not really believe it.

The cheese he munched was dry. Looking out from the tent he could still see some men drowsing in their pup tents, and it enraged him. But there was no time to fix that. Everything was getting out of control. The Major felt as if he were holding a dozen packages in his arms and the first few were beginning to work loose already. How much would he have to juggle?

And the artillery. That would have to be co-ordinated too. He groaned. The machine was coming apart, gears and springs and bolts were popping out at every moment. He hadn't even thought of the artillery.

Dalleson held his head and tried to think but he was blank. A message had come through that the advance elements of the reserve were already at E Company's new positions. When the rest of the battalion got there, what could he do? The Jap supply depot was back of a hill, stored in caves. He could send the battalion on to there, and then what? He needed still more men.

If his head had been clear, he might have hesitated, but all he could think about was moving men. He gave an order for Charley Company to join the reserve battalion, its positions to be taken up by Baker Company on its left. It simplified things for him. Two companies would be holding down the normal positions of three, and so they could remain put. He wouldn't have to worry about them. And the right flank could attack frontally. Let it all pour down, let the artillery take care of itself. He could give them a battalion mission for the supply depot, and after that it would depend on liaison and targets of opportunity.

He phoned Div Arty and told them. "I want you to keep your liaison planes up all afternoon. Both of them."

"We lost one the other day, don't you remember, and the other one's grounded."

"Why didn't you tell me that?" Dalleson roared.

"We did. Yesterday."

He swore. "Well, then, assign your forward observers to Able Baker Charley and Dog Companies of the 460th and to Charley of the 458th."

"What about communications?"

"That's your worry. I got enough goddam things to think about." His back was itching from perspiration. It was one o'clock already and the sun was smoldering on the canvas slopes of the tent.

Slowly the afternoon wore by. It took until three o'clock for the reserve battalion and Charley Company to complete their movements, and by that time Dalleson hardly cared any longer. He had almost a thousand men posted at the jumping-off point and no real idea of where to send them. For a few minutes he thought of turning them to the left and having them bear down to the sea. It would isolate half of the Japanese line, but he remembered too late that he pulled out a company from his left flank. If he squeezed the Japs there, he might endanger his own front-line positions. The Major felt like butting his head against the desk. It was such a blunder!

He could send them to the right, toward the mountain, but after they cut off the Japs it would be difficult to bring up ordnance, and the troops at the end of the advance would have to be supplied over a long route. He had the same kind of panic Martinez had felt on his solo. There were so many obvious things he was forgetting.

The phone rang again. "This is Rock and Rye." (The commander of the 1st Battalion, 460th Regiment.) "We're going to be ready to jump off in fifteen minutes. What is our mission? I have to brief my men."

They had been asking him this for the past hour, and each time he had roared back, "It's a mission of opportunity. Wait, goddammit." And now he had to give an answer. "You're to proceed in radio silence up to the Japs' supply depot." Dalleson gave the co-ordinates. "When you're ready to attack, you're to send a message back, and we'll bring artillery down. Handle it through your FO. If your radio won't carry, we'll let go on our side in exactly one hour, and you're to go in afterward. You're to destroy the depot, and you got to move goddam fast. I'll tell you what after that."

He hung up, and stared at his watch. Inside the tent the heat hung in heavy draperies. Outside the sky was darkening and the foliage yawned flaccidly in the turgid suggestion of a breeze. The front was silent. On an afternoon like this, a half hour or so before a downpour, it was usually possible to hear every sound, but now there was nothing. The artillery was waiting, plotting their concentration targets, but he could not even hear a machine gun or a rifle. The only noise was the occasional jarring of the earth, the scattering of dust, when a tank moved by. He could not use them at the breach, for there were no roads, so he was sending them to cover up the weakened positions on his left flank.

Abruptly Dalleson remembered he had given the attack battalion no antitank support and he groaned aloud this time. It was too late to get them up in time for the attack on the supply depot but perhaps he could send them in time for a Jap counterattack if it were to develop. He alerted the antitank platoon of 2nd Battalion, sent them after the first units. How many other things would come to mind?

And of course he waited, swearing to himself as he grew more nervous. He was at the point where he was convinced everything would go wrong, and like a small boy who has kicked over a bucket of paint he hoped feebly that he would get out of it somehow. What bothered him most at the moment was the thought of how long it would take to get all these men back and reassorted after the attack failed. It would be at least another full day — two days lost on the road. That was what bothered Dalleson most. With surprise he realized he had mounted a complete attack.

Ten minutes before the hour was up, the radio silence was broken. The attack battalion was two hundred yards from the supply depot, still unnoticed. The artillery began to fire and continued for a half hour. At the end of that time the battalion moved forward and captured the supply depot in twenty minutes.

Dalleson picked up the story by degrees. It was discovered much later that two thirds of the Japs' supplies were captured that afternoon, but he hardly thought about that the first evening. The important news was that General Toyaku and half of his staff were killed in the same advance. His secret headquarters had been only a few hundred yards past the supply depot, and the battalion had overrun it.

It was too much news for Dalleson to assimilate. He ordered the battalion to bivouac for the night, and in the interim moved up every man he could find. Headquarters and service companies were stripped of everyone but the cooks. By the next morning he had fifteen hundred men behind the Japanese lines and the flanks were rolled up by afternoon.

Cummings returned the same day from Army. After much pleading, after giving his considered opinion that he could not end the campaign quickly without invading Botoi Bay, he was granted a destroyer. It had followed behind him, was supposed to reach the peninsula by the following morning. It would be impossible for him to order it to return now.

Instead, he had the staff working all night to divert troops from the jungle to the tip of the peninsula. When morning came he was able to send two rifle companies out in assault boats to invade Botoi Bay. The destroyer appeared on schedule, shelled the beach, and came in close to shore to give direct support.

656

A few Jap snipers greeted the first wave with an occasional shot and then fled. In half an hour the invading troops joined up with some units maneuvering behind the shattered Japanese front. By that evening the campaign was over except for the mopping up.

In the official history of the campaign sent to Army, the invasion of Botoi Bay was given as the main reason for breaking through the Toyaku Line. The invasion was aided, the history was to say, by strong local attacks which made some penetrations of the Japanese lines.

Dalleson never understood quite what had happened. In time he even believed that it *was* the invasion that had decided it. His only desire was to be promoted to captain, permanent grade.

In the excitement, everyone forgot about recon.

12

ON THE same afternoon that Major Dalleson was mounting his attack, the platoon continued to climb Mount Anaka. In the awful heat of the middle slopes they bogged down. Each time they passed through a draw or hollow the air seemed to be refracted from the blazing rocks, and after a time their cheek muscles ached from continual squinting. It was a minor pain and should have been lost in the muscle cramps of their thighs, the sullen vicious aching of their backs, but it became the greatest torment of the march. The bright light lanced like splinters into the tender flesh of their eyeballs, danced about the base of their brains in reddened choleric circles. They lost all account of the distance they had covered; everything beneath them had blurred, and the individual torments of each kind of terrain were forgotten. They no longer cared if the next hundred yards was a barren rock slope or a patch of brush and forest. Each had its own painful disadvantages. They wavered like a file of drunks, plodded along with their heads bent down, their arms slapping spasmodically at their sides. All their equipment had become leaden, and a variety of sores had farrowed on every bony knob of their bodies. Their shoulders were blistered from the pack bands, their waists were bruised from the jouncing of their cartridge belts, and their rifles clanked abrasively against their sides, raising blisters on their hips. Their shirts had long washed lines of white where the perspiration had dried.

They moved numbly, straggling upward from rock to rock, panting and sobbing with exhaustion. Against his will Croft was forced to give them a break every few minutes; they rested now for as long a period as they marched, lying dumbly on their backs, their arms and legs spread-eagled. Like the litter-bearers, they had forgotten everything; they did not think of themselves as individual men any longer. They were merely envelopes of suffering. They had forgotten about the patrol, about the war, their past, they had even forgotten the earth they had just climbed. The men around them were merely vague irritating obstacles into which they blundered. The hot glaring sky and the burning rock were far more intimate. Their minds scurried about inside their bodies like rodents in a maze, concentrating fruitlessly on first the quivering of an overworked limb and then on the smarting of a sore, became buried for many minutes in the agony of drawing another breath.

Only two things ever intruded on this. They were afraid of Croft and this fear had become greater as they grew more exhausted; by now they waited for his voice, plunged themselves forward a few additional yards each time he flicked them with a command. A numb and stricken apprehension had settled over them, an unvoiced and almost bottomless terror of him.

And in opposition to that, they wanted to quit; they wanted that more than anything they had ever hungered for. Each step they advanced, each tremor of their muscles, each pang in their chests generated that desire. They moved forward with a dumb blistering hatred for the man who led them.

Croft was almost as exhausted; by now he appreciated the breaks as much as they did, was almost as willing to allow each halt to drag out to double its intended length. He had forgotten the peak of the mountain, he wanted to quit too, and each time a break ended he fought a quick battle with himself, exposed himself to all the temptations of rest, and then continued. He moved on because somewhere at the base of his mind was the directive that climbing this mountain was necessary. His decision had been made in the valley, and it lay as an

658

iron warp in his mind. He could have turned back no more easily than he could have killed himself.

All through the afternoon they straggled forward, toiling up the gentler slopes, proceeding from rock to rock when the walls of the mountain became sheerer. They traveled from one ridge to another, stumbled painfully along the slanting inclines of minor knolls, slipped and fell many times when they passed over swatches of moist clay. The mountain seemed eternally to rear above them. They glimpsed its upper slopes through the fog of their effort, followed one another up the unending serpentines, and plodded along gratefully whenever their route was level for a time.

Minetta and Wyman and Roth were the most wretched. For several hours they had been at the tail of the column, keeping up to the men ahead with the greatest difficulty, and there was a bond between the three of them. Minetta and Wyman felt sorry for Roth, liked him because he was even more helpless than they. And Roth looked to them for support, knew in the knowledge of fatigue that they would not scorn him because they were only a little less prostrated than he.

He was making the most intense effort of his life. All the weeks and months Roth had been in the platoon he had absorbed each insult, each reproof with more and more pain. Instead of becoming indifferent or erecting a protective shell, he had become more sensitive. The patrol had keyed him to the point where he could not bear any more abuse, and he drove himself onward now with the knowledge that if he halted for too long the wrath and ridicule of the platoon would come down upon him.

But, even with this, he was breaking. There came a point where his legs would no longer function. Even when he stood still they were close to buckling under him. Toward the end of the afternoon he began to collapse. It was a slow process, dragging out through a series of pratfalls, a progression of stumbling and sliding and finally of dropping prostrate. He began to tumble every few hundred feet and the men in the platoon waited gratefully while he forced himself slowly to his feet, and staggered on again. But each fall came a little more quickly than the one that had preceded it. Roth moved forward

659

almost unconsciously, his legs buckling at every misstep. After a half hour he could no longer get up without assistance, and each step he took was doubtful, uncertain, like an infant walking alone across a room. He even fell like an infant, his feet folding under him while he sat blankly on his thighs, a little bewildered that he was not still walking.

In time he began to irritate the platoon. Croft would not let them sit down and the enforced wait until Roth was able to walk again annoyed them. They began to wait for Roth to fall and the inevitable recurrence of it rasped their senses. Their anger began to shift from Croft to Roth.

The mountain was becoming more treacherous. For ten minutes Croft had been leading them along a rocky ledge up the side of a sheer bluff of stone, and the path in places was only a few feet wide. At their right, never more than a yard or two away, was a drop of several hundred feet, and despite themselves they would pitch at times close to the edge. It roused another fear in them, and Roth's halts made them impatient. They were anxious to get past the ledge.

In the middle of this ascent Roth fell down, started to get up, and then sprawled out again when no one helped him. The rock surface of the ledge was hot but he felt comfortable lying against it. The afternoon rain had just begun and he felt it driving into his flesh, cooling the stone. He wasn't going to get up. Somewhere through his numbness another resentment had taken hold. What was the point of going on?

Someone was tugging at his shoulder, and he flung him off. "I can't go on," he gasped, "I can't go on, I can't." He slapped his fist weakly against the stone.

It was Gallagher trying to lift him. "Get up, you sonofabitch," Gallagher shouted. His body ached with the effort of holding Roth.

"I can't. Go 'way!"

Roth heard himself sobbing. He was dimly aware that most of the platoon had gathered around, were looking at him. But this had no effect; it gave him an odd bitter pleasure to have the others see him, an exaltation compounded of shame and fatigue.

Nothing more could happen after this. Let them see him weep-

660

ing, let them know for one more time that he was the poorest man in the platoon. It was the only way he could find recognition. After so much anonymity, so much ridicule, this was almost better.

Gallagher was tugging at his shoulder again. "Go 'way, I can't get up," Roth bawled.

Gallagher shook him, feeling a compound of disgust and pity. More than that. He was afraid. Every muscle fiber demanded that he lie down beside Roth. Each time he drew a breath the agony and nausea in his chest made him feel like weeping too. If Roth didn't get up, he knew he also would collapse.

"Get up, Roth!"

"I can't."

Gallagher grasped him under the armpits and tried to lift him. The dead resisting weight was enraging. He dropped Roth and clouted him across the back of his head. "Get up, you Jew bastard!"

The blow, the word itself, stirred him like an electric charge. Roth felt himself getting to his feet, stumbling forward. It was the first time anyone had ever sworn at him that way, and it opened new vistas of failure and defeat. It wasn't bad enough that they judged him for his own faults, his own incapacities; now they included him in all the faults of a religion he didn't believe in, a race which didn't exist. "Hitlerism, race theories," he muttered. He was staggering forward dumbly, trying to absorb the shock. Why did they call him that, why didn't they see it wasn't his fault?

And there was something else working. All the protective devices, the sustaining façades of his life had been eroding slowly in the caustic air of the platoon; his exhaustion had pulled out the props, and Gallagher's blow had toppled the rest of the edifice. He was naked another way now. He rebelled against it, was frustrated that he could not speak to them and explain it away. It's ridiculous, thought Roth in the core of his brain, it's not a race, it's not a nation. If you don't believe in the religion, then why are you one? This was the prop that had collapsed, and even through his exhaustion he understood something Goldstein had always known. His own actions would be expanded from now on. People would not only dislike him, but they would make the ink a little darker on the label.

661

Well, let them. A saving anger, a magnificent anger came to his aid. For the first time in his life he was genuinely furious, and the anger excited his body, drove him on for a hundred yards, and then another hundred yards, and still another. His head smarted where Gallagher had struck him, his body tottered, but if they had not been marching he might have flung himself at the men, fought them until he was unconscious. Nothing he could do was right, nothing would please them. He seethed, but with more than self-pity now. He understood. He was the butt because there always had to be a butt. A Jew was a punching bag because they could not do without one.

His body was so small. The rage was pathetic, but its pitifulness was unfair. If he had been stronger, he could have done something. And even so, as he churned along the trail behind the men there was something different in him, something more impressive. For these few minutes he was not afraid of the men. His body wavering, his head lolling on his shoulders, he fought clear of his exhaustion, straggled along oblivious of his body, alone in the new rage of his person.

Croft, at the point, was worried. He had not taken part when Roth had collapsed. For once he had been irresolute. The labor of leading the platoon for so many months, the tensions of the three days with Hearn, had been having their effect. He was tired, his senses rasped by everything that went wrong; all the sullenness of the men, their fatigue, their reluctance to go on had been causing attrition. The decision he had made after Martinez's reconnaissance had drained him. When Roth fell down the last time Croft had turned to go back to him and then had paused. At that moment he had been too weary to do anything. If Gallagher had not struck him, Croft might have interfered, but for once he was content to wait. All his lapses and minor failures seemed important to him. He was remembering with disgust his paralysis on the river when the Japanese had called to him; he was thinking of the combat since then, all the minor blank spots that had occurred before he could act. For once he was uncertain. The mountain still taunted him, still drew him forward, but it was with an automatic leaden response of his legs. He knew he had miscalculated the strength of the platoon, his own energy. There was only an hour or two until dark and they would never reach the peak before then.

The ledge they were on was becoming narrower. A hundred feet above them he could see the top of the ridge, rocky and jagged, almost impossible to traverse. Farther ahead the ledge rose upward and crossed the ridge and beyond should be the mountain peak. It could not be more than a thousand feet above them. He wanted to have the summit in view before they halted for the night.

But the ledge was becoming dangerous. The rain clouds had settled over them like bloated balloons, and they traveled forward in what was almost a fog. The rain was colder here. It chilled them and their feet slid upon the damp rock. After a few more minutes the rain obscured the ridge above them, and they inched along the ledge cautiously, their faces to the rock wall.

The ledge was no more than a foot wide now. The platoon worked along it very slowly, taking a purchase on the weeds and small bushes that grew out of the vertical cracks in the wall. Each step was painful, frightening, but the farther they inched out along the ledge the more terrifying became the idea of turning back. They hoped that at any moment the ledge would widen again, for they could not conceive of returning over a few of the places they had already crossed. This passage was dangerous enough to rouse them temporarily from their fatigue, and they moved alertly, strung out over forty yards. Once or twice they would look down, but it was too frightening. Even in the fog they could see a sheer drop of at least a hundred feet and it roused another kind of faintness. They would become conscious of the walls, which were of a soft gray slimy rock that seemed to breathe like the skin of a seal. It had an odious fleshlike sensation which roused panic, made them want to hasten.

The ledge narrowed to nine inches. Croft kept peering ahead in the mist, trying to determine if it would become wider. This was the first place on the mountain that demanded some skill. Until now it has been essentially a very high hill, but here he wished for a rope or a mountain pick. He continued along it, his arms and legs spread-eagled, hugging the rock, his fingers searching for crevices to latch upon.

He came to a gap in the ledge about four feet wide. There was nothing between, no bushes, no roots to which they could cling. The platform disappeared and then continued on the other side. In the gap there was only the sheer drop of the ridge wall. It would have been a simple jump, merely a long step on level ground, but here it meant leaping sideways, taking off from the left foot and landing with the right, having to gain his balance while he teetered on the ledge.

He slipped off his pack carefully, handed it to Martinez behind him, and hesitated for a moment, his right leg dangling over the gap. Then he leaped sideways, wavering for a moment on the other side before steadying himself.

"Jesus, who the fug can cross that?" he heard one of them mutter.

"Just wait there," Croft said, "I'm gonna see if the ledge widens out." He traveled along it for fifty feet, and discovered it was becoming broader again. This gave him a deep sense of relief, for otherwise it would have meant turning back to find another route. And he no longer knew if he could rouse the platoon to go up again.

He leaned over the gap and took his pack from Martinez. The distance was short enough for their hands to touch. Then he took Martinez's pack and moved a few yards farther away. "Okay, men," he called, "let's start coming over. The air's a helluva sight better on this side."

There was a nervous snicker. "Listen, Croft," he heard Red say, "is that fuggin ledge any wider?"

"Yeah, more than a bit." But Croft was annoyed at himself for answering. He should have told Red to shut up.

Roth, at the tail of the column, listened with dread. He would probably miss if he had to jump, and despite himself his body generated some anxiety. His anger was still present, but it had altered into a quieter resolve. He was very tired.

As he watched them pass their packs across and leap over, his fear increased. It was the kind of thing he had never been able to do, and a trace of an old panic he had known in gym classes when he waited for his turn on the high bar rose up to torment him.

664

Inevitably, his turn was approaching. Minetta, the last man ahead of him, hesitated on the edge and then skipped across, laughing weakly. "Jesus, a fuggin acrobat." Roth cleared his throat. "Make room, I'm coming," he said quietly. He handed over his pack.

Minetta was talking to him as though he were an animal. "Now, just take it easy, boy. There's nothing to it. Just take it easy, and you'll make it okay."

He resented that. "I'm all right," he said.

But when he stepped to the edge and looked over, his legs were dead. The other ledge was very far away. The rock bluffs dropped beneath him gauntly, emptily.

"I'm coming," he mumbled again, but he did not move. As he had been about to jump he had lost courage.

I'll count three to myself, he thought.

One.

Two.

Three.

But he could not move. The critical second elongated, and then was lost. His body had betrayed him. He wanted to jump and his body knew he could not make it.

Across the ledge he could hear Gallagher. "Get up close, Minetta, and catch that useless bastard." Gallagher crawled toward him through Minetta's feet, and extended his arm, glowered at him. "C'mon, all you got to do is catch my hand. You can fall that far."

They looked weird. Gallagher was crouched at Minetta's feet, his face and arm projecting through Minetta's legs. Roth stared at them, and was filled with contempt. He understood this Gallagher now. A bully, a frightened bully. There was something he could tell them. If he refused to jump, Croft would have to come back. The patrol would be over. And Roth knew himself at this instant, knew suddenly that he could face Croft.

But the platoon wouldn't understand. They would jeer him, take relief from their own weakness in abusing him. His heart was filled with bitterness. "I'm coming," he shouted suddenly. This was the way they wanted it.

He felt his left leg pushing him out, and he lurched forward

665

awkwardly, his exhausted body propelling him too feebly. For an instant he saw Gallagher's face staring in surprise at him, and then he slipped past Gallagher's hand, scrabbled at the rock, and then at nothing.

In his fall Roth heard himself bellow with anger, and was amazed that he could make so great a noise. Through his numbness, through his disbelief, he had a thought before he crashed into the rocks far below. He wanted to live. A little man, tumbling through space.

Early the next morning, Goldstein and Ridges set out again with the litter. The morning was cool and they were traveling at last over level ground, but it made little difference. Within an hour they had plummeted quickly into the same level of stupor as the day before. Once more they toiled forward a few feet, set Wilson down, and then strained forward. All about them were the gentle foothills rolling backward toward the mountain in the north. The country spread out in an endless peaceful vista of pale yellow, like sand dunes mounting into the horizon. Nothing disturbed the silence. They trudged forward, panting and grunting, bent under their burden. The sky had the pale effortless blue of morning, and far toward the south beyond the jungle a string of puffball clouds tugged after one another.

This morning their torpor had taken a new form. Wilson's fever had become worse, and he moaned for water continually, pleading and begging, screaming, abusing them. They could not bear it. It seemed as if hearing were the only sense left to them, and that was partial; they did not notice the humming of the insects or the hoarse sobbing sounds they made when they drew a breath. They could hear only Wilson, and his moans for water grated on them, burred stridently through their resistance.

"Men, y' jus' gotta gimme water." A pinkish spittle had dried at the corners of Wilson's mouth, and his eyes moved uncomfortably, erratically. From time to time he would thrash about on the litter, but without any real strength. He seemed smaller somehow; the flesh over his large frame had settled. For minutes at a time he would blink vacantly at the sky, sniffing delicately at the odors about him. Without realizing it he was smelling himself. Forty hours had elapsed since

666

he was wounded, and in that period he had soiled himself frequently, bled and sweated, had even absorbed the dank moist odors of the damp ground they had slept on the night before. He moved his mouth in a weak elaborate grimace of disgust. "Men, y' stink."

They heard him without much feeling, gasping again for breath. As they had got used to living in the jungle and being wet all the time, as they had forgotten what it was like to live in dry clothing, so they had forgotten now how it felt to draw an effortless breath. They did not think about it; certainly they did not think of when their journey would end. It had become all existence.

That morning Goldstein had roused himself long enough to contrive an aid. Their stiffened fingers had been slowing them most of all. They were unable to hold onto the litter for more than a few seconds before its weight would slowly force their hands open. Goldstein had cut the straps from their pack, tied them together and yoked the line over his shoulders onto the handles of the stretcher. When he could grasp them no longer with his fingers he would transfer the weight to the strap, and plow forward until his hands were able to hold them again. Ridges followed his example soon afterward, and they plodded onward in their harness, the burden of the litter swaying slowly between them.

"Water, goddammit, y' fuggin . . ."

"No water," Goldstein gasped.

"Y' goddam Jewboy." Wilson began to cough again. His legs ached. The air that played over his face had the flushed heated quality of a kitchen when the oven has been on too long and the windows are closed. He hated the litter-bearers; he was like a child being tormented. "Goldstein," he repeated, "always snufflin' around."

A thin weak smile formed on Goldstein's mouth. Wilson had hurt him, and he envied Wilson suddenly because Wilson had never been forced to think about what he said or did. "You can't have water," Goldstein mumbled, waiting in a rather delicious expectancy for Wilson's abuse to continue. He was like an animal so used to the whip that he found it a stimulus.

Suddenly Wilson screamed. *"Men y' gotta gimme some water."*

By now Goldstein had forgotten the reason why Wilson mustn't

667

drink. He only knew that it was forbidden, and was irritated that he could not remember the explanation. It caused him panic. Wilson's suffering had affected Goldstein oddly; slowly, keeping pace with his exhaustion, it had entered his own body. When Wilson screamed, Goldstein felt a twinge; if the litter lurched abruptly, Goldstein's stomach plummeted as if he were dropping in an elevator. And every time Wilson pleaded for water Goldstein was thirsty again. Each time he opened his canteen he felt a sense of guilt, and he would do without water for hours, rather than provoke Wilson. It seemed that no matter how delirious Wilson might become he would always notice when they took out their canteens. Wilson was a burden they could not leave. Goldstein felt as if he would be carrying him forever; he could not think of anything else. The limits of his senses were confined to his own body, the litter, and Ridges's back. He did not look at the yellow hills or wonder how far they had to go. Infrequently, Goldstein would think of his wife and child with a sense of disbelief. They were so far away. If he had been told at that moment that they had died, he would have shrugged. Wilson was more real. Wilson was the only reality.

"Men, Ah'll give ya anythin'." Wilson's voice had changed, become almost shrill. He would talk in long spates, droning on and on, his voice singsonging almost unrecognizably. "Jus' name it, men, Ah'll give it ya, any ol' thing, y' want some goddam money Ah'll give ya hundid poun' you jus' set me down, gimme drink. Jus' gimme it, men, tha's all Ah ask."

They stopped for a longer halt, and Goldstein lunged away and fell forward on his face, lying motionless for several minutes. Ridges stared dully at him, then at Wilson. "What you want, some water?"

"Yeah, gimme that, gimme some water."

Ridges sighed. His short powerful body seemed to have condensed in the last two days. His big slack mouth hung open. His back had shortened and his arms become longer, his head bent over at a smaller angle to his chest. His thin sandy hair drooped sadly over his sloping forehead and his clothing sagged wetly. He looked like a giant phlegmatic egg set on a stout tree stump. "Shoot, Ah don't know why y' can't have water."

668

"You jus' gimme it, they ain' anythin' Ah won' do for ya."

Ridges scratched the back of his neck. He was not accustomed to make a decision by himself. All his life he had been taking orders from someone or other, and he felt an odd malaise. "Ah ought to ask Goldstein," he mumbled.

"Goldstein's chicken . . ."

"Ah don' know." Ridges giggled. The laughter seemed to come from such a distance inside himself. He hardly knew why he laughed. It was probably from embarrassment. He and Goldstein had been too exhausted to talk to each other, but even so he had assumed that Goldstein was the leader, and this despite the fact that he knew the route back. But Ridges had never led anything, and out of habit he assumed that Goldstein was to make all the decisions.

But Goldstein was now lying ten yards away, his face to the ground, almost unconscious. Ridges shook his head. He was too tired to think, he told himself. Still, it seemed absurd not to give a man a drink of water. Little ol' drink ain't gonna hurt nobody, he told himself.

Goldstein knew how to read, however. Ridges balked at the idea of breaking some law out of the vast mysterious world of books and newspapers. Pa use' to say somethin' about givin' a man water when he's sick, Ridges thought. But he couldn't remember. "How you feel, boy?" he asked doubtfully.

"You gotta gimme water. Ah'm burnin'."

Ridges shook his head once more. Wilson had led a life full of sin and now he was in the fires of hell. Ridges felt some awe. If a man ended up a sinner, his punishment was certainly terrible. But the Lord Christ died for pore sinners, Ridges told himself. It was also a sin not to show a man some mercy.

"Ah s'pose y' can have it." Ridges sighed. He took out his canteen quietly and glanced at Goldstein again. He didn't want to be reprimanded by him. "Here, you jus' drink it up."

Wilson drank febrilely, the water splattering out of his mouth to trickle down his chin, wetting the collar of his shirt. "Oh, *man*." He drank lavishly, eagerly, his throat working with lust. "You're a good sonofabitch," he mumbled. Some water caught in his throat, and

669

he coughed violently, wiping the blood from his chin with a nervous furtive motion. Ridges watched a droplet of it which Wilson had missed. Slowly it spread out over the moist surface of Wilson's cheek, faded through progressive shades of pink.

"Y' think Ah'm gonna make it?" Wilson asked.

"Shore." Ridges felt a shiver. A preacher had once given a sermon about the way a man resisted the fires of hell. "Y' cain't avoid it, you're gonna get caught if you're a sinner," he had said. Ridges was telling a lie now, but nevertheless he repeated it. "Shore you're gonna be awright, Wilson."

"That's what Ah figgered."

Goldstein put his palms against the ground, forced himself upward slowly. He wanted so very much to remain lying on the ground. "I suppose we ought to go," he said wistfully. They harnessed themselves again to the litter and trudged forward.

"You're a good bunch of men, they ain't anybody better'n you two men."

This shamed them. At the moment, still enmeshed in the first pangs of setting out again, they hated him.

"It's all right," Goldstein said.

"Naw, Ah mean it, they ain't any two men like you to be found in the whole fuggin platoon." He was silent, and they settled into the stupefaction of the march. Wilson was delirious for a while, and then sober again. His wound began to ache and he abused them, screaming once more with pain.

Now it bothered Ridges more than Goldstein. He had not thought very much about the agony of the march; it was something he had assumed was natural, perhaps a little more extreme than any work he had ever done, but he had learned when he was very young that work was what a man did with most of his day and it was pointless to wish to do anything else. If it was uncomfortable, if it was painful, there was nothing you could do about it. He had been given the job and he was going to do it. But now for the first time he hated it genuinely. Perhaps there had been too many fatigue-products, perhaps the cumulative labor had dissolved and reshaped the structures of his mind, but in any case he was wretched with this work,

670

and as a corollary he understood suddenly that he had always hated the drudgery of his farm work, the unending monotonous struggle against an arid unyielding soil.

It was too much of a realization; he had to retreat from it. And that was not difficult. He was not accustomed to threshing out a solution with his mind, and now he was too blunted, too completely tired. The thought had come into his head, exploded, and shaken a great many patterns, but the smoke had cleared quickly, and there was nothing now but a vague uncomfortable sense of some wreckage, some change. A few minutes later he was merely uneasy; he knew he had thought something sacrilegious, but what it was he could not guess. He was fastened to his load again.

But this was mixed with something else. He had not forgotten that he had given Wilson the water, and he remembered the way Wilson had said, "Ah'm burnin'." They were carrying a man who was already lost, and that meant something. He was made a little uneasy by the idea that they might be contaminated by him, but that really was not what bothered him. The ways of the Lord are dev'us. It meant something else; they were being taught by example or maybe they were paying for their own sins. Ridges did not work it out for himself, but it gave him a mixture of dread and the variety of exaltation that comes with too much fatigue. We gotta git him back. As with Brown, all the complexities and cross-purposes canceled out into that simple imperative. He lowered his head, and bulled on for another few yards.

"Men, you might as well lea' me." A few tears worked out of Wilson's eyes. "They ain't no use y' killin' yourself for me." His fever was torturing him again, and it sent a leaden aching ecstasy through his body. He felt consumed with the desire to express something. "Y' gotta lea' me. Gowan ahead, men." Wilson clenched his fists. He wanted to give them a present, and he was frustrated. They were such good men. "Lea' me." It was plaintive, like a child weeping for something it will never get.

Goldstein listened to him, tempted by the same inevitable suite of rationalizations that Stanley had followed. He wondered how to suggest it to Ridges, and was silent.

671

Ridges mumbled. "You jus' shut up, Wilson. We ain't leavin' ya."

And therefore Goldstein could not quit. He would not be the first one; he was a little afraid that Ridges then would bundle Wilson on his back and continue. He was bitter and thought of fainting. That he wouldn't do, but he was angry with Brown and Stanley for deserting them. They quit, why don't I quit? he wondered, and knew he wouldn't.

"Jus' set me down an' gowan, men."

"We'll git ya back," Ridges muttered. He too was playing with the idea of deserting Wilson, but he pushed it away in a spasm of disgust. If he left him it would be murder, an awful sin if he left a Christian to die. Ridges thought of the black mark it would be on his soul. Ever since he had been a child he had imagined his soul as a white object the size and shape of a football, lodged somewhere near his stomach. Each time he sinned an ineradicable black spot was inked onto the white soul, its size depending upon the enormity of the sin. At the time a man died, if the white football was more than half black he went to hell. Ridges was certain that the sin of leaving Wilson would cover at least a quarter of his soul.

And Goldstein remembered his grandfather saying, "Yehuda Halevy wrote that Israel is the heart of all nations." He lunged along, carrying the litter through habit, not conscious of the torments of his body. His mind had turned inward; he could not have concentrated more intensely if he had been blind. He just followed Ridges without looking where they went.

"Israel is the heart of all nations." It was the conscience and the raw exposed nerve; all emotion passed through it. But it was more than that; it was the heart that suffered whenever any part of the body was ill.

And Wilson was the heart now. Goldstein did not say this to himself, he did not even think it, but the idea worked through him beneath the level of speech. He had suffered too much in these past two days; he had traversed all the first nauseas of fatigue, the stupors that followed, the exaltation close to fever. There were as many levels to pain as to pleasure. Once his will had forbidden him to collapse,

672

Goldstein burrowed deeper and deeper through exhaustion and agony, never quite plumbing the pit of it. But he was in a stage now where all the banal proportions were gone. His eyes functioned enough for him to notice automatically where he walked; he heard and smelled isolated little events; he even felt some pain from his racked body; but all this was separate from him, like an object he might hold in his hand. His mind was both blunted and exposed, naked and stupefied.

"The heart of all nations." But for a few hours, after two days and fifteen miles of staggering forward under a tropic sun, after an eter-nity of wrestling Wilson's body through an empty and alien land, this could be true for him. His senses dammed, his consciousness reeling, Goldstein fumbled through a hall of symbols. Wilson was the object he could not release. Goldstein was bound to him by a fear he did not understand. If he let him go, if he did not bring him back, then something was wrong, he would understand something terrible. The heart. If the heart died . . . but he lost the sequence in the muck of his labors. They were carrying him on and on, and he would not die. His stomach had been ripped apart, he had bled and shit, wallowed through the leaden swells of fever, endured all the tortures of the rough litter, the uneven ground, and still Wilson had not died. They still carried him. There was a meaning here and Goldstein lumbered after it, his mind pumping like the absurd legs of a man chasing a train he has missed.

"Ah like to work, Ah ain't a goddam fug-off," Wilson mumbled. "If you're job, do goddam thing right, that's what Ah say." His breath was gurgling again out of his mouth. "Brown and Stanley. Brown and Stanley, shit!" He giggled feebly. "Little ol' bugger May when she's a kid, always crappin' her pants." He rambled through a cloudy memory of his daughter when she was an infant. "Smartest little devil." When she was two years old she would drop her faeces behind a door or in a closet. "Goddam, step in it, git dirty." He laughed, only it sounded more like a feeble wheeze. For an instant he recalled vividly his mixture of exasperation and merriment when he had discovered her leavings. "Goddam, Alice'd git mad."

She had been angry when he had seen her in the hospital, angry again when they discovered he was sick. "Ah always say a dose ain't gonna hurt a man a goddam bit. What the hell's a lousy little dose? Ah had it five times an' it never came to a goddam thing." He stiffened on the litter and shouted as if arguing with someone. "Jus' get me some pyrdin whatever the hell y' call it." He twisted about, managed almost to prop himself on an elbow. "If goddam wound gits y' opened maybe Ah won' need the op-per-ration, jus' gits rid of all the pus." He retched emptily, watching through dimmed eyes the blood trickling and spattering out of his mouth onto the rubber fabric of the litter. It was so distant and yet it sent a shudder through him. "Whadeya say, Ridges, does it git rid of it?"

But they hadn't heard him, and he watched the blood fall in droplets from his mouth and then lay back again moodily.

"Ah'm gonna die."

A shudder of fear, of resistance rippled through him. He could taste the blood in his mouth, and he began to tremble. "Goddammit, Ah ain't gonna die, Ah ain't gonna," he wept, choking on his sobs when some mucus clotted his throat. The sounds terrified him; he lay abruptly in the tall weeds, his blood sopping into the sun-warmed earth, the Japanese chattering beside him. "They're gonna git me, they're gonna git me," he shouted suddenly. "Jesus, men, don' lemme die."

Ridges heard him this time, stopped lethargically, set the litter down, and unyoked himself from the pack straps. Like a drunk proceeding slowly and elaborately to unlock a door, Ridges moved over to Wilson's head, and knelt beside him.

"They're gonna git me," Wilson moaned, his face contorted, his unconscious tears slinking out of his eye sockets, racing down his temples to become lost in the matted hair about his ears.

Ridges bent over him, fingering numbly his own scraggly beard. "Wilson," he said hoarsely, a little imperatively.

"Yeah?"

"Wilson, they's still time to turn."

"Wha . . . ?"

Ridges had made up his mind. It might not be too late. Wilson might not yet be damned. "Y' gotta return to the Lord Jesus Christ."

"Uh."

674

Ridges shook him gently. "They's still time to turn," he said in a solemn mournful voice. Goldstein looked on blankly, vaguely resentful.

"Y' can go to the Kingdom of Heaven." His voice was so deep that it was almost lost. The sounds quivered heavily in Wilson's head like the echo of a bass viol.

"Uh-huh," Wilson mumbled.

"Y' repentin'? Y' askin' forgiveness?"

"Yeah?" Wilson breathed. Who was talking to him, who was bothering him? If he would agree they would let him alone. "Yeah," he mumbled again.

A few tears mounted in Ridge's eyes. He felt exalted. Maw told me 'bout a sinner was caught on the deathbed, he thought. He had never forgotten her story, but he had never imagined that he too would do something so wonderful.

"Git out, y' goddam Japs."

Ridges started. Had Wilson forgotten his conversion already? But Ridges did not dare to admit this. If Wilson repented and then threw it away, his punishment would be doubly awful. No man would ever dare that.

"You jus' 'member what you said," Ridges muttered almost fiercely. "*Jus' watch yourself, man.*"

Afraid to listen any longer, he stood up, went to the head of the litter, rearranged the blanket over Wilson's feet, and then worked the strap over his neck and under his armpits. In a moment, after Goldstein was ready, they moved on.

They reached the jungle after an hour's march, and Ridges left Goldstein with the stretcher, and explored to his right until he found the trail the platoon had cut four days earlier. It was only a few hundred yards away. Ridges felt a feeble glow of pleasure that he had been so accurate. Actually he had done it almost instinctively. Permanent bivouacs, roads through the jungle, stretches of beach always confused him; they always looked the same, but in the hills he could travel with a sure and easy sense.

He returned to Goldstein, and they set out again, reaching the trail in a few minutes. The foliage had sprung up again considerably since it had been cut, and the floor of the path was muddy from the rains. They blundered along, slipping frequently, their thickened feet finding no hold in the slick mud. If they had been less tired, they might have noticed the difference; the fact that the sun no longer beat on them would have been noted with pleasure, and conversely the uncertain footing, the sluggish resistance of the bushes and vines and thorns would have angered them. But they hardly detected all that. By now they knew there was no way to carry the stretcher without travail, and the individual circumstances that obstructed them had no force.

Still they progressed even more slowly. The trail had been cut no wider than the breadth of a man's shoulders, and the litter became lodged in several places. Once or twice there was no way at all to carry Wilson through, and Ridges would lift him off, drape him over his shoulder and lumber forward until the trail widened. Goldstein would follow with the stretcher.

At the point where the trail reached the river they took a long break. It came about through no decision on their part; they had halted to rest for a moment, and the minute passed, stretched out to half an hour. Toward the end, Wilson became restless and began to thrash about on the litter. They crawled over to him, attempted to quiet his movements, but he seemed absorbed in something and waved his big arms, cuffing them feverishly.

"Rest a little," Goldstein said.

"They're gonna kill me," Wilson wailed.

"No one's gonna touch ya." Ridges tried to restrain his arms but Wilson wrestled free. Sweat laved his forehead again. "Oh, man," he whimpered. He made an effort to slide off the litter but they forced him back. His legs kept twitching, and every few seconds he would begin to sit up and then groan, fall back again. "Baawoowwwwwm," he mumbled, imitating the sound of a mortar, his arms protecting his head. "Oh, here they come, here they come." He whimpered again. "Sonofabitch what the fug 'm Ah doin' here?"

The memory frightened them all. They sat quiet beside him, averting each other's faces. For the first time since they had re-entered the jungle it seemed malign.

676

"Quiet down, Wilson," Ridges told him. "You'll be gettin' the Japs on us."

"Ah'm gonna die," Wilson mumbled. He started up, almost reached a sitting position, and then fell back. When he looked at them again his eyes were clear but very weak. After a moment or two he spoke. "Ah'm in bad shape, men." He spat tentatively but the spittle did not quite clear his chin. "Can't even feel the hole in mah belly." His fingers trembled toward the soiled clotted dressing of the wound.

"Fulla pus." He sighed, licked his tongue dryly over his lips. "Ah'm thirsty."

"You can't have any," Goldstein said.

"Yeah, Ah know, cain't have any." Wilson laughed feebly. "You're a goddam woman, Goldstein. If you wasn't so chicken you'd be a pretty good boy."

Goldstein made no answer. He was too weary to get any sense from the words.

"What you want, Wilson?" Ridges asked.

"Water."

"Y' had some."

Wilson coughed and more blood inched out of the crusted sticky corners of his mouth. "Mah ass's givin' blood too," he grunted. "Aaah, git away, you men." He was silent for several minutes, his lips working abstractedly. "Never could figger out if Ah'd go back t' Alice or t'other one." He could feel new processes going on inside himself. His wound seemed to have dropped through his body; he had the sensation he could put his hand in the hole and find nothing. "Oh." He looked blearily at the men. For an instant or two his vision focused, and he saw them clearly. Goldstein's face had drawn back so that his cheekbones stood out and his nose was beak-like. His irises had become a bright painful blue in the reddened ovals of his eyes, and his blond beard looked red and brown and filthy, was matted over the jungle sores on his chin.

And Ridges looked like an overworked animal. His heavy features hung even more slack than usual, his mouth open, his lower lip drooping. He breathed with a regular panting rhythm

677

Wilson wanted to say something to them. They were good men, he thought. They didn't have to carry him this far. "Ah 'preciate what you done, men," he mumbled. But that wasn't it. He had to give them something.

"Listen, men, they's a goddam little still Ah been wantin' to build out in the woods yonder some'eres, on'y damn trouble is we never stay put long enough. But Ah'm gonna git it goin'." A last facsimile of enthusiasm worked in him. He believed himself while he spoke. "Ain't any 'mount of money a man cain't make ifen he gits one set up. Jus' turn it out, an' have all y' want to drink yourself." He was drifting, and he forced himself back. "But Ah git one made soon as we git back, an' Ah'll give you men a canteenful of it each. Jus' a free canteen." There was no expression on their gaunt faces, and he shook his head. It wasn't much to offer for what they'd done. "Men, Ah'll give ya all y' want to drink anytime, don' matter a goddam. You jus' ast me for it an' it'll be yours." He believed all of it; his only regret was that he had not built it already. "Jus' all y' want." His belly dropped again, and then a spasm seized him, and he slid backward into unconsciousness, grunting once with surprise as he felt himself turning over. His tongue protruded, and his breath gave a last rasping sound. He rolled out of the litter.

They pushed him back. Goldstein picked up Wilson's wrist and searched for a pulse, but his fingers felt too weak to support the arm. He dropped it, and then prodded with his forefinger along the flesh of Wilson's wrist. But his fingertips were too blunted. He could not feel the skin. After a while he just looked at him. "I think he's dead."

"Yeah," Ridges mumbled. He sighed, thought vaguely of praying.

"Why, he was just . . . talking." Goldstein reeled through the shock, balanced for a moment in his mind all the unutterables.

"We might as well be goin'," Ridges mumbled. He stood up heavily, and began to fit the litter straps over his shoulders. Goldstein hesitated, and then followed him. When they were ready, they staggered out onto the flat shallow falls of the river and began moving downstream.

They did not think there was anything odd about moving this

678

way with a dead man. They were too accustomed to picking him up at the end of each halt; the only thing they understood was that they must carry him. Even more, neither of them really believed he was dead. They knew it but they did not believe it. If he had shouted for water they would not have been surprised.

They even talked about what they would do with him. In one of the breaks Ridges said, "When we git him back, we'll give him a Christian burial 'cause he repented."

"Uh-huh." And even so they talked without feeling the words. Goldstein did not want to realize Wilson was dead; he held his mind away from the knowledge rigidly, thinking of nothing, merely sloshing forward through the shallow water upstream, his shoes sliding on the flat smooth rocks. There was something he could not face once he understood.

And Ridges was bewildered too. He was not convinced Wilson had begged for forgiveness; it was all jumbled in his mind, and he fastened on the thought that if he could get Wilson back, get him buried decently, the conversion would take. And more, both of them felt a natural frustration with having carried him this far only to die. They wanted to complete their odyssey with success.

Very slowly now, more slowly than they had moved at any time, they shambled through the water, the litter swaying between them. Overhead the trees and foliage met; as before, the river wound a tunnel through the jungle. Their heads drooped, their legs moved stiffly as if afraid of collapsing if they were hinged at the knee. Now when they rested they would flop in the shallow water, leaving Wilson half submerged while they sprawled beside the litter.

They were almost unconscious. Their feet blundered along the floor of the stream, crunching on the river pebbles. The water flowing past their heels was chill, but they hardly felt it. In the dim light of the jungle aisle they stumbled onward, following the current dumbly. The animals chattered at their approach, the monkeys screaming and scratching at their haunches, the birds calling to one another. And then as they would pass the animals would be silent, and remain quiet for many minutes after they had gone. Ridges and Goldstein reeled forward like blind men, their bodies expressing a mute eloquence.

Behind them the animals were silent, passing a warning through the congested channels of the jungle. It might have been a funeral march.

They descended a waterfall from one flat waist-high rock to another, Ridges dropping down first, and standing in the foam while Goldstein slid the litter over, and flopped down to join him. They struggled through the deeper water, which lashed at their thighs, floating the litter between them. They worked along the riverbanks, splashed through shallow water again. They stumbled and staggered and fell many times, Wilson's body almost washing away. They could not go more than a few feet without halting, and their sobbing fitted into the murmurs of the jungle, was lost in the washing of the water.

They were bound to the stretcher and the corpse. Whenever they fell they would lunge first at Wilson's body, and become conscious only when they had secured him of the water pouring into their own mouths. It went deeper than any instinct they had ever had. They did not think of what they would do with him when they reached the end, they did not even remember any longer that he was dead. His burden had been the vital thing. Dead, he was as much alive to them as he had ever been.

And yet they lost him. They came to the rapids where Hearn had carried the vine diagonally across the stream. It had washed away in the four days that had elapsed and the water churned viciously through the rocks now with no support to guide them. They hardly realized their danger. They stepped down into the rapids, took three or four steps, and were upset in the swirling of the water. The litter ripped out of their enfeebled fingers, dragged them in their harness after it. They wallowed and tumbled through the rough water, glancing off rocks, choking and swallowing. They made feeble efforts to free themselves, tried desperately to stand up, but the current was too violent. Half drowned, they let the water carry them.

The litter split against a rock, and they heard the canvas ripping, but the sound was only an isolated sensation in the panic they felt at swallowing water. They thrashed once more and the litter broke completely in two, the harness ripping free from their shoulders. Gasping, virtually insensible, they washed out of the worst part of the rapids, and stumbled toward the bank.

680

They were *alone*.

A fact which obtruded slowly through their bewilderment. They could not quite grasp it. One moment they had been carrying Wilson, and now he had disappeared. Their hands were empty.

"He's gone," Ridges mumbled.

They staggered down the river after him, pitching and falling, and reeling on again. At a turn in the stream they could see for several hundred yards, and far in the distance Wilson's body was just disappearing around a bend. "C'mon, we gotta catch him," Ridges said weakly. He took a step and fell forward on his face in the water. He got up very slowly, and then began to walk again.

They came to the other bend and stopped. The stream spread out into a swamp beyond the turn. There was a thin ribbon of water in the middle and bog land on either side. Wilson had washed into it, was lost somewhere in the foliage and swamp. It would take days to find him if he did not sink.

"Oh," Goldstein said, "he's lost."

"Yeah," Ridges mumbled. He took a step forward and stumbled in the water once more. It felt pleasant lapping against his face, and he had no desire to stand up. "Come on," Goldstein said.

Ridges began to weep. He struggled to a sitting position, and cried with his head on his folded arms, the water swirling around his hips and feet. Goldstein stood over him tottering.

"Mother-fuggin sonofabitch," Ridges mumbled. It was the first time he had cursed since childhood, and the words pulled out of his chest one by one, leaving behind a vacuum of anger and bitterness. Wilson would not have his burial, but somehow that was not important now. What counted was that he had carried this burden through such distances of space and time, and it had washed away in the end. All his life he had labored without repayment; his grandfather and his father and he had struggled with bleak crops and unending poverty. What had their work come to? "What profit hath man of all his labour wherein he laboureth under the sun?" The line came back to him. It was a part of the Bible he had always hated. Ridges felt the beginning of a deep and unending bitterness. It was not fair. The one time they had got a decent crop it had been ruined by a wild rainstorm. God's way. He hated it suddenly. What kind of God could there be who always tricked you in the end?

The practical joker.

He wept out of bitterness and longing and despair; he wept from exhaustion and failure and the shattering naked conviction that nothing mattered.

And Goldstein stood beside him, holding onto Ridges's shoulder to steady himself in the current. From time to time he would move his lips, scratch feebly at his face. "Israel is the heart of all nations."

But the heart could be killed and the body still live. All the suffering of the Jews came to nothing. No sacrifices were paid, no lessons were learned. It was all thrown away, all statistics in the cruel wastes of history. All the ghettos, all the soul cripplings, all the massacres and pogroms, the gas chambers, lime kilns — all of it touched no one, all of it was lost. It was carried and carried and carried, and when it finally grew too heavy it was dropped. That was all there was to it. He was beyond tears, he stood beside Ridges with the stricken sensation of a man who discovers that someone he loves has died. There was nothing in him at the moment, nothing but a vague anger, a deep resentment, and the origins of a vast hopelessness.

"Let's go," he mumbled.

Ridges got up at last, and they wavered slowly through the water, feeling it recede to their ankles, become shallow once more. The stream broadened, rippled over pebbles, became muddy and then sandy. They staggered around a bend and saw the sunlight and the ocean beyond.

A few minutes later they staggered up on the beach. Despite their exhaustion they walked on for a hundred yards. Somehow it was distasteful to stay too near to the river.

As if in mutual accord, they sprawled out on the sand and lay there motionless, their faces on their arms, the sun warming their backs. It was the middle of the afternoon. There was nothing to do but wait here for the platoon to return and the landing craft to fetch them. Their rifles had been lost, their packs, their rations, but they did not think about this. They were too depleted, and later they could find food in the jungle.

682

They lay like this until evening, too weak to move, absorbing a faint pleasure from resting, feeling the sun upon them. They did not talk. Their resentment had turned toward each other and they felt the dull sour hatred of men who have shared a humiliating failure together. The hours passed and they drowsed, became conscious again, fell asleep once more, woke with the nausea that comes from slumbering in the sunlight.

Goldstein sat up at last, and fumbled for his canteen. Very slowly, as though learning the motions for the first time, he unscrewed the cap and tilted it to his mouth. He had not realized how thirsty he was. The first taste of the water in his mouth was ecstatic. He made himself swallow slowly, setting the canteen down after each gulp. When it was half empty he noticed Ridges watching him. Somehow it was obvious that Ridges had no water left.

Ridges could walk up to the stream, and fill his canteen but Goldstein knew what that meant. He was so weak. The thought of standing up, of walking even a hundred yards, was a torment he could not bear to face. And Ridges must feel the same way.

Goldstein was annoyed. Why hadn't Ridges been more thoughtful, saved his water? He felt stubborn and tilted the canteen to his mouth again. But the drink tasted suddenly brackish. Goldstein was conscious of how warm it had become. He forced himself to take one more drink.

Then, feeling an unutterable sense of shame, he handed it to Ridges.

"Here, you want a drink?"

"Yeah." Ridges drank thirstily. When he had almost emptied the canteen he looked at Goldstein.

"No, finish it."

"We're gonna have to rustle in the jungle for food tomorrow," Ridges said.

"I know."

Ridges smiled weakly. "We'll git along."

13

WHEN ROTH missed the leap, the platoon was shattered. For ten minutes they huddled together on the shelf, too stricken, too terrified, to move on. An incommunicable horror affected them all. They stood upright, frozen to the wall, their fingers clenched into the fissures of the rock, their legs powerless. Once or twice Croft tried to rouse them, but they shied away from the commands, petrified by his voice as though they were dogs terrified by a master's boot. Wyman was sobbing in nervous exhaustion, quietly, thinly, a small steady wailing, and into it fitted their own voices, a grunt or a small moan or a hysterical curse, random things, disconnected, so that the men who uttered them were hardly aware that they had spoken.

Their will recovered enough for them to continue, but they moved at a frantically slow pace, refusing to step forward for seconds at a time before some minor obstacle, clinging to the wall ferociously wherever the ledge became narrow again. After half an hour Croft finally brought them out, and the ledge widened and crossed the ridge. Beyond was nothing but another deep valley, another precipitous slope. He led them down to the bottom, and started up the next ascent, but they did not follow him. One by one they sprawled down on the ground, looked at him with blank staring eyes.

It was almost dark, and he knew he could not drive them any more; they were too exhausted, too frightened, and another accident might occur. He called a halt, giving approval to what was already a fact, and sat down in their midst.

On the next morning there would be the slope, a few gullies to traverse, and then the main ridge of the mountain to be crossed. They could do it in two or three hours if . . . if he could stir them again. At that moment he doubted himself seriously.

The platoon slept poorly. It was very difficult to find level ground, and of course they were overtired, their limbs too tense. Most of them dreamed and muttered in their sleep. To cap it all, Croft gave them each an hour of guard, and some of them awoke too early and waited nervously for many minutes before going on, found it difficult afterward to fall asleep. Croft had been aware of this, knew they needed the extra rest and knew it was virtually impossible there would be any Japanese on the mountain, but he had felt it more important not to break routine. Roth's death had temporarily shattered his command, and it was vital to start repairing it.

Gallagher had the last shift. It was very cold in the half hour before daylight and he woke up dazed, and sat shuddering in his blanket. For many minutes he was conscious of little, feeling the vast shapes of the mountain range about him as no more than a deeper border to the night. He only shivered and drowsed, waiting passively for the morning and the heat of the sun. A complete lethargy had settled over him, and Roth's death was remote. He drifted through a stupor, his mind almost inert, dreaming sluggishly of far-gone pleasant things as though deep within him he had to keep a small fire going against the cold of the night, the space of the hills, and the cumulative exhaustion, the mounting deaths of the platoon.

The dawn came slowly on the mountain. At five o'clock he could see the top of the mountain range clearly as the sky became lighter, but for a long half hour there was little change. Actually he could see nothing, but his body contained a tranquil anticipation. Soon the sun would struggle over the eastern ramparts of the mountain and come down into their little valley. He searched the sky and found a few tentative washes of pink streaming over the higher peaks, coloring the tiny oblong clouds of the dawn a purple. The mountains looked very high. Gallagher wondered that the sun could get over them.

All about him now it was getting lighter but it was a subtle process, for the sun still remained hidden and the light seemed to rise from the ground, a soft rose color. Already he could discern clearly the bodies of the men sleeping about him, and he felt a touch of superiority. They looked gaunt and bleak in the early dawn, oblivious to the approach of morning. He knew that in a short while he would be rousing them, and they would groan as they came out of their sleep.

In the west he could still see the night, and he recalled a troop train speeding across the great plains of Nebraska. It had been twilight then, and the night chased the train out of the east, overtook it, and passed on across the Rockies, on to the Pacific. It had been beautiful and it made him wistful now. He longed suddenly for America, wished so passionately to see it again that he could smell the odor of wet cobblestones on a summer morning in South Boston.

The sun was close to the eastern ridge-line now and the sky seemed vast, yet fresh and joyful. He thought of Mary and himself camping in a little pup tent in the mountains and he dreamt that he was waking with the velvet teasing touch of her breasts against his face. He heard her say, "Get up, sleepyhead, and look at the dawn." He grunted drowsily, nuzzled against her in his fantasy and then popped open one eye as a grudging concession. The sun *was* clearing the ridge, and while the light in the valley was still faint, there was nothing unreal about it. The morning was here.

In that way Mary ushered in the dawn with him. The hills were shaking off the night mists and the dew was sparkling. For this brief moment the ridges about him appeared soft and feminine. All the men scattered around him looked damp and chilly, dark bundles from which mist rose. He was the only man awake for a distance of many miles, and he had the youth of the morning all to himself.

Out of the dawn, far on the other side of the mountain, he could hear artillery booming. It shattered his reverie.

Mary was dead.

Gallagher swallowed, wondering with a dumb misery how long it would be before he would stop tricking himself. There was nothing now to anticipate, and he was conscious for the first time of how tired he was. His limbs ached and his sleep seemed to have done him no good. The character of the dawn changed, left him shuddering in his blanket, damp and cold from the night's dew.

There was still his child, the boy he had never seen, but that did not cheer him. He believed he would never live to see him, and the knowledge was almost without pain, a dour certainty in his mind. Too many men had been killed. My number's coming. With a sick fascination, he envisioned a factory, watched his bullet being made, packed into a carton.

If only I could see a picture of the kid. His eyes misted. It wasn't so much to ask. If only he could get back from this patrol and live

686

long enough for some mail to come with a picture of his kid.

But he was miserable again, certain he had tricked himself. He shivered from fright, looking about him uneasily at the mountains reared on every side.

I killed Roth.

He knew he was guilty. He remembered the momentary power and contempt he had felt as he bawled at Roth to jump, the quick sure pleasure of it. He twisted uncomfortably on the ground, recalling the bitter agony on Roth's face as he missed the step. Gallagher could see him falling and falling, and the image scraped along his spine like chalk squeaking on a blackboard. He had sinned and he was going to be punished. Mary was the first warning and he had disregarded it.

The mountain peak before them seemed so high. Gone now were the gentle outlines of the dawn; Anaka mounted before him, turret above turret, ridge beyond ridge. Near the peak he could see a bluff which encircled the crest. It was almost vertical and they would never be able to ascend it. He shuddered once more. He had never seen country like this; it was so barren, forbidding. Even the slopes of jungle and brush above them were cruel. He would never be able to make it today; already his chest ached, and when he slung his pack and began the climb again he would be exhausted in a few minutes. There was no reason to keep going; how many men had to be killed?

What the fug is it to Croft? he wondered.

It would be easy to kill him. Croft would be at the point and all he would have to do would be to raise his rifle, take aim, and the patrol would be over. They could turn back. He rubbed his thigh slowly, absorbed and uneasy from the force with which it appealed to him. Sonofabitch.

It was no way to think. His superstitious dread came back; each time he thought like this he was preparing his own punishment. And yet . . . It was Croft's fault that Roth had been killed. He really couldn't be blamed.

Gallagher heard a sound behind him and started. It was Martinez rubbing his head nervously. "Sonbitch, no sleep," Martinez said softly.

"Yeah."

Martinez sat down beside him: "Bad dreams." He lit a cigarette moodily. "Fall asleep . . . eeeeh . . . Hear Roth yell."

"Yeah, it hits ya," Gallagher muttered. He tried to reduce it to a more normal frame. "I never liked the guy particularly, but I never wanted him to get it like that. I never wanted nobody to get hit."

"Nobody," Martinez repeated. He massaged his forehead tenderly as if he had a headache. Gallagher was surprised how bad Martinez looked. His thin face had become hollow, and his eyes had a blank lusterless stare. He needed a shave badly, and dark streaks of grime had filleted all the lines in his face, making him appear much older.

"This is a rough deal," Gallagher muttered.

"Yah." Martinez exhaled some smoke carefully and they watched it glide away in the early morning air. "Cold," he muttered.

"It was a sonofabitch on guard," Gallagher said hoarsely.

Martinez nodded once more. His watch had come at midnight and he had been unable to sleep since then. His blankets had chilled; he had shuddered, twisted nervously for the rest of the night. Even now in the dawn, there was little release. His body still held the tension that had kept him awake, and he was bothered by the same diffused dread he had suffered all night. It had lain heavily on his body as though he were in fever. For over an hour he had been unable to rid himself of the expression on the face of the Japanese soldier he had killed. It was extremely vivid to him, and it reproduced the paralysis he had felt as he waited in the bushes with the knife in his hand. The empty scabbard clanked against his thigh, and he trembled delicately, a little shamefully. He fingered it with a twitching hand.

"Why the fug don't you throw the scabbard away?" Gallagher asked.

"Yah," Martinez said quickly. He felt embarrassed, meek. His fingers shook as he worked the hooks of the scabbard out of the eyelets in his cartridge belt. He tossed it away and winced at the empty clattering sound it made. Both of them started, and Martinez had a sudden gout of anxiety.

Gallagher could hear Hennessey's helmet spinning in the sand. "I'm gone to pot," he murmured.

Martinez felt automatically for the scabbard, realized it was gone,

688

and with a sudden congealing of his flesh saw Croft telling him to be silent about his reconnaissance. Hearn had gone out believing . . . Martinez shook his head, choked by relief and horror. It wasn't his fault that they were on the mountain.

Abruptly the pores of his body opened, discharged their perspiration. He shivered in the cold mountain air, wrestling against the same anxiety he had suffered on the troopship the hours before they had invaded Anopopei. Against his will he stared up at the tessellated stones and jungle of the upper ridges, closed his eyes and saw the ramp of the landing boat going down. His body tensed, waiting for the machine-gun fire. Nothing happened and he opened his eyes, racked by an acute frustration. Something had to happen.

If only he could see a snapshot of his kid, Gallagher thought. "It's a goddam trap goin' up this mountain," he muttered.

Martinez nodded.

Gallagher extended his arm, touched Martinez's elbow for a moment. "Why don't we go back?" he asked.

"I don't know."

"It's fuggin suicide. What are we, a bunch of goddam mountain goats?" He rubbed the coarse itching hairs of his beard. "Listen, we'll all get knocked off."

Martinez wriggled his toes inside his boots, extracting a bleak satisfaction.

"You wanta get your fuggin head blown off?"

"No." He fingered the little tobacco pouch in his pocket where he kept the gold teeth he had stolen from the cadaver. Perhaps he should throw them away. But they were so pretty, so valuable. Martinez wavered, then left them there. He was struggling against the conviction that they would be an effective sacrifice.

"We ain't got a fuggin chance." Gallagher's voice shook, and as if he were a sounding board, Martinez resonated to it. They sat staring at each other, bound by their common fear. Martinez wished dumbly that he could assuage Gallagher's anxiety.

"Why don't you tell Croft to quit?"

Martinez shivered. He knew! He could tell Croft to go back. But the attitude was so foreign to him that he shied away from it fearfully.

He could just ask him, maybe. A new approach formed for him naïvely. For a moment as he had hesitated before killing the Japanese sentry he had realized that he was only a man and the entire act had seemed unbelievable. Now the patrol seemed ridiculous. If he were just to ask Croft, maybe Croft would see it was ridiculous too.

"Okay," he nodded. He stood up and looked at the men bundled in their blankets. A few of them were stirring already. "We go wake him up."

They walked over to Croft, and Gallagher shook him. "Come on, get up." He was a little surprised that Croft was still sleeping.

Croft grunted, sprang to a sitting position. He made an odd sound, almost like a groan, and turned immediately to stare at the mountain. He had been dreaming his recurrent nightmare: he lay at the bottom of a pit waiting for a rock to fall on him, a wave to break, and he could not move. Ever since the Jap attack at the river he had been having dreams like this.

He spat. "Yeah." The mountain was still in place. No boulders had moved. He was a little surprised, for the dream had been vivid.

Automatically he swung his legs free of the blanket and began to put on his boots. They watched him soberly. He picked up his rifle, which he had kept beside him under the blankets, and examined it to see if it was dry. "Why the hell didn't you wake me earlier?"

Gallagher looked at Martinez. "We go back today, huh?" Martinez asked.

"What?"

"We go back," Martinez stammered.

Croft lit a cigarette, feeling the pungence of the smoke in his empty stomach. "What the hell you talkin' about, Japbait?"

"Better we go back?"

This was a shock to Croft. Was Martinez threatening him? He was stunned. Martinez was the only man in the platoon whose obedience he had never doubted. Croft's next reaction was rage. He stared quietly at Martinez's throat, restraining himself from leaping at him. His only friend in the platoon threatening him. Croft spat. There was no one you could trust, no one except yourself.

The mountain ahead had never looked so high and forbidding.

690

Perhaps a part of him did want to turn back, and he flung himself from the temptation. Hearn was wasted if they turned back. And again the flesh on his back writhed under a play of nervous needles. The peak still taunted him.

He would have to go easy. If Martinez could do this, then the situation was dangerous. If the platoon ever discovered . . . "Goddam, Japbait, you turnin' on me?" he said softly.

"No."

"Well, what the hell's this talk? You're a sergeant, man, you don't go in for crap like that."

Martinez was caught. His loyalty was being questioned, and he hung sickly on Croft's next speech, waiting for him to say the thing he dreaded. A Mexican sergeant!

"I thought we were pretty good buddies, Japbait."

"Yah."

"Man, I thought they wasn't a damn thing you was afraid of."

"No." His loyalty, his friendship, his courage were all involved. And as he looked into Croft's cold blue eyes he felt the same inadequacy and shabbiness, the same inferiority he always knew when he talked to . . . to White Protestant. But there was even more this time. The undefined danger he always sensed seemed sharper now, closer upon him. What would they do to him, how very much would they do to him? His fear almost stifled him.

"Forget it. Japbait go with you."

"Sure." Croft's wheedling had hung awkwardly on him.

"Whadeya mean, you're goin' with him?" Gallagher asked. "Listen, Croft, why the hell don't you turn back? Ain't ya got enough fuggin medals?"

"Gallagher, you can shut your hole."

Martinez wished he could sidle away.

"Aaah." Gallagher pirouetted between fright and resolution. "Listen, I ain't afraid of you, Croft. You know what the fug I think of you."

Most of the men in the platoon had awakened and were staring at them.

"Shut your mouth, Gallagher."

"You better not keep your back to us." Gallagher walked away, trembling in the reaction from his courage. Any moment he expected Croft to come up behind him, spin him about, and strike him. The skin along his back quivered with anticipation.

But Croft did nothing. He was having a reaction from Martinez's unfaithfulness. The resisting weight of the platoon had never pressed more heavily upon him. He had the mountain to fight and the men dragging upon him. It accumulated in him for that moment, left him empty and without volition.

"All right, men, we're gonna move out in half an hour, so don't be fuggin around." A chorus of mutterings and grumblings answered him, but he preferred to single out none of them. He was extracting the last marrows of his will. He was exhausted himself and his unwashed body itched unbearably.

When they did get over the mountain what could they do? There were only seven of them left, and Minetta and Wyman would be worthless. He watched Polack and Red, who munched their food dourly, glaring back at him. But he forced these considerations away. He would worry about the rest of it once they had crossed the mountain. Now that was the only important problem.

Red watched him for several minutes afterward, noticing every move with a dull hatred. He had never loathed any man so much as Croft. As Red picked at the breakfast ration of tinned ham and eggs, his stomach rebelled. The food was thick and tasteless; when he chewed there was a balance between his desire to swallow it and his desire to spit it out. Each lumpful remained heavy and leaden for an interminable time in his mouth. He threw the can away at last, and sat staring at his feet. His stomach pulsed emptily, sickeningly.

There were eight rations left: three cheeses, two ham and eggs, and three beef and pork loafs. He knew he would never eat them; they were merely an added load in his pack. Aaah, fug this. He took out the ration cartons, slit the tops off each with his knife and separated the candy and cigarettes from the food tins, the crackers. He was about to throw the food away when he realized that some of the men might want it. He thought of asking, but he had an image of passing from man to man with the cans in his hand, having them jeer

692

at him. Aaah, fug 'em, he decided, it's none of their goddam business anyway. He threw the food into some weeds a few feet behind him. For a time he sat there, so enraged that his heart was beating powerfully, and then he relaxed and began to make up his pack. That'll be lighter anyhow, he told himself, and his rage began again. Fug the Army anyhow, fug the goddam mother-fuggin Army. That stuff ain't fit for a pig. He was breathing very quickly once more. Kill and be killed for this lousy goddam food. So many images blurred in his mind, the mills where they stamped and pressured and cooked the food that went into the tins, the dull *thwopping* sound of a bullet striking a man, even Roth's shout.

Aaah, fug the whole goddam mess. If they can't feed a man, then fug 'em, fug 'em all. He was trembling so badly he had to sit down and rest.

He had to face the truth. The Army had licked him. He had always gone along believing that if they pushed him around too much he would do something when the time came. And now . . .

He had talked to Polack yesterday, and they had both hinted about Hearn, both let it lay. He knew what he could do, and if he skipped out on it he was yellow. Martinez wanted them to go back. Since he had tried to convince Croft, Martinez must know something.

By now the sun was shining brightly on their slope, and the dark-purple shadows of the mountain had lightened to lavender and blue. He squinted upward toward the peak. They still had a morning's climb ahead of them, and then what? They would drop down among the Japs and be wiped out. They could never come back over the mountain again. On an impulse he walked over to Martinez, who was fixing his pack.

Red hesitated for an instant. Nearly all the men were ready, and Croft would shout at him if he delayed. He still had to put his blanket in his pack.

Aaah, fug him, Red thought again, ashamed and angry.

Before Martinez he paused, uncertain what to say. "How you doin', Japbait?"

"Okay."

"You and Croft couldn't work it out for a little while, huh?"

"Nothing the matter." Martinez averted his eyes.

Red lit a cigarette, disgusted with what he was doing. "Japbait, you're kind of chicken. You want to quit and you ain't even got the guts to say so."

Martinez made no answer.

"Listen, Japbait, we been around quite a while, we know what the hell the fuggin score is. You think it's gonna be fun goin' up that hill today? We're gonna have a coupla more men droppin' off on one of those ledges, maybe you, maybe me."

"Leave me alone," Martinez muttered.

"Let's face it, Japbait, even if we do get over, we'll just get a leg or an arm blown off on the other side. You want to stop a slug?" Even as he argued Red was bothered by a sense of shame. There was another way to do this.

"You want to be a cripple?"

Martinez shook his head.

The arguments filed naturally into Red's mind. "You killed that Jap, didn't ya? Did ya ever know that brings your number a little closer?"

This was a powerful point to Martinez. "I don't know, Red."

"You killed that Jap, but did you say a goddam thing about it?"

"Yah."

"Hearn knew about it, huh, he walked into that pass knowing there was Japs?"

"Yah." Martinez began to shake. "I tell him, I try tell him, big damn fool."

"Balls."

"No."

Red was not completely certain. He paused, took another tack. "You know that sword I got with the jewels back at Motome? If you want, you can have it."

"Oh." The beauty of the sword shone in Martinez's eyes. "Free?"

"Yeah."

Croft shouted suddenly. "Come on, men, let's move out."

Red turned around. His heart was churning and he massaged his hands slowly against his thigh. "We ain't goin', Croft."

694

Croft strode toward him. "Made up your mind, Red?"

"If you want to do it so fuggin much, you can do it alone. Jap-bait'll take us back."

Croft stared at Martinez. "Changed your mind again?" he asked softly. "What are ya, a goddam woman?"

Martinez shook his head slowly. "I don't know, I don't know." His face began to work and he turned away.

"Red, get your pack ready and cut out this shit."

It had been wrong to talk to Martinez. Red saw it clearly. It had been disgusting, as though he had been arguing with a child. He had been taking the easy way and it wouldn't work. He would have to face Croft. "If I go up that hill, you'll be draggin' me."

Some of the men in the platoon were muttering. "Let's go back," Polack yelled, and Minetta and Gallagher joined him.

Croft stared at them all, and then unslung his rifle, cocked the bolt leisurely. "Red, you can go get your pack."

"Yeah, you would do somethin' when I ain't got a gun."

"Red, just get your pack and shut up."

"It ain't me alone. You gonna shoot all of us?"

Croft turned and gazed at the others. "Who wants to get lined up with Red?" None of them moved. Red watched, hoping numbly that one of them might pick up a rifle. Croft had turned away from him. Now was the time. He could leap at him, knock him down and the others would help out. If one man would move, they all would.

But nothing happened. He kept telling himself to jump at Croft and his legs wouldn't function.

Croft turned back to him. "Awright, Red, go get your pack."

"Fug you."

"Ah'm gonna shoot ya in about three-four seconds." He stood six feet away, his rifle raised to his hip. Slowly the muzzle pointed toward Red. He found himself watching the expression on Croft's face.

Suddenly he knew exactly what had happened to Hearn, and the knowledge left him weak. Croft was going to shoot. He knew it. Red stood stiff looking at Croft's eyes. "Just shoot a man down like that, huh?"

"Yeah."

695

It was worthless to temporize. Croft wanted to shoot him. For an instant he had a picture again of lying on his stomach waiting for the Japanese bayonet to strike into his back. He could feel the blood thumping in his head. As he waited, his will drained away slowly.

"How 'bout it, Red?"

The muzzle made a tiny circular motion as if Croft were selecting a more exact aim. Red watched his finger on the trigger. When it began to tighten he tensed suddenly. "Okay, Croft, you win." His voice croaked out weakly. He was making every effort to keep himself from trembling.

About him he could see the platoon relaxing. He felt as if his blood had slowed down, halted, and now had begun to flow again, outlining every nerve in his body. With his head down he strode over to his pack, rammed in the blanket, buckled the straps, and stood up.

He was licked. That was all there was to it. At the base of his shame was an added guilt. He was glad it was over, glad the long contest with Croft was finished, and he could obey orders with submission, without feeling that he must resist. This was the extra humiliation, the crushing one. Could that be all, was that the end of all he had done in his life? Did it always come to laying down a load?

He fell into line and trudged along in the middle of the platoon. He looked at nobody, and no one looked at him. All of them felt a wretched embarrassment. Each man was trying to forget the way he had been tempted to shoot Croft and had failed.

As they walked, Polack cursed continually in a low sullen voice, filled with self-loathing. Dumb yellow bastard. He was swearing at himself, frightened, a little shocked. The moment had been there, and he had let it go, had had his rifle in his hands, and had done nothing with it. Yellow . . . yellow!

And Croft at this point was confident again. This morning they would cross the mountain peak. Everything and everybody had tried to hold him back but there could be nothing left now, no obstacle at all.

The platoon climbed the slope, crossed another ridge, and descended over a stretch of scattered rocks into one more tiny valley.

Croft led them through a small rock gorge onto another slope and for an hour they toiled upward from rock to rock, crawling sometimes for hundreds of yards on their hands and knees in a laborious endless progression which skirted the edge of a deep ravine. By midmorning the sun was very hot, and the men were exhausted once more. Croft led them much more slowly, halting every few minutes.

They topped a crest-line and jogged feebly down a gentle slope. Before them was a huge amphitheater, bounded in a rough semicircle by high sheer bluffs covered with vegetation. The cliffs of jungle rose almost vertically for five hundred feet, at least the height of a forty-story skyscraper, and above them was the crest of the mountain. Croft had noticed this amphitheater; from miles away it looked like a dark-green collar encircling the neck of the mountain.

There was no way to avoid it; at either side of the amphitheater the mountain dropped for a thousand feet. They had to go forward and climb the jungle before them. Croft rested the platoon at the base, but there was no shade and the rest had little value. After five minutes they set out.

The wall of foliage was not so impossible as it had appeared from a distance. A crude stairway of rocks bedded in the foliage and zigzagged upward like a ramp. There were bamboo groves and bushes and plants, vines, and a few trees whose roots grew horizontally into the mountain and whose trunks bent upward in an L toward the sky. There was mud, of course, from all the rains that had trickled down the rocks, and leaves and plants and thorns restricted their passage.

It was a stairway, but not a convenient one. They carried the weight of a suitcase on their backs, and they had to climb what amounted to forty flights of stairs. To give an added fillip, the stairs were not of equal height. Sometimes they would clamber from one waist-high rock to another, and sometimes they would scrabble up a slope of pebbles and small rocks; sometimes indeed each rock was of a different height and shape than the one that had preceded it. And the stairway, of course, was littered, so that often they would have to push aside foliage or cut through vines.

Croft had estimated it would take an hour to ascend the wall of the amphitheater, but after an hour they were only halfway up. The men struggled behind him like a wounded caterpillar. They never traveled all at once. A few would advance over a rock and wait for the others to catch up. They advanced in ripples, Croft toiling ahead a few yards and the rest of the platoon filling the gap in a series of spasmodic lurches which traveled like a shock impulse. Often they would halt while Croft or Martinez hacked slowly through a tangle of bamboo. In a few places the stairway leaped upward in a big bound of seven or ten feet of muddy earth up which they climbed by clutching at roots.

Once more the platoon dropped from one layer of fatigue to another, but this had happened so often in the past few days that it was almost familiar, almost livable. With no surprise they felt their legs become numb, trail after them like a toy which a child drags on a string. Now the men no longer stepped from one high rock to another. They dropped their guns on the shelf above, flopped over and dragged their legs after them. Even the smallest rocks were too great to step over. They lifted their legs with their arms, and placed their feet on the step before them, tottered like old men out of their beds for an hour.

Every minute or two someone would stop and lie huddled on the rocks, weeping with the rapt taut sobs of fatigue that sound so much like grief. In empathy a swirl of vertigo would pass from one to the other and they would listen with a morbid absorption to the racking sounds of dry nausea. One or another of them was always retching. When they moved they were always falling. The climb up the rocks slippery with mud and vegetation, the vicious thorns of bamboo thicket, the blundering of their feet against the jungle vines, all blended into one vast torment. The men groaned and cursed, stumbled on their faces, reeled and skidded from rock to rock.

It was impossible to see more than ten feet ahead, and they forgot about Croft. They had discovered that they could not hate him and do anything about it, so they hated the mountain, hated it with more fervor that they could ever have hated a human being. The stairway became alive, personalized; it seemed to mock and deceive them at every step, resist them with every malign rock. Once more they forgot about the Japanese, forgot about the patrol, almost forgot about

698

themselves. The only ecstasy they could imagine would be to stop climbing.

Even Croft was exhausted. He had the task of leading them, of cutting trail whenever the foliage became too thick, and he prostrated himself trying to pull them up the mountain. He felt not only the weight of his own body but the weight of all their bodies as effectively as if he had been pulling them in harness. They dragged him back, tugged at his shoulders and his heels. With all his physical exertion his mind fatigued him as greatly, for he was under the acute strain of gauging their limits.

There was another strain. The closer he came to the crest of the mountain the greater became his anxiety. Each new turn of the staircase demanded an excessive effort of will from him. He had been driving nearer and nearer to the heart of this country for days, and it had a cumulative terror. All the vast alien stretches of land they had crossed had eroded his will, pitched him a little finer. It was an effort, almost palpable, to keep advancing over strange hills and up the flanks of an ancient resisting mountain. For the first time in his life he started with fear every time an insect whipped into his face or an unnoticed leaf tickled his neck. He drove himself onward with the last sources of his endeavor, dropping at the halts with no energy left.

But each time the brief respite would charge his resolve again and he could toil upward a few yards more. He, too, had forgotten almost everything. The mission of the patrol, indeed even the mountain, hardly moved him now. He progressed out of some internal contest in himself as if to see which pole of his nature would be successful.

And at last he sensed that the top was near. Through the web of jungle foliage he could perceive sunlight as though they were approaching the exit of a tunnel. It spurred him on, yet left him exhausted. Each step he took closer to the summit left him more afraid He might have quit before they reached it.

But he never had the opportunity. He reeled over a rock, saw a light-tan nest shaped something like a football, and in his fatigue he smashed into it. Instantly, he realized what the nest was, but too late. An uproar burst in it and a huge hornet, about the size of a half dollar, fluttered out, and then another and another after it. He watched dumbly as dozens of them flickered about his head. They were large and beautiful with great yellow bodies and iridescent wings; afterward he exhumed the memory as something completely apart from what followed.

The hornets were furious, and in a few seconds they raced down the line of men like a burning fuse. Croft felt one of them flutter at his ear, and he struck at it with a grunt, but it had stung him. The pain was maddening; it numbed his ear like frostbite, and traveled through his body with an acute shock. Another stung him and another; he bellowed with pain and struck at them frenziedly.

For the platoon this was the final unbearable distress. Perhaps five seconds they stood rooted, flailing dumbly at the hornets that attacked them. Each sting lashed through a man's body, loosing new frantic energies of desperation. The men were in delirium. Wyman began to bawl like a child, holding feebly to a rock, and swatting at the air in a tantrum.

"I can't stand it, *I can't stand it!*" he roared.

Two hornets bit him almost at once, and he hurled away his rifle, and screamed in terror. The shriek detonated the men. Wyman began to run down the rocks, and one by one they followed him.

Croft shouted at them to stop, but they paid no attention. He gave a last oath, swung impotently at a few of the hornets and then started down after them. In a last fragment of his ambition, he thought of regrouping them at the bottom.

The hornets pursued the men down the jungle wall and the rock ramp, goading them on in a last frenzy of effort. They fled with surprising agility, jumping down from rock to rock, ripping through the foliage that impeded them. They felt nothing but the savage fleck of the hornets, the muted jarring sensations of scrabbling from rock to rock. As they ran they flung away everything that slowed them. They tossed away their rifles, and some of them worked loose their packs and dropped them. Dimly they sensed that if they threw away enough possessions they would not be able to continue the patrol.

Polack was the last man ahead of Croft as the platoon poured into the amphitheater. He caught a quick glimpse of them, and the platoon was halting in confusion now that they had escaped the hornets. Polack

700

threw a glance over his shoulder at Croft and burst among the men shouting, "WHAT THE HELL ARE YOU WAITING FOR? HERE COME THE BUGS!" Without pausing he ran past them, let loose a scream, and the platoon followed him, bolted in a new panic. They scattered over the floor of the amphitheater, continued on in the same spasm of effort over the next ridge, and down below to the valley, to the slopes of the rise beyond. In fifteen minutes they had fled beyond the point where they had started that morning.

When Croft finally caught up with the platoon, gathered them together, he discovered there were only three rifles and five packs left. They were through. He knew they could never make the climb again. He was too weak himself. He accepted the knowledge passively, too fagged to feel any regret or pain. In a quiet tired voice he told them to rest before they turned back to the beach to meet the boat.

The return march was uneventful. The men were wretchedly tired, but it was downhill work on the mountain slopes. Without any incident, they jumped the gap in the ledge where Roth had been killed, and by midafternoon descended the last cliffs, and set out into the yellow hills. All afternoon as they marched they heard the artillery booming on the other side of the mountain range. That night they bivouacked about ten miles from the jungle, and by the next day they had reached the shore and joined the litter-bearers. Brown and Stanley had come out of the hills only a few hours ahead of the platoon.

Goldstein told Croft how they had lost Wilson, and was surprised when he made no comment. But Croft was bothered by something else. Deep inside himself, Croft was relieved that he had not been able to climb the mountain. For that afternoon at least, as the platoon waited on the beach for the boats that were due the next day, Croft was rested by the unadmitted knowledge that he had found a limit to his hunger.

14

THE BOAT picked them up the next day and they started on the journey back. This time the landing craft had been equipped with eighteen bunks along the bulkheads and the men put their equipment in the empty ones and stretched out to sleep. They had been sleeping ever since they had come out of the jungle the preceding afternoon, and by now their bodies had stiffened and become painful. Some of them had missed a meal that morning but they were not hungry. The rigors of the patrol had left them depleted in many ways. They drowsed for hours on the return trip, awaking only to lie in their bunks and stare out at the sky above the open boat. The craft pitched and yawed, spray washed over the sides and the bow ramp, but they barely noticed. The sound of the motors was pleasant, reassuring. The events of the patrol had receded already, become a diffused wry compound of indistinct memories.

By afternoon most of them were awake. They were still terribly fatigued but they could not sleep any longer. Their bodies ached and they felt no desire to walk about the narrow confines of the troop well, but still they were subtly restless. The patrol was over and yet they had so little to anticipate. The months and years ahead were very palpable to them. They were still on the treadmill; the misery, the ennui, the dislocated horror . . . Things would happen and time would pass, but there was no hope, no anticipation. There would be nothing but the deep cloudy dejection that overcast everything.

Minetta lay on his bunk, his eyes closed, and dawdled through the afternoon. There was one fantasy he kept indulging, a very simple one, a very pleasing one. Minetta was dreaming about blowing off his foot. One of these days while cleaning his gun he could point the muzzle right into the middle of his ankle, and press the trigger. All the bones would be mashed in his foot, and whether they had to amputate or not, they certainly would have to send him home.

Minetta tried to add up all the angles. He wouldn't be able to run again, but then who the hell wanted to run anyway? And as for dancing, the way they had these artificial limbs he could put on a

702

wooden foot, and still hold his own. Oh, this was okay, this could work.

For a moment he was uneasy. Did it make any difference which foot it was? He was a leftie and maybe it'd be better to shoot the right foot, or were they both the same? He thought of asking Polack, and immediately dropped the idea. This kind of thing he'd have to play alone. In a couple of weeks, on a day when nothing was doing, he could take care of that little detail. He'd be in the hospital for a while, for three months, six months, but then . . . He lit a cigarette and watched the clouds dissolve into one another, feeling agreeably sorry for himself because he was going to have to lose a foot and it was not his fault.

Red picked at a sore on his hand, examining maternally the ridges and creases of his knuckles. There was no kidding himself any longer. His kidneys were shot, his legs would begin to break down soon, all through his body he could feel the damage the patrol had caused. Probably it had taken things out of him he would never be able to put back again. Well, it was the old men who got it, MacPherson on Motome, and then Wilson, it was probably fair enough. And there was always the chance of getting hit and coming out of it with a million-dollar wound. What difference did it make anyway? Once a man turned yellow . . . He coughed, lying flat on his back, the phlegm gagging him slightly. It took an effort of will to prop himself on his elbow and hawk the sputum out onto the floor of the boat.

"Hey, Jack," one of the pilots on the stern hatch yelled, "keep the boat clean. We don't want to scrub it after you guys."

"Aaah, blow it out," Polack shouted.

Croft called from his bunk, "Let's cut out that spittin', men."

There were no answers. Red nodded to himself. It was there, all right; he had waited a little anxiously for Croft to say something, had been relieved when Croft had not scolded him by name.

The bums in the flophouse who cringed when they were sober and cursed when they were drunk.

You carried it alone as long as you could, and then you weren't strong enough to take it any longer. You kept fighting everything, and everything broke you down, until in the end you were just a little

703

goddam bolt holding on and squealing when the machine went too fast.

He had to depend on other men, he needed other men now, and he didn't know how to go about it. Deep within him were the first nebulae of an idea, but he could not phrase it. If they all stuck together . . .

Aaah, fug. All they knew was to cut each other's throats. There were no answers, there wasn't even any pride a man could have at the end. Now, if he had Lois. For an instant he hovered over the idea of writing her a letter, starting it up again, and then he threw it away. The least you could do was back out like a man. And there was the thought that maybe she'd tell him to go to hell. He coughed once more and spat into his hand, holding it numbly for several seconds before he wiped it surreptitiously on the canvas of his bunk. Let the boat pilot try to wash that out. And he smiled wryly, shamefully, at the satisfaction it gave him.

The sneak. Well, he'd been everything else in his time.

And Goldstein lay on his bunk with his arms under his head and thought dreamily about his wife and child. All the bitterness and frustration of losing Wilson had been tucked away in his brain, encysted temporarily by the stupor that had followed. He had slept for a day and a half, and the journey with the litter seemed remote. He even liked Brown and Stanley because they were a little uneasy with him and seemed afraid to bother him. He had a buddy too. There was an understanding between Ridges and him. The day they had spent on the beach waiting for the rest of the platoon had not been unpleasant. And automatically they had selected bunks next to each other when they got on the boat.

He had his moments of rebellion. The goy friend he got was such a goy — a peasant, an outcast himself. He *would* get somebody like that. But he was ashamed for thinking this, with almost the shame he felt whenever a random caustic thought about his wife slipped through his head. It ended by his being defiant. For a friend he had an illiterate, but so what? Ridges was a good man. There was something enduring about him. The salt of the earth, Goldstein told himself.

The boat wallowed along about a mile offshore. As the afternoon wore by the men began to move about a little, and stare over the side. The island skidded by slowly, always impenetrable, always green and opaque with the jungle skirting the water. They passed a small peninsula which they had noticed on the trip out, and some of them began to calculate how long it would be before they reached the bivouac. Polack climbed up on the rear hatch where the pilot was steering the boat and rested under the canvas canopy. The sun shifted over the water, reflecting brightly from each ripple, and the air held a subtle bouquet of vegetation and ocean.

"Jeez, it's nice out here," Polack said to the driver.

The man grunted. His feelings were hurt because the platoon had been spitting in the boat.

"Aaah, what's eatin' ya, Jack?" Polack asked.

"You were one of the wise guys who was giving me some lip before."

Polack shrugged. "Aaah, listen, Jack, you don' wanta take an attitude like that. We been t'rough a lot, our nerves are up in the air."

"Yeah, I guess you did have a rough go."

"Sure." Polack yawned. "Tomorrow they'll have our ass out on patrol, you watch."

"It's only mopping up."

"Where do ya get that stuff, moppin' up?"

The pilot looked at him. "Jesus, I forgot you men were out on patrol for six days. Hell, man, the whole fuggin campaign blew sky high. We killed Toyaku. In another week there won't be but ten Japs left."

"Wha . . . ?"

"Yeah. We got their supply dump. We're slaughtering them. I saw that Toyaku Line myself yesterday. They had concrete machine-gun emplacements. Fire lanes. Every damn thing."

Polack swore. "The whole thing's over, huh?"

"Just about."

"And we broke our ass for nothin'."

The pilot grinned. "Higher strategy."

Polack climbed·down after a while and told the men. It all seemed perfectly fitting to them. They laughed sourly, turned over in their bunks, and stared at the side bulkhead. But soon they realized that if the campaign was over they would be out of combat for a few months at least. It confused them, irritated them, they didn't know whether the news pleased them or not. The patrol should have been worth something. In their fatigue this conflict brought them close to hysteria and then shifted them over to mirth.

"Hey, you know," Wyman piped, "before we went I heard a rumor they're going to send the division to Australia to make MPs out of us."

"Yeah, MPs." They roared at this. "Wyman, they're sendin' us home."

"Recon's gonna be personal bodyguard for the General."

"MacArthur is gonna have us build him another house at Hollandia."

"We're gonna be Red Cross girls," Polack shouted.

"They're puttin' the division on permanent KP."

Everything mixed in them. The boat, which had been almost silent, quivered from the men's laughter. Their voices, hoarse, trembling with mirth and anger, carried for a long distance over the water. Each time one of them said anything, it provoked new spasms of laughter. Even Croft was brought into it.

"Hey, *Sergeant,* I'm gonna be a cook, I hate to leave ya."

"Aaah, get the hell out, you're a bunch of goddam women," Croft drawled.

And this seemed funniest of all. They held weakly onto the stanchions of their bunks. "Do I have to leave now, Sergeant? There's a lot of water," Polack bawled. It rushed through them in a succession of confused waves like water ripples spreading out from a stone only to be balked by other wavelets formed by another stone. Every time someone opened his mouth they roared again, wild hysterical laughter, close to tears. The boat shook from it.

It died down slowly, erupted again several times like fire licking out from under a blanket, and finally wore itself out. There was nothing left but their spent bodies and the mild pleasure they found in releasing the tension upon their cheek muscles, soothing the ache of laughter in their chests, wiping their freshened eyes. And it was re-

706

placed by the flat extensive depression which overlay everything.

Polack tried to revive it again by singing but only a few of them joined him.

> *"Roll me over*
> *In the clover.*
> *Roll me over,*
> *Lay me down*
> *And do it again.*
>
> *Ha' past three*
> *I had her on my knee.*
> *Lay me down,*
> *Roll me over,*
> *Do it again.*
> *Roll me over in the clover . . ."*

Their voices piped out feebly, lost in the flat placid washes of the blue sea. Their boat chugged along, the motors almost smothering the sound.

> *"Ha' past four*
> *I had her on the floor.*
> *Lay me down,*
> *Roll me over,*
> *Do it again."*

Croft got out of his bunk and peered over the side, staring moodily at the water. He had not been told the date on which the campaign had been won, and he made the error of assuming it was the day they had failed on the mountain. If they had been able to climb it, the campaign would have depended upon them. He did not even question this. It was a bitter certainty in his mind. His jaw muscles quivered as he spat over the side.

> *"Ha' past five*
> *We began to jive . . ."*

They sang as if they were playing chimes, Polack and Red and Minetta, gathered together at the stern. At every pause Polack would blow out his cheeks and go "Waah-waaaah," like a trumpet when it is fanned with a mute. Gradually it was catching the others. "Where's Wilson?" one of them shouted, and they all stopped for a moment. They had heard the news of his death but it hadn't registered. And suddenly he was dead. They understood it. The knowledge shocked them, loosed the familiar unreality of war and death, and the song wavered over a syllable or two. "I'm gonna miss that old sonofabitch," Polack said.

"C'mon, let's keep going," Red muttered. Guys came and guys went, and after a while you didn't even remember their names.

"Roll me *over* in the clover."

They passed a bend in the island and saw Mount Anaka in the distance. It looked immense. "Boy, did we climb that?" Wyman asked.

Some of them scrambled up the side, pointing out slopes of the mountain to each other, arguing whether they had climbed each particular ridge. They had a startled pride in themselves. "It's a big sonofabitch."

"We did okay to go as far as we did."

That was the main sentiment. Already they were thinking how they would tell it to their buddies in other platoons.

"We just got lost in the shuffle. Everybody's gonna have a story to tell."

"Yeah."

And that pleased them too. The final sustaining ironies.

The song was still going on.

> *"Ha' past six*
> *I had her doin' tricks.*
> *Lay me down,*
> *Roll me over,*
> *Do it again."*

708

Croft stared at the mountain. The inviolate elephant brooding over the jungle and the paltry hills.

It was pure and remote. In the late afternoon sunlight it was velvet green and rock blue and the brown of light earth, made of another material than the fetid jungle before it.

The old torment burned in him again. A stream of wordless impulses beat in his throat and he had again the familiar and inexplicable tension the mountain always furnished him. To climb that.

He had failed, and it hurt him vitally. His frustration was loose again. He would never have another opportunity to climb it. And yet he was wondering if he could have succeeded. Once more he was feeling the anxiety and terror the mountain had roused on the rock stairway. If he had gone alone, the fatigue of the other men would not have slowed him but he would not have had their company, and he realized suddenly that he could not have gone without them. The empty hills would have eroded any man's courage.

> Ha' past seven
> She thought she was in heaven . . .

In a few hours they would be back, pitching their pup tents in the darkness, getting a canteen cup of hot coffee, perhaps. And tomorrow the endless routine of harsh eventless days would begin once more. Already the patrol was unfamiliar, unbelievable, and yet the bivouac before them also was unreal. In transit everything in the Army was unreal. They sang to make a little noise.

> ". . . roll me over
> And do it again."

Croft kept looking at the mountain. He had lost it, had missed some tantalizing revelation of himself.

Of himself and much more. Of life.

Everything.

Mute Chorus:

ON WHAT WE DO WHEN

WE GET OUT

(Sometimes spoken, usually covert, varying with circumstance.)

RED: Do the same fuggin thing I always did. What else is there?

BROWN: When we hit Frisco, I'm going to take my pay and throw the biggest goddam old drunk that town ever saw, and then I'll shack up with some bitch, and I won't do nothing but screw and drink for two whole goddam weeks, and then I'm going to take it easy going home to Kansas, just stopping off whenever I damn feel like it, just throwing the damnedest old binge you ever saw, and then I'm gonna look my wife up, I ain't gonna let her know I'm coming, and I'm going to give her the surprise of her life, and have witnesses along, by God, and I'll throw her out of the house, and let people know the way you treat a bitch when we're stuck over here God knows how long, never knowing when you're going to catch something, just waiting and sweating it out, and finding out things about yourself that, by God, it don't pay to know.

GALLAGHER: All I know is there's a fuggin score to be paid off, a score to be paid off. There's somebody gonna pay, knock the fuggin civilians' heads in.

GOLDSTEIN: Oh, I can just see it when I get home. I'm going to get back in the early morning, and I'm going to take a taxi from Grand Central, and ride all the way out to our apartment house in Flatbush, and then I'm going to come up the stairs, and ring the bell, and Natalie'll be wondering who it is, and then she's going to come, and she's going to answer it. . . . I don't know. So much time ahead.

MARTINEZ: San Antonio, see family maybe. Walk around, nice Mexican girls San Antonio, big wad money, ribbons, go to church,

710

kill too many goddam Japs. Don't know, re-enlist, Army no goddam good, but Army okay. Nice pay.

MINETTA: I'm gonna walk up to every sonofabitch officer in uniform, and say 'Sucker' to them, every one of them right on Broadway, and I'm gonna expose the goddam Army.

CROFT: Waste of time thinking about it. The war'll go on for a while.

PART FOUR

Wake

THE MOPPING UP was eminently successful. A week after the Toyaku Line had been breached, the remnants of the Japanese garrison on Anopopei had been whittled into a hundred and then a thousand little segments. Their organization broke completely; battalions were cut off, and then companies, and finally platoons and squads and little slivers of five and three and two men hid in the jungle, attempted to escape the flood of American patrols. Toward the end the casualty figures were unbelievable. On the fifth day two hundred and seventy-eight Japanese were killed and two Americans; on the eighth day, the most productive of the campaign, eight hundred and twenty-one Japanese were killed and nine captured for the loss of three American lives. The communiques went out with a monotonous regularity, terse and modest, not wholly inaccurate.

"General MacArthur announced today the official end of the battle for Anopopei. Mopping up continues."

"American troops under Major General Edward Cummings announced capture today of five enemy strong-points and large concentrations of food and ammunition. Mopping up is in progress."

Astonishing reports continued to come in to Cummings's desk. It was discovered from questioning the few prisoners that for over a month the Japanese had been on half rations, and toward the end there had been almost no food at all. A Japanese supply dump had been destroyed by artillery five weeks before, and no one had known it. Their medical facilities had been exhausted, there were portions of the Toyaku Line which had been in disrepair for six or eight weeks. Finally they discovered that the Japanese ammunition had been almost depleted a week before the last attack had begun.

Cummings searched through old patrol reports, read again all accounts of enemy activity on the front for the past month. He even digested once more the puny findings of intelligence. In all that, there was no hint of the actual Japanese situation. From the reports, he had made the only possible assumption — that the Japanese were still in strength. It bothered him, terrified him; this was the most powerful lesson he had ever derived from a campaign. Until now, while he had partially discounted any patrol information he received, he had nevertheless given it some weight. The information here had been worthless.

He had never quite freed himself of the shock Major Dalleson's victory had given him. To leave his battle front on a quiet morning and return the next day to find the campaign virtually over was a little like the disbelief with which a man would come home to find his house burned down. Certainly he had handled the mopping up with brilliance. The Japanese, once staggered, had been given no opportunity to regroup but that was a hollow triumph, the salvaging of a few sticks of furniture. It enraged him secretly that Dalleson's blundering should have exploded the campaign; the collapse of the Japanese had been due to his efforts, and he should have had the pleasure of detonating the fuse. What irritated him most of all was that he must congratulate Dalleson, perhaps even promote him. To snub Dalleson now would be too patent.

But this frustration was replaced by another. What if he had been present, had directed the climactic day himself? What really would it have meant? The Japanese had been worn down to the point where any concerted tactic no matter how rudimentary would have been enough to collapse their lines. It was impossible to shake the idea that anyone could have won this campaign, and it had consisted of only patience and sandpaper.

For a moment he almost admitted that he had had very little or perhaps nothing at all to do with this victory, or indeed any victory — it had been accomplished by a random play of vulgar good luck larded into a causal net of factors too large, too vague, for him to comprehend. He allowed himself this thought, brought it almost to the point of words and then forced it back. But it caused him a deep depression.

If only he had conceived that patrol a little earlier in the cam-

716

paign, had had time to work it out more completely. It had been a botch, and Hearn was dead.

Well, one could not really call it a shock. Still, for a little while, Hearn had been the only man in the division who was capable of understanding his more ambitious plans, capable even of understanding him. But Hearn had not been big enough. He had looked, become frightened, and crawled away, throwing mud.

He knew why he had punished him, he knew it was not accidental that he had assigned Hearn to recon. And his end had not been unforeseen. Cummings had extracted at first a fragile grain of pleasure from it.

Only . . . for an instant when he first heard the news of Hearn's death, it had hurt him, wrenched his heart with a cruel fist. He had almost grieved for Hearn, and then it had been covered over by something else, something more complex. For days whenever Cummings thought of the Lieutenant he would feel a mingled pain and satisfaction.

In the end the important thing was always to tot up your profit and loss. The campaign had taken a week more than had been allowed for it, and that was not going to count too effectively for him. But there had been a time only a week or two ago when he would have settled for an extra month. Besides, as far as Army was concerned, the campaign had been won by the side invasion of Botoi. That would be undeniably in his favor. Altogether, he had not been either fundamentally hurt or benefited by Anopopei. When the Philippines came up he would have the entire division to employ and a chance to achieve some more striking results. But before that the men would have to be shaken up, given vigorous training, and their discipline would have to be improved. He had again the same anger he had felt in the last month of the Anopopei campaign. The men resisted him, resisted change, with maddening inertia. No matter how you pushed them, they always gave ground sullenly, regrouped once the pressure was off. You could work on them, you could trick them, but there were times now when he doubted basically whether he could change them, really mold them. And it might be the same thing again in the Philippines. With all his enemies at Army, he did not have much chance of gaining an added star before the Philippines, and with that would go all chance of an Army command before the war ended.

Time was going by, and with it, opportunity. It would be the hacks who would occupy history's seat after the war, the same blunderers, unco-ordinated, at cross-impulses. He was getting older, and he would be by-passed. When the war with Russia came he would not be important enough, not close enough to the seats of power, to take the big step, the big leap. Perhaps after this war he might be smarter to take a fling at the State Department. His brother-in-law certainly would do him no harm.

There would be few Americans who would understand the contradictions of the period to come. The route to control could best masquerade under a conservative liberalism. The reactionaries and isolationists would miss the bell, cause almost as much annoyance as they were worth. Cummings shrugged. If he had another opportunity he would make better use of it. What frustration! To know so much and be hog-tied.

To divert his balked nerves, he carried out the mopping up with a ceaseless concentration on details.

Sixth Day: 347 Japanese — 1 American
Ninth Day: 502 Japanese — 4 Americans

The patrols filtered along the trails behind the Japanese lines. In great numbers they threaded all the aisles of the maze, hacked through the jungle itself to find any survivors who might have crawled up a game trail. From early in the morning until twilight the patrols were out and always with the same mission.

It was simple, a lark. After months of standing guard at night, of patrolling up trails which could explode into ambush at any moment, the mopping up was comparatively pleasant, almost exciting. The killing lost all dimension, bothered the men far less than discovering some ants in their bedding.

Certain things were SOP. The Japanese had set up many small hospitals in the last weeks of the campaign, and in retreating they had killed many of their wounded. The Americans who came in would finish off whatever wounded men were left, smashing their heads with rifle butts or shooting them point-blank.

But there were other, more distinctive, ways. One patrol out at dawn discovered four Japanese soldiers lying in stupor across a trail, their ponchos covering them. The lead man halted, picked up some pebbles and flipped them into the air. The pebbles landed on the first sleeping soldier with a light pattering sound like hail. He awakened slowly, stretched under the poncho, yawned, groaned a little, cleared his throat, and stretched with the busy stupid sounds of a man rousing himself in the morning. Then he poked his head out from under the poncho. The lead man waited until the Jap saw him and then, as he was about to scream, the American sent a burst of tommy-gun slugs through him. He followed this by ripping his gun down the middle of the trail, stitching holes neatly through the ponchos. Only one Jap was left still alive, and his leg protruded from the poncho, twitching aimlessly with the last unconscious shudders of a dying animal. Another soldier walked up, nuzzled the body under the poncho with the muzzle of his gun, located the wounded man's head, and pulled the trigger.

There were other variations.

Occasionally they would take prisoners, but if this was late in the day and the patrol was hurrying to get back before dark, it was better if the prisoners did not slow them. One squad picked up three prisoners late in the afternoon, and was delayed grievously by them. One prisoner was so sick he could hardly walk, and another, a big sullen man, was looking for a way to escape. The third had gigantically swollen testicles which were so painful that he had cut away his trousers from his groin the way a man with a bunion slits the toe off an old shoe. He walked pathetically, hobbling along and groaning as he held his testes.

The platoon leader looked at his watch at last and sighed. "We're going to have to dump them," he said.

The sullen Jap seemed to know what he meant, for he stepped off the trail and waited with his back turned. The shot caught him behind the ear.

Another soldier came up behind the prisoner with the swollen

719

genitals and gave him a shove which sprawled him on the ground. He gave a single scream of pain before he was killed.

The third one was half in coma and had no idea of what happened.

Two weeks later Major Dalleson sat in the newly finished operations and training shack and ruminated pleasurably about the past, present, and future. Now that the campaign was over, the division's headquarters had moved back almost to a cool pleasant grove not far from the sea. At night the breezes made sleep quite enjoyable.

The training program was going to begin the next day, and this was the part of military life that the Major found most congenial. Everything had been got ready. The troops had set up their permanent bivouacs in squad tents, the walks through the bivouac had been graveled and every company had finished building racks over each man's cot to hold his equipment neatly. The parade ground was finished and the Major was proud of it, for he had supervised it personally. It had been a considerable feat to clear three hundred yards of jungle and level the ground in only ten days.

Tomorrow there would be the first parade and inspection, and the Major anticipated it eagerly. He obtained a simple childish joy from seeing the troops march past in clean uniforms, in picking a file at random and inspecting their rifles. Before they moved on to the Philippines he was determined to get the division marching decently again.

His days were quite busy. There were any number of details to be carried out and the training schedule gave him a lot of difficulties. Without the proper facilities it was going to be troublesome to give all the courses he wanted. There would be rifle marksmanship, of course, and the care, nomenclature, and operation of the machine gun. There could be a class in special weapons, and one in compass and map reading, another in military discipline. And of course he was going to keep them busy with inspections and parades. But still there were many other things they should have. In any case, he could always fill the gap with hikes.

This training was what he liked; there was no getting away from

720

it. Even making up the schedule for each company was a problem, but a good one. It was a little like filling out a crossword puzzle. The Major lit a cigar and stared out past the galvanized-iron walls of the operations shack across the hundred yards of jungle to the ocean that lapped delicately against the beach. He breathed deeply, savoring the pungent fish smell of the water. He always did his best, no one could deny that. A rosy satisfaction eddied through him.

At this moment he got his idea. He could jazz up the map-reading class by having a full-size color photograph of Betty Grable in a bathing suit, with a co-ordinate grid system laid over it. The instructor could point to different parts of her and say, "Give me the co-ordinates."

Goddam, what an idea! The Major chuckled out of sheer pleasure. It would make those troopers wake up and pay some attention in map class.

But where was he going to get a life-size photograph? The Major chased a coil of ash with the tip of his cigar. He could ask quartermaster but he was goddamned if he'd make a fool of himself filling out a requisition for that. Maybe Chaplain Davis, who was a good egg — but, no, he'd better not ask him.

Dalleson scratched his head. He could write a letter to Army Headquarters, Special Services. They probably wouldn't have Grable, but any pin-up girl would do.

That was it. He'd write Army. And in the meantime he might send a letter to the War Department Training Aids Section. They were out for improvements like that. The Major could see every unit in the Army using his idea at last. He clenched his fists with excitement.

Hot dog!